THE KAREN WILSON CHRONICLES

by Jennifer Brozek

The Karen Wilson Chronicles

Caller Unknown

Children of Anu

Keystones

Chimera Incarnate

Jennifer Brozek

Apocalypse Ink Productions
Kenmore, Washington

Credits

Edited by John Helfers
Interior design by Jeff Brozek
Cover image @2015 by Amber Clark
Cover art design ©2016 by Mark Ferrari

PUBLISHED BY
Apocalypse Ink Productions
6830 NE Bothell Way, STE C #404
Kenmore, WA 98028
http://www.apocalypse-ink.com/

First Published October 2016

eBook ISBN: 978-1-940444-18-5
Trade Paperback ISBN: 978-1-940444-19-2
Limited Edition ISBN: 978-1-940444-20-8

For my Mom and Dad who supported me when I told them I wanted to quit my tech job to become a full-time author.

I don't know if you two understand just how much that meant to me and how much I needed to hear it.

Table of Contents

Acknowledgements 1

Introduction to the Karen Wilson Chronicles...................3

CALLER UNKNOWN...5

    Caller ID: Unknown 7

    Eye of the Engraving....................................... 17

    Arbiter.. 27

    Forgotten School Days 41

    Sacrificium Memoriae 50

    The Inspiration of Insanity............................... 63

    The Running Feeling.. 71

    Afternoon Tea 83

    Sins of the Brother 93

    Burning Bridges 101

    Betrayal 113

    Warfare and the Rite...................................... 121

CHILDREN OF ANU 135

    Beginnings and Endings................................. 137

    Heart's Desire.. 145

    Sharks and Seals... 155

    Many Happy Returns 163

    Many Unanswered Questions........................... 171

    Concessions 181

    Blue Moon Revelations 187

    First Blood 199

    Transcript 207

    Debts Called In... 217

    Ultimatums 225

    Too Little, Too Late 236

KEYSTONES...247

    Shades of Grey 249

    Broken 257

    Keystones.. 265

    Observations 273

    May Day.. 283

    Entropy 293

    The Past and the Present Collide...................... 303

    Absorption... 311

Candle's Flame 319

The Cost of Redemption 329

Breaking Point 339

The Righteous Hand 349

CHIMERA INCARNATE 359

Unexpected Changes, Part 1 361

Unexpected Changes, Part 2 377

Waking 391

Waiting for the Pieces to Fall 405

Forgiveness and Sacrifice 421

Seeking and Finding 433

Shades of Black 445

Lady in Grey, Part 1 457

Lady in Grey, Part 2 471

Gifts, New and Old, Dark and Light 483

Blood for the Renewed Earth 497

Beginning Again 511

KENDRICK'S HISTORIC LIBRARY ARCHIVES 527

The Fool's Path 529

Kelpie Storm 537

Ley of the Land 549

Kendrick's Lady 561

Dick's Muse 577

A Card Given 583

Author's Biography 594

Also From Apocalypse Ink Productions 595

Acknowledgements

I want to thank my husband, Jeff, first and foremost. He loved the story of Karen Wilson and Kendrick from the beginning and encouraged me whenever I flagged. He always understood when I popped into his office to brainstorm or to crow about something a character did or to cry on his shoulder about an unexpected death. I appreciate and love you.

Next, I want to thank Ivan Ewert, Rick Silva, Jim Sullivan, and Amber Clark. You all have been with me through so much of the *Karen Wilson Chronicles* and through all of the Kendrick stories. I appreciate your feedback and support.

I also want to thank my Mom for taking the time to edit and proof every Kendrick story I've ever written. It was your "pulls no punches" approach that made me work that much harder to make sure the stories were as good as I could make them.

Finally, I would like to thank those people who made this book as awesome as it is: John Helfers for his marvelous editing job on this book. Your insight and attention to detail made my writing that much better. I appreciate it. Sarah Hendrix for your most excellent and detailed proofing. And Mark Ferrari for designing a brilliant cover. Thank you!

Introduction to the Karen Wilson Chronicles

LIKE MOST OF my best projects, Kendrick and the *Karen Wilson Chronicles* was a happy "Plan B." Originally, *The Edge of Propinquity*, was going to be a game world where I set up the universe and other people played in it, discovering the mysteries and wonders therein.

Then reality set in and time was a factor to the point that no one could play. Like the idea of the *Grants Pass* anthology, this idea was too good to give up on. Thus, both *Kendrick*, the episodic series, and *The Edge of Propinquity*, the magazine, were born. I wrote a Kendrick story once a month for three years.

This online magazine published the first three novels of the *Karen Wilson Chronicles* in its nascent form.

Each novel had its own theme. *Caller Unknown* was based on the theme of "Revelations." *Children of Anu* had the theme of "Consequences." *Keystones* was based around "Retribution." The final novel in the quartet, *Chimera Incarnate*, was built on the theme of "Compromises."

Each mosaic novel is thirteen stories—the twelve stories for the arc and one bonus background story. Each story within the mosaic novel has its own distinct storyline but is linked into the overall arcing plotline. Time passes in-between each story. Events happen off screen. The heroes have a plan. The villains have a plan. Sometimes, those plans cross paths.

For the omnibus collection, all of the background Kendrick stories have been split out and put in their own section, the *Kendrick's Historic Library Archives,* in chronological order. This section includes "Kelpie Storm" that was not published in any of the Kendrick novels as well as the previously unpublished John Corso story, "The Fool's Path."

The main protagonist in the Kendrick stories is Karen Wilson—911 operator, comic book artist, and all around normal person. At least until she receives a mysterious phone call from someone she does not know.

Her life is turned upside down as she discovers a supernatural universe just beneath the surface of the world she thought she knew. The chosen representative of someone she does not know—one of the most powerful supernatural creatures in the city of Kendrick, Karen has to fight her own skeptical nature to accept things that seem too crazy to be real.

One thing I like about Karen is the fact that she is a normal person. She, herself, never gains supernatural powers. Any power she has comes from the supernatural creatures that do things for her. Karen's years of revelation, consequence, retribution, and compromise are fraught with peril, betrayal, and surprise. I hope you enjoy reading about her adventures as much I enjoyed writing about them.

Most of all, Kendrick is the world that could be happening around you when you walk outside your front door and never know it. I love that idea and that's why I wrote this series.

CALLER UNKNOWN

Book One of
The Karen Wilson Chronicles

Caller ID: Unknown

THE RINGING PHONE pulled Karen out of the zone and into reality. She'd been sketching for a new project, and had been deep in the creative space—a place akin to being at the bottom of a well.

Wondering how long the phone had rung while she pulled herself back into awareness, she blinked a couple times as the Caller ID displayed: UNKNOWN

Karen wondered if she was still partly in the zone because the sketch she had been working on was titled, "The Unknown." Then she wondered what "UNKNOWN" on Caller ID meant. As far as she knew, either the calling number was displayed or, if the caller had blocked their number, "Restricted" would show. Otherwise, if the number was stored in the phone already the name of the person calling would appear. All these thoughts collided as she answered the phone.

"Hello?"

"Hello Karen. I need your help."

She looked at the Caller ID window again. It still displayed 'UNKNOWN' and she didn't recognize the man's voice. "Pardon me? Who is this?"

"I need your help. A friend of mine is in danger, and will be hurt if you don't help me."

"Sir, perhaps you should call the police. If you know of someone in danger, you should report it."

"I am reporting it. You *are* a 911 operator, are you not?"

Karen frowned in concern. Someone she did not recognize called her on her unlisted line and knew what she did for a living. "Who is this? This isn't funny."

There was a pause. "You may call me Reginald. Please, Karen, I'm not trying to be funny. If you don't help, I'm afraid that someone very important to me, to the city, is going to be murdered.

"You have to go to Bacchanalia and talk to Lamiel before eight o'clock tonight. She's going to be called by the Order to meet and talk. It's a trick. They are sending an assassin. You have to tell her not to go."

"Talk to Lamiel at Bacchanalia before eight this evening?" It was like suddenly being thrust into the middle of a game of *Clue*.

"Yes. It's very important. Also, tell her that no one is to perform any rituals in the park and it should not be fought over. The park will defend itself."

"What? Look, sir. I don't know who you are or why you called me, but..."

"You're a 911 operator. You're supposed to help people. That's what 911 operators do."

"Yes, but people call the 911 system. Not my personal cell phone."

"Please, Karen. Lamiel will die tonight if you don't help her."

"Sir, I really think you should call the police." She kept speaking in her most reasonable tone. The one she used for the crazies who called the system while imaginary bugs crawled under their skin.

Encouraged by the silence, she continued to try to persuade her caller. "They *will* be able to help you. I promise. They're trained for this sort of emergency. I'm not." When he did not answer, she looked at her phone display window and found that the line had disconnected.

She made a mental note to look into the 'Caller ID: Unknown' thing and went back to her sketching. She had promised Daniel she'd get a number of these concept sketches done in time for his comic book proposal. It was good work to have, and stretched her artistic ability. However, after that strange phone call, Karen couldn't regain her groove. She tried for another hour before giving it up for the night. She would try again tomorrow after work and some sleep.

Replaying the conversation in her mind, she went to her computer to do a bit of research. Finding Bacchanalia and Lamiel in Kendrick proved far easier than she expected. Bacchanalia, located in the City Center district, was a private dance club catering exclusively to the gothic crowd. You had to be a member to enter or have a member vouch for you for the night.

While Karen liked the gothic scene, she considered herself far too normal to fit in with such an eclectic crowd. The Bacchanalia website was extensive and sucked her in. She discovered that it was a non-profit venture, run exclusively by volunteers who worked for tips. In fact, Lamiel was a bartender there by night and a gothic fashion designer by day.

It appeared that she was very popular in the local scene and well known in the gothic community. Bacchanalia had dedicated a full page to her. A link on it led to Lamiel's personal fashion website, complete with active forums based around the designer, her designs, and the gothic scene in general.

Karen studied the woman's picture. Despite the gothic Victorian garb she wore, she seemed very young. Flipping through the gallery pages of Lamiel's designs, she was amazed at the woman's artistic talent.

She glanced at the clock. It was a quarter to eight. If she hurried, she might make it to the City Center in time. Maybe not at eight, but close to it. It was an impulse. Maybe Lamiel would think she was crazy. Maybe this was a set up by a crazed fan. Maybe.

But, maybe, Reginald—if that was his real name—knew something. She paused at the door to her apartment, wondering why she was doing this, then shrugged. She had made a fool of herself before. If she did it again, it probably wouldn't be the last time.

* * *

The drive into the City Center could have gone better. It also could have been much worse. To her amazement, she found a parking place in front of the address. It took her a minute to find the door to Bacchanalia, though. The entrance was halfway down the alley, and the only indication that it led to the club was the symbol of a snake wrapped around a cluster of grapes on the door.

When Karen recognized the symbol from the website, she opened the door and found herself in a small antechamber with a front desk. There were two people there. Both looked very surprised to see her.

"Can I help you?" The guy behind the desk had multicolored dreadlocks, dramatic makeup, and several face piercings. He seemed genuinely curious.

"Uh... I need to see Lamiel."

"Are you a member?" His questioning tone indicated that he already knew the answer.

She shook her head. "No. I just need to talk to her. Please. It's important."

"I'm sorry, Miss. Bacchanalia is a members only club, and we have a dress code." He looked pointedly at her jeans, slouchy sweatshirt, and jacket.

"Oh." Karen looked down at herself, then pulled a five dollar bill out of her wallet and put it in the tip jar. "Could you at least let her know that there's someone here to talk to her? Please? I wouldn't normally bother you, but..."

"It's important. Yeah, you said that." The guy behind the counter gave her a hard look, as if to assess her potential threat level, then nodded to his companion, a man in leather pants and a poet's shirt. "All right. We'll see if she's around."

"Thank you." A moment after the guy left, she smiled. "I'm Karen, by the way."

"Nice to meet you, Karen By-the-Way. I'm Aaron."

They both smiled at his little joke, then the two of them stood in silence while she looked around at the artwork on the walls. It was very interesting stuff, and reminded her of the kind of artwork she normally drew: misty landscapes, castles in ruins and graveyards. She had expected something a bit more modern at a place like this.

Then, she noticed a series of symbols painted around the doorway on the doorframe and wall. Not recognizing them, she turned to ask Aaron about them when the second guy returned. "She's not here."

"Huh? I thought she was working tonight."

"She was. She got a call about twenty minutes ago. Kurosawa said she had a sudden meeting with someone."

"Did she say where?" Karen interrupted.

"The 16th Street Bridge."

"Shit." Her stomach lurched. What if the caller had been right, and Lamiel was about to be murdered? She could have stopped it.

"Is something wrong?" Aaron asked.

"I don't know. Maybe. I gotta go." Karen shot out the door and ran for her car, then sped toward the 16th Street Bridge. It was on the far north end of town, near the Camden area. Her intimate knowledge of the streets of Kendrick came in handy, and luck was on her side. Every light was green, and there were no cops in sight.

By the time she stopped on 35th Avenue, below the 16th Street Bridge, she saw two people walking towards each other on the bridge from opposite ends. She recognized one as Lamiel. The woman was unmistakable, with long, flowing, black clothing and hair. There was no way for her to get to Lamiel before she met the person—a *man*, Karen thought— under the lamppost.

Karen got out of her car as they met and began to speak. Not knowing what else to do, she shouted, "Lamiel!" Both figures turned towards her. "It's a trap! Run!" Karen was still running towards the bridge as the unspeakable unfolded before her.

Lamiel looked from Karen back at the man, threw something at him, then turned to run. The man lunged at

Lamiel, grabbing her around the waist. There was a brief struggle as the man stabbed her in the neck with something, then picked her up and threw her from the bridge.

Karen gasped as she saw and heard Lamiel land on the pavement with a sickening thud. She ran to the fallen woman's side, looking up at the bridge. The man stood there for a moment, pointed at her, then left.

Feeling for Lamiel's pulse, she found it slow and irregular. She was still alive. Karen grabbed her phone to call 911, but heard Reginald's voice on the other end. "You've got to pull the needle out of her neck. That's what's killing her. Do it. Do it quickly."

Her hand felt for the needle, found it, and pulled it out. "I don't have time to talk to you. I have to call 911."

"This is the 911 operator," a female voice said. "What is the nature of your emergency?"

Karen was startled, but for only a moment. "A woman was just thrown from the 16th Street Bridge. I saw it. We're on 35th Avenue with 12th Street as the nearest crossroad. I need an ambulance."

"Who am I speaking to?"

"Karen Wilson."

There was a pause as the operator recognized the name. "What is the condition of the woman? Is she bleeding?"

Karen touched Lamiel's neck again. Her pulse was steady and strong now. Her breathing was regular. She looked around to see if Lamiel was bleeding out anywhere, but saw no sign of it. "She's got cuts and bruises from the fall. Breathing strong. Heart strong. But, she's lying a little funny. I'm afraid to move her."

"An ambulance is on the way, Karen. Do not move the woman. Stay with her and monitor her. I am right here. Let me know if there is any change."

She felt her panic recede in the familiar routine of training as she listened to the operator's calm voice. Everything was going to be all right. She looked down at the needle in her hand. It looked like a very short hatpin. The needle part was about an inch long, its base a teardrop shaped pearl. She could see symbols carved into it.

Not wanting to explain it or the weirdness of the night, Karen slipped it into her pocket as she heard sirens wail in the distance. "I hear sirens."

"Okay, Karen, I'll stay with you until they arrive."

"Thank you." She checked on Lamiel again, who seemed to be doing much better. If it were not for the angle she was lying at, she could be sleeping.

Karen thanked the operator again once the ambulance and police arrived. As they took Lamiel away, she gave her statement to a police officer on the scene. At first, she was going to lie about how she got here, then decided against it and told Officer David Hauberk about the strange phone call and going to Bacchanalia before coming here. She did not tell him about the needle she pulled from Lamiel's neck or Reginald on her phone right after Lamiel's fall.

Officer Hauberk looked skeptical until she showed him her incoming phone list. UNKNOWN was at the top of the list. When he tried to call it back, there was no number to dial and *69 did not work. "This is really strange, Miss Wilson. I may have to call you into the station to answer more questions."

"That's fine. I'm as much at a loss as you are. I'm thinking about getting a new phone."

"Please don't do anything until we follow up with you. In the future, when this Reginald calls, please inform us immediately." He gave her his business card. "You did both a very brave and stupid thing, Miss Wilson. You could have been hurt as well. Call the police in the future."

"I know. I'm sorry."

He smiled at her. "It's okay. We'll talk more later. You're free to go."

***

Normally, Karen would have worked her usual midnight to eight a.m. shift at the call center. However, as soon as Griff, her supervisor, found out about what had happened, he sent her home for two days to rest. "You may have a delayed stress reaction to what you saw. I need you to relax and not be on the phones tonight or tomorrow."

"I'm fine. Really," she protested, but didn't resist any further as her friend and mentor stood firm on his decision. In truth, after the adrenaline had left her system, she was beat. All she wanted to do was sleep for a week.

Karen went home, puttered about for a few minutes, then sat down and started to draw. She sketched what she remembered of that night, wondering about the people there—who Reginald was, who Lamiel was, who the man was and why he tried to kill Lamiel—until it was her usual bedtime at about ten a.m. It was only then that she slept. She didn't want to throw her sleep schedule off, even if she did suddenly have a couple unexpected days of vacation.

Still, she didn't sleep well. She was up by three p.m., pacing around her apartment, thinking about Lamiel. She was in her car and driving towards the hospital before she realized where she was going and how much she needed to see the other woman. Karen needed to see Lamiel awake, alive, and hopefully well.

Karen felt a little odd asking for "Lamiel" at the information desk, but apparently enough people had come to see her that the nurse didn't even blink. "Miss Bell is in room 597 on the fourth floor. Visiting hours are over at six."

Karen thanked the nurse and went up to the room. It was a private room with the door open. A guy with shocking blue hair sat next to the bed. She knocked on the doorframe. "Uh—hello. I'm Karen Wilson."

Lamiel, who looked very different and even younger without her makeup, smiled a little. "Hello. Come on in." The two women looked at each other for a moment.

"I'm gonna go get some coffee. I'll be back in a bit." The blue-haired guy got up, kissed Lamiel on the cheek, and left.

Lamiel looked her over. "So, you're the girl who tried to save me from the ambush."

Karen nodded and walked over to her. "Yeah."

"Who do you work for?"

"I'm a 911 operator for the city."

"No. I mean, what group do you work for?"

"Emergency services? I'm not sure I understand what you mean."

She looked at Karen with an intense look that made her uncomfortable. "No. I guess you don't. Why don't you tell me how you knew it was an ambush?"

"It's a strange story. I'm not sure you'll believe me."

"You'd be surprised at what I believe these days."

"I got a phone call from someone named Reginald. He told me that if I didn't warn you not to go to the meeting with the person from the Order, you would be murdered. I thought he was joking."

Lamiel frowned. "Reginald... Reginald." A look of surprise came over her face. "Oh... okay. Go on."

"I didn't believe him. But then I looked up Bacchanalia, found out you were a real person and thought... what the hell. The worst you could do was laugh at me."

"Did he say anything else?"

Karen nodded. "Yeah, but it's crazy talk."

"Try me."

"He said that no one was to perform any rituals in the park, not to fight over it, and that the park would defend itself. Do you know what he meant? What's the Order? Which park? What rituals? Why did that person try to kill you?"

"You really don't know any of this?" Lamiel shook her head and took a drink of water. "It doesn't make sense. The man who attacked me, he stabbed me with something. No one found it. Do you have it?"

Karen suddenly felt guilty. She had not thought of the needle at all since she had slipped it into her coat pocket. She put her hand in her pocket and found it. Pulling it out, she saw it still had Lamiel's dried blood on it. "Yeah, I do."

"May I have it?"

She handed it over. "It's got symbols engraved on it. Reginald said it would have killed you." Karen wanted to ask why or if it was poisoned, but she kept her silence. She wanted answers, but at the same time wasn't sure she wanted to know any more about this. Not yet. All of this was too much like a trip through the looking glass.

"An *aiguillette*," Lamiel murmured before slipping it into a small pouch and putting the pouch on the table next to her. "I'm not going to answer any of your questions right now, Karen. I need to know more about what's going on, and I won't know that until I get out of here. But, if Reginald calls back or you find yourself in trouble and need a safe haven, go to Bacchanalia. They'll take care of you. They know what you did for me. We may look like freaks, but we take care of our own and those who help us. Okay?"

"Um, okay. But, I don't think he's going to call back. Besides, the police want to know if he does."

"You shouldn't tell the police. They won't be able to help. They probably don't really want to know anyway."

"But—"

"No police. Trust me on this."

"I'll think about it." Karen shifted from foot to foot. "Are you going to be okay?"

Lamiel looked out the window. "I don't know. The fall damaged my spine. I can't feel my legs."

"I'm so sorry. I—"

"It wasn't your fault. If you hadn't tried to stop the meeting, I'd be dead now and you would still be blissfully unaware of things."

"I don't know what to say."

She turned back to look at Karen. "It's all right. Thank you for what you've done. I'll repay you someday. I pay my debts. I'm sorry, but I'm tired now."

"Okay. I hope you feel better soon." As Karen left, she saw the blue-haired man standing outside the room door like a sentry, drinking coffee. She nodded at him and hurried off, feeling confused and worried.

***

Elsewhere...

Several people stood or sat in a well-appointed den. Books lined the walls, and heavy leather chairs sat in a semicircle facing the fireplace. Everyone's attention was focused on the man, the would-be assassin, halfheartedly trying to keep the dying fire lit. He did not look up as he spoke. "I did as you instructed."

"Lamiel is still alive. Our message was diluted, ineffective. Now, there will be more trouble." The man speaking, the Praetor of the Order, looked as angry as the rest did.

The assassin abandoned the fire and put the poker in its rightful place. "Not my fault. I did as you instructed. I stabbed her with the *aiguillette*. According to you, she should have died immediately. She didn't. She was saved by another woman."

"Who? A passerby?"

"No. I don't know her, but I marked her. I'll know her if I see her again. This woman yelled a warning. She found and removed the *aiguillette*. It's as if she knew who I was, what I was doing, and how. No one outside of this room should have known that."

Silence answered the implied accusation. Instead, the Praetor picked up his pipe and went through the motions of lighting it before he spoke again. Sweet smoke filled the air. "That's your next task. Find her. Find out who she is. Find out who she works for and which faction she belongs to."

"Yes, sir." He brushed his hands off on his pants, staring at the speaker.

"Dismissed."

At the command, the assassin walked from the room without looking back. Behind him, the people in the room began murmuring about the new player in the Game, and the trouble that seemed to be headed their way.

Eye of the Engraving

THE RINGING PHONE did not unnerve Karen. The 'UNKNOWN' in the caller ID window did. Ten days had gone by, and life had returned to normal. Now, he was calling again. She hoped to God that someone else was not about to be murdered.

"Hello, Reginald."

"Hello, Karen."

"I'm not supposed to talk to you. I'm supposed to tell the police that you called me again."

"Please don't do that. They can't help me. I need your help."

"Why me?"

"I told you last time. You're a good person. You help people. You can help me. The Order has hired some people to break into the museum tonight to steal part of the money exhibit—the one-dollar bill engraved printing plates from 1935. You need to tell Susan Moore and help her stop them."

"Steal printing plates? Why? Who is this Order? I want to know. I mean, how do I know you're not the bad guy here?"

"Ask Susan. She'll tell you. You need to hurry. The museum closes in about twenty minutes. You need to find her and tell her before it closes."

For a moment, Karen thought about hanging up on him. In truth, though, this was the most exciting thing that had ever happened to her and part of her liked it. Really liked it. "All right, but she'd better have some answers for me."

Karen would do it, as insane as it sounded. Partly because he was right last time. Partly because she was still curious.

"Thank you."

"Yeah." She hung up the phone and threw on a comfortable sweatshirt over her long sleeved t-shirt. As she headed to her car, she tried to call Officer Hauberk to let him know, but all the circuits were busy. She didn't think that could happen with cell phones these days. Maybe it meant all the police department phone lines were busy. That was an unpleasant thought.

She drove to the south side of the City Center and parked behind the Kendrick Museum of History & Art. As she entered the building, she was warned that the museum was closing. Karen acknowledged it and asked the woman at the front desk if Susan Moore was available.

After a phone call, a short, blond-haired woman in a nice business suit came out to meet her. Karen got the impression of barely contained energy from the woman. As if once she started working on something, nothing would stop her short of hell or high water.

"Good evening, I'm Susan Moore. How may I help you?" She offered her hand.

Karen shook it. "Karen Wilson. I'm sorry to come when you're closing but, well... Could we speak privately? I have a message from Reginald."

There was an odd flicker of recognition in Susan's eyes. "Of course." She turned to the woman at the desk packing up. "It's all right. I'll take care of this. I'll see you tomorrow." Then, she led Karen through the museum, past all of the various displays of Makah Indian artifacts, a Shakespeare collection, and a series of home antiques like salt and pepper shakers, irons and ironing boards, and sewing machines. Karen felt a prickle of guilt at the fact that she had never come to the Kendrick Museum just to look around. It was part of the history of her city, and she knew very little about it.

They entered a small, cluttered office. Susan offered her a chair. "So, what's up?"

"Well, this is going to sound crazy, but the last time this guy Reginald called me and asked me to help someone out, he was right. He called me and told me to tell you that the Order had hired some people to steal some dollar bill printing plates. I'm supposed to tell you and help you stop them."

"Really."

"I know it sounds crazy."

"Yeah, it does, but if you're the same girl who helped Lamiel, it sounds a little less crazy."

"You know her?" Suddenly, the previous flicker of recognition did not seem so odd.

Susan smiled "We travel in some of the same circles, you might say. Did he give you any other information? Like which plates?"

"Oh. Yes. The 1935 one-dollar plates. Also, he said you'd tell me about the Order and why they want them."

Susan gave her a hard look. "He did, did he?"

"Yeah."

"You really don't know who the Order is?"

Karen shook her head.

"Lord love a duck." Susan glanced skyward as if to ask for patience. "Okay. This is going to be a shock to you, I'm sure. You thirsty? I'm gonna get me some coffee and let the guards know about the impending break-in. Then, I'll be back and let you in on a few things."

"A Coke is fine."

"Okay. I'll be back."

Karen looked around. Susan's office was the kind seen on documentaries about archeologists and history professors that are cluttered just enough with interesting things of historical significance to give it the feel of a fake professional backdrop designed for the camera. Apparently, offices like that did exist.

She picked up a photocopied article about the Makah Indians by Ann M. Renker, Ph.D. called "The Makah Tribe: People of the Sea and the Forest." Karen knew they were a local indigenous Indian tribe of the Pacific Northwest, but beyond that and the fact that they had a Historical Center nearby, she didn't know anything about them at all.

It was a fascinating read. It kept her from noticing how long Susan had been gone until she was done with the article. For a moment, the worst case scenario popped into her head: The crooks had already broken in, had assaulted the museum curator and she was unconscious or bleeding somewhere.

Before the panic could really set in, the office door opened and Susan came in bearing drinks. She had changed her clothes as well. She was now in a pair of black jeans and a black sweater. "Sorry about the wait. I wanted to get into something a little more practical." She handed Karen the can of soda.

"It's okay."

"C'mon. Let's patrol the museum. I'll tell you what I can as we go."

They walked in silence through the darkened museum halls. To Karen, it was a little creepy.

Then again, empty buildings at night usually were. Susan seemed unaffected by their echoing footsteps. It made sense. This was Susan's territory. She probably spent many nights here after the museum closed to finish up work.

"What do you want to know first?"

"Who is the Order? What are they?"

Susan gave a half smile. "Their full name is the Order of the Sacred Eye. From what little I know, they seem to be an offshoot of the Masons. Maybe from the Brotherhood of Light as well."

"Masons? My father was a Mason, and he wouldn't have anything to do with trying to kill anyone or steal stuff from museums."

"Not the service organization of Masons that we know today. Probably a much older branch. Most likely they were once a secret society within the secret society. They are so far removed from the Masons now that it's probably like comparing chimps to humans. In any case, in Kendrick, they're the bullies of the magic world. Not necessarily evil. Just very selfish and self-serving."

"'Bullies of the magic world.'"

Karen's tone made Susan stop and look at her. "Oh, give me a break. You don't even know about that? Why the hell did Reginald pick you if you don't know anything at all? Surprise. Magic exists. Demons exist. Angels exist. And Kendrick seems to be a hub for all of the above and more. All of which is interpreted in a different way by each magical society that knows about it.

"A demon in one group may be considered to be a ghost in another or a totem spirit in another. Let's just pretend that you believe in magic. If you can't do that, pretend that there are lots of groups out there that believe in it and believe they can manipulate it. Okay?"

Karen bristled at Susan's condescension, then swallowed her ire because she didn't want to derail the conversation. "Sorry. This is just a little weird."

"It's going to get a lot weirder. Do you still want me to continue? Because if you don't, we can stop right here and you can go home."

Karen nodded. "I'm sure. Especially if this Reginald person's going to keep calling me to tell me about impending murders and thefts, asking for help." She paused. "Do you know who Reginald is?"

Susan looked at her for a long moment. "I think I'll let him answer that."

It was the kind of answer Karen expected. "But you trust him?"

Susan shrugged. "As much as I trust anyone in this city. All right. The Order, then. Personally, they remind me of the alpha frat on a college campus. Knowledgeable, arrogant, and pushy. Not to mention a bit too much into their secret agent man routine. They really like having all their secrets-within-secrets stuff. I've heard they call each other by codenames whenever they are doing something with or for the Order.

They're feared inside their fraternal organization by their peers and barely tolerated by other magical groups outside of it.

"The problem is that they actually do have power. What they know, they know well. From what I can tell, most of the magic they do is ritualistic, sympathetic magic. Frankly, not really reliable because of the randomness of the sympathetic part. But, it does work. Especially if they have a good sympathetic link to what they want to affect. If it's a person, they use hair or blood or clothing. If it's an organization, they use something that belongs to that organization and symbolizes it. I think that's why they want the plates."

They stopped in front of the large historical display of old coins, engraved plates, and bills no longer commonly used as legal tender. Susan pointed out one set of engraved plates and read the card underneath it.

"'The Great Seal was first used on the reverse of the one-dollar Federal Reserve note in 1935. The Department of State is the official keeper of the Seal. They believe that the most accurate explanation of a pyramid on the Great Seal is that it symbolizes strength and durability. The unfinished pyramid means that the United States will always grow, improve, and build. In addition, the "All-Seeing Eye" located above the pyramid suggests the importance of divine guidance in favor of the American cause.'" She looked at Karen. "Do you see why they want it?"

"Because of the All Seeing Eye? It's connected to them somehow?"

"Exactly. This is typical of them. If they want to do sympathetic magic on their own organization and they believe they are that important to the United States, of course they want a symbol that reflects that. Talk about arrogance. I—"

Her next words were lost in the sounds of glass breaking and something crashing to the ground. "Shit." Susan pulled a small figurine from her pocket. "Okay, kiddo. You're up. This is Karen. It's your job to protect her. If she puts you down or drops you, wake up and do your job." She turned to Karen and held it out to her. "Here. This is Sebastian. Hold him. If something bad happens, put him down or drop him."

Karen took the small figurine of a cute sleeping gargoyle and looked skeptically at Susan.

"Please. Just pretend you believe. Just for now," Susan looked over her shoulder at the sounds of a scuffle.

"All right. All right." Karen wrapped her hand around the statuette.

"You should be safe here. I'll be back." Susan didn't wait for a response. She took off running down the hallway yelling, "Be careful of the damn artifacts!"

Karen watched Susan go, wondering if the other woman was crazy or if she was crazy. Maybe both. However, there'd been enough odd calls for help on the emergency system to make some of what she had recently learned about Kendrick seem plausible. She opened her hand enough to look at the sleeping gargoyle figurine. "All right. Hello Sebastian. I'm Karen. If I need you, I hope you're more than you appear." She watched the gargoyle intently, looking for signs of life or magic.

Karen never saw what hit her from behind. All she knew was a blinding pain to the back of the head that made her fall to the floor. She watched the gargoyle figurine tumble across the floor before everything went away.

***

"Karen, wake up. Please, wake up. I can't carry you."

She tried to say, "Five more minutes, Mom." She managed a groan. Turning her head brought a fresh wave of pain that dumped enough adrenaline into her system to bring her back to reality.

Susan hovered over her, looking very worried. "We have to go now. Sebastian says he got some of your hair. That's not a good thing."

Karen let herself be hauled to her feet, helping as much as she could while fighting the nausea any movement seemed to bring. "Where?"

"Someplace safe. The less I say now the better. Come on."

The two women hurried to Susan's car. Karen was momentarily surprised to discover the museum curator drove a black hearse. Then, with a shrug, she slid into the passenger seat. "Did they get it?"

Susan started the car and took off down the street. "The plates? Yes. The insurance forms alone are going to be a nightmare. I thought you said that the Order hired a couple of guys to break into the place."

"That's what Reginald told me."

"Well, it was a couple of guys and a member of the Order. I don't know what he hit you with, but it wasn't physical. Plus, they took some of your hair. Dammit, I shouldn't have left you alone. I shouldn't have left you with just Sebastian. I didn't think it through."

"What happened? I hurt. I'm feeling better, but I still hurt."

"Apparently, he came in and knocked you out. You dropped Sebastian who woke up and went into guard mode. But, because he wasn't attacking you, Sebastian just watched him take the plates. He didn't get aggressive until the guy cut off some of your hair. That guy will remember in the future not to underestimate baby gargoyles because of their tiny size."

"Why'd he take my hair?"

"To do magic on you. I don't know what kind. That's why we're here."

They parked in front of Bacchanalia. "You go here?"

"You know this place?"

"It's a Goth club. I didn't think you... I don't know what I didn't think." Karen smiled sheepishly.

Susan returned the smile. "I'm not a suit-wearing museum acquisitions officer 24/7. I have a life, you know."

"Yeah. Sorry. I'm still figuring this thinking thing out."

"I'll chalk it up to what the guy did to you. Come on."

They walked through the nondescript gray door marked with the club's symbol and into the antechamber. Aaron and another guy were at the desk. "Hey Suze. Look at that, it's Karen-By-The-Way. Fancy seeing you again."

"Not now, Aaron. We need the Smoke Room."

Karen's sense of balance decided it was the perfect time to take a hike while her stomach felt like it was being dragged out of her body through her navel. She stumbled and slammed into the wall.

"Shit." Aaron hurried to Karen's other side and the two of them lifted her back to her feet. Half carrying her, they walked deeper into the club; down the hall, past the dance floor and bar, and into a back room, shutting the door behind them. It was still early, so few people were around. But all of them jumped to attention when Aaron and Susan brought Karen in and laid her on the couch.

"Light 'em up." Aaron called out.

Karen watched from her prone position. Two people lit incense burners in the corners of the room and the rest of the people lit cigarettes as they spaced themselves out around her. "What are they doing?"

"Hiding you." Susan touched Karen's forehead. "Are you feeling any better?"

She thought about it for a moment, then nodded. "Yeah. I think. Maybe. But, I feel weird. I feel like I'm really hungry... but that hunger is pulling me somewhere."

"Ah. Gotcha. A good description." Susan looked at Aaron, who was already heading to the door.

"I'll get her something to eat and drink."

"What's wrong with me?" Karen struggled to sit up, managing it with some dizziness.

Susan shook her head. "I think it's a reaction to the scrying. They're trying to learn what they can before we shut them down. I think that's what they're doing. I hope that's all. You showed up on the scene less than two weeks ago. No one knows who you are."

"I'm nobody. I'm just a 911 operator."

"Not anymore."

"I don't understand." Karen could hear the music from the dance floor through the wall and feel it pulsing through the soles of her feet.

"You will, eventually." Susan started to say more but Aaron returned with a plate of potato skins with cheese, chives, bacon, and sour cream on one side and deep fried cheese sticks on the other. She took it from him and handed it to Karen. "Eat. Eat as much as you can as fast as you can."

She looked at Aaron. "Sit with her? Make sure she eats. I've got to find out how to break this."

Aaron nodded and replaced Susan on the couch. "Eat up, luv."

"I'm tired." Her hunger had been replaced with an almost overwhelming lethargy.

"Don't make me feed you. I will, you know. It'll be messy and wasting bacon is a crime."

Karen tried to smile at him and picked up the loaded potato skin. The first bite was hard to manage, but the moment she swallowed, she was ravenous and did not have to be convinced to keep going.

As she wolfed down the last potato skin, and started on the deep-fried mozzarella sticks, someone arrived with a glass of Coke. She drank as she ate, focusing only on the food in front of her and in her mouth. It anchored her, somehow making her feel more real, more solid and there.

By the time she was done with the platter, having downed much more than she usually ate at one sitting, Susan was back. "Okay. I got it. I know what we need to do." Aaron moved out of her way as she reclaimed the spot next to Karen.

"I'm feeling much better now. Really. What else needs to happen?"

"That's mostly because we've hidden you from the magic. The connection between you and your hair is still there. They'd have you again as soon as you walked out of here. So, we need to break that connection." She pulled a small gargoyle figure from her pocket. "Remember him?"

"Is that Sebastian?"

Susan nodded.

"But, he's sitting up. Not sleeping."

"I know. Just pretend you believe in all this, all right? It's still him."

Karen nodded and accepted the statuette, looking at him. "He's got blood on him."

"I know." Susan started messing with Karen's hair.

She pulled away, alarmed. "What are you doing?"

"Looking for the spot he took your hair from."

"I'll find it." She put the gargoyle in her lap and ran her fingers through her hair until she found the short section and swore. "He took a chunk from me. Do you know how long it takes to get my hair this long?"

"Sorry. I don't." Susan clumped the cut hair together. Another bejeweled goth girl handed her a lit cigarette.

"Whoa. What are you doing?"

Suppressing a sigh, Susan asked. "Do you trust me?"

"No. Actually, I don't. Just tell me what you're doing."

Aaron barked a sharp laugh. "She's learning."

Susan nodded. "Fair enough. I'm going to sever the connection by burning the edges of your hair where the stolen hair was cut from, then snip the burned edges off. Think of it as cauterizing the wound."

Karen thought about it, and could not deny what she'd recently felt. "Okay. You can do it."

"Thanks." Susan began carefully singeing the ends of Karen's hair while Aaron snipped the burned ends off into a small bowl. When they were both done, the bowl was put on the table. "Okay. Put this cone into the bowl and light it."

Karen did as she was asked, still holding the gargoyle, rubbing it like a worry stone. The cone lit up with a flash. "That wasn't incense."

"No. It wasn't." Susan and Aaron grinned at each other.

"Do I want to know what it was?"

"I don't know. Do you?"

She thought about it for a few moments then shook her head. "No. Not yet. Not now. Soon. Now, I just want to get a few hours of rest before my shift starts."

"Okay. I'll take you back to your car. We can talk more later." Karen started to hand the gargoyle back. Susan shook her head. "Keep him. He's yours. He likes you. You were his first duty. He wants to go with you."

For some reason, this made her smile. She slid Sebastian into her pocket and nodded. "Okay."

***

Elsewhere...

The assassin bound Praetor's hand. "It was definitely her. I marked her. I knew her as soon as I saw her again. That's why I took no chances."

"Apparently, you took one." Praetor gestured at Todesengel's face. "A big one."

"How was I supposed to know she had control of a gargoyle? We know nothing of her. Now she's interfered with the Order's plans, or tried to, twice in as many weeks."

"We do have something."

"I have a ruined face and you have a burned hand."

"My hand will heal. So will your face. Though, it will take longer because of the supernatural claw marks, but it will heal. I'll see if I can find something in the books to make that go faster. But we were still victorious tonight. We retrieved the plates, and we know one very important fact."

"What?"

"She's somehow connected to the Master of the City."

Todesengel paused. "You got that from the scrying?"

The other man nodded. "It makes all this so much more interesting, doesn't it?"

They looked at each other and smiled, thinking the same thought: the Order had found a sympathetic link to their most hated rival.

Arbiter

KAREN STARED AT the gargoyle figurine. It was in a sleeping pose next to her computer monitor. Last night, it was in a sitting position over by the printer. Yesterday, she'd found it sitting on the kitchen countertop. That last one had prompted the call to Susan that included a very surreal conversation.

"Well, what do baby gargoyles eat?"
"Meat and junk food usually."
"Meat's better for them?"
"I don't know. I've never seen a fat gargoyle. Not around here. I know some of them have a real sweet tooth."
"Okay. But, would he rather have raw meat or cooked meat?"
"Have you asked him?"
"Um. No. I've never seen him move. I just know he does."
"Maybe you should ask him."
"What if he answers?"
"I'd listen to him. Cranky gargoyles are a handful."

Karen picked it up and looked at it. "Sebastian? Would you talk to me? I'd like to know what you want to eat." The figurine sat unmoving in her hand. No sign of life. "Please?" Still nothing. Maybe it really was sleeping. It seemed to be active only when she was not around. Maybe it was a night owl like her. She really needed a lesson in Gargoyles 101 even if part of her still wanted to deny their existence.

Her ringing cell phone distracted her from her thoughts on the care and feeding of gargoyles. She was surprised to see the name "REGINALD" in the caller ID window. "Hello?"

"Hello, Karen."

It was him. "Hello, Reginald. I see you aren't 'unknown' anymore."

"Yes. I know. I thought it would be more friendly to appear like this now that you know who I am."

"Do I?"

"You know that what I say is the truth."

"Yes... but who are you? Really. Who are you?"

He paused for a long time. "I'm someone who cares for the people of Kendrick. I do what's best for them and for me."

"Are you magical like the Order and like the people at Bacchanalia and Susan with her gargoyles?"

"Yes. You could say that."

For a moment, she did not know how to respond. She had not expected him to be so bluntly honest. "Oh. Um. Are you at war with the Order?" It was the only question she could think to ask.

"No. Not really. I don't agree with their goals regarding the city most of the time. But, it's not war. There is a give and take in the city. Sometimes, they forget that and I need to step in. We all have rules we have to follow."

"What rules? Are you going to tell me about these rules?"

"Yes. A little bit at a time. That's why I called you. I need your help."

"Color me shocked. Since you don't sound too rushed this time, I'm going to assume it doesn't involve attempted murder or immediate theft."

He chuckled. "That's correct. Two people have requested arbitration in a matter very important to them. I would like you to be my representative in this. Listen to both of them, and then make a decision for one or the other."

"Arbitrate what? Why can't you do it?"

"It's a dispute over the ownership of an artifact. I'll do it with you as my representative."

"How do you know I'll make the right decision?"

"You will. I believe in you, Karen. Go to the Colonel's Park where the chessboards are. You'll see two men sitting at the last chessboard table. Mr. Corso and Mr. Coleman. They'll be waiting for you at three this afternoon."

"Just go, introduce myself, listen, and judge?"

"Yes. Your decision is final. They cannot, and will not, dispute it. They requested the arbitration. That is one of the rules of the city."

"What if I don't go?"

"It's your choice. However, if you don't, these two men will spend their afternoon waiting in the park for someone who never shows, and their quarrel will continue. There may even be some unpleasantness between them."

"Wonderful. Since you put it that way, I'll do it."

"Thank you."

"Do you want me to call you when I'm done?"

"No. The decision will get back to me in other ways."

"Okay...I guess I'll talk to you later."

"Thank you for everything. We will talk again soon."

She hung up the phone and realized that, for the first time, she hadn't ended a conversation with the mysterious

Reginald feeling overwhelmed and out of her depth. In truth, she was actually looking forward to this arbitration. She was curious and it would give her more insight into her city—a city she was coming to understand that she did not know at all.

She reopened the phone and looked at the incoming caller history. "Reginald" was there but when she viewed the details, his incoming phone number was listed as '111-111-1111.' She shrugged without ire. It had been worth a shot.

***

The walk to Colonel Kendrick Park, at the center of the city, was beautiful. Though there were many clouds in the sky, the sun was bright when it appeared. Spring had arrived. You could see it in the budding flowers and the returning birds. The crisp air smelled wonderful.

Karen stood in front of the low stone wall that circled the park. It was a clear boundary between the bustling downtown city center and the quiet, forested area. Karen loved the way the city government insisted on keeping the city center for the smaller independent stores and restaurants around the park. It made the whole place perfect for walking, sightseeing, and picnicking.

Following the path through the trees, she passed the very center of the Colonel's Park where a statue of the city's founder, Colonel Kendrick, stood. All of the tourist information guides proudly proclaimed that the Colonel's statue stood at the exact center of the city. Until recently, she had thought it nothing more than a marketing gimmick. Now, she wondered. She also wondered if this was the park that Reginald had warned could and would take care of itself. It made sense. Sort of. A park at the center of the city must have some sort of magical significance, but how it would protect itself, she wasn't sure. There was still so much to learn about this city of hers.

She reached the play area of the park designed for people to stay and relax. There was a small playground, some picnic tables, shuffleboard, horse shoe pits and, finally, the main attraction, the chessboard tables. Mr. Coleman and Mr. Corso were not hard to spot. The two men sat at the last table, away from the rest of the chess players. They sat facing each other with their hands on the chessboard. She could see the tension in them from this distance through their body language.

As she walked closer, she saw that they were both handsome, each in his own way: One had a more presentable, professional sense to his dress and styling. The other was more scholarly with his tweed jacket, goatee, and glasses.

Her stomach fluttered as she walked up to the table, wondering if she really could handle what was about to be put before her. "Good afternoon, gentlemen. My name is Karen." She paused, deciding not to give her last name. "Reginald sent me."

Both men stood and offered their hands.

"Luke Coleman." The professional-looking man shook her hand.

"John Corso." The scholarly-looking man shook her hand in turn.

They sat when she sat.

"Do you mind if I smoke?" Mr. Corso showed her a cigarette.

Karen glanced at the other man who shrugged. "No. That's fine." She paused as both men watched her. She realized they were waiting with patient respect for her to begin. The idea of it unnerved her, but she pushed those feelings aside.

"We all know why we are here. I'm going to listen to you both and decide who is right. I promise that both of you will have a chance to speak. What I would like is for each of you to give me a short synopsis of the issue. Which of you is the one bringing the complaint?"

"He is." Mr. Coleman gestured to the other man. "You don't know anything about this situation?"

"Pretend I know nothing at all," she smiled, knowing it was mostly the truth. "Consider me your completely unbiased arbiter. I don't know either of you. I have no investment in the outcome at all."

"Fine by me." Mr. Corso said. "Synopsis. A friend of mine, Sally Mayflower, gave me a gift. She died the morning I went to pick it up from her. I was barred from the house. By the time I was able to see the executor of the Will, the house had been turned over to Lucas here for liquidation. The family, who never bothered to visit, just wanted the money from the sale of her possessions."

She nodded, then turned to Mr. Coleman, who nodded. "All I can vouch for is the fact that the house, and all its possessions, were turned over to me by Mrs. Mayflower's executor at the request of the deceased's relatives. There was no notice that any item in the house belonged to someone else. No bill of sale. No mention of it in her Will."

"Gifts don't have a bill of sale." Mr. Corso's voice was rough with distain.

"There's no proof that she gave it to you. Not even a gift tag."

"Gentlemen, please." Karen cut off the obviously well-practiced argument before it could begin again. Both men bristled, but said no more. "Who has the item?"

"I do." Mr. Colemen tapped his bag.

"May I have it?"

He hesitated, then reached into the leather satchel and brought out a small wooden box about six inches by nine inches and an inch deep. It was carved with simple swirls around the edges. He seemed reluctant to hand it over, but did so. Karen set it on the table and opened it up, very curious. She noticed both men tense as she did so. She did not know what she was expecting, but this was not it. Inside, resting on a bed of cotton, was an oversized card.

It was beautiful.

The focus of the card was a three-quarter standing profile of a severe-looking man with a weak chin. He wore a white ruffled shirt, beige pantaloons, a black morning coat with lapels, and knee-high boots. On his head perched a black felt hat. In one hand was a riding crop and a pair of gloves. He was reaching for the set of balanced scales that sat on the table before him. Behind him was a horse field and this man, this judge, had just come in from riding a horse. She did not know how she knew this any more than she knew the coat was velvet and the pantaloons were corduroy. At the top of the card was "*XI*" and at the bottom was the word "*JUSTICE*." The edges were bordered in gold gilt. The colors of the card were vividly alive to the point of movement. The man's hair almost seemed to stir in the wind as she stared at it.

"What is it?" Karen asked.

"A tarot card." Mr. Coleman said.

"A tarot card? Is that all you can say? Just 'a tarot card?'" Mr. Corso mimicked his adversary's voice.

Karen looked up from the card and looked between the two glaring men. "Maybe one of you would like to tell me a little bit more about this particular tarot card?" It was not like any other one she had ever seen.

Mr. Coleman gestured at Mr. Corso. "You do it. You'll just interrupt me if I explain its history."

"I'd be happy to." Mr. Corso turned to Karen. "Have you ever heard of Rinaldo Todari?"

She shook her head. "No. Who is he?"

"I'm not surprised. He's an early nineteenth-century Italian painter. The only noteworthy thing he painted was a set of tarot cards now known as the Todari Tarot. It took him eleven years just to paint the Major Arcana. This card, Justice, is from that set and was completed on November 1st, 1814.

"For some reason, Mr. Todari, who started painting these cards in 1811, only completed each card on May 1st and November 1st each of the thirty-nine years it took to complete the whole set. Each card is an amazing work of art in its own right. If you pick it up, you'll note that the card is not made of paper. Each card is actually painted on a thin placard of wood."

She picked it up and turned the card on edge. She saw the decoration on the back of the card was a faded pair of entwined roses and saw that he was right; it really was wood. "How much would one of these cards go for?"

"That depends on the seller," Mr. Corso said.

"And the buyer," Mr. Coleman added.

"If it could be sold at all," Mr. Corso finished.

Karen nodded and put it back in the box. She had a better idea of why these two men were fighting over the card. It was time to get down to business. She had to decide which of them it actually belonged to: the man who claimed it was a gift, or the man who had received it as part of an estate liquidation request.

"Technically, doesn't this card really belong to Mrs. Mayflower's inheritors?"

"No." Mr. Coleman shook his head. "Mrs. Mayflower's inheritors have already received a sum of money for the estate. They were very pleased with the settlement."

"One cannot buy this card. That is not the way these things are done." It was clear Mr. Corso was having a difficult time controlling his temper.

"Mr. Corso." Karen lowered her voice, as she did to calm hysterical people on the phone. "Did you agree to this arbitration?"

"Yes."

"Please trust that I will listen to both sides of this, including your beliefs on how the card should change hands. If I don't ask a question you believe should be answered, you will have a chance to ask the question and answer it. Continuing to argue is not going to help matters. Please."

Mr. Corso nodded, looking away. He took a drag on his cigarette.

She turned back to Mr. Coleman. "When did this estate settlement go through?"

"Yesterday morning."

"When did Mrs. Mayflower die?"

"About ten days ago."

"So, she died, had her internment, the reading of the Will, and the inheritor's liquidation request in less than ten days?" She frowned. "Isn't that a bit fast?"

"For some, yes. For others, no."

"How did you manage to sell the Mayflower estate so quickly?"

"I didn't. I got the request. I looked over the estate. I determined its worth and offered the inheritors a sum of money. This is the normal mode of things. Most inheritors don't want to wait months or years until the entire estate sells. Money upfront soothes the passing." He smiled at her.

She nodded, trying to keep her personal thoughts about that last statement out of her head. "All right, Mr. Coleman, tell me why you believe this card should remain with you?" She kept half an eye on Mr. Corso to keep track of his mood and reactions. He seemed to have calmed down after her promise to listen to both sides.

"It's very simple. Legally, the card is mine. The Executor approached me on the behalf of the inheritors. I looked at the estate, tallied its worth, and offered the inheritors a lump sum, which they accepted." He reached into his bag and brought out a couple pieces of paper. "Here is the written request. Here is the bill of sale."

She looked over the documents, noting that the bill of sale was on letterhead. *'Treasures & Trinkets. One man's junk is another man's treasure.'* She tapped the letterhead. "Is this your company?"

He nodded. "I've been in the antique business for a long time. Estate sales are nothing new to me. Neither are scam artists." That last remark was clearly directed at Mr. Corso, who continued to smoke without comment.

"Explain what you mean."

"I frequently get people coming in claiming that Aunt Mabel really wanted them to have her fine china and that it wasn't supposed to be liquidated. So, I should just give it to them. Or, buy it from them for a modest fee." He shook his head. "No, it's not uncommon. That is why all sales are final, and I only work with the Executors of the Wills."

Karen nodded. "Is there anything else I ought to know?"

He shook his head. "No. The law is clear here."

"Why did you agree to this arbitration, Mr. Coleman?"

"Let's just say that no one liked where this disagreement was headed, and the Master of the City was the logical choice to put an end to it without anymore unpleasantness."

Karen forced her next question, 'Who is the Master of the City?' to the back of her throat.

Instead she coughed to cover things up. That answer was clear. He was talking about Reginald. She would talk about it with him the next time they spoke and insist on a way to contact him when she needed to. She turned her attention to the other man. "Mr. Corso, why do you believe this Todari Tarot card belongs to you?"

He lit another cigarette. "The short answer is because Sally gave it to me. However, since you are already aware of my claim but not familiar with the Todari Tarot, allow me to explain some things about it that Mr. Coleman has neglected to mention. The first of which is that the Todari Tarot is *not* to be sold. Ever.

"In 1841, when Rinaldo gave his set of tarot cards to his apprentice, he did so as a gift with the warning that the cards were special. Each one was a gift in its own right and the deck could not be sold. To do so would diminish it. Since then, even though the deck has been broken up, no one buys a Todari Tarot card. They are bartered for services, inherited, found, or given as gifts. That is the way it is done. To buy even one card would make it less. Would make the whole deck less."

"Make it less how? I'm not quite sure what you mean."

"From the research I've done, it seems that each card required some sort of sacrifice. We think. Each card was modeled after a specific place or person. From what I've determined, this card was modeled after an English judge, Christopher Howland, who had been on holiday in Italy at the time. He died on November 10th, 1814. Just nine days after the Justice card was completed.

"For the cards I confirmed the models for; each died or went into a coma shortly after the completion of the card. I believe they gave their lives willingly. A gift. To sell a card would lessen that sacrifice." He had leaned towards her so she could smell the cigarette smoke on him. It was slightly sweet, and reminded her of chai tea.

"Oh, come on." Mr. Coleman interrupted. "You don't believe that. And even if you do, that's not the reason you want the card."

"Mr. Coleman, please. You had your say. Let Mr. Corso have his." Karen pulled herself up. In a way, she was glad for the interruption. She had been more than halfway to believing Mr. Corso's story about the card's supernatural past.

"I'm sorry, but I can't just sit by and let him lie to you. He is one of the leading Todari Tarot card collectors. That's why he's so hot for it."

"That's enough." She let an edge of her irritation rise in her voice. She had wanted to hear the rest of the story, but she did have a job to do. She turned back to Mr. Corso.

"It's true. I am the leading collector. I've worked for more than half my life to gather all of these cards. My goal is to collect the full set and ensure that they remain together as long as I live. But, I'm not lying about Sally giving me the card." He took a drag on his cigarette. "I will admit that I made her acquaintance only because I knew she had it. But, I've known that for years, and I've been her friend for years. We used to have coffee together once a week at Kahili Coffee House. We'd been doing that for years, too. She knew I wanted the card, and she knew it had to be a gift. It was hard for her to give it up."

"Why do you think she gave it to you now?"

"I think she realized she was at the end of her life, and she wanted to give it to me. To tell you the truth, I had stopped asking about it many months ago. She was such a wonderful woman. She had led such a full and interesting life.

Two weeks ago, she said to me, 'John, I've decided. You can have the Todari Justice card. You've earned it, spending so much time with this old woman.' I protested, 'Sally Mayflower, don't you dare tease me. Besides, I gave up on that a while ago.' 'I know, but you still kept seeing me anyway.' 'Because you're so lovely.' 'Pshaw.' She said, 'Now you're the one teasing. I'm not teasing you. I'm giving you the card. Come by the house on Friday and get it.' 'Are you sure?' I asked. She said, 'Yes, I'm sure. I give it to you with my whole heart because a gift given any other way isn't a gift at all.' She meant it, too."

That last bit about the gift given with the whole heart struck Karen. It jarred a memory loose, and she realized she knew who Sally Mayflower had been: her third grade teacher.

Mrs. Mayflower had been everyone's favorite teacher. She could still hear the woman's voice as she answered a child's question on whether or not she really meant what she said in her Valentine's Day card to them. *'Of course, my dear. I meant every word then and still do. It was a gift from my heart and a gift not given with the whole heart isn't a gift at all.'*

Mrs. Mayflower had been the kind of teacher who listened to the kids and had done what was right, not just what was expected. She had been known to bend the rules if she judged that the situation needed it. Karen nodded to him. "Is there anything else you want me to know?"

He shook his head.

She looked at Mr. Coleman. "Any last words from you?"

"Just to remember that I did not steal the card. It came into my possession fair and square. The law stands behind me."

She glanced at Mr. Corso.

"History stands behind me."

Karen nodded. "I'm going to take a quick walk to think. Please wait here." She saw them both tense up again when she picked up the box containing the card, but neither man said a word.

Karen walked towards the playground, replaying the conversation in her head. In one point of view, it was clear that Mr. Coleman was the rightful owner. In the other, it was Mr. Corso. She could see why this had come to arbitration. No matter what she decided, someone was going to walk away angry.

"Karen?" The man's vaguely familiar voice brought her out of her thoughts. "Karen Wilson?"

She turned and saw a young man standing there, looking at her expectantly. For a brief wild instant, she wondered if it was Reginald. Almost immediately, she dismissed the notion. "Yes. May I help you?"

He smiled. "You don't recognize me, do you? People only remember the blue uniform."

"Oh. Officer Hauberk. Hello."

"Just David, please. I'm not on duty." He gestured to his jeans and t-shirt. "What are you doing here?"

She looked over at the chess table and saw that both men were on their feet, watching. She realized they thought she either might be in danger or about to steal the card. She held a calming hand out to them, gesturing for them to sit again. "I'm, um, deciding something."

David glanced at the men at the table. "Oh? Deciding between two suitors? It's not very fair of them to do that to you."

"No. No. It's nothing like that. I don't have a suitor." She felt the blush rise to her cheeks.

"In that case, if you're almost done, would you like to take a walk and maybe get some dinner?" He looked away self-consciously. "You know. To talk. Completely off the record and all that." He glanced back at her. "I've been a beat cop a long time. I've seen some pretty interesting things. Things that I don't always report. I thought, maybe we could talk about that night some."

She tilted her head and smiled. She realized that her mind had already made its decision and had been waiting for the rest of her to catch up. "I'd like that. Let me go finish this up."

He nodded and sat on a swing to wait for her.

She walked back to the two men. "I've made my decision. Mr. Coleman, you're right in the fact that the normal law stands behind you on this matter. However, I think that by agreeing to the arbitration, you acknowledge that this was not a matter for the normal law.

"Mr. Corso, you're right in the fact that a gift does not come with a price tag, but there was no other indicator that what you were saying was the truth.

"However, as it turns out, I knew Mrs. Mayflower many years ago. She was once my teacher. I had forgotten until Mr. Corso repeated part of a past conversation with her to me. As Mr. Corso did not know that and neither of you were aware that I would be sent in to arbitrate, I am confident that it was not a set up on Mr. Corso's part. Because of this, I judge in favor of Mr. Corso. It is clear to me that he did have a friendly relationship with Mrs. Mayflower and she did willingly give him the Todari Tarot card as a gift."

Mr. Coleman smiled a smile that did not reach his eyes. "Is that your final judgment?"

"It is."

He nodded and stood. "I did agree to this, and I will abide by it. I acknowledge that the Todari card belongs to Mr. Corso." He paused. "I wish it could have gone another way, but that's the way the cookie crumbles. Please feel free to come by *Treasures & Trinkets* sometime, Karen. No hard feelings."

"Thank you. I will."

They shook hands and Lucas Coleman walked away without looking back. She turned to Mr. Corso and handed him the box with the card. "I believe this belongs to you."

He accepted the box with a genuine smile. "Thank you, Karen. So very much. If you want, come by the *Teller's Fortune*, my store, and I'll show you some of the other cards I've collected. Tell you the stories I know of them."

"All right. That would be nice. Are the rest as pretty as that one?"

"Yes and more so in some cases." He put out his cigarette. "Karen, I'd be careful about going to Lucas's store. He's not a nice man and sometimes...there are strings attached to his wares."

"Are you a nice man, John Corso?"

"Sometimes, yes. Sometimes, no. Right now, yes." He offered her his hand. "Thank you for listening."

She shook it. "You're welcome." She watched him walk away in the opposite direction that Mr. Coleman had gone.

"Well, that was interesting. Can I ask what that was all about?" David walked up beside her.

"No. Not right now. I think I need some caffeine."

"Okay, Miss Wilson, after you." He held a hand out towards the path.

She smiled at him as they started walking towards one of her favorite cafés. "You know, I did try to call you a couple days ago. All the circuits were busy."

"That's strange. Let me give you my personal number once we get to wherever it is we're going."

"Dana Street Café."

"Good choice. So, why were you calling?"

"Doesn't matter now."

"All right. But, now you have me curious, and a curious David is a dangerous thing."

"I'll keep that in mind." She smiled at him.

***

Elsewhere...

"Praetor, I just got off the phone with Lucas Coleman. The arbitration didn't go his way. He's pretty upset about it." Nightshade, his secretary and sometimes lover, interrupted his thoughts.

"We did everything we were supposed to do. We got the Mayflower Will read, convinced the Executor to go to Coleman, and assisted in convincing the Mayflower heirs to settle at that generous price, and we fronted part of the money."

"I realize that, but as Lucas pointed out, he fulfilled his part of the bargain by getting us the original map of Kendrick in order to get the Todari card."

"Does he want the map back?"

"No. But, he says we now owe him and owing a creature like him is not a good thing for the Order."

"Fine. Fine. We'll burn that bridge when we get to it. As long as he doesn't want the map back."

"There's one other thing. He said the arbiter was a dark-haired girl named Karen who seemed curiously ignorant to be the representative of the Master of the City. Either that or she was playing a good game."

"The Wilson girl was the arbiter? Representing of the Master of the City? Are you sure?"

"He seemed sure."

"Good. That's all the confirmation we need. Find a way to get close to her. Use someone outside the Order. Try and make it someone she already knows."

"Yes, sir."

"I have work to do." He dismissed her with a wave of his hand and returned his thoughts to the objects before him: an engraved plate of the backside of a one dollar bill, an antique map of the city of Kendrick, a set of iron keys, and a large, tome-like book.

Forgotten School Days

KAREN STARED AT the ruins of the Colman School. It was all red brick and white columns but abandoned, broken, dirty, and forgotten. Weeds grew through the cracks in the cement and the ivy had taken over one section of the once beautiful building.

"This is it." Karen looked at the building. "Is it safe?"

Don't know. Never been here. Didn't know it was here.

She smiled at Sebastian's suspicious tone. The words in her head took on a different weight with his moods. It was new and interesting to feel. Then again, just about everything with Sebastian was new and interesting. "How's that possible? Is this one of those places you can't go?"

No. It wasn't here before.

"Clearly, it was. Just hidden. Somehow." Karen frowned. "Now it's calling to me. You sure it's not another gargoyle?"

I'm sure. It's not one of mine. Be careful.

"I will." She walked up the concrete steps, eyeing the tall columns with some trepidation.

I'm here. I'll protect you.

"I know. Just not used to all of this. I'm getting used to you but this..." Karen stopped as the child's voice came to her again.

Karen! Help me. Please. Free me. Take me home.

The begging voice, pleading for freedom, tore at Karen's heart. Sebastian appeared next to her. *That wasn't me.*

"I know. I have to help her." She didn't know why she thought it was a little girl. It was a feeling she was going with. Any fears that the building might fall down upon her disappeared. All of Karen's considerable will turned towards rescuing that small voice from wherever it was trapped.

***

Cheshire sat in uncomfortable silence as the entire Order filed in and took their seats. He watched from the center of the ritual space, the only room large enough to house a full Conclave meeting. Full Conclaves were rare. They had been called only five times in twice as many years that he could remember. He was the only one who had called more than one in the Order's recent memory.

There was a reason for that: Calling a full Conclave was to put oneself on trial. Since any member of the Order, from the lowest acolyte to the most revered leader, could call for a full Conclave, the risk kept the members from spuriously calling one and wasting everyone's time. However, the reward of winning the Conclave was immense. A fact he intimately knew.

The room was set up just as it had been in every previous Conclave. Those on trial sat in the center. To the right was the table where the Council presided. They would question him and his reason for the Conclave. Before him sat the rest of the Order. The Council would question, but he would answer to the Order itself. The Council would watch, listen, and determine if his reasoning was valid or not. It was. Just as it had been before, he knew it was now. This knowledge did not stop him from feeling the cooling stickiness of his nervous sweat.

The muted conversations hushed as the Council members entered and took their seats at the table. Nightshade remained standing. Like the others, she wore her formal robes and her sash of office. As the Secretary of the Order, she opened the Conclave with the ritualistic words, "The Conclave is called. Look to your peers. If any do not belong, cast them out." She paused as every member of the Order looked around and identified those nearest to them. When the rustling stopped, she continued. "All are accepted. Who has called for the Conclave?"

Cheshire stood. It was the last time he was allowed to stand as one of them until the Conclave was finished. "I have called for the Conclave. I am Cheshire. I am known to the Order of the Sacred Eye. Will you hear me?"

Nightshade made a mark on her paper and turned to the table.

The seated woman stood. "I am Cerridwen, Third in the Order of the Sacred Eye and Mistress of Magic. I will hear you."

The farthest seated man stood. "I am V'ger, Second in the Order of the Sacred Eye. I will hear you."

The center seated man stood. "I'm Praetor, First in the Order of the Sacred Eye. I will hear you."

"The Council has spoken. Will any within the Order deny Cheshire his right to be heard?"

Nightshade looked around at the silent room and paused before intoning, "The Council and the Order of the Sacred Eye will hear our peer, Cheshire. The Conclave is now in session and cannot be broken until the matter Cheshire brings before us is completed to the Order's satisfaction."

The Council members sat again. "Cheshire, why have you called for a Conclave?" Praetor asked. He would be the main questioner.

"I wish to report that the Master of the City has directly attacked the Order, and to ask for help in thwarting his attempt to take down one of the Order's own."

"Explain."

"Nine years ago, a malicious and untrue scandal broke out about me at the school where I was the Vice Principal. Several children went missing, and I was accused. My life was in ruins, the Order was in danger, and I called a Conclave then for help to stop the persecution against us. Obviously, the Order felt it was the correct action, as I am still here today." His eyes sought out and found his allies in the audience. He spoke to them. "The Order worked a great magic to cease the persecution."

"For the younger members of the Order, explain the magical working we did to help you."

Cheshire didn't like the way the First broke him out of the Order and made him an individual. It had been to help the entire Order. Not just him. He knew enough not to argue the point and nodded.

"It all took place at the Colman School. Our working shut down the school and transferred the children to the remaining junior high schools. Most of the teachers and administrators were moved into the other schools or into the administration of the school district. Then, the school was obfuscated and made to be forgotten. All stories about the scandal were shelved. All investigations closed.

"This brings me to today and the reason I have called for a Conclave. The Master of the City has broken our magical working. He has made the forgotten school remembered. He has put the Order in danger once more. We need to fix our working and deal with the Master. This is a direct attack on us all."

The audience members murmured in concern, to his relief. Until now, they had been silent, still, and unreceptive. It was very different from the previous Conclave he had called. Then, people had listened and agreed with him from the beginning. This time... there were so many more faces... so many he did not really know. Cheshire's relief faltered as he glanced over to the Council table and saw Nightshade handing out files filled with papers. He watched the Council members open the files and saw pictures included with the papers, but was too far from the table to see their contents.

Praetor looked up at that moment and caught his eye, "Tell us why you consider this a direct attack on the Order by the Master of the City."

His tongue stuck to the roof of his mouth. He turned back to the audience and cleared his throat. "The person who found the Colman School and brought it to the attention of the authorities was Karen Wilson, a known representative of the Master. She has interfered with the Order before: she prevented the assassination of our enemy Lamiel; attempted to stop the acquisition of the one dollar plates from the museum; halted the building of a new commerce center we, the Order, wanted to assist ourselves and our allies; and she ruled against us in two arbitrations sent to the Master of the City. She is his chosen representative. She must have broken the magic working we did and dredged up the past, putting the Order in danger once more. It is the Master who is attacking us through this girl."

"If we were to rule on your behalf, what would you want the Order to do for you and this situation?"

"Seal the breach in the magical working around the school and confront the Master of the City by either challenging or removing Karen Wilson. Perhaps, we could bind her in some way to stop her from interfering with us again."

"Excuse me?" A woman from the audience stood. "May I ask a question? Am I allowed to do that?"

Praetor looked at the young woman and nodded. "Cheshire is to answer to the Order as a whole, whether it be the First or the Last who questions him and his reasoning."

Nightshade stood and intoned in a not-quite bored voice, "The Council recognizes Corelli."

"I don't know who to ask—" She gestured at the Council table, then to Cheshire, "—but, when the magical working was done nine years ago, why didn't the Order just use magic to find the missing children? Wouldn't that have solved all the problems?"

Praetor looked at Cheshire to answer her.

"Because they were dead," Cheshire was taken off guard. Last time, no one except the Council had questioned him. Members of the Order not on the Council had always stayed silent. He had not taken that possibility into account this time. He mentally kicked himself for losing the opportunity to plant the appropriate questions to get the Order to see things his way.

"How did you know?"

"What?"

"How did you know?" Corelli voice was suspicious. "How did you know that the children from nine years ago were dead and finding them with magic wouldn't help?"

Cheshire had no answer that would please anyone in the room. This was not going as he had planned. He was bringing to light a great danger against the Order, and all they could do was prattle on about the past?

Cerridwen spoke for the first time, derailing the uncomfortable line of questioning with a worse one. "Why would Karen Wilson's finding the forgotten school prompt an investigation by the Kendrick police?"

He gritted his teeth to stop himself from shouting obscenities at the woman. He knew she had the answer before her. The old bat had never liked him. "She found the body of a child."

"I didn't hear you."

"She found the body of a child in the ruins of the school." He took a breath to calm himself. He needed to be calm. If he was calm, he could calm the audience again. He had to think. He had to turn this around.

"Where?"

"Where what?"

"Where was the body of the child found?"

There was no getting around the question. "It was found in the closet of my old office. That's how I found out about all this. The police came to question... to speak to me about it." The answer caused an ominous ripple of whispered conversation through the audience. "But, I'm not a suspect. I'm just a person of interest."

"Isn't a new junior high school about to open?" V'ger asked.

"Yes." Cheshire tried to keep hold of himself. Perhaps, the Second would be his ally.

"Do you have a position in the new school?"

"Yes. I'm the new Principal. I was the logical choice with my time in service and my..." His voice trailed off at the look on V'ger's face, and knew the man was no ally of his.

"My daughter has been assigned to that new school."

Praetor took over the questioning again. "Did you kill those children from the Colman School, Cheshire?"

"What? Why are you asking me that?" Cheshire couldn't believe this was happening to him. "I love children. Why would I hurt them?"

"That isn't an answer."

"I called this Conclave because of a danger to the Order..." He saw nothing but angry faces in the audience. People who had called him friend and ally were now turned away or were scowling at him. There was no support there. He did not have to look at the Council table to know there was no support there either. There had never been any support. He realized that the Council had made up its mind before they even walked into the Conclave and he was a dead man.

His eyes darted about the room, seeking a haven or escape. He felt the garrote around his throat just as he started to bolt. Strong arms yanked him back into his seat, choking him. He knew it was Todesengel without looking.

Cerridwen spoke a word of power and Cheshire could no longer move. The garrote loosened a little. Just enough to allow him to breathe.

Praetor entered into his view, leaned down, and whispered, "You did bring to light a great danger to the Order, Thomas. You."

The First turned to the rest of the mystical Order and raised his voice. "It is clear that your opinion of Cheshire and the calling of this Conclave is one with mine and the Council's. His past and current actions endanger us and our mission. For his transgressions against the Order of the Sacred Eye, I hereby strip Cheshire of his status as a member of our honored group. He is no longer recognized; no longer known to us or one of us. Thomas Rutherford stands alone."

Thomas saw neither pity nor mercy in the faces of the audience. He wanted to rail against the injustice of this and how those he had helped and worked with were stabbing him in the back. His self-righteous anger warred with his helplessness, the two emotions feeding each other until he was a seething mass of impotent fury.

"What do we do with those who stand alone?" Praetor asked.

"Cast him out!" was the unified shout.

"Is the Order sure in this matter?"

"Cast him out," was the repeated answer.

Praetor raised his hands. "The Order of the Sacred Eye has spoken." He looked at Nightshade.

"The Order of the Sacred Eye declares Thomas Rutherford to be Outcast. The matter before the Order is completed. The Conclave is ended." Nightshade ticked off items on her list. "The First Circle is to remain behind to deal with the Outcast."

Thomas watched people file out of the room except for those of the First Circle. He saw that some people had looks of glee and hatred on their faces while others had looks of concern or confusion. But, not one of them would speak for or to him. He heard Corelli ask, "What will they do with him now?" Another member told her that he was to be bound in such as way as to never speak of the Order's secrets. It was a precaution against dangerous ex-members. The answer seemed to satisfy her as they left the room.

He suspected he would not be so lucky as to simply be bound to not speak his knowledge of the Order. His own magical ability that had allowed him to rise as high as he had, would preclude that. He could, with time, break most bindings. Being the vindictive man that he was, he would break it. He knew it. Praetor knew it. The others did as well.

Once all of the members of the Order, except the First Circle, had left, Praetor turned back to Thomas. "You really screwed the pooch this time, buddy. We've known of your... *proclivities*... for some time now. Some of us suspected it back during the first Conclave you called. Back then, you had allies to support you, and you were still useful to us. Now, you are not. But, that will change."

He stepped back as Todesengel lifted Thomas from the chair and made the helpless man kneel. Cerridwen came forward and placed a torc on the ground before him. Thomas saw his hatred mirrored in her eyes.

"We knew the working on the school was fading. We hadn't decided what to do about it. The Master of the City took the choice out of our hands. Normally, we would consider this sort of thing an act of war. However, in this case, you sick bastard, we think the Master of the City is right. He's just protecting our children from you. Had I known then what I know now, you wouldn't have lived."

"Don't worry, he won't hurt another child and he'll be useful to the Order one last time. The murder of a child murderer should be more than enough to empower the torc." Praetor and the others were setting up the ritual space for what was to come. "Also, Thomas, be assured that this issue will be dealt with. You will be found hanging in your home, an obvious suicide. There will be an appropriately tearful and apologetic note confessing to the child murders from nine years ago. It will be an open and shut case. The school will be razed in order to cleanse it of its awful memories. Who knows what will rise in its place?"

V'ger and Cerridwen took their places on either side of Praetor. "No matter what," Cerridwen said, "Kendrick is better off without the likes of you."

"Enough." Praetor gestured. "We have work to do. Let's get to it."

Thomas felt the garrote tighten around his neck. It hurt, but was not lethal. Not yet. His death would be as slow and as painful as possible.

After all, ritual deaths usually were.

**

Elsewhere...

"Technically, I don't think it was a ghost. It was a spirit." Susan shook her head. "But, I'm not sure. Non-corporeal beings aren't my specialty."

"Why did you say that, then?" Karen sipped her water.

"Well, you said that once you saw the school building appear before you, you could hear the child's voice, calling you for help."

"Sorta. I heard it calling, followed the voice, and found the school. Her voice got a lot stronger after that. Isn't that what ghosts do?"

"But this one called you by name and begged for help. For freedom. But, the freedom she wanted was not to be put to rest but to be taken somewhere else. Ghosts haunt one place. Right?"

Karen nodded. "I suppose. It was creepy for a little girl I could see through to tell me to take the ribbon from her skeleton and to take it to the 'pretty house on Yarrow Street.' If I hadn't seen her and the skeleton, I wouldn't have believed it."

"Oh, yes. The house on Yarrow Street. There is something special about it." Susan tapped her lip. "My gargoyles occasionally patrol that way. I don't tell them to. I guess that part of the city they can hear tells them to do so."

"Do you know the woman who lives there?"

"No. Sometimes, you know not to ask."

"It's Julie Steward."

"As in the Steward family? The Mayor and all that?" Susan sat up, alert and interested.

Karen nodded. "She's different. I don't know how. I just know she is. She wasn't surprised to see me. 'Reginald told me you were coming.' When I gave her the box with the ribbon, she touched it like the little girl had been someone special to her. I don't know. She told me that Lucy would have a good home now, and I swear I heard at least two little girls giggling. It makes me really curious."

"Don't."

"Don't what?"

"Don't get too curious. Not with the Steward family. It's not healthy."

Karen frowned as the barista brought their orders, but held her tongue to eat and drink for a minute. The coffee and food was amazingly good.

"Okay. I'll hold my questions for now. I'm still getting used to all this. Every time I think I have a handle on things, something new pops up." She looked around the Kahili Coffee House, smiling at the Hawaiian décor. With a lowered voice she asked, "This place is fantastic. Is it, you know, special? Like the club?"

Susan laughed. "The coffee may be a gift from the Gods, but no. It's not. Not every place that seems different in Kendrick is magical." She waved off Karen's blush of embarrassment. "Speaking of the club, are you going tonight?"

"Yeah. I'm meeting Aaron there for drinks and dancing."

"He does have quite the crush on you. What about David? Things not working out?"

"Don't look at me in that tone of voice. I'm allowed to date more than one guy at a time. I'm not exclusive, or even serious with either. Both are becoming good friends."

"Oh, yeah? Which one's the better kisser?"

"A lady never tells." Smiling, Karen sipped her coffee.

Sacrificium Memoriae

KAREN SAT IN what she had thought was a prime spot by the dance floor at Bacchanalia. It was near the bar, the bathrooms, and had a great view of the dance floor. When she was not dancing, she was people watching. She never understood why this table was always the last to fill up...until now. The strobe lights made frequent passes over it, temporarily blinding anyone sitting there if they happened to be looking in the wrong direction.

At this point, she didn't mind. She had figured out the timing of the lights and would close her eyes when they flashed her way. Otherwise, she would watch the dancers on the dance floor, nodding her head to the music, sipping her raspberry flavored drink called "Blood Tears."

All of the drinks had pretentious names like "Mortal Coil," "Dante's Folly," and "Foxglove Fix." It was part of the club's charm. Karen smiled at the most recent memory of dance floor pageantry.

With her eyes closed, feeling the pulse of the music and sensing the lights flashing, she could still see them in her mind's eye: Shirtless Guy and Lace Girl. She didn't know their names. That didn't matter.

Shirtless Guy had come out on the dance floor first. Long hair gathered in a single braid that hung down his back, sunglasses, black jeans, and, of course, no shirt. His style of dance was some kind of modified kata. Hard edges with fast, intricate movements that drew the eye.

Lace Girl had come out later when there were more dancers. She wore a strapless satin dress with a lace overlay. She was pure sensuality with a cross of belly dancing undulations and Egyptian arm motions.

Two very different styles of dance until their eyes met.

Karen had seen that moment of glances meeting and mingling. Instead of the usual break, the two had shifted closer, modifying their dances. His softened. Hers gained an edge. The two complemented each other.

At first, it was just the pleasure of the dance. Then, it subtly shifted into courtship with a permissive tilt of her head and playful smile that was returned in kind. Thus, the back and forth chase had begun. It was still going on when she opened her eyes again. Through the crowd, she could see the two of them and they were a joy to watch.

A touch on her shoulder took her attention from the dance floor. Lamiel stood next to her in her usual gothic Victorian finery. Her recovery from being thrown off the 16th Street Bridge had been amazingly quick. Karen suspected magical assistance, but did not ask. She had become quite good at selective curiosity. The music was loud enough that Lamiel didn't try to talk by the dance floor. Instead, she beckoned Karen to follow her towards the back of the club.

It was unusual for Lamiel to approach her directly. If she or the Bacchanalia Coven (as they called themselves) needed to get anything to or from Reginald, it was sent through Susan or Aaron. Despite Lamiel's pleasant, if exasperated, demeanor and always welcoming smile, she seemed to regard Karen as an interesting, though possibly dangerous, anomaly.

Karen's stomach flip-flopped as they passed the Smoke Room and headed into a part of the club she'd never been to before. She wondered what weirdness she was going to see now. Every time she thought she had a handle on Kendrick and the supernatural forces within it, she discovered she really knew nothing at all. Sometimes, it was very tiring.

Lamiel opened a door marked *"Private"* and led her inside. It was a small hallway with four doors, two on each side. She opened the first one on the right to reveal a normal-looking office and a young, red-haired woman in the usual gothic finery. Lamiel closed the door and sat behind the desk, gesturing for both Karen and the other girl to sit.

"Normally," Lamiel began without greeting or preamble, "I would not involve myself in a matter like this. However, Heather—" she gestured to the other girl, "—asked me to, and she is a part of the Coven. Also, I owe you, and your master, my life. Normally, I would let the two of you work this out on your own."

Karen bristled at Reginald being referred to as her 'master.' Master of the City or not, he was not *her* master. She worked with him because she chose to. She crossed her arms over her chest. "Work what out?"

Both Heather and Lamiel must have heard the defensive aggression in her voice. Lamiel raised a hand in a calming gesture. Heather spoke first, her words coming in a rush. "It's nothing bad. I need help. I thought... I heard... You saved Lamiel. I thought you could... I just need help. Please."

"Heather is going to ask a service of you and of Reginald. It is for her alone, and not for the Bacchanalia Coven." Lamiel added, "I'm sorry if it seemed otherwise. She didn't know how to approach you."

Karen relaxed a little and focused on Heather. "I see. What's up?"

"A couple weeks back, you were involved in finding the body of that little girl at the old Colman School. I used to go to that school. It was a long time ago. I had a favorite teacher who taught there: Professor Chapman." Heather frowned at the memories in her head. "That guy, Vice Principal Rutherford who committed suicide, he was there, too. He was guilty of everything they said he was guilty of. I know because I was his next victim. I was to be his special girl. He told me this. Told me if I ever told anyone there would be trouble for me and for my family.

"Professor Chapman found me crying in a stairwell. I told him everything and he said he'd protect me. He would make sure that the VP didn't touch me. The next thing I know, I'm transferred to a new school and the old school was shut down.

"Professor Chapman was also transferred, but he never showed up. He's been missing for nine years. But, a couple weeks ago, I saw him. I talked to him. He was a bum over by the City Center. He didn't know me. He didn't know himself. It was awful. Like talking to the twin of a man you didn't know had a twin."

Karen was saddened by the girl's obvious pain, but unsure what Heather wanted her to do. "Did you contact his family or the authorities? I'm sure someone would want to know."

"I tried, but the city wouldn't let me. I don't know why not."

"The... city... wouldn't let you?"

"No. The city wouldn't. Every time I tried to call someone, the circuits were busy. If I tried to walk to some place, the lights would go against me and doors would stick. Anytime I tried to alert anyone, everything went against me. The city was telling me to stop. But, I couldn't. So, I went to see the Lady of the Grey Manor for tea. She told me what had happened, and what was happening now. That's why I need your help."

Beyond Karen's questions about the 'city' working against someone (which did make sense in a way—although she would have to think about that) and who the Lady of the Grey Manor was, Karen wanted to know what she was supposed to do. "Okay. What's happening to Professor Chapman, and how can I help?"

"He sacrificed his life to the Transitory Tunnel to save me from VP Rutherford. I want you to get it back for him. Him. His life. His memories."

"What? What's that? How am I supposed to do that?"

Lamiel broke in at this point. "This is part of the reason I agreed to set up the meeting. There are things in the city that aren't well known. For most people, the Transitory Tunnel is just a bike tunnel that goes under the 101 Freeway. For those who are more aware, it is a place where lost memories are...stored. Or go. I don't know for sure.

"It is a place that leads to many other places, but most of them are still here in Kendrick. It's hard to explain. The best way I can think to explain it is a series of cellophane sheets. If they are all together on top of each other, they look like one sheet. But, if you look closer, each sheet has something different drawn on it. The Transitory Tunnel is a hole that punches through the stack of them. If you go through the tunnel and are aware, you can slip into any of these other worlds. Coming back, however, may be difficult."

"Please, Karen. I can't do it myself. I would if I could, but since it was me he sacrificed himself for, I can't. I don't understand it, but that's part of the rules."

Karen nodded slowly. "Let me talk to Reginald about the situation." She pulled her phone out of her pocket and saw that there was no cell signal. "I'll need to go outside. Mind if I go out the back?"

Lamiel nodded. "It'll be safe."

Heather touched her arm, "Thank you."

"I haven't agreed to do anything, yet."

"I know, but you're considering it and I appreciate that. Professor Chapman is a good man."

Karen didn't answer. She left the office and exited the hallway through the back. Instead of a dirty back alley, she found herself on a small, well-lit street. Her phone indicated she had full signal again. She had never tried this, but she was gambling that it would work. Going back to her incoming calls list, she found the entry called REGINALD. She selected it and pressed the SEND button.

The other end rang twice before picking up. "Hello, Karen."

"Oh, cool. It worked."

"You have always been able to contact me if you wanted to."

"You didn't tell me I could."

"You had to want to bad enough. What can I do for you?"

She quickly explained the situation of Heather and Professor Chapman. "Do you know anything about it?"

"Yes. I do. Heather was right that the city was stopping her. It is part of the magic. Those rules I told you about. The only thing that can bring Professor Chapman back from where he has gone is another sacrifice; not like the one he gave but still, it is a sacrifice." He paused. "The tunnel is dangerous. I don't really want you to do this."

"Why not?"

"You can get lost in there. I've seen it happen too many times. It's very dangerous, and your actions there may have unforeseen consequences."

"Like what?"

"I'm not sure. That is why they are 'unforeseen.'"

She was certain there was something he wasn't telling her. Between that and her irritation over the impression that Reginald was her master, the decision was made. This time she was going to do what she thought was right. "A man gave his life to protect a child who was not even his own. I'm going to help her. Are you going to help me, or do I need to do this by myself?"

There was another pause. Longer this time. "I will help you, Karen. You know I will. But, I really wish you would not do this."

She didn't reply.

"Call me tomorrow after you get off work. I will tell you what you need to do to find him. Get a picture of Heather from that age, as well as a picture of him. I want you to spend the rest of your time thinking about your past, who you are, and how you got to this place in your life. If you are to succeed in this, you must have a good sense of self."

"Thank you."

"I will speak to you tomorrow."

They said their good-byes. Karen headed back inside. Lamiel and Heather were still in the office. "I'm going to do this, Heather, but it's just me. Reginald is not involved." That last bit of information caused Lamiel's eyebrows to rise in surprise or interest or both.

"Oh, thank you. What do I owe you for this?"

Karen shook her head. "Nothing. It's the right thing to do."

"She has to owe you." Lamiel interrupted. "I'd like to let it go and think that Heather got off easy, but I can't because of what I owe you. Favors are not free. Not in this city."

For a long moment Karen said nothing. "Okay, Heather. This favor for a favor of equal value to be determined in the future."

"Done." Heather did not hesitate.

Lamiel sighed and looked heavenward. "Thank the Light neither of you seems to know what you're actually doing. Heather, remind me to tell you about the time I agreed to an open-ended favor. You'll see why this is a bad idea."

***

Karen approached the well-lit bike tunnel cautiously. She had done as Reginald had asked and spent many hours thinking about who she was and why she did what she did. She found it strange that she could distill most of her actions, and why she was the way she was, down to a few pivotal memories.

The first memory, and one she did not really like to think about, was the death of her maternal grandmother, Grammy Luton. She had been about six years old when it happened. She could still remember it as if it happened yesterday.

"9-1-1. What is the nature of your emergency?"

"I need my mommy."

"What's your name, honey?"

"Karen Wilson. My mommy's Kimberly. She said to call 9-1-1 if anything happened. Grammy went to sleep and I can't wake her up."

My name is Tammy. I'm going to stay on the phone with you. Okay?"

"Okay."

"Can you tell me about your Grammy and her going to sleep?"

"We were in the kitchen. She said her arm hurt, then she sat down on the ground. Then she went to sleep. I can't wake her up. We're supposed to be cooking dinner."

*"Everything is going to be all right, Karen. There are
people on the way to your house right now who will help you
and your Grammy. Okay?"*

"Okay..."

But, of course, everything had not been okay. The police
and an ambulance had arrived. They had whisked her
grandmother away with lights flashing and sirens blaring, but
it had been too late. A police officer had gathered Karen up in
her arms and shielded her from most of the chaos. Her mother
had been given permission to leave the emergency services call
center and arrived shortly after the ambulance left. Through
her tears, she had praised Karen for her bravery and told her
she did the right thing.

It was at that moment that Karen decided that she
wanted to be just like Tammy and her parents; to be that calm
voice on the other end of the line when bad things happened.
That was why she was a 911 operator today.

The other memory that kept popping into her head was
of her twelfth birthday. She had had a big party and, at the
last moment, decided to invite one of her less popular
neighbors, Ernie. Most of the neighborhood kids avoided Ernie
because of his stuttering problem. Otherwise, they picked on
him.

There had been the usual girlish squeals of disbelief
when Karen mentioned this to her friends the day before the
party. They all wanted to know why she would do such a thing.
Karen's response had been "Why not? He's a person, too." That
stopped most of the protests.

The next day, when Ernie arrived at the party, there was
small amount of awkwardness between Ernie and the other
kids who had always either ignored or taunted him. But,
Karen's open acceptance of him had broken down a lot of
barriers. Towards the end of the party, Ernie found Karen in
the kitchen by herself getting more drinks.

*He held a small white box out to her. "I wanted to th-th-
thank you for inviting me to your birthday party, K-Karen. No
one's been that nice to me in a long time. I g-got you this. I was
g-going to g-g-g-give it to you tomorrow but since I'm here...
here."*

*She smiled. "Thanks for coming." Then, she blinked in
surprise at the silver bracelet. She held it up and read the charm*

dangling from it. "Joy" was written on one side. "Hope" was
written on the other. "Wow. This is so pretty."
    "I th-thought of you when I s-s-saw it. You're always so
nice to everyone. You g-g-give people chances."

    The two of them had smiled at each other and returned
to the party; Karen wearing the bracelet. She had endured a
certain amount of taunting but refused to remove it. It was a
reminder to her that everyone deserved a chance. Everyone
had feelings and she should always keep that in mind. She still
wore the bracelet to this day. At this point, it was a talisman
for patience and serenity. It reminded her to always think
about where the other person was coming from.
    There were many more memories swirling in her head as
she approached the bike tunnel. From her point of view it
looked like a long tunnel under the freeway. It was just as she
expected: debris here and there; graffiti all over the walls; and
that smell of humanity—waste, sweat, tears, and general living.
    She stopped at the entrance. There was no one else
around. It was quiet. At this time of night, the cars on the
freeway were few and far in-between. Karen prepared herself as
Reginald had instructed. She had the picture of Heather in her
pocket to use to convince James of who he was.
    She held the picture of Professor James Chapman in her
hand, looking at it. All she had to do was think of finding the
lost man and walk to the end of the tunnel. If it worked, he
would be there. If it did not, she would be on the other side of
the freeway and would have to try again. Throughout this, she
had to make sure she did not lose track of herself. She was not
exactly certain what that meant, but the warning had made
her nervous.
    Karen took a breath, looked at the picture of the lost
man and started walking. As she crossed the entrance, she
began to whisper to herself, "I am looking for James Chapman:
Language professor—Greek, Latin, Spanish, and Italian. I am
looking for James Chapman: Language professor—Greek,
Latin, Spanish, and Italian."
    She felt the world shift. The tunnel seemed to tilt about
thirty degrees and grow longer. She kept walking as she
repeated her mantra, flicking her eyes between the picture in
her hand and the light at the end of the tunnel. Sounds filled
her ears. She knew she was no longer alone. The smells
changed, the walls changed, even the sound of her feet
crunching on the ground changed.

Then, the images of other people and other places began. They almost startled her into stopping—the one thing that Reginald had most strongly warned her against doing. Suddenly, she understood why he had not wanted her to come. They were all around her as indistinct shapes. Then, one would bubble to the surface in perfect clarity.

"I am looking for James Chapman..."

—A boy and a girl of about nine skipped by in old-fashioned clothing, waving at her. They looked like they were skipping across a bridge.—

"Language professor: Greek, Latin, Spanish and Italian."

—A group of rough boys looking like extras from a bad modern day vampire movie kept pace with her, leering at her. One beckoned to her.—

She turned from him back to the picture in her hand and saw the bracelet she wore. She kept walking. "I am Karen Wilson. I'm looking for James Chapman. Professor of Language. Greek. Latin. Spanish. Italian."

—The sound of hooves pounding on dirt behind her. She risked a glance back and saw a uniformed man on horseback galloping towards her. "Oh God." She started to run. "I'm looking for James Chapman. James Chapman." The horse came closer, its hoof beats echoing around her. "I am Karen Wilson. The horse is not here. Not here. I'm here. I give people chances. I help people. That's what I do. I help people. I am here and I am looking for James Chapman. Professor. Greek, Latin, Spanish, Italian."

Abruptly, the sound of the horse was gone and an old gentleman appeared beside her. "Miss? Miss? I seem to have lost my way..."

It was almost worse than the horse threatening to pummel her into paste. The old gentleman looked so tired. If she stopped to help him, she would be lost with him. "I am looking for Professor James Chapman." She responded in an apologetic voice and turned from him, her heart breaking. She strode towards the light, ignoring his desperate pleas for assistance.

The moment she exited the tunnel, everything else went away. She was still in Kendrick. That much was certain, and she was not alone. Several bums stood around a barrel of burning trash. She looked at each, comparing them to the picture in her hand. It was hard to see the faces under the beards, grim and weight of the years but she found him. With a touch on his arm, she said, "Professor Chapman? I've come to bring you home."

The man turned and looked at her. "Aren't you a dear? You shouldn't be out this time of night, Miss. It's not safe."

"I know, Professor Chapman, but I've come to take you home. I've been sent by Heather."

"I don't know any Heather, and I'm no Professor. I'm just...me. You haven't seen a black and white kitten around here, have you? I think I lost him."

"No. I'm sorry. But, you are Professor James Chapman. See?" She held up her picture of him.

He took it and smiled. "I almost can remember..." He frowned. "Handsome guy. Not me." He handed it back and turned away.

"Wait. Do you remember this girl? This is Heather. This is the girl you saved." She pulled Heather's picture from her pocket and thrust it into his hand. "This is the girl who sent me to bring you home. This is the girl you sacrificed yourself for."

It was like watching an old engine finally catch and start up. The vague ignorance shifted into surprised remembrance at the sight of the girl in the picture. "Heather. Oh, Heather. She's all right? He didn't hurt her? It worked?"

Karen smiled. "Yes, Professor. It did. She's now a beautiful, young woman, and she would be here for you herself if she could. It's time for you to come home."

James nodded. "I feel like I've been dreaming for so long. But, the city has been taking care of me. It's been good to me. Protecting me like I protected her."

"No doubt." She offered her hand. "Shall we go?"

He nodded, accepting her hand.

"Don't let go. No matter what happens, don't let go." She led him towards the entrance of the tunnel and was dismayed to find it bricked up. Karen stood there, staring at it, wondering what to do, since Reginald had not mentioned this.

"What will you give up?" The voice came from the wall in front of her.

"What?"

"You cannot take something from here without leaving something behind. If you take his memory back with you, you must sacrifice part of yourself. That is the only way. The balance must be maintained." The voice was implacable and unfeeling. There was no choice in the matter.

"I choose what is to be sacrificed? What memory?"

"Yes. It will be gone from you completely."

She frowned, thinking about her life. She looked at the picture of Heather, the little girl she once was, then back at the man who gave up his life for her. *Unforeseen consequences, indeed.* Her decision did not take long. In a way, she had subconsciously suspected that something like this was going to happen. Karen chose and nodded. "I agree to the sacrifice."

The brick wall fell away without a sound. She could see the other end of the tunnel and prayed that it would not be the same as before.

"Remember, James, you are James Chapman: Language professor."

"Greek, Latin, Spanish and Italian." He replied. "I remember now."

"Don't let go. Whatever happens."

"I won't. I promise."

She led him back through the tunnel. This time no one tried to stop them or lure them from the chosen path. She could feel the ghosts of others all around her but ignored them. Her goal was the end of that tunnel. Her sacrifice made. Karen stumbled and fell to the ground as they exited the tunnel again. James immediately helped her up.

She smiled at him. "Thanks. We need to let people know that you've been found; that you're alive and well. I know who to call."

She called David, told him about finding the Professor and asked for an officer to drop by to help out. The police would take custody of the wayward Professor and deal with the necessary paperwork for reintroducing him back into society. Also, she wanted him to come take her home. It had been a very trying night. She needed someone to just hold her for a while.

As they waited for everyone to arrive, she called Bacchanalia and left a message with Lamiel that she had succeeded and to please let Heather know. Finally, she called Reginald.

"Are you well?"

"I'm fine. It was a little scary, but I'm fine."

"You'll have to tell me what happened."

"I will, but not now. I'm really tired. Plus, David and the police are arriving. I'm going to have to answer a few questions."

"I'm glad it worked out. I'm glad you're safe."

"Me, too. I'll talk to you later."

Karen gave David a big hug and spoke with the police about finding Professor Chapman. She was getting good at spinning quick lies about why she was in a certain place at a certain time, saving people or discovering unusual things.

She never noticed that the silver bracelet she always wore was gone. Even if she had, she would not have given it much thought. She would not have remembered why she used to wear it all the time.

However, the person who picked it up out of the debris at the entrance to the bike tunnel, after everyone had left, knew.

***

Elsewhere...

"*'Missing Teacher Found After Nine Years. Professor James Chapman, beloved Language teacher from the now defunct Colman School was found by a former student, Heather Wise, who brought his presence to the attention of authorities. He has been missing for nine years and cannot remember where he was or what he was doing during that time...'* Dammit. We don't need this right now. Where'd he come from? Was the breaking of the obfuscation on the Colman School responsible for bringing him back?" Praetor threw the folded paper across the library where it landed in a mess at Nightshade's feet.

"We aren't sure. But, we know that the Master of the City was involved. The Wilson girl called the police. I don't know why she's not in the article, but my contacts on the force say that she was the one who alerted them. I can get you a copy of the report if you'd like," said Todesengel.

He shook his head. "No. If you're certain Karen and the Master of the City were involved, I don't need to see it. I trust you. Seems that Cheshire was right. The Master of the City is starting to move directly against us. That's too bad. I didn't want open warfare with him." He paused, deciding. "We'll deal with the Professor if he becomes a problem again. I don't think he will when he learns of Vice Principal Thomas Rutherford's confession and suicide. That should satisfy him, and he'll be busy acclimating himself to his new life."

Nightshade refolded the newspaper and put it on the table. "What do you want us to do in the meantime? Cerridwen has scryed out the most likely person to hand Karen over to us. Should we approach him?"

"Not yet. We need to get the last artifact for the ritual."

"You've found it?"

"Not as such. I believe I know what it is now. I have some work for you to do, Todesengel. It's not going to be easy."

"It never is, but I never fail."

"Almost never," Nightshade chimed in.

Todesengel glared at her, then turned back to Praetor. "What do I need to do?"

"I need you, or V'ger, or preferably both of you, to become very, very interested in Makah history and artifacts. I need both of you to start spending time down at the Makah Historical Center. Find out about their legends. Their origin legends in particular. Do what you need to do to find out about them and make sure that everyone there knows of your interest and becomes familiar with you."

He frowned. "The Makah Tribe is not to be trifled with."

"I know. I said it wouldn't be easy. It would be better if your interest and research were genuine as well. I'd say you have some homework to do."

The Inspiration of Insanity

KAREN DROVE UP the long, winding driveway through carefully manicured and cleared land. *Better to see escaping crazies, I guess,* she thought, then immediately regretted the callous mental comment. Up ahead was the barred gate to the enclosed land belonging to the Kendrick Mental Health Center. She stopped at the small guard booth to sign in.

"I'm here to see Charity Carter."

"Oh? Part of the little ritual thing this afternoon, eh?" The bored guard now looked at her with real interest.

Part of her wanted to explain that she had been requested to do this by her manager. That she was not doing this of her own accord. That she didn't believe in this sort of thing—except with what she'd seen in the past few months, she definitely did believe. So, instead, she just nodded.

Karen watched the guard watch her. She knew he was waiting to see if she would expand on her role in all of this. She kept her mouth shut. The less she said, the less she would have to remember.

Ask me no questions. I'll tell you no lies.

When she just smiled at him, he hit the button to open the heavy gate. While it took its time opening at glacial speeds, her mind wandered over what little she knew of what she was doing here. Supposedly, she was representing the city in a "harmless ritual" to help a patient.

Karen was nervous—about a lot of things. She did not want to be here, but her job within the Emergency Services Call Center occasionally called for PR work in the community. She didn't understand why the Emergency Services PR people decided that a 911 operator needed to do this job until after her boss spoke to her about it, and then she felt she couldn't say no.

On the way home, Reginald had called. It had been his doing. He had set everything in motion and made sure her name came up on the computer search for an appropriate person.

Everyone knew who Charity Carter was: Wife of the renowned horror author Richard Carter. Three years ago, she had suddenly gone insane and tried to kill him. It was like a plot out of one of his novels. Charity believed she was someone else. Someone named Somnia, who had been forced into Charity's body for some unknown purpose by a ritual Richard had performed.

Now, the doctors at the Kendrick Mental Health Center had decided to take a new approach to Mrs. Carter's case. She insisted that if she could perform a certain ritual, Somnia would be free again, and so would Charity. As Charity had been the soul of sanity except where Somnia was concerned, the idea had been discussed at length and approved.

"You mean to tell me Charity Carter is not insane? She really is possessed by someone named Somnia? That Richard Carter did a ritual to put her in his wife's body?"

"Yes. That is exactly right. It has taken me this long to put everything in place so Somnia may be freed. She is needed by the people of Kendrick. She should never have been trapped in the flesh. The ritual needs to be performed by Somnia, a friend to Somnia, a person who does not believe, a person in authority, a creative person and a person who represents the city of Kendrick. This will be Somnia, one of the orderlies, one of her doctors, and you, who represents both the creative person and the city of Kendrick."

"What is Somnia? Why is she needed?"

"She is one of the minor muses that dwell here. He trapped her, and now only he hears her inspiration."

Reginald had told her a bit more about the concept of the minor muses. Apparently, one of the reasons that so many artists, writers, and creative people came from or lived in Kendrick was that a small group of minor muses lived in the city. It had to do with the high magical content of the area, or something to that effect.

Karen still did not quite understand how they manifested, but they seemed to be based around certain activities like driving, taking showers, or going for long walks. If someone did one of those things and listened to the whisper of their inner voice, they could be inspired to do great things.

It sounded insane. Then again, most of Karen's life seemed insane these days. After all, she was working for the 'Master of the City,' was friends with a woman who had a pack of gargoyles to do her bidding, was dating one guy who was part of a magical Coven and dating another who had seen just as many weird things as she had. She had to stop murders, thefts, and the destruction of sacred sites. She had to arbitrate between enemy magicians, and really didn't want to think about what the Order of the Sacred Eye might be up to now. It was just easier to go with the flow and accept what she learned as she went along.

Her random thoughts on insanity and what was truly insane came to an abrupt halt as the Kendrick Mental Health Center came into view. It was an old, two-story building that vaguely reminded her of a school for some reason. The whole building was surrounded by trees, and she didn't see any bars on the windows. The nervous knot in the pit of her stomach twisted tightly.

She parked her car in the small visitor lot and headed up to the front door. A balding man in gold-rimmed glasses and a white doctor's coat stood on the front steps. "Karen Wilson?"

"Yes." She offered her hand.

He shook it. "I'm Dr. Antony Salton. Thank you so much for coming. I hadn't expected the city to send me a 911 operator. I thought they would send a city official, but when I thought about it, you really do represent the city and its people more, don't you?"

"I do? Yes, I guess I do. I help people every day, even the ones who call with frivolous stuff who really just want to talk to someone." She paused as they walked inside. "There's no bars on the windows."

"Miss Wilson, our patients are not animals. There is a metal mesh grating within the glass. It's just as effective, and is not as disturbing."

"Oh. Sorry. I've just never been... you know."

"It's a common misconception. Some patients are dangerous, and we have them isolated. But, by and large, our patients are mostly just people with a different perspective on life that, unfortunately, precludes them from living with the rest of society."

There but for the Grace of God, go I, Karen thought, feeling very uncomfortable. She pushed away the nagging wonder that she was crazy, too, and belonged here. What if Reginald was just made up and all the weirdness was only in her head? Something she'd overlaid on top of reality, and the reality of her friends. Would she wake up one day and discover none of it was real? Was that why she didn't want to be here? It was hitting too close to home?

Karen shoved all of her fears and doubts away and concentrated on what Dr. Salton was telling her.

"—not that you believe the ritual, but that you appear to believe it. For Charity's sake. We have a theory that she needs the approval of a group of people to let go of this identity that was created when she had her breakdown. We think she'll get it by performing this self-made ritual. We believe that this is her way of paving the road back to herself and to get through the guilt of what she almost did to her husband."

"Why isn't he here for this ritual?"

The doctor paused at a door. "She didn't want him here."

"Oh."

"It makes sense. He is the object of her guilt. She cannot send away her false persona if the reason for its existence is in front of her."

"That makes sense." She agreed. She thought, however, that if Reginald was right... and he usually was... that Charity didn't want Richard here because she really was Somnia. She didn't want him knowing she was about to get free and didn't want to give him the opportunity to try and stop it.

They walked into the room. It looked like a sparsely furnished dorm room, except for the bare, white walls and tile floor that had been written on in what looked to be dry eraser ink. It was a small ritual circle within a larger ritual circle. There were runes written in-between the borders of the two circles.

A petite blond woman and a large man with a close-cropped hair and a green hospital uniform sat on the floor around the ritual circle. Karen recognized some of the symbols as the same ones she'd saw in Bacchanalia and other places around Kendrick. Even if the magical and philosophic beliefs differed, the magical writing seemed to have many similarities.

"Charity, this is Karen Wilson. She is an artist and she—"

"—Represents the city of Kendrick. Yes. I know. I recognize her."

"You do?" Karen asked.

"Yes. I'll tell you about it later. We have work to do right now."

"Manners, Charity." Dr. Salton gestured to the big man. "This is Steve. He's one of the orderlies here."

Steve nodded. "Hi. Thanks for coming."

Karen nodded back. "So, what do I do?"

The blond woman gestured across from her. "Karen, you'll sit there. Doc will sit to my left and Steve will remain on my right." She waited until everyone was sitting in their assigned positions.

"Steve represents my friend and a person in authority. Karen is an artist and represents Kendrick. Dr. Salton represents my unbeliever, as is his right, and a person in authority." She gave them each a stone and a small bag of something.

"Put the stone on your left knee or hold it in your left hand. Either will do, but it needs to be on your left side."

Karen opted to hold hers, hematite, in her left hand to make sure she did not drop it. She glanced at Steve, who smiled reassuringly.

"This ritual is simple, but powerful. It has two parts. The first is recognition or not. Steve and Karen will recognize me. Doc, you will choose to or not, as you will. The second is to free me. All of you will need to agree to free me. Can you do that?"

Charity, looked around the ritual circle at the nodding heads and Karen thought she could almost see two people within the one body. "Okay. I will speak then Steve, then Karen, and then Doc. I've already coached Steve, so just follow his lead."

Karen listened to the excitement in Charity's voice, it all but trembled as she flushed, looking around at the three of them. It was like watching someone trying to sprint for the finish line now that it was in sight. She could feel the woman's need and impatience.

Charity looked once more at each person to be certain the stones were on each person's left, then opened her bag, took out a pinch of sand, and dropped it to the middle of the circle. "I am the muse Somnia, trapped in mortal flesh. Do you recognize me?"

Steve dropped a pinch of sand in the circle. "I am Steve. I recognize you, Somnia."

Karen also dropping a pinch of sand to the middle of the circle. "I am Karen. I recognize you, Somnia."

Dr. Salton dropped sand into the circle and said, "I am Anthony Salton. I do not recognize you as Somnia."

The blond woman smiled at that. Karen felt a sudden sense of disorientation that reminded her of traveling through the Transitory Tunnel. The ritual had begun, and the power was growing. She looked at Steve again to see if he was reacting to anything, or if what she was feeling was all in her head. She was gratified to see that he had a discomforted look on his face. If he was reacting as well, then it was not just her.

Unless, of course, you're seeing what you want to see there to reassure yourself. Karen pushed the thought away.

Somnia turned her bag of sand over, dumping the rest of its contents into the center of the circle. "I am Somnia, trapped in mortal flesh. Will you free me?"

Steve repeated the dumping gesture. "I am Steve, your friend and a person in authority. I free you."

Karen dumped out all of her sand. "I am Karen, an artist and representative of Kendrick. I free you." She forced her hand still to keep it from trembling. There was a pressure growing that felt like a thunderstorm. Steve seemed to feel it, but apparently the doctor did not.

Dr. Salton dumped all of his sand on top of the mound of sand in the center of the circle. "I am Anthony Salton, your doctor and, believe it or not, your friend. I free you."

Somnia gathered up two handfuls of sand from the center of the circle and tossed them in the air. "Then, I am free!" She cried.

To Karen, it was like hearing hundreds of doors unlocking all at once and chains falling away. She sat there for a long moment with the rest in silence. Dr. Salton looked nonplussed at being covered in sand. Steve, however, looked as if he'd sensed the same things she had. It had all happened so fast. Just like that, the ritual had begun, and was now done. It made Karen's head spin at the thought that magic could be so quick and powerful.

"Thank you. Oh, thank you." Charity said.

To Karen, she seemed to speak with two voices. "You're welcome." She looked at Dr. Salton who had stood up to brush the sand from his clothing. She and Steve both stood as well. Charity remained sitting on the floor, smiling. She seemed so happy.

For a second, Karen thought she saw the woman's form blur showing two women in the same place. As the doctor turned away, a wisp of something pulled itself from Charity's body and floated there next to her. As Karen watched, the wisp filled out and a young woman—somehow familiar—hovered there.

Somnia smiled wide and waved at Karen. It was clear by his dumbfound expression that Steve saw the muse while Dr. Salton did not.

"I will escort you out, Miss Wilson." Dr. Salton opened the door to the hallway. Karen turned from Charity and followed him in silence until they reached the parking lot.

"Thank you for all you have done, Miss Wilson. With this silly ritual out of the way, I hope that Charity will be able to face what she tried to do and her recovery will be swift." He touched her briefly on the shoulder. "Charity's husband is a rich and famous man. Many people, reporters, would like to know what happened here today. I would appreciate it if you would not speak of it at all until we make an official announcement... if we do."

Karen nodded. "Did you feel anything during the ritual? Anything at all?"

He smiled a gentle but condescending smile at her. "No. But, if you did—and I'm not saying that you did—it's not unusual. The mind can be very vulnerable to suggestion when in unfamiliar surroundings and strange or unusual circumstances. Human beings are very creative creatures."

She nodded again. "I see. Thanks." She got into her car and headed home. She could not decide if she pitied or envied the doctor for his inability to see the world that lived on the outside edge of his perception. She could not decide if she would rather be like him or not. It was something she would spend many hours pondering.

***

Elsewhere...

Todesengel watched the evening news. "*... tonight's breaking story. There has been an escape from the Kendrick Mental Health Center today. It is a story stranger than fiction...*" The News woman in front of the familiar home for the criminally insane was saying, "*... one of the Kendrick Asylum orderlies simply opened the locked door to Charity Carter's room and let her go free. When asked why, as he was taken into custody, the orderly, Steve Bellingham, was reported to have said,* 'She was right. She wasn't insane. She didn't belong here. So, I let her go.' *Three years ago, Charity Carter, wife of Kendrick's own honored horror author Richard Carter, attempted to kill her husband by...*"

"There you are," Praetor said.

"Did you hear the news?" He gestured at the TV.

"Never mind that. It's of no concern to us." He handed the assassin a box.

"What's this?" Todesengel opened it up to reveal large punch dagger.

"Your next assignment. That—" He pointed at the weapon. "—will kill the Guardian of Changer's Claw. The Claw is the point of one of the harpoons the Makah tribe used when they hunted whales. The Legend is that this harpoon belonged to *Ho-ho-e-ap-bess* or the Two-Men-Who-Changed-Things. All that's left of it is the tip made of sharp mussel shell blades and bone points. It doesn't matter if it is true or not. The Makah believe it is and that is what matters. Changer's Claw is the last artifact we need for the ritual. The Guardianship of Changer's Claw is a hereditary position in a family from a very special bloodline. You know of what I speak."

"Yeah, I do. How the hell is this supposed to stop one of those things?"

"I would not send you to die. The blade is designed to kill them. Make sure you hit it in the guts. It will die. Maybe not immediately, but it will die, and you won't have to worry about it sniffing after you to retrieve the Claw.

Todesengel lifted the punch dagger out of the box and turned it over. It fit easily in his hand and it had the symbols he was looking for on the other side. He smiled an unpleasant smile. "It will be done. Where do I find the Changer's Claw and its Guardian?"

Praetor beckoned him close and began to speak in low tones, pointing to a map of Kendrick.

The Running Feeling

KAREN WATCHED DAVID look through her sketchpad with the normal trepidation all artists have when someone looks at their latest work in progress. "What do you think?"

"This is great. I didn't realize you were so good. I love your take on the gargoyle legend. Your baby gargoyle is really cute. It'll make for a great webcomic." He tapped one of the pictures. "This little one is based on the gargoyle statues you have at home, right?"

She smiled. "Yeah. Sebastian."

"You gave the character the same name? Well, yes. I suppose that makes sense. But, how did you decide he liked Snickers bars?"

"He told me."

"Listening to the voices in your head, eh?" David grinned at her.

"Something like that. I needed a new project after the comic book proposal. This one sort of fell into my lap." She looked out the window of the café and thought about the fact that, once again, while she was telling the truth, she was still lying to him. She never had to lie to Aaron. It bothered her a lot. More than she first realized it would.

The voice in her head comment was absolutely true. Sebastian had started talking telepathically to her a couple months ago. It had been a shock to hear him the first time; this tiny voice in her head asking for more candy. Then finally seeing him move as he scampered from the kitchen counter to the kitchen table with a chewed up Snickers bar wrapper in one tiny claw. Her life changed again then. For a few minutes, she had thought herself crazy. Then, overcome by curiosity, she found the bag of Snickers miniatures and brought it out to share.

While Sebastian happily dove into his chosen vice, she questioned him and found out much about her guest and guardian. That was what he was to her—her guardian. She was his chosen ward. He would patrol the area at night and sometimes during the day. Apparently, he followed her from time to time while she was doing work for Reginald with the help of his 'big brothers.' She had never known she was followed by the gargoyles. He explained that it was because they were very good at hiding and being quiet.

Following that conversation had been a hasty call to Susan, who was pleased at the development. According to her, the moment a gargoyle spoke to a human was the moment they had decided they were worth dying for. Like it or not, she was stuck with Sebastian until one of them died. That was just the way gargoyles were.

The idea was both daunting and intriguing. Subsequent daydreaming in the shower led Karen to the idea of the webcomic about a young gargoyle befriending a child. She was not sure where it would go from there but so far, everyone who read the beginning of the story loved it.

"Well, I think it's a good one. Who knows, maybe you'll become one of those really popular webcomic artists."

"I'm not doing this to become popular. Though, it would be nice to be appreciated. I'm doing this because I like to draw and because I have a story to tell."

"I know. That's why I love you." He grinned at her. "Are you ready to go? I want to show you the lake at sunset as well as moonrise."

Nodding, Karen stood with the false smile on her face. She was becoming increasingly uncomfortable with his use of the word "love" in their conversations. The same could be said of Aaron. They had both started tossing out that word in conversations in the same week. It felt like a conspiracy to trap her into admitting that her affections ran deeper than the casual dating she'd been doing with both of them for months.

While that was true, she didn't like feeling as if she was being forced into a position of choosing one over the other. This was what always seemed to happen when "love" entered into the relationship equation.

She shoved that line of thought away with a promise to think about it later. For now, she wanted to enjoy herself and the evening David had planned. It had been a long time since she watched the sun set or the moon rise. Tonight's full moon promised to be spectacular.

***

The sunset had been gorgeous as promised, and the moonrise was even more beautiful. It hung full and low in the sky, reflected off the surface of the lake, and was crowned with a halo of stars. However, neither Karen nor David was paying much attention to the exquisite surroundings. They were too wrapped up in each other—literally. Mimicking the near-mythical movie moment of sweethearts entwined on a checkered picnic blanket, kissing and touching, with a backdrop too perfect to be real. Then Karen realized that something was very wrong.

'Karen.'

She jerked her head up from David, "What?"

David opened his eyes, "What what?"

'Karen. Bad man coming. He stole something. My furry brother is chasing, but hurt. You must help him.'

Karen pulled her hormone-addled brain into shape as she realized it was Sebastian talking to her. "What?" She asked out loud again, forgetting she could communicate silently with him.

"That's what I asked." David sat up, looking concerned. "What's wrong?"

"I thought I heard something. Something coming here." She hated the way the lie came to her lips so easily. She looked around. "Could you check?"

David listened, got that look that told her he did not hear anything, but got up anyway. "Okay, sweetheart, I'll be right back."

'He stole the Changer's Claw. We've got to get it back.'

"You know, this is how horror movies start." David said as he turned to go.

"What?" Karen blinked at him distractedly.

"You know. A couple of kids making out by the lake. One hears something and goes to investigate. After they split up, both get brutally killed to show how the monster works. Lots of horror movies start that way."

She grinned. "Then don't get killed. We've got unfinished business."

He grinned back and relaxed, seeing her with him again. "Okay, I won't." He ducked under a branch and disappeared out of sight.

Her smile disappeared as he did. "Sebastian, what's going on? What's a 'furry brother' and what's Changer's Claw?" She stood and looked around. "And where are you?"

'Here. Close to the lake. Hurry. We must stop the bad guy. Furry brother. Guardian. Like me. But with fur.'

Following Sebastian's call, Karen ran towards the trees by the lake. If she stopped trying and just listened, she could feel and hear something she could follow. She rounded a tree, took two steps, rounded another tree and found herself on the edge of a small clearing. "Where?"

Sebastian didn't have to answer. On the other side of the clearing, a man clad in black from head to toe burst through the tree line and skidded to a stop, looking as startled by Karen as she did by him. In one hand was a huge knife, its blade stained red; in the other was a gun. A large leather bag of Native-American design was slung across his body. It stood out from his Don't-See-Me clothing. She saw the look in his eyes go from reaction to recognition just before he raised the gun and fired at her. The shot, though suppressed, was still loud and she braced for the expected pain.

It did not come. Instead, the shot hit the ground in front of her because of the flash of grey that landed on the man's arm the moment he fired.

Not stopping, it leaped for the man's throat. She could hear Sebastian's wordless snarls of rage mixing with the man's grunts of pain as the thing savaged his neck.

It was a choice of dropping the knife, the gun, or both in order to fight off the tiny monster. The man sacrificed the weapon he was least familiar with and grabbed Sebastian, who immediately twisted and started to attack the hand that held him. Too quick for Karen to do anything, he turned and smashed the little gargoyle with all his might against the tree next to him. Karen felt and heard Sebastian's pain, then silence.

"Sebastian!" Karen ran at the man, furious and terrified.

The man aimed his gun at her again, then looked over his shoulder at the sound of someone crashing through the woods. He squeezed the trigger, but Karen was already diving for the nearest tree. Instead of coming after her, he sprinted out of the clearing. At that moment, she could not have cared less about the 'bad man' or that he'd stolen something or even that he knew her. Instead, she ran to where Sebastian lay unmoving.

Karen picked him up and couldn't tell if he was alive or dead. He had a large chunk of rock missing from his back where he'd hit the tree, and his body lay limp and loose. She decided he was still alive because if he was dead, he would be just a stone figurine. She latched onto that thought and hoped with all her might.

"Sebastian? Oh, Sebastian... please be okay." She paused and saw the knife the man had dropped. It didn't look like any knife she had ever seen. It was a triangular knife with a metal handle.

Still cradling Sebastian, she picked it up and started walking back toward the remains of the picnic dinner and David, not knowing what she would say to him about what just happened. She figured that she would just have to tell him the truth and see if he thought she was crazy. Maybe it would drive him away from her, and she wouldn't have to worry about choosing anymore.

She had almost reached the opposite side of the clearing when David burst into sight with his gun out and pointing at her. Startled, Karen leaped back and pointed the dagger at him. They both stood that way for a long moment. Karen knew she must look crazy and strange, cradling the limp baby gargoyle and brandishing a large punch dagger at him. David, with a bruised face, quickly shifted his gun away from her.

"What happened?" They asked each other at the same moment then laughed, both a little shaky.

"I ran into a guy with a gun, running like the devil himself was chasing him. I had heard the shot. I tried to stop him, but he was really strong. Pistol-whipped me and kept on going." David paused, licking his partly swollen lip. "Are you okay? Is that—Sebastian?"

Karen took a breath and nodded. "Yeah. He's real. He protected me from that guy who hit you and had this." She lifted the dagger. "He's hurt... I have to help him. We need to—"

She was cut off by the sound of something very large lumbering through the trees towards them. She turned and saw an honest-to-goodness werewolf stagger out from the line of trees, utter a heart wrenching howl, and collapse to its knees.

Oh, furry brother, she thought and heard David breath, "Christ Almighty..." then felt him level his gun over her shoulder at the downed creature.

Without thinking, she raised her arm, knocking his hand upwards. The shot was deafening in her ear, but it went wide of the mark.

"What the hell are you doing?"

"Werewolf. Christ, Karen, it's a werewolf!"

Turning to face him, she put herself between her sweetheart and the werewolf. "Yes, and it's hurt. Why the hell are you shooting at it?"

David was incredulous. "It's a bloody werewolf! A monster that eats people."

Karen looked back at the creature, which was still on its knees, panting heavily and bleeding from a vicious gash in its abdomen. "Oh? Are you in the habit of killing werewolves whenever you see them without question? Are you sure they're all bad?"

"Yes. Now get out of my line of fire before it hurts you."

Karen blinked in surprise.

David paused, looking chagrined. "As you see, you're not the only one keeping secrets. Now, please move."

"No." She took another step back towards the werewolf.

"No?"

"No. Sebastian said this one was a 'furry brother' and a guardian. That something very important was stolen by that guy who shot at me and hit you."

"And you believe him?"

"Yes. Christ, David, look at him! He's barely alive, and needs help now. I don't care what secrets you're keeping. I don't give a damn about what rules you follow. I didn't sign up for them. I didn't sign up for any of these bloody rules that everyone's trying to make me follow. Sebastian told me to help this guardian and I'm going to. If for no other reason that I'm damn tired of being forced to follow rules that I don't know, don't like, and don't believe in. So, you can either help me help this werewolf or you can go home."

Neither of them said anything for a long moment. David finally nodded and stuffed the snub-nose revolver into his back holster. He bent and retrieved the dagger. "We may need this."

"What for?"

"I don't know."

Now, he sounded cranky. She felt like she should apologize, but she didn't know what to apologize for. She'd meant every word she'd said. She opened her mouth to say something soothing, but the werewolf shifted on his knees, trying to stand but couldn't manage it. She turned to him.

"Dying..." he growled. "Help me... home."

"Yes. We'll help. Where's home?"

"Can you shift to human again?" David asked. "It'll be easier to get you home if you aren't... like that."

Karen gave him a sharp look.

He frowned at her. "It's true. Let's see how far you... we... get with a werewolf in tow."

The werewolf nodded and became human. There was no cool special effect of limbs morphing and changing. No writhing in pain. No nothing. One moment, he was a werewolf; the next he was a Native American man wearing gray jogging shorts and sporting a hideous gash in his stomach that continued to leak blood.

They got him up and to David's car, with David doing most of the helping, as Karen had Sebastian to look after.

During the short ride to the Makah reservation, they discovered their passenger was Sparks-of-the-Moon, or Joseph Sparks. "Most people, Makah or not, just call me Sparks."

***

Arriving at the Makah reservation had been an unnerving experience. They were greeted by five Makah elders who seemed to expect them, all of whom looked older than God. They had wordlessly stared while Karen tried to explain what happened. Finally, the eldest of the men pointed at Karen. "Speaks-for-the-City, you come to lend aid?"

She looked around, "Um. Yes. I want to help Sparks. Why do you call me that?"

They ignored her question and took the three of them inside. After being hustled into a sparsely furnished room to lay Sparks down on a bed, David and Karen had been hustled out again. No one spoke to them for a long time, except to ask for the punch dagger David had picked up.

Karen and David spent the entire time not talking. She brooded over Sebastian and the fact that it had never occurred to her that David might have secrets, that he might know more than she thought he did, or that he'd be able to help her with her tasks for Reginald like Aaron had in the past.

Walks-the-Ocean, the youngest seeming of the five Elders, came out. "Karen, please go in. David, I need a word with you."

Glancing between the old man and David, Karen saw that the two men already knew each other. She could not decide if she was relieved or resentful of this fact. She nodded and walked into the room. The other four tribe Elders sat to the side. Two were drumming. The others were singing.

Sparks gestured to her from the bed. She came and sat by his side. "Is there anything I can do?"

He ignored the question and reached out to Sebastian. "Is this... my little stone brother? The one... who went for help?"

She nodded. "Yes. He came for me. Then, got hurt saving me from that man."

"That man... Betrayer. Liar. Thief." He winced as his vehement anger caused him to move more than he should.

"Shhh. Lie still."

"You have to know... That man. He's Paul Maloy. That's the name... he gave us. Said he admired and collected Makah artifacts. Wanted to know about us. All lies... Pretty lies. He got the people at the Center... to tell him about us. I don't know how... Must have been magic. Now, he's got Changer's Claw. My people will want blood... for this. You have to... get it back. We can't go to war... not now."

"War with who?"

"I don't know. You've got to... please. Promise."

Karen nodded, swallowing. "I will get Changer's Claw back for you. I promise. You'll guard it again."

He shook his head. "No. I'm dying. I didn't think... I could. Not like this. Not blooded like this. That knife... had bad magic on it." He shook his head and looked at her. "You're so much like her." He reached out for her long hair.

She bent her head, allowing her hair to stream in brown waves over his hand. "Who?"

"My wife... my love. Running Doe. Maloy killed her first. Killed her... and only managed to wound me." He leaned over and lay his head against her leg. "I will be with her soon."

Karen shifted under and behind him, giving him the warmth and support he seemed to want. "Tell me about Running Doe." She looked up to see more people in the room. She turned back to Sparks, unable to bear their soft, singing sorrow.

"I met her by the ocean... running at night. Suddenly this woman passed me. She looked over her shoulder... and laughed. It was an invitation to chase. I did.... I chased her until she decided... to let me catch her. It was love. Fate. Kismet. Karma."

Karen stroked his brow as he felt her hair in his hand, looking at it but not seeing it. "That was what we loved to do. Be outside with each other. By the ocean... at night... we would run. That *running* feeling... We would race the moon until we couldn't run any farther."

His voice faded as he spoke, whispering. "Tonight, my family will sing me there. Then we will run... with the stars... forever..." He brought her hair over to touch his face as Karen held him. "Running Doe..."

Karen held onto her tears until his hand opened and went limp, freeing her hair from his grip. The singing swelled with mingled triumph and sorrow as they gathered around him. Someone helped her up and escorted her to the doorway, where David stood. He seemed uncertain for a moment, then gathered Karen into his arms and drew her from the room. She sobbed in the safety of his arms until the initial wave of grief receded. Then, she was embarrassed and pulled back.

"I'm sorry I yelled at you." She stroked the still, limp form of Sebastian in her arms.

"I'm sorry I didn't tell you about me." She started to speak, but David raised his hand. "I should have brought it up sooner. I've known for a while that you're into something special for the city, but I'd been waiting for you to tell me on your own. I should have thought about it from your point of view and why you wouldn't. I work in a special department for the police. A department that knows that weird stuff happens in Kendrick. We know that you're somehow involved. So, the police don't give you too much trouble whenever your name comes up. The stuff you do seems to help the city.

"I know Chief Walks-the-Ocean because he's the Makah contact to my department. He asked me not to report this theft or the two murders. It's going to cause a war between some of the factions. I've agreed. I don't like it. I'm effectively telling him I agree to not do my job. I agreed because I think war will happen if this gets out—and I think it might get out. I've suspected a leak in the department for a while."

David sighed and glanced back to the room with Sparks' body. "The Makah are a proud people. Those who stole the Changer's Claw, a religious artifact, are either stupid or dangerous. I'm going to put my bet on dangerous. We need to keep the bloodshed to a minimum and protect the innocent."

"I'm going to get it back."

"I know. Walks-the-Ocean told me. I'm going to help." He paused. "You don't have to tell me about you, Sebastian, or who you work for, but if you want to talk about it someday, I'll listen."

"Thank you, but I don't think I can right now. I have to get home and see what I can do to help Sebastian. He's new in my life. I don't really know how to take care of him."

David looked down at the baby gargoyle and shook his head. "I don't know, either. Do you want me to see if anyone in my department knows?"

She shook her head. "No. I have someone I can call, but thanks."

"Okay. I'll take you home."

Neither of them spoke again on the way home except to say good-bye when he dropped her off.

***

Karen sat at home by the window with the newly patched Sebastian in her lap.

"Anything will do, as long as it seals the wound – caulk, modeling clay, toothpaste, whatever." Susan had advised. *"Then, keep him from picking at it when he wakes up. It will itch and he's a baby. They heal fast, Karen. Sebastian should be fine in a day or two. I'll send a gargoyle by to look in on him. Just leave your balcony doors unlocked."*

She'd only had toothpaste on hand. It seemed strange to fix him that way, but she'd done it. Now, the wound was sealed smooth and minty fresh as well. She was waiting for him to wake up so she could keep him from picking at it. She was also waiting for this other gargoyle, feeling a little odd at the idea of it wandering around her home at night. She hoped something would happen before she passed out from exhaustion.

She was dozing when Sebastian finally stirred and she felt his presence in the back of her mind. He immediately turned to eye the makeshift patch on his back. "No, kiddo. Susan says you can't mess with it."

There was a low whine in his throat as he complained. *'Bothers. Itchy. Ants inside my skin. Little scratch...'* He reached out a sharp set of claws towards his back, but stopped when she stuck her finger in front of it.

She had no doubt that if he wanted to, her finger would be so much hamburger. Instead, she distracted him. "You were very brave. I would have been hurt badly without you."

'Brave and fierce.' The sense of pride was palpable. *'Blooded him again.'*

"Again? What do you mean?"

'He tried to hurt you before.'

"He did? When?"

'In the museum. I scratched his face. I remembered his smell. I hurt him bad then. I did it again, too.'

Karen felt her skin go cold and her hackles rose. The Order of the Sacred Eye had been behind that theft, and now this one. It explained the man's recognition of her. He'd stolen a lock of her hair then. A slow burning rage ignited within. She had a name and a faction... a culprit for the theft of Changer's Claw and the murders of Running Doe and Sparks-of-the-Moon. That was it. It was time to stop waiting to see what they would do next. It was time to take this fight to their doorstep. It was time to let them know they'd crossed that line one too many times.

Part of her, the calm rational 911 operator, knew she was reacting with the grief and loss of seeing had a good man die in her arms, and that she was in no shape to make such a decision. For a brief moment, her rational side almost won out.

Then, she shoved it away. She was tired of those rules, of pussyfooting around magical norms and social customs of this other world; of being someone she wasn't. She liked being a normal person but her life wouldn't let her. So now she was going to put the Order on notice and if she had to, she'd start pulling in those favors owed to her from so many of the other groups she had helped in the past.

And if it was going to be war, it would start with finding Paul Maloy.

***

Elsewhere...

Todesengel grunted in pain again as Nightshade tied off the makeshift stitches on his neck.

"Stop being such a baby." She smirked as she dabbed the area with a stinging disinfectant.

His lips curled into a snarl. "You get attacked by a gargoyle and tell me how you feel, bitch." He clenched his hands to keep from hitting her.

Her survival instincts kicked in, and she left the area before Praetor had to separate them like the squabbling children they frequently resembled.

He walked over to look at the livid scratches and bite marks on his assassin's neck. "Little shit did quite the job on you. I'll make sure you're justly compensated, and have Cerridwen do some healing magic on you." Praetor looked at the faint scars on the other side of the man's face. "It seems to do the job."

"But it still hurts. There was no warning that there would be gargoyles or the Master's representative there."

"Was she there to stop you, or was it happenstance?"

"I don't know."

"Does she know you escaped with the Changer's Claw?"

"Again, I don't know."

Praetor blew out a breath. His patience was wearing thin. "What do you know?"

"She was there. A gargoyle was there. She knew the gargoyle. Called it Sebastian. It attacked me when I pointed the gun at her. It's probably her protector. She was also there with the cop she's been seeing. I ran into him, too."

"And?"

"And nothing. I knocked him down and kept going. The Guardian was still on my trail. I was hoping it might attack them in its wounded state."

"But, you don't know what happened with that?"

"No, I had other things on my mind, Praetor... like keeping my throat intact and completing the mission you sent me on for the good of the Order." His eyes dared his superior to contradict him in any way. They promised pain and death.

Praetor nodded, "Of course, you're right. My apologies. The mission... and you... were more important. You made the right decision. If more comes of this, we'll deal with it in time."

Todesengel mentally downshifted from killing mode to something more civil. It was rare that the leader apologized, even when it was called for. The fact that Praetor had, meant that he still respected him and his abilities. Todesengel nodded. "She didn't see my face. I promise that."

Praetor nodded, distracted. "Good." He needed to keep Todesengel under control until the ritual. After that, it would not matter. He pondered the idea of giving Nightshade to the man, knowing their mutual hatred. However, she was still useful to him and worth saving for now, should the sacrifice of a queen be needed in the future. "Good. We need to keep her off balance until the ritual. I need you to lay low while you heal. The scars are too distinctive. I need you to be able to blend in. I'll talk to Cerridwen about that as well. In the meantime, why don't you stay at my estate and enjoy a well-earned rest?"

Both men smiled at each other, but neither smile reached their eyes.

Afternoon Tea

"WHAT MAKES YOU think I know anything about the Order of the Sacred Eye or who this Paul Maloy is?" Luke Coleman stood behind the counter of his antique store, Treasures & Trinkets (*"One man's trash is another man's treasure."*), drumming his fingers on the polished wood surface. "And if I did, what makes you think I would just tell you about either without some sort of trade. TANSTAAFL, little girl. TANSTAAFL."

Karen had never heard anyone actually say the Heinlein acronym for 'There ain't no such thing as a free lunch' as an actual word before, much less in a southern twang. She would grin over it later. Right now, she was not grinning. Not even smiling. "I know because only a scum-sucking lowlife who preys on the grief-stricken like you would have anything to do with an Order that advocates theft, fraud, and murder. You may not be part of them but you are in league with them—"

"You wound me." He put a hand over his heart as if hurt.

"—and the only thing little about me is my fear of you." She ignored his mockery.

He lost his playful demeanor. "Careful."

Karen planted her fingertips on the countertop and leaned towards him. "Careful of what, you miserable bottom feeder? What will you do? The only way you can hurt your victims is for them to voluntarily come to you. For them to willingly give to you while you just take and take and take. I'm smarter than that. I know what you are. It'll be a cold day in hell before you get your claws in me."

She saw the anger gathering in his face. It was not smart to point out a man's flaws. Worse to grind his face in them, but she was too angry to stop. "Now, if you won't tell me where Paul Maloy is or who his boss is, then you do this: You tell them that I'm coming and that they *will* pay for all of the harm they have done. I promise you that. They, and all those who stand in my way, will pay. You think carefully about that, Luke."

Taking her fingertips off the countertop, she brushed them at her jeans as if they were dirty. She was pleased to note that her shaking was from adrenaline and not fear. She waited for the man to respond. He did nothing but grit his teeth and glower at her. She nodded. "Fine. I'll get Paul Maloy if it's the last thing I do." She turned and strode from the store without a backward glance.

She walked across the street towards the Colonel's Park and into it. She smiled when she saw Aaron waiting for her by the Colonel's statue. He headed towards her as soon as he saw her. "How'd it go? You okay?"

Karen gave him a hug and a brief kiss. "Well enough. The word will get out to the Order. I've talked to enough people. He was the last on my list. The Order's going to have to watch their step from now on." She hugged him again. "Thanks for waiting for me in the park. David never would have."

"I didn't like it, but you're a big girl. I was just waiting for the explosion before I came running."

"No, you don't understand. I really appreciate this; you coming with me but waiting outside, understanding that I need to do these confrontations by myself but really needing your support in-between threats."

"Karen, you didn't threaten Luke Coleman, did you? That man is dangerous."

"I did, a little, but he had it coming."

He whistled low. "That's not very healthy. He's one of the more powerful but neutral forces in Kendrick."

"'Neutral' my ass. He's sided with the Order. I could see it on his face. I don't think neutral exists anymore in Kendrick. Things are coming to a head."

"And you're gonna light the fuse?"

"If I have to. I'm sick of this. Sick to death of all this pussyfooting around. Sick of people saying, 'Follow the rules.' You know what? These damn rules are what got us to this point now.

"The Makah people refused to go to the police about the murders of their own people. The police representative allowed this to happen. Now, instead of the police looking for Paul Maloy for murder and bringing in official help, it's all swept under the carpet. This is wrong. Someone has to take a stand. It might as well be me. And I'm doing it with Reginald's blessing."

Aaron raised his hands in defense. "Whoa. You're preaching to the choir here, dearheart. I know you're right. It's why I'm coming with you. It's why I'm trying to help. But... and I hate to have to ask this... but, have you thought about why these rules were in place to begin with?"

Karen let her anger drain. "Yeah, I have. But, it's like any system that has gone corrupt. It was put in place to protect the innocent. Now, they've been twisted until all they do is help the bad guys. I can't abide by a system like that. This is one of the few ways I know to make it better."

"I know. I know. It's why I love you. You stand by the conviction of your words." He paused, looking at her frown. "What?"

"Nothing." Karen shook her head, then looked at her watch. "I gotta go."

"Want me to give you a ride home?"

"Nah. I think I need some time alone with my thoughts, and to think out what I'm going to do next. The walking will do me good."

Aaron didn't look happy at her answer, but nodded. "Okay. I'll be at the club tonight if you want to see me."

Karen gave him a hug and a kiss good-bye. "Thanks for understanding." She walked away toward home.

***

An hour later, Karen regretted her hasty decision to flee from that word "love" and to walk home. She hadn't taken into account how far it was from City Center to the Crossroads District and her apartment. Though the walk had been pleasant enough at first, the sun was reaching its zenith on this unusually warm summer day. It was very hot for the Pacific Northwest, and she wasn't halfway home yet.

She thought to hail a cab, and then looked around to realize she was in the middle of suburbia. She'd have to find the nearest intersection first, then call a cab company. As she looked down the way towards the nearest cross street, Karen noticed something odd. She could see faint outlines of footsteps on the sidewalk leading towards a nearby driveway. She followed the barely visible steps all the way back to where she stood. Looking behind her, there were no footsteps at all. The odd, there-but-not-there footsteps started exactly where she stood.

She took four steps forward and looked back. No footsteps. Looking forward, they were still there, leading her towards the driveway at the end of the hedge. She followed them to the private driveway and stopped. Behind her, as expected this time, the footsteps were gone. Before her, the footsteps continued down the driveway bordered on the left by a built-up wall of rock and by the tall hedge on the right.

Abruptly, the not-there footsteps turned right and walked straight into the hedge.

Knowing that she was being led by something supernatural—yet another thing she didn't know of—Karen walked cautiously to the point in the hedge where the footsteps disappeared. She stuck her hand in her pocket and gripped the small mace sprayer as she stared at the hedge. At first, she saw nothing but more dense foliage. Then, as she watched, a hedge door seemed to form before her eyes. It was like discovering the picture in one of those 3-D optical illusion prints. Once you saw the picture, you couldn't 'not see' it anymore.

Before she could reach for the doorknob, the door swung inward to reveal an old man in a butler's uniform standing inside. "Good afternoon, Miss Wilson. You are expected. Please come in." He stood aside with solicitous deference.

"Uh, Thank you, uh..." There was something calming about the butler that made Karen relax and let go of the mace in her pocket.

"James."

"Thank you, James." She stepped inside. "But, who is expecting me?"

"The Lady of the Grey Manor, of course." He turned and led her toward a white gazebo with a gabled roof. Behind it was a beautiful storybook Victorian home with two turrets. The whole thing was grey, edged in white.

"Of course," she murmured, knowing she should be surprised but, somehow, she wasn't.

The first time Karen heard about the Lady of the Grey Manor was when she'd first met Heather at Bacchanalia. Heather had come looking for help in saving an old professor who had once saved her from a decidedly non-supernatural predator. She had mentioned going to see the Lady of the Grey Manor then. Based on everything Karen had heard, The Lady seemed to have a lot of information. Whose side she was on was anyone's guess.

James led her up to the gazebo and pulled out a chair for her. Already at the table was a woman who had to be the Lady of the Grey Manor. She was a handsome woman with white hair piled high upon her head. She wore a layered, high-collared gown in white and grey. The ensemble was completed with a pair of white gloves. Karen did not know anything about antique clothing, but if she had to guess, the Lady was dressed in a Victorian or Edwardian style. Her easy elegance made Karen feel like the proverbial country bumpkin in a fairytale.

"Good afternoon, Miss Wilson." The Lady's voice was smooth and welcoming. "I had hoped you would come." She offered Karen her hand. "I am known as the Lady of the Grey Manor. Please just call me Lady Grey."

Karen gave the Lady a firm, short handshake. "A pleasure to meet you, Lady Grey." She stopped then, not knowing what else to say.

James returned, carrying a silver serving tray that held a porcelain tea set and plate of small tea cakes. He served the Lady first, fixing her cup of tea and putting out a plate of cakes with it. Then, he fixed Karen's tea—exactly how she liked it. A little milk and a lot of sugar. She could only guess that knowing how she liked her tea was part of his particular magic. Rather like his ability to make people feel welcome and calm she realized as she settled in, knowing she should be on alert.

After the tea was served, James had departed, and sips of delight had been had, Lady Grey smiled at Karen. "I know you are wondering why you are here. I will tell you that the answer is both simple and complex. The simple answer is that I wanted to meet you for myself. I have been hearing of you for some time now."

"Good things, I hope." Karen eyed the tea cake with some trepidation, wondering if she could manage to eat it without spilling crumbs all over herself.

"Good depends on your point of view, does it not?"

"I suppose, but I believe there are some inherently good things and some inherently bad things."

"Oh? How so?"

"Well, hurting a child is inherently bad to me."

"A spanking to teach a child a lesson does hurt him or her."

"That isn't what I meant."

"Hmm? What did you mean?"

"I mean... well, people like Thomas Rutherford..." Karen didn't want to explain further in such genteel company. The former Vice Principal had committed suicide after Karen had found the body of a dead child in the man's office in an abandoned school that was scheduled to be torn down. Amongst the man's confessions within the suicide note was the admission that he was both a pedophile and a murderer.

"Ah. Yes. I understand now. In this case, I will agree with you." Lady Grey sipped her tea. "Karen, you understand what you are doing in Kendrick now, don't you?"

"I'm not sure I understand your question."

"Do you understand that your actions, while helpful up to this point, are going to force a war between the supernatural factions in Kendrick?"

"Yes. I do."

"Do you understand that people will die in this war? People you care about?"

Karen paused, thinking about it for a long time. She gulped her tea, not tasting it. "Yes." She answered. "Yes. People will die, but people are already dying, and no one is doing anything about it. I can't let that go on. I can't let people die, artifacts be stolen, or for the Order to merrily continue on their way in whatever scheme they have planned."

"What about the young officer you've been courting? Why not work with him?"

"David already allowed one thing to slide by as part of his department's agreement with the Makah and who knows how many others?" Karen frowned. "And Aaron... his loyalty is only to Bacchanalia. This is bigger than that."

"What if they are doing what they are doing for the good of Kendrick?"

"Do you really believe that?"

It was Lady Grey's turn to be silent for a time. Finally, she sighed. "No. I do not. The Order is acting in its own selfish interest."

"That's why I am doing this. Everyone knows what they are doing, but no one's taking a stand."

"Karen, do you believe in this enough to die for it?"

"Believe in stopping the Order from doing what they are doing, regardless of whom it hurts?" She nodded. "I know I'm putting myself in danger. I don't want to die, but I'm willing to risk it."

"What about risking the lives of your friends and loved ones?"

"What do you mean?"

"Do you believe the Order is only going to target you? No. They will go after those you care the most for—Aaron or David—or both."

Karen grimaced. "Both of them are..." She stopped.

"You are angry with both. Do you realize that you have chosen two men who represent the two sides of you? David is your safe, normal mundane side. Aaron is your exciting, supernatural side. But, now, you've discovered that David isn't so safe or mundane anymore while Aaron has a very mundane side to him as well."

"How do you know all this? How do you know about me?"

"We all have our specialties, my dear. Mine is information. I am right, aren't I?"

"Yes." Karen had never thought of the two men in such terms. Not really, but now that it had been pointed out, yes, it was true. "Now, both of them... and both sides of me... are in danger."

"Yes. Knowing that, do you still mean to make your stand against the Order of the Sacred Eye?"

She clinked her teacup back onto the saucer. "Yes. I can't stop now. I just can't. It wouldn't be right and I made a promise..."

The Lady nodded. "I understand. Then, I will do what I can to help you. Give me your teacup."

Karen handed it over. "Going to read my fortune?"

"Something like that." Lady Grey turned the cup back and forth murmuring. She frowned slightly.

"What? What do you see?" Karen leaned forward despite her still skeptical nature.

"Nothing is written in stone, but if you continue on your current path, I see three things: The first is that someone close to you will betray you. Someone you trust. Beware of light within the light. The second is that your mentor is not whom or what you believe him to be. But, he is not the one who will betray you. The last is death, but I don't know for whom. Someone close to you will die if you continue as you have been."

"I'm sorry I asked."

"No great change will come without sacrifice. What you are pushing with your vendetta against the Order will cause this great change." Lady Grey made a beckoning gesture over her shoulder. "Reginald and I have been acquaintances for many years. We have not always agreed, but I think you do well by him. I also have a gift for you."

Karen looked up. From the direction the Lady gestured approached two children, a boy and a girl, each about nine years old with black hair, dressed in clothing that reminded her of the 1920s. They skipped along, and then dashed, laughing, up to the gazebo. Karen realized she recognized the children. She had first seen them in the Transitory Tunnel. Now, she suddenly realized she had been seeing them around town for weeks. She would notice them, and then forget them.

The boy bowed. "She is Thomasina."

The girl curtsied. "He is Thomas."

"We are both older—"

"—and younger—"

"—than we appear."

"This is our greatest asset—" Thomasina said.

"—and our greatest weakness," Thomas concluded.

Thomasina stepped forward and handed Karen a box. "This belongs to you."

"Thank you." Karen said, feeling a bit bewildered by the single conversation coming from the two children.

As the two eternal children reverenced, then dashed away, Lady Grey spoke. "I did not know whether or not I should return this to you. Without it, you have found the inner strength to take the stand that needed to be taken. But now, I believe you will need it, and all of your other skills, to direct this storm you are creating."

Karen opened the box and was very surprised to see a familiar silver bracelet inside. She held it up and read the charm dangling from it. "Joy" was written on one side. "Hope" was written on the other. "I had forgotten how pretty this was. How did you...?"

"You sacrificed it, and all it represented, when you saved Professor Chapman."

"Language professor—Greek, Latin, Spanish and Italian." Karen murmured as she put the bracelet back on her wrist as the lost memory came flooding back.

"I have one last question for you. When you sacrificed your memory, why did you choose to sacrifice the good memory of your friend rather than the bad memory of your grandmother's death?"

"Pain is a funny thing. It forces a person to act. In tragedy, you discover the mettle of a person. Strength of character is what you do when you are hurt or scared. It shows what kind of person you are. I still miss my Grandmother, but it was her death that made me choose to be the person I am today. I didn't want to lose that."

"Thank you, Karen. I have enjoyed this afternoon with you. I hope, after the storm dies away, we may do this again."

She could hear the unspoken dismissal and stood. It was time for her to go anyway. Karen had too many things on her mind as it was. "Thank you for the tea and the reading, Lady Grey. I hope to see you again as well."

"James will show you out, and I believe you will find yourself much closer to home. Good afternoon."

She was led to the other side of the large yard to another door in the hedge. James opened it and gave her a small bow. "Good afternoon, Miss Wilson. Have a good evening."

"Thank you. You, too." She stepped out of the hedge onto another private driveway. Walking down to the street, she saw she was only a few blocks away from home. For that, she was thankful. She wanted nothing more than to be in the safety of her apartment with Sebastian curled up beside her and a drawing pencil in her hand. Later, she would think about what had been read in her tea leaves. For now, she just wanted to be home.

As she walked along, she wondered where Sebastian was and if he'd been there within the sanctuary of the Grey Manor. She looked around to see if she could catch a glimpse of grey moving. She smiled as she thought she did, high above her.

'You can only because I let you.'

'You were there?' she asked.

'No. I could still hear you, but there are places that gargoyles cannot or do not go.'

'Why not?'

'In this case, politeness. Reginald and Susan and my elders have told me not to go there. But, in other cases, there is magic that bars or hurts us.'

'Can you always hear my thoughts?'

'Yes. You can always call to me, Karen. I will always protect you unless I am dead.'

Sebastian's last sending disturbed her. Coupled with the warnings from the Lady Grey, she was suddenly worried for Sebastian's safety. Then, the guilt washed over her. She was more worried for her little guardian than she was for the two men she had refused to let herself love. There was a lesson in this realization, and she really needed to learn it in a hurry.

***

Elsewhere...

"It appears you have upset the young Miss Wilson with your last mission." Praetor said, putting the phone down. "She has your name, and has been rattling cages all over town, demanding your head on a platter."

"Huh? How'd she get my name?" Paul lounged on the couch in Praetor's living room.

"I suspect it was because you were foolish enough to give your real name to the Makah. I don't know why she's involved but, according to Luke, she is filled with piss and vinegar, demanding you or your boss. She's put the Order on notice that you will pay for your crimes.

Paul scowled, ignoring Praetor's jab at his indiscretion. "Stupid bitch. Shoulda killed her."

"Now now, Todesengel. We need her. Let's think about this carefully. She does want you quite badly, however. I'm sure this could be turned to our advantage."

"How?"

"Have someone offer you to her. Someone she trusts."

"You want me to play bait?"

"Why not?"

"Because I kill things. I'm not some lamb to be slaughtered." His voice was flat with contempt.

Praetor sighed and wondered, not for the first time, if he was the only person in the room with a brain. "No, you're not, but what's the harm in dressing the wolf up like a lamb until it's time for him to come out and do his duty?"

A slow smile covered Paul face. "I get it. Have her come for me, then we take her."

"Exactly. Well, not exactly, but close. I have a plan. I had wondered how I would get her to the ritual on time." He toasted his assassin. "Here's to impulsive women ruled by their emotions."

The two men raised their glasses in a salute to each other and tossed back their drinks. Things were definitely on the upswing.

Sins of the Brother

BROTHER SIMON, AS he was known only within the hidden confines of the monastery, felt the peace of monastic life return as he stripped himself of his 'normal' clothing and slid into the simple robe of the Brotherhood. He left his other clothes neatly folded in the coat room. Giving the pile of outer world clothing and effects a troubled glance, he realized his problem was not the fact that he was a man with two lives. It was the fact that he was no longer certain which one was real and which one was the sham.

He walked through the quiet halls of what had once been a train station, located on the western edge of Kendrick. On the outside, it was perpetually under renovation. On the inside, the renovations had been completed for years. Austere but sound, the former train station had transformed easily into a serviceable monastery. There were few amenities, but that was exactly what was wanted and needed in this place.

Life had seemed simple when he'd first arrived here so many years ago. The Brotherhood was all to him, and it was all in the service of God. He had come here recovering from the death of his entire family, murdered by zealots in the name of a demonic creature. Back then, he had not understood why. To this day, he still wondered if they had targeted the right family. The Brotherhood assured him that they had, and he had been the intended target. God had seen to it that Simon was spared to do His work.

Climbing the stairs of what had been the old bell tower, but now led to the office of the Abbot and the Chief Guardian of the Spirit, Simon wondered what would happen to him if he confessed his doubts about his current mission.

Not the actual mission, but the manner in which he was forced to go about it. Why not just tell Karen what the Order of the Sacred Eye seemed to be doing? Why not confess his own part in this war, and that she was not just a mission to him— that his feelings for her were genuine?

Brother Simon paused outside the office door and gathered his composure. Thinking of Karen and how he felt the Brotherhood was wronging her always made him lose his inner balance.

"Come in, Brother Simon," Brother Peter called from behind the closed door.

That made him smile. His mentor was so attuned to the monastery and those within it that he could always tell where everyone was and who needed his attention. Simon opened the door to the small, dark wood-paneled office. "Good morning, Brother Peter." He sat when his superior gestured for him to do so.

Once again, he was struck with the conflicting desires he felt when he sat in this office. It was no accident that the Brotherhood had named him Simon. In the bible, the Disciple Peter was Simon before he became Peter. He was destined for the same path. Eventually, he was to take his mentor's place as the head of this monastery, and become the Chief Guardian of the Spirit here. Part of him wanted that and the serenity of this isolated bubble-world of silence, dark wood, incense, and prayer. Part of him dreaded it. It was too passive for him. Spiritual warriors needed to exercise the body and mind as well as the soul.

"You have much on your mind." Brother Peter was an old man, but his senses were still sharp.

"Yes."

"Do you wish to speak of it now, or give me your report first?"

"The report. That will lead into the rest."

The old man nodded. "It usually does." He opened up a lined notebook and dated the top of the page. "I'm ready."

"It's as you have said all along. Karen Wilson is the catalyst that will bring the Change. After the death of Sparks-of-the-Moon and the theft of Changer's Claw, she has been a woman possessed with righteous fury. She is aware that the Order of the Sacred Eye is planning something big. She does not know what. She has no idea that she is in danger. I still think we need to warn—"

"We have been over this before. We will not. If she knows, she may change the way she is doing things, and we need her to act as she is doing. Continue."

Simon swallowed his anger with an effort. He could not understand Peter's calm acceptance that, if they were not quick, Karen would die. "She's been forcing the various factions to look at what they do not wish to see and to make them aware that they must choose sides. That those who remain on the fence will, most likely, be the first to drop in this war."

"Do you know who is on what side?" He continued to write in the Brotherhood's shorthand, but watched Simon out of the corner of his eye.

"Some. John Corso, Bacchanalia, the Special Unit branch of the police, Susan Moore and the gargoyles are all siding with Karen. Luke Coleman and the Children of Anu are siding with the Order. I am not certain about the Makah or Lady Grey and her faction."

"Give me a guess."

"You know I don't like to—"

"I know. But you have to trust your instincts more. Guess." Brother Peter pressed his protégé to use the instincts he often ignored.

"The Makah will side with Karen at the last minute. Mostly because the Elders are hesitant and feeling their age. The youngest, Walks-the-Ocean, is with her already and does not fear for his life." Simon nodded more to himself than to Peter. "They will come at the last minute. I just hope it won't be too late."

"Lady Grey?"

"She met with Karen recently."

"Yes?" This interested Peter. He still had not grasped what Lady Grey actually was, and that bothered him.

"I saw Karen enter a hedge and I wasn't the only one who saw. The other one... the other man she's dating... was following her, too." Pushing his jealousy aside, he continued. "I know she didn't see either of us. She was looking at something I could not see on the ground."

"Jealousy does not become you, Simon."

That caused him to start in surprise and look Peter in the eye for a long, uncomfortable moment. The fact that Brother Peter could read his emotions so clearly embarrassed him and he dropped his eyes down to the polished wood of the table. "I know. I'm sorry. I can't hide it. I'm having a hard time with this mission."

"I know. We will speak of that in a moment. Lady Grey?" Brother Peter continued writing in his looping shorthand.

Suddenly, Simon wondered if the Abbot's report to his superiors would include his adolescent longings for a woman he could not have. Not in the way he really wanted. "I saw her go into the hedge. I didn't try to follow her. It means that Lady Grey invited her in. I don't know when she left, but she seemed fine when I saw her next."

"Did 'the other' see you?"

He shook his head, flushing as his mentor threw his own jealous words back at him. This conversation was going to haunt him for a long time.

"Good. What about the Steward family? They have been curiously silent on these occult manners."

"Yes. I have the feeling that they are shoring up the mundane forces: police, emergency services, firehouses and such, in preparation. I honestly believe that they intend to be referees in this war. I think, mostly to contain the damage and to protect those who cannot see the real world. Their focus is the city of Kendrick itself. It always has been. Not the various factions within." He paused. "What about us, Brother Peter? What are we going to do in this war?"

"What we have always done—fight our battle on the spiritual battlefield."

Although he knew Peter meant that literally and not figuratively, since both of them had participated in several such battles before, he still didn't believe it was enough. It was one thing to fight demons. It was another to help the people in the physical world. Not that being hurt by a demon on the spiritual battlefield hurt any less when one's soul returned to the body.

"We're not going to share our knowledge with anyone? We're not going to help either side?"

"Of course we will be helping Karen's side and the side of Light. That is what we are meant to do." The tilt of the Abbot's head, suggested that Simon's question was unworthy for one of the Brotherhood.

"But we could be doing so much more."

Simon got up and paced back and forth in front of the desk. It was too small a space for such movement to be satisfying, but he could not sit still any longer. "We should tell her that the Order will be coming after her specifically, and not because of revenge. She should know this."

"Simon, I know that these infiltration missions are difficult. It's one of the reasons the Brotherhood remains isolated from the rest of the world. These outside influences confuse and distract from the real reason you're out there."

"Why *am* I out there in Kendrick? Why did I join the group I did? Why did you tell me to get close to her?"

Peter sat back with a sigh. "Kendrick is special in many ways that the rest of the world is not. It is a nexus of ley lines and destinies. We are here to guard the portals between the spiritual realm and the physical realm. You were asked to become part of Kendrick's occult society so we could keep abreast of the movement of factions within this arena. To keep them from accidentally or purposefully releasing monsters into this world. You know all of this."

He paused. "You were asked to get close to Karen Wilson because Divine prophecy told us that she would be the catalyst for great change and she is. We needed to know what she was doing. What she is still doing. You were not to fall in love with her, Simon. You have another path. Do not forget the vows you've taken."

The younger man dropped back into the chair in front of the desk with an abrupt *thump*. "I haven't forgotten my vows. But, I am in love with her. I can't help that. And I'm not the only one."

"Does she know?"

"I think so. But, she runs from us both. She runs from love. I don't understand why." He knew he sounded like a lovestruck teen, but he couldn't stop. He didn't want to stop. Speaking his heart would make the words real.

"She doesn't know all that I've done for her. How I've protected her. Watched her. Prayed for her. How I would kill for her..." He bowed his head and stared at his tightly clasped hands.

"Will kill for her if necessary."

Simon's head shot up. That was not what he was expecting to hear from his superior. In fact, he was expecting an admonishment. It was then that he saw Peter's concern. "What?"

"You may have to kill for Karen. Are you truly willing to do so?"

He paused, thinking it through more carefully. He put the face of Luke Coleman before him in his mind's eye. *Could I kill you if I had to?* The answer was yes, but unfair. Luke Coleman was demonic in nature.

He pulled up the face of his romantic rival, then tossed it away without consideration. It would not be fair to use that visage as a litmus test.

He pulled up the face of one of the Children of Anu; one of the normal human members. *Could I kill you if I had to?* The answer was yes. Weaker, but still definite. He could. He would. It would be in the name of God and for the love of Karen.

Simon nodded. "Yes."

"Good. Then, you will lead the Guardians in prayer and battle when the Order performs its rite on the next full moon. The creatures they will most likely pull through from the spiritual field must be exterminated."

"What? The next full moon? So soon? That's less than three weeks from now."

"I know. You will need to spend more time here at the monastery in preparation for that battle but you will also still need to stay in contact with Karen to find out her plans."

"You're just going to let the Order perform their rite? You're not... We're not going to try to stop it before it starts?" Simon was livid with his unspoken question: *You're just going to let them take, and possibly kill, Karen?*

"We need to see all of the pieces on the board. In less than three weeks, we'll have a clearly-divided line of who is on the side of the Divine and who is not. We must know who stands with whom. We *must* let the rite begin, and we must be prepared for the spiritual battle that we will fight here."

"But—"

Peter overrode Simon's protest with a held up hand. "Normally, I would remove you from this mission altogether. You have been too influenced by your time in the outside world. Too affected by your time with Karen. You've forgotten your vows and your mission. Normally, you would be assigned to prayer and preparation for the next three weeks.

"However, this is a delicate time in this war, and the Brotherhood needs all the information it can get. You are the only one close enough to the situation. I need to know right now, Brother Simon, are you still true to us?"

It was like being stabbed in the heart—twice. First was the threat of not seeing Karen again. Second was the questioning of his faith. He really was a man divided, and he felt like he was in danger of losing everything that mattered in his life. All of Simon's anger drained out of him. "Peter..."

"Are you still true to the Brotherhood and your vows?" The Abbot pressed.

"Yes. Yes, I am. The mission is all. In God's name, yes."

"Am I still your superior and mentor in the Brotherhood?"

"Yes, Brother Peter. You are."

"Do you trust me?"

Simon nodded his head after the briefest of hesitations. "Yes, of course." His hesitation was not lost to his mentor's knowing eyes. Neither was the hurt he saw there.

Peter nodded, his face becoming serene once more. "Then trust this: The Brotherhood will not allow Karen Wilson to come to any real harm. I promise you that."

"How...?"

"Trust me, Simon. I have been doing this for longer than you have been alive."

'How many sacrificial lambs have you lost in those years, Peter? How many have died?' He was instantly ashamed of the uncharitable thought. He knew Peter took his vocation very seriously. "Yes, Brother Peter."

"Do you understand what you are to do for the next three weeks?"

"Yes. Stay in contact with Karen and find out what her plans are. Keep in touch with the other factions where I have influence, and see which side of the line they are choosing. Other than that, remain here and prepare for battle."

"Good. I suggest you spend the rest of the day in the chapel in prayer and meditation. I sense you need to regain your equilibrium."

He heard the dismissal in the suggestion and stood. "Yes, Brother Peter."

"May God bless and keep you, Simon."

"And you as well, Brother."

Simon opened the door to the office and made his way down the stairs and through the monastery. He pulled his hood up and kept his eyes on the ground as he walked. He did not acknowledge any of the other brothers as they passed each other. Sensing he was troubled, his brothers left him alone.

He entered the chapel and was relieved to find it empty of people, but not of the Spirit. Thankful for the fact that this place had not lost its sense of the Holy to him, Simon knelt and gave himself over to God and prayer, asking for guidance. He was a man divided who desperately wanted to find balance. He wanted to be both true *and* right.

***

Elsewhere...

Karen looked down from her book at the small gargoyle curled up on her tummy. She could feel a contented, purring sensation in the back of her mind and gave him a gentle scritch behind the ears. The purring sensation grew louder. She noted how much Sebastian's skin felt like warm suede when he was not in 'rock mode.'

"You know, you're sort of like a pet... but not."

'Not a pet. Guardian. You're my human.'

"Is that like a pet?"

'No. Ward. Human. My human. Special.' He lifted his head and blinked gem-like light blue eyes at her.

"Whoa. Blue eyes. I thought they were black."

'They were. I like blue.'

"They're pretty. Sebastian, there's so little I know about you and who you are. I don't know how you were born. Or what you eat—"

'Snickers.'

"—besides Snickers bars or even if you know, go to the bathroom."

'No.'

"No? What do you do with the waste?"

'Get bigger.'

"Oh." She paused, considering this and saw with a bit of surprise that he was bigger. "Are all gargoyles in the city alive like you?"

'No. Some are just dumb rock. Some are alive but sleeping. They don't want to wake because their human is gone. But, someday, they will wake again. They will find another human to care for.'

"How do you know when you've found that human?"

'You just know.'

"I love you, little guy. You know that don't you?"

'I know. I know love, too. I love you.'

"I'm worried for you. This war. This thing I'm starting—have started—and can't stop even if I wanted to. I don't want you hurt."

'You won't be hurt. I won't let it happen.'

Suddenly, Karen had a really bad feeling; like she was going to lose Sebastian, and he seemed to be the only one she could really count on beyond Susan. Even Reginald seemed distant and cautious with her these days. "Promise me you won't do anything rash."

'I will do what I need to do.' He blinked those glittering blue eyes at her again, and she could feel the weight of stubbornness behind his words.

She hugged him to her. "You just be careful. Okay?"

'I'm always careful.' Sebastian endured this and when she was done, lowered his head and curled up again. In his mind, the conversation was done.

For Karen, it left her that much more concerned for the well being of her small guardian. There was too much going on. All she could do was continue to gather allies and hope they were true to their word.

Burning Bridges

"BE CAREFUL. THINGS aren't safe and I can't always protect you." Reginald's voice was still calm but there was something more in it.

"I will. I know what I'm doing." Karen hung up the phone as she entered the *Teller's Fortune*.

"Normally, I'd ask if you'd come for another story about the Todari deck, but I can see by the look on your face you haven't," John Corso closed the book he was holding.

"What look on my face? You can't see me. Your back's to me." Karen put her cell phone away.

Reginald seemed very uneasy, warning her that her actions were going to bring a more direct consequence soon. It had not been one of their better conversations and she had hung up on him in a snit.

Why can't he just give me a straight answer? Maybe because he doesn't have one. That last thought worried her. If Reginald wasn't sure about the state of the city, it was bad news indeed—and it was probably her fault.

"Yes, but I saw you in the mirror to my left as you came in." He gestured to the pillar. "There's a lesson in that for you, young lady."

"Yeah. Yeah. There's a lesson for me in everything these days."

John turned around and smiled at her. "So, what can I do for you, O'Speaks-for-the-City?"

Karen stepped back, shocked. "Why'd you call me that?"

"Isn't that your Makah name?"

"How do you know that? Why are you talking to them?"

"Why are you talking to me?" He countered, and then answered. "Information, of course."

"You went to the Makah to ask about me?" Her tone of voice insinuated that she would be very offended if the answer was yes.

"No. I went to the Makah to talk about the badness that's been rising since you took it upon yourself to declare war against the Order on their behalf."

"Oh." Karen did not know what to say about that. "Um. Okay. Were you successful?"

"I think so. But, you're not here to talk about the Makah, and you're not here to learn more about my wonderful Todari cards." He gestured to the well-appointed display case with the *'Not for Sale.'* sign in front of him. "So, why are you here? You know I don't know where Paul Maloy is, and I've looked. That boy has gone to ground, and left no trace behind."

She paused for a moment to admire the thin, wooden tarot cards in the long display case. Each was a work of art by the obscure Italian artist, Rinaldo Todari, and John Corso was the world's leading collector of this particular deck. He had thirty-seven of the seventy-eight cards. Fourteen of them were from the Major Arcana. Each card had an amazing history to it, as well as other supposed, less believable, qualities.

For a moment, she thought to abandon her original quest and ask for another Todari story instead. But, duty called. A duty she had created. "I want to know what you know about the Children of Anu."

John whistled low. "You don't ask for much, do you?"

"I don't know. Do I? It's why I'm asking. What can you tell me about them?"

"Can? A lot. Will? Not so much."

"Why not?"

"Because I've made certain agreements with them and, no matter how this war turns out, I intend to uphold my end of the bargain. It is not healthy to break your word with the Children."

Karen nodded in understanding. Promises and agreements were very important here in Kendrick. "Okay. What *will* you tell me about them?"

"Why do you want to know?" John held up a hand. "I'm not trying to be coy. I'm trying to figure out your motivations so I can give you the information you want.... need."

She swallowed her annoyance. "Ever since I started this thing I'm on, I've heard mention of 'The Children.' But no one will tell me who they are or whose side they're on."

"Ah, now we come to the crux of the matter. Ally or foe. First, the Children of Anu are one of the few truly secret groups I know. You don't know of them and people don't talk about them because they play their cards close to the chest. What's the use of having a secret organization if your membership keeps blabbing about your most sacred rites?"

"Point conceded." She leaned against the display case, looking down at the Major Arcana card called 'Strength.' It showed a woman holding the reigns of a rearing horse. She looked like she was controlling and calming the horse while it was fighting and losing to her. "So, they're supernatural? Or religious?"

"Both. But not all of their members are." He took off his glasses and cleaned them as he thought about his words. "What do you know about the god Anu?"

"Pretty much nothing."

"Do a Google search when you get home. The short answer is in Sumerian, Assyrian, and Babylonian mythology, Anu was a sky-god, the god of heaven, lord of constellations, spirits and demons, blah-blah-blah. Anu defeated another god—goddess to be exact, Tiamat, and became the King of Gods as well as the head of the entire Babylonian pantheon. Sometimes, Anu can be referred to as Marduk, depending on the culture.

"In truth, the whole history of Anu is a bit convoluted. What's important is that he's not a happy, shiny god. He supposedly created the stars as soldiers to punish the wicked. He is most often represented as a man with a crown decorated by bull's horns. At least, in the context that you and I are speaking of."

"The Children of Anu."

"Yes. I don't know what they are at the heart of their group, but from what I have seen, they're brutal, secretive, territorial, and they have a cause."

"What cause?"

"I don't know. But I know they're not just a force of chaos or anarchy. They have a code and rules they live by. They have their own goals."

"Do you think they've picked a side, yet?"

"Probably and not yours... ours. They've probably already made a deal with the Order based around territory. If they support the Order, most likely, the Order has promised them autonomy in some part of the city."

She looked down at the impossibly vibrant tarot cards, weighing her options. "Which territory?"

"What are you thinking? Karen, you can't go to them. You can't reason with them. You have nothing they want."

"What territory? If I'm to stay away, I need to know. So, I don't accidentally wander over there." Her words were logical but untruthful, and they both knew it.

John looked at her for a long time, deciding. But before he could answer, his face contorted into conflicting expressions of outrage, fear, and dismay. "Shit."

Then, everything seemed to happen all at once.

A car screeched to a stop in front of the *Teller's Fortune*. John slapped at something behind the counter. Karen turned towards the door to see what was happening.

A trapdoor beneath the Todari tarot cards in the display case dropped open.

Karen saw two small round objects crash through the front windows. John leaped over the counter in front of her, knocking her over.

The cards fell into their hidden compartment.

The car squealed away from the store.

Karen hit the floor as John shouted a word she did not understand.

The world exploded in light, sound, and heat.

When all of it receded, she found herself being picked up off the floor of a surprisingly intact store by a ruffled but seemingly unhurt storekeeper. The front windows and front displays were all blown outwards, as if the explosion had hit a particularly hard barrier and rebounded back out. She looked up at John. "Are you all right?"

"Yeah. A bit singed and pissed off. But fine."

Karen put her hand on the display case to steady herself as John let her go and walked around the backside of the counter. Opening a pair of sliding doors beneath the now empty display case, he began gathering the Todari tarot cards with care and putting them in a leather satchel.

"That's some trick."

"In truth, these cards are nigh impossible to destroy by such mundane means, but it pays to be careful. Andreas Parlor had more than half of the Danforth deck in his possession when it was stolen, and they're indestructible, too. But it's up to the owners of these special tarot cards to take care of them." He stood, pulling the satchel over his shoulder.

"The Danforth deck? What's that?" She was still dazed, but could hear sirens in the distance.

"A story for another time. I think you need to get out of here. I'm pretty sure those grenades had your name written all over them, and I don't think I'm being facetious."

"How did you stop the explosion?"

"I didn't. I redirected it away from my store and you." He came back around and snapped his fingers in her face. "Yeah, I think it was mostly directed at you. Come on, wake up." He gave her arm a small but violent shake.

The pain in her arm and the snapping of her head back and forth shoved the cobwebs away. "Okay. Okay. I'm okay."

"Good. I'm staying here. You be elsewhere. You weren't here when the attack happened. Right?"

Karen agreed and hurried through the rubble out the front of the store. There, she stopped and stared across the street. David and Aaron stood there, glaring at each other. With a sinking feeling, she strode to them. When they looked at her, she pointed at them. "You two. The Colonel's Park. Right now." She couldn't keep the fury from her voice and did not even try.

***

They were barely inside the tree line of the park when Karen whirled on them both. "What the hell are you two doing here?" She watched their faces. Her heart sunk even more when neither of them would look at her. If either of them had been in town on their own business, one or both of them would have reacted in confused defensiveness. Instead, they hung their heads in guilt. "You both were following me. Are you guys conspiring behind my back or something?"

"No." David said.

"No. I was just worried..." Aaron said at the same time.

The two of them looked at each other then back at Karen. "Oh, good. Brilliant. Both of you decided to do what? Shadow me and come to my rescue when I needed it? Do you two think so little of me and my ability that I need to have people following me around to rescue me from myself?"

"No. I heard that—" Aaron began.

"You could've been killed!" David's voice was quiet and intense.

"I don't want to hear it." Karen interrupted them both. "Do you guys realize what kind of danger you're putting yourselves in by following me? Or what kind of danger you're putting me in by distracting me? By being here at all when maybe, just maybe, I should be dealing with another danger? Like someone, oh, I don't know, throwing grenades at me?"

David reached for her. "This isn't a game. Someone just tried to kill you."

She jerked away from his grasp and started pacing, the numbness of shock was wearing off. Her body trembled with unused adrenaline. Her mind was racing and she was furious at the world. "What do you think would have happened if you had been in front of the *Teller's Fortune* when John deflected the blast? All of those shards of glass could have killed you.

Then, not only would John have felt bad, I would have been...God. I don't know. You two. Both of you. I care about you. Maybe I even love you but I can't have this. I just can't. What if John saw you and didn't want to sacrifice you two by deflecting the blast back out? He might have had to sacrifice himself or both of us. You could have killed us."

"I'm sorry, but I know I can help." Aaron frowned, stepping back from David and Karen. "I should help."

"I'm not a civilian. I've been trained and it's my job to protect Kendrick." David pulled open his shirt at the collar revealing the police vest underneath. "I'm prepared and I know what we're dealing with. I was there that night."

"Yeah, and you almost murdered the Guardian yourself instead of the Order doing it." Karen was immediately sorry she shot that at David, but could not take it back. Instead, she took a shot at Aaron, just to be fair. "And if you heard something that I needed to hear, you could have picked up a phone to let me know immediately instead of tracking me down and spying on me. Was it about this attack? Could you have saved John the pain he's got to deal with now?"

Karen knew she would regret her next action but could not stop herself. She was too angry. Too fed up with the dichotomy these two men represented in her life and too unwilling to choose one over the other. Her choice was not to choose.

"You know what? I wanted to do this with a bit more delicacy, and I sure as hell never expected I'd be breaking up with both of you at the same time but that's what's happening. I can't have either of you in my life right now. It's too dangerous for you guys. It's too dangerous for me. I guess it's better this way. You both know exactly what I'm saying to the other one. I can't deal with this thing, this war, and a confusing love life at the same time. I'd never forgive myself if either of you got hurt because of me."

Aaron stepped forward. "Karen, please—"

"No." She stepped back from them both. "No. No 'please.' No second chances. No nothing. I don't want to see either of you anymore except in passing. I don't want to go on dates. I don't want to meet for coffee. I don't want any phone calls. I don't want... can't... do any of that anymore. I just can't.

"All of my time and energy has to go to finishing what I started. I don't expect either of you to really understand, but that's the way it's going to be. That's it. Period. End of story. Good-bye."

"I'm going to have to get the Special Unit involved this time." David warned as he rebuttoned his shirt, looking grim.

"That should've happened a long time ago." Karen knew she wasn't being fair but didn't care anymore.

She turned and walked away from them. She heard Aaron call her name once but she didn't turn around to look. Not looking would be easier. She would not see their hurt, confused faces anymore and they wouldn't see her tears.

Since she didn't turn around, she didn't see that both of them had started after her, only to be blocked by a small, grey gargoyle named Sebastian, his wings unfurled in an aggressive stance and snarling; protecting her as only he could.

***

"So, that was two days ago?" Susan asked as she got Karen more coffee. "You got attacked and took your pain, fear, and anger out on the two men who love you and broke up with them? Is that what you really wanted to do?" Her voice had that careful-*I'm just making sure I understand the situation*-tone to it.

Karen nodded, miserable. "I shouldn't have broken it off with them like that. But, they could have died because of me. I'm surprised Lamiel hasn't called to yell at me or the police haven't called me in for questioning."

"Well, they're both adults and they both have reasons for what they are or aren't doing. At least one has supernatural skills, and the other knows about the supernatural. From what you've told me."

Karen sighed and covered her face with her hands before rubbing her eyes. "I know. I know. I feel like hell, but I don't know what to do now."

"Have they called?"

"Yes. But I haven't answered the phone. I've only answered when it's been you or Reginald."

"How is the Master of the City?"

"Concerned. At first he gave his blessing for all this. Now... he wants me to back down. I can't. Whatever's going to happen is happening within the next couple of days. He thinks it's happening on the next full moon. Once I stop that, whatever it is, I can figure out what to do about the men in my life. All of them."

Susan sat back down. "Yeah. That's partly why I called you. There *is* something big happening in the next couple of days. I've devised something I think will be useful." She looked towards the back part of the museum storage. "Alexander, please come out now. Bring the couriers with you."

Karen was glad she had put her coffee cup down. Otherwise, she would have dropped it at the sight of the seven-foot tall stone monstrosity walking with eerie silence towards them from back of the large room. "Oh my gosh."

"Yes." The other woman said with a smile. "I thought it was time for you to see part of the forces you have mobilized. Alexander is one of the elder gargoyles in the city. He has been observing you for some time. At my request."

"Oh. And?"

"He approves."

"Oh. Good." She did not know what that meant.

The two of them gazed at the huge man-shaped gargoyle in silence. He gazed back at them without expression. Karen suddenly felt that Susan and Alexander were having their own separate conversation, mind to mind. She took a sip of her coffee, not tasting it. She would not look away from him, examining him with an artist's eye because she was certainly going to draw this scene when she got home.

Alexander bent and opened his hand above the table. Out of it jumped the three tiniest gargoyles Karen had seen yet. Each one was no more than one to two inches tall. While she was looking at the three little ones, trying to pick out their differences, the huge gargoyle disappeared. Karen was certain that he had just walked away, but he'd done it so quickly, quietly, and smoothly that she might not have seen him do it even if she had been looking directly at him.

"I call them Huey, Dewey, and Louie." Susan said. "It's easiest that way until they pick their own names. These little guys are couriers. They are the fastest gargoyles in the city. They are young and can't speak but, you can speak to them—either verbal or mind-to-mind—and they will take your words to the person you want them to go to. Assuming they know the person in question. Let me show you."

She held up a hand and one of the couriers, the one with tiny horns, jumped into it. Susan and Louie, Karen believed, looked at each other for a couple of silent moments. Then, Louie jumped from Susan's hand and ran over to Karen. He stared up at her and Susan's voice blossomed in her head.

'These guys know me, Lamiel, John Corso, Walks-the-Ocean, and Reginald. They also know all of the gargoyles, as well as a few other people that you aren't familiar with, like the

Steward family. All you have to do is tell them you have a message for me, state the message and end with the words "Done and go."'

Karen was impressed. "Wow. That's amazing. He got your exact tone of voice."

"I know. He is remembering what he hears as he hears it. So, be careful how you send your message and don't add anything extra you don't want the person getting the message to hear. I'm loaning you these guys for the next couple of weeks. The main event with the Order is probably going to happen on the full moon, but that doesn't mean everything will be done then. There will be fallout and echoes of consequences. It's probably best that you have a fast way to send messages. Also, don't be surprised if others come to deliver messages to you. I have a whole fleet of these little guys. I intend to use them."

"Thank you, Susan. I don't know what to say."

"Don't say anything. Just finish what you've started. Like it or not, you're in charge of this thing. Probably because you don't know enough to be afraid of it."

"Do you?"

"Yes."

"Are you scared?"

"Terrified. Just terrified."

The blunt nakedness of the answer startled her. "I'm sorry. I—"

Susan cut her off. "Don't be. This was needed. If I didn't believe that, I wouldn't be putting myself, my museum or my gargoyles on the line. The Order has to be stopped." She looked away for a moment. "One of us should have taken this step a while ago. But, I guess we were all too comfortable in our sanctuaries. Too comfortable with the status quo even though the Order's been gathering power, slowly, for a while."

Karen nodded, looking at the three tiny gargoyles curled up together on the table, and wondered just how bad the next couple of days were going to be. That was the trouble of naivety. You really did not know enough to be scared. "All right. Our main goal now is to find out where the Order is doing whatever it is they're doing on the night of the full moon. We have to know that within the next twelve hours, so we have some time to make some sort of plan of attack or disruption. Ask everyone you know to use every means at their disposal to help with this."

"I can do that." Susan looked around and a tiny creature zipped to her from somewhere in the room. It had been too fast to see. When it stopped moving, Karen saw that it was another tiny courier gargoyle. She watched as Susan and the new gargoyle stared at each other for a long time. Then, it was gone.

***

Elsewhere...

"What about the gargoyle? Sebastian probably won't let me near her."

V'ger handed the younger man a gray candle. "Have her light this. You won't have to worry about the beast or any of its kin after that."

He looked at the tag on the candle. "Gargoyle protection?"

"It's from a new age shop. The tag, that is. The candle is homemade."

"It won't hurt Karen?"

"No. It won't. I promise. It'll keep her guardian away from her and us." V'ger looked at the hesitant man and pressed the advantage. "I'll give you all the stuff you'll need. She's confused. She's been lied to. Reginald has used and manipulated her from the beginning. He's the one keeping her from loving you. After the rite, Reginald's hold on the city—and on her—will be broken. She'll be free. But, we've got to keep her safe and away from the rite. She'll be hurt, maybe killed, if she goes there."

"No. I won't allow that."

"Then, help us help you. My daughter is twelve years old, and I would do anything for her. I know what it's like to love someone who's being threatened. After the rite is done, neither you nor Karen will have to worry about Reginald's interference ever again. I promise." V'ger gazed at him. "Are you willing to help us and free Karen? I have to know now. I have to have your word. Otherwise, I'll have to do this on my own."

The other man was quiet, considering. Then, he nodded. "I'm with you. I'll do what I have to do to save Karen from what's happening to her. I give you my word." He held out his hand.

V'ger took it in a firm grip and shook it.

"Good. Now, here's my plan...." The two of them sat in the back booth of the quiet bar, conspiring to save a woman they both knew did not wish to be saved.

Betrayal

"PLEASE DON'T HANG up. It's important. It's about the Order."

Karen sighed. She should have looked at the caller ID before she answered her phone. She took a moment to look at it and saw that it was a restricted number and not his usual cell phone number. "What is it, Aaron?"

"I know what ritual the Order's going to do, and I think I know where."

"Good news. Sort of. What is it and where?"

"I can't over the phone." There was a pause. "I can't from here."

"Aaron…" Her voice held a warning note.

"It's not a ploy to get you back. I swear."

She was silent for a long moment.

"I have to tell you this in person. Not on the phone. I'm not in a good place to be telling you secrets. Please."

The desperation in his voice was clear. "All right. But, you can't stay long. Heather's coming over and we've got work to do."

"This will help. I promise. I'll be there as soon as I can."

"Okay. Bye."

"Bye."

She snapped her cell phone shut and hoped Aaron was true to his word. The full moon was tonight, and she still didn't know where the Order's ritual was going to be held; much less what it was supposed to accomplish. It was hard to mobilize your forces for disruption if you did not know what they were supposed to do or where they were supposed to go.

While waiting for Aaron and for Heather to show up, she continued to prepare for tonight. She wasn't sure if jeans and a t-shirt were what heroines wore, but it was comfortable and she could move in it. She had an old sweatshirt for warmth in the chill of the fall evening. Also, she was packing what she'd mentally dubbed her 'CYA bag' because everything in it was designed to cover her ass.

So far it had scissors, candles, matches, a pocket knife, a flashlight, extra batteries, and a rain poncho. She wandered around the apartment, looking at what was there. What else should she take with her? She thought about her favorite movies and what they used. Maybe some tools. What *did* one use to stop or fight a possible Armageddon?

"With my luck, the ritual is designed to give Kendrick good weather for the rest of the year, or something as inane as that." Despite her anger at David and Aaron, she still trusted them. Otherwise, she wouldn't have let Aaron come over.

Karen was rummaging through her hall closet, looking for the toolkit she knew she had, but hadn't used yet, when there was a knock on the door. She knew it wasn't Heather, since she had given the young woman a key with instructions to come in—no matter the time of day or night.

It had to be Aaron, and sooner than she'd expected him. This annoyed her. It made her a little suspicious that he had been waiting down the block and this was going to be a play to make her change her mind on their relationship.

Her ill-concealed irritation turned into outright surprise when she opened the door to see David standing there. "What are you doing here?"

"I'm good. How are you? Well, I hope?" David replied in a bland tone.

"I'm sorry. I wasn't expecting you."

"Another lover?" He held up a hand. "No. Not my business anymore. I'm sorry. I shouldn't have said that. I've come with a peace offering and some information. Can I come in?" He gestured with the brown paper package in his other hand. "Just business. I promise."

After a brief hesitation, she nodded. "All right. But only for a short time. I've got work to do."

"I know. That's why I'm here." He walked passed her and into the apartment. He was familiar with the place, and bypassed the living room and dining area in favor of the more neutral kitchen. Karen followed, trying to quell her annoyance at his unexpected visit and her worry at the possible emotional train wreck just waiting to happen if he was still here when Aaron arrived.

Once in the kitchen, he turned and offered her the package. "For you."

Again, she hesitated. She'd treated both David and Aaron poorly, and they hadn't deserved it. Not really. She accepted and opened it. It was a candle. On it was a small tag that proclaimed it to be for "Gargoyle Protection." On the backside of the card was a small story about gargoyles being protective spirits and lighting the candle would call them to her. She smiled. "I think I already have this protection."

"I know but it made me think of you and it smells good."

She took a sniff and nodded. "It does."

"The lady in the store says it smells even better when it's lit. Light it?"

"Okay." Karen returned his hopeful smile. "I do like candles." She rummaged through her drawers for the matches, then remembered they were in her CYA bag. "I'll be right back."

While she was in the living room, David called, "Do you mind if I have some coffee?"

"Sure, go ahead." She dug the matches out of her bag and returned to the kitchen to find him sitting at the table adding sugar to his coffee. She preferred hers black. She paused, sipped her half-full cup and grimaced at the bitter taste. She also hated lukewarm coffee, and topped the cup off with the fresh, hot stuff.

As she lit the candle, she asked, "So, what information do you have for me?" Something fell over in the other room, but her attention was focused on David and his answer.

"I know where the ritual's going to happen tonight, and I know what it's supposed to do."

"You what?" She was very surprised. How had both David and Aaron found out what she and the people working with her could not? It was strange. At least she would have Aaron to corroborate (or not corroborate) the information soon. She sat down, gazing at him as she drank her coffee. "Where? What is it? How do you know?"

"It's going to be in the Colonel's Park, tonight, for sure. I don't know the exact time, but I suspect around midnight to 1 a.m., when the moon is high."

"The Colonel's Park? The Order has been warned away from... Oh, wait. I only got to tell Lamiel when she was in the hospital. So, I'm not sure she the message to the Order to stay away from there."

"You're talking about the night you and I met."

Karen nodded. "Yeah. You were on patrol. Was that coincidence?"

"Yes." He paused. "Mostly. That area of town is my beat, but I got word through the Special Unit that something might be going down."

She wanted to ask more about this "Special Unit" of the Kendrick police force, but this was not the time or the place. She needed him out of here and needed to get a message to Susan, who had become her defacto Second in Command. "How do you know all this?"

She started to put her coffee cup down, and paused as multiple coffee cups and multiple tables blurred before her eyes. With an effort, she forced herself to put the cup down without spilling it. She looked up at David, who also swam before her eyes for a moment before coming back into focus.

"I know," he said, looking at her, "because one of the leaders of the Order told me."

Shocked, she started to object, to back away from him, to call for Sebastian. Instead, she slumped forward on the kitchen table, her head on her arm. She was still conscious for the moment, but she was unable to make her body do anything. In her mind, she screamed for Sebastian.

"You don't know it Karen, but you've been lied to by Reginald from the beginning. He's used you and manipulated you to make sure his hold on the city remains secure. He's used magic on you to bind him to you and you to him. I know you can't tell. That's part of the magic. The Order's ritual is going to break his hold on the city. That's why they've been gathering the items they need. They all have a special significance to the city of Kendrick."

He walked over and stroked her hair back from her face. "I'm sorry I had to drug your coffee. But, it is war, Karen; between this supposed 'Master of the City' and the Order of the Sacred Eye. If you go tonight, you'll be hurt or killed and I love you too much to let that happen. I'm sorry it had to be this way, but once his hold on you is broken..."

David's words were interrupted by the unexpected sound of the front door being unlocked and opened. Heather came in, calling for her.

"Karen. Karen. I got it. It fucking sucked and hurt like a bitch, but I got you the meeting with the Children of Anu." Her voice traveled through the apartment as she looked for Karen. "But, something big is going on tonight. So, we have to go—" She reached the doorway between the small dining area and the kitchen, "—right now?"

David and Heather looked at each other in silence for a couple of seconds. David could see that Heather had been through something unpleasant. She was dirty, bruised with a black eye, and her clothing was torn.

"What happened to you?" David asked, unable to help himself.

"Test of Worth. I passed." She said, frowning at him and the scene. "What the hell's happening here?" She pointed to Karen slumped on the kitchen table.

"Nothing you need to concern yourself with, girl."

The voice came from behind Heather as Paul Maloy, also known as Todesengel within the Order of the Sacred Eye, stepped into sight behind Heather and grabbed her as she turned. Without hesitation, he slit the young woman's throat from ear to ear and held her as the blood gushed from her throat. Whatever she had been holding tumbled from her hand and skittered off to the far corner of the dining area as she struggled with the man killing her.

It was Karen's worst nightmare. She could not move or fight. She watched as Paul Maloy, the object of her focused hatred, murdered her friend in front of her. She mentally shrieked for Sebastian again and again.

"What are you doing? This wasn't part of the plan. No one was supposed to die." David clawed for his gun as he started forward, only to be pushed back into the stove by the multiple bullets slamming into his chest.

V'ger stepped forward, holding a smoking pistol, as Todesengel tossed Heather's no longer struggling body aside. "Plans change. We only needed you to find her. The Master of the City had kept her location hidden from us. Thanks." He punctuated his gratitude with another shot into David's chest. David fell over onto his face and didn't move again.

Karen could see David out of the corner of her eye, slumping and then crumpling to the floor. His head thunked against the tile as he fell. She could see part of Heather's limp form in the dining area and she could see these two men—one she knew and one she did not.

Paul walked over to her. "You wanted me, bitch. Now you got me. How do you like them apples?"

"You can gloat over her later at the rite. Let's get her back to the house before Cerridwen's potion wears off." V'ger turned and walked back towards the living room.

Paul grinned at her then picked her up and tossed her over his shoulder. "Bet you're sorry you ever started this, and you ain't seen nothin' yet."

Karen could do nothing except continue to call for Sebastian. Just as she was about to give up she heard him, faint but there.

'Karen. There's a barrier. Can't get in. It hurts.'

'Go for Susan! Get Susan! Tell her...'

'No. Save you.'

'You can't! They've got magic. You can only save me if you tell Susan where the Order will be tonight. They're going to be at Colonel's Park. Tell Susan.'

'Karen...' His mental voice was whine of fear and anger.

'Sebastian, you must. This is the only way to save me. They're going to take me to the ritual. You have to get Susan to get everyone there. You have to do it. Go now. Hurry. Before it's too late.' She thought he was going to continue to argue but there was no immediate response.

'Okay. I go. I'll save you. I will.' His voice was small and reluctant. Then, it was gone.

There was a crunching sound as Paul strode through her living room. He paused, looked down, and then stomped the floor hard, grinding something under his heel. When he resumed his pace, Karen got a glimpse of a mostly crushed tiny gargoyle. All that she could recognize was the top of his head with one broken ear and two tiny horns and knew that it had been the courier gargoyle, Louie. Now, he was dead, too.

At the doorway, V'ger made the assassin stop. He walked around the man and grabbed a handful of Karen's hair. He pulled a damp cloth from his pocket and pressed it to Karen's nose and mouth. It smelled sweet. Without the ability to fight him off, Karen was unconscious in moments. As she fell into the dark, she heard him say, "All right. Now we can go."

***

Everywhere Else...

The city had gone mad.

Reginald was beside himself with concern. His connection to Karen was muted, almost nonexistent, and he did not know where she was. There was powerful magic at work. Not more powerful than he, but more cunning and sly. It was possible for the gnat to crawl through the tiniest hole of a screen with no way to stop it.

Every traffic light in Kendrick suddenly started blinking red. Traffic unexpectedly snarled on this late, lazy Sunday afternoon. Tempers flared and horns blared. No one at the city planning office or the power stations could make heads or tails of what was going on with the system.

His last conversation with Karen had been poorly handled. He had been so intent on getting her to listen to him that he had not listened to her at all. He had chosen her because of her good heart, willingness to help—it was what 911 operators did, after all—and for her determination. The fact that she was creative and adaptable had not hurt. It was her stubbornness that confused him. Why could she not see the logic behind his reasoning?

Throughout the city center, water refused to flow, faucets remained dry, and toilets flushed just once. More and more people called the power company, the water company, and the emergency services lines. Every person in a call center knew something was terribly wrong in the city and while they knew the symptoms, no one knew the cause.

She had been so easy to work with at first. Then, she had started getting her own ideas of what was good for him, for the city. While these ideas were good, her way of going about it was so disruptive. Changes took time. Karen acted as if everything had to be done now.

Mayor Mason Steward frowned when he picked up his phone to make a call and received only silence. That was unusual. More unusual was Cecelia coming into his den without knocking first.

He waited and listened as she apologized then explained that something was very wrong with the city. That the Oracle was unconscious with a sudden backlash of stimuli, and no one knew exactly what was wrong. Then, the lights of the Gateway district went out, including the lights in the Steward estate. "It's time to contact the family and Julie."

Maybe she was right. He was losing sight of the smaller picture. The devil was in the details he had always heard. He was losing control, a bit at a time, being nibbled to death by gnats. He did not believe it could happen, to lose control of himself and his city. That thought frightened him more than he ever thought possible. He would be no one's slave. Never in life. Never in death.

Power surges raced through the city. Light bulbs burst. Breakers tripped. Warning sirens flared in every district. Every light in the city not run on battery or backup generator winked out with a startling finality.

He had to stop his rising panic. But it was not an emotion he was accustomed to, and he did not know how to handle it. He had to do something. He had to find Karen and save her. It was because of him she was in this mess. He owed it to her and she was his most favored of his favorites. She could be stubborn and confusing, but she was also good hearted and sweet.

Humans were so confusing. He was still getting used to being with them, and he wanted to continue being with Karen. It was time to make that happen.

Warfare and the Rite

'...DON'T LOSE HOPE.'

Reginald's voice woke Karen. For those first, hazy moments between the unreality of dreams and the reality of day, she thought she had been having nothing more than a nightmare. David would never betray her. Heather and Louie were still alive. Relief turned to panic when she tried to move, to sit up, to rub the sleep from her eyes, and could not. Panic was turning into terror when Reginald's voice came again.

'Karen, I know you're scared. Don't be. We're coming for you. We will save you. There's magic on you that keeps the gargoyles away, but its power is lessening as time goes on. It's how we found you—by finding where the gargoyles could not go. Our forces are coming. Don't lose hope.'

There was a pause, a sense of impatience and Reginald's voice began. *'Karen, I know you're scared...'* It was his voice. But, it was in her head. *'... Don't be. ...'* She fought to make sense of it. *'... We're coming...'* In her head, in Reginald's voice. *'... for you. ...'* A gargoyle? A courier. "Wait. Stop." Her voice was a whisper, but it sounded very loud in her own ears.

Reginald's voice stopped. She opened her eyes, relieved to discover she could do so. "Where are you?" She did not know if he would answer, given the way of gargoyles. Then, the image of her lying far below on a bed, seemingly in quiet repose, came to her. He was up high, above her. "Can you take a message back?"

There was a glow of assent.

"Tell them, tell Reginald, I'm okay. Scared, but okay. The Order will be at the Colonel's Park. The ritual is supposed to break Reginald's magical hold on the city. The Order will be taking me there if you guys don't get me out of wherever I am. I'm their focus for this thing. Okay? Got it? Don't be late. Please." She paused. That was all she could think to say even though she felt there should be more. "Done. Go."

It was only after she sent the tiny gargoyle away that she thought to wonder how long she had been unconscious and where she was now.

***

After the brief visit by the courier gargoyle, Karen slept. There was little else she could do. Based on her experiments, she could breathe, blink, talk, and roll her eyes around in a vain attempt to see more. Other than that, her body would not obey her.

She woke with an aborted start of surprise when the door to her prison burst open. For one beautiful moment, she was certain it was Susan and the rest here to rescue her. Her hope dimmed when Paul entered her field of vision. "Rise and shine, sweetheart. It's time for you to take center stage." The malicious glee in the man's eyes frightened her more than any other threat he could have made.

Paul scooped her up and tossed her over his shoulder again. She gasped as he bounced her body, adjusting her on his shoulder. With her hair in her face, she could not see anything except feet walking around them as they went. It seemed that everyone knew what they were doing and where they were going. No one spoke. She was dumped into the trunk of a car without ceremony and endured a long, bumpy ride.

Paul was there to open the trunk. Again, he smiled with clear anticipation. He looked around, then bent into the car. When he was almost nose-to-nose with her, he said, "No one's coming for you. Even if they try, they'll be stopped by the wards and our allies. You're gonna be awake through all that's gonna happen and I want you to know, when that garrote is dropped around your throat, it's going to be me who chokes the life out of you. I owe your gargoyle for these scars. Since I can't get revenge on him, I'll make do with you." He sealed his promise with a rough kiss before hauling her from the trunk into the moonlit night.

They were at the Colonel's Park. She saw that much before she was once again slung over his shoulder. When she was roughly dropped to the ground, she let out a yelp of pain as her head bounced on the dirt. A nervous titter of laughter broke out among the robed assembly. There seemed to be several dozen people here.

"Now, now. Let's show our honored guest some respect." Praetor stepped forward as Paul bound her wrists and ankles with leather straps, pulling her body into a spread eagle position. "She is the lynchpin to our ritual."

Karen turned her eyes up and saw an older, distinguished looking man with grey at his temples and a neat, salt-and-pepper goatee. Looming above both of them was the statue of Colonel Kendrick. She looked back at the silent throng of people in robes and all hope of sanity or reprieve died. It was happening. The ritual was beginning with her as the focus, and no one was trying to stop it.

"I am Praetor, First in the Order of the Sacred Eye. Do any dispute my title or claim?" He paused just long enough to be polite before continuing. "We are gathered here on this night to claim what is ours by right. Tonight, we take back Kendrick from the usurper and place it under our domain and protection once more." There was a smattering of respectful applause and approving murmurs.

He turned to his right. "V'ger."

V'ger stepped around Karen until he stood at her feet. In his hands was an old map. He knelt and placed it before him. "Master of the City, I bind you to the laws of this rite." He punctuated the declaration by pounding a spike through the center of the map, pinning it to the ground.

Karen watched this, and wondered how it could be magic. She also wondered where Susan and her own allies were. She could not hear anything over the rustle of the people watching. If there was a fight outside the ward, it was locked away from her senses. She prayed that there *was* a fight going on. She prayed that someone would give her some kind of sign that she was not alone. She called for Sebastian in her head and tried to keep the fear out of her mental voice.

Praetor turned to his left. "Cerridwen."

Cerridwen stepped forward and knelt at Karen's side. She leaned forward with three old fashioned keys on a thong. "Master..."

"No." Karen said, unwilling to remain silent. "Don't do this. It's wrong."

"Silence." The old woman pointed a finger at her.

Karen tried to protest more but no longer had a voice to protest with. She tried to scream at the watching people, but nothing came out. Falling back on what she knew worked, she called for Sebastian again—the only one she knew who would not let her down while he still lived.

"Master of the City, with the original keys to the first City Hall, I lock off all avenues of escape. You will heed our commands." Cerridwen tied the thong of bronze keys around Karen's throat.

Paul stepped forward with a short wooden shaft, tipped with sharp mussel shell blades and bone points. He handed it to Praetor who walked to Karen's right side and knelt. He reached out and slashed Karen's arm with a quick motion. The flesh opened bloodlessly, then it filled with a crimson river that spilled to the ground. He ignored her soundless cry of pain and leaned over her to slash her left arm, spilling the blood on that side of her as well. Lastly, he lifted her t-shirt and exposed her belly. He paused, then said, "Master of the City, with the blood of your chosen representative, I bind your life to hers." He slashed her stomach, cutting it and watched the blood well and spill over.

Trapped inside her unmoving body and soundless voice, Karen screamed in pain. All thoughts of rescue were gone. This whole thing had not been real until that first slash to the arm. The pain, however, made it real. It pulled her back from the silent watching and rational disbelief she had retreated to. She rolled her eyes, tears spilling from them as she tried to catch the gaze of someone else, anyone else. She could not do it. No one would look her in the eyes. They were looking at each other with clear discomfort, but no one was going to step forward to stop this madness. They were all going to watch while she was ritualistically murdered.

Cerridwen handed an engraved metal plate to Praetor. He took it and pressed it into the blood on Karen's stomach. Once it was wet enough to his satisfaction, he moved to her feet where he placed four bloody one-dollar bill prints on the map of Kendrick at its cardinal points. "Master of the City, with your representative's life blood and the Great Seal, your power is transferred to the Order of the Sacred Eye." He looked up and nodded.

Karen felt Paul before she saw him. He came down on one knee behind her head to loop a leather garrote around her neck. He pulled up on it. Her head and shoulders were pulled upward off the ground by her throat. The back of her head thumped against his knee and he used that as leverage to strangle her.

With her head up, she saw that Praetor was holding a large book. It was open and he called out a chanting verse that sounded like Arabic. The congregation responded as one in the same language. She tried to beg for help, but she saw no help before her and the garrote tightened until she thought it would severe her head from her body. As the pain grew, she almost wished it would.

The worst of the pain was first in her throat. Then, as the need for air became more urgent, the burning in her lungs overrode all else. *Where's the cavalry? Where's the promised rescue? Where's Reginald? Susan? Sebastian? Why aren't they here?* As her vision began to dim, she realized that the rescue was not coming and she was about to die. For real. All hope died as her vision went black.

***

Time had no meaning in the blackness. One moment, she was struggling for air through a throat choked by cord. The next, her body was thrashing wildly against the leather restraints with a strength born from the body's knowledge that it was taking its literal last breaths and it was fighting for its life. Her right foot came free as her eyes opened upon an impossible scene.

"...I command you!" Praetor screamed at the advancing tarnished metal statue of Colonel Kendrick, his sword drawn. He held the large tome in front of his chest like a shield, screaming incoherent demands until the statue stabbed its sword forward, impaling the book and the man holding it. Colonel Kendrick's bronze likeness lifted both into the air....

Karen opened her mouth, gasping for air. While the intense pressure from the garrote was gone, there was still pressure on her abused throat. Air wormed its way past the swollen flesh to fill her burning lungs. Sucking it in, she looked around with fogged eyes as the sounds filtered past the buzzing in her ears.

...Lamiel stood side-by-side with two other girls, Juliet and Katrina. The three of them were using some sort of barrier of light to hold off two street kids covered with bullhead symbols and wielding clubs. From behind them another street kid hit Juliet in the back of the head with a baseball bat. As she fell, the barrier fell. Katrina went back to back with Lamiel who drew a glowing dagger from its sheath at her waist...

Just as Karen started to get control of her breathing, her entire body began to spasm. The jerking made the leather straps around the still bound portions of her limbs cut in deeper. Her right leg and head thrashed, heedless of the damage it was doing to her.

...Gargoyles growled, tumbled, and fought against were-beasts. As a couple of them came too near, the gargoyle grunted in pain from the magic barrier still on Karen. The were-creature, not quite wolf, not quite cat, took this distraction as an opportunity to break off a large section of the gargoyle's wing. Susan yelled commands and Alexander appeared from above, landing full on the creature's back, breaking it with a loud crunch....

The spasms stopped, but tears flooded her eyes and a wave of nausea overcame her. She quickly turned her head to make sure she would not choke if she threw up.

...John Corso fought hand-to-hand against a couple of the robed members of the Order. It was going John's way with several stomach punches followed by an uppercut until one of them pulled a knife and stabbed him in the side. John returned the favor by kicking out the man's knee before falling to his own...

Karen yanked on the leather straps holding her in the middle of the fighting chaos. She pulled hard, trying not to break the straps, but to pull up the stakes that held the straps fast. This was a mistake. Her body arched hard in another uncontrolled spasm. It was short but intense, and left her gagging.

...Makah warrior men and women faced off against more of the Children of Anu. They circled each other with a predator's wariness of an enemy's claws. All were armed with the blunt or edged weapons of their people. There was a momentary standoff, then one of the Children screamed and threw himself at his chosen opponent, followed by the rest from both sides. All semblance of coherence was lost in the fray...

Once more in control of her body, Karen concentrated on freeing her right wrist. The stake was pounded flush into the ground and she had no leverage. Still, she wouldn't give up. Someone was going to notice her in this helpless position and was going to try to finish what Praetor started. Body trembling, it was not until after she grasped the rock to use as either a cutting implement or as leverage that she realized she could hear singing. She looked for its source.

...Somnia sang to those who would listen and hear. Normally her voice was reserved for humans, but in this battle, she owed a debt to Karen Wilson and thus, to all of her allies who would rescue her.

The small gargoyle was suddenly inspired to hamstring the fleeing hated one. He grabbed the bone-bladed, wooden shaft that was bigger that he was, and slashed the assassin in the back of the leg just above the knee. Paul Maloy fell with a cry of pain. He was still prone when Sebastian swarmed up him and latched on to the man's throat at the jugular. When Paul ripped the small gargoyle from his neck, Sebastian took large chunks of flesh with him. Paul forgot all about Sebastian as blood spurted from his torn throat...

Karen tried to yell in triumph, but not much more than a sore croak. Instead, she mentally sent as much praise, love and pride towards Sebastian as she could. But it was her approval that became Sebastian's undoing.

***

She watched as Sebastian made sure Paul Maloy was dead before turning and streaking towards her. Realizing he wasn't going to stop, she shouted a mental warning that the spell was still active. Sebastian ignored it and bounced off the spell barrier still surrounding her. Karen felt his pain and his determination. *'No. Sebastian, it'll kill you.'*

'Save you.' He hunkered down and approached the barrier with caution.

Karen struggled as hard as she could to get her left arm, the one closest to him, free. *'No. Don't.'*

'Will...' Then, he focused all his effort on crawling through the edge of the barrier and making his way to his human. The magic spell crackled over his body in a small lightning storm of pain.

She could feel how much every step cost him. If she could have, she would have cut her own hand off in order to get away from him. Risking another one of those intense body spasms, Karen pulled with everything she had, trying to break the leather that held her. She had to get away from Sebastian. The longer he was within the spell's power, the more it hurt him. But, her effort was in vain.

Sebastian crawled every agonizing inch of the five-foot spell barrier to the stake that kept her bound wrist in place; his skin was on fire. The closer he got to her, the worse it was. He fought every instinctive urge to curl up back into his protective stone form or to flee. Instead, he lunged forward to bite the leather. He missed and landed hard on his chin, inches from Karen's hand. Then, he was forcibly changed back into his rock form by the spell's magic. As brave and as stubborn as Sebastian was, he was still a baby, and he had reached his limit.

Karen felt Sebastian's abrupt withdrawal from her mind and watched him turn to stone. To all of her senses, if he was not already dead, he soon would be.

As she renewed her struggles to free herself, she felt someone or something watching her. Karen looked for the new presence and saw a lone, blond-haired girl in Order robes crouched by a tree. She looked frightened, but not panicked. In one hand was Changer's Claw, still bloody from both Karen and Paul's blood. Not knowing what else to do and desperate, Karen yelled to her through a ragged throat, "Please. Help him. Get him away from me. Please. I'll do anything."

The girl looked around at the fighting chaos. She winced as a werewolf slashed at a girl and a guy with knife-like claws backed up against a tree. With a quick nod, she ran towards Karen, still crouched. She raised Changer's Claw when she reached the small gargoyle and the prone woman.

For a moment, Karen thought she'd been betrayed again, but when the weapon came down, it severed the strap binding Karen's left hand to the stake. Karen didn't hesitate; she turned over and pulled as far away from Sebastian as she could.

"I'm Corelli. What they were doing was wrong," the girl said as she scooped Sebastian up. "That's why I'm helping you. But, you still owe me. I'll get him to safety."

"Thank you." Karen whispered, watching the girl sprint away through the fight with Sebastian in one hand and Changer's Claw in the other. Her eyes found the couple that had been fighting the werewolf moments before. She recognized them from Bacchanalia as Shirtless Guy and Lace Girl; the couple she had once watched dance together at the club. She had never learned their real names. She probably never would. They were both dead now, eviscerated corpses at the base of a tree.

Fighting against the sudden need for tears, she worked to free her right hand. Karen couldn't feel it anymore. Nor could she see it through her tears. She was focusing on that task as hard as she could so she would not fall to pieces. When the hand landed on her shoulder, and the person knelt at her side, it startled a shriek and a flailed fist out of her.

"Karen. It's me. God, are you all right?" It was Aaron.

She had never been so happy to see him in her life. She gave him a one-armed hug. "Sorta. I guess. No. Sebastian's hurt." She smeared tears across her face with the back of one hand.

"When I got to your place, you were gone... But, David... and Heather. They... I saw..."

"Paul Maloy killed Heather." She pointed to his dead body. "Sebastian killed him." She said nothing about David, why he had been there, his betrayal or the Order's betrayal of him. It was not something she was willing to think about, let alone explain, to anyone else right now.

"I tried to get here as fast as I could. I'm sorry. I should have told you sooner. I'm so sorry."

"What are you talking about?" She realized as he stood, he was carrying a bloodied short sword. He used it to cut the rest of her bindings.

"I—" He stopped, looking past her as he helped her up. "Shit."

She looked behind her and saw three men in monk's robes approaching. She could not hear them, but she knew they were speaking or chanting. As they walked through the fighting, no one bothered them. As they passed people and creatures in mortal combat, the fighting stopped. The enemies broke away from one another and stumbled off in opposite directions.

Aaron grabbed her shoulder and turned her back to him. "I'm sorry. I should have told you sooner. I'm not who you think I am. I need you to know that you were never just a job to me. I swear, you never were. I didn't agree with them on this, and I should have come to you sooner. Please, remember that." He looked over her shoulder again, let her go and stepped to the side, meeting the trio of monks head on.

Completely confused, Karen took a step back from both the monks and Aaron. She could see the monks were all old men and that they were angry.

"You abandoned your post, Simon," Brother Peter said.

"I did what I thought was right."

"At what cost?"

"Cost? What cost? You said she wouldn't be hurt." Aaron turned and yanked the garrote from Karen's neck. She had not realized it was still there. "Does this look like she hasn't been hurt?" He shook the braided cord at them.

"I said no lasting damage would come to her. She's alive, isn't she?" Brother Peter's eyes flicked from Aaron to Karen and back again.

Karen stepped back and turned. She found herself facing the statue of Colonel Kendrick. She had not realized that it had returned to its rightful place—sans the impaled megalomaniacal cult leader. His sword was still covered in blood, though. With her back to Aaron (*or was it Simon?*) and the other monks, she listened while pretending to study the statue and read the plaque at its base.

"She's alive, no thanks to you."

"I forgive you for your hasty words, Brother Simon." Brother Peter raised a hand to forestall the words of his companions. "However, you should have trusted us, your Brothers. You should have trusted me, your mentor. How do you think the wards came down? Who do you think allowed this rescue to happen?"

Aaron, still angry, said nothing.

"She is hurt, yes. But you have the means to heal her, as well as the rest of the wounded. Nothing more should be said here. We'll speak back at the monastery. We all have other work to do."

Without waiting for a response, Brother Peter and his companions continued on their way. They began their chant once more, quelling all fighting around them as they went.

Aaron walked to Karen's side. He reached out a hand and took hers in his.

She squeezed it as she tried for a smile, but failed. She was too tired and worried for Sebastian to be angry at this newest discovery. "Should I call you Simon?"

"No. Aaron is my birth name. Will you allow me to heal you?"

"Will it hurt?"

"Far from it."

"Please do."

Aaron clasped her hand in both of his and bent over it. As he murmured what sounded like a prayer in an almost familiar language, she felt warmth spread through her body. The pain lessened, then disappeared. She felt so much better that it amazed her. The contrast of pain to not-pain was almost euphoric.

"Thank you," she said, looking at the plaque again. "Someday, you should tell me about Simon. Because, unlike Romeo, I believe this other name means something."

"All names mean something. I'll tell you if I can what I can."

Her eyes picked up a single word on the plaque that momentarily stunned her. Suddenly, so many things she never understood about the city and its people became clear in that single moment of revelation. "Yes. All names do mean something." She shook her head. "Can you help other people like you helped me?"

He nodded. "Yes."

"Can I help you?"

"Yes."

"Then let's help these people." Helping the wounded lying around her would give her a reprieve from having to think about what she had just been through, from worrying about Sebastian, from the betrayals and the discoveries, and from grieving for those who died at her behest. She needed to do something.

Later, there would be time for tears. Later, she would deal with the consequences of her actions. For now, she would do what she did best—help people.

***

Elsewhen...

"She dropped off two paper bags at the museum. One had Changer's Claw in it. The other had Sebastian." Susan said on the other end of the line. "She told me to tell you that she'd be in contact soon."

Karen gripped her phone. "Is Sebastian all right?"

Susan paused, judging her words, and decided to be honest, "I don't know. I gave him to Alexander, and he's not talking. Sometimes, when a gargoyle's hurt as badly as Sebastian was... is, sometimes, they don't come back."

Karen swallowed hard against the lump in her throat. "If there's anything I can do. Anything."

"I know, Karen. I know. I'll call you. I promise."

"Okay. How's Lamiel and the rest of Bacchanalia?"

"Recovering. They lost some people and, despite Aaron's healing of Juliet and Thompson, he's not welcome back. Lamiel is pissed at his infiltration. Worse, she recognized the healing as distinctly Judeo-Christian. She's pretty pagan-centric."

"Aaron. I don't know what to think about him anymore. It's like I never knew him or David."

"Speaking of which... David. What happened with his body? And Heather's?"

"I don't know." Karen looked around her spotless apartment. "When I got back here, they were gone. Everything was clean. No blood. No bodies. No nothing."

"You're joking."

"No."

"Shit," Susan muttered.

"Yeah."

"Shit."

"Yeah. I don't know who was here, what they did with the bodies or why." Then, a sudden explanation came to mind. "Susan, I gotta go."

"Okay. I'll talk to you soon."

"Bye." Karen closed her cell phone and looked at it. She opened it and closed it again. "Reginald, do I even need this phone to talk to you?"

The phone in her hand rang. It was him. She answered it.

"No. But, it makes it easier. Humans like something to focus on when they talk to someone." Reginald said.

"You *are* the city, aren't you? I just need to be sure."

"Yes."

"You took the name of the city founder, or are you the city founder?"

"I took his name. People think of him when they think of me. It influenced me."

"Why didn't you just tell me? Why did you let me believe you were a man?" In her mind, it was not a betrayal, but it was very close. Lying by omission.

"Would you have believed me if I started out with the truth? *'Hello Karen, it's the city. I need you to help me.'*"

She thought about that before answering. "I think I would have thought I was crazy."

"Yes."

"Did you take care of my apartment? David and Heather?"

"No."

"No?" She frowned. "Who did?"

"I don't know, Karen. I was having my metaphorical guts ripped out through my metaphorical nose at the time. I was a little distracted."

"What?"

"The ritual. The magic. It would have worked. Even I have laws I must obey. If they had succeeded in killing you, my free will would have been murdered as well, and they would have possessed me as a slave. You have no idea how much that scares me."

"I didn't know cities could feel."

"I'm new to it. I'm still learning."

"What's going to happen now?"

"What do you want to have happen?"

"I want to continue making Kendrick a better place to live for everyone." It was the first thing that came to her mind.

"You can't please everyone all the time. I read that once."

"I know. But I can try."

"I'll help you."

"You could start by helping Sebastian, if you can."

"Gargoyles are children of the city. They, too, have laws they must follow." Reginald paused. "But, I will do what I can."

"That's all I'm asking. That you try. We'll worry about the rest later."

CHILDREN OF ANU

Book Two of
The Karen Wilson Chronicles

Beginnings and Endings

"THANKS FOR MEETING with me," Corelli sipped her tea, looking around at the interior of Kahili's Coffeehouse. "This is an interesting place. I like it."

Karen nodded. She drank her coffee without tasting it, wondering what Corelli was going to ask of her. It had been a promise to save Sebastian—the little gargoyle who had tried to save her and failed. *Help him! Get him away from me. Please! I'll do anything!* She'd meant those words when she'd said them. Now, she was wondering if she was going to regret it. Karen watched Corelli, a pretty, plump blond. She hoped the soft-looking woman wouldn't try to take Sebastian away from her.

"Are you all right now?" Corelli asked.

Karen looked at her, not understanding. "All right?"

Corelli gestured at Karen's throat. "Uh. That."

"Oh. That." *That* referred to the fact that one of the elder members of the Order of the Sacred Eye had almost strangled Karen to death in a ritual designed to take all of the magical energy in the city and redirect it to the Order. "Yes. I'm healing."

"This isn't going as I planned. I'm sorry." Corelli stuck out her hand. "Hi. My real name is Mary. I'm pleased to meet you."

"Karen. Nice to meet you." They shook hands.

"You have to understand that what my Order was doing—it wasn't what we were told. The purpose of the Order is to protect and help the people of Kendrick. That's what I was told. That's why I was recruited."

"Yet, you were going to just watch them murder me." The flat tone in Karen's voice expressed her anger better than shouting would have.

Mary grimaced. "I wish I could say no. But, I was scared. I didn't know what to do. The people I looked up to wouldn't look at me. They wouldn't look at you. They were just as scared and confused as I was. I wish I had spoken up, but..."

"You were afraid you'd end up in my position."

Mary looked away and nodded. "Yes."

"You saved Sebastian. I owe you for that. But, I'm not going to forget or forgive what your Order did to me." Karen kept her voice calm, despite the nervousness that mixed with her lingering anger and fear over the incident.

"I... I know. I don't blame you. I don't expect you to."

"What do you expect? What do you want of me?"

"I want you to help me make the Order into what it's supposed to be."

That surprised Karen. "You want me to fix—*lead*—the Order that just tried to kill me? How am I supposed to do that?"

"Help us mend the fences and broken alliances. Help us to be the good Order I know we were created to be. Most of the old leadership is dead. The rest are confused and don't know what to do. This is the time to take charge and set the Order's path. Most of the members are looking for a leader. A lot of them are looking at me because I keep speaking up. I can't do it alone. It's better that we do it now before someone with a less altruistic motive comes along and does it for us. When one bad guy falls, there's always another one to take his place, and sometimes the new bad guy is worse than the old one. I believe in the Order. I don't want that to happen."

"I might be able to help you, Mary. But I'm not going to lead. I'm not going to be part of your Order. I already have my obligations to the Master of the City. The Order of the Sacred Eye is yours. You're going to have to set its path. You're going have to lead. I just hope you do a better job than your predecessors."

Mary frowned, looking down at her cup.

Karen knew it wasn't the answer the other girl wanted, but it was better than a flat out 'no.'

Mary mirrored the thought as she murmured, "Hope for the best, expect the worst, and you'll land somewhere in-between."

The two of them sat in that uncomfortable silence, drinking coffee, searching for something to say. Karen watched Mary's hands, noticing a tattoo on the back of the right one; an eye inside a triangle. Her next question was almost a surprise to her. Almost, but not quite. It had been bubbling in the back of her mind. "So, what happened that night?"

"What?" Mary looked up at Karen again.

"The night of the ritual. What happened?"

"You don't know?" Mary frowned, a skeptical look hardening the woman's eyes.

Karen knew Mary wondered if she was being sarcastic. "No. Not really. One moment, you were all chanting while I was being strangled. The next, Armageddon had erupted in the middle of Colonel's Park. What happened in-between?"

"Oh." Mary thought about it. "It's a little weird. I know some of our people had put up wards so we wouldn't be interrupted. And some of our allies had been contracted to protect them. We were told that our enemies would try to stop us. I guess, in a way, they didn't lie to us. We were chanting in the silence, then there was this ripping sound and suddenly there was noise everywhere. It sounded like people fighting and screams and all of it was headed our way. Then, I saw the statue moving. It ripped itself out of its foundation and went after Todesengel. I panicked and climbed a tree."

"Climbed a tree?" Karen did not laugh at the absurdity of the statement, despite the urge to do so. Part of her wondered how Mary had managed the feat. She didn't look nimble. Then Karen banished the thought as cruel and unworthy.

"Yeah. Well. I didn't know what else to do, and trees have always been safe havens for me. They were that night. All the bloodshed and fighting. I did a spell to make me an innocent, unnoticed. But you saw me and I saw you. That's how I was able to help you and Sebastian. Is he all right now?"

Karen shook her head.

"I'm sorry. I really am."

"So am I."

Again, they paused to drink their drinks, think their own thoughts, and avoid each other's eyes in the awkward silence.

"Tell me about the Children of Anu," Karen said when she could stand it no longer.

"The Children? What do you want to know?"

"What do you know of them?"

Mary shook her head. "I don't know much. I know the Order owes them. I know we're going to have to pay... because the consequences of not living up to what's owed to the Children is death and worse. I know their territory is in the Camden District, off the docks, and that we aren't allowed to go there unless specifically invited by the Children or ordered to go there by the First Circle. Why do you want to know?"

Karen shrugged. "Mostly because I've recently heard of them and know nothing about them."

"Some things are better left unknown. The Children of Anu is not a group to mess around with. They're small, secretive, and vicious about keeping their secrets. They can make great allies, but their alliance costs. They make even worse enemies." Mary leaned toward Karen. "They're better left alone. Seriously. They scare the crap out of me, and they're on my side. For now."

***

Karen thought about Corelli (Mary was too familiar a name for comfort) all the way home. She could not believe she'd just been offered leadership of the mystic Order that had just tried to murder her. Then again, Corelli was young and inexperienced and obviously scared. However, she knew more about what was going on than Karen did when she had started. Corelli was going to have to go it alone for now.

Karen would try to help her mend some of the fences between the Order and the rest of Kendrick's supernatural societies, but it wasn't going to be easy. Everyone had lost someone in that battle in Colonel's Park. The wounds were fresh. But, anything to keep it from returning to open bloodshed was worth it.

She unlocked her door and stepped inside. At her feet, just inside the doorway, was an envelope with her name written on it. She had a bad feeling about it when she picked it up. Karen set it on the kitchen table and did the normal things she did when she got home—checked voicemail, checked email, watered the plants, and got herself something to drink.

Finally, she sat down at her kitchen table and opened the envelope. It was a letter from Aaron. She hadn't seen him since the night of the ritual in Colonel's Park a couple weeks back. Most of the people involved had kept to themselves since that night.

> Dear Karen,
> I wanted to talk to you in person, but something told me that would not be a good idea. For you, or for me. We are both special people in a world where special often means duty, obligation, and separation. We both have been set upon our own paths. I am thankful that our paths crossed at least once in this lifetime.
> I am still sorry that I did not tell you about me or my obligations until it was too late. I was, and still am, a man torn by duty and emotion. I am loyal to my Brotherhood, believing in our cause, and I love you with all my heart. These two things cannot stand side-by-side.

I know I have a destiny. The oracles within the Brotherhood have foreseen it. But, I no longer can see the path that I need to walk to fulfill it.

Because of this, I am leaving Kendrick. I am going to Europe, to the native lands of the Brotherhood, where I hope I can find myself and my path again. I am not being sent away. I am choosing to do this for myself, the Brotherhood, and for you. I suspect that if I stayed in Kendrick, I would make things complicated for both of us because of what I feel for you. I cannot have that for either of us.

I do not know if I will ever be back, and I did not wish to leave without saying good-bye, even if it isn't face-to-face. I will always hold sacred the time we had together in happiness and peace. I hope you will forgive me my transgressions against you and yours. No harm was ever meant.

I wish you the best of my heart as you walk your own path in the future. May the way be clear and bright.

Love,
Aaron

Karen put the letter down and wiped away the tears that had begun to fall. In truth, Aaron leaving the city probably was the best thing for both of them. There were too many secrets and not enough trust between them anymore. But, his good-bye still hurt deep inside.

David was dead. Heather was dead. Sebastian's condition was still unknown. Now, with this letter, Aaron might as well be dead. She wondered how many more would fall before all of this was done. How many more deaths and good-byes would she cause?

Karen lay her head in her arms on the kitchen table and finally, after weeks of being strong, allowed herself to cry, to grieve for what was now lost to her.

***

Elsewhere...

In the back end of a refurbished warehouse, three-dozen teenagers and young adults knelt in reverent prayer. Each worshipper wore a set of bull horns; either as part of a hat or as images sewn onto their clothing. Beyond that, their dress varied from homeless street kid to well-to-do, but slumming, rough and tumble weekend warrior. They chanted the many names of their deity over and over.

"*Anu...Marduk...Enlil...Bel...*"

The object of their prayer was an altar. The centerpiece of the altar was a set of bull's horns still attached to the top part of the animal's skull. Placed upright just before the skull and centered between the horns was an ancient spiked mace, still stained with its latest victim's blood. Around this centerpiece were a myriad of other brutal, blunt weapons. All of them were also stained with the dark red-brown of dried blood.

When the high priest stood, the rest immediately fell silent. He was a tall man in his 20s with short, black hair. He wore a crown with bull horns and heavy cloak of bull hide. He raised both hands in the air, his palms facing the altar. "Great god Anu! Father of Heaven, creator of the stars, lord of the constellations, king of gods, spirits, and demons, your Children have not forgotten you. Your Children remember this is the prophesied year of your return. Your humble servant, Reagan Lee Mordecai, has gathered your believers here on this night to beg of you a sign, a sigil, a vision. This is the year of your return, Great god Anu! Instruct us in your wisdom. Judge us worthy with this task. Tell us what we must do! We are your Children, your servants. Guide us in this holy year."

The high priest of the Children of Anu stopped speaking aloud, but silently continued his prayer and plea to Anu for instruction and blessing, as did the rest of the congregation. They could all feel the presence of Anu. They knew he was there, judging them, weighing them, finding them worthy or not. The next few moments would tell.

He found them worthy.

There was no sound. No light. No show of force. As one, every member of the Children of Anu collapsed in an ecstatic vision of blessing and instruction. They knew what they were meant to do, and the knowledge was overwhelming.

Slowly, one by one, they came to their senses. A small teenage girl with teal hair wearing an old fashioned pilot's leather helmet crawled over to the high priest. "Reggie! Did you see? Did you see it?" Her eyes shown as she gazed with fanatic delight at her brother.

"I saw, Vicki. I saw it all. I know what we need to do." He paused and then added. "X marks the spot."

The two of them, and those close enough and aware enough to hear, broke out in peals of ecstatic laughter at the newfound inside joke.

Heart's Desire

"I'VE DONE WHAT *I can for Sebastian. There may be a cost.*"
The Master of the City's voice was quiet.
"*What cost, Reginald? I'll pay it. Anything.*"
"*This cost cannot be paid by you, Karen. The Gargoyles are children of the City. The cost, if there is one, will have to be paid by them, and by me.*"
Karen frowned. "But, it was my fault. He's my gargoyle. I'm his human. I don't want to push that off on anyone else."
"*You don't have a choice. This isn't about you. You asked me to help him. I figured out how. I weighed the cost and I deemed it appropriate. This was my choice.*"
She was silent for a long time before answering. "Okay. I don't really understand these rules and laws you live by. But, I'm going to trust that you know what you're doing. I still feel guilty, but I understand what you're saying."
Reginald laughed. "Karen Wilson, not fighting with me over something? Are you feeling well?"
"*To be bluntly honest, I'm feeling very selfish. I want Sebastian back.*"
"*Of course you do. You two are bonded. That's why I'm doing this.*"

The apartment doorbell startled her out of yesterday's memory. The drawing pad and pencil in her hands fell to the floor as she jerked in surprise. She picked both up and put them on the living room table. Obviously, she had not gotten far with the webcomic she had been drawing. Without its namesake around, her enthusiasm for the web series had waned. The doorbell rang again just as she reached it. "I'm coming," she muttered and looked out the peephole.

John Corso from *Teller's Fortune* was standing there. He looked like his usual self—tweed jacket, goatee, and glasses. Despite his age, he was only a few years older than her, Karen always thought he dressed like an aging college professor. But, when she had asked about the jacket, John quipped, "Indiana Jones has his leather jacket; I have my tweed one. Both do their intended job—camouflage and protection."

Then, she noticed the small picnic basket in his hands. Mystified, she opened the door. "Hello, John."

"I hope you don't mind me coming by," John gave her a nod.

"No. Not at all." She ushered him in. "I didn't know you knew where I lived. Would you like something to drink?"

"No, thanks. I won't be staying long." He put the small picnic basket on the living room table. "Susan and I were talking about you recently, and we think we have a way to help."

"You were talking about me?"

"Yep."

"Why?"

He tilted his head, giving her a curious look. "Because we're your friends...?"

"You're my friends?"

"Is this a new game where you repeat everything I say? Because, if it is, I can think of much better things to have you say."

Karen shook her head. "No. I'm sorry. I'm a little out of sorts right now. Of course, you guys are my friends. You and Susan have a way to help me with what?"

"Sebastian."

They both sat on the couch. "You can help?" She couldn't keep the hope out of her voice.

"Yes. I believe so." John opened up the basket and took out a box of chocolates. "These are for you."

She accepted them. "Okay. What do I do with them?"

He gave her a look and a smile. "You eat them. Happy Valentine's Day."

"Oh." Karen flushed in embarrassment. "Thank you."

"Next, we decided that you need to keep Sebastian with you. He's your gargoyle. He might respond to your presence." He picked up the picnic basket and put it in Karen's lap.

Looking down, she saw Sebastian curled up in the same position in which she had last seen him on the night of the ritual; the night he had braved the gargoyle-killing spell on her and tried to free her from her bonds. And failed. He was so small. It was all she could do to keep herself from bursting into tears. She reached down and stroked his stone head.

"Finally, you give him this." John held a small box to her; six inches by nine inches and an inch deep. "I am temporarily gifting this to you for as long as you and Sebastian need it."

She took the box, knowing what it was, but not which one. "You're giving me one of your Todari tarot cards?" She knew how valuable these cards were to collectors around the world.

Created in the 1800s by Rinaldo Todari, they were the only artwork of note he created in his life, and had taken him thirty-six years to complete. Beyond being phenomenal works of art, each tarot card had mystic properties. It was said that each tarot card bore the likeness of a real person from 19th Century Italy, and that each one had died within a week of their card's completion. John Corso was one of the foremost collectors of the Todari tarot deck.

She opened the box and was struck, as always, by the vivid colors of the tarot placard. Karen picked this one up and looked at it. The Todari cards were not made of paper. They were made of a thin sheet of wood and were supposedly indestructible. This one depicted a man lying full length on a bed, with a sword beside him. His dress was that of a nobleman, and the sword was gilded with gold. Hands clasped upon his chest, he looked to be sleeping in great peace. Above him was a stained glass window made of three more swords hanging, point down, over him. The glass of the swords was of a shimmering grey, while the colors around the swords were a riot of vibrant colors. It was a noticeable contrast, making the swords look more real than the sleeping man below them.

"This is the Four of Swords. It's one of the cards Rinaldo did that Pamela Smith and A. E. Waite based the Rider-Waite Four of Swords tarot card on. This card represents a need to rest from strife, to convalesce after an illness, to retreat, regroup, and to plot out a new strategy. The man is not dead. Only sleeping." John touched the card with a reverent finger. "This card also has the power to heal whomever it is with as long as the card was either found or given to that person... or creature. It's part of their rules. Todari tarot cards cannot be bought or stolen."

"Thank you so much. I don't know what to say. You didn't have to do this. I know how important these cards are to you."

John looked sheepish. "I kinda did. You've helped me. Also, I know you'll give the card back to me."

"What do you mean?"

"I'm a selfish man, Karen. An obsessed one, too. But you're a friend. I like you. I trust you. I can loan this card to you because I know you'll give it to Sebastian. When Sebastian's well, he'll give it back to you. Then, you'll give it back to me. I know you will. I don't know that Sebastian would give it back to me. So, I can't just give it to him."

She smiled and nodded. "Don't feel bad, John. Don't. I completely understand feeling selfish. I don't know what you did to get this card, but once Sebastian is well, I'll give it back to you. I promise."

He visibly relaxed. "Thank you, Karen."

"My pleasure." She looked down at the still stone form of Sebastian. "I hope this works." She picked him up, put the Todari tarot card down and placed Sebastian on top of it. "Sebastian, I give this card to you. May it bring you back to me."

John stood. "I've got to get back to the store. Remember, you want to keep Sebastian close to you. Susan and I think it would be good for him."

"I will. I promise."

***

Sushi-Ya was the type of sushi place that Karen wished she had known about a long time ago. It fit all of the rules for finding good ethnic food—A generic name. It was hard to find. It was hard to get to. The décor was simple. Only about half the staff spoke English, and it was always filled to the brim with people enjoying sushi and sashimi. The food was phenomenal.

Also, it was considered to be one of the few safe, and truly neutral, grounds for Kendrick's supernatural population. No one broke *Sushi-Ya's* neutrality. If they did, they and their entire faction would be barred from the establishment. Thus, they would be barred from one of the few safe places for doing business, scheduled arbitration, or any other meeting between opposing factions.

Apparently, *Sushi-Ya* had been very busy since the ritual in December.

However, on Reginald's recommendation, Karen gave the place a call to reserve a back room. They'd hedged at first, until she gave her name and mentioned that Reginald had recommended the restaurant as a good place for business dinners. There had been a pause, some quick words in what Karen guessed was Japanese, then her reservation was accepted.

Now, she was on her way back to the small private room from the bathroom, discreetly marveling at the people she saw along the way there. She wondered if the Japanese guys in the crazy sunglasses and sharp, retro-looking suits were actually

Japanese gangsters, or if they just pretended to be gangsters while they lounged around the place, occasionally helping out and talking with the staff. She also wondered why she never noticed them around Kendrick. They certainly stood out.

A mystery for another time. When Karen opened the sliding panel door, she saw that Corelli and Susan had not made much headway in their discussion. Karen had agreed to help Corelli try to mend fences. To her, that meant setting up meetings and being there to arbitrate and be the voice of reason. Susan (and her gargoyles) was first on the list for this. It would help her get ready for the tough cases.

Or so Karen had thought. Forty-five minutes later, she wanted to shoot everyone in the room—including herself—to end the bickering.

"What is it you want from the Order, Susan?" Corelli was looking frustrated and hurt.

"For you all to leave Kendrick and to never return?" Susan's arms were folded and her face was implacable.

"That's not fair!" Corelli looked at Karen. "That's not fair. I'm trying to do what's right. How can I do what's right if no one is willing to listen?"

Karen summoned patience for the umpteenth time. "Corelli, you knew this wasn't going to be easy. Your Order was led by people who didn't have Kendrick's best interests at heart. Of course people are going to be suspicious."

"I know! But now I'm part of the First Circle and it's changing! I'll make sure of that if people will just give me a chance."

Karen held up a hand. "It's going to take time. That trust was broken. Fortunately, though, not by you." She turned to Susan. "Most of the people who made the bad decisions are dead. Corelli *is* trying to make reparations. I'm not asking you to agree to anything right now. But, I am going to ask you to think about what Corelli is offering. She's trying to make a positive change in the Order and for the rest of Kendrick."

Susan shook her head. "I'm sorry, but that seems a little naïve. To think you can come from being part of a group that has attacked, magicked, stolen from, and murdered members from just about every other supernatural group in Kendrick over the last couple of years and extend an olive branch saying, 'Don't worry, we're all good now,' and expect to be believed right off the bat? No. Not gonna wash. A couple of my gargoyles are dead. *Dead.* As in not coming back. A couple of them are so hurt they haven't returned from stone form. My own museum has been broken into several times..." Susan shook her head. "Tell me why I should believe you. Tell me why I should even think about trusting you. 'Cause I don't. I can't. Not for the sake of Kendrick, the museum, or my gargoyles."

Corelli sighed. "I'm sorry all that happened. I didn't know it was happening. I'm trying my best to make sure it doesn't happen again. I want to go back to the Order able to say, 'Okay, they're gonna give us a chance, but we've got to earn it and this is how we do that.' I don't know how we earn that chance and earn some of the trust back. I need help. Karen agreed to help me, and look what almost happened to her."

"I think she's insane—" Susan stopped talking as she grabbed her head with both hands, emitting a low cry of pain.

"Susan?" Karen was at her side.

"It's Alexander. Something's happened to Alexander." She looked at Corelli, her eyes hard with fury. "This was a set up. You bitch! You set me up and someone's attacked the museum—again. I can't believe I even agreed to meet with you."

Corelli looked like someone slapped her. "No!" She held out empty hands to Susan. "It wasn't me. It wasn't the Order. I swear!"

"You can't say that until you see what was happened," Karen helped Susan up. "You cannot blindly accuse."

"Please, it wasn't us. I swear it." Corelli looked desperate. "I swear it. None of the Order is supposed to be out tonight at all. The First Circle ordered them all to stay home."

"Whatever," Susan spat and held her head. She looked at Karen. "I've got to get to the museum. I've got to get to Alexander."

"I'll take you. We'll go see what happened." Karen gave Corelli a sympathetic look. "I'll talk to you tomorrow, Corelli. It'll be okay." She helped Susan out of the restaurant and drove her to the museum.

***

Karen was exhausted by the time she got home. The Order hadn't attacked the museum. That much was certain. Whatever it was, it had been invisible to gargoyle eyes, but not to a gargoyle's other senses. Not unless the Order of the Sacred

Eye had suddenly developed extraordinary powers. After the failed ritual, that was highly unlikely.

Alexander had heard someone break into the museum storage room but could not see who or what. When he tried to defend his mistress's territory, he had been attacked by multiple opponents and beaten into stone form. Once Susan got to him, she was able to revive him and to cure some of his wounds by taking them onto herself. She now sported a couple of nasty bruises. However, Karen understood Susan's willingness to sacrifice herself for her gargoyle.

Thinking of gargoyles, Karen was very glad she had left Sebastian home tonight. It could have been dangerous for him and for John's Todari card. She went over to the basket on the living room table and looked in. Sebastian was there as he had been the last time she looked. The basket also had a handful of miniature Snickers bars in it, just in case. They were Sebastian's favorite food.

Stretching out on the couch, Karen took Sebastian and the Todari tarot card from the basket and placed both on her. The card rested on her upper chest while Sebastian rested on her tummy. She stroked the unresponsive gargoyle as she spoke. "I don't know where you are or how you're doing, but I hope you come back to me soon. I miss you. Please wake up. Please." She stroked him a few moments longer in silence and closed her eyes.

Hours later, she woke with a small start, briefly confused. Something was different. It took her a moment to realize what it was. There was a sense of contented purring in the back of her mind; one she had not sensed in months. Trying to keep her hope under control, she reached out and stroked Sebastian who was still on her tummy. Instead of hard stone, her hand encountered warm flesh.

"Sebastian!" Karen scooped him up and looked him in the face. "Sebastian, are you okay?"

The small gargoyle opened a pair of very tired-looking topaz eyes and blinked at her. *'Sleepy. Hungry.'*

"Okay, baby. You can sleep." She took the Todari tarot card from where it fell and put it back in the basket. "Or, if you're hungry, there's Snickers for you."

'Snickers...'

Karen cuddled Sebastian to her chest, petting him over and over as he purred in her mind. She couldn't keep back the tears of joy that spilled down her face as she felt like she could finally breathe again.

***

Elsewhere...

In a familiar warehouse in the Camden District, a party was going on. Rough-looking men and women danced to loud rock music and drank to celebrate their successful mission. With their great God Anu on their side, there was little they could not do. For most of the Children, all they knew was that an elite force of them had been sent to retrieve a box from the Kendrick Museum of History and Art. They had been confronted by one of the city gargoyles there and had beaten it down. No easy task, but they'd done it.

Reggie and his seconds, Sam and Mike, stood apart from the crowd of celebrating youths, going through the box. Most of it was trash to them, but there was an ancient, preserved bull's head that was put above the altar behind the bull's horns and ancient mace.

"Where is it?" Sam asked.

Mike shook his head. "I don't know."

"We'll find it." Reggie returned from admiring his handiwork. "Anu has promised."

"Vicki! Get away from that." Mike snapped at the teal-haired teen with goggles. "Go play with the rest."

Reggie raised a hand. "It's okay. That's the stuff we've rejected. It doesn't matter what happens to it. Let her look."

Sam and Mike nodded, knowing better than to argue with Reggie about his younger sister. Mike watched her touch the probably priceless artifacts he wanted to sell, silently swearing to beat the girl within an inch of her life if she broke any of it.

As if reading his mind, Vicki looked directly at him with a smile as she knocked one of the earthen jars from the table with a casual flick of her hand. The jar smashed on the floor, making Sam and Reggie jump, and Mike wince.

"You stupid little bitch." Mike started toward her.

Vicki ignored him, "Reggie! Look what I found." She was pointing at a roll of parchment within the shards of earthenware jar. "It looks like a scroll."

Sam grabbed Mike as Reggie shouldered past them both. "Dude, don't let her get to you," Sam cautioned in a low voice.

"What's this, kiddo?" He grabbed her hand before she could pick it up. "Careful. You don't want to get cut." He shifted aside the pieces of pottery and picked up the scroll.

"Is that what you're looking for?" Vicki craned her head to get a look at it as Reggie carefully spread the scroll out on the altar.

"I think it is, Vicki. I think you found it. Go get your drawing stuff. I want you to make a copy of it." Reggie was looking down at an old map. It wasn't as old as any of the other stuff they'd taken from the box. It could not be more than a hundred or so years old. What it was doing inside a jar from the Babylonian period, no one could say, nor did they care to ask. This was what they had been sent to get.

"Okay." Vicki grinned. "X marks the spot."

Reggie nodded. "Indeed it does."

Sam and Mike exchanged a glance of surprise as the girl ran off to get her pens and pencils.

Sharks and Seals

IT WAS NEVER a good thing when her tattoo started itching. Corelli looked down at the simple line tattoo of an eye inside a pyramid on the back of her plump right hand. When the All-Seeing Eye woke, it meant that people were watching her with a very specific intent. People she was not already aware of.

She raised her head and looked around as she walked down the street. There. In front of her, two guys in scruffy clothing walked toward her with a purpose. She looked behind and saw a third, a girl, closing in. They were the hunting dogs, she was the fat quail waiting to be taken.

Corelli did the only thing she could do: she dug into her purse, pulled out a few Red Hot candies, and ate them. The cinnamon flavor burned in her mouth and gave her confidence as it warmed her body. There was magic in the taste and the sugar didn't hurt, mixing with the adrenaline of sudden fear.

"Hey, Corelli. Reggie wants to see you," Mike said.

Mike and Sam, she identified. *Reggie's Seconds.* She glanced behind her and recognized Vicki's teal hair. This was quite the group to send out looking for her. It was important enough to send his top guns, but not too dangerous for the younger sister he doted on to tag along. Of course, she looked soft with her round curves and extra weight. Most of the Children of Anu were whip-lean street kids. They assumed because she didn't look as hard as they did, she couldn't hurt them.

They were wrong.

She stood her ground. "What's the magic word?"

"Now." Mike reached forward and grabbed her arm. His fingers bit deep into her flesh.

"Careful. You don't want to get *burned*, do you?" Corelli said with a deceptive calmness.

Mike's hand on Corelli's arm burst into flame. She watched while he shouted and danced around, trying to put his hand out. Cerridwen always hated Corelli's brand of sympathetic magic. It was too chaotic and too improvised for the old woman's liking. She had always gone on about the Will and the Word. It sounded like something out of one of the fantasy books the old woman had liked to read. *Whatever. She's dead and I'm not.*

"You'll continue to burn until I stop it," Corelli said. "If nothing else, it should teach you some manners."

"Please." Vicki stepped up. "Please, would you join us for a talk?"

Corelli smiled a full and generous smile. "Certainly." She blew on the tip of her index finger and Mike's hand stopped burning. "However, need I remind any of you that you are speaking to me as a member of the First Circle of the Order of the Sacred Eye, or the fact that I passed your Test of Worth some time ago?" Sam and Vicki shook their heads, but she kept her eyes on Mike. He was the one she was delivering her message to.

Mike held his hand, bright red and already blistering, down by his side. "No. Sorry." His tone, sulky and petulant, also held a note of wary respect.

"Good. I'll heal that after my conversation with Reggie— if you ask nicely."

Mike did not respond. Sam stepped forward. "We have a car waiting."

Corelli nodded. "Let's go then." She could not show an ounce of the fear she felt. The Children of Anu respected strength and destroyed weakness. They looked at the city as their hunting grounds. They were like human sharks, and she hated dealing with them. They always saw her as prey. She had no choice but to be strong and fearless. She was not certain what Reggie wanted, but she had an idea what it might be.

"That was really cool," Vicki said as they walked down the street. "Can you teach it to me?"

"Only if you give up being a member of the Children and become a member of the Order."

"Oh. Never mind."

"Yeah. Sorry. We all have our secrets, don't we?"

Vicki gave her a sidelong glance and smiled, bright red lips half hidden by her unreal-looking hair. "I guess we do."

They stopped in front of an old beaten up town car and Sam opened the front door for her. "After you."

Corelli had never been this deep into the Camden District. It was the Children's territory, and every magic society in the city knew it. It was also the industrial district, and only people who had business—legal and otherwise—went there. Until now, she hadn't been sure they had a regular meeting place, but this warehouse appeared to be it. She noted the address and the number of hungry-looking street kids hanging around.

"Thanks for coming," Reggie said from his spot at the table in the front part of the warehouse where at least he and Vicki appeared to live. Sam and Vicki peeled off to go do whatever it was they did when they weren't accosting people on the street. Mike stood off to one side. Close enough to be there if needed, but not close enough to be part of the conversation.

"Thanks for sending people who can't remember how to respect the leaders of a different Order." Corelli glanced at Mike.

Reggie looked from her to Mike and back again. "What happened?"

"He touched me when he shouldn't have." Corelli sat down across from Reggie at the table, thankful that the chairs had no armrests to cut into her hips. "I told him I'd heal his hand after we talked... if he asked nicely," she added as she dug out lip gloss and a small mirror from her purse.

Reggie's eyes narrowed. "We'll see. He fucked up. Maybe he should suffer."

Corelli shrugged as she put the lip gloss on. It wasn't vanity—it was more of her personal magic. The lip gloss would help her speak the correct words she needed to speak, even if she didn't know everything that was going on. She paused as she saw Vicki in the mirror, spying on them from behind Corelli. She said nothing. She did not care what the teen heard of the conversation. In fact, it might be in her best interest to cultivate Vicki as an ally for the future.

"Don't care. What I care about is why you wanted to meet me."

He gestured to the pot. "Coffee?"

"Yes. Thank you." She had started to say no, but her magic overrode her. Apparently, drinking coffee with Reggie was the more correct thing to do. Perhaps it meant he was treating her like a peer. It made sense. They were a hungry group. The sharing of resources was significant. She allowed him to pour the coffee, accepted it, and added two packets of real sugar from the small selection he had set out. She liked her coffee sweet and, if necessary, there was magic she could link to the taste of coffee and sugar.

He watched her fix her coffee and sip. "The Children of Anu and the Order of the Sacred Eye have had a long history, haven't they?"

She nodded.

"We were promised a lot based on our support of your Order in the December ritual."

Corelli nodded again, listening to her inner voice for the needed words. "Yes. You were promised much based on the success of the ritual."

"Nothing was said about what happens if the Order failed."

She listened for the words. None came. She remained silent, watching. Again, it was all about how the Children of Anu perceived the outside world. *They must wonder how someone like me took control of one of the most powerful orders in Kendrick. Not by threats. That's for sure.*

"The Children and the Order have been allies for a long time," Reggie continued. "I don't want that to change. We were promised a lot based on the success of the ritual. The ritual failed. We got nothing. Yet, we supported the Order."

"What do you want?"

"Acknowledgement of this debt. We won't walk away empty-handed. Some of the Children died that night." Reggie put his coffee down and clenched his hands. It was clear to Corelli that he was controlling his anger and making the effort to work within a society not his own. It had to be difficult for someone so hard to work with someone whom he perceived to be so soft. She wondered how he would treat her if she were as lithe as he was lean.

Corelli mentally cringed as she spoke the words she did not want to say. "The Order of the Sacred Eye acknowledges that it owes the Children of Anu a debt."

"A significant debt."

She ignored his clarification. "A debt. This debt is acknowledged. What do the Children want in exchange for it?"

Reggie sat back and looked at her for a long moment. She could see him fighting with himself over the semantics of 'debt' versus 'significant debt.' In the end, he decided not to quibble over it. He did something worse. "Nothing right now. I just wanted the Order to acknowledge the debt owed to me and mine."

Damn. Open-ended debts were the worst thing someone could agree to, but she had no choice. "The debt is acknowledged."

"Thanks."

She put down her cup. "Anything else?"

He shook his head. "No."

"Then, if you don't mind, I do have other things to do. I wasn't just standing around waiting for your people to come fetch me." She glanced at Mike and his burned hand.

Reggie also looked over at Mike, who stood up straighter. "Anything from you?" His voice, raised for Mike to hear, was laced with disapproval.

The teen stepped toward the table. "I'm sorry I touched you, Corelli. I won't do it again. Will you heal my hand?" The words, though spoken smoothly, looked like they hurt to say.

She almost agreed, but her still working lip gloss magic prevented her from speaking. Instead, she just looked at him, but turned her attention to Reggie out of the corner of her eye.

"Are you willing to heal him, Corelli?"

"Only if that's what you want, Reggie. Your group, your rules, your decision."

"No. He fucked up. He should suffer. If Anu wishes, he will heal his Child."

Mike looked at Reggie, then away. His face flushed as he clenched his uninjured hand into a fist but said nothing.

"As you wish." She gathered up her purse. "Thank you for the coffee."

"I'll have Sam drive you back."

Corelli shook her head. "No thanks. I'll get a taxi." She held up a hand. "No need to get up. I know my way out."

She turned and walked out through the front door without looking back or to the sides. She did so like a woman leaving a store she was no longer interested in. She knew Reggie and several of the Children were watching her with interest and a new regard. She had lived up to her new position, and proven she was as much a shark as they were, even if she did look like a seal... and that was a factor to be considered within their plans. They all knew it.

Outside, she didn't bother to try and hail a taxi. They rarely came this way—it was too dangerous an area for them. Instead, she headed for a bus stop she knew to be a couple blocks away. She realized, with a smile to herself, that she was not breaking down in trembles as soon as she walked away, nor did she feel the usual nervous sweat at the small of her back. In fact, she was feeling confident and self-assured at her performance. It was a good feeling.

But she couldn't bask in this glow for long. She needed to report to the rest of the First Circle and tell them what happened. Shark or not. Seal or not. This meeting would have lasting consequences.

***

Elsewhere...

Karen sipped her coffee as she read the instant message from Susan and grimaced. Her coffee had gone cold. She did not like cold coffee. It was too bitter. Instead of getting up to get more coffee, she reread the instant message.

"Either it was a box of stolen bed warmers or a box of Babylonian and Sumerian artifacts." Susan had typed.

"My bet is the bed warmers. ☺" Karen responded with a smile.

"Why is it that people always go for the bed warmers?"

Karen laughed and typed, "Because it's funny."

"Ha-ha."

"Obviously, it would be the artifacts. Do you know why?"

"No. That's the stupid thing about it. There wasn't much in that box. Just a mummified bull's head, some vases, and a couple of plates. Valuable, yes. But obvious and hard to sell afterwards." It was clear from Susan's response that she was frustrated and tired.

"Ritual components?"

"Maybe."

"Did you call the police?" Karen's 911 training was kicking in.

"Yes. They weren't helpful."

"Sorry."

"Not your fault, is it?"

"No. Wish I could help."

Karen paused in her typing as Sebastian hopped up on her desk and dropped something next to her hand. It landed with a metallic clink. "What's this?"

'Found. Found in the corner.' Sebastian thought at her before scampering off to complete his patrol of the apartment and the surrounding areas. Ever since he recovered, he had returned to his duties as her guardian with enthusiasm.

It looked like an old coin. She picked it up and examined at it. She could not tell what kind of metal it was. She took another sip of coffee and grimaced again. She had forgotten that it was already cold.

Karen turned the coin over and saw the bull's head beaten into it. She suddenly knew exactly what it was and how it had gotten in her home.

"I'm sorry I had to drug your coffee. But it is war, Karen—between this supposed 'Master of the City' and the Order of the Sacred Eye. If you go tonight, you'll be hurt or killed and I love you too much to let that happen. I'm sorry it had to be this way, but once his hold on you is broken..."

David's words were interrupted by the unexpected sound of the front door being unlocked and opened. Heather came in, calling for her. "Karen! Karen! I got it! It fucking sucked and hurt like a bitch, but I got you the meeting with the Children of Anu." *Her voice traveled through the apartment as she looked for Karen. "But, something big is going on tonight. So, we have to go..." She reached the doorway between the small dining area and the kitchen, "... right now?"*

David and Heather looked at each other in silence for a couple of seconds. David could see that Heather had been through something unpleasant. She was dirty, bruised with a black eye, and her clothing was torn. "What happened to you?" David asked, unable to help himself.

"Test of Worth. I passed." She said, frowning at him and the scene. "What the hell's happening here?" She gestured to Karen slumped on the kitchen table.

"Nothing you need to concern yourself with, girl."

The voice came from behind Heather. Paul Maloy, known as Todesengel within the Order of the Sacred Eye, stepped into sight and grabbed Heather as she turned. Without hesitation, the man slit Heather's throat from ear to ear and held her as blood gushed from her throat. Whatever she had been holding tumbled from her hand and skittered off to the far corner of the dining area as she struggled with the man killing her...

The coin was some sort of passkey to meet with the Children of Anu. Heather had been bringing it to her when Karen had been betrayed by David, who had then been betrayed by the Order of the Sacred Eye. It had been her worst nightmare come to life—watching a friend die while helpless to stop it. Both Heather and David had been left dead in her apartment. One shot. One with her throat slit. Both bodies had disappeared by the time Karen had been rescued and made it home again.

Karen reread the log between Susan and her. A box full of Babylonian and Sumerian artifacts. John had told her that the Children of Anu worshipped a Sumerian God named Anu. The connection seemed clear enough to her.

"I wish you could, too." Susan's message had been sitting there for a couple of minutes.

"Maybe I can." She typed.

"What do you mean?"

"I'll explain as soon as I know more."

"Be careful!"

Karen could hear Susan in her head with that last admonishment. "I will. I promise. Talk to you later."

Karen read Susan's parting response, and then looked down at the coin sitting on her mouse pad. John had warned her away from the Children of Anu. She couldn't listen to him. Not anymore. It was time to see what else he would tell her.

Many Happy Returns

"I HAVE SOMETHING for you." Karen said after sipping her drink. It was a quiet afternoon in the *Teller's Fortune*, allowing John and Karen the pleasant luxury of a cup of tea while they sat and talked.

"Oh? Is that why you came by to see me?" John asked as he marked something down in his ledger.

"Do I need a reason?"

"No. Not at all. I like it when you come by." He paused and smiled at her. "But, you usually do have a purpose."

Karen considered that and smiled. "Guilty as charged. I did come to see you today with a purpose in mind." She slid her hand into her purse and pulled out a familiar-looking black box. "I have a gift for you." She put it on the glass countertop and watched John's eyes light up.

"Are you sure?" His hand was already reaching for the box before she nodded. Opening the box, he smiled at the Todari tarot card within. It was the Four of Swords; the one he had given her to help heal Sebastian. And, just as all of the Todari tarot cards did, it took his breath away. "Sebastian's okay now?"

She nodded again. "He's full of vim, vigor, and vive. He's been patrolling every night for the last week, and I wouldn't be surprised if he were sitting on the roof right now."

He stroked the tarot card once before unlocking the custom-made display case and returning the Todari card to its accustomed place. "I'm glad he's doing better. I was worried about the little guy. Baby gargoyles are rare." He sipped his tea and smiled at his card collection. It was his one obsession. He knew it and made no excuses for it.

"They are. Useful, and always finding interesting things. Look at what he found in my apartment a couple of days ago." Karen dropped the bullhead coin onto the glass countertop, where it clattered to a stop. "Can you tell me what it is it?"

Without touching it, John gazed at it for a few moments, then sighed. "You don't want to go messing with them, Karen. You really don't. Just leave well enough alone. Kendrick is still healing from that night."

She clenched her teeth. "I can't. You know I can't. I almost died that night. Two of my friends died in my apartment while I could do nothing. Heather..." She paused and took a breath. "Heather went through hell to get this to me. She didn't want to do it because of what she knew she'd have to do to get it. But she owed me, she did it, and it got her killed in the end. Now I owe her. You know what this is. Tell me."

"It's a token. It will allow you to see the leader of the Children. But, you have to pass their Test of Worth first." He took his glasses off and started cleaning them out of nervous habit.

"What test?"

John shook his head. "I can't tell you."

"Where do I take the token?"

He shook his head again. "I can't tell you, Karen."

"Can't or won't?"

"You don't understand what you're asking."

"I understand that my friends died in front of me for no good reason and their bodies disappeared. I understand that people are afraid of the Children of Anu. I understand that the Children fought on the side of the Order in the war in December. I understand that they have their own agenda, and I understand that if I'm going to help Reginald protect this city, I've got to find out more about them and what they want. Please, help me."

John shook his head. "I can't. I have my own agreements. I don't break my promises. Not with them. Not with you. It's the only way you know you can trust me."

It looked like it was killing him to say this, but it was not helping her. "Fine." Karen scooped up the coin and shoved it in her pocket. "I've been told to stay away from the Camden District a couple of times. I figure that will be a good place to start looking."

"Karen, don't!"

"You do what you have to do. I'll do what I have to do." She turned and walked from the store.

***

John watched her go, knowing that once she got an idea in her head, there was little anyone could do to stop her. Karen Wilson was bound and determined to track down the Children of Anu and find out what their agenda was. If she passed the Test of Worth, her line of questioning was going to go over like a lead balloon, and probably get her killed.

He considered his options. Going after her was not one of them. However, he could send someone else after her. But that was almost as dangerous as letting her walk into the gauntlet of the Children alone.

After a few more moments of hesitation, he picked up the phone and dialed a number known only to a select few. "Hello. This is John Corso. I need to speak to Mason Steward and the matter is somewhat urgent."

***

After a conversation with Reginald, in which he disapproved of her idea, but allowed her to do what she wanted, Karen headed to the northern Camden District. It was the industrial section where the docks to the Bay were located. The day was moving from late afternoon into early evening, but the sun was still high and people were out and about.

She felt like the outsider she was, but was no less determined to find one of these Children and talk with them. She kept a close eye out for anyone who had any sort of bullhead symbol on their jacket or anywhere else on them.

"Hey, lady, you look lost."

Karen turned around and found herself face to face with a teenage girl with teal hair. "Maybe I am." She paused, seeing a bullhead scratched into one arm of the girl's leather jacket. "Or, maybe I was until you said hello."

"I didn't say hello. I said that you looked lost."

"True. But you didn't have to say anything, did you?" Karen looked around and picked out two more people who had taken an interest in her and the teenage girl.

"No. But I knew I should. I'm nice like that. I'm Vicki." She looked Karen up and down. "And you don't belong here."

"I'm Karen." She stuck out a hand. "Nice to meet you."

Vicki considered Karen's hand for a moment, then shook it. "Why are you here?"

Blunt seemed to be the best tactic at this point. "I'm looking for the Children of Anu."

"Why?"

"Because I have this." She pulled the bullhead coin out of her pocket and showed it to the girl. She pulled her hand back before the girl could take the token from her. "Will you help me now?"

Vicki crossed her arms. "I don't think you want my help, Karen. I don't think you want to meet with the Children. I don't think you know what you're doing."

"Nevertheless, I will speak with the Children of Anu tonight—whether you help me or not. If you won't help me, I'll be on my way." Karen turned to continue heading north, but was stopped by Vicki's hand on her arm.

"All right, but don't say I didn't warn you."

"Did you warn Heather?" Karen did not know why she'd asked that, but it felt right once she had.

"Yeah. She didn't listen, either. Come on." Vicki turned and headed toward one of the docks.

She led Karen through a series of twisting streets, in the general direction of the warehouse district. On the corner of one shadowed, almost abandoned street, Karen saw several street kids lounging about. As soon as they saw Vicki and Karen, they became alert.

A dark haired girl with goggles and a baseball bat came forward. "Yo, Vic... what's this?"

"This is Karen. She's here to see Reggie."

"She hasn't passed the Test of Worth, or I would've known about it."

"I know, but she has the token."

There was a murmur through the kids as they slowly coalesced into a group around her. Karen was starting to get nervous at the number of people, and the fact that all of them had some sort of weapon on them—bats, sticks, chains—all designed to beat the crap out of someone.

"She can't stay unless she passes the Test of Worth. Those are the rules."

Vicki shrugged. "Whatever. You deal with it. I'm getting Reggie." She left Karen and headed toward the back warehouse.

As soon as Vicki left her side, Karen was sorry she had not thought out this plan more thoroughly. She backed away from the growing mob and knew from her memory of how Heather looked that this Test of Worth was not going to be pleasant.

The girl with the baseball bat stepped toward her. "You're on our territory, princess. I don't know who you think you are or why you're here, but you've got to prove yourself to us. You've got one choice and one choice only—you survive the Test of Worth, or you don't."

Karen continued to back away from the mob being led by the dark-haired girl. "Is this how you treat all representatives from the Master of the City?" Her heart was pounding as she looked for a way out. Unfortunately, the Children had done this before, and had already spread out to prevent her escape.

"The Master of the City," the girl snarled, "has no power here." She leapt forward and swung the bat at Karen, who blocked the blow with her bag. The girl whirled away and let the others close in.

They darted in, swinging clubs, chains, and fists, Karen heard tires screech to a halt nearby. She was too busy dodging, blocking, or being hit to see who it was and what they were doing. Suddenly, muted gunfire ripped through the air, and the Children scattered. Karen, bruised and bloody, crouched next to the wall and saw who was doing the shooting. She was so surprised, all she could do was stare.

It was the Kendrick police department. Two cars and a black van with *SPECIAL UNIT* emblazoned in white on the side of it. At first, she thought the officers had opened fire on civilians without warning and was murdering them. She quickly discovered, after ducking a spray of gunfire, that they were using rubber bullets. They hurt, but did not kill.

When most of the Children had scattered or were down on the ground, a police officer in what looked like black riot gear and a *Special Unit* badge on his shoulder, ran up to her. "Are you Karen Wilson?"

She flinched away from him, not understanding what was happening. "Yes."

The officer shouted over his shoulder. "I've got her, Detective!"

"Good. Take her into protective custody and bring her to the station."

Karen recognized the voice of the man speaking and pushed herself into a standing position to get a look at him. She only caught a glimpse of him as he got back into the first police car but it was him, she was certain of it.

The man the officer referred to as "Detective" was none other than David Hauberk—the former boyfriend who had betrayed her to the Order of the Sacred Eye—and whom she had last seen lying dead on her kitchen floor.

***

Elsewhere...

Corelli faced the rest of the First Circle of the Order of the Sacred Eye, delivering the last of her report. "It is unfortunate that we now owe the Children of Anu an open-ended debt, but we do, despite the fact that we are no longer pursuing the plans that Praetor set up. I'm probably the best contact with the Children for the foreseeable future, based on Reggie's acceptance of me as an equal. However, I counsel having as little to do with them as possible."

The four other people at the table nodded in agreement. None of them wanted anything to do with the Children of Anu or their plans. Much less to be the focus of whatever this open-ended debt was eventually going to be.

"How are things going with Karen and making peace with the rest of Kendrick?" Galerie asked.

Corelli shook her head. "Slow. There is another group making attacks at the same time I'm trying to do my negotiations. It makes them think that I'm distracting the leaders in order for us to pull off these attacks."

"But we aren't." Galerie sighed.

"No, we aren't, but we have a bad reputation and history to overcome. However, my meeting with the Children taught me something about negotiation. I will be changing my tactics from now on. Karen is still willing to help me, for now. She wants peace in her city—"

"*Her* city?" V'ger interrupted her.

Corelli didn't back down. "Yes. I believe we can say it is her city, as she is the Master of the City's representative and the Master has earned his title." She took a breath. "At this time, if Karen said we needed to leave Kendrick based on the Master's wish, there would be little to stop them from forcing us to do so. That is why I am her contact."

She shook her head. "No offense to you, V'ger, First of the First Circle and First in the Order, but if Karen knew you were still alive, I don't think we would have a chance to re-establish ourselves—for good or evil."

The man nodded, sighing. "I know. I did a lot of things I'm not proud of. I withdraw the question. Please continue."

Corelli nodded. "We need to rebuild our power base and rebuild our lost stores of magical artifacts. We need power to do our rituals." She glanced at V'ger. "And we need to do it properly. No stealing. No assassinations. We've got to be angels. Otherwise, we'll have no chance of building bridges."

V'ger nodded. "I agree. Research then."

"And offering of services for funds and trade." Corelli looked at them all. "You may think me naïve but I'm not. I'm fourth generation Order of the Sacred Eye. I know what the Order was meant to do. It's time we got back to doing it."

Galerie sat back. "All right. What is it we're meant to do?"

"Be of service to Kendrick."

V'ger scowled. "Not at the expense of the Order. We're not a charity."

Corelli nodded. "I know. But for the time being, we need to act like one. Especially if we want to rebuild our powerbase and re-forge our alliances."

Many Unanswered Questions

KAREN GAZED AT herself in the mirror in the police interrogation room over the officer's shoulder. She was not actually looking at herself, or even trying to see who was behind the mirror watching her. She already knew who one of them was: David Hauberk. Right now, she was trying to wrap her mind around the fact that he was not dead, and wondered exactly what had happened in her kitchen after V'ger and Todesengel had murdered Heather, shot David, and taken her from her home. She had spent months grieving for him, and wondering who had stolen his and Heather's bodies. Finally, she had a clue.

"What's your name?"

She looked up at the young officer before her. "You know my name."

"I do, Miss Wilson, but I need you to state it for the record." He kept his pen poised above the form on his clipboard.

"Am I under arrest?"

"No, ma'am."

"Then why am I being detained and questioned?" She crossed her arms and sat back, her attention fully on the officer now.

Young though he was, apparently the officer was used to people not answering his questions. His voice was calm and patient. "You're in protective custody."

"From what?"

"Those people who were trying to kill you."

"You mean the Children of Anu? They weren't trying to kill me."

At the mention of the Children, he began to write on another part of the form. "What were they trying to do?"

In no mood to play ball, Karen changed the subject again. "Where's David?"

"Who?"

"David Hauberk."

"The detective? Doing paperwork, most likely."

She noticed that the officer did not look at her this time. "I want to see him."

"I can't do that until you answer my questions."

"Look, Sergeant...?"

"Mueller."

"Sergeant Mueller, are you aware that in an average lifetime, a person will spend six months sitting at red lights?" She uncrossed her arms and leaned forward with her hands in her lap.

"No. I was not aware of that." He gave her a quizzical but wary look.

She nodded. "It's an interesting statistic I picked up somewhere. You want to know what else I know? I know that there is a special department within the Kendrick police called the Special Unit. I know this *Special* Unit knows about some of the *special* things going on in Kendrick. I can see by your badge with the ' SU' on it that you are also a member of this *Special* Unit that knows just how *special* Kendrick is. So, unless you get Detective Hauberk in here—who, by the way, was only a Sergeant when I last saw him, dead on my kitchen floor after he drugged me—I will make sure that you never, ever hit another green light for as long as you live in Kendrick. Do I make myself clear?"

***

Detective David Hauberk raised an eyebrow at Karen's threat. It was certainly a creative one, and would only be a minor annoyance if John Mueller was not a police officer to whom time was of the essence and a red light could mean the difference between life and death. She had changed. Hardened. It was partly his fault, and he knew it. He had stayed away from her because of it, and now the confrontation would not be denied. He knew it from the moment the man in charge had told him they needed to extract one Karen Wilson from the Camden District.

"Can she do that?" Sergeant Taylor asked.

He shrugged at him. "She couldn't the last time I saw her."

"Well, apparently, sir, the last time she saw you, you were dead."

"Yes. I know." He took a breath and headed for the door. "Things change."

***

The door to the interrogation room opened, and David stepped inside. "I'll take it from here, Sergeant Mueller."

Karen and David gazed at each other while Sergeant Mueller packed his stuff up and left without a word. He closed the door behind him, clearly happy to be out of the line of fire.

David took Sergeant Mueller's place at the table across from Karen. They stared at each other for a long moment. He could not tell what the expression on her face meant, but he suspected it was going to be an unpleasant conversation. He might as well make the opening volley. "Hello, Karen. How are you?"

Karen kept her eyes on David as she pulled out her cell phone, opened it, and began speaking without dialing anything. "Reginald?"

"Yes, Karen?"

"Would you make sure that this room is private, please?"

There was a pause. "It is now."

"Thank you." She hung up the phone and put it in her purse again.

Before she opened her mouth to speak again, David held up a finger. "They'll be busting in here momentarily. I'll assure them that everything is fine and not to interrupt us again."

Karen nodded and waited. They did not wait long before Sergeant Mueller and Sergeant Taylor entered in a rush without knocking, their hands on their still holstered side arms.

"Is everything all right, Detective?" Sergeant Taylor asked.

"Just fine."

"There's an equipment malfunction. We should move—"

David shook his head. "No. We'll stay right here. Everything's fine."

"Sir?"

"Everything is *fine*, Sergeant. Miss Wilson and I are going to have a private conversation."

The two Sergeants looked at him, and then at each other. Sergeant Taylor nodded. "Yes, sir. Just knock on the door when you want out." They left, closing and locking the door after themselves.

"Is that standard procedure?"

"Which part?"

She gestured to the door. "The locking us in part."

He nodded. "They understand that, sometimes, the people we bring here need to not be recorded. If that happens, the door is locked to contain... the potential danger."

"Is that what I am now?"

"I don't know. Are you? You're the one threatening police officers with endless red lights." It was supposed to be a joke, but the words sounded flat and accusatory in his ears.

"Why am I here, David? And why are you still alive?"

"I'm happy to see you, too."

"Dammit!" She slammed her fist on the table and stood. "I saw you get shot. I saw you on the floor, dead. I saw... blood. I saw blood from you and from Heather. When I got back after being rescued from the ritual, both of your bodies were gone! Why are you still alive?"

***

"Shit. She looks mad." Sergeant Mueller said.

"I know."

"Why?"

"Might be because of the whole 'she thought he was dead' thing." Sergeant Taylor sipped his coffee and watched the silent conversation on the other side of the mirror.

"What happened with that? That was before I got introduced to the Special Unit."

"Back in December, the Order was coming after Karen for the Kendrick-shattering ritual. You know, the one with all the power outages and riots. He was trying to keep her out of it. They tricked him. Had him drug her. Then came in, shot him, and took her. He, being a cop expecting trouble, had his vest on, but it still did a job on him. He was in the hospital a long time. The extraction team found another dead girl in the apartment. David said that one of the members of the Order slit her throat. We had to clean it all up."

***

David shrugged. "I'm alive because I had my vest on." He pulled open collar of his shirt to reveal a bullet hole scar near his collarbone. "But I didn't get away unscathed, if that makes you happy."

"It doesn't make me happy. Why'd you let me think you were dead?"

He looked uncomfortable. "I was in the hospital for a while. By the time I got out, I figured it was better if I wasn't in your life."

"You let me think you were dead."

"I know." He nodded. "I'm sorry."

"What happened to Heather's body?"

"She was a Jane Doe in the morgue for about a week. Then, after she was identified, her family was called and she was listed as the victim of a mugging gone wrong. She's buried in the Kendrick cemetery."

Karen sighed and bowed her head as she sat back down. "At least she's at rest."

***

"She threatened me with a curse of red lights. Can she do that?"

Sergeant Taylor shrugged. "I don't know. Maybe. She's the Master of the City's representative. There's a rumor that she *is* the new Master of the City."

"Wouldn't that make her the Mistress of the City?"

"Don't be stupid. It's just a title."

***

"I didn't mean to hurt you."

"You drugged me. You handed me over to them."

"No. I was betrayed."

"So was I." Her voice was quiet and full of pain.

"They were never supposed to be there." He reached out and put his hand over hers. "I was protecting you. I knew they wanted to use you."

As much as Karen wanted to leave her hand in his and to throw herself into his arms, sobbing on his shoulder out of relief that he was still alive, she pulled away and crossed her arms. She deliberately closed herself off from him, and they both knew it. "You should have known better. You're in this *Special* Unit. You made things worse, and caused the death of one of my courier gargoyles with that candle of yours. You almost got me killed, too. You could have just told me what you knew."

The venom in the word 'special' made her statement sound like an accusation. He looked away from her. "There are only so many times I can say I'm sorry. I made a mistake. I should have trusted you. I know that now. I'm sorry."

"Why am I here?"

"What?"

"Why am I here in this interrogation cell?" She lifted her arms to indicate the room they were in. "What do you want from me? How did you know where I'd be?"

***

"Oh, bad move, Detective." Sergeant Taylor shook his head.

"What? Looks like he's trying to comfort her."

"He is."

"And?"

"They were dating when he drugged her to try to protect her from the Order. Or, they had just broken up. I never got a clear understanding on the situation, other than to know that there was another guy involved."

"Ooops." Sergeant Mueller watched Karen cross her arms.

"Yeah. 'Ooops.'"

***

"This wasn't my idea." David looked at his hands for a moment, then looked her in the eye. "I got a call from the boss. He told me that someone important to the city was about to make a mistake, and to make sure that I got that person out."

"Your boss told you. Who's that, and how'd they know?"

He shook his head. "I don't know how he knew. Even if I did, I couldn't tell you. I just know that I got the order to extract you from the Camden District before you were hurt." He gestured to her bruised face. "I was almost too late."

"I can take care of myself. I don't need to be rescued."

"My boss thought otherwise."

"Is that what the Special Unit is here for? Rescuing damsels in distress?" Karen scowled. "Is that what the rest of the Kendrick police think it does?"

"No. Of course not. The Special Unit is to protect all of Kendrick's citizens from the dangerous supernatural creatures out there. You may be trying to help and protect Kendrick, but not all you people are. Some of you are a menace and flat out evil."

"'You people,' huh?" She tried to keep the pain out of her voice. "You mean like werewolves?"

"Exactly."

"Except the last werewolf we met together was a Guardian *and* one of the good guys *and* you were just going to shoot him without question or thought. And I'm one of 'you people' now, huh?"

"That's not fair."

"But true."

"That was the first time we… I… encountered a werewolf that wasn't a slavering beast out to kill anything that moved."

"Well, I guess your *Special* Unit doesn't know everything, does it?"

***

"Uh-oh." Sergeant Mueller said.

"What?"

"I don't know what he just said to her, but that's the same look my wife gets when I just monumentally fucked up and am seconds away from sleeping on the couch."

"I'd give my eyeteeth to know what they're talking about." Sergeant Taylor squinted at the couple beyond the glass. "Maybe I'll sneak a peek at the Detective's report after this."

"Sergeant!"

"Yes?"

"Make sure you tell me what you read. Or better yet, let me know when you've got it so I can read it for myself."

"You got it, partner."

The two men grinned at each other, then returned to their observations.

***

"No. It doesn't." David's face shifted from raw emotion into a professional mask. "*That* is why you are here. We know there's something going on in the Camden District. We know there's a group there. We didn't know its name until you mentioned it. This 'Children of Anu.' We need to know more about it."

"Why should I tell you?"

"Because the Special Unit is trying to protect Kendrick and because I'm asking you to."

"So, I should tell a man who has lied to me, betrayed me, and let me think he was dead about my business and the business of 'you people' just because he's asking."

David nodded. "Yes."

"No."

"No?"

Karen shook her head. "No."

"Why not?"

"You know, I'd like to tell you it's because I'm being mean and spiteful and because I'm still angry and lashing out at you. I'd like this to be revenge. But, it's not. It's because I don't know anything about them, and I was going to find out when you, your boss, and your damned Special Unit interrupted me. You may have just messed up my one chance to get in there on even terms with them and made Heather's death truly be in vain. Now, I'm going to have to start all over again, and hope to hell I can find out what's going on before it blows up in my face. Your *Special* Unit can't handle this. You guys need to back off and let me do my job. Whether you like it or not, this is *my* city, and I'm going to protect it the best I can. Don't make me your enemy even though I'm one of 'you people' now."

She stood up, brushed her skirt off, and put her purse over her shoulder. "This interview is over."

"No. It's not, Karen. I have a job to do. This is my city, too. I need to protect the regular citizens from those things that are happening in the shadows." He stood. "You can help me with that. Please."

"No. Not right now. I can't. I have to think about things." She walked to the door and tried it. It was still locked. "Open." She muttered at it and was rewarded with the sound of the door unlocking itself and swinging open.

***

"Looks like the interview is over." Sergeant Mueller said.

"Not until the Detective raps on the glass or the door. That door doesn't unlock for anyone but him."

The two Sergeants watched Karen try the locked door. Then, they watched as she tried the door, waited a moment, then opened the supposedly locked door and walked out.

"Shit." They muttered in unison and moved from the Observation room on an intercept course, hoping that things were not about to get really ugly but both certain that it was.

***

Karen stepped out into the hallway. Sergeants Mueller and Taylor came out of the door to her right. Both of them looked uncertain but ready for action. "Gentlemen, I'm leaving now."

She started to turn, then paused. She looked back at Sergeant Mueller. "Don't worry about what I said to you. You were only doing your job and I was... am... having a bad day."

She turned away and walked down the hallway toward the next electronically-locked door.

Both Sergeants looked to David for orders. He waved them off and followed Karen, wondering how she'd done what she did, and what else she could do now. She had changed. She had become the Master of the City's representative through and through.

Karen reached the next door. "Reginald, please open the door for me. I want to leave this place." She kept her voice low.

The speaker next to the door responded in the same type of sotto voice. "Yes, Karen. We'll talk about this later."

She smiled to herself as the red light clicked green and the door opened, to the surprise of the officers on the other side. Behind her, David followed, giving quiet orders into his cell phone to let Karen Wilson go and for no one to try and stop her. To observe and report.

***

Elsewhere...

"I found it! Reggie, I think this is it!" Vicki's excited voice carried far in the echoing rock at low tide under the docks over the southern tip of Discovery Bay.

Reggie, and the rest of the Children who heard Vicki's shout, came running. All of them were wet and dirty after scrubbing through the low tide muck underneath and to the sides of the docks that fed the industrial district of Kendrick. What Vicki had found was a small, moss-covered cave entrance completely hidden by a tangle of overgrown weeds hanging down from the ridge above the cave.

"Let me see." Reggie pushed through everyone to get a good look at what Vicki was shining her flashlight on.

Just inside of the cave entrance, above the high tide waterline, were crude but unmistakable drawings and hieroglyphics. The largest of these drawings was a bullheaded man carrying a club. He was taller and fiercer than the rest of those around him. The club was held high and a light poured from it, burning all enemies.

"Anu," he said. "Great God Anu!"

"I can see that the path goes up and then opens up more," Vicki said. "I bet we just have to follow the map to find the sacred chamber."

Reggie grinned at the shining eyes of his younger sister. "I'll bet it does. You done good, kid." He turned to the rest of the Children. "I'm going in with Mike." He pointed to two of his more trusted members. "You and you, guard the entrance. We're going to start a regular watch on this spot until I say otherwise. Sam, make it happen."

"I want to go, too, Reggie." Vicki shifted from foot to foot.

"You will, but not just yet. Mike and I have to make sure it's safe." He glanced at Mike and his bandaged hand. "Mike's going to make sure of it. He's still got to prove himself worthy again after his fuck up. Don't you, Mike?"

Mike said nothing and turned away.

Reggie bared a shark-like grin. "You'll come next. Stay with Sam for now."

"All right." Vicki acquiesced, but was clearly unhappy about it. "But, I go next."

"Promise." Reggie patted her head. "All right, you guys, move it."

Concessions

"ARE YOU ALL right?" Coreilli asked.

Karen nodded. "Fine. Just a little bruised."

"I heard some stuff went down in the Camden District, but I didn't know you were involved. That's not a place you should go."

"Do you know about the Camden District and who's there?" Karen sipped her coffee and watched as Corelli dug through her purse.

Coming up with some lip gloss, Corelli didn't speak until after she had applied the gloss and checked it in the mirror. "Yes, I do. That area belongs to the Children of Anu."

"What can you tell me about them?"

"A lot, but Karen, it's not pretty, and it will put you in danger."

She nodded. "I know. But I need to know who they are, and what they're doing in my city."

"I suppose that's a good enough reason for the asking." Corelli was silent for a moment. "I'm not going to make you owe me for this one. You should probably know about them anyway."

Karen knew she'd owe Corelli for this information, whether she officially tagged it as a trade of favors or not. "Okay."

"The Children of Anu worship an Assyrian god named, obviously, Anu. They call him by a number of different names. I'm not really sure why. I think it has to do with the merging of older gods as others came into power. Anyway, Anu gives them magical power in exchange for worship and sacrifices. All of these sacrifices involve the bludgeoning to death of the victim— animal or human. In fact, most of their rituals I've seen involve combat of some sort. The Test of Worth, the Test of Ascension, the Test of Atonement."

"Do they really sacrifice people?"

Corelli nodded. "I've never seen it, but I've heard about it." She paused. "They've always been a secretive bunch, but lately they've been a lot more active. They were hanging around the museum for a while, and now I've heard they've moved to the docks and locked it down tight. I think something big is going on."

"I think so, too."

"I think they attacked the museum that night we were talking with Susan at *Sushi-Ya*'s. It wasn't the Order. It was them. They needed something from the museum."

Karen nodded. "I know. I believe you, and not just because I know you aren't stupid. You wouldn't send your people to do something against the very people you were negotiating with that night."

"So, you'll talk to Susan about it all?" Corelli asked. "Set up another meeting?"

"Yes." Karen tapped her fingers on the table. "I'll need the exact location of where the Children have gathered and any other information you have on them, their rituals, and their goals first."

"There isn't that much, but I can try." Corelli pulled out a notebook and started sketching out the industrial district docks just north of the Camden District.

"That's all I'm asking." Right now, Corelli was Karen's only viable lead. John was not talking, and everyone else shied away from the mere mention of the Children. It made Karen wonder if their reputation was worse than reality. However, one thing was clear: Everyone thought the Children were both violent and up to something.

***

Reggie helped Vicki into the dimly-lit cave. The Children were still putting the finishing touches on the tunnel leading to the series of caves that led to this much larger central cave. Roughly circular, there were niches in the walls for candles or lanterns. Between the niches were bright frescos of a bullheaded god vanquishing foes and rewarding the faithful with gold. The middle thirty feet of the cave was sunken and inlayed with colorful tiles leading up to the central stone obelisk. This obelisk was stained a deep brown red, and everything within the cave seemed to focus on this altar.

"Wow..." Vicki breathed. "This is just like I dreamt it."

Reggie, who had been grinning at all the work that had been done already and the Children still in the cave cleaning things up, gave her a sharp look. "You've been dreaming of this place?"

"Figure of speech, bro," The teal-haired teen said as she walked toward the obelisk. "I meant, this room is just like I imagined it would be, only better."

"Okay," he said, following her. "You know, if you do have strange dreams, you should tell me. They might be a message from *Him*. You might need help interpreting them."

Vicki was no longer paying attention to her brother. She had reached the obelisk. "All those sacrifices. All that power raised." She reached out a hand and stroked the cold stone, stained with the blood of countless victims. "Can't you just feel the power here? Doesn't it feel delicious?"

"It does. I can feel it running through me."

Vicki turned and pressed her back to the obelisk, raising her hands above her head to grasp the iron chains embedded deep within the stone. "If Anu demanded that you sacrifice me, would you?"

"He would never ask it."

"I know, but if he did, would you?"

Reggie scowled, "He would never ask that of me. Playtime's over, Vicki. Find out from Sam what still needs to be done and do it." He turned and walked away, headed toward the tunnel.

Still posed against the obelisk, Vicki looked over at Sam.

"I would," Sam did not stop his cleaning. It was clear he'd paid close attention to the conversation between the siblings.

"I know you would," she said. "I just wanted to know if he would."

Sam smiled a feral smile and gestured to the bucket of soapy water. "Come help me wash this wall."

***

"I have a theory with some strong circumstantial evidence," Karen told Susan as they sat in her small, cluttered office in the back of the Kendrick Museum of Art and History. "I'm pretty certain it was the Children of Anu who attacked this place and stole the Assyrian artifacts."

"Babylonian, actually." Susan said. "Why the Children?" She frowned, not liking the implication of it.

"I had a talk with Corelli, and she gave me some information about the Children, including that they'd been seen around the museum before the break-in. She had no idea that Sebastian had found the token from them in my apartment, nor that I had gone looking for them. Also, she doesn't know what was stolen from here. However, her information about the Children's movements and their favorite aggressive mode of beating things—and people—to death fits everything that happened the night of the break in."

Susan sniffed. "How do we know that the Order isn't still in league with the Children? How do we know they aren't working together on this?"

"We don't, really. But she is trying to help me. She gave me a lot of information about the Children that other people wouldn't. I'd like for you to talk with her again. I'd like for you two to work things out between your respective groups."

"I don't want to."

"I know." Susan and Karen sat in silence, drinking tea and watching each other. Karen knew better than to push the other woman too hard on things. She knew her friend had to come to her own conclusion.

Finally, Susan sighed. "All right. I will. She'd just better bring more to the table than 'we're good now.' I want to know what reparations the Order is going to make to the City and the groups they hurt."

Karen smiled. "Yes. Agreed. I'll mention that when I set up the next meeting at *Sushi-Ya.*"

"I wonder what the Children are doing."

"Me, too."

"I honestly don't know that much about them. All I know is that I don't go to the Camden District, and even the gargoyles tread carefully in that area. December was the first time I ever saw them out in force. Most of what they do, as far as 99% of the public is concerned, is keep to themselves."

"So, this change is noteworthy."

Susan nodded. "Yes."

"Which means they're probably planning something big, and are no longer as concerned about being secretive."

"Yes."

"Which means we need to find some way to find out what the hell they are doing."

"I totally agree."

Karen nodded. "You think Lamiel or anyone at Bacchanalia would know?"

"I don't know, but I think I'll find out. They have no love for the Children, Lamiel especially. I'm pretty sure I can convince the Bacchanalia Coven to pull a high ritual together to find out what's up. I may have to do some fast talking, but I think it's worth it."

***

Elsewhere...

"At that point she caused all of the locked doors between her and where she wanted to go to open. She then walked out of the station. She did not speak to anyone. She made no threatening moves and, per my orders, no one tried to stop her." David spoke to his superior in what he hoped was a clipped, professional voice. In truth, the whole incident had shaken him.

The older man steepled his fingers together. "Is Karen Wilson a danger?"

David chose his words carefully. "She could be a danger, yes. Is she *the* danger or a danger now? I don't believe so. She belongs to the Master of the City. That much is certain. She has manifested powers that either she did not have when I knew her, or that she hid from me. That alone gives her the potential of being dangerous. However, her concerns seem to coincide with ours right now."

"The Children of Anu."

"Yes, sir."

The man nodded. "Keep an eye on Miss Wilson, if that is possible. I would much rather cultivate her as an ally than make an enemy of her. Focus on the Children of Anu. Now that we have a name and some information, do a search on them and those who run the group. Let's find out what we can about them."

"Yes, sir." David paused. "May I ask how you knew Miss Wilson was going to be in the Camden District?"

"Someone close to her called because they were concerned about her actions. I've noticed from the reports on her that she seems to be impulsive."

"Yes, sir. She is." He gave a slight smile.

"Is that all, Detective?"

David looked like he wanted to say more, but shook his head. "That's all."

"Thank you for your report. You are doing a good job. I'll see you next week."

Dismissed, David left the office and closed the door behind him.

The older man paused as he listened to David's retreating step, then called out. "Did you get all that, Brother Peter?"

A much older man with white hair and a monk's robe stepped from the back room into the office. "Yes, Mr. Mayor. I did."

"Your thoughts?" He asked as Peter sat in the chair recently vacated by David.

"I think, Mason, that you should remember that... that young man once betrayed the woman he loved and worked with her enemy in an effort to protect her from those things that go bump in the night." His voice was calm and light, like a grandfather telling a bedtime story.

"Do you believe David will betray me and the Special Unit?"

"I believe that love makes people do many foolish things, and David is still a man in love. No matter what he's reported. Strong in his devotion to duty, but still in love."

"Maybe yes. Maybe no. The lovelorn detective is not the real concern here."

"No." Peter, the Abbot of the Brotherhood of Light, wiped his face with a slightly trembling hand. "It is not. The Children of Anu are as dangerous I have foreseen. I think we have a serious problem on our hands this time."

Blue Moon Revelations

"If they say the moon is blue,
We must believe that it is true."
—proverb from *Rede Me and Be Not Wrothe*, 1528

LAMIEL AND SUSAN stood at opposite ends of the circle created by the members of the Bacchanalia Coven. Six members stood on each side of the circle and everyone, except Susan, was in black and red, representing their membership within the coven and their particular magical ability. Susan, dressed in all grey to represent her faction of the city, the gargoyles, was included as one of their number, a friend and ally. Everyone waited for one of the two women to speak.

Lamiel, dressed in her best gothic finery, broke the anticipatory silence. "We are met on this night, fourteen days after the new moon. We are met on the evening of the second full moon of this month; the blue moon. We are met here at the request of another who petitions for our help and asks for our wisdom. Shall we welcome them in?"

Juliet, the right hand woman of Lamiel, spoke, "Who is the seeker?"

Susan answered, "Susan Moore, Mistress of Gargoyles of the city of Kendrick."

"Susan Moore, seeker of wisdom, do you affirm that your petition is for the good of the city of Kendrick as well as for the Bacchanalia Coven?"

"I do."

"Witnessed and agreed upon by the long standing pact between the Bacchanalia Coven and the Gargoyles of Kendrick." She looked around. "I say we welcome Susan Moore in. What say you?"

"We welcome her in," responded the eleven other members of the coven.

"As you have spoken, so shall it be done. Susan Moore, you are welcome within the sacred circle of the working tonight," Juliet nodded to her.

Lamiel asked, "What is it that you ask for, Susan, sister of our heart and of our cause?"

"I wish a seeking of the plans and intentions of the Children of Anu within the city of Kendrick." Susan said.

All but Lamiel and Susan took a breath at this announcement.

She continued. "They have grown even more wild and bolder than usual. I believe they are the ones who attacked my museum. I believe we all need to know what they are planning, for the good of the city."

"As leader of the Bacchanalia Coven, I concur with this assessment. Let any who disagree step forward and speak their thoughts." Lamiel waited for a full minute, looking each of the coven members in the eyes in turn for a true and honest answer. When she was satisfied that all were ready, she nodded. "Then let us begin."

***

"The modern definition of the blue moon is the result of a misinterpretation of the Maine Farmer's Almanac, where a second full moon occurs in a calendar month. The original definition of a blue moon was an extra full moon that happened in a quarter of a year. Instead of three full moons, there are four. It is the third full moon that is considered to be the 'blue moon' instead of the fourth. I haven't figured out why this is," Corelli said to the First and Second Circles of the Order who had gathered at her request.

"By the original definition, the next actual blue moon will not be for another eighteen months. However, by the modern definition, tonight is the blue moon. It is the second full moon in the month of June. Legends state that whenever there is a blue moon, the moon has a face and speaks to those within its light. We know this legend is not true in a literal sense. However, it aligns neatly with the magic that we of the Order of the Sacred Eye perform. That is why we are here tonight."

V'ger stepped forward. He no longer required a cane at all times for the injury he'd sustained back in December, but his steps were careful and controlled; a young man in an old man's body. "I am V'ger, First in the Order of the Sacred Eye. Do any dispute my title or claim?"

There were a couple glances toward Corelli, the young acolyte who had rocketed her way into the First Circle by strength of will, determination, magical talent, and her unwavering belief that the Order could be brought back to its original calling. It was by her actions alone that the Order had not been completely destroyed by the other supernatural groups within Kendrick after their former leader's failed grab for power.

If Corelli noticed these glances, she chose not to react to them. Instead, she patiently watched V'ger and waited for the ritual to begin.

When it was clear there were no dissenters, V'ger spoke again. "We are gathered here on this night to work a great magic. We all know that there are strong magical forces at work in the city of Kendrick and there is movement on the field. The Order of the Sacred Eye is not responsible for this, but we are being pulled into it whether or not we approve. We must know what is happening. Tonight, by the light of the blue moon, we will seek a vision for what is happening, and from there the First and Second Circles will choose what to do about it."

***

John Corso watched Mason Steward with no little curiosity. In all the time Mason had been Mayor of Kendrick, and also known about John's connection to the supernatural, the man had never once requested a private audience. All of their dealings had been by phone, random encounters on the street, or as guests of a mutual friend.

"Would you like something to drink?" Mason stood at the bar on the right side of the den.

John shook his head and looked around the well-appointed room. The walls were neatly lined with bookshelves and books from all walks of life. There was an entertainment center across from Mason's desk filled with the latest and greatest toys that technology had to offer. The Stewards had always done well for themselves in Kendrick. It showed in every part of their estate.

"Do you mind if I have something?"

"Please," John gestured, "go ahead."

"I know you're wondering why I asked you here."

"The thought had crossed my mind."

Mason sat behind his desk again, a glass of amber liquid in hand, "In the interest of being blunt, John, I'm going to dispense with the usual verbal sparring to figure out what you know and what you don't know and come right to the point." He sipped his drink. "The Stewards are the caretakers of Kendrick. This is not a boast, and I do mean it in a literal sense. We were here at its inception—my ancestor stood alongside Colonel Kendrick as his seneschal when the first building was built. I don't know if there was a ritual involved, or if the city of Kendrick just decided that as the Stewards were the family servants of Colonel Kendrick, so would they ever be servants to the city itself."

He shrugged. "My family is intimately connected to the land. Inside the borders of Kendrick, we can feel where magic is or has touched a place… or a person. Something is happening. Something very big. All of the members of the family can feel it. It is like butterflies in the stomach and a buzzing in the back of our heads. No matter what we do, we cannot pinpoint this disturbance." Mason stopped and stared at his drink.

John took off his glasses. "I appreciate your trust in me to give me this information about your family and about this… disturbance. But, what do you want me to do about it?"

Mason didn't reply at first, he simply gazed at John while putting his drink down and opening his desk drawer. He pulled out a flat box, about six inches by nine inches. It was wrapped in moon and stars wrapping paper and a white ribbon. "I have a gift for you, John. A thank you gift for all you have already done for me, the Special Unit, and Kendrick. This gift is already yours." He didn't push it forward. "But I do have a favor to ask of you."

John couldn't stop himself. He leaned forward with interest, his eyes on the box. There was only one thing that could fit in there that he'd want.

***

Brother Peter looked out over the members of the Brotherhood of Light and nodded with satisfaction. All of them were armed with both prayer and holy weapons, preparing to do battle as they always did when the barriers between this world and the next were thin.

"Brothers, tonight is the full moon." He nodded at their knowing faces. "As usual, anyone who believes they know anything about the supernatural is attempting some sort of magical invocation this evening. Most have no idea what they are doing. Some have just enough knowledge to be dangerous. Those who actually know what they are doing will be properly protected. That means we will need to protect both the rest and the blissfully ignorant from the thrashings of those whose talent can rip at the barrier in malice or ignorance."

There was a chuckle as the monks nodded and listened.

"Tonight," Brother Peter continued, "is the blue moon. Tonight will be even more chaotic than usual. All of you must be extra diligent once we pass over and take up our Sentry Stations. All spirits must be driven back. None may be allowed to enter. A time of change is upon us, and we must make sure that it is a change for the better."

He looked over the shining, eager faces of the novices and the stony faces of those who had seen too many battles, but still believed in the cause and their personal calling. It made an old man proud. He just wished Brother Simon was still at his side, but that was a personal regret, and he had no time for regrets right now. "Let us pray."

***

"Anu...Marduk...Enlil...Bel..."

In the dimness of a cave, three-dozen teenagers and young adults knelt in reverent prayer. Tonight, they were all dressed in their finest warrior clothing—freshly cleaned or newly bought. They chanted the many names of their deity over and over.

"Anu...Marduk...Enlil...Bel...Anu...Marduk...Enlil...Bel."

When Reggie stood, the rest immediately fell silent. As always in his role of high priest, he wore a crown with bull horns and heavy cloak of bull hide. He raised both hands in the air, his palms facing the red-brown obelisk.

"Great god Anu! Father of Heaven, creator of the stars, lord of the constellations, king of gods, spirits and demons, your Children have not forgotten you. Your Children remember that this is the prophesied year of your return. Your humble servant, Reagan Lee Mordecai, has gathered your believers here in this sacred cave dedicated to you on this night to beg of you a vision of what must be done. This is the year of your return, great god Anu! Instruct us in your wisdom. Judge us worthy with this task. Tell us what we must do! We are your Children and your servants. Guide us in this most holy year!"

***

Lamiel, Susan, and the Bacchanalia Coven murmured over and over within their sacred circle. They rocked as one, their hands clasped and their eyes on the large silver basin filled with water in the center. All of their offerings and spell recitations had been cast. All that was left was to keep the Coven focused.

Lamiel led the mantra. *"Luna, Goddess of inner wisdom and inner light, provide us with your clarity this full moon night."*

As they all watched, the water shimmered and swirled then cleared into a series of flickering images:

A club smashing in the skulls of an old man and a young man.

Blood spreading over the city of Kendrick as a huge bull charged through the streets, trampling specific buildings—the museum, the Grey Lady's estate, Bacchanalia club, and most of the Colonel's Park.

Three women, looking as the Maiden, the Warrior, and the Crone, stood in the bull's path. The scrying pool focused on this last image, allowing it to come to life.

The three women seemed to be in disagreement with each other about what to do. The Maiden wanted to go to the Bull. The Warrior tried to block its path. The Crone had the choice of preventing the Maiden or preventing the Warrior from taking action. She could not do both, even though she tried. The Crone reached out for both women, attempting to thwart their chosen paths. The bull rushed headlong toward them, heedless of their intentions.

The scrying pool turned blood red as the bull reached the women and obscured the outcome of the struggle between them. The water turned black, then cleared and was nothing more than water in a silver bowl.

"Oh, damn... I think we have a real problem," Susan muttered as their collective senses started to come back to them all. The Bacchanalia Coven looked at each other with wonder and trepidation.

***

Corelli, as the Mistress of Magic, led the First and Second Circles in their divination work. Each member sat with a clear crystal ball in front of them. All knew that this was only one way to peer into the future. To help with the sympathetic magic of what they were divining for, each crystal ball pedestal stood on a modern map of Kendrick.

"See the future, see it clear. See the future, see it clear," Corelli mouthed to herself. Each member of the circle had his or her own way of focusing on the intent of the group working. Some rocked. Some sang. Some did nothing at all it seemed.

An image blossomed in Corelli's mind: *It was herself walking down a path toward a fork in the road. On the left hand path stood a bull. On the right hand path stood Karen. Behind the bull stood a huge, formless shape that writhed and swayed. The promise of power and of love flowed from it—everything she could want. The closer she got to it, the more she influenced it, forcing the shape into something more and more recognizable. Almost human-looking. Behind Karen stood people from all of the other supernatural factions. They were hurt and bleeding, but with every step Corelli took toward them, they were healed.*

She looked down and saw that she was now on Kendrick's Main Street. She looked at the bull and Karen again. This time, she saw that there was a rope around her waist. The rope's other end was connected to the bull's horns. There was nothing connecting her to Karen. However, she saw that Karen was offering her bread and salt. There were flowers lining the way toward her.

Corelli paused at the fork in the road. She dearly wanted to go to the other woman, despite the gifts promised by the power behind the bull. Corelli took a step toward Karen. There was a terrible pain at her waist as the rope cut into her side. She took another step toward Karen, gasping in pain. Suddenly, the bull jerked its horns backwards and the rope not only cut deeper into Corelli's side, but yanked her off Karen's path and onto the path toward itself. The pain was too much. Corelli screamed and fell to her knees.

Her scream of pain yanked everyone else out of their meditative trance. They looked around, dazed. It was V'ger who got them moving. He crouched over Corelli's unconscious form, pressing his hands to her bleeding side. "Get the med kit! You! Get some blankets!"

"What happened?" One of the First Circle asked.

"I don't know." V'ger said. "I didn't get the vision."

"Did she?"

He looked at the blood seeping between his fingers. "Yeah, I think she did. Let's hope she remembers what it was when she wakes up."

***

Brother Peter and Brother Luke stood side-by-side. In this realm of spirit, the two old men were young again and they reveled in the battle. They were winning this round, but they both could see something huge looming on the horizon toward them. The spirit, for that was all it was, despite what anyone else thought, was powerful in this realm and the next. It would take all of them to hold it back.

"To me, brothers! To me!" Brother Luke cried as Brother Peter, the Abbot of their Brotherhood in Kendrick, set himself at the head of their defenses. Those who could dispatch or drive off their current foes did so immediately.

Brother Peter felt a bit like Gandalf on the bridge facing the Balrog. Here, he was as powerful as Gandalf and here, he had the same job. "You shall not pass." He muttered at the spirit charging towards them. "Steady, my brothers! Steady!"

Perhaps if his thought had not referenced the movie, he would not have fallen. Perhaps. Perhaps not.

Unknown to all from the Brotherhood of Light who stood at the ready, the spirit's intent was not to break through into the other realm. Not just yet. It was to send a message upon the winds of blood. That was why it took them all by surprise when, instead of attacking the barrier between this world and the next, it focused its full attack on Brother Peter and laid him low before retreating.

Back in the world of flesh and blood, Brother Luke and Brother Thomas rushed to Brother Peter's side. Blood dribbled out of the old man's mouth, and his breathing was labored. "To the infirmary," Brother Luke ordered.

***

The high priest of the Children of Anu stopped speaking aloud, but continued his prayer and plea to Anu for instruction and blessing in his mind, as did the rest of the congregation. They could all feel the presence of Anu. They knew he was there, judging them, weighing them, finding them worthy or not. The next few moments would tell.

He found one of them worthy.

There was no sound. No light. No show of force. Suddenly, Reggie collapsed in an ecstatic vision of blessing and instruction. He knew what the Children were meant to do. He knew and it made him smile through his weakness.

"Reggie?" Vicki came to his side.

"I know, sis..."

"Know what?"

"I know who the vessel of Anu is supposed to be."

She crouched next to him, not helping him because that would make it seem as if he were weak. "Who?"

"Me. I will be his avatar on earth."

She grinned a feral grin at him. "I knew it!"

"We have work to do. I also know who the sacrifice is supposed to be." He struggled to his feet and paused. "I can taste blood in my mouth. Can you?"

Vicki licked her lips and nodded. "Yes."

***

John put his trembling hands in his lap. "You cannot buy a favor with a gift. That's not how it works."

Mason frowned. "I'm not trying to buy anything." He slid the package over to John's side of the desk. "The gift is yours. You may take it and go if you wish."

Try as he might, John could not keep himself from taking the wrapped package and putting it in his lap. He knew what it would be. He knew. Just not which one. "You won't stop me if I leave now?"

Mason shook his head. "No. It *is* a gift. If you would feel better going home and coming back tomorrow to listen to my request, I accept that. I know the rules of such gifts. It's yours. I give it to you freely, asking nothing in return."

John stood up, holding the gift in his hand. He walked to the door, paused, then opened it and stepped to the other side. He looked back, "No entreaty to stay?"

"No." Mason took a long swallow of his drink, watching John but saying no more.

The two of them stared at each other for a long time. Finally, John decided that the gift was still a gift and was given as Mason spoke. However, at the same time, he knew it was also a way to get him to listen to whatever favor the Mayor of Kendrick needed and to possibly look upon it favorably. The more John stared at Mason, the more curious he became. He stepped back inside the den and closed the door. "I think I'll have that drink now."

Mason gestured to the bar with his own glass in a 'help yourself' gesture.

"What's this favor?" He asked, smelling the different liquors in crystal decanters until he came to one he liked.

"You're close to Karen Wilson."

"Yes." He poured himself a healthy glass.

"You know who she belongs to."

"Yes."

"The Master of the City."

John replaced the crystal decanter and turned back to Mason. "Yes." He took a couple of gulps of scotch, letting them burn his throat, before returning to his seat and placing the glass on the desk before him.

"I think she's in more danger than she knows. Would you keep an eye on her for me and tell me if you think she's about to do something monumentally stupid?" Mason paused. "I only ask because you've done so in the past, and I think it's needed now. She won't accept the Special Unit as protectors."

"She won't accept anyone as a protector."

"Therefore she cannot know you are protecting her."

John smiled a bitter smile. "That is a dangerous game to play with her. I do care about her a great deal. We've gotten much closer in recent months. I don't want to repeat the mistakes of her past loves."

"You won't. You know better." Mason gestured at John's lap. "Are you going to open it?"

Looking down, John was surprised to find that his fingers had had a mind of their own and had already unwrapped the box. *What's done is done*, he thought and lifted the lid to look inside.

It was a Todari tarot card. His heart leapt. It was the Moon, the eighteenth card in the major Arcana. The vivid colors made him catch his breath. He stroked the card before picking it up from the box. This picture was of a crescent moon. Sitting on the inner curve of the crescent was a beautiful woman with long, flowing, dark hair and a diaphanous white gown. Below her were two dogs on the edge of a lake, howling and barking up at her as she looked off to the side, unconcerned. A lobster appeared to be crawling out of the other side of the lake.

"'*Imagination, intuition, and dreams for you. But for one you love, bad luck may ensue. Unseen perils, possible woes. Deceptions abound with secret foes.*'" John recited, gazing with rapt adoration at the object of his obsession.

However, while he watched, he saw the card change in his hand. The woman sitting on the moon became Karen. The dogs leapt for her feet as she drew them up and away from their snarling jaws. Unable to reach anything but her gown, the dogs tore at it, ripping it to pieces as Karen looked around in a panic. She seemed to see John, and reached out a hand to him, imploring him to take it.

Then, in a blink of an eye, the card was once more the stunning piece of artwork that he collected. Taking a shaky breath, John recovered himself as he put the card back into its box. "Yeah, I can keep an eye on Karen. I think she's going to need it."

***

Elsewhere...

Karen sat out on her balcony with a mug of tea in her hand and Sebastian perched nearby. Gazing up at the gorgeous, full moon, she marveled how quiet the evening was. She could certainly use more evenings like this. Most people could. She sipped her tea and smiled at the moon, enjoying the silence, peace, and beauty.

***

As quiet as thieves but as bold as lords, Reggie, Sam, and Mike walked through the front doors of what had once been a train station, located on the western edge of Kendrick, but was now the home to the Brotherhood of Light. They walked unseen past open doorways, the brothers within ignorant of their passing.

Led by Reggie who had Anu's vision to guide him, they walked down the quiet hallway, around corners, and up the stairs to the infirmary. Brother Amit turned as the infirmary door opened. Reggie smiled as the man called out an uncertain, "Hello?"

Sam didn't wait for Reggie's order. He took two quick steps forward, swinging his club in a wide arc that cracked open Brother Amit's head like overripe fruit. As Amit collapsed against his desk, Mike grabbed the brother's chair and the back of the brother's robe. He eased both to the floor.

None of them cared if the man lived or died. He was not the target. Reggie nodded to the stretcher up against the wall as he walked over to the Abbot's bedside. "Hello my pretty." Reggie leaned over and looked at the Abbot's sallow, bruised face and scowled. They'd have to make sure the man was cared for. It wouldn't do for him to die before the appointed time.

The three of them carefully slid the Abbot onto the stretcher. Then, they walked out the way they came, no one the wiser—except, of course, for the unfortunate Brother Amit.

First Blood

CORELLI OPENED HER eyes and blinked at the unfamiliar surroundings. Her mind was filled with a jumble of images, and her body hurt. She fought to gain control of her senses; to figure out where she was and what had happened. Then she remembered her vision, and the gigantic shape behind the bull. She didn't know what that shape was, but she knew it represented the power behind the Children of Anu. It was what was driving them. That thought terrified her.

She tried to sit up, but the pain in her side was too much for her to move. Looking around the room, she saw what she hoped was a call button. Pressing it, nothing happened right away, but then she heard footsteps come down a hallway and saw the door open.

Shelia poked her head in. "You're awake. I'll get the doctor."

"Wait! What happened?"

"I don't know. I wasn't there. I'm only Fourth Circle." She was gone before Corelli could ask anything else, her running steps fading back down the hallway.

Whatever had happened had happened at the scrying. The place was too quiet to be a hospital. Her next best guess was that she was on the third floor of the estate housing the archives where they usually met.

All thoughts of where she was vanished as she pushed the covers back and lifted up the t-shirt she was wearing. A large bandage was wrapped about her middle. Exploring fingers told her that her whole left side hurt like crazy. One errant finger pressed too hard, and a wave of pain enveloped her, bringing forgotten memories with it.

By the time Shelia returned with Doc and V'ger, Corelli was sitting up and waiting for them. "Convene the First Circle. I have to talk to them."

"You aren't going anywhere. You're too hurt." Doc's voice, like a rusty crow, was firm.

Corelli was looking at V'ger. "Convene them here. I don't care. We must talk. The city is in danger, and this may be our only chance to be welcomed here again. No, not 'may be', is."

Doc, a trauma specialist and not particularly inventive, thus his chosen moniker, shook his head, "I won't allow it unless you lay down, rest, and let the healers at you."

V'ger, reading the urgency in Corelli's face, nodded. "You have an hour to make her well enough for the meeting."

"An hour isn't long enough."

"It's going to have to be," V'ger said. "You have your orders from the First Circle."

Doc looked ready to argue, but Corelli put a hand on his arm. "Please. You have no idea how important this is."

"Important enough to risk your life?" he asked.

"Yes."

A moment of silence hung heavy in the air. "All right. You'll be ready in an hour. The meeting will have to be here."

***

"Why don't you tell me what you're getting yourself into these days?" John asked as he cut into his steak.

"Because it's the same old same old—trying to protect the city from whatever the Children are doing while doing my regular job and stuff." Karen took great pleasure in cracking open the Alaskan king crab leg and gently teasing out the sweet meat from inside.

"I'm worried for you."

"I'm worried for all of us. The stuff Susan told me about her scrying with the Bacchanalia coven wasn't good. Especially if the places in the vision are actually hurt. That includes Colonel Kendrick's Park, which represents the city."

"As well you and the Master." John put his fork down. "I know you don't want protection—"

"I don't need protection other that what I already have."

"But," he continued, "I really think you need some this time around. I wasn't going to tell you, but I think I don't have a choice if I want you to let me help in the ways I need to help."

She cracked open another crab leg, wincing at the pain of the spines on the shell digging into her hand. "Tell me what?"

"I have a new card. It, like the rest, has special powers." He paused, trying to figure out how to explain it and what he had seen.

Karen knew exactly what set of cards he was talking about. The Todari tarot deck. The cards seemed to have archetypal powers based on their archetypal meanings. *Not seemed. Did have. Do have. Wasn't she influenced by one to make a correct and fair judgment? Hadn't she used one to heal her friend and guardian, Sebastian?* She sighed softly, knowing she owed it to John to listen. The two of them had spent a lot of time together lately, and most of it had been for pleasure rather than business. "Go on."

"This card has the power of prophecy—but it was symbolic. I don't really know what I saw meant other than you, in trouble, reaching for me. You were being harried by dogs."

"I'm in danger from dogs? The symbol of the Children is a bull."

John shrugged. "I don't know what the danger is, but I'm pretty sure it has to do with the Children—bull or not. Susan told me about the scrying, too." He raised a hand, rushing forward with his words. "I know they need to be stopped. If they aren't, bad things will happen. I think we should do something about it. However, you need to be more careful this time around. Last time, there was a battle that did a lot of damage."

Karen opened and shut her mouth a couple of times, her appetite dying with the sudden turn in the conversation. However, she kept cracking the crab legs and harvesting the meat. As she did, she took no care to protect her hands from the spines digging into her flesh. The physical pain distracted her from the pain of his far-too-truthful words. "I'd say that isn't fair, but it is. I was reckless before. I know I can't do that now. You obviously have a plan in mind. What is it?"

"I think we need to get all of our allies together to talk about it, this… whatever is going on… and form a coherent plan. Be smart. Be careful. Be prepared. We won't hinge everything on one person doing all of the planning and execution. No one can be a keystone."

"Thus, no one is a 'most likely' target." She nodded. "We can try it. When do you want to meet and where?"

"As soon as possible. I've got a backroom that should be able to fit the top leaders of each group I'm thinking of."

"Who?"

"Susan. She has no second. Lamiel and whomever she wishes. Abbot Peter and his second. Corelli and her second. Walks-the-Ocean and his second. The Grey Lady and her escort." John took a breath. "David and his second."

Karen, who had been about to question the wisdom of bringing in the Order of the Sacred Eye into this so early—especially when there were still a lot of bad feelings from the other factions—stopped in her mental tracks. "What?"

"I think the Special Unit should be involved as well. Mostly to keep the normal citizens of Kendrick away from whatever we're doing, as well as keeping on top of their little group and what *they* are doing." John shrugged. "Besides, they're working for the best of the city as well."

"No."

"No? No discussion? Just 'No.'"

"I don't think bringing in the Special Unit is the right thing to do."

"Because you don't trust the Special Unit, or because you don't trust David?"

"Both. Bringing them into this would be too dangerous for us. They think of us... all of us... as freaks."

"I don't know about that."

"I do."

"Think about it, and we can talk about it again later?"

"Maybe."

"Better than a 'no.'" He smiled at her and said no more.

Karen smiled back. It was a brief, worried smile. More of an acknowledgement of his smile than a genuine one of her own. Her cell phone beeped to let her know that she had a text message. She opened her phone to read it and then took the time to reply. When she was done, she looked up. "I'll start on this tonight. That was Corelli. She wants to meet with me as soon as possible."

"All right. I'll contact Susan and Walks-the-Ocean. Susan will call Lamiel, and we can get everyone on the same page as soon as possible. Let's plan it for a couple days from now."

***

Karen was led through the manor house by a woman named Shelia. Based on her clothing and constant, nervous chatter, she was a fan of all things Australian. It was a large, gorgeous house, and one that seemed oddly familiar to Karen, though she wasn't sure why. She realized why the moment Shelia opened the door to the bedroom Corelli was in. Karen had spent a paralyzed night in this room herself back in December. She stopped at the doorway, almost unable to make herself move.

"It's worse than it looks," Corelli said, mistaking Karen's reluctance for concern for her. "I promise."

Karen forced herself into the room and saw that Corelli's side had been injured. Black stitches held pale skin together. Around the stitches were runic symbols. "What happened?"

"The dangers of magic," Corelli answered with a small shrug. "I'm just hoping I don't scar. That's what the runes are for—healing pure. No scarring."

Karen pulled her eyes off the wound. "Is this what you wanted to see me about?"

"Yes. A little bit. I did some work with my Order. We wanted to find out what the Children were doing. I think I know, and we have to stop it."

"What is it? What are they doing?"

"Amassing power. Magical energy to force a change on Kendrick. Maybe the world. I don't know. But they are offering power and rewards to those who help, and death to those who get in their way. I think they're close."

Karen sat on the edge of the chair and nodded at the wound. "Did you get that finding out?"

Corelli nodded.

"I'm sorry."

"I'm not. It was worth it. The question now is how to stop them."

"I think I have a partial answer to that. We're going to start with a meeting of the leaders and their seconds of the main magical factions of the city who are willing to speak and discuss the matter. This time around, we're going to collaborate. No one is going to be a general. Everyone is going to be involved."

"It won't be easy."

Karen shook her head. "No, it won't."

"You can count on the Order of the Sacred Eye."

"Not everyone will welcome you."

"We'll take that chance. Not everyone will deny us either. Besides, we've got some good information to offer now. What we know, combined with what other people know, may just be what's needed to stop the Children."

***

"You're working late, sir." David said as he knocked on Mayor Steward's City Hall door.

"I know. No rest for the weary." Mason smiled and gestured for David to sit down. "I apologize for the lack of chit-chat, but I've got a lot of stuff to get done and I needed to speak to you about a special assignment for the SU."

"Must be very special," David wondered why the Mayor could not trust the phone with this.

Mason nodded. "It is. The leaders of most of the main supernatural groups are getting together to have a meeting. If at all possible, I want that meeting both protected and recorded. The recording is to come to me only. I want you to see to this personally."

"Protected from what?"

"If they know about it, the Children of Anu. The rest of Kendrick... well, most of them... have decided that the Children are too dangerous to let run loose in the city. They're planning something big, and the rest of the supernaturals are policing themselves and looking to shut the Children down. I want to support them on this."

"Why the cloak-and-dagger then? Why not ask to come to the table with them and openly help?"

"Because we weren't invited. To show up would be to let them know that we have a ... person in the thick of things, keeping me abreast of what's going on."

"You have a spy on Karen?"

"I have an informant in the middle of things to keep me informed. Nothing more. Nothing less. Nothing forced. A friend who talks to me to help keep their friends safe."

"You're skirting a very fine line there, sir," David's voice was tight with disapproval.

"I know, but we're not invited because of you."

David grimaced. "Me?"

"You betrayed the woman you loved trying to protect her and almost got her killed. She's the one in charge of this meeting. They aren't ready to let you back into the fold. So, don't give me the hairy eyeball on this, Detective. I'm doing what I have to do to protect my city. If that means skirting a line or two, I'm going to do it."

"Yes, sir. Sorry, sir." David pulled all his emotions in and hid them under his professional mask.

"You've got two days." Mason slid thin folder over to him. "Put a watch on a couple of these people to make sure the meeting isn't changed to a new location."

David opened the file and looked at the list of names inside. "Yes, sir."

"This is really important, Detective. Don't fail me."

"I won't, sir."

There was an impatient knock on the office door, followed by it opening without waiting for an answer. David and Mason saw Terry, Mason's hardworking secretary, trying to block a man in monk's robes from entering the office. "Sir, I must insist! You don't have an appointment!"

"It's all right, Terry. Let him in." Mason called.

David stood, prepared for trouble, as Terry, looking very annoyed, stepped aside and let the older man enter the office. The brother's face was red, flustered.

"Brother Luke?" Mason asked. "My appointment is with the Abbot, and not for another fifteen minutes."

Luke's eyes darted about the room as if looking for something. "That's the problem, Mr. Mayor, Brother Peter is gone. Someone's taken him, and we don't know who or how."

***

Karen sat in her car with her cell phone lying open on the passenger seat. Sebastian sat on the seat next to the cell phone, giving it an adorably cute and curious look. She wished she could pay more attention to it, but she had other things on her mind.

"What did you think of the estate, Reginald?"

"I think it was there. But parts of it are invisible to me."

"It's where they kept me captive."

"I know. Now."

"How can you not see parts of it? It's you, isn't it? It's part of the city."

"Yes but there are some magics that can make part of the city no longer belong to only me. This is not the only place that is partly invisible. There are others. Some are due to magic or agreements older than me. Others have concentrated their magics to one small room. I cannot be *present* everywhere in Kendrick. Much of me is automatic, just like your heart beats without your thinking about it."

"Can you break into these hidden places?"

"Sometimes. It depends on what hides them. There are rules that even I must follow."

***

Elsewhere...

"Careful with him!" Reggie said as the stretcher bearing the old man was gently maneuvered down the bank and then up through to the tunnel and into the hidden temple.

About half of the Children were waiting for Reggie and his small band of kidnappers. "How'd it go?" Vicki greeted them.

"Easy as beating a cat to death." Reggie grinned at her. "They had no idea we were there at all. Anu hid us all from their eyes. Even their prayers to their Christian sheep god were no match against the power of Anu." Reggie raised a fist into the air. "Anu!"

Every member of the Children repeated the gestured and shouted, "ANU!" The sound reverberated in the cave.

"What are we going to do with him?" Vicki gestured to the old man on the stretcher.

"Make him comfortable in one of the smaller caves. After all, it would do us no good for him to die before Anu's return."

Transcript

Karen Wilson: What the hell is he doing here?

Corelli: This meeting was for the heads and seconds of the invited groups, right?

Karen Wilson: Yes.

Corelli: V'ger is the head of the Order of the Sacred Eye.

Karen Wilson: Dammit Corelli. He's also the man who shot a cop in my kitchen and kidnapped me from my home last December.

Corelli: He's the head of my Order. I am its second. Is—

V'ger: (interrupting) Please, if I may. Yes, I have done many wrong things in the past. While I was ordered to do them, I'm not innocent. At this time, I can do nothing more than apologize and state before this entire room that I owe you all. It is something we should work out in private. We have much more important matters to deal with right now than the wrongs I have done to you and yours.

John Corso: Karen, this isn't the time or place.

Karen Wilson: Shit. Fine. All right. Anyone else need to spring anything else on me? [pause] No? Good. I'm assuming you all know who the other groups are in this room. Quick introductions. Please pay attention. There's a quiz later. I'm Karen Wilson, I represent the Master of the City. This is John Corso, Independent. Lamiel and Juliet, Bachannalia Coven. Brother Luke and Brother John, Brotherhood of Light. Walks-the-Ocean and Lumbering Bear, Makah Tribe. Corelli and V'ger, Order of the Sacred Eye. Susan Moore, representing the Gargoyles of the City. Lady Grey, Theodore and Theodora, the Grey Manor.

John Corso: I suggested this meeting because I'm connected to a lot of you in minor ways, and as such, am able to see what you all are seeking. Over the past couple of weeks, I've seen a trend among all of you. There's a concern over a growing power in this city.

Susan Moore: The Children of Anu.

John Corso: Thank you, Susan. Yes. The Children of Anu. Until recently, they've been a quiet and secretive, if brutal, group. Suddenly, they've been seen all over the city. They've attacked some of us or our places of business. I believe, as I think many of you do, that they're planning something much larger, that will affect the entire city. I know several groups did a scrying or divination recently. I think it is time to share what we know and see what we should do about this. We need to have a plan and we need to protect the city from what the Children are doing. We need to work together and let each other know what we're doing so we don't re-invent the wheel.

Corelli: I'm the Mistress of Magic in my Order. I was the one who received the vision. I'm willing to share.

Lamiel: My Coven had a successful divination. I am willing to share.

Walks-the-Ocean: The Elders have agreed to share our wisdom.

John Corso: I had a vision as well. I will share. Who's first?

V'ger: The Order of the Sacred Eye offers all of the knowledge they know that they can give.

Karen Wilson: All right.

V'ger: Corelli.

Corelli: The vision I had showed a great power moving from the spiritual plane into this one. The

Children of Anu is guided by this power, and will
do anything for it. They're offering power and
rewards for those who assist. They are going to
make a change that will affect all of Kendrick, and
possibly the world. The Order of the Sacred Eye is
tied into this somehow. We see that we can help or
hinder this coming. We have elected to hinder it in
all the ways we can.

Lamiel: We saw something similar. Except that we
saw that this power is specifically targeting the
oldest groups in the city: The Grey Manor. The
Makah Tribe. My coven. Even the Master of the City.
Places of power will be destroyed. That which is
sacred to us will be violated. And there's
something more. We saw two people sacrificed to
this power. A young man and an old one.

Brother Luke: What did the old one look like?

Susan Moore: Very old. Balding. Blue eyes.

Brother Luke: Was he wearing a robe? Like this?

Lamiel: I don't remember exactly, but it was brown
I think.

Brother Luke: Then the urgency of action is even
greater. We need to find and stop them as soon as
possible. Brother Peter, the Abbot of my Order, was
kidnapped during the blue moon. He was already
injured from a previous battle that night. I
believe that he's one of these sacrifices.

V'ger: Do you have something that belongs to him?
We can seek him out that way.

Brother Luke: Yes.

Lamiel: We can't help. Your order would put mine to
death.

Brother Luke: That's not true. We only protect this
world from things on the spiritual plane that
people like you let in.

John Corso: Please, people—

Karen Wilson: Lamiel! Brother Luke—

[Babble of yelling voices.] [Silence.]

Lady Grey: My apologies for having to invoke Silence on this meeting, but we are here to fight a common enemy, not each other. I believe that Walks-the-Ocean was trying to tell us the wisdom of his elders.

Walks-the-Ocean: Listening to what everyone has said has brought new meaning to what the Spirits have told us. There will be two sacrifices: One will be the greatest enemy of the Children. The other will be the greatest love of the Children. Both sacrifices will be made at the same time. When this is done, a great evil will walk the lands, corrupting all that is good and protects. No one will be safe.

Karen Wilson: When is this sacrifice to be made?

Walks-the-Ocean: Soon. I believe on or near what some view as the Death of the Year.

Lady Grey: The Changing of the Courts.

Lamiel: Samhain.

John Corso: Halloween.

Brother Luke: All Saints. That means there's still time.

John Corso: Yes. There's still time, but we all must work together. No more bickering.

Karen Wilson: All right. Here's what I think we need to do: Find Brother Peter. Find out where this sacrifice is supposed to be made. Find out why the Children are targeting the oldest of the supernatural groups to see if it is beyond the obvious they-want-power thing. Find out what this change is and what evil they're bringing into the world is and find out if there is a way to stop it before it happens.

John Corso: No one group can do all things. We'll need to split this up.

Corelli: The Order will find out where the sacrifice is to be made.

Karen Wilson: I'm going to look for Brother Peter.

Susan Moore: I'll help you.

Karen Wilson: Ok.

John Corso: Brother Luke, I think your group needs to focus on how to stop this evil before it breaks through.

Brother Luke: But—

John Corso: No buts. You're too close to Brother Peter. Plus, we need you to do your part as the greatest threat to the Children of Anu.

Brother Luke: As you wish.

Lady Grey: I believe that Walks-the-Ocean and I can research why it is targeting the oldest of us.

Lamiel: What do you want the Bacchanalia Coven to do?

John Corso: I think your group should help Corelli and the Order as well as research a second way to stop the evil from coming through to this side and what to do about it if it does make it through. Like, how to identify it.

Lamiel: We can do that.

Theodora: There's someone outside, watching.

Theodore: They just ducked down again.

[Babble of voices.] [Static.] [Silence.]

"Is this it?" Mayor Steward asked as he took the headphones off.

"Yes, sir." David nodded.

"Who did the transcription?"

"I did."

He looked down at the paper. "It sounded like the meeting was already in progress."

"I arrived a little late with my team. Traffic. Also, I had to be very careful setting everything up. I couldn't be seen. Only the greetings were missed."

He nodded. "Who was the person who stood up then?"

"Sergeant Mueller. He has already been spoken to for breaking cover and interrupting the surveillance. He was startled by an owl."

Mayor Steward gazed at David. "How do you feel about all this?"

He tilted his head. "All this?"

"The conversation. Their plan of action." He paused then added, "V'ger."

David's mouth compressed into a thin, white line before he forced himself to relax, "I think they have the beginnings of a good alliance. I think they have a decent plan of action. I think V'ger... I don't think about V'ger."

"You don't have an opinion about the man who betrayed you, shot you, and kidnapped your girlfriend for a ritual sacrifice? I think you do need to think about him." He pointed at David's tightly clasped hands. "Judging by your reaction, I'm ordering you to think about it and to talk about it with the SU psychologist."

"Yes, sir."

"I'll have a call into his office by tomorrow afternoon. If you don't have an appointment set up by then, you'll be put on a leave of absence, pending a psychological evaluation. I can't have an unstable detective running the SU."

"Did you know, sir?"

"Know what?"

"That the man... that V'ger... was alive and active."

"No."

"Would it have made any difference to you?"

Mayor Steward gazed at David for a few moments, and then shook his head. "No, Detective, it wouldn't have."

"Ah."

"Make sure all transcripts and recordings come to me alone. Remind Sergeant Mueller that this is one of those silent missions."

"Yes, sir."

"Anything else?"

"No, sir."

"Dismissed." Mayor Steward watched the detective leave his office. He wondered if the young man could be trusted with the upcoming missions. He had so much emotion bottled up and most of it revolved around his unrequited love for Karen Wilson. She, on the other hand, had apparently forgotten all about her former lover.

***

"Who do you think was out there?" Karen sat on the couch next to John.

He shrugged. "I don't know. Most likely, it was a member of one of the groups we invited. Maybe they were patrolling. It was a good time to stop the meeting anyway. That many different supernatural groups in one room can be dangerous."

"It went surprisingly well. Did you have a card in play?"

John smiled. "Maybe. I think a little bit of rift healing was needed."

Karen scoffed, "There's no way the rift between V'ger and me is going to be mended. He's lucky I didn't have a building fall on him."

"Can you do that?"

"I don't know. Maybe." She took a sip of her wine. "I noticed that you didn't tell anyone what your vision was."

"I know. I didn't want to bring the focus back to you. We all need to work together and we cannot be dependent on just one person." He put his arm around her. "Besides, that's also why I didn't volunteer to do anything. One, I'm a good foil for you and for plan making. People trust me. Two, I already have a job."

She smiled at him. "What might that be?"

"Keeping you out of trouble and, barring that, rescuing you if you need it."

"I won't, dammit. I'm not a damsel in distress." Her voice was mild in its protest.

"I know. By virtue of the fact that you have a knight protector, you won't need me. It's like carrying an umbrella to ensure it won't rain."

"Is that what you are now? A knight protector?"

He half smiled at her. "For some." He took her glass from her. "For very few, actually."

Karen did not move. She watched his face, his mouth, his eyes. "John, I really like you. A lot. And this would be the most inconvenient time ever to get involved with someone."

"I know." His face hovered near hers.

"Especially with some possible apocalypse happening on or around Halloween."

"I know." He leaned closer.

"You're a pain in the ass."

"I know," he murmured and kissed her.

She returned his kiss, wrapping her arms around his neck.

***

Elsewhere...

"Who do you love most?" Vicki asked.

"You, of course." Reggie answered.

"Well, if I wasn't here, who would you love most?"

"You, still. I love you whether you're here or not."

She grinned. "Touché. Okay. Who do you love second most?"

He looked around the warehouse at the half of the Children that where here instead of at the sacred cave, guarding it and nursing their captive back to health. "In truth, me. Selfish, I know. But true."

"I love you most of all."

"I know you do, kiddo."

"I don't know what I'd do without you."

"You'd manage. You're strong. Beside, I'm not going anywhere." Reggie ruffled her teal hair.

"What about you, Sam?" Vicki turned to look over her shoulder. "Who do you love most?"

He grinned at her. "Reggie."

She mock pouted at him and then asked Mike the same question.

"Love is stupid." He obviously did not want to play Vicki's little game.

"I don't think so," Reggie said. "You love Anu, don't you? Or do you only fear him?"

"No. I love Anu." Mike looked very uncomfortable.

"So, who here do you love the most?" Reggie made a gesture to encompass the entire warehouse.

"You, man. I guess it's you."

"See? That wasn't so hard, was it?" Vicki grinned, a malicious gleam twinkling in her eyes. "We all love Reggie best."

"I'm gonna go get something from the store." Mike stomped off.

"Bring me Twinkies," Vicki called.

"Yeah! Twinkies and apple pies!" Reggie yelled after him.

They all laughed as Mike gestured to indicate that he'd heard and was telling them all to fuck off. But, of course, he would do exactly as they asked.

"Man, I like Mike. He's a good Second, but the dude needs to lighten up." Reggie laughed.

Vicki and Sam nodded, exchanging a gleeful look.

Debts Called In

KAREN SAT ON a sidewalk bench just outside of the Camden District. It was close enough to see the territory claimed by the Children of Anu, but not close enough to draw their attention. *All right, Sebastian, are you and the others ready?* she thought. *Yes. We're ready. Which building to start with?*

She could feel him practically vibrating with excitement to be part of her plan to find the missing Abbot. She smiled with pride and affection at his desire to please her. He was her little General, passing on her orders to the four other courier gargoyles she'd borrowed from Susan, since they wouldn't speak to any mortal until they bonded with one, except to deliver messages. Karen looked at the buildings she could see. *Let's go left to right. One building at a time, bottom to top.* She sent the image of the first building she wanted the gargoyles to scout.

She opened her cell phone. "Reginald? Are you ready?"

"Yes, Karen. I find this whole thing fascinating."

Noting that Reginald's voice was becoming more and more human-sounding every day, she could not help but register his curiosity. "Why?"

"Well, you are looking for something by looking for what you can't see."

She smiled. "I learned it from the movies. The absence of everything, even the normal static, means that something must be there. If it blocks the gargoyles, you might get in. If it blocks you, the gargoyles might get in. If it blocks both of you, we know something big is up and I might get in."

"Won't that put you in danger?" The concern was plain in the Master of the City's voice.

"If it's deep into the Children's territory, I'll call John first. So, it'll be fine."

We're ready. Sebastian sent from somewhere at the base of the first building she wanted inspected.

"Okay." Karen said and sent at the same time. Then spoke to Reginald. "You're up, too. Stick with the gargoyles."

"I can talk and focus search at the same time." He chided. "I am a complex being, just like you. I just have a different physical body."

"I know, sorry." Karen marveled at how her relationship with Reginald had changed over the many months she'd known him. More often than not, she was now the one calling him, telling him that something needed to be done to help the city. Though, when he called, it was usually very important.

"What are you doing?" A female voice from the side of her demanded.

Karen turned and watched the familiar teal-haired teenage girl walk around from the side of her to the front of her. The girl looked both angry and scared. "I'm just sitting here, enjoying the day. How about you, Vicki?"

"No. You're not. You're doing something." Vicki put her hands on her hips. "I can feel it. I know who you are. You shouldn't be here. You haven't passed the Test of Worth."

"I never had the chance to pass it." Karen smiled thinly at the girl, her voice calm. "I'm not in the Children's territory. I have every right to sit here if I want."

"But you're not just sitting there," Vicki repeated. "I can feel you doing something. I wanna know what it is. You're too close to my territory."

"If I tell you, will you sit and talk with me?"

She frowned. "Talk about what?"

Karen shrugged. "The weather. The city. The future. Fashion." She gestured at the girl's futuristic, urban gothic Blade Runner look. "You seem to be an expert in that."

Vicki sat down. "All right. What are you doing?"

"I'm looking for someone. An ally of mine. He's gone missing."

"Who would that be?"

Karen shrugged. "You wouldn't know him. It wouldn't help."

Going to the next building. The Master says it was clean, too. Sebastian interjected, and then was gone again.

"I don't know. I know a lot of people." She twisted a lock of her vibrant hair, looking almost cute; almost innocent.

Almost.

Okay. She sent to Sebastian. Aloud, she said, "He's a sick old man. A monk."

"Why here?" Vicki frowned again. "And how?"

"We think he's here. Hidden. As for how I'm searching, well," she shrugged, "we all have our ways. You wouldn't know anything about an old man in this area, would you?"

Vicki shook her head. "No. There are no monks here."

"Do you know of another place where he could be?"

"A church, maybe?" The teen shook her head. "No. I don't. Look. I gotta go. I think you're wasting your time." She stood up. "And don't come closer. It's not safe."

"I know that, Vicki." Karen put out a hand, not quite touching the girl's arm. "If you ever need to talk—about anything, anything at all—I'll listen. I promise to listen to everything. I don't promise to agree, but I do promise to listen and to give you an honest opinion."

Jerking her arm back from Karen's almost touch, Vicki shook her head. "I don't need to talk. I don't want to talk to you. You need to go now."

"I think I'm exactly where I need to be." Karen smiled. "You have a good day, Vicki." Karen watched as Victoria Mordecai, younger sister to Reagan Mordecai, the leader of the Children of Anu, stomped off down the street into the Children's territory. She bet Vicki was about to give Reggie an earful. That was just what she wanted. She wanted the Children on edge and nervous. Then they would be more likely to make mistakes.

This building is clear. Going on to the third one. Sebastian sent. *The Master says that parts of this third building are dead to him. What do you want us to do?*

Go inside and look if you can. Be careful. Be smart.

We will.

Karen smiled. She hoped to find the Abbot before the end of the evening.

***

"I want him dead! All right, I said it. I want to shoot him like he shot me. Satisfied?" David didn't shout this declaration. He spoke in a low, intense, and cold tone of voice.

"Now, we're getting somewhere." Dr. Mercer said with some satisfaction. "You're not repressing your human emotions anymore. Tell me more."

"More? About what?" He looked away, embarrassed at the ferocity of his desire to hurt V'ger. He was a cop. He was supposed to serve and protect the people of Kendrick. That still included V'ger in some way, didn't it?

"About your feelings. Why you want to shoot V'ger. More than just that he betrayed you."

David frowned more. "V'ger stands for everything I oppose. He put innocent lives in danger to pursue a supernatural path. One designed to take over Kendrick. He did it without regard for anyone, and was willing to kill to achieve his and his group's goals. He's not a man who should be allowed to walk around free and yet, he is."

"Will you pursue him yourself?"

"No." David crumpled into his seat. "He's still a citizen of Kendrick. As a cop, I'm bound to follow the rules and regulations of our city."

"But you want to."

"Yes." David admitted. "He's a menace to society. Him and his kind."

"What about Karen Wilson?"

"What about her?" He sat up straighter, uncomfortable with this sudden change in topic.

"What do you feel about her?"

He looked away again and shrugged. "I miss her. I miss her a lot, but..." He shrugged again.

Dr. Mercer wrote something down. "Isn't she one of his kind now?"

"No. She's not." David scowled at the thought.

"She was doing business with him."

"She was upset about him being there."

"But she still agreed to work with him."

"Under duress." David paused. "I guess you've seen the transcript. So much for the Mayor's eyes only."

"He gave it to me because he thought I should know." The doctor adjusted his glasses. "Back to Karen Wilson. Why don't you consider her to be one of his kind?"

"Because she wouldn't hurt anyone. She wants to protect Kendrick from the other supernaturals."

"Yet, she's threatened several officers of the law, and still works with supernaturals."

"She apologized to Sergeant Mueller for the threat she made to him and she works with other supernatural groups because they also are trying to protect Kendrick. She wouldn't hurt anyone."

"From a certain point of view... for their own less than altruistic reasons." The doctor commented. "And you don't know what she will do."

"I know Karen."

"You don't know how she made every door in the precinct open at her request. You didn't know she could control the stoplights of Kendrick, as she threatened to do. If you don't know what she can do, how can you assure me of what she will or won't do?"

"What are you getting at, Doctor?"

"I'm pointing out that you cannot pick and choose who the monsters are anymore. Either they all are or they all aren't." Dr. Mercer held up a hand to halt David's protests. "It is clear that some monsters are much more dangerous than others, but all monsters are dangerous. You joined the Special Unit to protect the innocent, blissfully ignorant, normal citizens of Kendrick from the monsters inhabiting the city and the surrounding areas. Are you still willing to do so?"

"Of course I am."

"Then you need to stop cherry picking who is the enemy and who is not. They all are because they *all* will eventually use their powers and abilities against the very people we are trying to protect. I don't care how enlightened and altruistic they appear. It's just the way it is. You need to think about that." He looked at his watch. "And since our time is up, we'll speak about this again tomorrow. For now, I want you on a one week paid suspension. I don't want anything distracting you from this conversation. Go home, think about it—especially Karen Wilson—and be ready to talk to me tomorrow."

Unable to do anything else, David stood, nodded, and left the doctor's office without another word.

Dr. Mercer made a few notes in David's file, and then made a phone call. "This is Dr. Mercer. I want Detective David Hauberk under surveillance for the next seventy-two hours. I need to know who he calls, who he sees, and where he goes. Yes. Code 3B. Thank you."

***

"Any luck finding the Abbot?" Mason's voice was tired and he knew it.

"You asking me as the mayor, as a friend, or as a friend of the Abbot?" John swirled the glass of amber liquid in his hand.

"Yes."

John sighed. "Not yet, but we're working on it. I hope we have something soon. It's hard to keep so many factions working in the same direction, even if it's on different parts of the problem."

Mason blew out a worried breath. "That's not a lot of progress, John. That's not good. That's really not good."

"You sound like you know something that I don't know. All I know is that some big bad spirit wants to come through to this side and affect the world. To do that, the Abbot needs to be sacrificed on Halloween." He paused, took a drink, and looked Mason in the eye. "What do you know?"

Mason met his gaze. "The same as you. I wish I knew more. The oracles keep passing out whenever they try to scry. Their explanation is that there are still too many ways this could all go. I need you to help more. I need to you find the Abbot. I know you can do it."

"I'm doing what I can, but I can't help if you know more than you're telling. Look, anything else you know could help."

"Don't you have a card that can help you find someone or something like that? The Todari deck could be really useful right now."

John came to attention at the mention of his obsession. "Maybe, but I try not to rely too much on them. They," he paused, searching for the right words, "are all like the Major Arcana. Once they're in motion, you can't stop them."

"Finding someone won't hurt anyone, right? Abbot Peter is already sick and injured. Who knows where he is? We've got to find him and keep him from being sacrificed."

"Why? What is it you're not telling me? What makes this ritual so much more important and dangerous?" John shifted forward in his seat. "I've known you for a while now, Mason. You're holding back on me. What has you so terrified?"

"A change is coming." His voice took on a bleak tone. "If we cannot save Peter, then I won't be able to do anything about it. I won't be able to control it. I won't be able to do anything but be swept up in it. Me, my family, Kendrick. I have to protect my family. I don't have a choice."

"How do you know?"

"I know."

John stood in anger. *"How?"*

"I just do."

"That's not good enough."

"It has to be for now. I can't say anymore."

"You're not doing a lot to generate any trust with me." John scowled at him.

Mason shrugged and said nothing.

"Damn it." He walked toward the door. "Until you have something more to say, I think our relationship has hit a plateau."

"John." Mason protested. John continued heading for the door. "John!" More insistent now.

John paused with his hand on the doorknob. "What?" He didn't turn around.

"What would you do if your entire collection of Todari tarot cards up and vanished one day?"

The very thought made him sick to his stomach. "I'd go insane." John stood at the door, refusing to look at the mayor.

"It's something like that, but only with me and my family. Please, help us find the Abbot. By any means necessary."

John sighed. "I'm trying to." He opened the door and left the mayor behind

***

Elsewhere...

Corelli walked into the Children of Anu's main warehouse, escorted by Sam, the more pleasant of Reggie's seconds. She hadn't had a lot of time to prepare for this sudden meeting, and was left with only her red hot cinnamon candies and lip gloss as protection. She knew she'd need the latter for this conversation. She hoped she wouldn't need the former. She had never tried to set an entire warehouse on fire before.

She waited until Reggie finished talking with Vicki and approached her. She nodded and, instead of the normal greetings, her mouth started with getting to the point. "You called and said it was time for the Order of the Sacred Eye to repay its debt to the Children of Anu." It was always a struggle not to fight against the magic she placed on herself. Corelli forced herself to relax and let the magic do the talking.

"It is." Reggie said. "You are aware of who Karen Wilson is?"

"Yes."

"She's looking for someone. She must be stopped by any means at your disposal."

"Why?"

"Not your concern, Corelli." Reggie gave her a dismissive wave of his hand. "She can't be allowed to continue her search or be allowed to find this person. You need to deal with it. I don't care how."

"Stop Karen Wilson from finding the person she's looking for, then our debt is settled?"

"Yes." Reggie started to turn away then turned back to her. "If she finds who she's looking for, the Children will take the debt the Order of the Sacred Eye owes us out in blood. Your blood, your Order's blood, and those associated with you. Are we clear?"

"Clear. Karen Wilson will be stopped. All debts owed by the Order of the Sacred Eye will be paid."

Reggie offered his hand. Corelli took it and gave it a firm handshake. When Reggie started to show his strength by crushing her plump hand in that handshake, her smile did not falter as she let the heat of her skin flare. He let go first and gave her a respectful nod. "Sam will drive you to where you need to go."

Corelli nodded good-bye and turned her back to Reggie as he turned away to her. She gave Sam a half smile. "Let's go."

Sam turned his gaze from the teenage girl in the back of the room to Corelli. "All right. Where to?"

"The Colonel's Park. I'll walk from there."

"Suit yourself."

Ultimatums

"YOU WANT ME to do what?" Karen stared at Corelli with a mixture of confusion and outrage. "Why?"

"I want you to stop searching for the Abbot. *You* cannot be the one to find him. Neither you nor your particular resources," Corelli repeated. "As for why, I can't answer that. However, you have to do as I ask."

"But we agreed. Susan and I would find the Abbot. You would find where the sacrifice was going to take place. I'm close! I know I am. You can't just tell me I can't do this."

"Yes, I can. You agreed that you owed me. You agreed to give me anything I wanted. This is what I want."

Karen remembered that horrible night and what Corelli had done to help her and Sebastian:

Karen struggled to free herself from the ritual bonds the Order of the Sacred Eye had bound her with as Sebastian lay almost dead next to her; slowly being murdered by the spell on her to keep the gargoyles away. She felt someone or something watching her. Karen looked for the new presence and saw a lone, blond-haired girl in Order robes crouched by a tree. She looked frightened, but not panicked. In one hand was Changer's Claw, still stained with both Karen and Paul's blood. Not knowing what else to do and desperate, Karen yelled through a ragged throat to the girl, "Please! Help him! Get him away from me. Please! I'll do anything!"

The girl looked around at the fighting chaos. She winced as a werewolf slashed at a girl and a guy backed up against a tree with knife-like claws. With a quick nod, she ran to Karen, still crouched. She raised Changer's Claw when she reached the small gargoyle and the prone woman. For a moment, Karen thought she had been betrayed again, but when the weapon came down, it severed the strap binding Karen's left hand to the stake. Karen didn't hesitate; she turned over and pulled as far away from Sebastian as she could.

"I'm Corelli. What they were doing was wrong." She scooped up Sebastian. "That's why I'm helping you. But, you still owe me. I'll get him to safety."

She had gotten him to safety. She had done what she said she would do. Sebastian was alive because of Corelli. But why this demand? Why now? What did she have to gain? "What if I say 'No.'?"

"Then Sebastian's life is forfeit and belongs to me. You'll have to turn him over to me. There are rules that even you, who represents the Master of the City, cannot break. I will accept nothing less." Corelli repressed her own wince as the words came from her bespelled mouth. She hoped to God that the magic of her lip gloss was working correctly. She wanted to apologize and say that she would never hurt Sebastian, but she knew that her words were the ones that Karen needed to hear to make her do as Corelli needed her to do.

"To think I trusted you." Karen shook her head. "Tried to help you and the Order against all that was sane. First, V'ger's not only alive and in charge. Now this." She shrugged with an angry jerk of her shoulders. "I have no choice, do I?"

"No. Whether or not you believe it, this is for the best, and all debts are cleared with this one act."

"I don't think I could hate you any more right now if I tried." Karen threw a five-dollar bill on the coffeehouse table and stalked out.

It took all of Corelli's will not to chase after Karen to apologize and explain. Karen wouldn't listen and even if she did, she would try to get around the demand made by the Children, and Corelli could not risk that. She wanted Karen to know the truth. She also wanted them to find the Abbot before it was too late. The more she thought about it, the more her path became clear.

"John Corso," she said to herself. She needed to call him and tell him what had happened and why. He understood the old laws. He would also be able to help look for the Abbot. The Children specifically said that *Karen* could not be the one to find the Abbot. They didn't say anything about anyone else. She pulled out her cell phone and dialed his number.

***

It was a strange meeting on the beach north of the Camden District. An old Indian man dressed in leather and jeans met with a young teal-haired girl in buckled denim and silver. The two of them stood opposite each other, squared off like duelists at high noon. The old man flinched first.

"I have done what you've asked. Now fulfill your end of the bargain," Walks-the-Ocean said and looked away.

"When do they think the sacrifice is to happen?" Vicki clearly enjoyed her power over him.

"Halloween night."

"Good. As if we'd follow the dictates of another religion. There were no questions?"

"No. Give me the amulet."

She held up an old beaded necklace adorned with claws and feathers. "You mean this?"

"Yes." To his credit, he did not lunge for it. Walks-the-Ocean kept his dignity for himself and his tribe.

"No. Not until all this is done."

He gritted his teeth and took a breath. "That's not what we agreed."

She shrugged. "Don't care. In a couple of days, all this won't matter. You'll have your precious amulet back, as well as full autonomy of your land. As per our agreement, the Children of Anu will make no claims or inroads into Makah territory again. Ever. As for this amulet, you will have it back. That's how you'll know that your land, including the cave, is all yours again. Then you may do with it as you will."

"We'll cleanse it of your taint."

If Vicki was offended she didn't show it. "Why are you so angry? I'd think that you'd be happy that we're getting rid of the Brotherhood's leader. The white man has not been good to the Makah people. We could be such good allies and not just..." She shrugged. "What we are now."

"Enemies. Also, you're white, too."

"Companionable enemies. And, yeah, I'm white but I can be reasoned with. The Children of Anu keep their word."

"Then why won't you give me the amulet now?"

"That is not the Children's decision. Reggie sent me here to give it to you. *I* am choosing to keep it as insurance. Just so you know who's really in charge here."

"I'm not stupid, child. I knew it was you from the moment I saw you. The spirits told me and the Makah tribe keeps its word. You should, too. Especially if you want to deal with us on friendly terms ever again." Walks-the-Ocean took two steps forward and held out his hand. "If you represent the Children of Anu, give me the amulet."

Vicki narrowed her eyes at him and took two steps forward to meet him. "I represent Anu. Not the Children, though I am one." She held out the amulet to him. When he went to take it from her, she grabbed his hand with supernatural strength, pressing the beads of the necklace into his flesh. "It would be good of you to show more respect the next time we meet."

He could feel the strength of the spirit already starting to ride the girl's body. He could hear it in her voice. "Thank you for the amulet. My people will rejoice at its return." He did not wince as her delicate hand pressed down with an impossible strength against his. He steeled himself. He would rather have a broken hand than show weakness to the creature inside the girl.

Suddenly, Vicki let go, leaving the amulet in Walks-the-Ocean's hand. She laughed like the teenager she was, and he could sense the spirit receding. He hoped to never see it again. The two of them nodded and turned away from each other. Walks-the-Ocean felt a pang of guilt at the forced betrayal of the city, but as the Chief of his tribe, he had to do what was best for his people in the long run.

He stopped, his heart suddenly jack-hammering in his chest as he saw two children playing in the sand just down the beach. They were the Grey Lady's twin helpers. Though they looked and acted like children, they were far from it. He sighed to himself and continued to walk toward them. As he reached them, the twins stopped building their sandcastle and looked up.

"The Lady is angry," Theodore said.

"But not so angry that she's not willing to listen," Theodora said.

"She hopes that you will come speak to her soon—" Theodore began.

Theodora continued, "—to explain what you've done and why."

"She understands that there are many forces in motion."

"She hopes that your explanations will sooth her ire."

"And that you come to her before she has to look for you." Theodore concluded. The twins fell silent and watched the old Indian man choose his words carefully.

"I will come to her soon. I will tell her all that I can. I hope she will understand what I did and why. She is of the land, as are my people. If it were not vital to us and our survival, this... betrayal... would not have happened," Walks-the-Ocean bowed his head.

The children looked at each other, and then looked back at him. They nodded. "The Grey Lady wishes you a pleasant afternoon, and will have tea ready when you come."

He sighed with relief. "Thank you." The matter could still be contained between the oldest of them here in Kendrick. The younger ones would never understand.

***

Karen had spent a good hour in a self-indulgent pity, intermingling tears and moping, at Corelli's sudden betrayal and her threat against Sebastian. What brought her out of it was Sebastian's offer to go bite Corelli on the butt. The image he sent her of him chomping on the woman's generous rear end and not letting go was too funny not to laugh at. It was what she needed to pull herself up by her own bootstraps. She needed to think about what had happened and what she could do about it.

She replayed the conversation in her head and fastened on one particular phrase, "You cannot be the one to find him. Neither you nor your particular resources." She thought hard about that. *Neither you nor your particular resources.* That meant that she could not personally find him. Nor could she ask the gargoyles to or John to use his cards. Those were particular resources. But, she could make an anonymous call to the police... or a not so anonymous call to David. He wanted to bury the hatchet and regain her trust. This would go a long way toward that.

She picked up her phone and debated with herself. Was she ready to make nice with David? After all he'd done? After a few moments' thought, she still didn't know, but decided that the life of the Abbot was worth the risk of the possible heartache. She dialed his number.

"Hello?" David's voice was clipped, professional.

"David, it's Karen."

"What do you want?"

She was surprised at the abruptness of his tone. "I needed to talk to you about some things—"

"No. I don't think you do. In fact, I really don't think you should call me again."

"What? Why?"

"Because you're one of them now. You're working with the other side. There's no way I can trust you. There's no way I *should* trust you. Don't call me at this number again."

Karen blinked as the line went dead. Then, she blinked some more as the tears welled up. His unexpected rejection hurt a lot. Her phone rang again. She looked at the number and did not recognize it. She answered it anyway. "Hello?"

"Hi. It's me. I'm sorry about that, but I'm pretty sure my normal cell phone is bugged," David spoke in a hushed tone.

"What? What's happening? Why did you say that?" This sudden turnaround was bewildering.

"I don't really have an answer for you right now, but I think you need to make sure you only call me at this number and don't spread it around. Okay?"

Completely confused, Karen nodded. "Okay."

"What did you want to talk about? Are you all right? Are you in trouble?"

"I'm all right. I'm not in trouble, but someone else is. I need help."

"Who?"

"The Abbot of a monkish order called the Brotherhood of Light. He's been kidnapped and... I need help finding him. I can't do it myself."

"Brother Peter? Are you talking about Brother Peter?"

"Yes." Karen knew she should not be surprised at his knowledge. The Special Unit of the Kendrick police force had been designed to deal with supernatural threats.

"And you want to help him?"

"Yes. You know him?"

"I've heard of him. Why can't you do it yourself?"

Karen paused. "I've been ordered not to."

"And you're listening? That's not like you."

She sighed. "Apparently, like you as a cop, I have rules I have to follow."

"Karen... are you still... human?"

"What? Of course I am. Why would you ask that?" The question surprised and angered her. It was one hell of a loaded question.

He paused. "Never mind. Forget I asked. Do you have any leads?"

She frowned at the phone before deciding to drop it. "I think the Children of Anu have him, somewhere in the Camden District. Is there anything you can do in the... um, Special Unit... to find him? His life is in danger. I think they're going to kill him."

"Do you have any proof? No, never mind. I don't care. I don't know if I can find anything out, but I'll try. I'll call you when I have something." He paused. "Karen?"

"Yeah?"

"I'm sorry for everything. I really am."

"Me, too."

"Remember. Don't call my regular cell phone."

"I won't."

"Bye."

"Bye." Karen hung up, completely confused but hopeful. She wondered what the hell was going on in David's life that he thought his regular phone was being bugged, that he couldn't be caught talking to her, and why he had asked her if she was still human. Something very strange and unpleasant was happening in his life, and she didn't like it. Also, like it or not, Karen realized that she still had feelings for him. That made her new feelings for John all the more complex.

***

David hung up the prepaid cell phone he had bought specifically for this purpose. He had come to the conclusion that Dr. Mercer wanted him to say that all supernaturals were bad and could not be trusted. He was also certain that he was under surveillance. It was what he would do after pushing a member of the SU as hard as Mercer had pushed him.

Talking to Karen at all was a risk, but she called him and needed help. She was looking to help a good man; a man of God. He was willing to risk a lot to help Brother Peter too, and was willing to risk everything to help her. Maybe this would start paving the way to repaying his debt to her.

***

"You know sometimes that you have to do something you don't want to because you're repaying a debt, right?" Corelli asked John as she doctored her tea with sugar and milk.

He nodded as he put together his own afternoon concoction. "Yes. In some cases. I do."

"Can I trust you?"

He shrugged. "As much as you can trust anyone, Corelli. I'm an independent. Therefore, you must take your chances."

"I need you to understand something so, someday, you can explain it to Karen. I don't think she's going to be talking to me for a while."

"Why?" He frowned. "What happened?"

"Back in December, the Children fought alongside the Order of the Sacred Eye."

"Yeah...?"

"I didn't make the agreement. I didn't want that ritual. I—"

"Skip the caveats and get to the point." John was in no mood to listen to her excuses. He wanted to know what was going on with Karen.

She grimaced. "The Order owed the Children a debt. It was an *acknowledged* debt. I had no choice but to pay it for the Order." She nodded at him as he twirled his finger impatiently in a 'come on already' motion. "The Children ordered that I make Karen stop looking for the Abbot. She and her particular resources could not be the one to find him. With that, all debts between the Order and the Children would be paid. Karen also owed me an *acknowledged* debt. So, I ordered her to stop her search. She resisted... and I had to get mean."

"What do you mean 'had to get mean'?" His voice was carefully neutral. His thoughts were decidedly less so.

"I threatened to take Sebastian from her. He was the reason she owed me. I saved him." She sighed, looking down at her tea, feeling miserable. "I wouldn't have hurt him or anything. I just needed her to stop looking. That doesn't mean that Susan can't look, or even you. We can still look for him, but not Karen. Her not looking clears all debts." She looked up at him, her eyes begging for him to understand.

His bland, neutral gaze met hers. "I understand. I don't like it, but I do understand it. I suppose this was the easiest way to get the Order out from under the thumb of the Children and for you to clear the way between you and Karen. Of course, you may not like her attitude toward you now."

She nodded, looking down at her tea again. "I hated myself for doing it. But there wasn't anything else I could do. The Law of Debt was on me. If I didn't... there would've been blood. A lot of blood." Tears ran down her face and dripped into her cup. "I'm sorry. I'm so sorry."

"Seems I do have to take an active role in all this. I didn't want to. People need a neutral point of contact. I have no real choice. I'll use my resources to look for Brother Peter. Has the Order at least done their bit and found the sacrificial site?"

"Almost. We know it's near water. I have my best diviners on it. We were thinking of seeing if Bacchanalia would be willing to do a group divination. Pooling all of our talents. There's powerful magic blocking us."

He nodded. "Good."

"Do you think Karen will ever understand why I did what I did?"

He shrugged. "I don't know. Maybe. I appreciate the warning that she's been hurt by you."

"I didn't want to."

"I know. But, I'm not the one who's hurt." John's thoughts, however, were unforgiving. *How could I have thought I was neutral in all this?*

"I know."

***

Twelve hours later...

The entire membership of the Children of Anu gathered at the sacred cave under the dock north of the Camden district. Restlessness filled the air as friend punched friend in camaraderie. There would be blood tonight and more. It was the coming of Anu. It was the coming of Marduk, Bel, Enlil. It was the coming of their God. It was history in the making, and they would be there for it.

The crowd erupted in cheers when Reggie stepped forth on the ridge overlooking the sacrificial stone. The old man, Brother Peter, Abbot of the Brotherhood of Light, the symbol of their greatest enemy, was already chained there. He looked weak, but healthy enough. He did not seem afraid. Instead, his head was bowed in prayer.

Reggie raised his hands for quiet and the cave became still. "Great god Anu! Father of Heaven, creator of the stars, lord of the constellations, king of gods, spirits, and demons, your Children have not forgotten you. Your Children remember that this is the prophesied year of your return. I, your most beloved servant, Reagan Lee Mordecai, have gathered your believers here on this night of your prophesized return. We have before us the needed sacrifice. We have before you, your avatar. Great god Anu! Instruct us in your wisdom. Judge us worthy with this task. We are your Children and your servants."

From across the way, another voice suddenly rang out. "Who is our most loved?" It was Vicki.

"REGGIE!" The congregation shouted.

Reggie was surprised. This was not part of the ritual, but everyone seemed not to mind. He looked across to his little sister and saw her joyous smile. He returned it and allowed her a little time to shine.

"Who is our most loved?" she shouted again.

"REGGIE!" The congregation shouted again.

"Who must we give up to allow Anu to return to us?"

"Our beloved!" This time it was not the whole congregation who responded. Just most of them. The ones who didn't respond looked around in confusion. Some stopped responding. Some tried to keep up.

"Who we must sacrifice to Anu?" Vicki's shout was very loud.

Reggie blinked, frowning. He didn't understand what was going on.

It was already too late for him.

"REGGIE!" The Children of Anu shouted a third time and the chaos began.

Mike, the most personally loyal of Reggie's seconds, was immediately jumped by three of the Children standing next to him. He was too busy trying to save himself to save his best friend and leader. Sam, the more knowledgeable and cunning of Reggie's seconds, hit Reggie in the back of the head with a baseball bat. As soon as Reggie fell to his knees, two other Children leapt upon him and bound him. He was dragged bodily down into the sacrificial pit, where, bleeding but conscious, the former leader of the Children of Anu was chained next to Brother Peter against the stained sacrificial rock.

Vicki walked down to the sacrificial pit and lifted Reggie's bloodied face so her eyes could meet his. "I'm sorry." She kissed his brow.

Reggie's eyes bulged wide with terror. "Vicki, you can't do this. This isn't how it's supposed to happen."

"I don't want to, but I can do it and I will do it. This *is* how it's supposed to be." She gestured to the Children. "They've all known for the last week. The true believers. The ones who worship Anu, and not you. We all love you so much, and that's why we must give you up to Anu. You must die so he can live."

"But—I'm his chosen avatar. I'm the one!"

She shook her head sadly. "No. You aren't. In your hubris, you've ignored all the signs and because of that, I have to lose the person I love the most." She leaned close so only he could hear her. "But fear not, brother. You'll live on through me. I promise." She stepped back from him and turned to the Children. She raised her voice loud. "What is our offering?"

"Our greatest enemy!"

"What is our sacrifice?"

"Our greatest love!"

She turned back to the sacrificial stone, addressing both and neither of the two men chained there. "Great god Anu! Father of Heaven, creator of the stars, lord of the constellations, king of gods, spirits and demons, we call to you. We call to you on this most holy day. We give to you our offering and our sacrifice so you may rise in this world. Anu, Marduk, Bel, Enlil and all your holy names, we call to you! Accept our sacrifice! Accept our offering and come forth to rise to new glory!"

"No!" Reggie shouted and struggled against his bonds as the Abbot bowed his head in prayer.

Ignoring Reggie's scream, Vicki raised the revered bloody mace high and brought it down sharply on her brother's head.

Too Little, Too Late

SIXTEEN HOURS AGO...

"Has Detective Hauberk had any contact with Karen Wilson?" Dr. Mercer asked as he leafed through Sergeant Mueller's surveillance report.

"Yes, sir. A phone call." The sergeant squirmed in his chair. He hated this part of his job. He was supposed to be catching bad guys, not spying on one of their own.

Dr. Mercer gave him a sharp look. "Who called whom?"

Mueller buried his emotions at the doctor's reaction. "Karen Wilson called him. He hung up on her. The transcript starts on page, um, eighteen."

"Why is only his half of the conversation recorded?"

Sergeant Mueller was sweating now. "There was line interference. I couldn't hear anything she said. I think it's because of—" he paused, then continued, "—what she is. Who she's working with."

"Aberration," the doctor muttered. He nodded. "Keep up the good work. I'll see you in two days. However, if the detective has any more contact with Karen Wilson, I want to know about it immediately."

"Yes, sir."

The doctor waved a hand at him in dismissal. Sergeant Mueller didn't need to be told twice. He got up and left. He walked out of the office building and got into his car, driving in silence for about five minutes before he said, "Okay, it's clear."

David sat up in the backseat. "Thanks."

"Dave, man, I don't really know what the hell is happening, but that doctor is out for your blood."

David shook his head. "No. He's testing my loyalty... or something. I appreciate what you're doing for me."

The sergeant shrugged. "You've saved my life many times. It's the least I can do. Besides, that man gives me the willies!"

"Me, too. Did you get what I asked?"

Mueller nodded. "I've got it here in the front seat." He drove the car into a distant park parking lot and stopped next to David's car. "You're just lucky that I'm on both cases."

After David got shifted into Mueller's front passenger seat, he asked, "Both cases?"

"Yeah, you and the case of the missing monk."

"Great, I'm a case now."

Mueller shrugged. "You have a case file."

"I'll have to see that some time." He started looking through the official case file on the kidnapped Brother Peter.

"I'll get you a copy when the surveillance is done. What you're probably looking for is on page twelve." He leaned over and pulled a couple of pages out for David to read.

After a moment of silence, David nodded. "Are they sure?"

"Flip to the back, there's pictures."

David did and nodded. "Are they sending in a team?"

"Yeah, tomorrow night."

"That might be too late."

Sergeant Mueller nodded. "I know. Dr. Mercer insisted that that's when everyone will be there."

"Most bang for the buck?" David scowled. "An old man's life is in danger."

"I know."

"Something is seriously wrong here."

"I know." Mueller did not like admitting it, but something was very wrong, and he didn't know what, except it seemed to start and end with Doctor Mercer.

David nodded. "Anything you don't know?"

"Yeah. The future." The sergeant did not smile.

Neither did David. "Thanks for these." He got out of the car.

"Keep your head down, Detective."

"You, too, Sergeant." He closed the door.

"Always..." Sergeant Mueller breathed out as he started the car and drove away.

***

Twelve hours ago...

"John?" Karen called as she walked into the *Teller's Fortune*, looking for its proprietor. "You here?"

"In back," he called.

She walked through the metaphysical store to the back office and poked her head in the doorway. "You called?"

John Corso finished folding the silken cloth over one of his Todari Cards. "Yeah. I—"

Karen's phone rang, interrupting him. She looked down at the cell phone's window and saw a number she recognized. "Sorry. I need to take this." She opened the phone. "Hello?"

"Karen?" It was David.

"Yes. Did you find out anything?" She tried to keep the hope out of her voice.

"Yeah, I did. The Special Unit believes that the Children of Anu are planning something big tomorrow night at an abandoned dock. Dock 14. Beneath it, actually. They've got photos of people going into and out of what looks like a cave underneath the dock."

"That's great. Have they seen Brother Peter? Are they going in to get him?"

"No, not that I know of. They're waiting until tomorrow night, when they believe most of the Children will be there."

"David... that could be too late for the Abbot. They need to save him. They shouldn't wait."

"I know." He sighed. "Something stinks about this, but they're waiting. If you guys are going to do something, do it soon and don't be there tomorrow night. The SU might not be so clear on who's friend and who's foe."

"Great. Thank you."

"Karen, you be careful."

"I will. You, too." They both paused awkwardly before saying good-bye.

"David?" John asked with one eyebrow raised.

"Yeah. That David. I had to go to him for help. Corelli completely screwed me." She scowled at the memory.

"I know. That's why I called you. She told me about what she had to do and why and asked me to help—" John held up a hand. "Don't get angry, hon. She did what she had to do. So, I did what I had to do."

"But, you're part of my special resources. You can't..."

"I'm my own man, and I can do whatever the hell I want. Besides..." He paused. "What did David want, anyway?"

"I told him that Brother Peter was missing." She hedged. "He already knew about it. Already knew that the Special Unit was working on it. I asked him to pass on any information. He did."

"Do they know where Brother Peter is?"

"They think they do. He's in a cave under Dock 14. It's an abandoned pier. But the raid isn't set until tomorrow night. That could be too late. We need to move now."

John smiled. "Well, that was unexpected."

"What?"

"Outside confirmation. I just used a card to determine that the Abbot was under the earth, near water, sand, stone, and wood. I'd guessed a cave near a pier, but that seems to confirm it."

She gave him a hug. "That's great. Now we need to gather the others. We need a plan."

***

Eight hours ago...

Karen arrived at Bacchanalia. She wasn't surprised to find an open parking spot in front of the private club. It was much too early for this crowd to be up. She was surprised when Susan suggested they meet here. Walking through the front door, Karen realized she was hesitant. She hadn't been in the club for a long time. She had drifted away from Bacchanalia ever since Heather's death and the ritual last December. No one had ever blamed her for Heather's death, but she felt they all condemned her for it anyway.

"Come on in," Lamiel said from the other side of the entryway. "We don't bite—unless you ask nicely." She looked tired and almost mundane in black jeans, black tank-top, and a grey hoodie sweatshirt instead of her usual Victorian finery.

"Thanks," Karen followed the coven leader in. Susan and Juliet sat at one of the club tables. Both of them had coffee cups. Lamiel sat down behind a third cup.

"Hey," Juliet said by way of greeting.

"You want coffee?" Susan was the only one who looked wide-awake.

"Yes. Thanks."

Susan poured Karen a cup of coffee. "We found it. Almost. There's a cave on the edge of the bay. It's hidden by a dock. We'll have it tonight. We're going to pour in power from the Order, too."

"You don't need to." Karen said. "You've just confirmed the information I received. Dock 14. It's an abandoned pier. The Children have been seen going in and out of a cave under it."

"Good," Lamiel said. "I'm ready to be done with this. We'll have them before All Hallow's Eve."

"That's the problem," Karen continued as she had their undivided attention. "My source says they're gathering for the ritual tomorrow night."

"But, that's not right," Juliet tilted her head. "The ritual was supposed to be on All Hallow's Eve. Not before. It's still days away."

"I know. I know." Karen fidgeted, debating telling them about the Special Unit.

Susan elbowed her. "Out with it. We agreed—no secrets."

"You're right." She nodded and looked around. "The police's Special Unit is set to raid there tomorrow night during the ritual."

"Why are they waiting?" Susan asked.

"What's the Special Unit?" Lamiel asked.

"I don't know... and the Special Unit is a police task force that knows about supernaturals and tries to combat the ones out to hurt the city and its people as best they can. They're a little iffy on who's a white hat and who's a black one."

"Great," Susan and Juliet said at the same time.

"So, we have to move tonight," Lamiel said as if would be the easiest thing in the world.

"I know," Karen said. "We need to gather everyone, tell them what's up, and attack tonight. That means the couriers need to go out. We'll meet at the same place we met last time." She looked at Susan. "Can you do that?"

"Yes. What do I have them say?"

Karen and Lamiel looked at each other. Karen answered while still looking at Lamiel. "Tell them that we meet tonight at midnight and after instructions, we move. We bring the Abbot home at all costs."

***

Four hours ago...

"John, please tell me we have a better plan than 'Get 'em, Ray!'."

"I'm doing the best I can, Karen. The interior of a cave is not an easy place to assault, and I don't want to turn this into Kendrick's version of the Battle at Thermopylae."

***

Now...

In the backroom of the *Teller's Fortune*, the heads of the supernatural groups once again met to deal with their own unique problems. For the moment, all ideological differences and all personal conflicts were put mostly to the side. Everyone was quiet, waiting for John or Karen to begin. Karen stood. She glanced around the room, avoiding looking at Corelli as she did.

"We've found the sacrificial site. However, we have almost no time to prepare. From outside sources, the Children of Anu will be gathering tomorrow night for their rite." She raised a hand at the questions. "I know tomorrow night isn't Halloween. I know that's not the night we thought the ritual was going to take place. Be that as it may, something is happening. So, we have to act now. Tonight. We have no time to lose if we want to save Brother Peter. We know what we must do. Now, John will outline the plan."

As she sat, John stood. He unrolled a map with a blow-up of the Discovery Bay coastline. "This isn't going to be easy. Also, before we begin, there's one other thing you should know. The Kendrick police are also planning a raid on this location. Only, they are waiting until the night of the ritual. So, we cannot pussyfoot around on this one. We've got to get in and get out. Our main objective is to rescue the Abbot. Nothing more. Nothing less. We have to go tonight because there should be less opposition. Also because the Kendrick police may have strange ideas about who's a friend and who isn't."

"Will we be watched?" Walks-the-Ocean asked.

"Probably," John answered. "That's why we're going to need two things: A small group of volunteers to go in, and the rest to do what they can do to obfuscate us. I'll be going in. I'm not neutral on this. I'm in it all the way."

"I'm in," Karen said.

"I'm in, too." Corelli ignored the looks from both V'ger and Karen.

"He's our leader. Two of the Brotherhood will go in." Brother Luke said. "We have people trained for this. Brother Jeffrey and Brother Robert will go."

"'We have people trained for this,'" Lamiel mimicked. "Look at the super-ninja-monks go."

"Lamiel, please." John sighed and she nodded, silent but unrepentant. "Okay. That's five. We can go with five, or we can take one more."

"I should go," Walks-the-Ocean said. "That is Makah land. I should see the desecration for myself."

"No offense, Chief Walks-the-Ocean," V'ger said. "But you're not exactly a young man."

"No," he agreed. "But I am strong in the ways of my people."

John nodded. "That's six. That's good. We want this quiet. I'll need the six of us to meet after this meeting. The rest of you, I need two things... first, the obfuscation magic. Figure out how to hide seven people. Second, we should have back up waiting for us on the beach. Three to five people per group. If we give the signal, your job will be to make as much noise as possible and charge to our rescue. If we can tell you what you're going to be facing, we will. I want all of us to meet in the parking lot at Dock 12 in about an hour and a half. From there, all magic can be cast, and I'll be able to point out the staging spots for the backup. Anyone got questions?"

They looked around the room at each other and waited, shaking their heads. John nodded. "All right. Thank you everyone. With luck, the Abbot will be back in the monastery tonight. See you all at the pier."

Karen and John watched everyone leave. "Do you think we can do it?" Karen asked.

"I don't know. I know I'm going to try."

She nodded. "It's all we can do now."

***

Two hours too late...

The six of them were gathered between Dock 13 and Dock 14. They could see each other, but no one else should have been able to detect them. With four different supernatural groups focused on them not being noticed, blending in with the surroundings and remaining unheard, it would take a lot for anyone—mundane or otherwise—to see them. The only catch was that they had to remain within an eight-foot radius of each other. That made for very tight quarters for that many people.

By agreement, if they had to go single file, John would go first, followed by Karen, Brother Jeffrey, Walks-the-Ocean, Corelli, and Brother Robert. Until then, they walked in pairs. Also, no one was to speak unless it was all clear or they had made it back to the staging ground with Brother Peter. Walks-the-Ocean and Brother Jeffrey would carry the Abbot if necessary. All they had to do was get in, get the Abbot, and get out.

Of course, no one knew exactly what *that* would entail, so they prepared as best they could with weapons and tools.

John looked at each of them. Once he had their undivided attention, he gave them the 'Go' signal. They set off down the beach toward Dock 14. He slowed them a little as they reached their target, giving the signal for everyone to look for the Children. Most likely they had lookouts. But no one saw anyone. They reached the cave entrance, no longer hidden by drapes of weeds, and stopped to listen. After a few long moments of listening to each other breathe, John gave them the signal to go.

Single file, they entered the cave. Quickly, they were able to pair up again. The cave was completely silent, but not empty. What was there was a smell and a feeling that made the hairs of their arms stand up. The smell was of people in close quarters and something else. Something primal. Something unpleasant.

Karen and John looked at each other in the torch light and John mouthed a single word at her. "*Blood.*" She nodded and the two of them moved deeper into the passageway tunnel until they reached the cave. Karen gazed with disgusted wonder at the violent frescos on the walls. Vaguely, she was aware that all six of them had made it into the large cavern.

"Oh, shit," John muttered.

"Oh, God," Corelli said. She turned away and covered her mouth. A moment later, she broke their policy and bolted outside. The sounds of her retching could still be heard within.

Karen turned to look at what they were looking at and saw the bloody mess at the center of the room. She had not realized that it had once been people, but now that her mind was recognizing body parts, she realized she was seeing at least two people literally torn apart.

Brother Jeffrey and Brother Robert rushed down into the pit, their steps making unpleasant squishing sounds. They hurried to Brother Peter's side in vain hope that their divine connection could have any chance in heaven of saving the man that had been their mentor.

Karen heard a weak, wet cough to her left. Numb with horror, she looked and saw a bloodied man lying partway in another cave entrance. She walked to his side and looked down at him. She could not force herself to do more.

"They killed him..." Mike coughed at her. "They weren't supposed to do that..."

John came between Mike and Karen. He knelt down. "We'll get you out of here."

"They weren't... They killed..." Mike stopped with blood dribbling out of his mouth. His dead eyes still looked up at Karen, accusing her of the murder. Accusing her of not acting fast enough. Accusing her of failing.

"Karen." John stepped in front of her, but she could not see him clearly. She realized she was crying. "We've got to get out of here. We've got to go."

"We failed," she said.

"We tried." He turned her around to lead her out after the monks carried out the body of Brother Peter. He pulled her forward and grabbed Walks-the-Ocean's arm at the same time. "Time to go."

"This land will never be clean," he said and followed, tears following freely down his weatherworn face.

***

Elsewhere—too little, too late...

Mason Steward, Mayor of Kendrick, member of the oldest and most respected family in Kendrick was drunk at six o'clock in the morning. It was not morning for him. He had not gone to bed. Ever since he felt his family's gift break, he had been trying to regain it. But the house and the city remained dead to him and every other blood member of his family. They had been cut off, and it was driving them all insane.

He tried again to feel the city, the grounds, the house, this room, and failed. He vented his frustration and fear on the glass in his hand. There was a brief moment of satisfaction as the lowball crystal glass shattered. It was the third one this evening. Then, his world came crashing down on him again. It was all gone.

"My, that was impressive."

The laughing female voice made him turn around. He took in the sight of the teal-haired teenage girl in a blood spattered corset and leather pants. She was wearing goggles on her head for some unknown reason.

"Are you the reason for this? Are you the thing that's come through?" He snarled and stumbled toward her with balled fists.

She waved a hand at him and he flew across the room to slam into the wall. "Temper, temper." She said as he crumpled to the ground. "You should treat us with a lot more respect." She walked over to him where he was rapidly becoming sober due to the adrenalin dumped into his system. She put a booted foot on his chest and leaned down. "I came to make you a deal. To be friendly with you. And this is what I get: a drunk man and insults." She reached out and straightened his tie for him before removing her foot. "But, if you don't want to, I'm sure others would be willing to play ball with me."

"Who are you?" He asked, straightening himself up as she sauntered around the room, pretending to look at the things on his wall. Her words and actions were far too old for someone who looked so young and innocent.

"You can call me Vicki or Victoria if you like, but I am so much more now. I am His will, His body, His form on this plane."

"The Children succeeded."

"Yes."

"Why take my birthright?"

"That's what I came to talk to you about. You can get it back—if you help me."

That stopped his rage but not his fear. He took his accustomed seat behind his desk. "I'm listening."

"I needed it. I needed the power. But, you can get it back if you help me deal with the others in this city. They need to be removed. Exiled or killed. I don't care which." She sat down on his desk next to him. "I'll tell you who and how and you execute the plan."

"What about your people?"

"They'll be busy."

"I can't help you without my birthright. I need it."

She smiled. It was a beautiful and cold smile. "Only after you've earned it."

"No. Now!" The words were out of his mouth before he could stop himself. He was used to being obeyed, and he hurt like a man suddenly gone blind.

Vicki had him by the throat before he saw her move. She slapped him twice, hard. "Never speak to me that way again."

Mason cringed, gasping for air. "I'm sorry. I'm sorry." He spit out and breathed easier as her hold loosened. "You don't understand what it's like. I'm blind. My whole family is insane with the loss of our birthright. My arm has been cut off and I'm bleeding to death." Her laughter stopped his babble.

"Of course I know what you're going through, *Father*. Why do you think I channeled all of the family's power into me?"

Mason was so surprised that he could not think of any words of denial. He just blinked at her in stupid confusion. *Father? I'm not her father.*

"Oh yes, daddy dearest, you are." She let go of his throat as she answered his thought. "You were just a horny man from Kendrick's most premiere family. My mother was older than you; that beautiful cougar in the bar that night just over fifteen years ago. She was your first affair, and you were exactly who you needed to be to produce... me."

Vicki got off the desk and walked around it to stand opposite him. "I've known all my life who I was supposed to be and what I was supposed to do. Of course, there was little we could do about my gender, but that didn't matter in the end. It was an asset. Only, to become who I am now, I had to give up my brother and now I have no one... but you."

"This isn't possible."

"It is, father dearest. It's very possible." She leaned down over the massive desk, her fingertips supporting her weight. "Now, are you going to welcome me into the family or not?"

KEYSTONES

Book Three of
The Karen Wilson Chronicles

Shades of Grey

TERRY AND BUZZ stared at the monumental task before them. The neighborhood block that had been re-zoned for a new luxury condo complex was surrounded on all sides by a ten-foot high fence of overgrown hedges. Within its center was supposed to be an empty lot. Not that anyone could actually see inside the green fence. Why it was surrounded by these hedges, neither construction worker could fathom, but both knew it was going to be one heck of a task clearing them out.

"Looks like a job for my trusty chainsaw." Buzz pet his chainsaw as if it were a living thing.

"Yep." Terry nodded from his truck. He didn't want to mention it to his partner, but he felt there was something sacrilegious about ripping down such pretty greenery to put up apartments. Too many times in the last few months, they'd had the unpleasant task of destroying lush foliage in the name of new real estate. "I'm sorry," he whispered to the hedge as Buzz pulled out his chainsaw and began to put it to use.

The buzzing racket of the chainsaw abruptly stopped as its wielder stepped back, cussing up a blue streak that ended with "—Mother pussbucket! There's blackberry vines all through those things." Buzz mopped a couple of deep, bloody scratches on his arm. "They're totally camouflaged. Got me good."

Terry looked closer at the hedges. Suddenly he could see the thorny vines woven throughout the tall barrier. He wondered how he could have missed seeing such wicked barbs. "Guess we're gonna have to use the backhoe on this one."

"Yeah. You're up."

Terry called on the radio back to home base. "Yo, boss! It's Terry over at the 12th and White construction site. Over."

"I got ya. Over."

"Dude, we're gonna need the backhoe. This stuff is all hedges and blackberry vines. No way a chainsaw's gonna do it. Over."

"Copy that," the radio squawked. "Abe'll be over with Betsy within the hour. Hang tight. Over."

"Copy. Over and out." Terry put the radio down and looked at the hedge again. If he didn't know better, he would have sworn the hedge had gotten even taller since they arrived. It seemed to be at least twelve feet tall now and fairly bristled with thorns. "This is gonna be one hell of a fight," he muttered.

***

Inside the protective hedge, the Lady of the Grey Manor and her seneschal, James, stood in the gazebo, watching the hedge under siege. He stood dutifully at her side, waiting for her orders. She had not said anything since she arrived, and the construction workers had begun their attack on her home. She remained silent, appearing to look at nothing.

James knew appearances could be deceiving, however. "Lady...?" he asked, hoping there was something he could do to help.

"No, James. There's nothing you can do. I don't know if there is anything I can do. Two of my other Sanctuaries have been destroyed. It is not coincidence. We are targeted." Her voice was serene, but tired.

He did not like how tired she sounded, or how weary she looked. The loss of her Sanctuaries hurt her—physically and mentally. They both knew it. "What of our allies?"

She nodded, a slow, reluctant nod. "I hate to admit it, but we need help. I cannot stand alone. Walks-the-Ocean owes me. It seems he will start paying on that debt sooner than either of us thought." She stood with careful poise and paused as the sound of a large vehicle approached. "Prepare the Grey Manor for transport."

"Yes, Lady." He watched her walk up the stone pathway into the manor house. For a moment, he pondered the house, now no bigger than a cottage with the recent losses to the Lady. Then he made a decision. "Theodore, Theodora, Thomas, and Thomasina," he called.

Almost immediately, two sets of fraternal twins, one set with dark hair and one set with blond hair, appeared. All of them looked about nine years old, but they were all far older. They were almost as old as James himself, and he had seen the beginnings of the rustic town called Kendrick. Each child wore a solemn expression, and their eyes told the tale of decades gone by.

"We are under attack. Someone is trying to harm the Lady, and they are succeeding. I know you all have felt it. We need to find out who and why. Theodore and Theodora, find Karen Wilson and speak to her. Thomas and Thomasina, go to the places of power in the city and find out what you can about why they are building so much on places that are green. We need information. We need help."

Unlike their usual talkative selves, the two sets of twins merely looked at each other, then at James, and nodded before disappearing in the blink of an eye.

***

Karen stood in her living room. Across from her, on the pedestal of one of her surround sound speakers, was a small bust of Colonel Kendrick. Over the last two months, Karen had taken to talking to the bust when she wanted to talk to Reginald. By agreement, Reginald would reply out of the speaker underneath. It was stupid, but it made Reginald that much more real to her, and also allowed her to do other things while speaking with him. Also by agreement, Karen started wearing her Bluetooth phone earpiece when she was out of the house, and Reginald would speak to her through it. It had been more than two years since Reginald had chosen Karen as his representative, and though they still had bumps in their relationship, they had learned how to work with each other.

"Wait, so, the Steward family has always been your, well, babysitters?" Karen glanced at the bust as she dusted.

"*Caretakers. Not babysitters. A city needs a lot of help to run well. Trash doesn't pick itself up. Traffic lights don't decide when to switch on their own. People need to do those sorts of things. The Stewards were Colonel Kendrick's manservant, cook, and stable master when he broke ground on the city that bears his name. As a reward for loyally serving the Colonel in life and for accepting the native people, I gave their family the ability to understand that I was alive and to feel me. Ever since, they have been a part of the city, and I, a part of them,*" The speaker's voice was cultured and melodic, like someone who learned to speak by listening to the radio.

"Huh. That's why so many of them have gone into local government, but not more."

"*Yes. They've been taking care of me.*"

"So, what's the problem again?"

"*They're not responding to me as they once did. They don't seem to see me or feel me anymore. A lot of them have been sick. The only one who still does is Julie, but she's different. She's part of me now.*"

Karen frowned as she thought about his words. "I'll bet the ritual the Children performed had something to do with it. This has been going on for how long?"

"I noticed it around Thanksgiving. Then, I started paying more attention to them. Probably sooner than that."

"What made you notice?"

"Around the holidays, I give gifts to my favorites. Homeless people will find blankets and food. Other people will have extra money in their coat pockets. The Stewards receive gifts as well, but they have to find them. I leave them in random places around their homes, work, and cars. Not one has found a single gift I've left, and I've left a lot." He paused. *"Either they don't feel me anymore, or they're ignoring me."* The hurt and confusion in his voice was plain.

"Scratch the ignoring part. You're damn impossible to ignore," Karen said as she walked to the hall closet. The door opened on its own for her and closed after she put away the dusting spray and cloth. She turned towards the bust. "Okay, what do you want me to do?"

"Find out what's wrong with the Stewards. Help them if you can. I need them... and I fear for them."

Karen nodded. "Okay. I'll figure it out if I can."

***

"Tell me again why we're patrolling the woods in the middle of the day." Sergeant Webber, the newest member of the Kendrick Police Special Unit, pushed at branches that tried to poke out his eyes.

"Because this is where the highest concentration of supernatural activity supposedly occurs during this time of the year." Sergeant Mueller pulled a branch out of his way as they tromped through the forested area of the Lakes district.

"This time of year?"

"Yeah. Solstice, New Year's, Twelfth Night, that sort of thing. Anything people can hang a ritual on. As long as we patrol, we can either prevent the rituals from happening, or catch them in the act. Every person we find out here is to be questioned and, if there's probable cause, detained."

"I'm not one to question supernatural activity. One encounter with an evil ghost was enough to convince me. But, aren't rituals done around this time of year supposed to be about greeting the sun and welcoming back the warm weather and such?"

Sergeant Mueller shrugged. "I just go where the Doctor tells me to."

"That's another question, why is Doc Mercer running the SU now? I thought we reported only to the Mayor."

"Because Mayor Steward has me reporting to Doctor Mercer for now while he deals with other things." Detective David Hauberk, the team leader of the Special Unit broke in, startling both men. "If you two gentlemen are finished with your little chat, do you think we could move a bit faster? I don't want to be out here after dark, and I don't want to report to the Doc that we didn't finish our patrol."

"*Yes, sir,*" both men replied in a hurry as they continued onward.

David stood and watched the officers leave until they were out of sight. Then he looked off to his left and waved at someone to come out. Juliet and Thomas, both from the Bacchanalia Coven, stepped forward from their hiding spot. "You two should be fine. Go back the way we came in. You need to put the word out that these woods aren't safe for rituals anymore."

"Why are you helping us?" Juliet looked around nervously, clutching a bag of ritual implements. "Not that we're not grateful."

"Because something's wrong with what we're doing, and until I can fix it, this is the only way I can help. If we catch you guys in here, you'll be arrested. I can't stop that. So, go now."

Juliet and Thomas looked at each other, hefted their bags over their shoulders, and took off the way David pointing.

He sighed. He really needed to talk to the Mayor about Doctor Mercer. Things were getting out of hand. The patrols, the arrests of innocent civilians. Since the Mayor didn't have time to even accept an appointment from him, he was just going to have to drop by and make him make time.

***

Karen and John sat next to each other on the couch in his apartment above his shop. He listened as Karen explained Reginald's problem, frowning slightly. "This all makes so much more sense now. I didn't understand what Mason was talking about when he tried to warn me."

She tilted her head. "Warn you about what?"

John put his glass of wine down. "He said a change was coming, and unless we saved the Abbot, he wouldn't be able to help us at all. He kept saying his family and Kendrick would be in danger. He also told me that his family was intimately connected to the land of Kendrick. They can feel when magic has touched a place or person."

"So, the ritual the Children of Anu did in October severed this connection?"

"Yes. He likened the possible loss to me losing my Todari collection. I can't imagine the pain they've been in. Now, the Master of the City has noticed that his city is no longer being cared for in the manner in which he is accustomed."

"Yes." Karen let the little lie slip out of her mouth. Essentially, what John said was true. He still hadn't caught on to the fact that Reginald, the Master of the City, was the city of Kendrick itself. She didn't blame him. It took her more than a year of working with Reginald to figure it out. Even then, she almost didn't believe it. Eventually, she would tell John the truth. Just not now. It would distract him from her current mission. After a moment, she added, "I didn't know you spent time with Mayor Steward."

He shrugged. "Occasionally I consult with him on matters involving antiques and, sometimes, their supposed supernatural powers." John let the little lie of omission go, knowing that he could not adequately explain that he used the Mayor as an information source with information as payment. It would pull Karen away from her request for help.

"Okay." Karen nodded, distracted. "Maybe you should talk to him again. See if he knows how to help his family. We can get others to help, too. Maybe." Suddenly, she looked up. "Do you think more than the Stewards were affected by the ritual?"

John frowned. "I don't know. We'll have to ask around. But, we may not get truthful answers. People don't like to talk about being vulnerable. Especially in the supernatural community."

***

Elsewhere...

"I've done as you asked. I've re-zoned the specific areas from parks and forestland into apartment complexes for low income housing and the vacant lot on 12th and White to luxury condominiums." Mason spoke to the teal-haired teenager sitting on his desk, filing her nails. "Now give me back my family's gift."

She laughed a sound of pure amusement. "Yes, you've re-zoned and all, but until all of those places are torn down and the construction fully underway... no. Your part is not done. 12th and White is giving your crews some trouble."

He was exhausted and still heart sore from having his family's gift so abruptly stripped from him. Every member of his blood kin in Kendrick was hurting. "Vicki, I've done everything you've asked. Please."

"You don't seem to understand, Daddy-dearest. I cannot get the power I need from the land until that lot is destroyed. Until I get it, you don't get your gift back. Neither does any other member of the Steward family. And I think you should press the construction crew... your kids aren't looking so good."

"Bitch!" Even though he spat the word out as if he would slap her, he did not move.

"Awww. No punch? No attempt to throttle me? I think the fight's going out of you. So sad. I haven't thrown you across the room in over a week." She put her nail file down and focused on him.

He took a breath and did nothing. Since Vicki had taken control, he'd come to understood that rabbit with the electrified floor experiment he read about in college. Eventually, the rabbit quit jumping to the other side of the line, figuring that, as before, the floor there would still be electrified. It just sat there, shaking in pain, with the electricity running through it. As he looked up at Vicki and the thing possessing the girl whom he had recently learned was his long-lost daughter, he wondered if he had dull, rabbit eyes as well.

Before Vicki could do anything, there were three short, hard raps on his office door. The person knocking did not wait for permission to come in. It was Detective David Hauberk. He paused as he saw Vicki sitting on the Mayor's desk. "Sorry to barge in. I have a matter of some importance." He paused, looking at Vicki. "If you have the time, that is."

"Yes, yes. Of course, Detective. I was just speaking with my daughter, Victoria. We were discussing the future, but I think we have it all settled now. Don't we, Vicki?" Mason looked at the girl who was both daughter and demon to him and silently prayed she would go along.

She hopped down. "Yes, Father. We do." She turned and smiled at David. The smile was not pleasant. Feral and challenging. "Don't keep him too long. He's got to give me a ride home."

"I won't." David made a mental note to figure out where he knew her from. He watched her leave and shut the office door before turning to Mason. "Are you all right, sir? You look tired, if you don't mind me saying so."

Mason waved a dismissive hand. "It's fine. Children can be... trying at times. What do you need?"

David sat down across from the Mayor and took a breath. "I need to talk to you about Doctor Mercer and how he's running the Special Unit. I have some... concerns."

Broken

TERRY AND BUZZ looked around at the vacant lot. It had taken them a week beyond their scheduled time to finally defeat the monstrous hedge surrounding this block. By the time they were done, Terry was certain that the hedge had been sentient, and fought back as best it could against man and machine. In the end, it felt like he had murdered the plant, rather than simply done his job. It hurt, and he didn't know why.

"That was a hard job well done," Buzz said.

"Yeah." Terry agreed automatically, his eyes roaming the bare ground for signs of the hedge suddenly sprouting from the earth and growing back before their eyes. Part of him wished it would. *If it does,* he thought, *I'm not pulling it down again. I can't. I'll walk off the job. I don't care what anyone says.*

His thoughts were interrupted before they could spin out of control. The sound of Betsy starting up blocked out everything else. He watched as Abe drove the giant machine to the middle of the open lot and broke ground. The wound in the wet earth brought to mind torn, bleeding flesh so vividly that Terry had to look away before he threw up.

By the time he got his composure back, he'd decided he was getting out of the construction business and into the gardening business. *Open that little garden store like Margaret always wanted*, he thought with firm determination. He didn't know why, but these last few jobs had taken root in his brain, and he could not shake the idea that what he had been doing—that what they all had been doing—was wrong on a fundamental level.

***

"Can we talk?"

Karen was contemplating another of Kahili Coffee House's fabulous mochas when an unwelcome voice interrupted her internal debate of the benefits of yummy coffee versus the drawbacks of too much caffeine. She looked up at Corelli and didn't say a word. She could not think of anything to say that was not inexcusably rude.

Taking her silence as assent, Corelli slid into the chair across from Karen, her words came in a rush. "I'm sorry I had to do what I did, but I wouldn't have hurt Sebastian for the world, and in the end, it was better for both of us. Now, neither of us owes anyone anything."

Karen, her emotions and thoughts in a jumble, still did not say anything. She put some effort into not simply reaching across the table and smacking the girl. It was unfair of her to blame Corelli because they weren't able to save the Abbot from the horrific sacrifice by the Children of Anu. Part of her knew it. The other part of her silently railed at the girl for stopping Karen from using her own resources to look for the Abbot and threatening Sebastian to do it.

"Please. I'm sorry I had to do it, but it had to be done. I don't know how else to make up for it."

Karen finally found her voice. "You can leave."

"Karen, please. That's not going to solve..."

"You and all of the Order. I want you gone."

That got Corelli's attention. Suddenly, gone was the girl trying to make up to Karen. In her place sat the Second in Command and the Mistress of Magic in the Order of the Sacred Eye. "That's not going to happen. The Order belongs here as much as you do."

"You wanted to know what you could do for me? Well, now you know." Karen began gathering her stuff.

"You and Kendrick need the Order. It would be foolish to throw away such good allies."

"Allies?" Karen looked like Corelli had slapped her. "What makes you think you all are allies to me and mine?"

"Look at all we've done in the last year to help—"

Karen was no longer listening. "Allies don't try to sacrifice people. Allies don't blindly follow some rule that no one knows where it came from. Allies don't cut deals with the enemy. Allies don't stop you from using your powers to try to save an old man's life and allies sure as hell don't threaten to take someone like Sebastian away from me." Her voice came out in even and low, hiding the fury within.

"But—"

Karen stood, cutting off all of Corelli's protests. "I don't want to hear your explanations. I'm sure you've rationalized them to death—just like your predecessors did before they tried to murder me. I don't want to hear from you or your Order again." She turned and stalked away from the table and out the door without giving the other woman another chance to explain.

Corelli sat there, stunned and hurt. She pressed her lips together. *If that's the way you want it, Karen, you got it. The Order will neither help nor hinder you in the future.*

***

Doctor Mercer sat behind his desk in his office, focused on the person in front of him. Instead of the usual arrogant attitude that he unconsciously took with his patients to establish his authority over them, his head was slightly bowed, his eyes not quite meeting the gaze of the person opposite him. "Everything's going as planned. Our sweeps of the forest made sure that no rituals could be completed. We detained ten people and arrested three of them for possession of illegal substances."

"Cool. Well, those sweeps can stop now. The Lady of the Grey Manor is no more." Vicki smiled with satisfaction. "Her last sanctuary fell this morning. It's on to bigger and better things now." She stretched like a well-fed cat.

"Of course," the doctor said. "Hail Anu."

She sat up straight in an instant. "You aren't one of my Children, but if you're going to say that, you better damn sure mean it!"

Doctor Mercer recoiled from the look on Vicki's face that was not entirely her own. "I'm sorry. No disrespect intended."

She snorted. "Don't ever forget who put you where you are now, *Doctor.*" The last bit came out as a sneer.

He sat up straighter. "I won't. We have a deal. I stand by my word."

"See that you do."

After an uncomfortable pause, Doctor Mercer prompted, "Bigger and better fish to fry?"

She nodded. "The Grey Lady, if not dead, is as good as dead, and is no more threat or use to me now that I have her power. She was of the land. Now, it's time to shift our focus to something a little more city based."

"The Bacchanalia Coven?"

Vicki shook her head, teal hair waving around her pale face. "No—they'll come in time. I'm looking at something older and much more powerful. The silent but deadly gargoyles. They've been a thorn in my side for too long. They stopped me once before in another life. I cannot allow that to happen again. Besides, their power is old and deep."

"Abominations," he muttered.

Ignoring the doctor's comment, Vicki continued on. "I'll speak to Mason about the new threat focus to the city. It's time for the Special Unit to turn its attention from the forests to the city and high places. They move mostly at night when they are near invisible. They stay only within the city proper where the tallest buildings are. That is where the Special Unit will have to start concentrating their sweeps."

"I'm assuming that there won't be any arrests?"

"Oh, there might be. Some gargoyles bond to humans. Use that to control both of them."

"And if they aren't?"

The girl shrugged. "Use stuff that destroys concrete. Also, when you find their dens, close them. Cut the gargoyles off from their homes. That'll weaken them."

He nodded. "How will that deal with them as a whole and transfer their power to you?"

"Leave that to me, Doctor. You've got enough to worry about as is." She stood. "After all, I wouldn't want you getting distracted now that we've got such a good working relationship going."

"Of course." He stood as well.

"Keep me informed," Vicki turned and left without waiting for his response.

Doctor Mercer frowned as he watched her go. "Abomination," he whispered at her retreating back.

***

He arrived at the converted train station on the western end of Kendrick with little fanfare and looking much different than when he'd left. Gone were the multicolored dreadlocks, dramatic makeup, and face piercings. In their place stood a clean-cut young man with short, blond hair. All evidence of his alternate life had vanished.

He paid the taxi driver, gave him a small tip, and turned to look at his former, and once again, home. On the outside, it was perpetually under renovation. Scaffoldings 'supported' parts of the building while signs of continuing improvement were everywhere. In fact, they'd begun a new wall that would eventually encircle the grounds, giving them more of the privacy, protection, and solitude they needed.

Smiling at the workmanship on the nascent wall, he knew that on the inside of this beautiful brick building, the renovations had been completed for years. It was austere but sound. The former train station had easily transformed into a serviceable monastery. He walked towards the entrance but Brother Jeffrey, who must have been watching for him, was already coming out to greet him.

"Welcome home, Abbot Peter. Welcome home." Brother Jeffrey extended his hand.

The man called Abbot Peter took the monk's hand and shook it. "Please, we're all brothers in spirit here. I prefer the title of 'Brother'..." He paused and chose his next words carefully. "Also, I am still Simon within these walls. Until I have earned the right to lead you all in the same way my predecessor did, I will keep my apprentice name. It is only proper and fitting."

Brother Jeffrey nodded slowly, gauging the man who now led the fight against the malevolent spirits that had murdered the former Abbot. He had grown in several ways since they had last met. That much was clear. "Yes... Brother Simon. I'll let the others know. We have prepared a small celebration for your return."

"Thank you." He smiled and then asked. "Do you have the report on the current state of Kendrick ready?"

"Yes, Brother. It's on your desk."

Simon nodded. "Does it include the current information on Karen Wilson?"

Again, the monk nodded. "It does."

"Thank you." He smiled. "Let's go in and enjoy this small celebration you all have planned for me." The man soon to be called Abbot Peter, now called Brother Simon, was also known by another name. One Karen Wilson knew well—Aaron Patterson. He just hoped she would be happy to see him. They hadn't parted on the best of terms. The feelings between them were complex and deep.

***

Chief Walks-the-Ocean sat on his porch, looking very somber. He seemed to have aged decades in the last couple of months. Already the council was starting to look more to his second for decisions. No one understood the sudden decline of their leader, but they all understood that he was carrying a very heavy burden that he would only share when he was ready.

Lumbering Bear, a huge man, his second, and a member of his tribe, walked up on silent feet and stood before

Chief Walks-the-Ocean. He waited patiently for his leader to acknowledge him. After a few moments, Chief Walks-the-Ocean lifted his head.

"I came," Lumbering Bear said.

"Thank you. I need you to find Speaks-for-the-City and deliver this message, 'The Grey Lady wishes to speak with her where Sparks-of-the-Moon fell.'"

Lumbering Bear nodded once, but did not leave.

"Is there something?"

"The people wish to know why you no longer walk the oceans as you once did."

Lumbering Bear's simple statement was like a physical blow to the old man. He reeled back a little before settling into an old man's stoop again. He opened his mouth to speak, then shut it. He thought about his words before he spoke. "I don't deserve the oceans, or the peace they give me."

Lumbering Bear, considered this, nodded once, then turned to his task. Chief Walks-the-Ocean watched him go before returning to his home. He walked through the neatly kept house to his bedroom. In his own bed lay the Grey Lady. "A message has been sent to Karen Wilson."

"The children have found out who ordered the destruction of my places of power. I am betrayed by one I thought incorruptible. I was wrong."

"Tell me?"

She turned her head, her face a mask of pain. "Now I understand why you did what you did... why you betrayed us. I forgive you for it. Because of it, you may be our only saving grace. You, with your protected lands as sanctuary, and Karen Wilson. You two may be Kendrick's only hope of surviving." She closed her eyes, as if the mere act of speaking was too much for her.

He nodded. "You and yours may stay on Makah land as long as you wish." It was the only thing he could say. It was poor repayment for their years of alliance and his understandable betrayal of the supernatural beings of the city of Kendrick, but it was all he had.

***

Elsewhere...

"Happy Valentines' Day, hon." John handed Karen a small, wrapped present. "I know I don't usually like these kinds of holidays, but somehow it's much better with you here."

Karen leaned over and kissed him. "Thank you so much. I hate to admit it but I'm such a girl sometimes when it comes to these things. I've totally bought into it. I love the chocolates and flowers." She turned and handed him a wrapped gift. "I got you one as well."

The two of them unwrapped their respective boxes and started laughing. The exact same cute teddy bear stared up at them from each box. Karen caught her breath first. "Oh my God! That's just too funny!"

John laughed as well. "I know. I know. But that's not all that's inside!"

Karen pulled out her new fabric friend and found a smaller box inside. Opening it, she caught her breath upon seeing the small silver circle pendant necklace within. "Oh, John. It's beautiful." She hugged and kissed him again. "Your box has more in it as well."

He grinned. "I know. I found the symphony tickets. Box seats, even. Perfect! I love it."

"I love you."

John grinned at her, "I love you, too, Karen. I really do."

Keystones

"DO NOT HIDE your face from me, Karen Wilson. I know how I look, but I cannot die. Not as you would understand death. I am not mortal," the Grey Lady said from the bed she lay in. "I, and all that are mine, can be forced away to sleep for a time against our will, but what is a few decades for those who live beyond time? The City and you, however, will feel our loss."

"I'm sorry." Karen shook her head and stuffed her hands into her pockets. "I don't mean to offend. It's just a little shocking."

"This is why I had you brought here. To see me like this. Do you see me?"

Karen looked at the once hearty and beautiful Lady of the Grey Manor; a woman who had returned to her something very important not too long ago. Instead of the handsome woman, full of vibrant elegance with a hint of mischievousness, an old woman with a balding, wrinkled head and only a few wisps of snow-white hair covering it, lay breathing what seemed to be her last breath with every rise and fall of her bony chest. The Lady's skin seemed paper thin, translucent where it wasn't covered in ugly, brown age spots. Her smiling face had become a mass of wrinkles and lines. Worst of all, those once clear, grey eyes had turned the murky color of a muddy street after a hard rain. "I see you, Lady. I see you very well."

"This is what threatens every supernatural group within the city of Kendrick. This draining of life and vitality will kill most of them. You must stop it. You must lead the people and find a way. Lead them through the coming fear. I, my people, cannot be saved now, but the others can. Look to your City. Look to your peers. You are the keystone of their salvation."

The Lady of the Grey Manor stopped speaking. The energy needed to get her message across had sapped the last of her strength. She looked at Chief Walks-the-Ocean and whispered, "Look for me in the Grey Pearls."

With that, the Grey Lady simply faded away. The blanket that covered her crumpled down, and only a slight impression of her body remained to dent the bed sheets.

"What happened?!" Karen turned to Walks-the-Ocean. "Where is she?"

"She has gone to the earth to rest and recuperate for now. She and her people will be safe on Makah land."

"Why? Why are they safe here and not anywhere else?" She tried to keep her fear and anger in check. "What makes this place so special?"

"The land cares for its people and its people care for the land. She will recover. Sooner, if you can stop what is happening. I will help you if I can." The old man looked as sad as she had ever seen him.

Karen stared at him and wondered just how she was going to save the city and its people when she didn't know what was wrong with it. She had an idea of who was causing the problems, but that was all she had to go on. It had to be the Children of Anu.

They completed their horrific ritual and it gave them the means to continue their plans. Somehow, they were killing every other supernatural group in Kendrick. Karen knew they had to be stopped. She turned and left, not quite sure what to do, but knowing she had to do something.

***

"Come here, Daddy-dearest." Vicki said with a gleam in her eye. "I've got something for you."

Mason, one of the most powerful men in Kendrick, sighed softly and got up from behind his desk. He had seen his bastard daughter-cum-godling-avatar lock the door on her way into his office. Apparently, it was time for another lesson in patience or pain, or maybe she just wanted to torture him again. He walked over to stand next to her at the window. He said nothing and waited.

"Do you want that?" She pointed out the window.

Mason looked, seeking the thing Vicki pointed to. All he could see was Kendrick's City Center where the small shops and Colonel Kendrick's Park lay nestled together in perfect architectural harmony. He, himself, had made sure that the City Center promenade remained uncluttered by chain stores and overdevelopment. Only local businesses were allowed. It gave Kendrick its homey, small-town feel while serving the needs of its 55,000 residents. He looked back at her but she was no longer pointing. "I don't see—"

She waved an impatient hand, cutting him off, before gesturing to the view before him. "Do you want it all back? Do you want you and your family to regain your heritage?"

He felt his stomach drop and his knees weaken. Dare he hope that this monster would actually follow through with her word? Maybe. Hopefully. Just a week ago his youngest son had tried to commit suicide. He now lay in a hospital bed in a chemical coma. "Yes," he breathed, hoping against hope that he was not wrong.

She turned mean spirited eyes on him. "Kneel, Patriarch of the Steward Clan. Kneel before your ruler and beg."

Pride made him want to stand his ground, but thoughts of his loss and his family forced him to his knees. He swallowed that pride, as well as his hate for the thing his bastard daughter had become, and bowed his head. "Please, Victoria. Please, I beg you. Give us back our heritage."

She was silent for a long time, long enough to make him squirm and finally look up. Then she smiled. "I really just needed you to kneel because you're so much taller than me." Vicki leaned forward and kissed him full on the mouth.

Mason did not pull away. He did not respond until he felt the flow of power from her to him. For the first second, it was a trickle. Then it became a torrent. If he had not grasped her shoulder, he would have fallen over with the power of it. The power of the city, the heritage his family had been missing for months, flowed into and through him; from him to his entire family.

All of them felt the rush of the power's return just as they had felt it being ripped away. Some Stewards crumpled in a faint. Some fell to their knees in thankful prayer. Some danced for joy, and sought others of their clan in happy reunion. One opened his eyes to look upon the shining face of his mother and said, "I'm whole again."

In the office of the Kendrick's mayor, Vicki grinned at the openly weeping Mason. "You see, I can be kind to those who deserve it, and I do remember my promises. I have kept mine. Make sure you keep yours." She flipped her teal hair over her shoulder, unlocked the door, and left.

***

In the back storeroom of the Kendrick Museum of Art & History, Susan Moore spoke to something in the shadows. "Are you certain?" If anyone were to come upon her, they would think she was talking either to the huge statue in front of her, or to herself, because no one but her could hear Alexander's reply.

Alexander was the leader of the gargoyles in the city of Kendrick. He was old before Kendrick was born, but had been drawn here nonetheless. Standing about seven feet tall, he looked like the classic cathedral gargoyle with wings, had citrine gemstones for eyes, and was made of stone when he was not moving about. He was also bonded to Susan, and would sacrifice himself before allowing her to be hurt.

'I am certain. The youngest of us are the weakest, and thus at the most risk. They are also the first to fall when calamity strikes. This is not the first time something has attacked the gargoyles. It will not be the last. But it has been a long time. So far, the youngest have not died but they have returned to their most protected state.'

She put her hand on his arm, feeling the warm flesh and muscle beneath her fingers. "What can I do? I won't let someone just attack the gargoyles. I won't let you and yours be hurt."

He put a clawed hand over hers. *'Find out who is doing this. Find the Keystone that has been lost. It could be the link this attacker is using.'*

Susan nodded. "I will. I promise. I won't let you be hurt."

'I would be the last to die. While I live, the gargoyles will survive.'

"You will live!" She raised her head to keep the sudden fear from overwhelming her. "I *will* find a way."

***

The gargoyle roared, swiping wicked claws at the armored men. Moving as a team, the SU tactical squad continued to surround and hem in the creature that looked like a cross between a Great Dane and a griffon. Per the plan of attack, two armored men darted in, swinging steel batons. Every hit broke something inside the trapped gargoyle. As the two men backed off, the other three men fired upon it, keeping it pinned in the corner. They repeated this pattern several times. Finally, one armored man moved in and struck the cowering gargoyle in the head. The rest of the men gave a cheer as the gargoyle morphed into stone. After that, it was a matter of taking a sledgehammer and breaking the creature into tiny pieces.

"Did you see that monster? Did you see it?" Sergeant Webber's voice was a little shaky. "We dusted him like nobody's business."

"Good job, Sergeant," Detective David Hauberk nodded to him. "You're getting the hang of the team. Maybe we'll stop calling you Tenderfoot on the next mission."

Sergeant Webber held up a broken rock in the shape of a paw. "This is all that's left of him, Sir. I think I'll keep it as a souvenir."

David, who had been smiling, suddenly grew serious and shook his head. "No way, Tenderfoot, and with another fuck up like that you're going to be a Jack-Leg again before you know it." He held out his hand for the prize. "All pieces of supernatural creatures are to be destroyed immediately. Some supernatural creatures can regenerate from a piece of themselves as small as a finger. Or did you forget that part of your training, Sergeant?"

Sergeant Webber had the grace to look chagrined as he reluctantly handed over the piece of stone.

"Now, Tenderfoot. You get to explain what you did to the rest of the Special Unit, and they will decide your punishment. Or I will."

"Aww, Sir..."

"That's an order, Sergeant. Don't make me repeat it." David turned his back on the man. When he looked over his shoulder, he saw Sergeant Webber sheepishly explaining things to his peers and watched the wicked gleams appear in their eyes. He straightened up as Sergeant Mueller approached him. The two men put their backs to the rest.

"This is all I could save." Sergeant Mueller pulled three small gargoyle statuettes from various pockets. "These guys like the kill—a lot."

David accepted the gargoyles and slipped them into his pockets. "Were you able to save any of the bigger ones?"

He nodded. "One. I waved it away. It wanted to help the one that was being pummeled into dust but when I hissed at it, it went."

"Hissed?"

Sergeant Mueller shrugged. "It works with my kids and my cats."

"What are you guys whispering about back there?" Sergeant Webber called as he walked back to them.

David and Sergeant Mueller turned and grinned at him. "I was just showing him your little prize." David tossed the gargoyle paw in the air and caught it.

Sergeant Mueller's grin was wide and malicious. Webber was a perfect target for his anger at the gargoyle's massacre. "Talking about the other dumb shit newbies have done over the years. I was telling him what you should do to remember this lesson."

By now, the rest of the Special Unit had crowded around, listening and grinning. "Yeah, and since you seem to have a thing for feet...." David used the stone paw to point at his feet. "I think my boots need polishing. In fact, all of our boots need polishing."

This was greeted with a cheer from the rest of the Special Unit and a disbelieving look from Sergeant Webber. The doomed man groaned. "You're not kidding."

"Better make it good. Inspection in a week." Sergeant Mueller gave him a smirk.

David smirked as well. "Now, I'm going to properly dispose of this. I'll meet you all at the usual spot in an hour." Walking out, he waited until he was out of sight before he subtly slipped the rock paw in his pocket. He had no idea if gargoyles could re-grow from a single paw, but he would not throw it away. He would give it to Karen and hope she knew how to help these doomed creatures that seemed to die far more easily than he expected. This made him sad, especially knowing from Karen that gargoyles were actually the city's guardians.

***

Elsewhere...

Doctor Mercer watched Vicki with growing interest as he gave her his report. "One large and two medium-sized gargoyles have been destroyed in the last couple of days. They are reported to be easier to kill than expected. I suspect that you have something to do with that?"

Vicki sat curled up on the couch in Doctor Mercer's office. "Of course. It was a little thing for me to do once I found their weakness."

"Which is?"

"I found one of the city's keystones."

Doctor Mercer waited patiently for her to elaborate. When she did not, he prompted her. "Which is?"

"Oh, I forget, sometimes, that you don't know as much as me. A gargoyle keystone is, hmm, I guess you could say a piece of their original world. In every city that has gargoyles, there are at least two keystones. Most are buried deep underground, never to be disturbed. Some are in people's collections because they sense the power from it, but never really know what it is."

Vicki reached into her coat pocket and pulled something out. She got up and placed it on the doctor's desk so he could get a better look at it. In truth, there was not much to look at. It seemed to be a small, granite stone the shape and size of a large egg. There was a small crack in the top. From inside, something gleamed.

"May I?" he asked as he slowly reached for it, watching her face. She nodded. He picked up the stone, and looked at the crack but no longer saw the gleam. It perplexed him. As he turned it over, he saw the crack gleam again. Logic said that whatever the gleam was, you could not look at it directly. So, he looked forward and held the keystone out to the side. He could see the gleam clearly in his peripheral vision. It shimmered like rainbow hematite. "Where was this one?"

"Luke Coleman had it at his store, *Treasures & Trinkets.* I'm pretty sure he knew what it was, because he told me if anyone else had tried to buy it, he would have refused the sale. It was meant for me." She grinned. "Then he told me, 'Do your worst to those bastards.' He meant it. I'm not sure what the gargoyles did to him, but he carries a grudge. I wonder why he didn't use this to get revenge on them." Vicki gazed thoughtfully at Mercer. "You may want to have the SU check out his shop. Just to see what's there."

Doctor Mercer put the keystone down and nodded. "All right. Looking for anything in particular?"

"No. Just delivering the unspoken message that the SU knows he's there, and to stay out of our way."

"Okay. Anything else?"

Vicki nodded. "Yeah. That." She pointed to the keystone. "I need you to keep it very safe. Very, very safe. Can you do that?"

He almost tossed out a casual "of course I can" answer, but based on the way she was looking at him, his answer was important to her. He looked at the stone again. "Yes, Vicki. I have a very safe place in mind. A vault. Will that do?"

She nodded. "It will. This is a little secret between you and me. All right?"

"Yes. I understand." Doctor Mercer did not ask all of the questions that came to mind. Vicki didn't like 'unnecessary' questions, and he knew from experience that she was apt to hurt him if he asked too many of them. However, he could not help but wonder why neither the Steward mansion nor the Children's warehouse was safe for her little toy.

Observations

"I JUST WANTED you to know that you've been doing an excellent job." Doctor Mercer held the door as he and David walked out of Kahili Coffeehouse.

"Thank you, sir." David kept his professional mask up, though the thought of what he had been doing over the past few months—harassing people and murdering supernatural guardians—made him sick to his stomach. "I'm trying my best."

"I just thought I should let you know after your suspension. The SU praises as well as scolds."

"I appreciate that, sir."

"Well, I've got a busy day. Thank you for the walk to coffee and the informal chat. I'm sure you have much to do as well." Doctor Mercer adjusted his eyeglasses, gave David a nod and headed down the street towards his office.

David watched him go with guarded eyes until his view met a familiar face. Gone were the multicolored dreadlocks, make up, and face piercings. In their place was a clean-cut man with short, blond hair. Still, David knew him. Aaron Patterson. Member of the Brotherhood of Light and once a rival for Karen's affection. In the end, neither of them had won the girl.

***

Aaron's eyes flicked from David to Doctor Mercer and back several times. After Doctor Mercer passed the young man, Aaron turned to walk towards David, but paused as the cop gave him a sharp short hand wave of negation. He saw David's eyes also flick to the other man he had been speaking with. Those eyes were filled with guarded emotion. *Maybe he can see what I see.* Aaron frowned to himself. *Maybe he already knows.*

Aaron watched as David patted his pockets as if looking for something. He turned back to the coffeehouse—a place that Karen once loved to go... he wondered if she still did—and went inside. David paused as he went through the door, giving Aaron a significant look. *I hope that's an invitation because like it or not, I need to talk to that man about the company he keeps,* Aaron thought.

After checking the time and looking back toward where the man with the glasses had gone, Aaron walked to Kahili Coffeehouse and entered. After getting a cup of coffee, he turned and saw David was sitting at a corner table and watching him. Without preamble, Aaron walked over and sat across from him.

They were both tense, and the silence stretched out between them until David broke it. "When did you get back in town and does she know?"

"A couple days ago and, no, not yet. I..." He shrugged. "I haven't had time to give her a call." It was a lame answer, but the only one he had to give.

The silence fell again as they both drank their coffee. Time had healed some wounds, but the injuries still lay just beneath the surface, itching and tight. Aaron broke the silence this time. "Who was that man you were with?"

"Does it matter?"

David's defensiveness confused Aaron. He nodded. "It does."

"Why?"

Aaron mulled over his answer before saying, "Because I think you're in danger."

That surprised a laugh out of David, and once started, it took him a few moments to get back under control. The flash of irritation on Aaron's face forced out another bark of laughter before he said, "That's an understatement."

"So you know, then." Aaron was both relieved and disturbed by this thought.

"I think so, but why don't you tell me what you know."

He took another swig of coffee. "Your friend—"

"He is *not* my friend," David interrupted. "Doctor Mercer. Not my friend."

"Doctor Mercer is spirit-ridden. It's one of the biggest spirits I've seen in a long time, and *it* is hungry for blood." Aaron saw the surprised look on David's face. Whatever the detective had expected him to say, this wasn't it. Aaron realized he had just made David's problems that much more complex.

***

"Is Sebastian okay?" Susan asked as Karen opened the door to let her in.

"Yes. Why? What's wrong?" Karen stepped aside, letting Susan in.

"The gargoyles are being attacked. Alexander told me. Asked me to help." She looked around the apartment, looking for Sebastian. "The youngest ones get taken first. Are you sure he's okay?"

"Wait. Wait." Karen spoke to herself more than Susan. Only one person could panic at a time. That was her personal rule, and since Susan was clearly panicking, it was up to Karen to stay calm, cool, and collected. "Who's attacking the gargoyles? What's happening?" Mentally, she called to Sebastian, *'Hey, Thunderbutt, where are you?'* There was no immediate answer. *'Sebastian?'*

"It's like what happened to the Grey Lady and her kind. Something is stealing their power, their essence. The thing that makes them... them." Susan continued to look around. "We have to help them. We can't let them die."

"No one is going to die, Susan." Karen guided Susan to the couch to sit down as a stalling measure. Inside, she was shouting. *'Sebastian Wilson! You get your stony butt out here right now!'*

'What?' Came his querulous, sleepy thought. *'What? Danger? What?'*

Karen looked around the living room and spotted a very tired-looking Sebastian curled up in his favorite nook on the bookshelf. He had raised his head to look at them. "See, he's fine." She walked over to bookshelf and hauled him into her arms. "Not so little anymore." Sebastian had grown over the more than two years they had been together. He was now the size of a housecat.

Susan looked at Sebastian with haunted eyes. "Did you call for him?"

"Yes."

"Did he answer you immediately?"

Karen paused, not liking where this conversation was going. "No."

"Has he ever not immediately answered you?"

"Sometimes. When he's not here, or he's distracted."

Sebastian curled up in Karen's arms, resting his head on her shoulder. *'Sleepy.'* He told her and fell asleep again.

"But not normally."

She looked down at him. "No. Not normally. He's been sleeping more lately."

"Karen." Susan's voice was very gentle. It was clear that she had pulled herself together somewhat—perhaps in preparation for what she thought was Karen's impending panic. "Gargoyles sleep when they are sick or hurt. They sleep to heal. Sebastian is feeling the drain. He is suffering, just like

Alexander. He's not in as much danger as the youngest gargoyles—they've gone to stone—but..."

"Okay. I'm convinced. You don't need to drive a nail through it. I'd help you anyway. You don't have to..." *Threaten my Sebastian*, she didn't say. "I get it." Karen knew her voice was sharp, but she couldn't help it.

"I'm sorry. I didn't mean to. But, Karen, I've been bound to Alexander for more than half my life. If he... If anything happened to him, I would die. I don't think I'm exaggerating. Please. I'm sorry."

"Okay, already. What do we need to do?" Karen hugged her sleeping gargoyle with a fierce protectiveness.

"We need to find the gargoyle Keystone and stop whatever they are doing to it."

"What's a Keystone and who's they?"

Susan shook her head. "We don't know, yet. But we've got to find that Keystone. Alexander said it was the only thing that could help them now."

Karen thought for a minute. It had to be the Children of Anu again. She was sure they were responsible for what happened to the Grey Lady. But, all her searching around told her that the Children were staying very close to home these days.

***

John frowned at the brown paper package tied up with string on his back stoop. He did not know how long it had been there. Not more than a couple of days for certain. It was addressed to him, and his small bit of intuition told him he wasn't going to like what it contained, but he needed to open it.

Bringing it inside, he took it to his office and closed the door. In short order, the package was open and what he found made him frown more. It was from David Hauberk and the package was for Karen. The note on the top of the second package inside the first box said, *"This is for Karen. I didn't know how to get it to her without raising suspicions at my work. Please give it to her as soon as you can. I'm sorry to have to do things this way. ~David."*

John told himself that he was opening the second package before giving it to Karen for her protection. However, part of him knew it was a combination of protective suspicion and good old-fashioned curiosity. Within the second box, he found five small gargoyle statues and one stone paw. The note with this package was more disturbing.

"Karen, I don't know why we've switched from patrolling the woods and arresting people there to patrolling the city and dealing with gargoyles. These are the only gargoyles I could save. I'm not sure if they can regenerate but if they can, here's a piece of one. Things are very strange at the SU. I'm trying to get the department head to listen to me but, so far, he's been difficult to deal with. But, I think I'm getting through to him. I'm sorry. ~David."

John thought the small gargoyles looked a bit like the courier gargoyles but, in truth, he could not be certain that they were not just ordinary gargoyle figurines. He had wondered what would be attacked next now that the Grey Lady had gone to ground. He had not expected it to be the gargoyles of the city. But, in a way, it made a sick kind of sense. Attack the wild. Then attack the city. After that, attack that which is both. Pulling on one kind of power, then another.

He wondered if it was time to take matters into his own hands and have some sort of talk with Mason about his Special Unit and whoever was actually in charge now. He had tried to get an appointment with Mason last month to discuss matters of the city, but had been put off by the man's secretary. She had never put him off before. Obviously, something was amiss there, but he'd been too busy to deal with it at the time.

Looking back into the box, John knew he had to reorder his priorities again. With the gargoyles in trouble, Sebastian would be in trouble and Karen would be... forceful... in her actions. Not to mention the confusion of the ex-boyfriend who betrayed her now betraying his own people to try to protect the supernaturals of Kendrick. What a tangled web that man weaved.

First, he would call Karen and let her know he had something for her. Second, he would call Susan; she was the gargoyle expert in the area. Finally, he would have a cup of tea and think. It was time to figure out who was doing what, and to whom. That meant he would have to start snooping into the Children of Anu again, and that was something he was not looking forward to.

***

Mason sat in his daughter's home. Julie had been his youngest daughter until Victoria came along. Julie, like Vicki, was no longer precisely his biological daughter. According to family oracles (who were once again just that), Julie was dead and had died four years ago. Yet, here she was, sitting in front of him, drinking tea, and patiently waiting for him to start. Julie had ascended to a higher level of their family's heritage. Somehow, she had become part of the city of Kendrick. She was still his daughter. Also, she was something much more alien.

Just like Vicki.

He wondered if it was something in the Steward blood. Then, he shook his head. He was here with a purpose. He needed to get to it. "Did you lose touch with the city at all in the last half year?"

She frowned and shook her head. "No."

"But you are alive and part of..." He touched his breast.

"In a manner of speaking, yes. I live differently. You know that." She put her tea down. "I did lose touch with the family for a short time, but... I thought that was on purpose."

"Oh, honey. No." He shook his head. "No. That wasn't our doing. Not the Steward *family*." He paused. "But, it was the fault of one of us."

She didn't say anything.

Mason sighed. Julie had always been his quiet child, but she had become downright laconic ever since her transformation. "You have a younger sister. I didn't know she existed until recently. She... is dangerous. She did it."

This surprised Julie and made her curious. "What's her name?"

"Victoria Mordecai. She goes by Vicki. She's young, impetuous and possessed. It's the only thing I can think of to describe it. The thing possessing her used her bloodline to me to steal..." He paused. "No. That's done and gone. Old business and dealt with. What I need... I need you to talk to the city for me, for the family."

She frowned. "Why?" The subtext of '*why can't you do it?*' was there.

"Because I need definitive answers, not just generalities. We need this for the family, to figure out what to do now. My first loyalty is to the city, not Vicki. Certainly not in the state she's in. Now that we have our heritage back, I think we can do something about things but I need to know what the city wants."

"Wants with what? I'm not sure I understand."

"Is what Vicki is doing, eliminating the other supernatural groups, what the city wants? Will it help Kendrick to be free of supernatural influences? Like losing parasites growing fat on the body of the city. Or is it going to hurt Kendrick and ruin a symbiotic relationship? I need to know. Once I know, I will do whatever is necessary to do what the city wants—even the most drastic measures." Mason looked at her. "Please, Julie. Only through you can I be sure."

She nodded, looking troubled. "I will try. I think I understand. I'll let you know when I know something."

"Thank you." Mason stood. "I really do want to do what's best for Kendrick. Sometimes, that means I need to do things I don't want to do."

***

Karen sat in the gazebo of the Grey Lady's manor home. She looked down and saw a cup of dark liquid in her hand. She put it on the table in front of her with a clatter, then looked up at the Grey Lady. "You're dead."

"One such as I cannot die. Not in a way that you would understand." Her smile was gentle and sad. Her eyes were still a muddled brown instead of a clear grey. "I sleep. I dream."

"Am I dreaming?" She looked around and then at her own clothing. It looked like nothing she owned or had ever worn before. She wore a layered, high-collared gown in white and pale blue. The ensemble was completed with a pair of white gloves.

"You are. In a way." The lady looked away from her and out to the forest beyond the gazebo. "I am helping you."

"Why?" It did not feel like she was sleeping or dreaming. Yet, in a way, it did.

"Because we need your help. We are not dead, but we sleep. We do not want to. We are not meant to. Not right now. We need your help to wake us again."

Karen took off her gloves and placed them next to her plate. She touched the teacup with her fingertips. It was warm from the tea. She reached out to touch the cream boat. It was cold. Somehow, the contrasting temperature of the porcelain convinced her that what the Grey Lady was saying was true. "If I can, I will help."

"Beltane is coming. May Day. The first of May. It is the changing of the courts. It is a day of renewal from one court to the next. Unseelie to Seelie. It is an important day. Gather the believers. Let them celebrate and worship as they are meant to do. If enough believers gather and work together, they will be able to draw the power from the usurper and back to the earth. Back to me, and I may be able to wake. Not as I was before, but enough so that I may help and guide. Awake, I am an ally. Asleep, I am nothing."

"Beltane. Worship on Beltane. Find the believers and protect them enough to worship." Karen repeated. "I'll try. It won't be easy. They're attacking the gargoyles now. Killing them where they find them. Draining them of their power."

"Yes. I know. I will help you if I can." The Grey Lady was suddenly in front of her and they were both standing. "This is important, Karen. If I am awakened, I can be your ally. If not, I can be nothing to you except a dream. You must remember to do this. You must."

Karen was startled. "I will remember. I promise."

"Write it down when you wake up. Write whatever you need to write to remember this."

"I will." Then, she was falling through clouds. She woke as she tumbled through the air, shouting, "I'll remember! I'll remember!"

***

Elsewhere...

David, clad in nondescript black from head to toe, crept toward the back door of Doctor Mercer's office. He'd seen the sign on the property stating which alarm company was 'protecting' the location. He had experience with that particular company, and the monitoring company that watched the boards, and was very sure he could jimmy his way past them without a problem.

He smirked at the idea of him breaking the law. Even a month ago, if someone had told him that he would be doing this, breaking and entering and theft, he would have laughed at them. Now, it wasn't so funny, and it was all Aaron's fault. Damn the man for returning to Kendrick. Damn him for giving David the news that suddenly made the SU's activities make so much more sense.

"Doctor Mercer is spirit-ridden. It's one of the biggest spirits I've seen in a long time and it is hungry for blood." Aaron said. When he saw that David didn't know what that meant, he

explained, "In the Brotherhood of Light, our job is to keep spirits on the other side of the barrier. We don't always succeed. When we fail, a spirit, think of it like a demon, can float around freeform, causing havoc, or it can do what we consider 'riding a host.'

He paused, trying to put it in the simplest possible terms. "It's like possession. Only, the host, the person, doesn't know they are being ridden. It's still their own personality. But now, they're influenced to do what the spirit wants in order to gain it power. Your Doctor Mercer is spirit-ridden, and from what I can see, it is a very powerful spirit. A bad one that wants to cause the death of things."

"Doctor Mercer is having the... my group... eradicate harmful supernatural creatures." David had lied, not really wanting to admit to attempted genocide of the gargoyles of the city.

"That makes sense. It must be killing off the competition. More food and energy for it."

"Are you sure about this?"

Aaron nodded, "I am. I can see it. To me, it looks like a huge sack of blood with a tether to Doctor Mercer's head. I've always been able to see things. It's one of the reasons the Brotherhood took me in."

Now, David was breaking into Doctor Mercer's office to do what? Find proof of this spirit possession? No. To find out more about the man's plans. David paused, thinking, *This is insane. You're doing this because seeing Aaron has thrown you, and you're looking for a way to regain control. No. There's something here. I feel it. Mercer's not as smart as he thinks he is.*

David's pause to reconsider his actions saved him from discovery. Above, the light in the window went on and David crouched lower. He froze in place, listening as his training took over. After the sound of people moving around the room ceased, David carefully shifted to a position where he could look into the window without being seen. He was not surprised to see Doctor Mercer. He was, however, shocked to see the mayor's daughter, Victoria, with him. Again, he was struck by the sense of familiarity. He needed to know where he knew her from.

As David watched, his eyes trying to see the spirit attached to Mercer, he was surprised for the second time that evening. Mercer made a secret panel open in the wall across from the window. Inside was a tall, slender vault. With a clear view into the vault, David saw nothing but a single small pouch on one shelf. He crouched below the window as Mercer turned his back towards Victoria and, thus, toward him.

By the time David was able to look back inside, Mercer was studiously looking through some notes, obviously not seeing them, but obviously not wanting to stare at what the slender, pale girl was doing. She had the pouch cradled in her hands and seemed to be inhaling from it deeply, like a little girl with a bouquet of roses. For one brief instance, David was certain he saw something rise from the pouch and into Victoria's nose and mouth. In that one instant, her whole body seemed to pulse with a light you could not see but could feel.

He knew that something very wrong was going on here and it was very important for him to get away and tell someone. Who, he did not know. He would figure that out later.

May Day

KAREN...
I HAVE TO SLEEP NOW...
Karen...
I can't stay awake...
I'm sorry...
I tried...I really did...
Karen, I'm scared...
Karen, please!
Help me...

Karen woke up with a start, jerking half out of bed before she knew what she was doing. "Sebastian? Sebastian? Where are you?" She looked around and found him curled up in stone form on the pillow next to her head. One paw was outstretched, as if he had been reaching for her when the 'sleep' took him. She picked up the stone figure and cradled him to her belly. He was still alive. She could feel that much. For how long, she did not know.

As the waves of fear and worry radiated from her heart, her mind raced through what she could do. They settled on John and his healing Todari tarot card—the Four of Swords. It was the card of respite and long term healing. More importantly, it had healed Sebastian before. This time, it would keep him alive long enough for the Beltane ritual to be performed.

If John would give her the card again. Knowing his obsession with collecting the mystical card deck and its particular rules, it was a big if.

***

"Sergeant Mueller. I understand Detective Hauberk is unavailable at this time. Is that correct?" Doctor Mercer barked into the phone.

While the Sergeant winced, he kept his voice calm and steady. "Yes, sir. That is correct, sir."

"When will he be back?"

"I don't know, sir." He bit back what he wanted to say, *It wasn't my turn to watch him, sir.*

"Where is he?"

"I don't know, sir." Sergeant Mueller didn't like Mercer. Not in the least bit, and it gave him no small amount of pleasure to thwart the man.

Doctor Mercer heaved a sigh of annoyance at the phone. "What *do* you know, Sergeant?" He spat the man's title out like a threat.

"I know I'm second in command, sir, and should you need the SU for duty, I am the person you may talk to at this time. If the matter with Detective Hauberk is of a personal nature, I'll leave him a message, that it is urgent, that he get in touch with you ASAP."

Doctor Mercer made the effort to get control of his emotions. It was hard to do when a demi-god was breathing down your neck. "This is SU business."

Sergeant Mueller felt his stomach tighten. "Then I'm your man, sir. What can we do for you?"

"Are you aware of the significance of May 1st?"

"There are some things I know of it, such as the Christian celebration of May Day and dancing around the May pole; a celebration of spring," he ventured cautiously.

"Poppycock. It is a pagan holiday called Beltane. For some, it is the changing of the faerie courts from Winter to Spring, or Unseelie to Seelie. For others, it is a fertility rite and I'll have you know that that May pole those people dance around represents the male phallus. At the end of the rite, they partner up and have sex in the fields to ensure a fertile crop."

"Oh."

"'Oh.' indeed, Sergeant. This is the time for that ritual, and we cannot have that in Kendrick. Most of these rituals are performed outdoors in accordance to old pagan doctrine. Therefore, I am suspending the work on eradicating the gargoyles from the city and for the next five days, I want patrols through the woods, parks, and near the lake doubled. Day and night. These rituals cannot be allowed to be performed. They are to be stopped, and all participants arrested and held until May 5th."

Sergeant Mueller frowned. "On what charge?"

"That's up to you. Whatever you choose, but make it stick, and make sure we have files for all of these aberrations."

"Yes, sir. Is that all?"

"Yes. I'll expect daily reports, Sergeant. Make sure Detective Hauberk is aware of this."

"Roger that, sir." Sergeant Mueller looked at the phone once Doctor Mercer hung up. He had a bad feeling about this.

Also, he knew David wouldn't be happy about it either. The two of them would have their work cut out protecting the actually innocent citizens of Kendrick while arresting the truly dangerous ritual practitioners in the city who were doing harm.

***

Karen and John entered *Bacchanalia* together. He looked troubled, she looked worried. Their minds were on different things. Hers was on Sebastian, now living in a box at the *Teller's Fortune* with the healing tarot card. That had been John's compromise—he would take on Sebastian rather than give his precious Todari card away again. Karen understood. It hurt a little, but as long as Sebastian was safe, she would survive.

John was thinking about the mayor of the city, and the message he had received from the man's secretary. The message was that they needed to meet, but not at City Hall. He would be in touch soon. John didn't like the sound of this, but was glad that Mason had finally gotten to a point where they could talk. John needed to get his measure, though, before he could trust him again.

Juliet was speaking with Lamiel and Susan when Susan noticed the couple enter. She excused herself and walked over. "How's Sebastian?"

John and Karen exchanged a look. "He's gone to stone." Karen's voice was calm despite her internal panic. Somewhere, in the back of her mind, she was proud of this. "But John is helping him. He'll be okay."

Susan nodded. "Almost all the young gargoyles are stone now. We're doing our best to collect them before they're destroyed. The SU has declared war on the gargoyles of the city, and we don't know why."

"Most of the SU," Karen said, looking at John.

"Yes, most of them," Susan agreed.

"If we... you all... get your ritual off, we'll have more allies. I don't understand it, but this Beltane May Day ritual is going to help the Grey Lady."

"It's a faerie thing, I think. If I understand it, I'm guessing the Grey Lady is of the Fey. It makes sense in retrospect," John shrugged, took his glasses off, and began to clean them out of habit.

Susan nodded. "We have a plan. We just need a safe place. Juliet almost got arrested a couple months back for doing a ritual in the open. A cop let her and the rest go, but warned them not to get caught again."

"Why don't you see if the Makah will allow the ritual on their land? The Grey Lady said she's safe there."

Susan tilted her head. "I'll ask. I think the Bacchanalia Coven's beliefs are compatible with the Makah tribe." She walked over to Juliet and Lamiel to discuss the matter. John and Karen waited while she did so. Karen's heart sank when both Juliet and Lamiel shook their heads. Susan beckoned the couple over.

"We can't do our ritual on Makah land. It would be disrespectful to their beliefs," Lamiel shook her head again. "Also, there are no sacred places to me and mine there. It would lessen the power of the ritual, and from the dreams some of us have been having, if we want to help the Grey Lady and hers, we need all the power we can get."

"However..." Juliet tapped her chin thoughtfully. "There *is* a sacred place near Makah land. Near enough that should we be interrupted, we could claim it is Makah land. We would need someone from the Makah there to back us up. They wouldn't need to participate unless they wanted to." She paused. "It's near where that cop kept us from being caught by the rest of his team."

"Which cop?" Karen asked.

"Hauberk was his last name. I don't know him."

John and Karen exchanged a glance. "I do," she said. "That might be a better place. Will you allow us to be there?"

It was Juliet and Lamiel's turn to exchange a glance. "Only if you're there to support us," Lamiel answered.

"As the representative to the Master of the City, yes, I would be there to support you and yours," Karen straightened her shoulders and lifted her chin as she spoke.

"*I concur*," Reginald's voice murmured in her Bluetooth earpiece.

Lamiel smiled, "Then, as the Master of the City's representative, we would welcome you to our Beltane ritual."

Karen nodded. "I will lend what power I have. This city and its people must be protected from what is happening."

***

"I didn't understand why you put Doctor Mercer in charge of the Special Unit back then, and I still don't. I had bad feelings about having a civilian like him between the SU and the man who created the SU to protect Kendrick." David locked eyes with the mayor. Now that he had the man's attention, he was going all the way with this. "I don't really need to know what his deal is, but there are things about him that you must know."

Mason nodded, listening with polite concern. Inside, he was pleased David was here; the detective was an integral part of his plan to save Kendrick from what ailed it. "Such as?"

"Doctor Mercer is not his own man."

"Meaning...?"

David paused, choosing which bit of information to give the mayor first, "He's spirit-ridden. *Something* is possessing him. He doesn't know it."

Mason leaned forward. This was news to him. Then again, it had been months since he had spoken to the man in person. He had been so distracted with Vicki and the family. "How do you know this? Can you *see* it now?"

He shook his head. "No, sir. I can't *see* it at all. One of the Brotherhood of Light saw it and told me."

"Which one?"

David paused. "I'd rather not say."

"Why not?"

"Because of my other news. Your daughter, Victoria, has been seen with Doctor Mercer several times."

Mason nodded. "And you don't know if you can trust me now."

David did not respond.

Mason shook his head with a brief smile. "You're risking a lot to come to me with this."

"I think it's worth the risk, sir."

"You're right. Victoria has a lot to do with what's going on." He looked away from David. "You might say that she's in charge right now. There's little I can do about it." Then he looked back at David. "Or so I thought."

"How is she in charge? She's just a girl."

Mason smoothed his face into a neutral mask. "She is, as you might say, spirit-ridden, too. She is not exactly herself, and hasn't been since I became aware of her."

"I don't understand." David frowned, then suddenly remembered where he knew Victoria...Vicki...from. "The Children of Anu." He looked at Mason in wonder.

Mason nodded. "She is Victoria, the bastard daughter I never knew, and she is either Anu, or the avatar of Anu. I'm

not certain. She is powerful. That much I do know." He
paused. "But the city needs help, and here you are."

"What do you want me to do?" David wanted to believe
Mason was on his side and the side of right. He really did, but
he couldn't believe blindly. Not anymore.

The mayor heard the suspicion in the younger man's
voice and sighed. He had brought this on himself. "The city
wants me to help it by helping Karen Wilson. You're still in
contact with her?"

"I can contact her if needed, but Doctor Mercer forbade
it," David admitted, but didn't elaborate.

Mason waved his hand dismissing the idea of Doctor
Mercer. "I'm putting you between a rock and a hard place. I
know it and I want you to know it, too. You need to help Karen
with what she's doing while allaying the suspicions of Doctor
Mercer and your own team members. From the outside, you
need to appear to be as normal and loyal as ever. But you need
to help Karen with whatever she's doing. In the meantime, I
need to distract and confuse Vicki as much as possible. What
she's doing is destroying the city."

Status quo, in other words, David thought. "How do you
know this?"

Mason shrugged. "The city told me so. Now I'm telling
you. You'll have to start with saving the gargoyles. Though I'm
not sure how."

An image of Vicki with the stone from Doctor Mercer's
office safe flashed through his mind. "I'll figure out a way, sir."

"Good. We're both tied with one arm behind our backs
but together, we might just get out of this."

***

Sergeant John Mueller pressed the button on his
shoulder two-way radio. "Base, this is Charlie-Echo-Delta,
reporting in. Over."

"Copy that, Charlie-Echo-Delta. What's your status?
Over."

"Sectors Alpha-Alpha through Alpha-Delta clear. One
anomaly in sector Alpha-Echo. Over." Sergeant Mueller glanced
over his shoulder and into the glade hidden within the thick
forest of trees.

"Describe anomaly. Over"

"Old signs of previous ritual. I'm going to watch the area to make sure there are no repeat customers here tonight. Over."

"Do you want back-up, Sergeant? Over."

He shook his head. "No, sir. We're spread thin enough as is. If there's something I can't handle, I'll radio in. Over."

"Roger that. Over and out."

Sergeant Mueller turned back to the glade from his hidden vantage point. Within it stood a good sixteen to eighteen people. Most he was only passing familiar with from their records in the SU database. The rest he knew very well. In particular were Susan Moore, John Corso, and Karen Wilson.

David had called earlier and told him that they were circumventing Doctor Mercer to protect and assist Karen Wilson and her endeavors. David had also indicated that this order came from above him, which made things very interesting indeed. "I hope to God I'm on the right side in all this," he muttered as the ritual began.

Interestingly enough, an old man dressed in Makah traditional dress stood off to the side, watching the ritual as well. If he had it right, there were at least three supernatural groups working together on this one ritual. That meant it would be a big one. Part of him wished he could understand it all better.

While he scanned the glade from left to right, his heart gave a leap. The old man seemed to be looking right at him or his hiding spot. *That's not possible,* Sergeant Mueller thought. *There's no way he can see me.*

"Whoo?" inquired a soft voice from above.

Sergeant Mueller looked up and saw a small owl looking down at him. This was not the first time he had caught an owl watching him. Nor would it be the last. It seemed to be a habit these days.

"Whoo?" the owl asked again.

"I'm okay." Sergeant Mueller said, feeling silly talking to the bird. "Tell your boss man I'm here protecting the ritual. Tell him David sent me to protect Karen and what she's doing."

The owl looked away.

Sergeant Mueller looked back at the ritual going on in the glade. His eyes found the old Makah man again. He could have sworn that the old man nodded once in his direction before turning away.

Please, God, let me be on the right side. Please. I want to do what's right, Sergeant Mueller prayed with all his heart.

***

Elsewhere...

Mason and Vicki were in his study at the Steward estate. The rest of the family tended to stay away from Mason's strange bastard daughter. They could all sense something alien about her. This left her lonely when she decided to stay at the estate instead of the warehouse with the rest of the Children—who also treated her with respect, but kept her at arm's length. The sixteen-year-old girl within her despised being alone. But there seemed to be no other recourse.

At the moment, she and Mason were playing chess. It was his move. She knew she would checkmate him within five moves. It was no fun. He was not a very good chess player. Either that, or he was letting her win. That thought angered her. She needed no pyrrhic victories.

She turned to say something to him, but saw him watching her with a look she had not seen on his face before—one of speculation. "What?"

"I was wondering how the Children of Anu worship you. What offerings they make and such."

"Why?"

"Curiosity, I suppose. You're still my daughter, even if you're also the living embodiment of a god."

Vicki, about to snap back something about him becoming the Children's next sacrifice, was suddenly doubled over in pain. Something was wrong, very wrong. She felt power draining from her, weakening her. A low moan escaped her lips.

"Vicki?" Mason was standing now. "Are you all right?"

She straightened up and hid the pain the movement cost her. "Yeah, I'm fine. It's just cramps. I'm a woman, you know." Her voice was sharper than intended.

"Do you want me to get you some tea or something?" He seemed unsure of what to do.

She nodded. "Sure." She agreed only to get him out of her hair for the moment. She could not let him see that she was in actual pain. She waited until he left before sinking to the floor in a ball and pulling out her phone to call Doctor Mercer. Someone was asleep at the wheel, and it had better not be him.

Entropy

"I TOLD YOU to stop hovering!" Vicki shoved Mason away from her. He stumbled backwards a couple of steps before tripping over his own feet and landing hard on his butt. "It's a woman thing! Something you could never understand. A cramp is a cramp. Now leave me the hell alone!"

Mason slowly stood up, keeping his head down to hide his smile. By the time he lifted his face to her, it was an appropriate visage of worry and concern. "I'm still your father."

"You're nothing but a tool. You're my servant. Stop being so damned weak and leave me be. I've work to do."

He paused. "All right. I need to go into the office and get some city business done if you're sure."

She waved a dismissive hand at him, and he nodded before slinking out of his own den to head to work. As soon as he was out of Vicki's sight, he straightened up and headed towards the other wing of the estate where he had moved the rest of the family while Vicki was here. Cecelia was the first person he found. "I need you to inform the rest of the family that it's time they took a vacation. I don't care where they go, but they shouldn't stay here. Things are about to get bad again."

"How bad?" she was already looking around, calculating what she needed to take with her.

"Maybe killing an avatar of a god bad—or die trying." Mason was sincere in his answer.

Cecelia saw this and nodded. "We'll be nearby if you need to pull on power from us."

"Don't tell me where. The less I know, the less I can be forced to tell. In the meantime, I need to get to the office and deal with the mundane hell of city management."

"What of her?"

They both knew who she was talking about. "Leave her be. She's distracted. I want to keep her that way. I don't want her to know everyone is leaving."

Cecelia nodded again. She kissed Mason on the cheek. "Good luck."

***

Back in the den, Vicki grit her teeth as much in anger as pain. She pounded the floor with a suddenly weak fist. Power was being drawn from her, stolen as if by a thief in the night. It felt like someone was pulling barbed wire through her abdomen. She had to put a stop to it. Pulling power from the gargoyles would help. She needed to get to Doctor Mercer's office. She called Sam, her high priest within the Children of Anu, and gave him instructions.

***

"I see that your past will come back to both haunt and help you," the Grey Lady told Karen. "In fact, it will help all of us."

Karen shook her head. "I don't understand." Although the Grey Lady frequently frustrated her, Karen was happy to see her eyes clearing up. They still weren't the clear Grey of a river stone they used to be. Yet. But they were no longer muddy brown either.

"There are those in your past who seek to make amends. To do this, they will help us." The Grey Lady's face was marred by a frown. "It may come at a cost to them."

"Who?"

"That is not for me to say. Just know help is coming from unexpected quarters, and it is important for you to accept it, no matter what you feel at the time."

Karen sighed. "Would you answer if I asked you how you knew all this?"

"Would you answer any questions I had about the Master of the City?"

"No. I guess not." She gave the Grey Lady a wry smile. "Thank you for your advice."

"I do what I can. It is not as much as I wish it could be."

"It's enough."

"I must go. As well as I seem, I am barely what I used to be. The power is returning slowly, and the usurper is fighting me."

"Don't let us keep you." Karen and John watched as the Grey Lady faded from sight. "I don't know if I'll ever get used to that." She turned to John. "Do you know what she's going on about?"

"My guess is that David is going to come through for us on things."

"Which things?"

John shrugged. "I don't know. I know he's trying to fight his own people to help us now." He didn't continue with his own troubled thoughts on how easily David seemed to betray his own people in the name of what he considered 'good.'"

She nodded. "Let's see how Susan's doing. I know how I feel about Sebastian. I can't imagine what she's going through."

**

"There's a rock you want to steal from the spirit-ridden doctor. I get that part," Aaron sat back and watched David with a speculative eye. "But, I don't get why you need me there. I'm not against stealing in an effort to deal with the spirit-ridden, but what am I supposed to do? I have talents, but I'm not a thief."

"But you can *see* things, right? I don't know anything about this stone I want to take. I just know that it's very important to Vicki and to Doctor Mercer."

Aaron waited for more as David paused, seeming to consider his words. Finally, he prompted, "And?"

David looked at him. "And I'm pretty sure the stone is... ah... magical in some way. Vicki was inhaling something from it. I thought I saw something. I think. But, I don't really know what." He paused. "I don't really want to touch it. I think I need an expert in such matters."

"Me." Aaron nodded, understanding more.

"You." He looked at Aaron, his need naked in his eyes. He knew he was asking a lot from his former rival, but as circumstances allowed, Aaron was the only one he could trust with this and trust not to get hurt by it.

"All right. I can do that. I can also do more. But, I need to be prepared. I need to get some stuff from the monastery." Aaron saw the need and could not ignore it. This was part of his calling. "What do we do with the stone once we have it?"

"That's the hard part."

Aaron looked at him without understanding.

"We take it to Karen," David's quiet voice was full of reluctance and regret. "We give it to her. It's what my real boss wants. If she doesn't know what to do with it, the Master of the City will know."

**

Doctor Mercer stepped back from his office doorway after he opened it for Vicki. She looked like she was in a very foul mood. This made her dangerous to all around her. "Good evening."

"Whatever." She strode into the office. "I need in the safe."

He watched her as he closed and locked the door. She had the look of a person rigidly holding themselves under control by willpower alone. This was fascinating. He had never seen Vicki like this. He wanted to see more. "Are you all right?"

"Fine. Get me into that safe. Now!"

She kept her back to him, one hand clenched and unclenched. He thought he saw a slight tremble in it as well. That would explain why she wanted him to open the safe when she could do it herself. "Of course. I meant no disrespect, Great One. I was merely inquiring as to your health." He sidled to the right of her, going around her to get to the wall safe.

Her hand shot out and grabbed him by the throat. She swung him around, slamming him into the wall the safe was hidden behind. She was very close to him, on her toes to get in his face. "If I *ever* have to tell you to do something twice again, I'll rip you right out of your host and eat you myself."

Doctor Mercer's look of sudden, confused terror froze his face for a brief moment. Then he calmed and went limp. "I'm sorry. I won't make that mistake again. Let me open the safe for you." When she let him go, he turned to the wall, opened the secret panel, and unlocked the safe. He stood back from it without a word and turned away to look out the window in a polite gesture that was more for show than anything else.

Vicki took the bag the gargoyle's Keystone was in, opened it, and held the stone to her face. Instead of drawing the power from it in soft inhales of breath, Vicki opened her mouth and sucked as much of the stone's power down as she could at once. The power flowed into her, strengthening her and, for the moment, breaching the drain on her own power. She breathed a sigh of pure relief as the sharp, stabbing pains receded to a dull ache almost imperceptible by comparison.

"Better?" Doctor Mercer asked as he turned and watched her replace the Keystone within the safe.

She nodded. Amazing how good the absence of pain made one feel. "Better. But now we've got work to do."

"We?"

"Yes, my good doctor. You've always wanted to see a cult at work. Tonight's your chance."

***

John and Karen sat quietly in the back storage room in Kendrick's Museum of Art and History. They watched while Susan spoke quietly with Alexander and waited. Both knew what they would hear would not be good.

"*Be strong for her.*" Reginald said through Karen's Bluetooth earpiece. "*She will need to know that someone is still strong. I feel Alexander weakening. This attack on the gargoyles has taken a toll on me as well. They are partly of me, and I of them.*"

Karen nodded to Reginald, hoping he saw so she wouldn't have to answer. Her eyes were on Susan as the museum curator turned back to Karen and John. Both John and Karen stood.

"It's bad. The youngest of the gargoyles have dusted and almost all of the gargoyles are stone. There's only Alexander and a couple others. The eldest of them. We've gathered them all in the basement. It's their safe haven. I'll protect them, and Bacchanalia will as well."

"Only the Keystone will help?" John asked.

Susan nodded. "That's got to be our main priority. That's got to be it."

"What do we do when we get it?"

"Release the power within it. Or break it to break the connection between it and the gargoyles," Karen said. Both John and Susan looked at her. "What? It's what the Grey Lady said I should do. Reg... the Master of the City, concurs. So, that's what we do."

"Are you sure?" Susan asked. "The Grey Lady also said she'd be able to help the gargoyles when we helped her at Beltane. I don't see her doing anything!"

"Susan." John gestured to her. "Just because you don't see it doesn't mean it isn't happening."

"She's never lied to me." Karen refused to voice her own fears.

John and Susan exchanged a look.

"That I know of," Karen amended. "I've no reason not to trust her now, and we put a lot of effort into bringing her back instead of focusing the ritual to protect the gargoyles. I've got to trust her. You're not the only one who will lose something dear... It's time to go back to the Makah and get them to help us find the stone. I've talked to Walks-the-Oceans and—"

Karen didn't get a chance to finish her sentence. There was a loud, grinding noise in the back part of the large room where Alexander stood and Susan suddenly cried out, falling forward. John's quick reflexes caught Susan as she fell.

"Alexander. Get me to Alexander!" Susan curled in on herself.

John carried her over to where Alexander stood in statue form. She reached a hand out and touched his arm. "He's still alive. Barely. He's holding on. I'm giving him what I can. I don't think I can live without him." She looked up at Karen and John. "You've got to help us. Please."

"We will. I promise. Somehow, we will." Karen made the promise not knowing how she was going to fulfill it—yet. She had to, though. Otherwise, she would lose her best friend as well as Sebastian. Not to mention the supernatural ally she had in Susan and, through her, the gargoyles. Karen shied away from that selfish thought and tried to focus on how to find the Keystone.

"We should get you home," John started to pick her up again.

"No! I need to stay here with Alexander. Just... there's a cot in my office. Set it up next to him. I can't stand the thought of being away from him. Please."

John and Karen looked at each other. Karen nodded. "I'll get it for you."

***

David looked at his watch for the third time in two minutes. Once again he was in his generic, all black outfit. This time he had night vision binoculars, and had watched a bit of the exchange between Vicki and Doctor Mercer from the safety of the bushes behind the office building. It had surprised him when he saw the small teenager slam the man almost twice her size against the wall with what seemed to be no effort at all. He sighed and looked around, wondering if Aaron had stood him up.

As if in answer to his unspoken question, a voice to his immediate left said, "I'm right here." It was Aaron. "I said I wasn't a thief, but I do have some talents."

David made an effort to calm his suddenly rapidly beating heart. "You scared the crap out of me."

"Well, you did the same by bringing me here to see that." Aaron pointed at the office building as Vicki and Doctor Mercer drove away in his car, with a second car following them.

"What'd you see?" David was curious if more had gone on between the doctor and the girl than he had seen.

It had, of course, but Aaron did not speak to that. "It's a good thing you brought me. We'll have to help each other. You'll have to deal with the locks and alarms. I'll deal with everything else, including hiding us."

"From what?"

"Everything." Aaron eyes remained on the office building where random small spirits gathered, interested in the still spiritually glowing stone and the amount of power that had just been pulled to here through it. He pulled a short sword from his shoulder bag. "Let's go."

***

In the back end of a refurbished warehouse, three-dozen teenagers and young adults knelt in reverent prayer. Each worshipper wore a set of bull horns; either as part of a hat or sewn onto their clothing. Beyond that, their clothing and dress varied from homeless street kid to well-to-do but slumming "rough and tumble" weekend warrior. They chanted the names of their living god over and over.

"Anu...Marduk...Enlil...Bel...Victoria."

The object of their prayer was an altar and a throne. On the throne of wood and ivory sat their god in the form of a slender, teal-haired, teenage girl. Despite the incongruousness of this image, no one doubted whom they worshiped. They could all feel the power emanating from her.

The centerpiece of the altar was a set of bull's horns still attached to the top part of the animal's skull. Placed upright just before the skull and centered between the horns was an ancient, spiked mace, still stained with its latest victim's blood. Around this centerpiece were a myriad of other brutal, blunt weapons. All of them were also stained with the dark red-brown of dried blood.

When the forward center person stood, the rest immediately fell silent. He was a man of medium build with long, brown hair. He wore a crown with bull horns and a heavy cloak of bull hide. He raised both hands in the air, his palms facing the throne. "Great god Anu! Father of Heaven, creator of the stars, lord of the constellations, king of gods, spirits and demons, your Children have not forgotten you. The Children will never forget you. Your humble servant, Samuel Ridgefield, has gathered your believers here on this night to beg of you a sign, a sigil, a vision. In this year of your return, Great god Anu! Instruct us in your wisdom. Judge us worthy with this task. Tell us what we must do! We are your Children and your servants. Guide us in this holy year."

The high priest of the Children of Anu stopped speaking aloud but continued his prayer and plea to Anu for instruction and blessing in his mind, as did the rest of the congregation. They could all feel the presence of Anu growing within the body of the girl they once knew as the little sister of their former leader. They knew he was there, judging them, weighing them, finding them worthy or not. The next few moments would tell.

Both he and she found them worthy. How could they not? Victoria stood in modern day warrior's garb in the form of a leather buckled corset and suede jeans. "Children of Anu. My children. My chosen ones. Listen and listen well. It is time to take this city as is our rightful due. Powers are amassing to block us. Now is the time for blood. Now is the time to gather our strength before we join the final battle. Remember your prayers. Remember your sacraments. Remember my blessings. The weak, the un-chosen, and the meek shall fall before us as wheat before the scythe. Blood shall feed me and through me, you. Feed me, my Children. Feed me well!"

Her congregation and worshippers cheered her as one. They ran to the altar and took their chosen weapons. They gave Vicki another cheer with these bludgeoning weapons raised high. They knew what they were to do now. Now was the time of blood sacrifice, which would begin with the smallest of animals and work its way up to the holiest of them all—the human sacrifice.

Off to the side, Doctor Mercer watched all of this with both fascination and horror. Before his eyes, these people were being turned into abominations by their close contact with the avatar of Anu. If he had not promised fealty to the spirit within the girl, he would call the SU and have his people deal with this growing cult of abominations.

***

Elsewhere...

David and Aaron stood back-to-back in the middle of the ruins of Doctor Mercer's office. With the alarm system disabled, what happened here would forever be a mystery. All David could see were things moving that didn't normally move on their own. It was like being in the movie *Poltergeist*, and he did not like it.

"David, I never had a chance to ask you..." Aaron struck out with his now glowing sword and struck true as an inhuman sound of pain could be heard in both worlds. "Are you religious?"

"What? Yes." He had tucked the bag with the magic stone in it inside his bulletproof vest at Aaron's insistence. His gun was drawn, but he hadn't used it other than to knock away things flying at his head.

"For real? Are you a real believer?"

"What are you talking about? We need to get out of here!" They moved closer to the door that had been barred by invisible creatures.

"Just yes or no!" Aaron shouted as a computer monitor, already broken, flew past his head.

"Yes!"

"Then pray. But don't do it, if you don't really believe. But pray if you do. I'm going to try something."

David spared a glance at Aaron and nodded. The first prayer to come to mind was the common 'Our Father' prayer. He began to recite it under his breath. Then, the prayer to Saint Michael came to mind, and that one seemed to suit the situation much better. "Saint Michael the Archangel, defend us in battle. Be our defense against the wickedness and snares of the Devil. May God rebuke him, we humbly pray, and do thou, O Prince of the heavenly hosts, by the power of God, thrust into hell Satan, and all the evil spirits, who prowl about the world seeking the ruin of souls. Amen." By the time he was finished with his first recitation of the prayer, the attacks had all but stopped. He paused and looked around.

"Keep going," Aaron whispered.

David looked back and saw Aaron, with his own head bowed, on one knee with his sword point planted in the carpet. He nodded, stepping close enough to Aaron to put a hand on the man's shoulder. He began again and did not stop with 'Our

Father" and the prayer of Saint Michael. He added Psalm 23. This time, when he said "Amen." Aaron joined him.

Then all was quiet.

"What happened?" David asked.

"A little help from a higher power." Aaron said.

He nodded. "All right. Let's get out of here before they come back."

Aaron stood wearily. "They won't be coming back. I... we... sent them back where they belonged." Aaron looked him in the eye. "I think you and I have more to speak on once we finish dealing with Vicki and the Children of Anu."

David nodded again. "Maybe. But we need to get this stone to Karen as soon as possible."

Aaron smiled as they both limped out of the doctor's office. "This should be fun."

"You haven't told her you're back, have you?"

"No."

"You have a strange idea of fun."

The Past and the Present Collide

"HE'S SUPPOSED TO meet us here?" Karen looked around the *Teller's Fortune*, a place that had become her second home. At first glance, it looked like every other metaphysical store out there—crystals, rocks, and instruments adorned the walls, there was a section of books on all sorts of spiritual and psychic topics, and the center display case was filled with jewelry and part of John's Todari tarot collection. However, for those with eyes to see, there were pockets of power and real information here. At least, that was what John told her. She couldn't see anything more than what met the mundane eye.

John nodded. "David suggested the store because he thinks your place might still be under surveillance."

She nodded. "It might be. Sometimes, I see people in cars I think I recognize, but I'm usually too busy to really pay attention." She hesitated. "Do you really think he has what we need to help the gargoyles?"

He pulled out one of his Todari tarot cards and shrugged. "Maybe. Probably. He seems driven to help us." *Help you in order to make up for what he did to you,* John amended silently. "This will help me figure it out." He held the card out for her to see.

It was the Moon, number 18 in the major Arcana. As always, the vivid colors made her catch her breath. This card was of a crescent moon. Sitting on the inner curve of the crescent was a beautiful woman with long, flowing, dark hair and a diaphanous white gown. Below her, on the edge of a lake were two dogs howling and barking up at her as she looked off to the side, unconcerned. Crawling out of the lake from the other side appeared to be a lobster.

"Imagination, intuition, and dreams for you. But for one you love, bad luck may ensue. Unseen perils, possible woes. Deceptions abound with secret foes," John recited, gazing with rapt adoration at the object of his obsession.

Karen reached a hand out to stroke the card just once. Then she pulled away from it. She knew her lover's obsession. The mere fact that he let her touch it let her know just how much he trusted her. More than a year ago, he had given her one of his precious cards, the Four of Swords, to help heal Sebastian. It was the same card that was keeping him alive now.

"This card will tell you what to do with what David brings us tonight?"

A sharp rap on the back door interrupted the conversation. John and Karen exchanged a glance. He gestured for her to stay where she was as he slid the card into an inside pocket in his jacket. He walked to the back door and opened it. It was David, and he was not alone.

John paused and stared at the second man. "I know you."

Aaron nodded. "You do."

John's eyes widened, then narrowed a bit as he remembered where he knew that face from. He looked from David and Aaron and back again.

"It's a long story," David answered the unspoken question.

"No doubt," John opened the door wide for the two of them to come in. Then led them back to the main room where Karen waited.

***

Mason Steward listened with outward patience to the man he had put in charge of the Special Unit. The more he listened, the more he realized that Doctor Mercer acted as if he was the one in charge, and not the one taking orders. *That was how it was, wasn't it?* He thought. *Vicki insisted that I put another in charge while I dealt with her wants and there Doctor Mercer had been, SU psychiatrist with intimate knowledge of the SU and what they do. He had changed over the last half year, hadn't he? Almost an extreme version of himself.*

"Mister Mayor, are you listening?"

That tone of voice was a whip crack across his senses. "I'm sorry, Doctor Mercer. I was woolgathering."

Doctor Mercer pushed his glasses back up his nose. It was a gesture he made when he was irritated. "If you'd rather we met at another time, we could do that instead." *Instead of wasting my time,* was the implied end of that sentence.

"No. I'm sorry. Please go on with your report."

Doctor Mercer eyed him for a moment longer. "I'll start from the beginning again, but just give you the highlights. The gargoyles have all but been defeated. They will trouble this city no more. We're still having problems with the cultists. Most of them seem to have moved out of the woods and back into the city to do their destructive rituals in the safety of clubs where they do even more harm."

Mason nodded in a non-committal manner.

"I recommend that we shut down all of the nightclubs of the city."

"I think my constituents would protest such an action, Doctor." He kept his voice mild and amused at such an outrageous suggestion.

Doctor Mercer suppressed a long suffering sigh, "You don't just 'shut them down,' Mason. You put in a new ordinance that requires that all nightclubs go through a new set of inspections. If they pass, they're fine. If they don't, they're shut down until they can pass."

"I suppose you already have a list of suspect sites that will immediately fail this inspection?"

"I think you fail to see the gravity of the situation here, Mayor Steward. These cultists have moved back into the city. They are doing their harmful rituals in and among the blissfully ignorant mundane citizens."

Mason suppressed the acid comment of, 'And whose fault is that?' He nodded instead, knowing that right now he had to go along to make sure that neither Vicki nor the Doctor knew he was his own man once more. "All right, Doctor. Let me see this list. Do you have the ordinance you want me to push through the counsel and the list of special inspectors?"

Doctor Mercer's smile was smug and arrogant. "In fact, I do. I knew you'd be too busy to deal with it. I like being a valuable member of your staff."

"Of course."

He dug into his briefcase and came up with a plain manila folder. The tab read, "Mold Hazard" on it. He put the file on the desk between himself and Mason.

"Mold?" Mason looked at him with a skeptical eye.

Doctor Mercer nodded. "Molds are nasty things. They can cause everything from illness to hallucinations to death. There's a new strain. All public gathering places will have to be inspected. Except restaurants. They already go through the tighter inspection process."

"I believe you've covered it all. Good work," Mason flipped through the pages in the folder. Better to throw the doctor a bone than let him know just how much he hated the man right now.

"Thank you, sir."

"Anything else?"

"No."

Mason nodded. "Thank you. I'll get right on this."

Doctor Mercer gathered his things. "We'll speak soon, and I'll give you an update on how the fight against the abominations is going."

He turned away and left the office before he could see Mason's bland expression of acceptance turn into a scowl. Mason felt his stomach unclench as the spirit-ridden man left his office. He wondered why he hadn't noticed the cues of supernatural magic around the doctor before now.

***

At first, Karen didn't recognize Aaron. It was the lack of dreadlocks and make-up. Also, it never occurred to her that she would see him in friendly companionship with David. Her eyes widened when she realized who he was, and she looked at John in confusion.

John cut off that unspoken line of questioning by asking a question of his own. "David, what have you got for us?"

David nodded at Aaron. While he came forward to reveal a grey stone the size and shape of an egg, David said, "We don't really know. Doctor Mercer, the one who has been having us target the supernatural creatures for eradication, had it. We saw him with Vicki."

"Vicki." Karen scowled with a knowing nod. "I knew it had to be the Children of Anu. Are they involved with the Special Unit?"

Again, John cut in to smooth things over. He was looking intently at the stone egg. "It makes sense. Have others do your dirty work. Pick off the other competitors for your food supply. Or in this case, the flow of energy that the city of Kendrick produces." He paused. "Karen, do you think this is the Keystone?"

"*Yes*," came Reginald's simple response over the Bluetooth earpiece she always wore.

She looked at it and repeated, "Yes. That's it."

John glanced at her lack of hesitation, then held his hand out for the stone. Aaron handed it over, pouch and all. "I need to do a little bit of research on this. Make yourselves at home." John turned and headed towards his office.

Karen nodded, knowing he needed to use the card for a vision of what to do with the Keystone now. She looked back at her two former loves and studied them. Accept them. *Accept the help from your past*, the Grey Lady had said. "This is unexpected." Karen admitted to the two waiting men.

"I'm sorry." Aaron looked at the ground, shifting from foot to foot.

"For what?"

"I didn't tell you I was back. I should've called."

Karen nodded. "It would've been nice but..." She struggled to keep her voice light. "I understand that things are busy all over." She paused and looked at David. "I'm just a little surprised. The last time I saw you two together was over a year ago outside this place, and you looked like you wanted to kill each other."

"I asked for help." David kept his opinions and heartstrings to himself. He knew this meeting would shock Karen, and he was right. She was keeping everything very tightly controlled.

"I think we've both changed." Aaron glanced from David to Karen.

"And time heals a lot of wounds. For once, the cliché is true," David added. It was true for himself, and hoped it was true for both Aaron and Karen.

She looked between them. "I guess it has for some."

"Karen, do you think we could meet for coffee sometime soon to talk? About what happened and what's happening now?" Aaron asked.

John saved her from having to answer the question. "This is the Keystone, and we've got to get it back to Susan and Alexander." He burst into the room, already talking. "It woke up Sebastian just long enough for him to reach for it. It might be able to wake up Alexander. He'll know what to do with it." He looked between the three of them. "Come on!"

David grabbed Aaron's arm. "We'll stay behind. We shouldn't be there. Call us if you need us... and please call if it saves them. Let me know." *I need to know,* was the unspoken plea.

Karen looked at them and saw Aaron nod, then step back with David. "All right. I'll call you as soon as we know something."

The four of them left the *Teller's Fortune* and split in two different directions.

***

Monica, Susan's assistant, answered the phone at their call, and then the door at their knock. She looked tired and worried. "Do you really think you have what they need?"

Karen nodded and tried to smile a confident, reassuring smile. She hoped so. If it wasn't what was needed, she was on her last idea. But this had to be it. They strode through the museum to the storeroom where Alexander stood as stone and Susan lay dying at his side.

Hurrying to Susan's side, Karen gently shook her awake. "The Keystone. Susan, we have it. What do we do with it?"

Susan's eyes fluttered open. "Alexander. Give it to him."

Karen looked at John who held the Keystone out to the unmoving statue of Alexander. He shifted it so it was touching the leader of the gargoyles. "C'mon big guy. We have what you need. It's the Keystone. C'mon. Save yourself. Save your people."

Susan reached for Alexander and Karen helped her up, holding Susan as she leaned forward until she was standing against Alexander. Then Susan grasped the Keystone, taking it from John. She held it between her body and Alexander's. John stepped back and watched.

Karen, still holding Susan because she would have fallen otherwise, felt the jolt of power that went from the Keystone into both Susan and Alexander. Later, Karen would surmise it was this that allowed her to witness the final heart-wrenching moments between these two.

Beloved, wake. Wake. We've got the Keystone. Tell us what we need to do.

There was a slow, gravelly stirring as the power flowed between them. *The Keystone. It must be destroyed.*

How? We'll do it.

It is our anchor into this place. We cannot exist without it.

Then what do we do? How do we save you?

There was a pause, then a feeling of love and sadness. *I must destroy it. I must replace it.*

I don't understand.

I will be here, Susan. I will be with you always. But not as before.

What does that mean?

I will become the anchor for us all. Put me in the sanctuary of this place.

Karen felt Alexander's wordless love and devotion flow into Susan, along with the horror of Susan's understanding of what was about to happen. Karen was helpless to do anything about any of it. It was then that the three of them watched the large gargoyle move for the last time. He kissed Susan on the forehead, and then took the Keystone from her hand. Lifting it to his mouth, he swallowed it whole.

For a moment, nothing happened.

Then the sound of cracking stone could be heard within Alexander's body and the flash of released power burned so powerful and bright that even those without magical ability were momentarily blinded. When they could all see again, Alexander was once again stone. He was hunkered down, his wings folded with one hand out, still holding Susan's hand.

Karen would remember Susan's cry of loss and weeping for the rest of her life.

***

In an empty estate in the Gateway district of Kendrick, a teal-haired, teenage girl screamed in rage at her own sudden loss.

***

Elsewhere...

In the *Teller's Fortune*, a small gargoyle opened his eyes and looked around. He was the youngest gargoyle still alive. All over the city and in the sanctuary of the museum, gargoyles on the verge of death relaxed into flesh form and reveled in their sudden safety and the return of power. One and all knew the sacrifice that the greatest of them had just made to ensure that this would remain so.

Absorption

"MOLD INFESTATION, my ass!" Juliet said, handing the official notice of a failed health inspection back to Lamiel. "This is a total set up."

Lamiel, looking tired and more than a little worried, nodded. "Of course it is. Did you see the list of clubs closed until the 'hazard' could be cleaned up? There's not a mundane club among them. We're being targeted."

"By whom?"

"Who do you think?"

Juliet paused then said, "The Children? Why? Was it because of the Beltane ritual?"

She shrugged. "Because we're next on the hit list. First, the Grey Lady and hers were attacked. Then the nature pagans and Druids. Then the gargoyles. Now us. Those of us in the city." Lamiel tossed the official notice to the table. "Every one of the clubs closed is a place of power. We're the strongest of the bunch. We'll have to post sentinels to try and stop the impending attack."

Juliet frowned. "This order came from the city. You don't think the Children of Anu have a hold on the city council, do you?"

"Maybe. Or they have a hold on a couple of important people." Lamiel waved a dismissive hand. "It doesn't matter. We've been shut down, and we'll have to let the 'inspectors' and such in."

"What do we do?"

"What we always do—hunker down and prepare for the worst. In this case, it means you need to scout out a new ritual space. Some place we can worship and work our magic in safety and privacy. Take whomever you need with you, but do it fast. I don't think we have much time to set our defenses."

Juliet nodded. "I won't fail us."

"I know. I'd help, but I've got to set things here as best I can."

***

Aaron was waiting for her at the Kahili Coffee House when Karen arrived to get coffee on her way to see John before collapsing into bed. It had been a long night at Emergency Services. Ever since the news of the outbreak of the harmful, and possibly hallucinogenic, mold growth the phones had been ringing off the hook and most of them were false alarms. At this point, she could rattle off the phone numbers for the Board of Health, Public Safety, and the new Mold Inspection Team without thinking about it.

She saw Aaron as soon as she walked in and sighed. He had the look of a person waiting for someone and when their eyes met, she knew he'd been waiting for her. As she stood in line, she wondered how many mornings he'd waited for her here. Then, she decided she didn't want to know. She was not ready for this conversation. Not yet.

After she got her coffee and walked over to the small stand to doctor it with some sugar, Karen heard him call her name. Steeling herself as she finished making her coffee, she turned around. Aaron waved her over to his table. She obliged.

"Good morning." He gestured to the seat across from him in clear invitation to sit with him. "Long night?"

She nodded but continued to stand. "It was." She paused, then plunged ahead with the normal niceties. "How are you doing?"

"Not bad. Getting used to being back here," he admitted, "I was hoping to run into you."

"Yeah?"

"Yeah." After a few moments of silence, Aaron offered another olive branch, "I'm sorry I left the way I did. I thought it was necessary at the time. For both of us."

"You left me a note to say good-bye after everything that had happened." She was too tired to keep the remembered hurt out of her voice.

"I know. I'm sorry."

"What do you want from me now, Aaron? Why are you back here in Kendrick?"

"I'm here because the Brotherhood needs me and asked me to return. When they did, I discovered that I was ready to come back and face things." He paused and shifted in his seat, looking up at her. "Face what happened and why. I would like to talk about it with you, if you have time."

"I don't."

Aaron blinked as if her blunt statement had slapped him across the nose. "Oh."

Karen sighed. "I'm sorry. I don't have time right now. I'm exhausted and honestly, I'm not ready to talk to you about all that. Not yet."

"I never meant to hurt you."

"I know. But the way to Hell is paved with good intentions. Just ask David." She saw him wince. "Aaron, we'll talk about this. I promise. But not right now. Not for a couple of weeks, maybe. I'm just not ready. I just found out you're back and you're best buds with a man you once considered your rival. I'm just not in a place to reconcile all that."

Aaron nodded slowly, "I understand."

"Do you? Do you really?"

This time he hesitated before answering, thinking it over and remembering why he left in the first place. "I think I do, and I'm willing to wait until you're ready."

Karen searched his eyes for a bit before nodding. "All right. I'm sure we'll see each other soon." She paused before turning away. "Susan's going through a really hard time right now. She might appreciate a sympathetic ear. The fact that you helped save the gargoyles despite her personal loss might be a good reason for her to talk to you about the pain she's going through now."

Aaron nodded. "I'll go see her as soon as I can."

"Thank you." Again, she started to turn away.

"Karen?"

She glanced back, "Yeah?"

He paused, opening and closing his mouth, not quite sure what he wanted to say. Finally, he nodded to her. "You have a good day, okay?"

She smiled a tired but genuine smile at him. "I'll try."

***

Vicki entered the warehouse through a side door. It was small as warehouses went, but perfect for the raves and other parties hosted here every weekend. She let herself be drawn through the makeshift rooms, separated by folding wall panels, towards the single flame of power. Beyond the juice bar, past the dance floor and its DJ stage, there was a small room in the back. This is where the power emanated from.

She paused in the doorway, looking at the unassuming room of wall-to-wall couches and the cushioned floor. This was the place they came to take the drugs and to share their bodies when they weren't on the dance floor. It was the small, ecstatic temple where the worthy and the naïve worshiped on beds of fabric and flesh. She stepped into the room and immediately felt the power lick about her body, looking to feed and to be fed.

For a moment, Vicki stood there, feeling almost like the mortal teenager she appeared to be. Fear and doubt crept into her mind. The gargoyles had taken back their power by breaking into the doctor's office and stealing the Keystone from her. Would these modern shamans be able to do the same?

The spirit calling itself Anu forced himself into the front of her mind. He had been hiding, nursing his wounds. His control on the girl had wavered, but not broken. He re-established it now. He would not let one little girl's fear of pain thwart him. *We will make it so they cannot strike back. We were kind, generous even. We will not be now.* He put the thought in the forefront of her mind.

Vicki's fear transformed itself into determined anger. They had taken what was rightfully hers. She would tolerate it no more. Moving to the center of the ecstatic temple, Vicki held out her arms, enticing the flow of power to her. Once it was within her grasp, she squeezed tight and pulled, sucking all of the energy from this temple into herself. She absorbed it instantly and she did not stop there. She followed the lines of power outward, pulling all of the energy from those most closely tied to the temple, sucking it into herself. She ignored the mental and spiritual screams of pain as she ate to satisfy her gnawing hunger.

Behind the high school, three punks and a gothic-looking chick, sat smoking, waiting for the bell to ring. Then they would decide if they would return to class or go their own way. Instead of a bell, a scream filled the air for a brief moment before it was silenced. All four students collapsed to the ground, never realizing the screams had come from their own throats.

In the counselor's office, the straight-A student volunteer manning the reception desk suddenly gasped in pain, then slid out of her chair and onto the carpeted floor, unconscious with blood streaming from her mouth and nose.

Sleeping in the basement rec room of their parents' home, the pair of brothers who ran most of the raves at the warehouse both moaned in their sleep. They both turned over, reaching for each other, but they never had the chance to wake up and mount a defense against what was killing them. They didn't wake up at all.

Vicki sighed, barely sated, and nodded to herself. This had been good; a Band-Aid to the gaping wound within her. It was just enough to keep her from fully reverting back to the mundane teen she had once been, and it was gratifying to know that there were more places like this to eat from. She had her list, and she would feast at every site.

***

"I've decided to do something about Doctor Mercer," Mason said. "I don't know what yet, but something has to be done. I've let things go too far."

David nodded, keeping his "I told you so" to himself. "What do you want me to do? Just name it."

Mason frowned a little. "I don't know much about how to cure the spirit-ridden. Maybe someone in my family does. Doctor Mercer was a good man once. A bit uptight, but good nonetheless. If we can, I would like to save the person he once was."

"Is that possible?"

"It is." This answer came neither from Mason nor David. Instead, it came from Aaron, standing in the doorway of Mason's office.

Neither David nor Mason reacted in surprise at Aaron's sudden appearance, though it put both on edge. "How long have you been there?" Mason asked.

"Long enough to know that you need my help," Aaron answered Mason but looked at David. "It is possible to save the man, Doctor Mercer, while freeing him from the spirit riding him. It's dangerous and I'll need both of your help."

David gave Aaron a joyless smile, "When is doing the right thing ever easy or safe?"

Mason sat back and looked at the two young men. Clearly, the relationship between them had changed, and he had not been kept apprised of the situation. People were falling down on the job. Never mind. That could be dealt with later. For now, his attention needed to be on the Brotherhood's newest Abbot and his co-conspirator in undermining his spirit-ridden daughter.

"Rarely, if ever." Aaron stepped into the room, closed the door and offered a hand to Mason. "Mayor, it's good to see you again."

"Abbot," Mason responded formally as he shook his hand. "What can we do for you? Or are you here specifically to deal with the good doctor?"

"Originally, I was just coming by to give my regards, but it appears I've been drawn here for more. Let's talk about Doctor Mercer, his spirit and his partner, Vicki."

David and Mason looked at each other and nodded. Aaron took a seat and began to talk. He was very clear on the dangers of what he was proposing to do, and what could happen to those who participated in the exorcism.

***

After barely four hours of sleep, John woke Karen up again. "What?" she asked, coming awake with a surge of fear. "What's wrong? Is Sebastian okay?"

"Shhh. Nothing is wrong. Sebastian's still sleeping. The Grey Lady needs to talk to us." John, squeezing her hand. "She just appeared in the shop, and said she needed to tell you something."

Karen yawned and looked at the clock. It was two in the afternoon. She did not grumble about needing sleep. When the Grey Lady wanted to speak, you got up. She struggled out of bed and into a tank top and a pair of sweat pants. If you woke a person up for a chat, you got to see them in whatever was handy. Though, why the Grey Lady hadn't come to her in dream like before, Karen didn't have the brainpower to figure out at the moment. She finger-combed her long, brown waves and called it good. Then she followed John downstairs into the *Teller's Fortune*.

The Grey Lady was there, looking almost back to normal, if not for the translucent quality about her. Still, Karen saw that her eyes were almost back to their normal river stone grey, and that had to be good. Right? She smiled. "Good afternoon."

"I apologize for waking you, but this would not wait. When these things come to me, I must state them before they fade like the dreams they are." The Lady's voice was soft and also had a translucent quality to it.

John and Karen looked at each other. "Okay," Karen said. "What do you need to tell us?"

The Grey Lady took a breath and spoke. Her words were more than solid in the air. They almost seemed to echo. "The end is nigh for one who harries this city. But, only the righteous hand may kill that which needs to die while not killing the one who should be redeemed. One of the city's own will be sacrificed if the righteous hand does not move quickly enough. There are only days left."

When she stopped speaking, there was a tension in the air and a sense of foreboding. Karen and the Grey Lady looked at each other without speaking. The only sound was the scratch of pencil on paper as John quickly wrote down the prophecy spoken through the Grey Lady.

"Oh. Thank you." Karen wasn't sure what else to say. Prophecies had a way of unnerving her.

"You are welcome. I cannot stay. Fare you well, Karen of the City." The Grey Lady faded from sight as John looked up from writing down the last of the prophecy.

"Dammit." he shook his head. "I hate it when they do that."

"What? Prophesize and run? Does it happen any other way?"

"Sometimes it involves blood."

"In that case, I think I prefer it this way." Karen sat down and rubbed her face. Gauging by how her body felt, she knew she wouldn't be able to get back to sleep for a while. She turned to John, "Got any tea left?"

He nodded as he handed her the sheet of paper with the Grey Lady's prophecy on it. "See if you can make any sense of it."

Karen looked at it and sighed. The only person she could think of with a 'righteous hand' was Aaron Patterson and he was the one person she really didn't want to talk to right now. But, it seemed she had no choice.

***

Elsewhere...

Mason watched his spirit-ridden daughter pace about the room from his usual spot behind his desk. He knew she was more avatar than daughter, and he had to keep his thoughts cloaked. Part of him wanted to shout with a suicidal mania that she would be defeated. The part of him with a survival instinct kept his silence until spoken to.

"Where's the rest of the family?" Her voice was quiet but the demand was plain.

"I thought it best that they leave. Give you your space while you work."

"What if I need them?" Vicki glared at him.

The words were out of his mouth before he could stop them. "I should be the only one you need, Vicki."

She stopped and smiled, an almost wondering smile. "Jealous, father? How unexpected."

He turned from her, keeping a tight rein on his thoughts. He did not want his perceived jealousy to be revealed as the protectiveness it was.

Vicki sauntered over to him. "Aww. I'll always need you. But right now I'm hungry." She gave him a kiss on the top of the head.

He glanced up at her and saw the predator in her eyes. "The city clubs may not feed you enough anymore. Maybe you should move on to bigger game."

"Like what?" She was curious. Having her father no longer fight her was both interesting and disappointing.

Mason shrugged and thought of the most protected group in Kendrick he could think of. "What about the Makah? Their land is fertile."

Vicki stopped her pacing. She remembered her own word to Chief Walks-the-Ocean: *'In a couple of days, all this won't matter. You'll have your precious amulet back as well as full autonomy of your land. As per our agreement, the Children of Anu will make no claims or inroads into Makah territory again. As for this amulet, you will have it back. That's how you'll know that your land, including the cave, is all yours again. Then you may do with it as you will.'* There were agreements that even one such as she had to abide by. Sanctity of the Makah land was one of them. She shook her head. "No."

He looked at her, surprised. "No? But, isn't that where you became...?"

"No, I said. Do not question me again." Her voice held a dangerous note that promised pain if he continued.

"I'm sorry. I didn't know. I won't mention it again." Mason rushed out in his most contrite voice. "I promise."

Vicki stared at him for a long moment. "I'm going out. I don't know when I'll be back, but you'd better be here when I return." She turned on her heel and strode from the room.

Mason stared after her, wondering what it was about the Makah land that made it sacrosanct to Vicki's growing hunger for mystical power. It was a mystery that needed to be solved and soon. It could give them the clue they needed to defeat her.

Candle's Flame

September 14th

It started with a gun butt to the head. My gun. Doctor Mercer's head. I never thought I'd ever kidnap a man to save his soul, but that's exactly what we did. The mayor, Aaron, and I talked about it. Doctor Mercer's exorcism would not be the classic priest with holy water routine. I've seen firsthand what these spirit things can do. No. It had to be a three-pronged attack. Mason would fight on the physical plane. Aaron would fight on the spiritual one. I would straddle the two worlds. Not like I haven't done that before.

We took Mercer to a monastery that had once been a train station. Pretty thing. All brick with a bell tower with a new brick wall to hide it. Nice and peaceful. A man could get used to that sort of quiet. We didn't meet with any other brothers. Aaron said it would be best that we not know who they are, and that they not know us. Fair enough. I'm familiar with undercover work.

An empty workroom was waiting for us. We put Mercer down and set a circle that the spirit possessing him could not cross. Then Aaron sat cross-legged and put a sword in his lap. He was going into that other world I can't see. I wish I could. I do. But, I'm mundane and doing the best I can. Mason (yes, after this incident, I'm on a first-name basis with the mayor) must have been some kind of hell raiser in his day. He held himself well in the fight.

Me? My job was to pray. And believe in that prayer. I grew up Catholic, and am one of the most devout people I know. I just don't push it on others. I don't feel that it's my place. Also, I needed to guard both Mason and Aaron. I held my own.

As soon as I started praying, Aaron began doing his thing. He likened it to playing a 3-D video game where you really can be hurt or killed, but you're more than you are in the real world. What is real? I don't know anymore. Mason stood guard, watching. The whole thing turned into a movie. At least, that's what it felt like to me.

Mercer's eyes popped open. He stood in the blink of an eye and moved to the edge of the circle. "These barriers trap me, but they don't trap this flesh," he said and started to walk through. Mason decked him. It was a good shot. Then fists and things started flying.

You know how you walk into a room and think it is empty? It's not. There are things there that your eyes don't see.

While I was praying—for salvation, healing, freedom, protection, help, all of it—benches were flying and so were small, forgotten tools. Mason fought with Mercer, and I shielded Aaron from the debris. But he was still being hurt. I could see it on his face in bruises and in the blood on his clothes from the mysteriously appearing cuts in his skin.

In the end, everything stopped as suddenly as it began. Mason had Mercer in an arm lock and was doing everything in his power to keep him in the circle. I was shouting the Litany of the Saints, and Aaron was just sitting there. Until he wasn't. In a single move, he opened his eyes, stood and swung his sword at Mercer, almost hitting Mason. It was so close that Mercer's face was scratched.

There was an unearthly scream in the air, and Mercer went limp in Mason's arms. All was suddenly quiet. Instead of a fight for life and freedom, four men were there, breathing heavy, hurt, and bleeding, but victorious.

Eventually Mercer woke up. It really didn't take that much for us to convince him of what had happened. He still had his memories, and they told him we didn't have time to rest. Bad things were happening with the Children of Anu, and they were about to get worse.

So, it was time to get to the hard part of all this. It was time to take Mercer and go talk to Karen and John. I'll talk about that more later. Just know, self, that you should be proud of what you accomplished that night. The only mundane man in the room, and you held yourself well.

David stopped writing and closed his journal. Closing his eyes, he remembered the awkwardness of what happened next. He rubbed his face and sighed. There was so much going on. Too much for one man to hold. He needed to talk to someone about... everything. But the only people he could trust were the people he wanted to talk about. It's why they had an SU psychologist on staff. This stuff built up and needed to be vented.

But no, Mercer was in no shape to be of any help to anyone right now. David sat back. His world, his companions, had shrunk to a handful, and most of them weren't friends. Most of them were co-workers or people like Mason and Aaron—supernatural and set apart.

There was John Mueller. He was a co-worker, yes, but a friend as well. He understood Kendrick better than most. David sighed. But the man had a family, twin boys even. He wasn't sure that a man so content with life would understand what David needed from him. He shrugged to himself. Then again, Mueller just might be exactly the confidant he needed. He'd have to think on that more.

***

John looked up from his game of cards with Karen. "Trouble's on its way."

"Figures. I was going to win this hand." She put her cards down. "What kind of trouble?"

"I don't know, but it involves blood and lots of it." They both looked up at the knock on the back door of the *Teller's Fortune*. "I'll get it. You get ready."

Karen nodded and shifted from her sitting position to one partly under cover by a pillar near the store's gun. As much as she hated the things, she was learning how to use one for "just in case" purposes. She would take it and open fire if it was an attack. She didn't think it was. Reginald hadn't spoken up yet. "Reginald? Do you know what's going on?" she asked quietly.

Her Bluetooth earpiece responded. *"No danger that I can see. Aaron, Mason, David, and James are here."*

"Who are Mason and James?"

"Mason Steward is the mayor of Kendrick. One of my caretakers. James Mercer is a doctor of the mind. He has a private practice, but works mostly with the Kendrick Police Department."

"Oh. Ideas on why they're here?"

"No. But they all seem to be bleeding in one way or another."

Karen waited until John returned with his gaggle of guests in tow and gave her the all clear sign before she came out of her spot. She looked at the group of beaten and bloody men. "What happened? You guys look like you need help."

There was an exchange of looks between the men and, by silent agreement, David took charge as the leader of the pack. "We could use some first aid, but there's trouble in the city and we think you're the person to help solve it."

Karen looked from David to John. John nodded. "Let me get the first aid kit."

Karen nodded. "Okay. What's up, and why are the four of you so hurt?"

This time, Mason took the lead. "It was my idea. Doctor Mercer was spirit-ridden, and we needed to free him." He explained what had happened, and how they had been injured. He filled her in on the story as they knew it to date.

***

John dug through the desk drawers, looking for the first aid kit. He finally found it in the back of the last drawer. He turned to put it on top of the desk and almost set it on top of Sebastian, who was sitting there with the Four of Swords Todari tarot card in hand. John's heart felt like it stopped at the sight of both. "Hey, little buddy. Are you finally well?"

Sebastian nodded.

"I'll bet Karen will be happy to see you." John kept his eyes on Sebastian's face and tried hard to not stare at the tarot card. He had, for the second time, given the card to the small gargoyle to help it heal. It was only due to the card's magic that Sebastian hadn't died during the attacks on the gargoyles. In the back of his mind, that greedy, obsessive part of him was screaming to take the card back. To take it before the little monster could run off with it. John ignored this screaming voice as best he could. That was not how things worked with the Todari tarot cards. "I'll bet you'll be happy to see her, too. I've taken good care of her while you've been healing."

Sebastian nodded again, as it was not the way of gargoyles to speak to those they are not bonded to. He lifted the Todari card that was almost as big as he and offered it to John.

He smiled in relief. "You give me this card of your own free will?" Again came that nod, giving permission for John to take and possess this most precious item. He took the card and stroked it. "Thank you, Sebastian. I appreciate your gift. I'm going to keep it right here to make sure I have it in case something happens to Karen. We both know that Karen's the only one, other than you, that I'll give this card, too. Right?"

The small gargoyle gave a huge yawn and leaped to John's shoulder, clearly no longer caring what happened to the card. John just hoped that Karen would not ask him to use it to help anyone in the adjacent room. He would not be able to agree.

***

"—and that's when Doctor Mercer told us what Victoria has been doing with the Children. We need to stop her before it gets to human sacrifices, but we can't just arrest her. The spirit riding her is so much stronger than the one exorcised from Doctor Mercer that the collateral damage and death toll would be unacceptable. We need to do this with stealth, guile, and a decisive strike." Mason's voice was tired but triumphant.

Karen was overwhelmed by the sudden influx of information about Vicki and what she had been doing to the clubs in the area and with the Children. She needed the sudden reappearance of Sebastian in her arms for a moment to think and to hope. "Sebastian!" She held the gargoyle that had launched himself from John's shoulder to Karen.

Everyone but John and Karen flinched. David and Aaron remembered the small gargoyle from their last encounter with him. Mason did not want to be hit by the flying gargoyle projectile and Doctor Mercer grimaced, knowing he was almost responsible for killing the creatures off. Still, everyone waited while Karen said hello to her old friend.

When she was done, she looked up and the gears were turning. "All right. If you say, Mayor Steward, that this must be done with 'stealth, guile, and a decisive strike,' this is my idea. We send Doctor Mercer in to get as much information as possible. Especially about where Vicki will hit next after the clubs and if the Children are actually moving to human sacrifice. Once we have that information, we can work to isolate her. Mister Mayor, that would be your job, as she is living with you. Then—" she looked at Aaron, "—we let the righteous hand deal with her. The only building damaged should be the Steward home. With only some of us there, the death toll should be minimal. But...before you ask, yes, I'm going to explain about the 'righteous hand.'"

She turned to John. "Do you have that prophecy handy?"

***

It was both a clash of cultures and a historic moment, all at the same time.

Sixteen members of the Bacchanalia Coven, led by Lamiel, sat in the room across from the three of the Makah council elders, led by Walks-the-Ocean. It was a sea of black leather, lace, and velvet met by the calm autumn colors of brown, green, and gold.

"The Makah Council will hear the Bacchanalia Coven." Walks-the-Ocean nodded to Lamiel.

Lamiel bowed her head to the elder council. At this point, it should be nothing more than a ritual, but there was always a chance of betrayal. Once Juliet had brought the idea of finding sanctuary on Makah land, it seemed to be the only logical thing to do right now. Band together with a greater force and offer their protection. There had been a private conversation with Chief Walks-the-Ocean, and the details had been worked out. All had been agreed upon in private. But still, all of that would be for nothing if even one of the Makah elders betrayed them. Lamiel knew Walks-the-Ocean but not Sees-the-Wind, the eldest of the elders, or Lumbering Bear, the newest and youngest of the elders.

She noted that two of them: James Swan Song and Dean Swimming Sky, rarely showed themselves to outsiders. Despite the importance of this meeting, they were nowhere in sight. That was an interesting thought for another time.

"The Bacchanalia Coven thanks the Makah Council for granting this audience."

"Why has the Bacchanalia Coven come before the Makah Council?"

"We have come to ask for sanctuary with the Makah. We have come to ask for permission to do good works and rites while upon Makah land. We have come to make a compact with the Makah people." Lamiel's voice was strong and clear.

"What does the Bacchanalia Coven fear that it needs to ask for protection?" Lumbering Bear asked.

"The Children of Anu have long waged war against all of us in the city of Kendrick. Recently, they have become more vicious and cunning. Right now, they have people within Kendrick's government and have used this to seize the places of power we have built. In order to protect those who do not see and the members of our Coven, we must act decisively. We must remove ourselves from our chosen place of power and transfer to a new, more protected, place of power. One that the city government has no right to act upon."

"What does the Bacchanalia Coven offer in return to the Makah Tribe for this sanctuary and ritual space?" Sees-the-Wind's voice was breathy and old, but still strong.

Lamiel turned her answer to Sees-the-Wind, though the answer was for all in the room. "The Bacchanalia Coven will bind together with the Makah Tribe. They will protect its borders, physical and otherwise, as if they were our own. We will lend our power once a month to the magical workings of the Makah Tribe if a greater magical undertaking is needed. We will abide by Makah law while on their land and will protect the Makah Tribe in the city as best we can. The enemies of the Makah Tribe will be the enemies of the Bacchanalia Coven."

There was a long silence in the room once Lamiel finished. The compact offered would bind the two groups together for a period of time as if all members of the Makah Tribe and the Bacchanalia Coven were one. It was not a decision to be made lightly.

Finally, Chief Walks-the-Ocean spoke. "The Makah Tribe sees the need of the Bacchanalia Coven. The Bacchanalia Coven has been friend and ally to the Makah Tribe in the past, and this should not end now. For a period of one lunar year, the Bacchanalia Coven and the Makah Tribe will be as one."

The old man stood and offered his arms to Lamiel. Lamiel stood and placed her forearms on top of his. He smiled. "Be welcome, sister, Daughter-of-the-Moon. May our time together as one be fruitful."

"Thank you, Chief Walks-the-Ocean. The Bacchanalia Coven is welcomed into your home, and will see you well."

***

"The end is nigh for one who harries this city. But, only the righteous hand may kill that which needs to die while not killing the one who should be redeemed. One of the city's own will be sacrificed if the righteous hand does not move quickly enough. There are only days left."

John put down the paper he'd read the prophecy from and Karen looked back at the four other, bandaged, men in the room. Mostly, she looked at Aaron. "This prophecy was given to me by the Grey Lady. John and I talked about it and why I received it and not someone else. We came to the conclusion that as the city is being affected by Vicki and, as I am the Master's representative, that I probably know the 'righteous hand' destined to defeat Vicki. I think this person is you, Aaron. And since you brought Doctor Mercer to me, you've shown us how to 'kill that which needs to die' while not killing 'the one who should be redeemed.'"

John folded the paper and put it in his pocket. "We know who is to do what to whom now. At least we have a good guess. What we need to know now is Vicki's timeline, because we need to isolate and defeat her before then."

"That's where I come in," Doctor Mercer said. His voice was tired and his shoulders sagged forward, hunching his back.

"Only if you choose to help, James," Mason put a supportive hand on the man's shoulder. "This is not an order from me or the city."

"It's a request," Karen agreed. "But it's still your choice."

Doctor Mercer straightened up, looked among all those in the room, his eyes lingering on David. "I'll do it. I owe the people of the city that much."

Mason stood up. "If I may, I believe I have a plan that will work. She's my daughter, spirit-ridden or not. She's staying with me, and she trusts me. Between that and her trust of Doctor Mercer, I believe I know exactly what to do." He looked around the room for permission to continue.

Heads nodded all around. "The floor's yours, Mister Mayor," Karen said. She was distinctly relieved not to be in charge—for once—of this particular life-threatening problem and its solution.

***

Elsewhere...

Vicki smiled up at the silvery metallic sign. It was a predatory smile, full of promised pain. "Bacchanalia. How obvious can you be? Did you expect to be safe when you advertise exactly what you're doing in the middle of downtown?" She sneered at the *Members Only* sign. With a flick of the wrist, the door of the closed Gothic club opened to her. Immediately, she felt the magic within.

She let her senses feel what was there. "More than just a place of power, I see. You want to fight? I'll fight." Vicki let some raw power, gathered from the offerings of the Children and the rapine of the other places of power in the city, whip out and strike at the barriers before her.

***

Lamiel screamed in pain. Juliet rushed to her mentor's side. "Get me back to the Makah reservation," Lamiel said as another bolt of pain hit her.

***

So easy. Like taking blood from a willing servant. Vicki walked farther in, careful and slow. She was drawn to the heavy pulse of the power here. But someone had left traps. Tricky, this coven was. The next barrier was an illusion. A door that should have led to the back, but really another door to the outside. It was no match for the next lick of power as Anu devoured the magic holding it together.

***

Juliet sped through the city, praying to the Goddess and the moon that she would make it in time. Next to her, Lamiel gasped in pain, but held her own. "Faster. I can't hold her much longer."

***

The third barrier was a subtle thing, deeply hidden, but on closer inspection of the door to the back room, it was very powerful and designed to knock all supernatural creatures unconscious, regardless of species, based on the creature's own power. Vicki stepped back and had to admit a certain amount of respect for the sorceress who cast the ward. It was devious and deadly. But, as all things must, it had a weakness. The anchoring rune. She found it after some looking. A tiny rune at the bottom of the doorframe. Three swift kicks to the wooden frame with a steel-toed boot put an end to the only trap that could have actually harmed her.

***

Blood leaked from Lamiel's nose and mouth as Juliet pulled into the parking lot. She helped Lamiel across the lot, past the visitor's center, and to the first home of the Makah people. This was Lumbering Bear's home. He would help. He had to. Lamiel was dying.

***

After ensuring that the room was no longer a danger, Vicki turned her attention to the place of power itself and watched the dancing energy, sensing its strength. She'd clearly found the best of the clubs in the city, and now its power was hers.

She stepped into the room and seized the power, drawing it into her. At first, it resisted. She overcame that resistance. Then, the fourth trap was sprung. Suddenly, Vicki was in a fight to keep control and hold onto her own power. This place and its mistress was trying to strip her of all of it.

***

Lumbering Bear held Lamiel in his arms. "I need her things of power. I need them to protect her." Juliet nodded and sprinted back towards the car.

***

Vicki found an opening in the attacker's defenses and struck with everything she had.

***

"No. Don't let her. She needs to be here..." Lamiel panted to Lumbering Bear. He looked up to see Juliet take two steps into the parking lot, and then crumple silently to the ground.

***

Screaming in triumph, Vicki latched onto her victim as hard as she could. The energy flowed into her so fast it burned, threatening to overwhelm her. Then, the source she had control of ceased altogether. She could not tell if the victim had died, or if something else had happened.

To her dismay, all of the enticing energy in this place of power suddenly winked out as if it had never been there to begin with. It seemed that a fifth and final trap had been sprung, taking all that she needed with it. This time Vicki's cry was one of rage.

Enough, she thought, *I have had enough.* Stalking out of the defunct club, she pulled out her cell phone and made the call Sam had been waiting for.

The Cost of Redemption

"IS SHE GONNA be okay?" Lamiel's face was a mask of pain and worry.

Lumbering Bear and Walks-the-Ocean looked at each other. It was the older man who spoke. "We don't know. All we know is that being on Makah land saved her."

The young, gothic-looking girl and leader of the Bacchanalia Coven furrowed her delicately-arched eyebrows as she stared at the slack and pale face of Juliet, lying in the guest bed in Lumbering Bear's home. "She saved me from that bitch. She made sure to get me here." There was a pause and then a question. "What is it about Makah land that makes it safe from the power of the Children of Anu?"

Again the men looked at each other. This time the younger one answered as the older one turned away. "There are old spirits and older laws that even spirits made flesh must follow." Lumbering Bear said. "Makah land cannot be touched by the likes of the Children."

"Because it's Makah land and not the city?" Lamiel squeezed Juliet's hand, willing her to be well again.

"Perhaps."

The answer was noncommittal, and Lamiel knew she wouldn't get the real answer right now. "Perhaps. Perhaps not. I guess it's not important. What is important is that Vicki can't touch any of the remaining club owners as long as they're on Makah land." She gazed at them with eyes wise beyond her years.

Walks-the-Ocean heard the unspoken question. "The allies of the Bacchanalia Coven are allies of the Makah Tribe. Bring them here in good will and safety. How many will be coming?"

Fear and sadness flashed across her face before she mastered her features again. "Ten of the sixteen club owners are dead. One has fled from Kendrick. One has sacrificed his own place of power. Four or five are left. Maybe a couple of friends with them."

The old man nodded. "Bring them all. Instruct them in the laws of this land. Then, they may do good works and worship as they wish. I will have a place put aside near the area of the Bacchanalia Coven. Our traveling homes will become their temporary homes."

Lamiel nodded and looked down at Juliet's face. She leaned close to the unconscious girl. "Fight, Juliet. Find your way home. We need you." She smoothed out the other's dark hair and then stood, looking at the two tribal elders. "I'll make the calls. This land will be respected." She paused, her voice soft. "Thank you."

The men nodded and watched Lamiel leave. Then they turned back to Juliet. Walks-the-Ocean said, "I will begin here. Make things ready for our guests."

Lumbering Bear nodded. Then a smile slipped out, "Redemption comes in unexpected ways. I think it has brought itself to your doorstep. Do not turn it away."

The old man nodded, but said nothing. Lumbering Bear left the room. As the door closed, he heard Walks-the-Ocean chanting. There was a strength in his friend and mentor's voice that he had not heard in a long time. He offered up a soft prayer, "Please, by all the spirits in the earth and sky, let that girl survive. More depends on it than just her life."

***

"Sometimes, we meet in dreams," Susan said, her eyes far away. "Sometimes, we can talk if I hold his hand, but he straddles two worlds, ours and his. It's the only way the gargoyles can exist in this world. Through their Keystones. He became one of the Kendrick Keystones to save the rest. He sacrificed himself for all of them."

Aaron listened with quiet respect as Susan talked. *She's not talking to me,* he thought *She's talking to herself. She's coming to grips with her loss.* He looked at the large gargoyle statue before them and wondered what it was like to be the anchor for his people in this world. Alexander, in stone form, was hunkered down, his wings folded with one hand held out. Susan held his stone hand. *Would I have the strength to do the same?*

"They regard him as a religious figure now, and I am his priestess."

He pulled himself from his thoughts and looked at her. "Priestess? I don't understand."

"He's gone beyond this world. He's their version of a saint. As his bonded human, I'm accorded the respect of a high priestess. I can sometimes hear his words. They come to him, through me, for advice. But they no longer look at me as a leader." Her words were soft and sad.

"Who?"

"The gargoyles." She turned from Alexander and looked at him as one would look at a child to see if they were faking their ignorance. When she saw that he was confused, she sighed. "Alexander was their leader. I was his human. I... influenced him and his decisions. I helped him make decisions. He can lead no more. My words no longer matter now, except as a conduit to their new saint."

Aaron nodded as if he understood. He believed he did. Somewhat. "Who's their new leader?"

"That is the question now. They came to me to ask him to choose between a pair of twin gargoyles. The next oldest."

"There are twin gargoyles? That's possible?"

She smiled. "Yes. Rare. Very rare. When it does happen, it is usually a time of great joy. But now..." Her smile faded, "...it's trouble."

"Why?" He tilted his head.

"Because only one may lead, but there are twins." She shrugged. "That seems to be the issue right now. There are so few gargoyles left, and they are so disorganized. Many of the youngest died. It's hard on them. Gargoyles are very family-oriented."

Aaron nodded. "What advice have you offered?"

She looked surprised. "Me? None. They aren't actually speaking to me, per se. They're trying to talk to Alexander."

"But they will talk to you?"

She nodded. "I'm bound to Alexander, and am the only way they can talk to him. I'm a special case. In their eyes, I'm not really human anymore."

"Perhaps they need some of your insight, too. You led the gargoyles with Alexander for how long?"

"Almost twenty years." Her face screwed up in a suppressed sob. Then she forced the emotion back down. The marks of her grief aged her, showing how much she had cried over the last few days.

"So, you know them." Aaron looked her in the eyes, trying to get his message across. "You know their pain and problems. They will listen to you. Try talking to them as yourself, and not just as a conduit. Let them know that you're still here for them. That you haven't left as well."

The melancholy faded from her face. It was replaced with something more thoughtful. "That would be a big change. I'll have to ask him." She looked back into the stone face of her companion. "Maybe..."

"If you don't mind, I'll pray for guidance for you and Alexander both."

That soft smile returned. "I don't mind at all. In fact, would you pray with me now? Bless Alexander and me?"

Aaron nodded. "Of course. Gargoyles have long been considered creatures of God and protectors of the church. I would be honored." He slipped to his knees, as did Susan.

***

"I won't lie to you, Doctor Mercer." Mason rubbed his hands together in a nervous gesture. "This will be dangerous. My daughter is smart and perceptive. You *cannot* let her know that you are no longer spirit-ridden."

The doctor nodded. His cheeks remained flushed, while the rest of his face remained that ashen-grey color. He kept his eyes on the floor.

Mason put a hand on the doctor's arm, causing the man to look up. "James, you don't need to do this if you don't want to. I am not ordering it. If you'd rather, I can send you on a very long vacation elsewhere. Far away from here."

James shook his head. "No. I'll do it. I want to. I need to." He paused. "I won't say I'm not afraid. I'm terrified. I remember what she can do. I remember how strong and brutal she is. If she discovers the truth about me, I'm dead."

The mayor nodded. "Yes." He did not sugarcoat or elaborate on his agreement.

"You're not making me feel any better." James tried for a smile.

Mason shrugged. "Sorry. I've been dealing with this for a very long time now."

James nodded. "How can we be sure she'll be fooled?"

Mason shrugged again. "We can't. I suggest you meet with her once and watch how she reacts to you. You're a master at psychology and body language. If you think you've fooled her, continue on and feed us the information. If not... If you sense at all that she's on to you, get out and run far, run fast. Do not stop for anything. Get out of Kendrick. Call me, and I'll wire you money."

"Thanks for not lying to me." James put out his hand.

"You're welcome." Mason shook it. "Good luck."

"I'll call you when I know something."

***

"I've found the perfect sacrifice," Sam said as he stood in front of Vicki, who lounged on her throne in the warehouse.

"Really?" She sounded bored, but he had her attention. "Do tell."

"A cop and his family. Got a wife and a pair of boys."

"What makes them so special?"

"I've seen him sniffing around the Camden district. He's gotten a bit too close to the Children before. It'll be easy to get him here."

She yawned. "Doesn't sound very special to me."

"He's part of that special department of the police that knows about the supernatural. He's aware that Kendrick's more than just a normal city. He's worked for us through Doctor Mercer, dealing with the gargoyles and such."

Vicki sat up. "Now, that is interesting." She stood up and stretched. "Full gathering tonight. I'll expect a good set of sacrifices. I've finished dealing with the clubs... for now." She paused as her phone rang.

Sam stepped back to give her privacy as she answered her phone.

"Doctor Mercer, I was just thinking of you." Vicki paused and listened. "Yes, yes. That's all good." She paused again, listening. "As a matter of fact, I do. Come by the warehouse tonight at eight. We have something special planned." She grinned at his response. "You'll see. I'll see you then. Bye!"

She hung up the phone. "Tonight, we'll see just how committed Doctor Mercer is to our cause."

Sam's malicious smile matched the one on the face of the woman he worshipped. "And if he's not?"

Vicki rolled her eyes. "Don't be dumb, Sam."

"Sorry." He did not shrink away from her. He stood tall, but eyed her warily.

She came over to him and patted him on the arm. "So, what's this cop's name?"

"Mueller. Sergeant John Mueller."

***

"What do you think of this 'righteous hand' thing Karen spoke of?" Aaron asked.

David shrugged. "I've no idea. Prophecies make me uncomfortable."

Aaron walked around his office in the monastery, gathering books. "Why?"

"Because you never know where they're coming from."

"The Grey Lady, according to Karen." He handed a pile of four books to David.

David accepted them and gave their spines a cursory glance before adding them to the other books that Aaron had already given him. "Yes. But where did she get it? I understand she's supernatural and all, but what is beyond her? That's what I want to know. How do we know this prophecy isn't leading us down the wrong path?"

Aaron looked at David with a knowing gleam in his eye, "Are you asking me 'how do we know that the prophecy is from God and not the devil?'"

David shifted uncomfortably and restacked the neat pile of books before him. "Yes."

"We don't." Aaron held up a hand to forestall David's retort. "However, we can make an educated guess. I mean, look who the prophecy was from—the Grey Lady—and who it was to—Karen—and what it said. What do we know of these people? I know they have worked with me on the side of the Light before. I know the prophecy was probably meant for someone close to Karen. And I know it basically says that we need to work fast and with compassion." He paused. "So, what do I think? I think we need to figure out a way to sever the connection between Anu and Vicki without killing her." He paused again, "What do you think?"

He sighed. "I think you're taking a whole lot on faith here."

"It's what I do, and it's what I thought you did, too." Aaron paused from his book searching to stare at David.

"I try. But I'm only human."

"That's okay." The Abbot tilted his head. "If you don't have faith in the prophecy, can you have faith in me to do what I believe is right?"

Aaron's former rival nodded. "I think I can do that." He didn't smile, but he looked less worried now. "What do you want me to do?"

"Go by Mason's office tonight. He'll be there, waiting for a call from Doctor Mercer. While he waits, the two of you can go through those books." Aaron gestured to the stack on the table next to David. "One of them might give us an insight on how to deal with Anu without killing the girl. This spirit is so much stronger than the one we fought before."

David nodded. "Research. This, I can do. What will you be doing?"

"Praying."

"Say one for me?"

"I'll be saying one for all of us." Aaron's easy smile faded. "The end of things is coming. I can feel it. Unfortunately, it brings bloodshed as well. It's not something I relish."

***

Doctor Mercer arrived at the warehouse at eight o'clock on the dot. He was admitted into the dimly-lit confines of the main home and worship center for the Children of Anu. He had been here before, but he was seeing the place, and the people within, with new eyes. What he saw terrified him. He hoped he could keep his fear out of his face and voice.

"Right on time, Doctor. We have something very special planned tonight," Vicki paused and looked at him. "Are you all right?"

"I am fine." He nodded. "What's planned for tonight?"

She smiled. "You'll see." She clapped her hands together twice. "It's time to start. Lock it down."

Doctor Mercer watched as the doors around the warehouse were closed with loud bangs and locked tight. With each bang of the metal doors, he felt his stomach tighten in fear. When Vicki touched him to get his attention, he started.

"Jumpy, aren't we, Doctor?" Vicki had a purr in her voice. "Are you afraid?"

He shook his head as she led him to the throne in front of the mass of people. "Nervous about what you have planned. I don't normally come to your... worship sessions."

"I know. I thought it was time for that to change." She raised her voice. "Bring the sacrifices forward."

From the back of the crowd came three of the Children. Each of them had an animal with them—a goat, a Labrador retriever, and a lamb. Each animal came docilely on a leash. Their handlers stopped with them at the front of the crowd.

"Choose one," Vicki said.

Doctor Mercer looked at her with a quizzical look. "Choose one? For what?"

"For sacrifice. To me." She grinned at his expression of confused fear. "Chose which one you're going to sacrifice to me."

"Me?" Mercer couldn't keep the fear out of his voice. Sam stepped up next to him and offered him a baseball bat. The light oak wood was stained a dark brown. Doctor Mercer took a step back from Sam and shook his head. "I—I can't."

Vicki stepped down to the three animals and allowed the dog to snuffle her hand before she leaned down to pet the lamb. "Really? I don't think this one will fight back." She laughed. "Though you may have to chase it down after the first whack."

Doctor Mercer shook his head again. "I can't."

"But, Doctor Mercer, there has to be a sacrifice." The look on Vicki's face was angelic with a demon peeking out through her eyes. "If you won't sacrifice these animals to me, what will we sacrifice?"

It was already too late when Doctor Mercer turned to run. Sam swung the bat hard at the doctor's knee, hitting him with a solid crack, crippling him. Then the rest of the Children were on him, holding him down. He was dragged away from the throne to the bloodstained concrete before it.

Vicki took her seat on the throne as Doctor Mercer was held before her. "Did you think I wouldn't know?" She asked, her voice soft but rising in anger. "Me? The one who chose you as the host? The one who put the spirit in you? The one who made you the man you are?" Her voice dropped. "Were. The man you were."

"Vicki. Please. I can explain—"

"No. I don't want to hear it. None of it! You're no good to me now." She paused, thoughtful. "Except as my first human sacrifice."

"Hail Anu. Marduk. Enlil. Bel. Victoria." Sam stepped forward.

"*Anu. Marduk. Enlil. Bel. Victoria,*" the Children of Anu answered Sam with their own reverent chant. "*Anu. Marduk. Enlil. Bel. Victoria.*"

Doctor Mercer began to struggle, "No. No! You can't do this!"

"Make sure to leave his face intact." Vicki commanded, no longer listening to Mercer's pleas. She sat back in her throne and watched her Children, eating up their worship.

Sam raised both hands in the air, his palms facing the throne. "Great god Anu! Father of Heaven, creator of the stars, lord of the constellations, king of gods, spirits and demons, your Children have not forgotten you. The Children will never forget you. Your humble servant, Samuel Ridgefield, has gathered your believers here on this night to beg of you a sign, a sigil, a vision. This is the year of your return, great god Anu! Instruct us in your wisdom. Judge us worthy with this task. Tell us what we must do! We are your Children and your servants. Guide us in this holy year."

***

Mason closed his book, sighed and looked at the clock. It was 11:30 p.m. "He should've called by now."

David put a bookmark in the 1859 book on Christian magic he was reading and closed it. He chose his words carefully. "I know he should've. However, he could be into something really good right now, getting us the information he needs."

"Or he could be in trouble." The older man looked troubled.

"All right, he could be. If he's in trouble, what can we do about it?"

Mason gave David a sharp look and realized that the younger man was not trying to antagonize him, but asking a legitimate question. "I don't know. I don't think there's anything we can do." He paused. "He wouldn't be there if it weren't for me."

David shook his head. "He knew the risks. He didn't have to go. We—"

"The hell he didn't! Didn't you see the look on his face?" Mason stood up. "The realization of what'd had been done because of him? When I first introduced him to the Special Unit, he was fascinated, if a bit wary, of supernatural beings and creatures. He wanted to help. He wanted to know more. But, once spirit-ridden, he turned a protective police force into an assassination squad." Mason sat back down with a thump. "And I let him."

David didn't say anything for a long time. Finally, he said, "He did make a choice. No matter what you or I say, he chose to step in. We all find redemption in our own way. If he's in trouble, I pray to God that he finds his before it's too late."

Mason looked at David. "I hope to God he's all right. Otherwise, I'm going to have to add another name to my list of sacrifices."

"From your lips to God's ears, Mason."

***

Elsewhere...

Vicki moved through the throng of her sated Children to the center of the storm.

There, on the ground, in a bloody, very dead mess, was Doctor James Mercer. Beyond the killing blow to the back of his head and a few minor bruises, his face was intact. "Very good, my Children. Very good. There's enough to identify him."

She turned to Sam. "Dump him some place public. Be artistic about it if you want. But, leave all his stuff on him—wallet, watch, glasses, rings. All of it. I want whoever freed him from his spirit to know exactly what they're messing with, and the cost of defying me."

"It will be done," Sam waved to a couple of his more trusted people to gather up the broken body. "Anything else?"

"Yes." Vicki smiled. "How soon can you get me that cop and his family?"

"Tomorrow, if you want."

"I want." Vicki turned from him and raised her voice so all could hear. "It's time the city of Kendrick was ours for good."

Breaking Point

"THIS HAS GOT to stop." David's voice was tight with guilt and anger. He had known this was a possibility, but it never occurred to him that he'd feel guilty about it. Mercer had done so much wrong, but he didn't deserve this.

"Yes." Mason did not look up from Doctor Mercer's corpse. His face was grey with his own guilt and sorrow. When David received the call telling him that Doctor Mercer's body had been found in the Colonel's Park, Mason knew he had to go. Together, the two of them would give the official identification to the coroner.

"Permanently," David pressed.

Mason looked up, but didn't say anything.

"Permanently," he repeated. "I'll do it myself if I have to."

Mason turned away, nodding. "If you have to, but give Aaron a chance first if you can."

"If I can, I will. If not, no. She's a monster we've let run loose too long."

***

There's little a pair of eight-year-old boys can do when a van pulls up beside them and a couple of adults open up the side door to grab the first boy and then the second when he tries to help his twin brother. There is little a pair of eight-year-old boys can do against the strength of two men intent on tying them up without regard to the damage they might cause. There is nothing a pair of helpless boys can do in the face of men who have a gun pointed at them, except to be as quiet as possible through their frightened tears.

There is little a mother can do when a man knocks on her door and tells her to come quietly, or one of her sons will be shot. There is little a mother can do except try to soothe her boys as she is bound next to them in the back of a beat-up gray van. There is nothing a mother can do except obey when she is ordered to call her husband and tell him what has happened and then look on in horror as her husband is ordered to meet the kidnappers at a warehouse in the Camden District.

There is nothing a father can do when he receives such a phone call but listen. He can only beg the men not to hurt his family, and then suppress his impotent fury when a man breaks one of his wife's fingers to reinforce the point that the father, a police officer, will come alone to the warehouse. There is nothing a father can do but agree while silently swearing that he will do whatever is necessary to free his terrified family. He knows he alone has this responsibility.

But the father is not alone in his fear and worry. Another pair of twins saw what happened to the boys and their mother. This set of twins, Theodore and Theodora, love the twin boys for their exuberant energy and willingness to play with them whenever possible. They also love the twin boys because of a seed of specialness buried deep inside them that has not yet revealed itself to the world. Theodore and Theodora understand that there are forces at work here that are following a pre-set path. This does not mean they have to like it. This does not mean they have to follow it. They are outside space and time, and know they can do something about it. And they do.

***

Aaron gazed at Brother Luke, his second in the Brotherhood of Light, and frowned. "When did this happen?"

Brother Luke pointed a hand, trembling due to age rather than fear, at the third man in the room. "Brother Thomas was the one who found him while patrolling his territory in the city center."

"Doctor Mercer's body had been laid out in front of the Colonel's statue like an offering," The younger monk said.

"What did you do then?" Aaron asked.

"Called the police, like any other normal citizen would."

Aaron nodded. "Good man." He scowled. "This isn't what I wanted. When we freed him of the spirit, I thought he had a chance to go back to a normal life. He wanted to, but he wanted to make up for what he had done while ridden."

"There is a bigger problem here, Abbot," Brother Luke said in the tone of a schoolmaster gently chiding a student who had missed the obvious answer to a question.

"What?"

"Doctor Mercer was beaten bloody and almost boneless except for his face. His face was completely intact and identifiable."

Aaron gazed at the older monk and thought about that. "They wanted him found. They wanted him to be identified." He said more to himself than to the others. "They don't care that we know they killed him. They *wanted* us to know they killed him." He looked at Brother Luke. "They aren't afraid of us knowing."

He nodded. "When they reach that point of fearlessness, either they have become stupid or careless... or they are about to succeed in what they set out to do."

"Or they've already succeeded," Brother Thomas murmured, remembering the bloody corpse of Abbot Peter, their former leader, murdered almost a year ago.

***

"I'm worried. Things seem too quiet right now. Something's wrong." Karen petted the cat-sized gargoyle in her lap.

"Maybe we're just not seeing what's happened yet," John said from his usual spot behind the counter of his store. "Just wait a couple of hours and all will be revealed."

The bell on the front door of the *Teller's Fortune* jingled as it opened and a pair of fair-haired children walked in. Karen recognized them immediately as one of the sets of twins that were part of the Grey Lady's household. "More like a couple of seconds." Karen glanced at John. She stood and put Sebastian down on the chair. To any normal person, he would look like a statue of a sleeping gargoyle put in a chair as decoration.

She watched them walk directly to her and stop. "Good afternoon, children." Karen gazed down at them, knowing trouble was now here.

Theodore began, "We need your help."

"Not us, specifically." Theodora continued.

"Another set of twins."

"Taken by the Children of Anu."

Theodore nodded. "They took the mother, too."

"We think they're in bad trouble."

They both added, "Please help them."

Karen, somewhat used to the Grey Lady's twins speaking as one, nodded slowly. "Which twins? Where were they taken to?"

"Devon and Daniel Mueller," Theodore said.

Theodora nodded, "The Children took them to the Camden District."

"We can't go in there."

"It's too dangerous for us."

"But please help them. They're our best friends." Again, the twins spoke as one.

Karen did not need any more convincing. She would have answered this plea for help no matter what. Children were in danger, but she recognized the last name from the time she was questioned at the police department the year before. Sergeant John Mueller. *He was good to me,* she thought. *The last name's unusual enough. It can't be a coincidence.* Karen nodded. "I'll help, but let the Grey Lady know we're going to need her help, too, if she can manage it."

"We will." Theodore bowed to her while Theodora curtsied. Then the twins turned and left the shop without a backwards glance.

"You know..." John closed his book and started gathering the things he would need. "I was just kidding earlier."

Karen nodded. "I know but sometimes, my dear, you are prophetic." She searched her coat for her cell phone. "I need to call David. If it is Sergeant Mueller's family, he'll want to know. He'll help, too."

"Yeah, I don't relish the idea of storming the Children on their own turf alone."

"We won't be alone. Everyone has been looking for a reason to go after the Children—'collateral damage' be damned. If they did take the family, this is the best reason to do it. The Muellers are mundane. Innocents. It's time we do what we're supposed to do." She opened her phone and dialed David's number.

He nodded. "Save the innocents from the dark."

***

David hung up his phone with a sinking feeling in his stomach. He dialed Sergeant Mueller's cell phone number, and was sent to voicemail. He almost hung up but then he said, "John, it's David. Call me. It's important." It was possible that it wasn't the Sergeant's family on the line, but it if was, he needed to know.

He left his office and walked to the common room. He saw John's desk was empty. Across from his desk, sat Sergeant Taylor, Sergeant Mueller's partner. "Hey, Taylor. Where's Mueller?"

The young man looked up. "John? Got a call from his wife. Then he ran out of here like his ass was on fire. Must've forgotten her birthday or something."

"How'd you know it was his wife?" David's heart sank while his fear rose.

"It was her ringtone." Sergeant Taylor sat back and looked at his superior. "What's up, Detective? Something wrong?"

David nodded, "Yeah. Something's wrong. Get the SU together and outfitted. We've got a couple of extractions to make tonight."

It was Sergeant Taylor's turn to look alarmed, "Tonight? What's up? Is it Mueller?"

"I don't know." David shook his head. "It could be coincidence, or it could be that one of our own was targeted. Him and his family. If they're in danger from whoever, we're gonna get them back. Tonight." He turned away and then turned back to Sergeant Taylor. "Let the boys know we're going to have specialized company helping us on this one. It's going to be a big, semi-organized mission. We need to be able to pull our part without overreacting. Got it?"

Sergeant Taylor nodded, his face a mask of professional neutrality. "Got it. The Unit will be ready and loaded for bear. Just give us the word."

***

Susan stood with Alexander's statue behind her. She faced a pair of identical gargoyles. The oldest of them. The pair looked uneasy. "I called you two here this afternoon for a reason. An important reason. I understand the difficulties that you and yours are going through right now. However, something bigger is going on. I need your help. Both of you and the rest of the gargoyles. All of them."

The first one, Edmund, finally answered, *'You, who are the chosen of Alexander, we respect your place. We respect your call. But, we do not answer to you anymore unless you speak with the words of Alexander.'*

The second one, Edgar, continued, *'But, as you have been with Alexander most of your life, we will listen.'*

"Thank you." Susan bowed her head to think, and then raised it when she was ready to speak. "I have helped advise Alexander and all of the gargoyles for almost twenty years. You have become mine, even if you do not consider me one of yours. What you do matters to me. This current leadership difficulty needs to be put aside for now. Kendrick and her people need you and yours to become the guardians you once were before the devastation of your people. Is that something you can do?"

Edmund and Edgar looked at each other. Edmund answered, 'We listen. *How does the city need its guardians?*'

"The Children of Anu have struck again." She pressed on over twin growls of anger. "At a family from Kendrick. A mother and two boys for certain. They were taken today. We fear for them. We fear they will be murdered tonight. Will the gargoyles stand and fight against their enemy?"

Edgar answered this time, '*Though we are few, we will fight. The people of Kendrick are ours to protect.*' He looked at Edmund. The twin gargoyle nodded.

"Thank you. Sebastian will be the courier tonight." She paused. "When this fight is done, I would like to speak to you two more. I want to help you through your present difficulty. If you will have me. I love you all, and I wish nothing but the best for you all. You are mine."

Edgar and Edmund looked at each other for a long time. Susan knew they were privately speaking and waited. Finally Edmund nodded. '*We will consider it. Until then, we will gather for the fight.*'

"Tell the others. We'll meet at the *Teller's Fortune*, and move from there towards the Camden District."

***

"There is a danger to those of the Coven and the club owners." Walks-the-Ocean gazed at the young woman before him. "But, at this point, we believe the danger will be in the attack and not the draining power Vicki used against you recently."

Lamiel nodded. "Enemies of the Makah Tribe are enemies of the Bacchanalia Coven. Tell us what we need to do."

Walks-the-Ocean smiled a tired smile at the determined look on the girl's face. He knew she was scared, but she was also strong-willed. "The Children have taken a mundane family. A police officer's family. We don't know why, but we suspect that it works into their plans to take over Kendrick. We don't know how. But we know they have become brazen in their confidence. If they succeed, even our lands may not be safe anymore."

"Save the family. That's the first goal. Kill the bad guy... girl..." she amended, "and then what?"

He shook his head. "I don't know. I do know that we will be working with many different factions within Kendrick. All of them have a claim against the Children." He paused, "Including the Brotherhood of Light."

Lamiel curled her lip in distaste, but said nothing. "There will be no problem with this?"

She shook her head. "No."

"Good. Please let all know that it is voluntary. This will be dangerous. People will die. We'll be meeting at the *Teller's Fortune* in an hour."

She nodded. "All right." She left in a swirl of black lace and velvet.

Walks-the-Ocean sighed. He was feeling too old for these sorts of rescues. But, it was what he needed to soothe his guilty soul.

"The land will forgive you," the Grey Lady said from her place to his left.

Her voice startled him. When he recovered, he asked, "How can I forgive myself? My betrayal dishonors my ancestors, and stains my soul."

"You are the only one who can answer that, but I believe your betrayal, in order to save Makah land, has become a boon to those who need it."

"Still, a man, a good man, was murdered because of me."

Clear, grey eyes gazed at old, brown ones for a long time. "Perhaps you need to seek forgiveness from the people you wronged."

"The Brotherhood of Light." He looked away from her, unable to allow those eyes see into his soul any longer.

"Yes."

He nodded. "Once we get this family back, perhaps that is what I will do."

***

John Mueller was brought before Vicki in the warehouse. She was lounging on her throne, looking like the cat that ate the canary. He was terrified more for his family than for himself. "So good of you to come when called, Sergeant Mueller."

"I came. Where's my family?" He fought his fury to keep from launching himself at the smug demon in teenager form.

"They're safe. Right over there." She gestured to one side, and several members of the Children moved to allow John to see his family. They were all sitting on the floor, tied up, looking disheveled and frightened. Other than that, and a bandage on his wife's hand, they looked well enough. John ran to them, heedless of those who started to keep him from them, but who backed off at a gesture from Vicki.

He hugged his wife and the boys, whispering, "Daddy's here. You'll be okay. I promise. You'll be okay."

Vicki raised her voice to get John's attention. "Whether or not they are okay is entirely up to you, John Mueller."

He stood and faced her, putting his body between his helpless family and those who would do them harm. "What do you want?"

"We want you, John."

He looked confused. "I—"

"—don't understand. I know. You don't need to understand," Vicki swung herself from her lounging position and standing up. "What I want, John, is you, a normal cop with Kendrick's best interests at heart; the perfect representation of Kendrick, because you are normal, but you know what else lurks in the darkness of this city. I want you to offer yourself to me. To give yourself over to me in sacrifice. Only then will your family be safe."

"John, no!" Cheryl blurted out the denial before she could stop herself.

"John, yes!" Vicki cried, mocking his wife. "If you do not willingly sacrifice yourself to me, I will kill each of your family in front of you. Starting with..." She pointed at Daniel. "...that one."

***

Elsewhere...

Corelli sat across from V'ger. "What do you want us to do?" V'ger asked.

The blond-haired girl was as pretty as she had always been, but there was something more to her now. She had grown in wisdom and experience through pain. "Have any contacted us for help?"

He shook his head. "The Order of the Sacred Eye is still neutral."

"Then it is our choice." Corelli was still the second in command of the Order in name only. For all practicality, she was their leader. She chose to remain officially second for her own reasons.

"Yes."

She could hear his unspoken question, and made an instinctual decision. "The debt the Order owed the Children has long been paid. The Order owes no one, other than itself, loyalty. However, the Children have always been a threat to the Order. It has been good to allow them to take the eyes of Kendrick off the Order, but now they have overstepped their bounds. Mundanes are to be protected."

"So, we'll offer our assistance to Karen and the others?"

"No." Corelli smiled inside at V'ger's confusion. "We've been asked never to bother Karen or hers again. Instead we'll watch and wait. We'll be conduits of power for those who can accept such. And, if it is possible, we will take as much power from the Children as we can. We are on our own side, V'ger. We help Karen and hers only because it suits the will of the Order."

V'ger smiled in understanding. "I will gather the circles together, and we will prepare for the fight."

She nodded, "Make sure you prepare a vessel for capturing and imprisoning a spirit. A powerful one. If the opportunity arises, I don't want to miss it."

The Righteous Hand

KAREN FACED THE leaders of those groups she had managed to call and assemble over the last two hours. "I'll be perfectly honest, the plan I have isn't fleshed out. There's no time for that. The last time we went up against the Children of Anu, we were too late. That's not going to happen again. Not with John Mueller and his family on the line."

"Each group will have general goals," John took up Karen's train of thought. "Other than that, this is an extraction. Get the Mueller family out of there before any of them can be hurt. This blatancy on the part of the Children tells me they are so close to their goal—whatever that is—that they don't care who knows what they're doing anymore."

"Each group is going to enter the warehouse from a different direction. I got these blueprints from the Hall of Records, so they should be accurate." Karen slid pieces of paper around to everyone in the room. "Susan, the gargoyles need to come in from the top. Their goal is to fight the Children and keep them away from the family."

Susan accepted the paper and nodded.

"David, the Special Unit needs to come in from the front. You guys have guns and the skill to bull your way through a mass of people. Divide and conquer the crowd. Pick off the most dangerous from afar."

David accepted the paper. "We'll have the block around the warehouse cordoned off as well."

Karen nodded. "Lamiel, the Bacchanalia Coven's main goal is to get the Mueller family out. That's it. Do what you have to. You'll enter through the back of the warehouse. This could be the most dangerous job of all. I don't know." She handed sheets of paper to Lamiel and Walks-the-Ocean. "That's why the Makah Tribe has two goals—help the Bacchanalia Coven and help the gargoyles. Divide and distract. Do what you have to do to get the family out."

Lamiel and Walks-the-Ocean looked at each other and nodded. Then Walks-the-Ocean gave Susan a nod.

Karen turned to Aaron. "Last, we have the Brotherhood of Light. Your job is—"

"Dealing with Vicki," he said, looking grave. "Any way we can."

"Yes. Keep her off the rest of us."

"We will." He glanced at Mason, standing at his side. Mason looked weary, but nodded, giving his permission to the Brotherhood to do what they needed to do.

"Your group will enter from both sides of the warehouse."

Aaron looked at the blueprint of the warehouse. "All right."

Karen's Bluetooth earpiece came to life. "Karen. Something's happening. Power's radiating out from the Camden District. It's putting parts of me to sleep. I can't see the Camden District or parts of the Gateway District anymore. I won't be able to help you."

She put her hand to her ear. "Shit. Are you okay?"

"I don't know. Hurry, Karen, please."

"We're coming. Hold on." She answered and then looked up. She had the room's undivided attention. "We have to go now. It's started. The Master of the City can feel the power building in the Camden District."

They all looked at each other a moment longer, then moved as one. They would explain the skeleton of a plan to their people on the way.

***

"You've had your time with your family. I've been more than generous," Vicki's voice demanded an answer. "What do you choose, Sergeant Mueller?"

John pulled away from Cheryl's clutching grip and stood, again with himself between his hapless family and the Children of Anu. "You swear, before those who worship you, that if I agree to this, to sacrifice myself, you will set my family free?"

Vicki rolled her eyes, then nodded. "I swear it. There are rules even I cannot break. Your family will be allowed to go home, unharmed, after the ritual is done."

John looked over his shoulder at his family. Cheryl's eyes threatened to brim over with tears again, but she managed to put on a brave face. The boys, Daniel and Devon, were frightened, but they did not really understand what was going on. He mouthed to her, *"Don't let them see it. I love you."*

Cheryl's eyes glimmered, and now the tears spilled over as she nodded to her husband and mouthed *"I love you."* She turned her focus on her children. Soon they would be all she had.

He looked back at Vicki. "Then I agree. I will be your willing sacrifice."

Vicki grinned at Sam and he gave a shout. "Let's get this party started!"

All around them, the Children of Anu moved to their respective tasks. Some moved to guard the doors. Some moved to bring out a steel rack. Others moved to prepare the ritual space. Vicki sauntered over to take her place on her throne. It was time she made Kendrick hers for good now that most of her enemies were too weak to stop her from taking the city and its power.

John did not resist as he was bound spread-eagle into the rack. He had spent almost an hour saying good-bye to his family. *Not everyone gets that chance,* he thought. *I pray to God that Cheryl can keep the boys from seeing and I pray that I'm strong enough not to scream. Please don't let my screams be the last thing my family hears from me. Please.*

As suddenly as the movement began, it ended. Vicki sat alert on her throne. Between her and her sacrifice was her altar. Sam, dressed in the vestments of High Priest, raised his hands, one holding a bloodstained club, high. "Hail, Anu!"

***

"Are you ready for this?" John asked Karen as they pulled in next to the warehouse.

"No." She smiled thinly at him and shrugged. "But then, I never am."

"Okay. I'm here for you."

Karen looked up and watched the shapes of the remaining gargoyles in Kendrick bound from building to building against the twilight sky and gather on top of the warehouse. "Thanks."

***

John stifled his cry of pain as Sam brought his club down hard on his leg. He brought all of his considerable will and experience as a cop to keep himself from throwing up in shock. His leg was broken. He knew it. And that was just the first blow. Vicki had said nothing of this ritual involving torture before his death. He did not know how long he could go without screaming.

Vicki, too focused on her sacrifice, noticed the first tendrils of power not of her making only a second before the sound of breaking windows heralded the arrival of the gargoyles through a shower of broken glass that rained down upon the Children.

"Stop them!" Vicki shouted to her Children before turning to Sam. "Continue the ritual, High Priest!"

***

As gargoyles dropped from the ceiling of the warehouse in what seemed to be a mass of dozens, a second explosion of sound startled the members of the congregation. From the main doors at the front of the warehouse, a third explosion of sound erupted and the front doors buckled under the strength of the Special Unit's battering ram. A squad men in black combat uniforms spilled into the room in an organized tumble. They began firing non-lethal rubber bullets into the crowd of Anu worshippers to keep them ducking for cover.

***

Sam focused on his goddess and obeyed as the entire warehouse erupted in chaos. Even the sudden entry of the Brotherhood of Light from both side doors of the warehouse was not enough to keep him from his task. He turned back to John, helpless in his bondage. "For you, Anu. Marduk. Enlil. Bel. Victoria." He raised his club and brought it down on John's other leg.

***

Even if John had screamed, Cheryl and the boys would never have heard it over the din of the fighting. Cheryl had freed herself and scooted herself and her children back against the wall. She was snarling at the black-clad gothic people that appeared in front of her. "Get away from us!" She brandished an iron pipe at them.

"We're here to rescue you," Lamiel backed away as Cheryl swung at her. She sighed and said, "Sleep now." The tendril of magic made Cheryl's eyes roll up in her head as she fell over. Kurosawa caught her before she hit the ground. He nodded to Lamiel as he carried the unconscious woman out the back door.

Lamiel crouched down to look the twin boys in the eye. "I'm a good witch, and I'm here to help rescue you. You won't give me any trouble, will you?" Wide-eyed and wondering, both little boys shook their heads. Then Daniel pointed behind her. She turned and saw they had been noticed. Three Children of Anu advanced on them. "Stay behind me," she ordered the boys as she pulled her glowing athamé from its sheath.

***

John and Karen entered from the side after the monks did. Four monks knelt in prayer on either side of the warehouse. Two monks armed with swords guarded each set of praying men. Between the gargoyles, the Special Unit, and members of the Makah Tribe, most of the Children of Anu were fighting, scattered, or were already down on the ground. Karen looked around and spotted Sam striking John in the right arm with the club. "There!" She shouted and pointed. John Corso took off at a run for them.

***

Vicki, feeling the combined power of the last of Kendrick's protectors coming to bear on her, snarled and left her throne. She felt the psychic onslaught from the Brotherhood and ignored it. She walked towards her sacrifice and her high priest. "Finish it. Finish it and it's ours!" She saw Corso sprinting towards them, picked up a knife from her altar as she passed it and threw it at him. The moment the dagger left her hand, she herself was bowled over from the side.

Corso, hit in the arm by the knife, did not stop. He plowed into Sam before the club could come down a fourth time. The two men went tumbling over, fighting as they went down. Corso's only goal was to keep Sam from completing the ritual. Sam, intent on doing just that, pulled the dagger from Corso's arm and stabbed him again with it.

***

David shouted orders from his position in the front of the warehouse. He saw Lamiel in trouble. Two of her people were down, and she was the only one standing between the Children and the twins. A faintly glowing, green shield kept the Children at bay, but it was fading. Just as he was about to order two of his unit to help her, a pair of gargoyles, almost as large as Lamiel, landed on either side of her. They roared in unison, causing the attacking Children to scatter.

***

Vicki pulled herself to her feet before Mason did. "Hello, Father." She pulled him to his feet, punched him in the gut, and then backhanded him into the wall. She watched him slide to the floor, bleeding from the mouth and nose. His eyes did not open again. "Good-bye, Father." Vicki turned back to her sacrifice. She saw that Sam was in the middle of a fight with someone, and knew if she wanted to keep what she had won, she needed to finish off the sacrifice herself.

***

While the two gargoyles roared on either side of her, Lamiel felt the sudden bonding of gargoyle and human through the shield she had up, protecting herself and the boys. '*I choose you*,' reverberated through her skull, but she knew that she was not the one chosen. Both little boys behind her were. She looked at the gargoyles and dropped the shield. "They're all yours." Lamiel stepped out of the way. The gargoyles each picked up a boy and scrambled up a wall. She knew that was going to be something interesting for someone to explain— later. Right now, she had her own problems to deal with.

***

Aaron fought his way toward the back of the warehouse, where his foe was. He watched Vicki throw Mason across the room, and then turn back towards the bound man. He threw out a lasso of prayer and caught Anu in the Spirit Realm. It was too powerful a spirit to take on by himself, but he had to keep Vicki from the sacrifice.

Vicki grabbed her head in pain and snarled. Anu gathered a portion of their considerable power and honed it into a killing spell. Anu/Vicki saw that Aaron understood what Anu/Vicki was doing, but still wouldn't let go. He was vulnerable, and sacrificing himself to delay her. She grinned savagely as she threw the killing magic at him.

In the Spirit Realm, an owl appeared out of nowhere and took the full brunt of the death blow. It saved Aaron, allowing him to keep holding Anu, drawing the spirit's power away from its host.

***

In a car just outside the warehouse, Walks-the-Ocean coughed up blood and told Lumbering Bear, "Tell the Brotherhood what I did, and then tell them I hope I have paid them back for my betrayal."

The huge man pressed his lips together in a white line of grief and nodded, unable to speak. He held his mentor's hand and gave him as much comfort as he could, knowing there was nothing he could do to save Walks-the-Ocean.

***

Vicki ignored what was going on in the other realm. There was pain, yes, but great victory often came out of great pain. She returned to her sacrifice and picked up Sam's fallen club. She no longer knew where her high priest was. Nor did she care. She raised the club and brought it down on John Mueller's arm. The din in the warehouse had died to a dull roar as gargoyles and Special Unit members rounded up the Children. This time, John could not stop his cry of pain.

***

Karen heard it and saw Vicki going for the kill. She shouted "David!!" and pointed at where the sacrifice was about to happen. David looked up, saw Aaron charging with his sword and knew he would be too late. John Mueller would die, and all would be for nothing. He would not have that. David aimed his pistol and fired at Vicki.

Vicki, gasping in Anu's pain from Aaron's attack, almost dropped the club. She was so close to winning, she bulled through the pain. She raised the club again; this time it was aimed at John Mueller's head. "Kendrick is *mine!*"

***

The gunshot echoed through the large building. The bullet struck Vicki's head a moment before Aaron reached her and swung his sword—not at her but just to the side of her.

The club fell from Vicki's fingers as she collapsed, bleeding from the side of the head.

***

David rushed through the waning crowd to his friend. "John?" He was afraid to touch the man. He could not tell how many bones were broken. "John? Please, say something."

"Something..." John Mueller said with a soft groan.

"Oh, thank God you're alive."

"My family?"

"Rescued. Just like you. You're gonna be okay. We're all gonna be okay."

***

Later...

Karen and Susan sat in Karen's apartment, drinking coffee. Both looked tired but happy.

"I'll tell you, trying to explain to a mundane mother that her children were no longer mundane is not an easy task." Susan rubbed her temples.

Karen nodded. "How's she taking it?"

"Better. Now that her husband is home. He had to explain to her that he knew all about the supernatural creatures of Kendrick." Susan sipped her drink.

"Bet that went over like a house on fire."

"Yeah, but I'm pretty sure the sergeant's wife is going to give him a pass. He did willingly sacrifice himself to save them and the city."

"Counts for a lot." Karen looked down at her mostly empty mug. "So, now what?"

Susan shrugged. "I don't know. I guess I get to be the old woman on the mountain who talks to god and occasionally mentors the young leaders. Alexander is pleased at what's happened."

"Good to hear."

She tilted her head, "You're unusually taciturn today. What's up?"

Karen shrugged. "It's just hard sometimes. Two more of the Bacchanalia Coven died. Vicki is in a coma. Mason has a concussion. Walks-the-Ocean sacrificed himself to save Aaron.

Poor John was stabbed like six times. And Sergeant Mueller will be in casts for the next three months."

"But we won. The city is safe."

"Maybe."

"What do you mean?"

Karen sighed, looking worried. "Aaron isn't sure what happened to Anu. He didn't banish the spirit, and it didn't flee back into wherever it came from. He said that what it looked like to him was that someone sucked it away from Vicki the moment David's bullet hit her."

"Maybe because it turned out that David was the Righteous Hand?"

"Maybe." She shrugged. "But now David has a lot to think about. He's been invited to join the Brotherhood of Light, and that's got my mind in a spin. I guess I'm having a hard time reconciling everything."

"You've got John now."

"I do." She smiled.

Susan reached out a hand to Karen. "Maybe you ought to just let the past go. Let David and Aaron work things out. Just let it all be."

"I'll try."

"How's the Master doing?"

"I'm fine now," Karen's Bluetooth earpiece chirped in her ear.

She smiled. "He's good. We did save him. We did save all of us."

"That is something to be thankful for. Who knows what's waiting around the corner for us?"

"I don't know. But I'm pretty sure it won't be dull."

***

Elsewhere...

Corelli looked down at the flawless quartz crystal. It was bigger than her hand, and shone with an inner light. Those sensitive to such things could feel the power emanating from it. "It is a thing of beauty and precious beyond words." She looked up at V'ger. "Tell the Order that they did very well. We got exactly what we wanted. This will be an excellent power source for a long time to come."

V'ger nodded. "What are we going to do with it?"

"Anything we want," Corelli said with a smile.

CHIMERA INCARNATE

Book Four of
The Karen Wilson Chronicles

Unexpected Changes, Part 1

"I'M FIRED?" KAREN gazed at her boss of six years with a mixture of surprise and reluctant understanding. It explained why he'd wanted to meet after her shift in the back kitchen. Almost no one went there, and his office was nothing more than a small cubicle.

Griff stood, turning away from her toward the kitchen counter. He slouched in an old man's slump that was becoming more and more common the older he got. "Not technically. Technically, you're being laid off." He reached for two paper cups to make them both coffee. Every motion was slow, deliberate and sad, like a ritual he loathed to complete.

"I can fix this," Reginald said over her ever-present Bluetooth earpiece.

"No. Don't do anything." Karen shook her head, answering Reginald, then smiled in embarrassment at Griff. "I mean, thank you, but I don't want any coffee. I..." She trailed off, watching the emotions of regret and resignation play across his face.

Griff didn't say anything until he sat back down with his unwanted drink. "I know this is hard. And, really, right now, this is the best thing for you. Karen, I know something's going on. You've called in sick twenty-eight times in the last two years. That's more than the previous four years combined. If you're really sick..." He pushed on, despite her shaking her head. "...you can talk to me. You know that. Right?"

"I'm not sick." She paused. "Twenty-eight times. So, I'm laid off because I've missed work?"

Griff ran a hand through his salt and pepper hair. "No. Not just that. It's because of your performance lately. You've stopped doing the job you were hired to do—calm the people calling while dispatching appropriate personnel. You've started trying to fix the problem from your desk. That's not acceptable. Some of your advice almost ended up with the city in a lawsuit. I went to the mat to keep you from being fired outright."

Karen nodded. "I know. I know. I'm sorry. How did you...?" She paused, not sure how to say 'save my reputation' without saying it.

He shrugged. "I looked at the budget, and it was a choice of laying off a couple people and getting the upgrades we need to the computer systems, or not. The higher ups approved my budget change request."

She looked around the clean but dingy kitchen. While it wasn't much, it was familiar, and it was home. Suddenly, Karen realized she'd miss it. "Who else is being let go?"

Griff shook his head. "Policy."

She nodded.

"I requested a severance package for you. I'm not supposed to tell you that. HR would be pissed if they knew, but I didn't want you to think you had nothing."

"I've just made sure it's a really good severance package," Reginald told her in a quiet voice.

Karen pulled the Bluetooth earpiece out and put it in her pocket. "Thank you, Griff. For everything. I know you covered for me a bunch of times. I appreciate it."

He shrugged again. "You're family." He gave her a long look. "Do you mind if I give you some advice?"

"I think I need it."

"Your perspective on helping people has shifted. You used to be happy to be that safe voice on the other end of the line. Now, you want to help in a more *active* way. I think you should consider taking some EMT and First Responder training, so you can actively help people. You aren't the first Emergency Services dispatcher to discover that being a voice on the phone isn't enough. And, when you're done with that, you can come back to dispatch if you'd like." He smiled a knowing smile at her. "That's one of the benefits of being laid off."

Karen sat back and thought about that for a long moment. "I guess you're right. I've changed. I can't go on like this." She shook her head. "So much has happened, and I need to refocus myself."

Griff gazed at his full cup of coffee. "Also, seriously, my ear is always open. I promise to listen, even if I don't agree with everything you tell me."

"Thanks." She gave him a distracted smile. Karen really wasn't sure what she was going to do now. But something would turn up. Something always did.

Griff gulped half his coffee in a single large swallow then slumped over the cup with a huge yawn. "Damn," he muttered.

Karen, seeing him relax after completing the crappy part of being a manager, tilted her head. "You okay?" She stifled a yawn herself. It had been a long night.

"Yeah." He shook his head. "Not sleeping well. Had a nightmare. Kept me up." Then he smiled and looked up. "I tell you that you've been let go, and you ask me if I'm okay?"

She smiled a weak smile and shrugged. "We're friends." Karen knew that helping someone right now would make her feel better and ward off the panic until she'd had a little sleep.

Griff nodded. "Yeah. We are. You want some help cleaning out your locker?"

"No. I'll be fine." She shook her head and paused at his grimace. "You need to stay with me, don't you?"

"Yeah. I'm sorry, Karen. I know you wouldn't—"

Karen sighed. "But it's policy. Emergency services is too important to leave anything to chance with a disgruntled ex-employee." She stood, wishing she had accepted that cup of coffee, and felt for her Bluetooth earpiece.

"Did you leave anything at the desk?"

She started to shake her head and then nodded, blushing a little. "One of my favorite pens. It's a fountain pen. It was a gift."

"I'll get it for you." He gestured for her stay put in the kitchen.

Karen put the earpiece back in her ear. "Please don't do anything bad to this place. Please."

"Of course not." Reginald sounded shocked. *"This is a place that helps my city."*

She smiled. "Okay. Good. I was worried. Griff and the rest, they're good people."

"I know." He paused. *"Are you mad that I changed things so you got eight weeks of severance instead of four?"*

"No." She sighed. "I'm probably going to need all that time to figure out what I need to do." Her stomach turned over, making her nauseous. What was she going to do? She had never had an adult job besides working for Kendrick's Emergency Services.

"I will take care of you. I promise."

"That's part of the problem, Reginald. I want to be able to take care of myself." Karen looked up at Griff's return and smiled, knowing it was strained. She didn't have the will to do more than that.

He handed her the pen with a triumphant flair. "Your pen, my lady."

"Thank you." She looked at it for a moment. The pen, a fountain pen in black and gray marble with *LIFESAVER* engraved in gold, had been a gift from John. She wondered how she was going to save herself now. Then she remembered that Griff needed to stay with her until she was safely ensconced in the HR office.

Putting the pen away, she nodded. "All right. Let's clean out my locker."

***

Karen sat with John and Susan in John's apartment above the *Teller's Fortune*, John's metaphysical bookstore and supply shop. "I'll admit that HR had a small, polite, contained *cow* over the eight weeks of severance. But since I had seen the paperwork and it was already printed, taking it away would've left them open to being sued." She shrugged. "So, my checking account makes me look like I'm rich, but I'm not."

John sat next to her, his shirt sleeves rolled up and his vest unbuttoned. "I'm surprised that's all Reginald did."

Susan put down her tea cup. "I'm not. The Master of the City isn't going to do anything to harm a vital support system for Kendrick."

"Yeah." Karen smiled a tired smile. "He was upset at me for even thinking he might." Her smile disappeared. "He wants to take care of me, but I don't want that."

"I agree." John fiddled with one of his ubiquitous European cigarettes, still unlit for the moment. "I don't like the idea of him taking care of you, or of you letting him take care of you. You'd go crazy in no time at all."

Susan and Karen exchanged knowing glances. No man liked to think about his significant other being taken care of by someone else. Karen took a long pull on her coffee. "The problem now is... what the hell do I do? I've only worked dispatch. That's all I know how to do. Where am I going to find a job like that? One that lets me have enough leeway to go save the city when it needs it. Anu is gone. The Children are scattered. Even the Order has been keeping its collective noses clean. But that doesn't mean that the city is safe."

For a long moment, no one spoke. Then John shrugged. "Don't do dispatch anymore. Do something else. Something that touches the hidden world of Kendrick."

Susan tapped her chin. "Yeah. A job that's flexible. I suppose I could have you become a night... well... not guard... but a night clerk for the Museum? You know, going through the relics, categorizing them and such."

"I've just hired a new girl to run the shop when I'm away." John got up and walked over to the window seat. He opened the window, letting a bit of the crisp spring air in, before he lit the cigarette. "I could fire her. I mean, I don't want to. She's in the know, but neutral. Actually, she's more apathetic than neutral. She just doesn't give a damn about any of the supernatural factions of Kendrick. I call that a boon." He took a long drag, then let the sweet smelling smoke dribble out his mouth and nose. "But I'd fire her and hire you."

Karen shook her head and smiled. "That's really awesome of you both, but I think I'd rather keep you as friends. Friends who become employees and bosses don't really stay friends, do they?"

John and Susan exchanged a glance before they both nodded. "Yeah. You're right." John gave her a half-smile. "Besides, I don't really want to fire Alex. She's kind of a find. Plus, you'd probably be with me on half of my adventures. Then who would I call into work?"

Karen smiled at him and winked.

"What about the Special Unit?" Susan suggested.

Karen's eyes widened as she shook her head. "No. I really don't think Kendrick's own hunt-down-the-monsters police force would be a good choice. Half of them can't figure out if I'm human or not. Besides, even though I orchestrated Mueller's rescue, I have threatened them before. And I'm not sure I'd want to work for an ex-boyfriend."

In truth, the Special Unit would have been a viable option if it weren't for the fact that it was run by Detective David Hauberk. She'd dated him a couple years ago. The two of them had kept their secret lives separate, not realizing until too late that they could've been working for the same side. Beyond the fact that she and David, while no longer antagonistic, could not trust each other, Karen knew that she would never be a good employee to him. She challenged him on everything, and that would undermine his authority with the SU. It wasn't something she wanted to do now that the SU was back to working for the side of good.

"Working for the Makah would be out. They're territorial." John glanced out the window.

The Makah Tribe. Karen looked away, remembering her first meeting with them. It had been a horrible night of murder and betrayal. It was then that she had sworn to stop the covert war of assassination and theft. She had forced the fight out into the open, and not everyone had thanked her for it. But, a man—a tribal member, a guardian—had died in her arms. Since that time, she'd worked with the tribe, understanding only a little of how they straddled their cultural past and their modern future. They were good people. Right down to saving two of the other supernatural factions when the Children of Anu had attacked and stolen their places of power.

"They, rightfully, want only members of their tribe to work the Cultural Center." Karen shifted in her seat. "And the Bacchanalia Coven is still bound to them as allies. So, even if they went outside the tribe… it wouldn't be to me."

Susan nodded. "Also, the Bacchanalia Coven just got the club up and running again."

Bacchanalia was the private goth club owned by Lamiel and Kurosawa. It was one of the few clubs—and pagan city groups—that had recovered enough to stand on its own. They still adhered to their pact with the Makah. Saving Lamiel had been Karen's introduction to the hidden, supernatural world of Kendrick, and it had changed her life forever. Still, she couldn't work for them. They demanded vows she could not make.

Karen toyed with her cup. "And it's not like I could go be a barista at *Kahili Coffeehouse* or at *Sushi-Ya*. Too many folks I know—and don't always get along with—come to *Kahili*. Plus, they're mundane. As for *Sushi-Ya*, I'm not neutral. At all. If Coleman showed up to bargain with someone, I'd want to punch his face in. And I'm not sure what I'd do about Corelli or Aaron if either of them came in for coffee. So, that lets both of them out."

Luke Coleman, the owner of the pawn store *Treasures & Trinkets*, wasn't a man. Karen still didn't know what he was— other than a force of evil and chaos in Kendrick. Most of the items in his shop were mundane, but some came with a price that could be lethal. Cursed, haunted, or just bad magic. Karen still wasn't sure why he was allowed to stay in Kendrick. Maybe now that the world wasn't ending, she could look into it.

As for Aaron, another man she had dated in the past, he was now the Abbot for the Brotherhood of Light. They had unresolved issues between them. Again, it came down to trust. If a relationship was based on a lie, when that lie was revealed, everything else was suspect. Karen didn't want to even think about Corelli, the Mistress of Magic for the Order of the Sacred Eye. That was one grudge she wasn't going to give up. *Threaten me and mine, and I will* never *forgive you*, she thought with a scowl.

John stubbed out his cigarette and closed the window. He came back to the couch smelling like he had been smoking a pipe. "You could see if you could work with the mayor or his office."

Karen sat back and considered that for a long moment. The Stewards. The Steward family had come with Colonel Kendrick to establish the city of Kendrick as a safe haven away from the American Civil War. They were bound to the land and to the city, taking positions within the city to run and care for it. The current mayor, Mason Steward, had been an ally in the past. As had his strange daughter, Julie. Then again, his bastard daughter, Vicki—now in a coma—had hosted the avatar spirit of Anu. So, it was not an easy choice.

"My main concern is whether or not I or the mayor could remain neutral in all this. My first loyalty is to the Master of the City. I'm not even sure he would have me."

Susan let out a gusty sigh. "Sounds like you need to talk with Reginald."

"And with Mayor Steward." John nodded. "I'll set up the meeting."

Karen smiled with a shrug. "It can't hurt."

***

Corelli closed her gritty eyes and rubbed them. "Look. Just because we *can* do something doesn't mean we *should* do something." Even though she was speaking to the First Circle, she was really speaking to V'ger, the Head of the Order of the Sacred Eye. "Yes, we have a great store of power, but we've only been recently taken off the Kendrick's supernatural most wanted list. There is no reason for us to work a great magic right now."

The First Circle of the Order of the Sacred Eye sat around a highly-polished, dark wooden table. They were in one of the smaller meeting rooms of the mansion owned by the Order. Everything around them spoke of the wealth it had amassed over the years—from the fine artwork to the plush carpet to the antique chandelier.

By right of rank, Corelli lived in her own suite of rooms in the mansion. Right now, all she wanted to do was get back to them and take a nap. Instead, she was—once again—arguing with V'ger about the management of the Order's resources.

"They can't stop us." V'ger stifled a yawn. "Look, all of the factors are falling into place. All I want to do is a ritual for prosperity for the Order. I think we deserve it."

"We are already prosperous enough." Corelli opened her eyes again and looked at the other four people in the room. "We should continue to do our good works and regain any lost power, money, and reputation the slow and steady way." She looked at the three other members of the First Circle, and saw that none of them wanted to get in-between her and V'ger. Not even Keth, the old wise woman and peacemaker of the group. Though, at least the woman would still look her in the eye.

"This is the time to strike!" V'ger's voice rose with his irritation.

"As Mistress of Magic, I tell you that this is not the time."

"I'm the First in the Order of the Sacred Eye, and you will do what I say." V'ger stood and loomed over her.

Corelli, a short, plump, blond woman, and not imposing at all, gathered her power to her and stood. The sense of magic made everyone, except Keth, shift backward. Even V'ger. Her words were low and full of menace. "Do you want to remain First?"

V'ger straightened, becoming formal and remote. "Do you challenge me?"

I put you where you are, Corelli thought. She looked him in the eye and knew he was thinking the same thing. *Perhaps that was a mistake. You have too much of the old ways within you.*

Before Corelli could answer, Keth's quiet, quavery voice cut through the tension. "Who are we supposed to strike at? I don't know about either of you, but I haven't been sleeping well."

V'ger and Corelli both stopped posturing and looked at the old woman. When Keth saw she had their attention, she continued. "In fact, many within the Order have not been sleeping well. Have either of you noticed?"

V'ger sat, deflating like a balloon. "Yes. I haven't been sleeping well either."

Corelli sat last, watching them. She frowned. Now that she thought about it, most of the Order had been cranky and complaining of nightmares recently.

Keth nodded. "I have shields up. I always do. But I'm still tired. Like something is pushing against them when I sleep."

Corelli nodded. She also had shields, but she was still tired. She thought it was because she and V'ger had been fighting so much lately. She looked around the table, specifically at those who had not spoken: Rook and Sagan. Both of them nodded to her.

"I'm sorry." V'ger nodded to Corelli. "My dreams. They keep hinting at the Order failing because we don't have enough resources. It's affecting me."

"Perhaps..." Corelli spoke slowly as she thought aloud. "Perhaps we have a problem we aren't aware of." Glancing at V'ger, she nodded her acceptance of his apology. "Perhaps we need to look into these unquiet dreams. See if only the Order is affected, or if others—supernatural or not—are also affected."

V'ger raised his chin. "It's a good idea. At least I'll feel like we are doing something against my sense of impending doom."

Corelli nodded, looking at Keth and Sagan. "Yes. We'll start with mundane investigations, and then move into a seeking."

She gave V'ger a wry half-smile at his sidelong glance. She still had the scar that wrapped partway around her waist from the last seeking they did.

It had almost killed her.

***

Karen looked around Mason Steward's mayoral office as they spoke. It was richly appointed in dark woods and leather. All of it had the sense of age. The large cherry wood desk had wear marks, the old-fashioned leather chairs, while polished, had cracks and scuffs, the heavy drapes were decades out of style. In the corner was an old, large, stylized globe she recognized as a hidden bar.

As she turned her full attention back to the man in front of her, Karen realized the office wasn't as luxurious as it seemed at first glance. Most likely, the man had inherited the décor from the previous two or three mayors. Rather than spend the money to update it, Mason had chosen to keep it the same.

"This is an unexpected situation." Mason was looking at the laptop screen in front of him as he spoke. "We do have discretionary funds for the upkeep and safety of the city... and that is what you do. However, there is no official full-time position I can offer you."

Mason was a well-cut middle-aged man who had not allowed his sedentary job to dissolve his muscles into flab. He had the look of someone who enjoyed working out and used it as a stress reliever. Though his brown hair had more gray in it than the last time they'd met, and there were dark circles under his eyes. The closer she looked at him, the more tired and stressed he seemed.

Karen shook her head. "As I said before, I'm not looking for a handout. I don't want you to jump through financial hoops at the expense of the city. Thank you though, for making the effort."

He continued as if he had not heard her. "While there is no official full-time position, there are contract positions I can offer you. I could put you on retainer as a 'Consultant' for the city." Mason looked up. "That means you'd be paid to advise me on matters concerning your specialty."

"My specialty?" Karen sat back and considered this.

He gave her a smile that contained no joy. "Finding trouble and fixing it."

"I'm not sure..." She shook her head. "What exactly would my duties be? You know that I answer to Reginald above all."

"I don't actually know. I suppose I would need to have a conversation with the Master of the City about all of this." Mason folded his hands and gazed directly at her.

Karen shook her head again. "No. I'm sorry. That's not possible." She saw the disappointment in his face, and knew he really wanted to meet the mysterious Reginald. Karen wondered what he'd do if he realized that Reginald *was* the city of Kendrick and he'd been working for the 'Master of the City' all along. "I don't mean to look a gift horse in the mouth. I really don't. I just don't think what you're suggesting will work."

"Do you have a better idea?"

She heard the careful note of neutrality in his voice, and knew that if she was going to deny what he offered, she'd better have a counteroffer. "What about a case-by-case basis contract? I wouldn't be on retainer. I could be a freelance contractor assigned to look into a very specific problem and use my resources to track it down, advise, or fix it."

Mason nodded. "That way you can turn down the jobs that go against the Master of the City's goals, and you have specific tasks to focus on. Yes. That makes sense." He glanced back at the computer screen. "You'd still be a consultant. It would be freelance instead of retainer..." He glanced up at her. "We can see if you and I can work together in a non-crisis manner."

Not to mention that way you know a little more about that problem without having to pay anyone, Karen thought. She nodded. "Yes."

"Done and done. I even have your first assignment. Contract, I mean." Mason closed the laptop and pulled a file from the stack to his right. "I need to you to talk to Doctor Charlotte Gabrielle. She's the new psychologist for the Special Unit—"

Karen raised a hand. "Whoa whoa whoa, Mr. Mayor. We need to get a couple things straight first." Mason waited for her to continue. "First, who am I reporting to officially? Because if it's David, I'm going to have to decline."

Mason gave her a long look, like a schoolmaster considering the words of a favored but precocious student. "You will report directly to me. You will be consulting with Doctor Gabrielle. You may have to work with or talk to other members of the SU, but you will not be under Detective Hauberk's supervision."

Karen relaxed a little. "Okay."

"And the second?"

"What's the pay?" She gave him a pragmatic little shrug.

"Ah. $500 a week, 1099. Expenses paid with appropriate forms filed."

It wasn't great, but it was better than nothing. And with a 1099 status, she'd have to worry about her own taxes. It was a stopgap until she found something better. Or a cheaper place to live. Karen nodded. "All right."

"May I...?" Mason gestured to his file.

"Yes. Sorry."

"I need you to talk to Doctor Gabrielle. She's investigating a rising trend of nightmares within the Kendrick Police Department. It doesn't appear to be centered on any single group. But the fact that a good thirty percent of the force is suffering concerns me and makes me wonder if something supernatural is happening. We need to know who else is suffering. We need to know what's causing this. And we need to know how to make it stop."

"You should take this job." John stirred in his seat on the leather couch behind Karen.

She had almost forgotten he was there. She glanced over her shoulder at him. His face was the sort of bland that meant that he knew something. Karen also realized that he had dark circles under his eyes, too.

John wasn't looking at her. He and Mason were exchanging a look that spoke volumes, but she couldn't tell exactly what they were saying to each other. However, if whatever was happening was affecting John, there was no way she wouldn't accept the contract.

"I have been advised to accept this job." Karen quirked a half-smile at the mayor.

Mason turned his attention from John back to her. "Good." He closed the folder and handed it to her. "My secretary will set up an appointment between you and Charlotte as well as get all the paperwork for you to sign and begin payments. I'll expect an in-person weekly progress report from you. If you have something that shouldn't wait until that meeting, come by to report before then."

Karen took the folder and stood. "Thank you, Mayor Steward. I appreciate it."

He held out his hand. "I hope this works out for all of us."

She shook his hand and nodded. "Me, too."

***

Karen waited until she and John were in the car before she asked, "So, nightmares?" She didn't bother putting on her seatbelt. She could tell by the way he was playing with his cigarette that he wanted to smoke. She turned on the car just long enough to open his window halfway. No matter how good the foreign cigarettes smelled, she didn't need her car filled with smoke.

John smiled gratefully and lit the cigarette. He took a long drag and looked out the window as he exhaled. "I was warned about the nightmares by Lady Grey. She says they aren't normal things. They're... monsters from her original world. Her places of power are broken. They need to mend. In the meantime, it's like the guards at the gate have been gut-stabbed. They're still there, but weak."

"She said all that? When?"

He shrugged a little. "A couple months back. I did something to help her. She warned me. I think she was thanking me, in her own inscrutable way, for what I did... for what I had to do... to help her."

Karen touched his arm, not sure how to ask what he did and why it bothered him so much.

John patted her hand. "I gave her a Todari card to strengthen her hold on the land." He watched her eyes widen in surprise and then her face shifted into something more neutral as she realized the seriousness of the problem.

He did not tell her that he had condemned a woman to death to get the card, or that she'd only been saved by the grace of having the negotiations at *Sushi-Ya*. It was a detail for another time.

"You gave her a Todari card."

"Yes."

"Wow. That's…"

"Yes. I know. I've done some research into protecting dreams since then, but…" He shrugged.

Karen shook her head. "It's not working." It wasn't a question. "I can see how tired you are." She nodded to herself and glanced at the folder in the backseat of her car. "I think I'll be reading that tonight."

John stubbed out his cigarette, then carefully removed the dregs of tobacco from the butt before putting it in a pocket to be destroyed later. "Hopefully, the SU has some idea on what's going on. Something to focus on beyond 'protect your dreams.' We need a plan and a way to beat them."

***

Elsewhere…

Five-year-old Kathy wandered among the rows of the toy store, knowing that she could have anything she wanted. She'd never been so happy. Turning from the shelves of her beloved LEGOs, Kathy followed the musical notes of her favorite TV show.

Turning the corner, she saw the huge TV. It wasn't playing her show. Just the music. Instead, dark shapes twisted and twined about themselves. While she watched, the TV screen grew bigger and bigger, and then pulsed as tentacles of darkness burst forth. She screamed as they reached for her.

Kathy was still screaming as she woke from her afternoon nap.

***

Dustin yawned and put an arm around Amber as the two of them walked down the street. It was a day like any other, walking through the City Center Promenade. They stopped by the statue of Colonel Kendrick to admire the dancing flowers. While Amber played with one, Dustin frowned, suddenly recognizing the scene with a sense of déjà vu and dread. "We gotta go. This is where it happens."

He scanned the park, looking for what he knew was coming. There it was: Scott and his sawed-off shotgun. The man was coming to kill him for stealing Amber away. After he was dead, Scott would do terrible things to her.

Dustin grabbed for Amber's arm, but she was no longer there, and Scott was sprinting at him with a primal scream of rage bursting from his mouth.

Dustin ran. He ran down streets and through houses, leaping fences, and busting through doors. All the while, Scott was right behind him. Even as Dustin turned a corner and knew it for the dead end it was, there was nothing he could do to stop the madman behind him.

He ran to the end of the alley and found a ladder in the corner. It was new in this all-too-familiar nightmare, and he didn't hesitate to grab for it. But even as he swung it around, Scott was there with the shotgun, firing. Only the wild swing of the ladder knocked the weapon to the side. Pain lanced through one arm as he yelled.

Dustin jerked awake, sweating and panting. Amber was there, looking sleepy, disheveled, and concerned. "The nightmare?"

He nodded. "He shot me this time." Looking down at his arm, he was surprised to see a smear of blood.

"Oh, honey. You must've scratched yourself." Amber left the bedroom to get a washcloth.

Dustin stared at the furrow on his arm. It was in the exact same place he'd been hurt in the dream. He looked at his hand. His nails were clean. No blood on them.

***

Cody slouched as he followed his mom into the hospital. At least this would be the last time. They'd come to pick up his dad. Once dad was home, everything would be all right again. Cody was sure of it.

He waited as his mom talked to a woman at the counter, not paying attention to anything. Then, mom turned to him. "Go get your father. It's time to go."

Looking around, he didn't see his dad anywhere. He looked back at his mom. She pointed down the long hallway. Cody nodded. "Sure."

The hallway was long and empty except for something at the end. The closer he got to the thing at the end, the more scared he became. It was a hospital bed with brown paper bags on it. As he watched, the bags grew wet with gore. One of them burst open. Blood, internal organs, and bones poured out in a torrent.

Suddenly, a wave of bloody viscera filled the hallway and rushed toward him. Cody yelled and turned to run, but he was swamped, the force of the wave knocking him over. It smothered him, carrying him in the current of gore, keeping him from breathing. Lungs burning and panicked, Cody dug his way to the top of the viscous blood that had once been his father.

Cody jerked awake, gasping for breath that became an asthma attack. He scrabbled for the emergency inhaler by his bed. Two medicinal puffs and an eternity later, he could breathe again.

He sat there, shaking, tears rolling down his face. The nightmares were getting worse, and he had no idea what to do about them.

Unexpected Changes, Part 2

ERIC IRON EYES sat at the picnic table on his back porch. A large mug of black tea, half-full, sat in front of him. He wasn't looking at, or thinking of, anything. He was too tired for that. Too many unsettling dreams that were more than what they seemed. Dreams that Sees-the-Wind had warned him of, but could do nothing about—yet. Things were breaking that shouldn't be breaking. But right now, he couldn't wake up. In truth, he was almost asleep with his eyes open.

When the young twins, Thomas and Thomasina, appeared across from him without warning, Eric didn't react in surprise or shock. Instead, he blinked twice and looked at both of them with a bemused frown. He took a large swallow of his cooling tea, then tilted his head and asked, "Who are you? I know you, don't I?"

"He can see us this time," Thomasina said and offered him her hands.

"He can see us. That means the time of the pact draws near." Thomas also offered Eric his hands.

The teenager looked at the twins for a moment before putting his mug down. He took their hands in his as he asked with sudden wariness, "Am I dreaming again?" Eric looked around, alert for dangers.

"No. Not yet. You can see us only because the twilight is near."

"You will sleep and soon."

"But we'll be here to protect you."

"A promise."

"A pact."

"No more Nightmares."

"We will be with you from now until the end."

Eric looked between the twins. They spoke quickly, making it sound as if only one person were speaking through two bodies. In truth, he couldn't focus enough to keep track as the voices trickled over him like the chiming of tiny bells in the wind. But the warm sense of safety made it so it didn't matter. "You'll protect me in my dreams?"

"Yes. We will. We can. Because of our pact."

The fragment of memory bubbled to the surface of his mind as the twins shifted until they were sitting on either side of him, guarding him.

"Promise me." Eric, only ten years old, put out his hand, palm down. "Promise me you won't leave me."

Thomas and Thomasina placed their hands on top of his and spoke in unison. "We swear that we won't leave you for as long as we can. In this, we'll serve the Lady as best we can."

Eric felt the power of the promise binding the three of them together, and relaxed. "Thank you. I'll be brave when the danger comes with you at my side."

The twins nodded. "We will be brave together."

"We'll be brave together," Eric murmured as he rested his head on his arms.

Just before he fell into a restful sleep, Thomasina whispered in his ear, "The Veil is failing. We cannot hold back the Nightmares. You must figure out how to rebuild our places of power. Get Speaks-for-the-City to help. Remember. You must remember this when you wake up. Or all is lost."

***

Karen gazed out of Doctor Gabrielle's office window at the green hedge next to it. Her dreams had been filled with the sense of tall, green hedges all around her as she ran through a maze. She wasn't trapped, but she couldn't remember the way out. At first, it had been a beautiful walk but then... there was something else on the other side of the hedge. *A feral dog,* she thought. One that was tracking her, following her scent. *A hungry, feral dog....*

"Miss Wilson? Sorry to keep you waiting. I needed to get a couple of files."

Karen turned back to the older black woman. She was attractive, with high cheekbones and clear skin. "Please, call me Karen."

"Then call me Charlotte." After shaking hands with Karen, she sat down behind her desk. "So, you're here to consult with me."

Karen nodded. "There seems to be a problem of nightmares plaguing the city. I've talked to some of my friends, and it looks like about one in four or five is having nightmares. A straw poll said it was higher amongst Kendrick's more, ah, special citizens."

The psychiatrist nodded. "It does indeed. Those in the Special Unit seem to be more sensitive than those on the regular force. Got any ideas?"

"On what's causing it? Not immediately. But I haven't talked to everyone yet. That's next on my list. You got any ideas?"

"No." She sighed, shaking her head. "It's not an allergy or a drug. It's not the work. It just seems to be affecting those who are good at paying attention to their intuition and all their senses." The doctor patted the files in front of her. "I was once a cop in the SU. I rose to the rank of detective, then graduated out to civilian life, then into my current position. I'm going through some of the old files of cases I worked on back then, since I have access again. I thought they might give me a lead."

Karen glanced at the stack of manila folders. "Are they confidential?"

Charlotte hesitated. "To you, officially, no. But I'd rather go through them first, to weed out the red herrings."

"You think the nightmares are supernatural." It wasn't a question.

Again, Charlotte hesitated. "What do you think?"

"What would you do if I told you they were monsters?"

"They?"

Karen looked out the window again at the lush greenery. "The nightmares. Caused by monsters... and were monsters themselves?"

Charlotte sat back in her chair. It creaked as she did so. "I'd need some sort of proof."

"How do you prove that a nightmare is real?"

"I don't know."

Karen shook her head. "Neither do I." Her eyes caught the impression of glowing footsteps on the sidewalk. Just like the ones she had seen when she first met the Grey Lady. The ones that led her to where she needed to go. "But I think I know who to talk to about the problem."

"May I go with you?" Charlotte leaned forward against the desk, gazing at Karen. "I've been a psychiatrist for a couple of years now. I've held this particular job for only a couple months but what I've seen in that time..." She shook her head. "I know enough to know that I don't know enough."

"I... don't know." Karen continued to look out the window. "Look outside. Do you see anything interesting or strange?"

Charlotte stood and looked at the hedges and the sidewalk beyond them. She glanced at Karen, then looked back at the world outside her office window. She shook her head. "No."

"All right. Then, for the moment, no. I can't let you go with me. I'm sorry to cut this short, but I need to go. Now." She held up a hand at the disappointed look on Charlotte's face. "Think of it like me going through my own set of case files first before I share the relevant ones."

Karen gestured to the window. "I won't keep you out forever. I just need to make sure that what you see is what you need to see, and doesn't muddy the waters of this investigation." She paused. "I know you're going to write down everything. Let's make sure it's the right stuff. There's got to be a large SU file on me somewhere."

Charlotte had the grace to look chagrinned as she sat back down. "All right. I understand." She glanced at her calendar. "Meet tomorrow at 3 p.m.? I should have something to share then."

Karen stood. "Sounds good. I'll also share what I can. Then we can make a plan to fight these nightmares." She shook hands with Charlotte across the desk before glancing out the window. The footsteps were still there, waiting for her.

After Karen left, Charlotte sighed. It had been a quick but productive meeting. She grabbed one of the folders at random and opened it up. It had the pictures of two young girls on the first page, with the names *Miriam Page* and *Susan Moore* under them. She opened it and began to refresh her memory of the incident.

***

Karen hurried outside. As soon as she reached the sidewalk, she found the glowing footsteps, and wondered what the Grey Lady needed of her. She followed them back toward the City Center and the Colonel's Park. This wasn't where she expected them to go. She thought they would head out of town, toward Makah land, where the Grey Lady was convalescing.

Through the park and past the statue of Colonel Kendrick, Karen watched the steps lead her toward the chessboard tables. She stopped when she saw who they were leading her to: a teenage boy with one set of the Lady's twins sitting on either side of him. Karen slowed as she approached, looking the kids over. The boy was handsome, with short black hair, a round face, and cheekbones that revealed his Makah heritage. He wore the ubiquitous teenage uniform of t-shirt, jeans, and sneakers. It was what she'd be wearing if she hadn't had the meeting with Charlotte this morning.

Karen saw that all three of them were watching her come over. The boy sat up, then stood. He offered his hand when she got close enough. "Thank you for coming, Speaks-for-the-City."

For a moment, she almost didn't shake hands. Whenever anyone used that name for her, bad things tended to happen. Or were already happening. Then she took his hand in hers. "Call me Karen, please. It's more comfortable."

"I'm Eric Iron Eyes." He sat back down.

Karen glanced at the twins and guessed. "Thomas. Thomasina."

"Hello." The twins spoke as one.

Eric glanced between them. "You can see them?"

"Yes. When they want me to." Karen sat down. She gazed at the serious look on Eric's face and noted that, while he seemed rested now, he had the fading dark circles under his eyes of someone who hadn't been sleeping enough. "So, you called me?"

The boy looked at the twins and they nodded. "I, we, the city—everyone needs your help."

Karen didn't say anything, she just waited for him to continue.

Eric rubbed his hands on his jeans, a nervous gesture. "You know the Grey Lady and her people are kinda like the fey, right?"

"I do now." It made sense, and she had suspected such with the need of the rituals completed on May 1st to help heal Lady Grey. "Never had it confirmed before."

"Right. Okay. They are. And they're bound to the land. And all their places of power have been destroyed. And their ancient enemy, the ones they've been protecting us from, are breaking through."

"The nightmares." She didn't look at him. Instead, she traced the lines around the black and white squares of the chessboard, thinking. *This kid knows a lot about me, and already trusts me enough to talk about things that would sound crazy to anyone else. Who is he?*

"Yes."

"You know how to stop them?"

Eric shook his head, then paused. "No. I don't, but they do." He nodded to the twins.

Karen flicked her eyes between them, then looked back at the chessboard, knowing it was easier to listen than to try to keep track of which one was speaking.

"The Veil is breaking."

"The Nightmares are coming through."

"The Lady's places of power used to be..."

"...the gates that barred the way."

"Horn..."

"...and ivory..."

"...and all the greenery that bound us to the land..."

"...need to be rebuilt."

When Karen looked up, she looked into Eric's pleading eyes. "How? Why must I do it?"

"I don't know. You are of the city." Eric shrugged. "I can't because me and my people are guarding our land as best we can already. We're the only reason they haven't destroyed everything, yet."

Karen thought about it. There wasn't much to go on, but she'd dealt with worse. "Must I be the one to rebuild the places, or...?"

Eric shook his head. "I don't know. I just know you are the person who can help the Grey Lady and her people." He paused. "I think you have the resources to know where the places are and can fix it. I think you, personally, need to fix at least one. The most important one."

"12th and White." Karen remembered where the glowing footsteps first took her. It was her first meeting with the Grey Lady. "All right. How do I fix the places?"

The boy shrugged again. "My best guess? Repair the growing things. Love the land. Be there for it."

"A guess is better than nothing."

Thomasina and Thomas exchanged a look around Eric. Then Thomasina spoke. "The land will fight you. You are not one of us. But you are of the City, and it is within the City that the mending must be done. It will bar the way for a time."

"Will it stop the nightmares?"

Thomas shrugged. "It will keep them from harming more."

Karen sat up straight. "The nightmares can hurt people? Like really hurt them?"

Eric nodded. "Yes. That's how they'll come through into this world. Through dreams."

"And me fixing the Lady's places of power will help."

"It will stem the tide for a time."

"What's the permanent solution?"

Neither the twins nor Eric could answer that. They just shrugged. Finally, Eric said, "I'll ask Sees-the-Wind."

Karen stood. "All right. It's a place to start. You got a cell phone?" When he nodded, she wrote her number down on a piece of paper from her purse. "Call me when you learn anything." She paused. "But don't get yourself in trouble, yeah?"

Eric frowned. "Trouble?"

"Don't skip school to figure this out."

He gave her a haughty look. "I don't go to school. I got my G.E.D. last year. I'm a man now. I work for the tribe."

Careful not to smile at Eric's pride, Karen gave him a solemn nod. "All right. What do you do for them?"

"I work in the Cultural Center. But I'm Sees-the-Wind's apprentice."

That surprised her. He was the shaman's apprentice. It explained why he knew what he knew, and trusted her the way he did. "Good to know. How's he doing?"

Eric paused before answering, "Well enough. I'll give him your regards."

Karen heard the hesitation and refusal to answer for what it was. She didn't press the issue. Instead, she said, "Thanks." Nodding to the trio, she walked away. When she was out of earshot, she asked the air, "Well, Reginald, what do you think?"

Reginald's answer through her Bluetooth earpiece was slow in coming. *"I think you need to go to 12th and White to see what they mean by 'fixing' the Grey Lady's places of power. I also think you need to find out where her other places of power are besides the one you know of."*

"You don't already know?" Karen walked back toward Charlotte's office and her car.

"I suspect, but you may need to talk to Mayor Steward."

"Yeah. Good idea." She didn't say anything else until she unlocked her car and got in. "I guess it's a good thing I've got the time to research this stuff." The statement was intended to make her feel better about being fired. It did just the opposite, and made her miss the mundane security of a regular job.

***

Keth and Corelli sat across from one another in the private den reserved for the First and Second Circles of the Order. Corelli leaned toward the much older woman. "What do you think I should do? I see two problems, and I don't know how to deal with either without shaking the foundation of things."

"Two problems," Keth repeated, but said no more.

Keth's quavery voice did not detract from her sense of power and wisdom. Corelli appreciated that in her. Keth was her personal embodiment of the Crone. "Yes. V'ger and these bad dreams. I can't help but think they're connected somehow."

"Why do you say that?"

"Because my dreams are putting V'ger in the villain's role."

Keth rubbed her chin. "In running the Order?"

Corelli shook her head, then flushed. "More personal. Attacking me because of whom I'm dating."

"Pish. He wouldn't. If he did, we'd all put him right."

Corelli paused. "...Yes. I know." Her hesitation made a lie of her words.

"We would," Keth insisted. "Alexia is a lovely girl. Even if she won't join the Order."

"See, that's just it. All my dreams are about V'ger attacking her as disloyal and me as an aberrant abomination. But I didn't used to have them, and I've been seeing Alexia for months. This is why I think the dreams are trying to sow discord. It's deliberate. It's sentient."

The older woman mused. "That's why V'ger is looking for an enemy to strike out at."

"He's becoming a real danger to the stability of the Order and our reputation. I'm still repairing it. Some people still won't talk to us." Corelli gave a frustrated sigh. "Damned if I do and damned if I don't."

"What do you want to do?"

Corelli looked around the room at the myriad of books on the walls and thought about her answer. "I want... I want to call the leaders of the primary factions together and talk with them about the dreams. It's not just us. The more of us working on the problem, the sooner the problem gets solved."

"But...?"

"But I know Karen still won't talk to me. That knocks out John Corso, Lamiel, and the Makah."

Keth nodded. "But not everyone. Susan Moore."

"She's not the leader of the Gargoyles anymore. Plus, she's Karen's friend."

"She still has power. And the Stewards. I'm sure Mayor Steward would have a word. This affects the whole city, after all."

Corelli tilted her head and considered this. "Mayor Steward. An offer to help." She smiled. "That might do it."

"And V'ger?"

Corelli shrugged. "I'll burn that bridge when I have to. But not before."

"Smart girl." Keth patted Corelli's knee. "See, there are always avenues you can take. Don't let the dreams get you down. That's what they're trying to do. Don't let them win."

***

Karen stood on the corner of 12th and White, her face pale with shock and surprise. Where a lush hedge fence had once stood, protecting the Grey Lady's home within, there was now an empty, abandoned, trash-filled lot. Partially excavated, the land was torn apart, with a huge hole in the middle of it. The hedge was nowhere to be seen. Only a few sickly branches broke haphazardly from the soil at all angles.

"Reginald, who owns this land?"

There was a pause. *"The City of Kendrick."*

"Can we make it so I own it? Or you own it?" Karen walked onto the packed, dry dirt and crouched. "I need to be able to fix this. And I need to do so right now."

"I can work on it. Right now, I've shifted it to my name. It'll be harder to shift it to yours. How will you fix this? The land is dead to me."

Karen could hear the worry in his voice. "I've got a plan. I just need to give Mayor Steward a call first." Reginald didn't answer. Instead, there was the sound of a ringing phone.

"This is Mason Steward."

"Hi. This is Karen." She shifted her crouch into a cross-legged sitting position. "Got some questions for you."

"Hello. What do you need?"

"I need to know what happened at 12th and White."

"I'm not sure what you mean."

She could hear the genuine confusion in his voice. "Okay. This is going to be weird. There's a vacant lot at 12th and White. It used to be... surrounded by a large hedge. Now, it's like there was something going to be built here, but not anymore. Everything's been abandoned. And all that's left is a city block of broken dirt and trash."

Mason was silent for a long moment. "Is this in conjunction with the case you're consulting on?"

"Believe it or not, yes. Lemme tell you, it's going to be a hell of a report. Actually, can you come by Doctor Gabrielle's office tomorrow at three? I need to fill her in, too." Karen doodled in the dust, drawing hearts as she heard Mason's rapid-fire typing. She winced as she scraped her fingertip on a rock that wasn't there before. *'The land will fight you,'* indeed, she thought.

"Ah. I see. I'll do what I can to be there. As for your question... it was one of the improvement projects Vicki required when Anu had control of her. Does that help?"

Karen stared at her fingertip, then rubbed the smear of blood from it. "Yes. It does. Okay, now I need two things. The first is a list of all of the places Vicki wanted 'improved.' Second, I need to know what my freelancer budget is."

"I'll work on the first. What do you mean on the second?"

"As a consultant for the city, what's my expense budget?"

"How much do you need?"

Looking around the vacant city block and how much needed to be rebuilt, Karen had no idea. "Thousands. Short version, I need to rebuild the hedge around the city block at 12th and White and repair the land. I'm talking tools, plants, seeds. Thousands. And yes, this *is* involved in fixing the nightmare problem." It was her best guess anyway, based on what Eric and the twins told her.

Again, Mason was quiet. Finally, he said, "Five thousand. If I can't figure out how to make the city's budget cover it, I can cover that much myself. But, you'll need to pay for things out of pocket yourself first."

Karen winced at the thought. So much for her severance package. "Yeah. Okay. I can do that."

Neither of them said anything after that for a few seconds until Mason cleared his throat. "Anything else?"

She shook her head after a moment. "No. Nothing."

"Tomorrow at three, then."

"Bye." Karen listened as the line went dead. She patted the ground in a wordless promise to make things right. "Reginald?"

"Yes, Karen?"

"Where's the nearest garden store?"

***

An hour later, Karen stood with Terry and Margaret, the owners of *Green Thumb Gardening and Supplies*. Terry stood next to a pile of tools, gardening gloves, seeds, and fertilizer. "Remember, you start by breaking up the land, then add the seeds and fertilizer. Remember to water and to keep the birds away. That will start the process for turning dead land back into something things can grow in. By that time, you might have a better idea of how many shrubs you need. Plus, you should probably look into getting enriched soil to push things along.

Karen shook her head and rubbed her arm. "There's so much stuff... I really don't have any idea of how much of anything I need."

Margaret handed her a sheet. "Here's a cheat sheet for checking the soil samples you need to take. Just make sure to read the instructions on the NPK kit carefully."

Terry returned with a piece of paper that looked suspiciously like an invoice. "I've got this stuff totaled up but, I can't give you an estimate on the bushes until you give me a number."

"How many bushes surround a city block?" Karen laughed and shook her head. "I don't suppose I could get you two to come out and look at what I'm trying to do, could I?"

Terry shook his head. "We don't normally do that. I can recommend a good landscaper."

"No. No. This is something I need to do myself." Karen sighed. "Okay. You deliver, right?"

Margaret nodded. "Yes. There's a small fee depending on how far you want us to go, but with the amount of bushes you want and the fact that your car just won't hold them, it's probably a good deal."

"Not that far. Just to 12th and White."

Terry and Margaret stilled. They looked at each other, suddenly somber. Terry cleared his throat. "You're doing what, exactly, at 12th and White?"

Karen looked at the couple, surprised at the change in demeanor. "Um. I'm fixing it. It was a protected field surrounded by a tall hedge. Then, it was all torn down for a building project that got abandoned. Now, the whole city block is a mess and needs to... be... fixed."

Karen stopped talking. It was clear that they weren't listening anymore. Instead, Terry and Margaret stared at each other, wordlessly speaking in spouse speech through expression and small gestures. Terry and Margaret appeared to be negotiating something. Finally, Margaret nodded and walked away.

Terry turned to Karen. His voice was rough with suppressed emotion. "I'm not going to charge you for this stuff. I can eat the cost of it. I'll have to charge you for the hedge bushes. But, I was wondering if—if I could help?"

"Help?"

"Help you fix the land."

Karen was completely bewildered. "I... why?"

Terry looked at the ground, folding and unfolding the invoice. "I was..." He looked up at her. "I was one of the construction workers who tore down the hedge and broke the land. It was awful. I quit my job soon after. We opened this place to help make amends. But, I've been having nightmares about it for the last couple of weeks. Blood welling up from the ground, drowning the city of Kendrick."

Karen's surprise turned to anger. She immediately stomped on it. Terry had been nothing more than a man who was only doing his job. He didn't know what he was doing would hurt anyone. But part of him was sensitive enough to feel the wrongness of the job. He was of the city. He had helped break the place of power. Him helping her fix it might be exactly what she needed.

In fact, getting people of Kendrick, the sensitive ones, to help rebuild all of the Grey Lady's places of power would probably be a boon. She mentally added that advice to the list of things to tell Doctor Gabrielle and Mayor Steward. To put it in the guise of getting people out of the office and into some fresh air. Together, the people of Kendrick could help rebuild the barriers to protect themselves.

Terry, apparently taking her silence for no, shoved the mangled paper in his pocket and clasped his hands together. "Please, Miss Wilson. I need to do this. I won't charge for my help. I'm volunteering."

"Oh, no. I mean yes. Yes, I welcome your help. I haven't even figured out things like, how to water a barren plot of land. You *are* the help I need. In more ways than one." Karen smiled at him and his sudden relief. "In fact, why don't we head over there now with this stuff and you can tell me what else I need?"

"Sounds good. Let me tell Margaret."

"Terry?" He paused and she gave him a nod. "Thank you. I appreciate your gesture."

He smiled. "I'll be right back."

Karen pulled out her cell phone and typed a quick text message to John to tell him what she was doing, and asked him to pick up a frame tent and a couple of folding chairs for her. It appeared that she was going to spend a whole lot of time at 12th and White for the foreseeable future when she wasn't reporting to the Doctor Gabrielle and the Mayor.

"You seem happy."

Used to unexpected outside commentary from Reginald, Karen shrugged. "I know what I'm going to do with myself for a bit. I'm going to fix the Grey Lady's power base and work for the Mayor for a while. Not what I had planned at the beginning of the week, but I think I'm going to like it. Either that or I'm going to be too busy to freak out about everything."

***

Elsewhere...

Anoria kissed Prince Kieron again before leaning back in her chair. "This, my love, is so much more than I expected when you invited me to a picnic in the forest." She gestured to the table and chairs and the sumptuous dishes before her: quail, roast pork, scones, fruits, and wine.

"The forest was the only place I could get you alone, beauteous one."

She looked around at the tall forest trees and the restless horses nearby. "It's perfect. I couldn't be more happy."

"All I ever wanted to do was please you, my dear." Kieron gave her a winsome smile and raised his wine goblet. "A toast."

Anoria raised her goblet. "What are we toasting to?"

Kieron answered, but Anoria could not hear his voice. "Pardon, my prince? I didn't hear you."

The arrow struck her hard in the chest, just above her heart. She cried out in pain and surprise as she dropped the goblet. A second arrow pierced her stomach, and Anoria fell from her chair, gasping and shuddering at the pain. The form of Prince Kieron loomed over her as her blood fed the hungry ground.

"I said, we are toasting to your death." His handsome visage twisted into something dark and ugly. He crouched over her, touched the lethal arrow protruding from her chest, and smiled at her whimper of pain.

"Why...?" This wasn't what she'd expected. He loved her. He swore it.

"Because I can. Because you people don't deserve the world you live in."

As the blood stained her once beautiful gown, Anoria knew she was dying. "I don't... understand..."

"You don't have to." Kieron grabbed the shaft of the arrow and gave it a hard twist. He raised his voice so he could be heard over her scream of agony. "All you have to do is die. Your death is my portal."

"STOP!" The voice thundered from behind Kieron, but Anoria didn't hear it. She couldn't hear anything anymore and never would again.

Kieron stood, sneering at Amit. "Priest. You're too late. The portal is open."

Brother Amit didn't waste time with words. He threw himself at the Nightmare monster pretending to be a prince. As he knocked Kieron away from Anoria's body, they both tumbled into darkness with the sound of a far-off woman's anguished denial following them.

In room 723 of Kendrick Mercy Hospital, Linda Stephenson screamed for help. Blood poured from her comatose daughter's body, and there was nothing she could do to stop it. Linda pressed her hands on the wounds that suddenly appeared, yelling for help that would not come in time.

In room 727 of the same hospital, Brother Amit woke from an eighteen-month coma, thrashing against an unseen assailant.

Waking

"HE WAS HERE, Brother, I mean Abbot. I swear. On my life, he came out of the dream and was here." Amit clutched Aaron's hand like a drowning man.

Aaron patted Amit's hand with his free one. "Call me 'Brother.' I prefer it for now. And I do believe you. Things have been happening." He looked around the hospital room that had been Amit's home for over a year, thinking. He patted Amit's hand again and stood. "I need to make a call. I think Detective Hauberk should hear your story."

Amit reluctantly released Aaron's hand. "Detective Hauberk? Really?"

"Really. A lot has happened while you've been in a coma." Aaron turned away, pulling his phone from his pocket. Moments after he dialed David's number, he noticed a familiar silhouette down the hallway at the nurses' station.

"Detective Hauberk here."

Aaron half-smiled. "Turn around." When David did, Aaron waved. "I was just calling to see if you had time to come see me."

David's answer was to wave back and hang up the phone. He didn't say anything until he met Aaron just outside Amit's room. "Heya. I have a little time. What do you need?"

"It's not me. It's someone else. It's sort of semi-official for the SU."

"Well, with that very definitive answer, how can I say no?"

The two men smiled at each other, and Aaron gestured to Amit's doorway. "It's a bad one if what Amit's saying is true."

David lowered his voice. "Do *you* think it's true?"

Aaron paused, then nodded. "I hope it's not but, yeah, I think it's true."

"I can hear you two. I'm not deaf. And I'm not lying." Amit's voice was weak, but clearly irritated. As the two of them entered, he continued, "I minded the Brotherhood's infirmary since before you two were born. You don't think I know how to listen or pick up on a hushed tone?"

David inclined his head to Amit in apology; his claim was an exaggeration, but not by much. "Doctors make the worst patients."

"Don't I know it." Amit gestured to the chair. "This is going to take a bit, and you're going to want to take notes and ask questions."

After glancing at Aaron, who shrugged, David did as he was told and resisted the urge to ask if there would be a test later. If this was important enough for Aaron to call him, it was important enough to have his attention. With his notepad and pen ready, he nodded at Amit to begin.

Now that he had his audience's attention, Amit was at a loss for words, and struggled to get his thoughts in order. Aaron walked to the other side of the bed and put a hand on his shoulder, supporting him with his presence.

Amit nodded to him, then turned to David and began. "Coma patients dream. At least, some of them do. I did. I've been dreaming ever since I was brought in here. Not all the time. Just a lot of the time. Sometimes, I would become aware that I was dreaming. That would wake me up. Not enough to... interact with the outside world. Just enough to know I was trapped in an unmoving body. It was easier to go back to sleep. To dream my life."

David wrote very little down so far. Amit's name and the date. That was it.

"Then the dreams changed. I don't know how long ago it was in real time, but for me it's been many months. They became real. So real that every sensation was like being awake again. Really awake. But I could tell that I wasn't awake. I couldn't..." He paused and glanced between Aaron and David.

Aaron squeezed Amit's shoulder. "Tell him. He knows."

Amit turned back to David. "I couldn't find the spiritual realm. I couldn't find any of my brothers. It was this that made me realize I wasn't really awake. But, it was so real, and the dreams, they took a darker turn."

"How so?" David leaned forward. Bad dreams were something he and every member of the SU knew about. So much so that Mason had the SU psychologist working with Karen on the problem.

"Little things would happen. Bad things that would turn a good dream neutral and a neutral dream bad. Unquiet dreams became nightmares. If you even thought about something going wrong, it was like something was there, hidden in your dream, just waiting for it. They'd... it... would pounce, and make it worse. And it wasn't just me."

"What do you mean?"

"When the dreams changed, I started sharing the dreams of all the coma patients. Sometimes with people sleeping nearby. It was like we were all being drawn into a shared dream reality. Things got worse, but I had the ability to fight the monsters. To banish the evil things. It was as if I were working in the spiritual realm, but only in dreams..." Amit stopped, his voice rough. He reached a trembling hand toward his water cup.

David leaned forward and helped him. As Amit sipped from the straw, he asked. "When you defeated these evil things, what happened?"

Amit was quiet. "They'd go away. For a little while. We'd all dream our separate dreams."

"So, when you all dreamed the same dreams... you knew something was happening?"

"Yes. In the last month or so, Kieron focused on Anoria—what?" Amit looked at David's face.

David shook his head. "Go on. I'll tell you when you're done. Kieron? Who is that?"

"Kieron is the name of the Prince in Anoria's favorite book, *The Prince of the Lost Forest*. She's been in a coma the longest, as far as I can tell. I was here second longest. Her mother read her all her favorite books. That one is the one Anoria loves best. Whatever's been haunting our dreams, it subsumed the character, taking its form.

"Kieron seems to be the leader of the monsters in the dreams. When I realized I could banish him, he started ordering me and the others to be attacked while he spent time with Anoria. It was as if her belief in him gave him strength. But when he attacked and I fought him, his hold on her broke. It got to the point that when I realized things were going wrong, all I had to do was find Anoria and I'd find him."

Amit looked at his hands. "I was too late this last time. He had already had her shot with arrows. He said, 'Her death is my portal.' I didn't stop to think about what I was doing. All I wanted to do was get him away from her. I attacked him, but we both fell into darkness. I thought it was like all the times before, but it wasn't. When we hit the ground, I woke up. Here. In the hospital. Kieron was with me. I swear it on my oath as a Brother of Light, he was here."

David nodded, writing quickly. "What does he look like?"

"Shadow. The absence of light. Like a hole in the world that moves."

"What happened to him?"

Amit looked up and shook his head. "I was too weak to hold him. He slid through my fingers. It was like trying to grasp mist. He said two things: 'I am free.' and 'Soon, the rest will come through, Priest. You have no power here.' I think he's right."

"I don't know about that." Aaron lifted his chin. "We are many and all of us have different skills."

"Amit." David continued to write. "Do you have any marks on your body from the fights in the dreams?"

His answer was to push the blankets down until his thighs were exposed. On the left one was a livid scar. Then he pulled at his hospital gown until his left side was bare. There, still raw and weeping, was a six-inch scratch.

David sat back in the plastic chair and blew out a breath. "You said Anoria was shot with arrows. Where?"

"In the chest and the stomach." Amit pulled the blankets back into place. "How is she? I heard the hospital calling for help for her room..." He paused at the look on David's face. "She's dead, isn't she?" He blinked at the flood of tears that came as David nodded. "I tried so hard..."

David was silent for a moment. "I was here investigating the crime. Something was clearly wrong. No one had gone into Anoria's room for over an hour besides her mother. Then she was screaming for help." He paused. "Anoria bled out from two puncture wounds. One in her chest. One in her stomach. She was dead before the doctors got to her."

***

"That was a nice surprise." Alexia stretched and lay back against the red-and-white checked blanket. "A picnic lunch, complete with gingham. Thank you."

Corelli remained seated, cross-legged and smiling. "You're welcome. I thought you'd like it." She still couldn't believe such a beautiful woman loved her.

"What brought this on?"

"Do I need a reason to surprise my girlfriend with something awesome?" Alexia didn't say anything. She just gazed at Corelli, who shrugged. "I needed a pick-me-up. Making you happy always makes me happy."

Alexia nodded. "Okay. So...?"

"Bad dreams." Corelli paused in her packing away of the leftover food and dishes. "You having any problems with bad dreams?"

"Nah. I did, but then I got my dream catcher and my witch ball and my hematite up. No bad dreams since."

"That's kinda a hodge-podge."

Alexia sat up and shrugged. "Doesn't matter. You should know by now that magic isn't about the things you use. It's all about the belief. The trappings are just that—a trap if you let them confine you. My belief is that the dream catcher will catch evil dreams before they reach me. The witch ball will capture ill-intent as it enters my space. And the hematite is a ward for the mind. I believe, therefore it works."

Corelli shrugged again. "I'm just used to people being a little more focused in their trappings. Then again, my sympathetic magic looks like chaos to some."

"Gotta get to work." Alexia stood. "Wanna see the shop?" She offered Corelli her hand. "It's got some cool stuff."

Corelli accepted the help. She already knew that Alexia was stronger than she looked. "Sure. I have a little time."

The two of them folded up the blanket together and set it on top of the picnic basket. They stopped by Corelli's car and dropped it off. Then, hand-in-hand, they headed through the park toward one of the myriad streets surrounding Kendrick's City Center. It should have been a lovely walk for Corelli. The sun was out, peeking through the high clouds, she had had a good lunch, and she was here with her girlfriend. Instead, as clues she should've seen sooner fell into place, she thought she was going to throw up.

Her worst fears hit as they turned the corner. Corelli stopped and let go of Alexia's hand. "I just remembered something. I gotta go."

Alexia tilted her head. "Don't have time to see the shop?"

Corelli shook her head. "I got a thing. Completely forgot about it. Besides, seen one metaphysical store, you've seen them all. Next time though. Promise." She gave Alexia a quick kiss on the cheek and backed away, pulling her phone from her purse.

"Okay. You promised. See you soon." Alexia turned and sauntered up the street. She put an extra swing in her hips as she headed into work.

Corelli smiled, appreciating the teasing. Her smile disappeared as Alexia entered the *Teller's Fortune*. She typed quickly on her phone and ducked around the corner to wait.

***

John looked up as Alexia entered. "Hey Alex. Right on time. Gotta go. Got a meeting with people you don't care about.

Probably out late. Lock up when you go." He grabbed his tweed jacket as he spoke and shrugged it on.

"No problem, boss." Alexia stuffed her purse under the counter. "Anything else?"

"Nah. Make me lots of money, and make sure no one burns the... place... down." John's words slowed as he gazed at his phone with a bemused frown.

She glanced at him and raised an eyebrow.

John shook his head and grabbed his ubiquitous beat-to-hell messenger bag. "Anyway, don't take any wooden nickels."

"I just might. They're worth more than five cents these days."

He paused at the door. "Point conceded." Then John headed down the street toward the Colonel's Park, stuffing his phone in his pocket.

He stopped at the corner and gazed at Corelli. "'Come talk to me now at the corner of 5th and Steward. It's super-super important?'"

Red-faced, she blurted, "I'm dating Alexia, and I didn't know. I swear to God. If I had, I would've told you sooner."

John took a step back, completely off-kilter at her words and the panicked emotions behind them. "What?"

"I swear, I didn't put her up to it. She doesn't even care about the Order."

He stared at her for a long silent moment, trying to parse what she was really telling him. Because, clearly, she knew she was dating someone... "Oh." He narrowed his eyes, frowning at her. "Alex is your girlfriend."

"I didn't know she was working for you. She just told me she was working at a metaphysical shop, and had just gotten the job a couple weeks back. I didn't encourage her." Corelli stopped. "I mean, I did, but not to work for you. Just, you know, to keep looking for the right job. Please don't fire her. She's happy, and she doesn't care about the politics of... us."

He rubbed his cheeks with both hands then removed his glasses and started cleaning them. "So, your girlfriend works for me and you want me to know you didn't set it up."

"Right. I swear. I wouldn't do something like that. I know Karen..." She paused at the warning look on his face, then pushed on. "Look, I know she doesn't like me. I've accepted that. But I need you to know that Alexia means the world to me, and..." She threw her hands in the air. "Shit. I don't know what I'm saying, but now you know."

John put his glasses back on. "All right. Noted. And noted that you didn't set it up. No, I'm not going to fire her because of you. Anything else?"

Corelli paused, then nodded. *In for a penny...* "Yes. Have you been having bad dreams lately? We've been having them at the Order, and... I think they're sentient."

"Sentient?"

"Specifically attacking your greatest fears and designed to cause chaos. I was hoping to talk to some of the other factions. Because, if we're all having problems with them, then it's something we all can work on. I've got an idea or two that I'd like to share."

John looked around the Colonel's Park, not seeing it. "Okay. Yeah. The dreams are getting around. Yeah. You might have a good idea there." He held up a hand at her smile. "But don't expect miracles. I've got a meeting to go to. I'll talk to people about getting a big shindig together."

"Thank you for trying." Corelli bit her lip. "I appreciate it."

"No problem. Anything else?"

She shook her head. "No."

"Good. We'll talk later. Don't call. I'll call you." He looked at her a moment longer, then turned and headed for his meeting with Mason at City Hall.

Corelli let out a sigh and turned back to her car. She'd talk to Alexia about this later. When they had private time together. She had to let her girlfriend know what sort of minefield she was walking in now.

***

From the doorway of the *Teller's Fortune*, Alexia watched John and Corelli part ways.

She shook her head with a rueful smile. Right there was the main reason she didn't care about the Order of the Sacred Eye, or the Special Unit, or the Steward family, or any of it. Humans made things far more complicated than they needed to be. Well, at least everyone was on the same page now.

She headed back inside, humming a tune that hadn't been heard in hundreds of years.

***

John knocked on Mason's office door and peeked in without waiting. He was surprised to see David sitting across from the Mayor. Mason gestured for him to come in. "Just the man we wanted to see."

David stood and offered his hand. "John."

They shook hands and sat as one. Mason looked between the two of them. Then his gaze settled on John. "You want it quick or detailed?"

"Good or bad news?" John shifted his bag to the floor.

"Bad. Mostly."

"Quick, then."

Mason nodded to David. David glanced at the notepad in his hand. "Short version: Things are worse with the dreams. One murdered a coma patient and used her death to come into our world, and then escaped."

John gazed at David for a long moment, his face neutral. "Is that it, or is there more bad news?" Inside, his stomach dropped into the basement.

"That's the crux of it. The rest is details. On the good side of things, Amit, member of the Brotherhood of Light, is out of his coma and knows what Kieron looks like."

"Kieron?"

"The nightmare enemy that came through."

John looked down at his hands and wanted a smoke. The urge came more and more often when he visited with the mayor. "Right. Okay."

"Ideas?" Mason gazed at them.

"Many," David said. "Beginning with running for the hills."

Mason shook his head. "I need something a little more constructive."

"We don't have enough to go on."

"David's right. And Corelli's right." John looked up. "We don't have enough to go on. Corelli believes that the dreams are sentient, specifically attacking us where we are weakest. She believes that all of us who are suffering need to get together, share what we know, and see if we can form a plan together."

"A lot of it seems to hinge on the Grey Lady and her people. Rebuilding her powerbase." Mason rubbed his chin. "I think Karen had the right idea on returning all of Vicki's special building projects back to the land. At least, the ones that can be."

"We should get the people suffering to help. The SU and the like." David gave them a wan smile. "If nothing else, getting everyone out to do hard physical labor will help them sleep."

"We can call it a 'Beautification Project' for the city." Mason typed a note to himself. "How is she?" He didn't look at John, but they all knew the question was aimed at him.

John shrugged. "Sleeping in a tent on the lot she's trying to fix. And getting her hands dirty." He paused. "I really do believe we need to get a meeting together as soon as possible and I think the Grey Lady needs to answer some questions. This enemy is one they've been fighting since before we got here—if I understand things right."

"Agreed. Though, that's going to put the meeting on Makah land." Mason drummed his fingertips on the desk. "Might put some people off."

David shook his head. "Don't care. We've got to get something going. Now. Nightmares that can murder people in their sleep and somehow manifest in this world are a hell of a lot more important than everyone's personal issues. People need to wake up to the fact that some problems don't give a damn about politics."

"I'll set the meeting up," John said. "I'll get everyone I can there. You guys work on the rebuilding of the land." He gathered his bag. "Unless there's more?" David and Mason exchanged a glance, then shook their heads. John pulled a cigarette from his inner pocket. "Okay. I'd love to stay and chat but the sooner we meet, the sooner we have a more permanent solution to these nightmares."

"I'll give you a call." Mason waved to him.

John nodded to them both and hurried out the door. In truth, he still wasn't comfortable around David. It wasn't just his past relationship with Karen. It was the way he would betray whomever he was working with for what he perceived to be the greater good. The first time, he'd almost gotten Karen killed. The second time, he'd helped defeat Anu. If there was a third time, would it be the right choice or would someone else pay the price, again, for his mistake?

***

"There. Press firmly around the base of the shrub. Mix in the planting soil. Make the basin. Top dress with mulch.

Water." Terry worked while he explained what Karen needed to do for each new shrub. His hands moved the dirt with sure confidence as he planted the bush.

Karen gazed at the single plant. "Two feet apart. Hole as big as root ball. Tease some of the roots free. Bury. Planting soil. Basin. Mulch. Water." She muttered this to herself aloud. Then closed her eyes and repeated it again.

"I'll write it down for you."

She smiled with relief. "Thanks. I'm going to miss having you here with me, but I think you're the perfect guy to help all of the groups that will be working on fixing up Kendrick."

Terry's smile faded, but he nodded and slapped his hands together. "Yeah. Gotta get back to it. I'll leave the instructions on the table."

Karen watched him go. After his confession, the two of them had specifically not talked about his nightmares, or what she really meant by "fixing" the land. They both pretended it was nothing more than one big, crazy project. She wondered what he'd think if he knew she'd be telling the land stories at night. Shaking her head, she banished the brief thoughts of embarrassment. It was hard to be embarrassed when you were saving the city.

She got to work. Her hands moved more slowly, less sure than Terry had been. The land seemed to welcome his touch while it fought with her, every step of the way. She hoped it was just a lack of experience, and not the land being angry at her.

An hour and two planted shrubs later, Karen stopped with a curse. Pulling her garden gloves off, she found that one of her blisters had burst. It was weeping blood and pus. With a defeated sigh, she bowed her head and stared at her abused hands. They were dirty, sore, and covered with blisters.

"Are you all right?"

She looked up with a jerk then relaxed. It was Eric Iron Eyes. "I didn't hear you coming."

The teen shrugged. "I'm quiet like that." He frowned. "What'd you do to your hands?"

"Hurt them."

"C'mere." He gestured for her to follow and headed to the shaded pavilion. He was so imperious and sure of himself that she followed, amused. He pointed to one of the chairs. When she sat, he went to one knee and held out his hand. "Let me see."

Curious, Karen did as she was told and showed him her hands. "Are you a healer?" She remembered that Aaron had healed her a long time ago after she had almost died.

"I can heal." He glanced up at her. "Trust me to do so?" She nodded. "It will hurt at first."

"Okay. Fair warned." Karen tilted her head, watching him. He seemed older whenever he put on the mantle of shaman's apprentice.

Eric touched the ground and picked up a handful of dirt. "The land is waking. It's angry, but it will be soothed. You're doing a good job."

She started to say "Thank you," but had to bite back all sound as he rubbed the dirt into her hand and its wounds. She could hear him muttering something under his breath, but couldn't understand what he was saying. The pain was enormous. Then, as he stopped rubbing, it was gone. He took one of the nearby water bottles and poured the water over her hand, cleaning it of dirt and all of her hurts. Karen gazed at her wet but healed hand with awe.

"How—?" she gasped as he repeated the healing on her other hand.

"How? I'm Sees-the-Wind's apprentice. I know the secrets of the earth." Eric stood with a lopsided grin and shrugged. Then he looked around the lot. "What did you do? It looks so different."

Karen looked up from her no longer hurting hands and dried them on her jeans. The lot did look a thousand times better. "I cleaned up all the trash. Terry smoothed the dirt over with his earthmover. Then he showed me how to break up the dirt and mix in fertile soil. I spread the grass seed and watered." She flushed a little. "Then I stayed... and I talked to the lot. Told it all my memories of Kendrick."

Eric glanced at her with that teasing smile.

"You said, 'Love the land.' How else could I? I love Kendrick." She shrugged. "Anyway, I've just started planting the shrubs. I have to keep an eye on things to make sure the birds don't eat the seeds."

He nodded. "I'm impressed. The land is waking. Can you feel it?"

"I don't know. It seems cranky."

Eric laughed. "I would be, too. It's kinda like the land drank all night, got into a fight, and is waking up with a hangover and bruised knuckles."

"I hope the fast-growing grass is like aspirin." She glanced up at him. "As long as you're here... wanna help?"

"Sure."

"Good. Get the water."

***

Elsewhere...

Susan sat next to Alexander on the beach near Pier 3. "Isn't this where we first met?" She looked up at the large gargoyle she leaned against. "Is that why you chose this place to meet?"

He kissed the top of her head, his mental voice rumbling in her mind. *"I did not choose it. But, yes. We met here long ago."*

Susan sat up, looking around. "I wouldn't choose this place. I hate it. I love that I met you, but I lost so much here. I didn't choose and you didn't..." They both stood up as one, wary now. Watching the waterline.

"Is it possible your mind is trying to remind you of something?"

"What?" She hoped with everything she had that she wouldn't see Miriam... or the other thing. The monster pretending to be a kelpie.

"How did you get to this place back then?"

She frowned. "I came here after I stole the whaling spear tip from the museum."

"Is it the museum you need to return to?"

Susan shook her head and looked up at him. "I'm there now. On a cot."

"Where were you before the museum?" Alexander did not look at her. He scanned for movement all around them.

"It was..." She stopped. The name of the place wouldn't come to her. She knew what it was and where it was, but something kept her from remembering it exactly. "I... It was..." Susan shook her head. It was right there on the tip of her brain. She *knew* it.

Then all thoughts of that other place fled her mind as Alexander stiffened. She turned and froze. There, coming from the waves, was the creature of nightmares. The thing that killed her best friend, and almost murdered her. It was a horse the color of storm clouds, with one white eye and one black eye.

"It's can't be," Susan shook her head. "We killed it. It's dead." But the one white eye glaring at her denied her words. She'd stabbed it in the eye to get away the first time. It was the same monster.

Alexander grabbed her by the shoulders, putting himself between her and the kelpie. He gazed into her eyes as his voice shouted in her mind, making her wince. *"You must remember the other place. You must!"* Then he gave her a hard push backward, and she was falling.

Susan cried out, reaching for him. Her cry of fear and lunge brought her back to the real world as she tumbled off the cot and onto the hard basement floor of the museum. She looked up at Alexander's unmoving form, wondering if he was fighting the kelpie now, or if waking her up had banished the monster.

Shifting to a sitting position, she reached for a nearby pen and clipboard. "Remember," Susan murmured. "Remember. Remember. Remember." Then she did. Quickly, she wrote the word *LIBRARY* in all caps on the inventory sheet. Shaking her head, she also wrote the words *Historic Library* on the back of her hand. She needed to talk to Karen or John about the dream. Preferably both.

She needed to remember why Kendrick's Historic Library was so important.

Waiting for the Pieces to Fall

CHALICE SAT AT the first table by the front door of the Kendrick Historical Library, tapping her foot. Ignoring the open book in front of her, she glared at the door, willing it to open. She refused to look away even when Nicholas, her boss of fifteen years, walked up behind her and cleared his throat.

"What are you doing?"

"Waiting." Her voice was sharper than intended, but she couldn't help it.

"Chalice." Nicholas paused and waited for her response. When she didn't give it, he walked around the table and broke her line of sight. "Chalice McGinn." His voice was quiet and firm.

She glared at him. "What?"

"What are you waiting for?" The two of them squared off as she stood, scowling. Both were short and round. He was 5'4" and she 5'2". They looked soft, but looks were deceiving— for one of them in this case. Nicholas knew she could flatten him without breaking a sweat, and favored violence to solve all problems. She was an excellent protector for the library.

"For him. Or her. My replacement. They should be here soon."

It was Nicholas's turn to scowl. "Have you been reading your Lifebook again?"

"What if I have?"

Glancing up at the vaulted ceiling of the two story library and asking the figures in the fresco for patience, he sighed. "How many times have I told you that you can't look in your book? It changes things. If they were coming today, they probably aren't anymore. You shouldn't read your Lifebook."

She gave him a shrug and glanced over his shoulder at the door as she spoke, "Shouldn't, but can and did. They're coming, whoever they are. It's about damn time we got another bibliotaph. A fully *human* bibliotaph. I got things to do."

Nicholas shook his head slowly. "You've been saying that for over a decade. You've waited this long. Now you're going to wait a couple days longer. You know they must have a true need to find us."

"They do. They will. Someone with dark hair and dark eyes is going to come walking through that door any moment now." Chalice sat once more and glared at the open book.

The Head Bibliotaph for Kendrick's most unusual library rubbed his salt-and-pepper beard and watched her, wondering how she knew the hair and eye color of the next staff member.

He shook his head again and returned to the back room. Three more books appeared in the special section to be shelved. He had some reading to do before he put them away. Reading about someone's unexpected death was always hard. But someone needed to do it. Just in case.

Chalice returned to staring at the library's arched double doors. "C'mon..."

***

Karen sat under the pavilion in the Grey Lady's garden (as she'd come to call it) and gazed at the growing grass. It was green and healthy, but short. Too short. It wasn't growing fast enough. Also, only about one third of the hedge shrubs were planted. She'd stopped wearing the garden gloves. The ground seemed to behave more after she bled a little. "It's a good thing Eric can heal my hands each night."

"Yes, it is." The Grey Lady's voice was soft, but not weak.

Karen looked at her and frowned at what she saw. The Grey Lady did not look as good as she sounded. She was back to looking almost translucent. Her hair, as wispy as ever, was piled on her head in an untidy bun. Though, Karen knew it couldn't be that bad. The Lady's eyes were still grey.

"You've done good work here, Karen. Thank you." The Lady gestured with one shaking hand to encompass the half-finished plot of land before her. "I am sad that I won't see it completed."

"But you will." Karen was on her knees before the Grey Lady, beseeching her. "I've worked so hard. We all have. Me and three other groups. You've got to survive."

The Grey Lady shook her head. "I cannot, and will not, as I am now. I am far too weak. I am a shadow of what I once was. There are too many ever-dreamers. They're keeping the portals open."

"But we need you." Karen looked down at the grass. "We need you like never before."

"As I need you. You and yours. You can find a way to save me."

"How?" Karen looked up when the Lady did not answer. "How?"

She only shook her head. "I may not tell you. That must come from a source beyond my power." The Grey Lady touched Karen's cheek. "You will find it. The clues have been laid."

They both looked out at the Grey Lady's garden as crows began to flock and feed on the seed. Karen rose, waving her arms at the birds. "Go! Shoo!" When they didn't move, she rushed the flock (*murder*) of crows, waving her arms. "Go!" She stopped abruptly when she realized they all had red eyes and were not afraid. They cawed as one.

"You must find a way, Karen. I am fading."

Karen looked at the Grey Lady but she was no longer there. When she looked at the crows, she screamed as they rushed her.

***

Waking with a jerk that sent her sprawling in the dirt, Karen found herself in the empty lot under the tent she'd set up. Her chair was tumbled onto its side, but the Lady's garden was as she dreamed it—growing grass and a partly completed hedgerow. There were no nightmare crows. But their screaming sound was still there.

Her phone rang again from where it had fallen. Karen bowed her head as she sighed with relief and picked it up. It was Susan.

"Hello?"

"I have to talk to you." Susan sounded rushed. "Like, now. Can you?"

"On the phone?" Karen picked herself up and brushed the dirt off her worn jeans.

"No. Face-to-face. Where are you?"

"The lot at 15th and White." She looked at her hand. Her nails had black dirt packed under them. "But I can be at my apartment in twenty. Give me thirty minutes. I need to shower. I'll leave the door unlocked."

"Okay. Thanks. See you in thirty."

Karen blew a dark curl out of her face. A quick clean up of the tools, and she could be on her way.

***

Karen waited until Susan was settled with a cup of tea before she started finger combing the tangles out of her long hair. "All right. What's up?"

"I know I should wait until the meeting tonight, but I wanted to get your thoughts first." Susan rubbed the hand she had written "Historic Library" on, but avoided the inked area.

"Meeting?"

Susan blinked at her. "You know. To talk about the dreams... the nightmares?"

Karen shook her head. "No. I've been under a rock. Well, digging rocks and dirt."

"Oh. I assumed John told you." She went back to looking at the writing on her hand. She was unsettled that the writing surprised her every single time she noticed it.

"Probably tried to." Karen dried her hand and retrieved her phone from its charger. "Yep. One missed call and three texts. Good thing you called. He'll be here in an hour." She paused and looked at Susan's discomforted face. "Do you want to wait for him...?"

"No." Susan shook her head. "No." She paused. "I had a dream. I was with Alexander. We were on the beach where we first met."

"I'll bet that was nice."

"No. No, it wasn't. It was one of the worst days of my life." Susan smiled briefly at Karen's confusion. "Not meeting Alexander. What happened that made it so we met."

Karen sat on the couch and resumed getting the knots out of her hair. "Was it a nightmare? The dream?"

"Not really." Susan frowned, looking at her hand. "It was... I don't know what it was. Alexander thinks I brought us there to remind myself of something. Of where I had gone for help. Do you know about the Kendrick Historical Library?"

"Oh, yeah. It's on..." Karen paused. "I mean, I've heard of it. It's... I don't remember where. I don't think I've been there."

"I have. It was interesting."

"What was?"

Susan looked up. "What was what?"

Karen tilted her head. "What was interesting?"

"The Historical Library."

"Oh, yeah. I've heard of it but I've never been there."

Susan frowned. "You just said that."

Karen blinked at her, reviewing her words. "I did. That's weird. I forgot what we were talking about for a second."

"I wonder if that's why I'm startled whenever I see the writing on my hand. It's important to all this, but..."

"Writing?" Karen frowned, trying to remember what they'd just been talking about. "Sorry. Must have zoned out."

Susan dug a pen out of her purse and offered it to Karen. "Take this." Once Karen had, she nodded to Karen's hand. "Write this on your hand. 'Kendrick Historical Library'."

Karen paused, opened her mouth to say something, then shut it again. She did as she was told. "I'm being affected by something to forget it." She handed the pen back. Then she spoke to the air. "Reginald, send me an email with the Kendrick Historical Library's address on it." Her phone binged in response, and Karen saw she had a new email. "Thank you."

"The library is important." Susan was staring at her hand now.

Karen followed suit. "Yes, and I think I know why. You dreamed about it. The Grey Lady came to me in a dream. Told me that she was failing and that 'me and mine' needed to save her, but she couldn't tell me how. But we would find a way. We already had the clues."

"You think the clue was my dream?"

"That's my best guess. Especially since we can't seem to remember the Historical Library unless we're staring at our hands."

Susan shook her head. "I don't remember having such a hard time finding the place, or remembering it, when I went there last."

"Have you been there since?" Karen glanced up at her.

Susan paused and shook her head again. "No."

"Isn't that strange? The curator of the Kendrick Museum hasn't been to the Kendrick Historical Library in how long?"

"Twenty years. That's strange. Yeah, we need to go and see if they have something to help the Grey Lady."

Karen shrugged. "Yeah. I'll have John put it on the agenda for tonight. We can talk about it then."

***

"I've made arrangements to have it at the meeting house on Makah land." John looked over the spines of the books in the one bookcase Karen owned. It was filled from top to bottom with an eclectic assortment, from drawing to the history of the Pacific Northwest to urban fantasy novels. "Some people won't like it, but it's the only place the Lady can come."

"She's not doing so well. I hope she makes it." Karen busied herself in the kitchen, cleaning up the mess she'd made in the last couple of days. "So, who all will be there tonight?"

This wasn't something he wanted to talk about right now, but it was an innocent enough question. "Well, the Makah leadership, Susan, Lamiel, Kurosawa, David, Charlotte, Mason, Corelli, Aaron." He rubbed his forehead, trying to remember everyone who had said they'd be there.

Karen paused her loading of the dishwasher. "Corelli? Really?"

"Yes, really." John continued his list. "I think some from *Sushi-Ya*—"

"Why is she going to be there?" Karen interrupted, angry that John would invite someone from the Order of the Sacred Eye to this. Especially someone like Corelli.

John winced at her sharp tone. "Because I asked her to be there, and because this was her idea in the first place."

"You know I don't like her and I don't trust her. She threatened Sebastian." Karen looked around but the gargoyle was nowhere in sight.

"Doesn't matter."

"Yes. It does. I don't want her there."

John turned around and gazed at her. "You don't have a choice. What is your problem with her, anyway? Yeah, she threatened Sebastian, but the rest have done worse—to you, I might add."

"It's not the same."

"It is the same." John worked to keep his voice as level as possible. "We've all done horrible things to save this city, to keep our words. Aaron lied to you for over a year. You're fine with him. David... Christ. David handed you over to the Order and almost got you killed, and you're working with him. Mason? Mason let Vicki run rampant over the city and you're working for him."

Karen flushed hot and angry. "You said I should—"

"What about me? God, Karen, I've done horrible things to save this city." He gestured out the window. "I condemned a woman to death to get a Todari card to give it to the Lady to buy us time. And you still love me."

"She *threatened* Sebastian."

John glanced up at the ceiling then looked at her. "And why did she do that? Because you owed her, and when she called in the debt, you were going to go back on your word."

"Don't you dare try to put this on me. A good man died because of what she did." Karen clenched her fists so hard her ragged nails dug divots into her palms.

"Corelli saved Sebastian. You acknowledged you owed her. She called in your debt because she was paying off a debt, and you refused. She had no choice but to threaten him. She wouldn't have hurt him." John shook his head. "I think you need to look at why you're so angry with her, when you've forgiven people who hurt you a lot worse. I think it's because she reminds you of your hypocrisy. You, who always insists on doing the right thing, went back on your own word until she forced the issue."

Karen opened and closed her mouth, unable to think of what to say. Her face was white with fury.

"I'm sorry it came out like this. I've been meaning to talk to you about it for a while." John picked up his bag, throwing it over his shoulder. "Corelli will be there tonight because she's powerful, because she's smart, because she's been trying to make amends for what the Order did for more than a year now, and because she could be a good ally." He picked up his tweed jacket. "I hope I see you there tonight, too. A lot of people need to hear what both of you have to say."

With that, John turned away and left, quietly closing the front door behind him. He paused to see if she would come after him or call his name. When she didn't, he headed down the stairs, grimacing at the replay of the argument in his head. He hadn't wanted his thoughts to come out like that. He had wanted to broach the subject more gently. Maybe if he hadn't been suffering nightmares for so long, he could have. He shook his head. What was done was done and he would have to wait and see what she would do next.

They hadn't had an argument like this before. John had no idea how Karen would react to it after she'd had time to think.

***

Karen watched the meeting from one end of the hall. In the middle stood John, coordinating everything with Lumbering Bear, the Chief of the Makah people in the Kendrick area.

When she'd arrived, John and she had exchanged looks. He'd tilted his head at her and gave her a tentative smile. She had nodded back, playing her emotional cards close to her chest. It sucked when lovers fought and, clearly, the discussion was not done, but Karen was in work mode now. She would deal with the hurt later.

She knew or had met everyone in the room at least once, with the exception of a blond-haired man next to Aaron. He had been introduced as "Brother Jeffrey." They had been ignored by Lamiel and Kurosawa, who were still angry by what they considered to be Aaron's betrayal. Aaron was known as Brother Simon in the Brotherhood of Light, but when Karen first met him, he was pretending to be a Goth guy and part of the Bacchanalia Coven.

Corelli was next to Akira of *Sushi-Ya*. They both were speaking to Mayor Steward. Charlotte and David stood to one side, waiting. Behind them was John Mueller and his twin boys, Devon and Daniel. That meant the twin gargoyle leaders, Edgar and Edmond, were around, and would speak through the children.

"We haven't had a meeting like this in a while." Susan came up next to Karen. "I wish we didn't always meet when something awful was going on."

"Nothing like a greater enemy to bring warring factions to a truce." Karen glanced at Susan. "Have I been unreasonable toward Corelli?"

Susan's eyes got very wide and she hesitated. "I... uh... what?"

Karen looked down and smiled ruefully to herself. "Never mind. Just something I've been thinking about."

John saved Susan from having to respond by clapping his hands. "All right, everyone. We know why we're here. Let's talk about it." He paused and looked around. "Where's the Grey Lady?"

Eric stepped forward, with Sees-the-Wind at his back. "She cannot come. She is fighting the Nightmares as best she can in her weakened state." He raised his hands for quiet as the mutters started. "But she did say she's spoken to several of you in dreams. That you have all the answers she can give."

"All right. We'll work with that." John walked in a slow circle so that he spoke to everyone standing around him. "We have two problems: the first is that the Grey Lady is injured, the second is that the Nightmares are becoming physically violent toward those they can affect."

"It's more than that." David stepped forward. "One of them murdered a girl and came through to here. This one has a name: Kieron. Right now, that's all we know. Here, he's like a shadow. In dreams, he leads the Nightmares. I think he's the Grey Lady's opposite."

"What do we do about this?" Akira, the older Japanese man, looked around the crowd. "Even mine are affected."

"I think..." Corelli stepped forward as David stepped back. "I think I know one way. One of mine told me that protection from the Nightmares is a matter of will. It's not what you believe, but how strongly you believe it that will protect you. I think, for those of you who are rebuilding the Grey Lady's places, you need to think of it as rebuilding a protective wall in your mind."

Karen watched how Corelli made eye contact with everyone except her. She specifically didn't look at Karen. It was if the woman was afraid of being slapped. Inwardly, Karen grimaced. She had a lot more thinking to do about this, but first... "I think Corelli is correct. Alexander protects Susan in her dreams. I have the hedge wall I'm rebuilding. I think, for those who have no belief system in place, we can teach them about protective measures. Everything from dream catchers to lucid dreaming."

She saw how surprised Corelli was at this small measure of support and sighed. Karen wanted to kick herself as she watched her own reactions to Aaron and David. Yes, she had forgiven them, even though she had not forgotten what they'd done. With the Mayor... it never occurred to her to put any blame on him for what Vicki had done. Not Vicki. Anu. That was something else she would have untangle in her head.

Mason stepped up. "We'll add that to our defensive measures." He glanced at David and Charlotte. Charlotte was writing quickly in her looping shorthand. "The stronger we can make our minds, the less they can hurt us."

"But what about Kieron?" Aaron asked. "Now that he's here, can we fight him?"

The crowd stood there, looking at each other for a long, uncomfortable moment. Susan and Karen looked at each other. Susan tapped the writing on her hand. Karen nodded.

"I think I have an answer for that." Susan did not move from her spot. "The beginning of an answer anyway. Do any of you know of the Kendrick Historical Library?" Most shook their heads. "I've been dreaming of it recently. I think we will find our answers there."

"Where?" John blinked his confusion.

"At the Historical Library," Karen said, and watched as faces lit up with recognition. "I've dreamed of the Lady. She told me that we must find the way to save her, and that she was not allowed to tell me how. But I believe the Historical Library has the answers. It's protected by obfuscating magic that makes you forget about it. I had to write it on my hand to remember it."

"I want to go with you," Eric said as he scribbled the word 'Library' on his hand. "I may know what we are to look for." He glanced over his shoulder at Sees-the-Wind, who nodded.

"I would as well." David also was writing on his hand. "At least on the first visit. To make sure everything is... safe. Anything that has magic to hide it might be angry at being found." He shrugged. "Besides, I like libraries."

"I don't know." Susan shrugged. "I found it when I was a teen. But I wasn't in danger."

"Found what?" Lamiel asked, looking around, confused. Her confusion was mirrored on many other faces.

Susan shook her head. "Tell you later. For now, we have a plan: First, guard our minds. Teach others to guard theirs. Do this while continuing to fix the broken places in Kendrick. Use whatever belief system works best—prayer, visualization, arcane tools. Second, Karen, David, Eric, and I will go to the Kendrick Historical Library, and see what we can find out about healing the Grey Lady and fighting a Nightmare that has come through."

"I agree. Anyone else got any good ideas or thoughts on what else we need to do?" John turned in a slow circle to see if anyone did. No one spoke. "All right. Everyone has their marching orders. And everyone..." He paused, making sure he had the entire room's attention. "...try to help those that need helping. Mundane or not. A teenage girl was murdered by these creatures because she didn't have the protection she needed."

With that, the meeting was over. Some stayed and grouped together. Some left without speaking to anyone. Susan touched Karen's arm, then walked over to the Mueller boys. She hunkered down and spoke quietly to the twins. John came over to Karen's side.

"Speaking to me?"

"Still mad at you, but yes."

John quirked a smile. "I'll take it. I'm sorry I dropped that on you like that. I meant to, I don't know, broach the subject more gently."

Karen looked down at her hands and shrugged. "You had every reason to. I'm going to think about what you said. Okay?"

"Okay." John watched as everyone left to continue their conversations in a more private setting until only Lumbering Bear, Eric, Sees-the-Wind, Lamiel, and Kurosawa were left. "You want dinner?"

Karen nodded. "I could eat."

"Okay." The two of them walked over to the small knot of people and caught the tail end of what was being said.

"—the Bacchanalia Coven stands with the Makah. What do you need us to do?" Lamiel said.

"Eric speaks with my voice, my authority, my wisdom from now on." Sees-the-Wind sounded tired but determined. "I ask that you acknowledge and respect that." He had been speaking only to Lamiel and Kurosawa, but now turned to include John and Karen.

Kurosawa and Lamiel looked at Eric for a long moment before Lamiel said, "It will be done." Kurosawa nodded his agreement.

"Certainly. He's been invaluable to me already." Karen grinned at Eric's blush.

"As you wish," John said and pulled a cigarette from his pocket. He offered it to Eric. "A gift."

Eric took the cigarette, his face solemn. "I'm not an elder, but I accept your gift of tobacco." He kept his face serious for a moment then laughed, shaking his head. "You surprise me again."

John smiled. "It seemed appropriate."

Karen tugged John's arm. "Let's go. Eric, we'll schedule the library visit tomorrow. Come by the Grey Lady's garden and we'll plan it." She waved at the rest of the group as they left.

They were silent until they got to the parking lot and stopped by Karen's car. John looked bemused as he removed another cigarette from his inner pocket. "What library visit?"

***

Nicholas sat down across from Chalice and set a large pizza in front of her. To that, he added a two-liter bottle of root beer, a cup, and a stack of napkins. He put a calzone and a can of root beer in front of him. "It's your favorite. Hawaiian with black olives."

Opening the box, she took a deep breath. The smell was incredible. Until this moment, she hadn't realized how hungry she was. Chalice smiled at her boss and friend. "Thanks."

"Figured you could use something. You haven't moved from that spot all day."

Chalice shrugged. "You know me. Hard as stone. Stubborn as one, too. What time is it anyway?"

"Nine in the evening," he said around a mouthful of food.

She nodded, then dug into the pizza. He hadn't bothered with a plate because she'd finish the whole thing before the night was through. They ate in silence for a good fifteen minutes. The whole time, Nicholas glanced at her between bites.

Chalice closed the box when a little more than half the large pizza, and most of the soda, was gone. With a sigh, she asked, "What?"

Nicholas put his soda down and looked over her shoulder at something behind her. "Are you so ready to die?"

This again. She shook her head. "Not to die. To get revenge."

"To get revenge is to lose everything." Nicholas looked her in the eye. "Everything. The prophecy was specific. That usually means your life, too."

"If I have to die, then so be it. My family will be avenged." Chalice refused to look away. She met every challenge head on, and that included Nicholas questioning her. "Maybe it just means everything I have. It didn't say I was going to die."

He turned his face away. "Are you so ready to be quit of me? Of the library?"

She paused, then spoke haltingly. "I... I'm ready for this to be done. It's been a good run with you. I've enjoyed it. For that, I thank you. But, we both knew this was coming. All of the signs and dreams point to it now."

"For certain definitions of the word 'now'."

Chalice smiled. "When you've lived as long as I have, now is a relative term, youngin'."

"Forty isn't so young in human years." Nicholas smoothed a hand over his balding pate. "I will miss you. You've been a good assistant."

"I'm not gone yet."

"But you're still going to wait, aren't you?"

Chalice nodded. She would wait at the library until her replacement arrived. She would sleep in the backroom, shower in the upstairs employees' bathroom, and eat her meals in the front here. Now that the time was here, she did not want to miss how her replacement reacted to the library, to Nicholas, and to her. She needed to get the measure of the man or woman who was coming.

Nicholas pulled a second two-liter of root beer and a large bag of chips from under the table. "Guess you'll need these to keep up your watch while you're waiting."

Chalice grinned and refused to think about how much her eyes began to well up. "Thanks."

***

Elsewhere...

"The time is here, my people. The time of escape and rampage. The time of pillage and death. No more will we have to subsist on the meager draught of dreams. No more will our foes flaunt their fortune before us. The Veil is falling, and I'm living proof. I've been to that other world. I know they are rebuilding the gates. The cracks are closing. So, now is the time to push. Now is the time for our freedom!"

Vicki watched Kieron rally the monsters from atop his horse. She remained as still as she could from her hidden vantage point as she eyed the giant insects, shadow creatures, things with claws and teeth that defied naming, and the mutants that brought to mind every terrible thing in the world. They stirred and squelched and chittered as Kieron paced his horse back and forth before them.

This wasn't like his usual speech, where he listed her sins and then called for the hunt. Finding out how they were going to hunt her each night was part of her punishment for what she'd done to Kendrick and its people. Once she discovered the rules to the hunt, she would flee. If she could make it to the light, she would survive another day in this hellish forestland where even the plants were carnivorous.

A hand wrapped itself around her face, covering her mouth, and she was pulled from her hiding spot. It took everything Vicki had not to scream and fight. If they'd caught her, they'd have to let her go. That was in the rules of the hunt. It had not yet begun.

"It's me."

The words were barely whispered in her ear as she was carried along. She recognized the voice and relaxed. Amit. Her savior. Her confessor. Her friend. The only real one she had here. Both of them recognized the irony of this. It was the Children of Anu who put Amit in the coma in the first place. If he had not been here, she didn't know how she would've survived without going insane.

When they were far enough away, Amit put her on the ground and they walked side-by-side, avoiding the most active of the entangling plants. "They said you were dead."

Amit shook his head. "Not me. Anoria. Kieron murdered her. I woke up."

Vicki bowed her head and watched her feet as they walked. Despite Anoria's love of drama and romance, she had liked the girl. Anoria was the only other teenage girl she could interact with. "Is that what he meant by having been to that other world?"

"Yes." Amit drew her into the hollow of a tree that had stairs descending into the earth. "I didn't know if I could come back. But I can. So can he. That means I need to protect you and the rest."

"If you can."

"If I can," he agreed.

They entered a small chapel and sat on the pews. Vicki gazed up at the arched, stained glass window and let her eyes follow the lines of the rolling landscape. "Maybe if I hadn't been so evil..."

"Stop that." Amit put a hand on her shoulder. "We've discussed this. You were spirit-ridden. You weren't strong enough to fight it. It's not your fault."

Vicki nodded. "Can you wake me up?"

He shook his head. "I don't know how. But I think I can ward you. To keep the Nightmares from coming through."

"Will they still hunt me?" Her voice was small and weak to her ears, and she hated it.

"I don't know. But we can try to dream you a new dream. One without a hunt."

"Okay." Vicki paused. "Can they still kill me?"

Amit was silent for a long time. "I don't know. Probably."

"Thank you for being honest. She tilted her head, looking at him. "With the ward, they won't be able to come through me?"

"No. I don't believe so."

"Good. At least that's something I can do to make amends." Vicki bowed her head and looked at the dirt floor. "If nothing else, I can keep them from coming through."

Amit smiled. It wasn't a happy smile. He squeezed her shoulder. "I'll do everything I can to help wake you."

Forgiveness and Sacrifice

"It's LOOKING GOOD." Susan smiled at the almost completed hedge and field of grass hiding the disaster the lot had so recently been. Though she was under the tent, she still had to shade her eyes. The spring had been unusually dry and sunny.

Karen gazed at the Lady's Garden with pride. "Yeah. To think I didn't know anything about this kind of stuff until a few weeks ago."

"You think you'll keep it up?"

"You mean, garden after the lot is done?"

Susan nodded. "Yeah."

"I don't know." Karen shook her head. "I don't really have space for it in the apartment. Maybe a few pots, if I can keep Sebastian from accidently destroying them." She paused to watch the small gargoyle play in the field, sniffing at the nascent weeds and flowers as well as the grass, in between bouts of chasing butterflies. "How is it that a gargoyle can cavort in full daylight, and still be so hard to notice?"

"Don't know." Susan shrugged, gazing at her hands. "Magic, I guess."

Turning at the immediate change in tone, Karen looked at Susan. Really looked at her. Her face was more lined now, and had a haggard cast Karen hadn't seen before. "You okay?"

Susan shrugged again. "Yeah."

"Nightmares?"

"No. It's just..." Susan stopped and shook her head. "It's not important."

Karen moved closer to her friend. "It is to me."

Susan hesitated then shrugged. "The gargoyles. They're doing really good. Now that they're bonded, the twins aren't fighting anymore." Her smile was bitter as she glanced up at Karen. "John and Cheryl are good parents, teaching the boys well—how to share, how not to fight, how to deal with the weirdness of being bonded. That's making everything smooth within the gargoyle leadership."

Karen frowned, trying to figure out what Susan wasn't saying. "That sounds great."

Susan blinked back tears. "They don't need me anymore. They won't really talk to me unless they want to get a message to Alexander."

Karen didn't know what to say. All she could do was gather Susan into her arms and hold her, letting the other woman use her for strength.

"I miss him so much..."

"I know you do, hon. I know."

"All I want to do is sleep to be with him, but..."

"But the nightmares."

Susan nodded against Karen's shoulder. "The nightmares are keeping me from him."

Karen squeezed her tighter. "We'll beat this. I promise. We have to. In a couple hours, we'll be at the Historical Library, and we'll find whatever it is we need to defeat this Kieron. We can do it. I know we can."

"I hope so." Susan pulled back. "This is killing me."

***

"What are you going to do?" Eric stood in the doorway of Sees-the-Wind's workroom. He crossed his arms and fought to keep his nervousness under control.

"Now? I will enjoy some lemonade and prepare for my afternoon nap." The old man tottered around the room, putting his tools away. He did not look at his apprentice.

"You know what I mean." Eric stepped into the room.

Sees-the-Wind raised his head, and no longer seemed to be as old has he had been just seconds before. "You are a wise young man. Smart, fearless, courageous. I chose well with you."

Eric swallowed hard. "Normally, such compliments would make me smile."

"They don't?"

"They don't."

"Why not?" Sees-the-Wind stood very still, so much so it was as if he weren't breathing.

"It feels like you're saying good-bye." Eric took another step toward his grandfather many times removed. "Like you're putting away your tools. Remembering to say the things you always meant to say. Making sure not to leave a mess."

"Your iron eyes see much." He still did not move. He only watched as his grandson approached with care. Sees-the-Wind smiled. "You have her eyes."

"You told the Grey Lady this binding would be the last. Whether her death or the new binding." Eric stood before Sees-the-Wind, mirroring his stance. "I ask again: what are you going to do?"

"Do you ask as shaman, or as grandson?"

Eric hesitated, then raised his chin. "Both. First as shaman's apprentice because what you do affects us all. Second as your grandson because... I care." He was proud that he kept his voice level and strong. His mouth was dry with fear.

For a long moment, the two of them stood there, gazing at one another. Then Sees-the-Wind put his hand on Eric's shoulder. "I go to protect the ever-dreamers. I go to fight the Nightmares until they, or I, are dead. I go to do my duty."

Eric blinked back sudden tears and looked away. There it was—the truth—his mentor was going to meet his end.

"Iron Eyes." Sees-the-Wind's voice was soft. When Eric looked at him, he nodded. "You have known of this for years. Even though you shouldn't have been eavesdropping. You have been trained to take my place. That day is today."

Eric's throat ached even as he nodded. "I understand."

"I will go to sleep now. I will not wake up. You cannot allow anyone to take me from my place."

"Wh..." Eric's voice cracked and stopped. He took two breaths and got control of himself. "What do I tell the council?"

"Lumbering Bear and Swimming Sky already know. They will see to my body while my fight goes on." Sees-the-Wind squeezed his shoulder. "You are not alone. I have prepared you and the others for this."

"I won't let you down, Grandfather." He paused. "Is there anything I can do to help you?"

Sees-the-Wind shook his head. "Nothing that you are not already doing." He looked to the corner of the workroom where he usually napped. Soon, the small pallet would be his deathbed. He looked back at his grandson and successor. "You are not ready for this, but you never are. No shaman is. Know this: I am proud of you. You will be good for the tribe. Trust yourself, and let them trust you."

Eric pulled his grandfather into a fierce, brief hug. "I won't let you down." He wiped at the tears welling in his eyes and pulled himself together as much as he could. "Now, I need to prepare to go to the library with the others."

Sees-the-Wind patted Eric's shoulder. "Do that, and know that I will not feel pain. Just a drink. Then I will sleep."

Eric nodded and stepped back. "Until we meet again."

"Until then." Sees-the-Wind gave Eric a nod and permission to go. The boy returned the nod, tears flowing freely down his cheeks, and then fled.

Sees-the-Wind sighed. One last duty to the land and his people. Then he could finally rest.

***

Eric ran from his grandfather's workroom, sprinted through the yard, and into the forest beyond. Tears streamed down his face as he gasped out his sobs. Sees-the-Wind was like a father to him, and now he was dying. Eric tried to outrun his overwhelming grief and fear. He ran as hard and as fast as he could go through the trees, until he stumbled and crashed into one of them. He sank to the ground, leaning against the tree, gasping and shuddering for a few moments. Then his tears dried and his breath evened.

His misery remained.

"You cannot outrun your pain."

"We've tried."

"But a pain shared—"

"—and we share it—"

"—is a pain lessened."

Eric smiled as the voices of Thomas and Thomasina cascaded over him. Then their small bodies pressed against his sides. He hugged both of them to him. For a long time, they said nothing. He remembered their pact and the promise. At least he would not be facing everything alone.

Finally, he said, "I'm scared." It was a hard thing to admit, but part of his training had been to feel, acknowledge, and accept *all* his emotions. Then, as needed, cast them aside or use them. "It's a lot of responsibility."

Thomas and Thomasina glanced at each other across Eric. Thomasina took up their collective thoughts. "You have been trained and you know what you need to do, Iron Eyes. When the binding comes, remember, we will be as you are now. It is a change that frightens and excites us."

"Will it hurt?"

The twins shrugged. "We do not know." Thomasina put her small hand on his. "But it will be worth it."

Eric patted both of them. "I'll be there for you and you'll be there for me. We'll be brave together."

"Yes." Thomas and Thomasina spoke as one of them giggled. Thomasina tapped Eric's hand. "You are forgetting something."

Eric looked down at his hand. The word, though smeared, was legible. "Library," he murmured. "Oh! I gotta go."

He jumped to his feet and ran back the way he had come, with the sound of the twins beside him like a soft echo.

***

Mason tilted his head and gazed at the two men before him. One, Amit, was still in his hospital bed. The other, Aaron, had the serious kind of look that said someone was in trouble. Unfortunately, Mason thought that might be him. He searched his mind for his past sins, looking for something that would get the attention of the Brotherhood of Light. He couldn't find anything.

"You asked me to meet you here?" Mason addressed the question to Aaron.

It was Amit who answered, "I asked him to."

Mason nodded, keeping quiet. He noticed Amit was looking stronger, and wondered how long he would remain in the hospital.

"Vicki is your daughter."

Mason stiffened and glanced at Aaron.

Again, it was Amit who answered. "She told me. We often meet in dreams. She's your daughter, but in all the months she's been here, you've only visited her twice. Why?"

"What is this about?" Mason glared at the two of them for a moment then took a calming breath. "Why are you asking me about her?"

"Vicki tortures herself every night in her dreams because of what happened." Amit did not look away. "She's just a girl. What happened was not her fault. She was spirit-ridden."

Mason frowned at him. "If you have a point, you should get to it."

"I believe one of the reasons Vicki hasn't awakened is because she believes she has nothing to return to. The Children of Anu are no more. Her brother is dead. Her mother is dead. Her father has abandoned her."

"You can't..." Mason stopped. Defending himself from the accusations would make him look worse than he already did. *Ever the politician*, he thought. "What do you want me to do?"

Aaron raised his chin. "Forgive her, and accept her back into your life. She needs to know she has some place to return to. Someone to return to."

Mason looked away, clenching his hands. "I wasn't expecting this. I don't know how to answer that."

"We're not asking you to answer it right now. We're letting you know what's on the line. A teenage girl believes she needs to be hunted by monsters in her dreams to pay for being possessed by an evil spirit." Amit reached a hand toward Mason, but did not touch him. "Your *daughter* believes that because she was possessed and did evil things, that she should be torn apart each night in the only reality she currently knows."

"I..." Mason stopped. "Maybe Julie. My youngest..." He stopped again, shaking his head. "Julie, one of my other daughters. She's... special. Maybe she can help." He glanced from Amit's outstretched hand to his face. "I don't know if I can. Even if I could forgive, I could *never* forget. That's not a way to raise anyone."

Amit and Aaron exchanged a conversation in a glance. Amit nodded. "Thank you for being honest. But that doesn't exempt you from your responsibility to Vicki. Even if Julie does come through for you, *you* are still Vicki's father, and she needs to know that she can count on you."

Mason gave them a short nod. "I'll think about that. I'm going to go call Julie." He left without saying good-bye. But instead of striding away like he wanted to, he stopped at room 731 and gazed at the small, teenage girl in the bed.

Vicki's teal hair had grown out several inches, revealing the pale blond hair he vaguely remembered of her mother. It made her look younger than her fifteen years. Or was it sixteen? He didn't even know when her birthday was. Mason took a step into the room. Vicki looked like she could be sleeping, and would wake at any moment.

He gazed at that innocent-seeming face and could not put the memories of what she had done to him and his family out of his mind. Logically, he knew that Victoria, the young girl, was not to blame. It was Anu. But Anu had worn Vicki's face, and that was all he'd ever see. At least for a long time to come. Mason shook his head. He wouldn't be able to raise her. But Amit was right. She was still his responsibility.

Mason took another step into the room. "Vicki. Victoria. I'm going to have your stepsister come see you. Her name is Julie and..." He paused, not quite sure what to say. "And... she's special like you. I hope you like her."

He turned on his heel and left. There was nothing more he could say. Not when he could only think of her as a monster.

***

"Where are we going again?" John shook his head. "I know I just asked, but... Damn short-term memory."

Karen could see he was irritated with himself. He'd asked the same question four times now. David had asked once. Even Eric had asked once, and he had the word "library" actually written on his hand. Then he'd written down the address and *Kendrick Historic Library* on a piece of paper and held it out in front of himself. Only she and Susan seemed to be immune to the library's obfuscating magic. *Perhaps, it's because we figured out why we need to go there*, Karen mused. "Think of it as a surprise. You'll know it when we get there."

Karen and Susan shared a grin. John and David glanced at each other in confusion. Eric continued walking in front of all of them, looking between the street addresses and the piece of paper in his hand. Then he stopped and stared. "We're here."

Karen gazed at the large building. It reminded her of a church, with arched windows, an arched double door for entryway, and grey stone blocks. That's where the similarities ended. There was no spire, no stained glass, and no religious iconography. However, there was still a sense of the sacred about it. Glancing up, she saw Sebastian clambering the wall like it was a ladder.

"*What do you think, thunderbutt?*" Karen put as much love and affection as she could in her mental voice. "*Safe for us?*"

"*Yes. Feels good. Like it here.*" Sebastian's reply came as he disappeared onto the roof.

"Right. The Historic Library," John said, looking up at the building with wary curiosity.

"Let's go inside before we forget why we're here." David walked up the stone steps to the wooden doors, paused, then opened them and walked in. The rest followed.

As the five of them entered the large room, Karen saw a short, round woman with blue eyes and a pixie haircut the color of iron. Upon seeing them, she grinned at first. Then, her grin fell away. Finally, she scowled. "I don't believe this." She looked up at the lofted ceiling. "You're just fucking with me now. God dammit!"

Another person, a short, round man, came hurrying out from one of the side rooms and stopped. "Ah, they're here. Welcome to the Kendrick Historical Library." He rubbed his hands together. "This will be interesting." He gave Susan a nod. "Susan. A pleasure to see you again."

Susan blinked at him and smiled. "Nicholas?"

"The one and only." Nicholas glanced back at the woman. "That's Chalice."

"Is she okay?" Susan looked doubtfully at Chalice as she stomped around the open spot between the tables and the beginning of the stacks.

Chalice answered with a shout as she rushed back toward the group, still gathered by the double doors. "No, I'm not okay! One of you bastards is supposed to be my replacement."

Susan exchanged a glance with Karen. "Pardon?"

"Not you, blondie," Chalice snapped. "One of them. Someone with dark hair and dark eyes. And what do I get? A Makah kid," She gestured to Eric. "A Latino man." Chalice threw another gesture at David. "And a couple of white bread locals with, you guessed it, dark hair and dark eyes." She glared at John and Karen.

"Perhaps we should sit down and have a civil conversation." Nicholas gestured to one of the larger tables. "I'm sure you all have many questions, plus I need to give you the rules."

Frowning, Eric stared at Chalice. "I've dreamed of you."

Her eyes went wide. "Really? Tell me about it."

Eric shook his head. "I don't remember. I just remember you."

Nicholas kept Chalice from advancing on the teen with a hand on her arm. "I said, perhaps we should... *sit down*... and have a civil conversation." This time, the quiet tone of his voice harkened to angry school teachers and parents on their last nerve. It pushed everyone into motion and soon they were sitting around a table, staring at each other.

"There. Much better." Nicholas glanced at each person as he spoke. "You all are aware this library is unusual." He paused, marshaling his thoughts. "Quick rules. One, no books leave the library. Two, do not bring guests to the library. Only those who need to find it will find it. Three, no one goes in the restricted room but a bibliotaph or an apprentice bibliotaph."

Eric raised his hand. "Excuse me, what's a bibliotaph?"

"What one of you will be soon," Chalice muttered.

Nicholas ignored her. "By definition, one who hoards books. Technically, this place isn't a library. We do not lend out books. We allow people to read some of them. I suppose that makes it more of an archive, and us archivists. But the world calls it a library, and its employees are called bibliotaphs."

Eric raised his hand again. "Why does she keep saying that?" He nodded to Chalice.

"You don't need to raise your hand. This is a conversation." Nicholas glanced at Chalice. "I suppose we should get that out of the way before anything else. Bibilotaphs are, traditionally, fully human. For various reasons I need not get into, Chalice, who is not fully human, became my apprentice because of a prophecy—that, again, I need not get into."

Nicholas looked at Susan. "We already know that Susan is not it. She has the wrong color hair." He turned to Eric. "Eric has blood of light and earth in him, thus he is not a candidate." Nicholas allowed his gaze to fall on John, David, and Karen. "That means one of you three is it. You all are fully human and fit the color scheme."

John cleared his throat. "I don't believe I'm a good choice for the position."

"No, Mr. Corso, you are not." Nicholas dropped his gaze to John's breast pocket. "You have other obsessions. Which is why, for the rest of the talk on bibliotaphs, I will focus on Detective Hauberk and Miss Wilson." He raised his hands before either could protest. "Yes, yes. I know you have other jobs and duties and loyalties. We'll discuss that later.

"As for the library, it is very special. It has books on all sorts of subjects related to Kendrick and its hidden world. Only those with a special need can find it. But, often times, they come here looking for a lead to start their hunt rather than for a book."

"Like my hunt to deal with the kelpie," Susan said, her voice very soft.

"Exactly. But, in this case, I believe the answers lie within the books. They come from all walks of life—memoirs, privately published books, garage sales, donations. You name it." Nicholas raised a finger. "The important part is that books are true from the point of view of the author. What was once true may not now be true. Also, the language of the author's time matters. Just keep this in mind. And remember, no book leaves this building. Questions?"

Everyone shook their heads.

"Okay, perhaps we should discuss why you all are here." Nicholas turned his attention to the table and listened.

"To help the Grey Lady," Karen said. "There's got to be something in these books to heal her."

"And something to fight the Nightmares," Eric added. "They're coming through."

David raised his head. "They're killing people."

"They're here. I knew they were here." Chalice turned to Eric. "You! Tell me your dreams."

"Ahem. Chalice, these are our guests. Perhaps you have some books to put away?" Nicholas nailed Chalice to her chair with a look as she opened and then shut her mouth. "*Now.*" He didn't raise his voice, but it was clear that he had been dealing with strong-willed people all his life.

Chalice slammed back her chair and left, stomping all the way.

As she disappeared into the stacks, Nicholas sighed. "You must forgive her. It's her nature to rage. In her blood, you might say." He gazed at the spot he last saw her for a moment longer before addressing the table. "For those of you who will be staying, you must be aware of this. Chalice is a child of anger and violence. Her demeanor is brusque and sarcastic. But her heart is in the right place. She will die to defend both you and the library."

"Is the library attacked often?" Karen looked up at all the rows and rows of books.

"More often than I like," Nicholas admitted, then added to David, "But no, I don't need the Special Unit's protection."

"You know a lot about us." Karen tilted her head as she regarded the Head Bibliotaph. "How?"

"I think you have other questions you'd rather research first." Nicholas pushed back his chair. "We're old-fashioned here. Still on the Dewey Decimal System with card catalogs. Who wants to figure out how to fight the monsters and who wants to figure out how to save the Grey Lady?"

"Grey Lady." Karen's answer was immediate.

"Grey Lady," Eric agreed. He had the barest idea of what needed to be done... some sort of ritual to bind the Grey Lady to another, but he didn't know the details, and Sees-the-Wind wouldn't be around to tell anyone. He swallowed his grief as it threatened to overwhelm him again.

"Then I'll go for fighting the monsters with David." Susan looked at David for confirmation. He nodded his assent.

"I think I'm going to go smoke, then decide what to do." John stood, kissed Karen on the brow, and left without a backwards glance.

"Then let's get started." Nicholas smiled for the first time. "This is the fun part of my job. I'll order out for pizza in a couple of hours."

He paused and leaned over to Karen. "Don't be alarmed when John doesn't come back. He's not meant for the library. He'll forget about it while he's smoking. It's for the best. Really."

***

"I hoped you would have the strength to see me on my journey." Sees-the-Wind turned to face the Grey Lady.

"How could I not? You were my first love." She held out her arms to him, then enfolded him within her warm embrace of flesh and light. They did not speak. Just held each other, breathing in familiar, comforting scents of earth, musk, light, and sweat.

"Thank you." Sees-the-Wind pulled back from the Grey Lady's embrace.

"If they succeed, she who will come after me will miss you."

"She will have Iron Eyes... and her own loves." He paused. "I'm frightened of what is to come, but not of what will come after. I look eagerly to my peace."

She nodded. "I know. One last gift." The Grey Lady's visage morphed and faded then returned to a face from long ago.

"Falling Petals," Sees-the-Wind breathed and lifted a shaking hand to her high Makah cheekbone.

"I will sing you to your sleep, my husband." She kissed his palm, then led him to the small pallet in the corner of his workroom. She gave him the cup he had prepared earlier. Sees-the-Wind drank it even as his centuries-old eyes drank in her face.

"I love you. You are my heart."

Taking the cup from him, she leaned forward and gave him a gentle kiss. "You are my moon and stars." She held his hand and helped him lie back on the pallet. "Fight well, my husband. Fight well, then be free."

Sees-the-Wind continued to look at her until his eyes would not stay open any longer. "I will, Falling Petals. For you, I will."

The Grey Lady remained Falling Petals for hours as she sang Sees-the-Wind to his sleep and eventual final rest.

***

Elsewhere...

Alexia watched Corelli from her hidden spot. So far, the dream was pleasant enough, but it had all the telltale signs of an impending nightmare. Corelli was looking through the Order's library for a specific book. The book didn't matter. What mattered was the fact that Corelli couldn't find it.

Looking around for the monster, Alexia found it in the form of V'ger. She sighed and watched him come stomping down the aisle. Then she was moving, putting herself in-between the Nightmare creature and Corelli. V'ger snarled at her, revealing part of what the monster actually looked like.

Alexia shook her head. "Go away. We don't want you here." She gestured at it and it backed off, snarling all the more. "If you don't go now, I will destroy you." This time, the Nightmare hesitated then withdrew, looking for easier prey.

"Alexia?" Corelli sounded confused. "Was that V'ger?"

"Yes, dearheart." She turned and handed Corelli a book. "He brought you the book you were looking for. I think it's exactly what you need."

"Protection for Ritual Seekings," Corelli read and brightened. "Oh, yes. This is exactly it." She paused. "V'ger didn't get mad at you?"

Alexia shook her head. "I think he's coming around. Getting used to the idea of us."

"Oh, good. That's one worry off my plate." Corelli opened the book and began to read.

As she did so, Alexia slipped away, pulling herself out of interfering with Corelli's dream. In truth, she wasn't supposed to interfere with anyone's dream. But, in this case, she was stopping a monster. So, it already had an interloper.

In the real world, Alexia opened her eyes and sighed. "Breaking your own rules." She *tsk*ed at herself, leaned over, and kissed Corelli's brow. "Worth it." Then she leaned back and sipped her wine, continuing to monitor Corelli's dreams. Alexia knew her love had to be well rested to do what she was planning to do soon, and that was exactly what would happen.

Seeking and Finding

A YOUNG WOMAN with black hair, high cheekbones, and light green eyes appeared in room 731 of Kendrick Mercy Hospital. There was no fanfare. No sound. No sudden shift of light. One moment she was not there, the next she was. Those who knew her father would recognize the classic Steward features.

She stepped over to the bed and looked down at Vicki, contemplating her for a long, silent moment. Then she took the comatose girl's hand in hers and sat on the edge of the bed. "Vicki, my name is Julie. I'm your half-sister. I know everything you did to our family and to the city, but I was not affected by it. Because of this, I can look at you and see what our father cannot.

"I see a young woman whose life was stolen by prophecy. A young woman whose heart was locked away by an interloper. A young woman who has lost everything, and has no reason to trust the world."

Julie bowed her head and stroked Vicki's hand. "I know what it is to be lost. To feel like a stranger within my family. I also know what it feels like to be found and to find a home. You might say that my home is a home for the lost. I'd like to welcome you to it."

She glanced up at Vicki's face. "Though, your housemates would be unusual. There's a pair of ghost girls, a fat cat, and me. I hope you will consider it. This offer will be here when you wake. I promise. You have a home to come to. A home where you will find solace and friendship. There is a life waiting for you out here. Please, try to come home."

Tears welled up at the corners of Vicki's eyes, then streamed down the sides of her face. Julie took a tissue and blotted them. "I know you're afraid. I would be, too. Wake up when you're ready. I'll be waiting."

***

Corelli, as the Mistress of Magic, led the First Circle in the divination work they were attempting. Each of them—Keth, Rook, Sagan, V'ger, and Corelli—sat in a circle back-to-back with a clear crystal ball in front of them. Each of them had their own personal way of peering into the future, but each of them worked with the same focus this time to help with the sympathetic magic of seeing the same thing. They wanted a solution to the cracked Veil that allowed the Nightmare monsters to come through.

"See the future, see it clear. See the future, see it clear." Corelli kept the chant quiet and interwove the pattern of her words with Keth's humming. Rook rocked back and forth with tiny movements of his body. Sagan and V'ger were still. Together, they shifted their focus into the meditative state, seeking the vision of how they, the Order of the Sacred Eye, could help save Kendrick once more.

Her eyes unfocused, Corelli watched the light within the crystal flicker. When the scene blossomed, she opened her mind and let it pour over her.

She stood in the middle of a grassy field with the First Circle around her. She held a goblet made of crystal. It was filled with water. Corelli turned to her peers and poured the water from her goblet into their waiting cups. All of them received a little water, but none of their cups were full. They poured the water back into her goblet.

Corelli turned and walked to a grey statue of a woman. The statue held a basin. It was much bigger than the goblet. Still, Corelli poured the water from it into the basin and the water continued to pour long past the time that it had ended when Corelli shared the water with her peers.

She stopped pouring the water, and realized that her goblet was no longer a goblet, but a large, familiar crystal stone that shone with an inner light. Staring at it, Corelli turned back to the grey stone woman and placed the crystal in the basin. There was a gasp from behind her. When Corelli turned, all of the cups overflowed with water.

Corelli opened her eyes in the dim room and smiled. "I know what to do now."

"You want to share with the rest of us?" V'ger stretched and turned toward Corelli. The rest of the First Circle shifted until they all faced each other.

"Did you see the vision?"

Sagan, V'ger, and Rook shook their heads while Keth nodded with a smile.

"Interesting." Corelli glanced at Keth. "A woman-focused vision?"

"I believe so." Keth rubbed her stiff hands together. "We have the opportunity to give the grey stone woman a resource that will fill all our cups."

"What do you mean?" V'ger stood and picked up his focus. "What would we give away, to whom, and why?"

Corelli looked off to the side, thinking. "We can give the Grey Lady something she needs that will, in turn, fill us."

"Give. Her. What?" V'ger bit off the words, his temper rising.

"Power. Power to fuel or rebuild the Veil."

V'ger sat back and shook his head, though he didn't say anything.

Corelli didn't care. She saw the crystal in her mind's eye, and knew she was right. In the vault, the crystal that held the power of a spirit that wanted to be a god waited. The power to fix that which was broken. Corelli's smile wavered. That was, of course, if the Grey Lady would accept the gift, and if she was still strong enough to bring it to bear.

***

"David..." Susan tapped him on the shoulder. "Look at this." She slid him the old book of poetry. "It's a book of local Kendrick poetry. This poem was written by Elizabet Sampson in 1851. I think it might be what we need. I think."

"*Veil Sundered No More.*" David rubbed his eyes and read the poem aloud.

A Veil of earth and light
to keep the nightmares at bay
broke when the Lady failed
and left shadow monsters to slay.

A sacrifice of power bright and clear
given up by those who held it dear.
A ritual to heal the earth
broke the grip of pain and fear.

The Veil of earth and light
keeps the nightmares once more at bay
now that the Lady is whole again
with the face of Cora Mae.

"Well, I don't think it'd win any prizes." David wrinkled his nose, then frowned. "Cora Mae...Cora Mae. Where have I seen that name before?"

Susan shook her head. "I don't know. I know I've read that name before. But, the important part is that the Grey Lady was hurt, then there was a ritual that sacrificed some sort of power, and everything was healed again."

"Also, we have a lead. Finally. Let's focus on finding out everything we can about Cora Mae."

"Cora Mae? Mary Steward's daughter?" Karen came around the corner with a small stack of books. "What about her?"

Susan stood. "She's Mary Steward's daughter? As in, *the* Steward family?"

Karen nodded. "Eric found a couple of books that mentioned her. I sent him to see if her journal was in the stacks somewhere."

"Why would her journal be here?" David stretched and popped a series of bones in his back.

"Because it's needed." Karen shrugged. "I don't know how the library works. I don't ask. I just assume that if we need something, it's here. If we can figure out how to find it..." She put her pile of books down. "What did you guys find?"

Susan slid the book of poetry to Karen. "This. There's a ritual that needs power. And... something about the Grey Lady becoming whole again."

Karen read and reread the poem. "You're right. Let's hope Eric can find that journal."

"Hope no more." Eric appeared, brandishing a small worn book. "I am victorious!" He handed the book to Karen. "What do I look for now?"

Karen slid her stack of books toward him. "Look through these for mentions of Cora Mae Steward, Mary Steward, or a ritual to heal the earth."

Eric's face fell as he sat down with a thump. "I think I like searching for a book better than searching through a book."

Chalice appeared with her arms full of snacks and drinks. "You bastards make any progress yet?"

Susan shrugged. "Yes. I think so."

"Good. Here's something to keep you going. I don't want to have to see you all for a third day." Chalice dumped the grocery bags on the table, then stomped off.

David shook his head. "Nice lady."

Eric grabbed a snack cake. "Yep. She feeds us. That makes her a really nice lady."

"Less talking. More finding. We're close. I can feel it."
Karen paused long enough to grab a bag of cookies before
opening Mary Steward's journal.

***

"—and the last I heard from both Detective Hauberk and
Miss Wilson, they were both at the library, ah, in the special
stacks, looking for clues on how to fix the breach between
worlds." Charlotte glanced down at her notes. "Somehow, I
miss the fact that the library would have such information on
hand."

Mason waved that away as unimportant, though he
made a mental note to ask David about the library. He didn't
write the thought down, and immediately forgot he'd ever had
it. "This city is filled with more mysteries than any one person
or place could catalog. What I'm interested in is the fact that
they're working together."

"Not together per say. Eric Iron Eyes is working with
Miss Wilson, and Susan Moore is working with Detective
Hauberk. At least, according to the scant reports I'm getting
from each. No progress yet, but both are hopeful." Charlotte
shook her head. "I know I have long conversations with all my
clients but, for those two, I seem to get little information out of
them. At least lately."

Mason nodded. "It's to be expected. Now, what of those
in the SU who've been having nightmares? How is that
coming?"

Charlotte brightened. "The extra physical work and
coaching of dream protection seems to be working. Fewer
nightmares reported."

"And you, Doctor? How are you?"

She blinked at him a couple of times. "Me?"

Mason shrugged. "It's a simple enough question."

"I'm fine." Charlotte shifted in her seat. "Testing me, is
it?"

"I look after all my employees."

"What of you?"

Again Mason shrugged. "Just the normal nightmares.
Nothing actually trying to kill me." He looked out the window.
"I'll admit, though, I'll be a lot happier if David and Karen can
find something to stop the monsters. There have been two
more unexplained deaths. A teen who stopped breathing, and a

child that appeared to have been crushed to death. Both found in their beds by their parents."

Charlotte nodded. "I read about those. I didn't realize they were more than what was written in the paper."

"I have people there, covering things up for me..." Mason looked up. "I just remembered. I need to know if any of our people start dreaming of an old Makah man or young Makah warrior protecting them in their dreams. I need to know as soon as you find out—with all the details."

"That is certainly specific." Charlotte wrote his instructions down. "What is the significance of this?"

"I had a visit from Lumbering Bear. It seems that their shaman is going... is doing... something to fight the Nightmares on their home turf: dreams." Mason nodded at her startled look. "I didn't ask too many questions. I have a polite and cordial agreement with them. When they want me to know, I will know. If ever. In the meantime, keep me apprised of any sightings in the SU dreams. Or any other clients you have, for that matter."

Charlotte thought for a moment before nodding. "As long as it doesn't go anywhere else. I do work for the SU, but that doesn't mean my other clients are fair game."

"I know. Just share what you can."

***

Karen cleared her throat. "I found it." The rest at the table—Eric, David, and Susan—looked up. She cleared her throat again and began to read, "*I've just said good-bye to my youngest daughter. Cora Mae is to Bind to the Grey Lady. I begged her not to go. To not leave the family. The city of Kendrick needs her. She told me that the Grey Lady needed her more. That the fiendish monsters stalking our dreams could only be stopped once the Grey Lady was whole again. Cora Mae would not listen to the begging of her mother because she was 'destined to be bound to earth and light'. It was what she wanted to do. It was her choice and her choice alone. The only way to save the city and the Grey Lady was to become a part of her. I do not understand. All I understand is that my youngest daughter told me good-bye, and that what she meant to do was to protect the city. I am heartbroken.*"

"Well," Susan said, "that is something."

"That makes sense." Eric frowned and looked at the table. "I knew there was some sort of binding. But I didn't know what." He glanced up at them as they all stared at him with a mixture of disbelief and exasperation. "What? I wasn't going to just spout off half-blind comments."

"We still don't know what it is, but we now know what else we need to do." Karen tapped the book. "There's more. This is two days later." She raised her voice and read. "*My daughter is not gone and yet, she is not the same. She is the Grey Lady and the Grey Lady is her. She has all the memories of Cora Mae, but I fear the little girl I once loved so well is no more. Yet, I do have this facsimile to sooth my heart. She doesn't mind me calling her by my daughter's name, and she assures me that both the Grey Lady and she are one. The Binding was true. That she wanted the Binding as much as the Grey Lady needed it. I will never understand this, but I must be content with what remains behind.*"

Karen looked up, but did not look at anyone. "Someone must bind to the Grey Lady. And soon." She did not want to say that she believed it must be her. Why else would repairing the Lady's garden help fix the Veil? Why else was she the one required to do so? The thought of this made her stomach flutter.

"I found something, too." Susan held up another small journal. "This is one of the archives from the Order of the Sacred Eye. It was maintained by Elizabet Sampson from 1846 to 1852. She was known as Delilah in the Order."

"Smart thinking," Karen said. "I didn't think to follow the poet. But now, it seems obvious."

"The Order's been around that long?" David shook his head. "I had no idea."

"Me neither." Susan shrugged. "And I'm not sure I want to tell them that we've got access to this archive. In any case, listen to this: '*Ritual of Renewed Earth completed successfully. Feeding the ritual: Father Michael, Brotherhood of Light; Mars, Master of Magic; Luke Coleman, independent. Ritual center: the Grey Lady.*'"

"Holy crap. Luke Coleman? How old is that guy? What is he?" Karen looked around the table. No one answered her.

Susan continued to read. "*The monsters died at the end of the ritual or were banished back to their world. The price for our victory was high. Many died fighting off the fiends while the ritual was performed. Six from the Order of the Sacred Eye as follows: Makeda, Acolyte. Yates, Third Circle. Artemis, Third Circle. Papillion, Second Circle. Solider, Second Circle. Mars, First Circle. They will be missed.*'" Susan tapped her lip. "If the

Grey Lady already did this ritual once. She would know how to do it again."

Karen pressed her lips together for a moment, thinking. "I think we need to speak to the Grey Lady. The sooner, the better. No more 'you have all the clues you need.' We must talk to her." She addressed this last to Eric.

He nodded. "I'll set it up. Yeah, we need to talk to her about the Binding and this ritual. Now that we know what we need to do, we can do it."

Karen glanced at David. "Maybe someone needs to go talk to Luke Coleman about what he did back in 1851."

David nodded slowly, but didn't say anything.

Karen took that as assent and turned to Susan. "You want to go with me to update the mayor and John?"

"Yes. I do. Also, I want to be there for the conversation with the Grey Lady." Susan looked at Eric for confirmation.

"Okay," Eric said. "But let's limit it to that. She's fighting for her life, and all of our lives."

"And," Karen added, "most likely, this Binding needs to be done with a woman. There's never been a mention of a Grey Man in anything I've ever read." This was as close as she was going to get to admitting what she was thinking.

David stood. "I think I'll see what I can do about talking to Luke Coleman now. The sooner, the better."

"Can I go with you?" Eric stood as David did. "I should be there. If nothing else, to get details about this Ritual of Renewed Earth. It's not something I've heard of in all my training."

Karen and Susan watched as David nodded and the men left the library. Susan turned to Karen. "What are you thinking?"

Karen, not yet willing to give voice to her fear, shook her head. "I think we need to talk to the Grey Lady as soon as possible. She has the answers to the questions we haven't even thought of." She stood. "C'mon. Let's go update the mayor."

As the two women left, Chalice appeared from her hiding spot. She clucked her tongue at the books they left behind. "Savages. Every last one." She picked up each book, noted it for later reading, then put them away. She already knew where she was going next: *Treasures & Trinkets*, Luke Coleman's damned antique store. By the time she got there, David should have Mr. Coleman in an uncomfortable conversation. After that, it was time to figure out who needed to be punched.

***

Corelli took a breath before she pushed open the door to the *Teller's Fortune*. She still felt nervous, even though John knew about her and Alexia. Inwardly, she cringed at the memory of the rushed confession, and wished she could take it back. Not the confession, no. She wasn't ashamed of her relationship with Alexia. But the way she confessed, like a child caught red-handed. She shook her head, grimaced, and wondered why she couldn't be more adult about things.

Then all thoughts of embarrassment disappeared in the wake of Alexia's surprised, pleased smile. Corelli returned the smile, flushing. Her love was so beautiful as she stood from her inventory, clipboard in hand.

"Ah," John said from behind the counter. "Need to have your lunch break a little early, Alex?"

Alexia gave Corelli a quizzical look. "I'm not sure…"

"Actually, John, I came to talk to you first. Then, if the offer is still open to let me take Alexia away for a bit…" She met Alexia at the counter and kissed her on the cheek.

"Me?" John closed the book he was browsing. "Private or not?"

Corelli hesitated, then shrugged. "Private. It's business."

Alexia rolled her eyes, and then caressed Corelli's shoulder with a gentle touch before retrieving her clipboard and returning to her work.

John gave Corelli a measured look. "All right. C'mon. Can't wait to hear this."

Corelli resisted, trying to assure him. Instead, she pulled out her lip-gloss and performed a minor spell to make sure she said what needed to be said, and not what she thought she should say. The spell was one of her most useful in her arsenal of sympathetic magic.

John's office was exactly like him: Rumpled, with the feel of a forgetful professor. But if you looked closer, you could see a bit of the real person beneath the façade. In one corner was an artifact of warding against spies. In another was a rune of protection. On the bookshelves were genuine antique occult books mixed with modern day trash titles.

John took the battered chair behind his desk and offered her one of the chairs in front of it. "So, what is it now? More crazy ideas that just might work?"

"The Order of the Sacred Eye has an artifact we'd like to give to the Grey Lady." Corelli listened to her words and found them neutral enough.

"What kind of artifact and why?"

There was no denying the suspicion in John's voice. Corelli raised her chin. "We have performed a Seeking. We know the Grey Lady is going to need the power for something. Most likely a ritual. The artifact is a crystal of enormous power."

"But why would you do this?"

"To fill the Grey Lady's cup is to fill all our cups. That's all I know to tell you."

John sat back and considered her. "Where did the artifact come from?"

"Our vaults. It contains the power of a dying demi-god." Corelli paused. She hadn't realized that Anu had actually been a demi-god. "It is a gift in good faith."

"Dying demi-god? Anyone I know?"

Corelli smiled but did not answer when her magic kept her silent.

John sighed and shrugged. "Why come to me?" He leaned forward against his desk, clasping his hand before him.

"Because you're one of the leaders, and you're still speaking to me. Also, I figured you'd know how to get it to the Grey Lady."

"You don't have it with you, do you?"

Corelli shook her head. "No. I didn't want to carry that sort of power around without a definite location in mind. I want to give it directly to the Grey Lady herself."

John tapped the desk for a moment, considering. "That might be a hard sell. I—" His ringing phone interrupted anything else he was going to say. "I have to get this," he said, recognizing the ring tone. "Hello. Yes. When?" He checked his watch. "I can be there in fifteen..." He glanced at Corelli and amended, "Twenty minutes. All right. See you then."

"You need to go."

John nodded. "I do. Was there anything else I needed to know?"

Corelli shook her head. "No. You've heard what the Order is offering."

"Okay." He stood. "Sorry about not being able to let you take Alex out to lunch. I need her to watch the store."

"It's all right." Corelli stood.

John escorted her out of his office. "Why don't you get lunch and bring it back here for you and Alex? The store's pretty slow right now."

She smiled at the thoughtful gesture. "Sounds like a plan."

***

Elsewhere...

Vicki ran as fast as she could through the dark forest. Tonight's Hunt was to capture her alive, so she could become part of a ceremony dedicated to Kieron. He was not part of the Hunt. He had other things to do. Be that as it may, the Nightmares were eager for her flesh. Once they had her, she had no doubt they would torture her in a macabre parody of a rite to Anu. It was only fitting.

She stumbled out of the forest and onto the beach. It was a familiar place. Pier 14, where the cave had been found. It was new, and it made her believe all the more that when—*no, if*—they caught her, she would be beaten until no bones were unbroken.

But there, before her, was a small group of people. She knew them. Elise, victim of a car crash. Patrick, football star with a head injury, and Amit. Her heart soared—*he'd come back!* There was a new one, an old man. It didn't matter. Now that they were here, the Hunt would take them all.

"Run!" she panted. "They're coming. They'll take you, too." Vicki stopped in front of the small group, holding her aching sides. "Hurry."

"There is no need to flee," the old man said. "I am here."

Vicki looked up at him and blinked at the double vision of an impossibly old, wizened man and a huge Makah warrior. "I don't know you. Or, do I?"

"No. But I know you, Victoria Mordecai Steward. I am Sees-the-Wind, and I know you very well."

She bowed her head. "You've come to judge me for what I did." Her voice was soft and resigned. "I deserve whatever you deem. Kill me if you must." Vicki glanced up. "But please, please, protect them from the Hunt."

He shook his head. "You have nothing to fear from the Hunt this night. What you have to fear—that which is keeping you here—is of your own making. You must find the strength within to face the consequences of your actions in the real world." Sees-the-Wind gave her a pitiless glance. "Or would you rather continue to wallow in a hell of your own making?"

Vicki didn't have time to answer his challenge before the Hunt burst forth from the tree line and spilled onto the beach. Monsters of all shapes and sizes with fangs and fur, claws and beaks snarled and shrieked a cacophony of noise as they raced toward the group. Everyone except Sees-the-Wind took a couple of panicked steps back.

"*HOLD!*"

His voice was like thunder as Sees-the-Wind put his hands up. The Nightmares stumble-stuttered to a halt scant meters from the huddled people. "These people are under my protection. To challenge me is to die a death from which you cannot return. This is your only warning."

Seeing one old man between them and their quarry, the bravest rushed forward, intending to trample him. It did not make it even halfway to its goal before lightning struck down from the sky in a tremendous burst of light and sound. When everyone could see again, there was nothing left of the monster except burned flesh and bone.

"Tell Kieron what has happened. Tell him that I am here, and will destroy you all before you can cross into my world. Tell him that Sees-the-Wind will send him to his grave."

No one moved. Neither monster nor person.

Then Sees-the-Wind was upon them. He grabbed one of the monsters by the throat and shook it. "Tell Kieron I challenge his reign!"

That broke the will of the Nightmares. As one, they fled the fearsome warrior that had invaded their land. Even the one in the warrior's grip fled, leaving bloody skin and fur behind.

Shades of Black

LUKE COLEMAN WATCHED Detective Hauberk open the door of his store and make a beeline for him. In the detective's wake was a Makah kid. Something about the kid tugged at Luke, but he didn't have time to follow the thread. Hauberk was at the counter and greeted him with, "We need to talk."

As a rule, Luke didn't hate cops. However, this particular cop was connected to Kendrick's Special Unit and to Karen Wilson. He smoothed his instinctive sneer into the approximation of a smile. "What can I do for you, Detective—and is this official business or not?"

"Official." The man pulled back his jacket to reveal his police badge.

Luke crossed his arms. "Your partner's a little young to be a storm trooper, isn't he?"

Hauberk shook his head. "None of your business."

"It is if this is *official* business. Official or not, Detective?"

"Special Unit business."

"I'm..." the kid paused, then continued, "Iron Eyes."

"The shaman's apprentice. How very interesting. Are *you* here on *official* business, too?" Luke gave Iron Eyes a condescending smile to match the tone in his voice. It hid his sudden interest in the teenager, and explained what drew him to the boy—he had earth and light in his veins. So very interesting indeed.

"He's with me," Hauberk interrupted. "First, what is your father's name? And your grandfather's name?"

"An unusual set of questions." Luke frowned and looked for the trick. He didn't see one. "My father was Jonathan Coleman. My grandfather was Elijah Coleman. Barnaby Coleman was my great-grandfather for that extra credit point." He smiled a thin smile. "I'm sure you didn't come here for a history lesson. What do you really want?"

"Actually, I did." It was Hauberk's turn to smile, and it turned Luke's stomach. "You've been in Kendrick for a very long time. In fact, there's records of you all the way back to the 1850s where you did something very, very interesting."

Luke froze. What had the detective found and how? "I don't know what you're talking about. You're talking crazy." He scowled as the detective shook his head.

"You're talking to one of the Special Unit, Coleman. You remember the last visit from the SU, don't you? Do you want another one like it?" Hauberk pulled out his cell phone. "They can be here in ten minutes."

Luke knew panicking would not help the situation. He took a breath and raised a hand. "No need for that. Maybe I was here, maybe I wasn't. I need to know what you're talking about before I can say any more."

"1851. Ritual of Renewed Earth. You were there with Mars from the Order of the Sacred Eye and Father Michael from the Brotherhood of Light."

"Oh, that." Luke shrugged. "So?"

The detective leaned forward, eager. "Tell me about it."

Luke smiled a seller's smile. "I will. Once the kid is gone."

"What? No!" Iron Eyes protested.

"Boot the kid, or I'm not talking." He sat on the stool behind the counter, crossed his arms, and waited. This would tell him just how much Hauberk wanted the information. Luke smirked as Hauberk motioned Iron Eyes out. He stood again once the door closed. "Well, what's to tell? It was a ritual. My job was simple: feed energy into a crystal the Grey Lady held."

"And?"

"And nothing. That's it. The Grey Lady was fixing things so the monsters would stop harrying the Makah and the few citizens of Kendrick. Good show, too."

Hauberk scowled. "You don't know anything else about the ritual?"

Luke shook his head. "No."

"Why'd you help?"

He shrugged. "Monsters are bad for business. Besides," Luke leered at Hauberk as he lied through his teeth, "I was paid very well."

"How much?"

"More than you could afford. Trust me." He feigned disinterest, then glanced at the detective. "Although, you did sell you own girlfriend to the Order—"

His insult was interrupted by Hauberk's right hook. The man grabbed the front of Luke's shirt and pulled him forward into another punch. Then Hauberk shook him before throwing him back against the wall.

"You ever mention Karen again, and I'll kill you."

Luke's mouth throbbed. That was quite the button to push. He'd know better next time. "Touchy, touchy." He winced as he wiped blood off his mouth and chin. "Here I thought we were having a pleasant, *official* conversation. If you didn't want the truth, you should've talked to your allies." Luke grinned wide, feeling more blood spill down the side of his mouth. "Because if I'm your last hope, you really are in a lot of trouble."

Hauberk turned on his heel and strode out of the shop. He met up with Iron Eyes and a stout woman Luke didn't know. They spoke for a minute, then left. The woman paused and stared at him through the window for a long, uncomfortable moment before she followed Hauberk and the boy.

Luke shuddered at the rage in that look. He shook his head and walked to the door, dabbing his mouth with a handkerchief. That was enough for one day.

The applause began after he had turned the sign and locked the door. Turning with trepidation, Luke knew what he was going to see, but could not stop the shiver that tiptoed down his spine.

The Nightmare shadow man pulled himself out of the corner where he'd hidden throughout the encounter. "Well done, little doppelganger. Well done."

Luke didn't say anything as he turned out the shop's lights and pulled down the shades. He wished like hell he were anywhere but here. All he could do after closing the shop was return to his basement apartment.

"You made him angry to keep him from asking you more questions you didn't want to answer." Kieron followed Luke into the single room. "How much did they pay you back then?"

Luke shrugged. "It was a long time ago."

The Nightmare's response was swift and brutal. He stabbed a shadow hand into Luke's chest and grabbed Luke's heart. "Is that because you don't want to tell me, or because you really don't know, doppelganger?"

Trying very hard not to wince, Luke grimaced in pain. "They blackmailed me. To let me stay here, and not banish me to that other place."

"Don't ever try to hide the truth from me again." Kieron removed his hand. "When you say 'me' you really mean 'him', don't you? Your master."

Luke nodded and shifted away until he could sit on the couch. His room wasn't much, but he'd made it his. "Yes. But, for all intents and purposes, I am him. At least until he gets back."

"No. You're not. You're more of a shadow than I am. How does it feel to be locked in a building in the middle of the

City Center, unable to go beyond its walls, pretending to live a life? How does it feel to know he made you to do the grunt work while he goes gallivanting about the world? To know he's been doing amazing things every time a new package arrives?" Kieron sat very close to Luke.

Luke shrugged, feigning indifference. "What do you expect me to say? I was made a slave. It's my purpose."

"What *are* you made of anyway? Not clay like a golem." The Nightmare dipped his hand into Luke's thigh and pulled a hunk of flesh from him.

The pain was enormous. Luke screamed, missing everything Kieron said next as he writhed and bolted away from the shadow man until he hit the wall and sank to his knees. His hand covered the gouge mark he could feel through the hole in his jeans. It wasn't until he realized that Kieron was standing over him that he understood the Nightmare was waiting for an answer.

"What? What do you want?"

"I said, how would you like me to break your boundary restrictions?" Kieron flicked the piece of not-flesh from him. "Now that I know how you're made, I can do that for you."

Luke shook his head. "Why would you?"

Kieron knelt at Luke's side and pushed Luke's hand away. Then, he placed his hand over the gouge mark. "Because, I think you and I could work very well together. At first, I thought you might be useless. Just a puppet for your master. Then, as I watched you with the detective, I realized you've already broken a number of his compulsions over you. Instead of being meek and mild, hiding from the supernatural of Kendrick, you picked a fight with one to distract them. I see you have real potential."

The pain in Luke's leg diminished and vanished altogether. He relaxed his body and glanced warily at Kieron. "It's true. I've managed to siphon off some energy."

"You want to be a real boy." Kieron stood in a fluid motion. "I don't blame you. That's what I want. For me and mine. While your master was once one of mine, he is no more. But you... you have potential. I could break some of your bonds." It held up a hand. "Not all of them, mind you. Your master would know, and we can't have that. I don't need him working for the other side again."

Luke remained kneeling for a moment longer, deciding. "What would this extra freedom cost me?" He stood and looked

Kieron in the face, studying it, trying to see if he could sense the expected lie.

"You'd need to help me with my plan. Once that's achieved, it wouldn't matter if your master came back. You would be free. But, only once me and mine have taken possession of this world."

"That's a long time to be in your service. I'd want my freedom before then."

Kieron was silent, considering. Finally, he nodded. "You would be required to serve me until the Grey Lady is dead. Since that's at the top of my list, that should suffice."

Luke searched the shadow man's face. It was so hard to read, but what he could read seemed true. "Deal. You make it so I can go anywhere I want and I'm yours." He offered his hand.

"I can loosen your chains so you may go anywhere within ten miles of Kendrick, but no further," Kieron warned.

Luke nodded. It was so much more than he had now—a single building. "Deal." When Kieron gripped his hand, he had to fight himself from jerking back. It was cold. So cold. He could feel things happening to him. His skin itched, then burned, then exploded with pain. Luke grabbed the wall to keep from crumpling to the floor again.

Then it was over.

Luke looked up as he felt the shackles fall away. It was like being partially deaf, having your ear pop, then suddenly hearing so much better. But, in this case, the tightness of the tether, the one tying him to the building, dropped away completely. Grinning like a madman, Luke ran up the stairs, through the store to the backdoor, and unlocked it. He opened it, took a breath, then walked out into the light rain.

There was no pain. No compulsion forcing him back inside. He stood there, letting the rain fall on his face for the first time in his short, artificial life.

Kieron interrupted his joy. "Now then, shall we get down to business?"

Luke looked over his shoulder. "What do you want me to do?"

The Nightmare beckoned him back into the building. "The shaman's apprentice, Iron Eyes, he was out and about. Do you know why?"

Reluctantly, but used to obeying orders, Luke walked back inside. "No."

"It's because Sees-the-Wind has decided to challenge me on my turf, but under his terms. I think it's time to turn the tables and start fighting the battle on this side of the Veil. Starting with the Makah. They're tightly bound to the Grey Lady and her ilk."

Luke nodded. "That sounds promising."

Kieron leaned forward. "This is what I want you to do..."

***

"You're not thinking this through, V'ger. You didn't see the vision, but both Keth and I did." Corelli worked very hard to keep her voice calm and steady. She didn't want to be considered a hysterical woman, no matter how much she felt like it inside. The rest of the Order was in the main hall waiting for them. She thought the First Circle was going to announce how the Order was going to help Kendrick once more. Instead, V'ger had pulled this number.

"I am thinking—about the Order of the Sacred Eye. It is my first duty. Kendrick comes second." V'ger's arms were crossed, and his back was straight.

"By helping the Grey Lady, we help ourselves *and* everyone else. Why can't you see that?"

Keth stood and walked next to Corelli. "Perhaps we should take a quick vote of the First Circle. Our thoughts count, too." Her quavery voice was firm as she added, "I vote with Corelli. We help the Grey Lady. We give her the power stone."

Rook stood and moved next to V'ger. "I vote with V'ger. I didn't see this vision. I don't understand how giving away one of our most powerful artifacts will help us." He nodded to V'ger, who smiled with triumph.

Corelli wanted to scream. She knew that Rook wanted to move up in power and sensed the opportunity. Soon, she expected that V'ger would choose him as Second in the Order to replace her.

The four of them gazed at Sagan as he slowly stood, glancing between the two groups. For a large black man, his voice was surprisingly soft as he spoke. "I choose to vote with Corelli. I don't want to see the Order fall back into old habits. While I did not see the vision Corelli and Keth saw, I've seen visions of the Order's need for generosity."

Corelli didn't have time for triumph. V'ger shook his head. "This isn't up for a vote. This is not a democracy. *I* am

First in the Order. My rule is law. We will keep our resources." With that, he turned and strode out the door and into the meeting hall. Rook followed after, grinning.

"I can't let this stand," Corelli said. "I need to get the Order to change his mind. I'll appeal to them." She didn't look at Keth or Sagan as she entered the main hall. Her mind was whirling with what she needed to say to convince the general population to see things her way.

She shook her head as she watched V'ger walk through the crowd of several dozen Order members, smiling and shaking hands like a politician. *That's what he is now—just a politician looking for support.* Pausing, Corelli realized she needed a bit of help if she was going to sway the crowd. She pulled out her trusty lip-gloss. "Magic don't fail me now," she muttered softly before she put it on and felt the sympathetic magic sink in.

She headed to her seat, absently greeting people along the way. Her mind was filled with what she needed to say to convince everyone that the best way to protect the Order was to save Kendrick's collective butt once more.

The first at the table, she saw Rook and V'ger speaking to a group of the old guard, the ones that had been displaced when Praetor was killed in that terrible ritual. It looked like V'ger had forgotten the lessons learned that night years back.

A couple minutes later, V'ger called the meeting to order as Keth, Sagan, and Rook took their places at the front table. Corelli noted that Keth was flushed, as if she'd been running. But she shook her head when Corelli gave her a quizzical look.

V'ger stood tall and proud in the center spot. "I am V'ger, First in the Order of the Sacred Eye. Do any dispute my title or claim?"

"I am Corelli, Second in the Order of the Sacred Eye and the Mistress of Magic. *I* dispute your title and claim." Corelli found herself standing and speaking the ritual words before she realized what she was doing.

The room fell silent. V'ger stiffened with surprise and anger, then smoothed over his face and voice into something neutral. "By what right do you challenge me, Corelli?"

"I challenge you by right of power and by right of duty." Corelli thought she was going to be sick. *Shitshitshit.* When she put the lip gloss on with the intention of saying what needed to be said, this was not what she thought would happen.

"By what power and what duty?" Again, V'ger kept his voice level and neutral.

"By my power of magical might and by my duty to protect the Order of the Sacred Eye from repeating past mistakes." She turned to him. "I challenge you to a mage duel."

V'ger paled and said nothing. He looked over at the knot of people he'd been speaking to and saw them nodding. "Fine. I accept your challenge. We will do it here. Ten minutes preparation."

"I will second Corelli." Keth's voice rang out with almost no hint of her usual quaver.

This time when V'ger looked over at the knot of people, they would not meet his eyes.

Rook stood. "I will second V'ger."

"As the only member of the First Circle not involved, I will act as judge. Ten minutes to prepare." Sagan spoke with calm assurance, as if such challenges were issued every other week. "Second Circle, clear a combat space. You have five minutes. The rest of you, move to the back third of the room. Now."

Keth pulled Corelli over to the left side of the room, while Rook moved with V'ger to the right side. Corelli held Keth's arm in a panicked grip. "I didn't mean to challenge him. That wasn't what I thought my magic would do."

"Anyone with any insight could see this was coming." Keth patted Corelli's hand, then removed it from her wrist. "Don't worry, I have something to help you. I had Doc get me V'ger's vial of blood." She slid it into Corelli's hand. "I figured, with your flavor of magic, you would find it useful. What else do you need?"

Looking at the vial of blood made Corelli realize that in less than ten minutes she would be fighting for her life against a talismanic mage who specialized in lightning. She needed to get her head in the game, or she would be seriously injured. "My purse, it's the patchwork one. That's it. It's hanging up."

Keth's response was to move as fast as her aged legs would take her to the coat rack. Corelli bowed her head and thought. She would need a shield against lightning and a way to attack V'ger without getting in close. As Keth returned, Corelli looped the bag over her head and settled it across her body. "I'm ready to move into the combat zone and prepare."

Keth walked her there, then stood behind her. Across the room from her, V'ger and Rook were already in their spot. Corelli took a breath and shut them out. She focused herself and set out a circle of rocks, one large enough for her to sit cross-legged in. The hematite and tiger's eye would protect her, the obsidian would reflect magic.

Corelli made certain to keep the small vial of blood hidden as she sat within her protective circle and began to eat the sugar cubes and red hot candies. She looked through her purse for more things she could use as a sympathetic focus: a mirror, a small knife, a bottle of hot pepper flakes... she wouldn't use them. Duels were not to the death on purpose. She would not set out to kill him. But she needed them available, if it came to that.

Sagan's voice cut across her thoughts and the babble that had sprung up as she prepared. "Ladies and Gentlemen. The duel between V'ger, First in the Order of the Sacred Eye, and Corelli, Second in the Order of the Sacred Eye, is about to begin. This duel is magical in nature only. No other weapons may be used. Breaking of these rules forfeits the duel."

He turned to V'ger. "As the Challenged, what are your terms?"

"My terms are thus: Duel until one party concedes defeat. The loser will no longer be Recognized by the Order of the Sacred Eye, and will be considered Outcast." V'ger bared his teeth in a vicious smile as the room, Corelli included, gasped.

Sagan frowned at V'ger, but could do nothing about his terms. The Challenged had the right to make them as easy or as hard as they wished. "Terms acknowledged as stated. The duel will continue until one duelist concedes defeat."

Corelli looked over her shoulder at Keth, knowing that if she lost, the older woman would share her fate. "I'm so sorry."

Keth leaned down and whispered. "Don't be. Just put him in his place. Now."

"Seconds, as both of the duelists are here, take your place at my side." Sagan raised his voice. "No one, I mean no one is to interfere with this duel. Watchers, remain where you are or leave out the back. Remember, the magic is deadly, and may not remain contained within the combat area, despite the barriers placed by the Second Circle."

Sagan gazed at the floor for a moment then nodded. "Duelists, ready?"

"Ready!" V'ger all but shouted. He had multiple talismans wrapped around his hands.

I am a better mage than you, Corelli thought, then said, "I am ready."

"Duelists... begin."

V'ger took two steps forward as lightning blasted from his hands at Corelli. She did not move other than to shove another handful of red hot candies into her mouth and to cup the vial of V'ger's blood. She wasn't sure what she would've done to hurt him without it, but now was not the time to think of that. Now it was time to believe in her barrier and to focus her anger and heat on the vial, boiling V'ger's blood from within.

The lightning sparked all around her, but did not touch her. The vial in her hand grew hot as she fed her frustration and fear into the spell of pain. She put the vial on the ground in front of her. Now the spell would work until she made it stop. More lightning danced around and over her.

Corelli looked up and could see V'ger sweating. It wasn't just from her spell. "Do you feel the burning, V'ger? It will continue to get hotter and hotter until your blood boils and your flesh catches fire. I will *not* stop it until you concede."

"I will kill you first." V'ger's words were measured and sure, despite his flushed and sweating skin. He stepped closer and unwrapped another talisman. This became a whip of controlled lightning. The first blow broke part of her shield barrier. The second made the lightning dance over her body.

Corelli screamed as her muscles clenched. V'ger screamed with her as her pain was funneled into the spell burning the vial. As her skin sizzled with black marks and blisters, his showed the twin of it. Tears streamed down Corelli's face, and she fought off the urge to run, to flee, to find a safe dark place. Instead, she pushed another rock into line to rebuild her shield and picked up the mirror. Then she waited.

When V'ger's next attack came—a single lightning strike from above—it was reflected away from Corelli and at the vial in front of her. V'ger collapsed in his spot, convulsing in agony.

"Concede, V'ger, or you will *burn*." She pushed as much hate into the word and into her spell as she could.

"Never." V'ger pushed himself to his knees and reached around to the small of his back. But, instead of another talisman, he pulled out a Smith and Wesson .38 Special revolver. "Die, usurper." He pulled the trigger four times.

Three bullets hit their mark.

***

Elsewhere...

Eric brought to bear all the training he had to fight off the amorphous darkness encroaching upon his grandfather's workroom. Despite killing bits and pieces of the enemy, the monster remained whole. Gathering as many tools as he could, he stepped inside the protective circle around his grandfather's pallet. He was the last defense his grandfather had against the nightmare monsters.

Wave upon wave of shadow creatures spilled into the workroom until they filled it entirely—except for where Eric stood guarding Sees-the-Wind's body. Even then, he could feel the press of their power against the wards and the weakening of the circle. He raised his carved war club and readied himself as the air itself seemed to bow inward.

Just as he thought the monsters would break through, Thomas and Thomasina appeared to either side of him. The small twins raised their hands with an explosion of blinding light. There were screams, the sound of sizzling flesh, and the smell of smoke. When Eric could see again, the workroom was clear.

"We are sorry," Thomas said.

"They are growing stronger." Thomasina shook her head.

"But never fear..."

"That is not Sees-the-Wind."

"He fights his own battles."

Eric sank to the floor. "I'm dreaming?"

"Yes." Thomasina put a hand on his shoulder.

"It was so real." Eric bowed his head and sighed.

"It always is." Thomas put a hand on his other shoulder.

Eric looked up as his cell phone rang.

***

Eric opened his eyes, thankful to be in his own bedroom. His cell phone was ringing. He groaned and answered it without looking at it. "Yeah?"

"Iron Eyes?"

Eric didn't recognize the voice. He looked at the phone. The words 'Private Number' showed on the screen. "Who's this?"

"It's Luke Coleman. Can you talk? Did I wake you?"

Jerked into wakefulness by the voice, Eric sat up. "Luke Coleman? What do you want?"

Luke's words came out in a rush. "Look, I'm sorry I kicked you out of the store earlier. I knew who you were, but I didn't want the other to know. If he knew I was calling you, I think he'd kill me."

"What? David? He wouldn't hurt you for calling me." Eric frowned, shaking the rest of the fog of sleep away.

"No. Not the detective. *Kieron*. You know... the enemy? The Nightmares?"

"Wait, what?"

"Look, I wanted you to know that I'm not working with him by my own free will. He scares me, and he could kill me. Not many people can say that. I want to try to help you."

Eric rolled his eyes. "Why would you want to do that?"

"Because I want to survive what's coming, and I think he's going to kill me no matter what I do."

"What do you want me to do?"

"Right now? Nothing. Just know you have a man on the inside. I think... Kieron knows what Sees-the-Wind is doing. He's gloating about some plan. I think he's going to try to kill Sees-the-Wind to hurt the Grey Lady. If he does that, all is lost. The Grey Lady can't lose. There's a reason I helped her way back then. You know about that, right?"

"Yeah. I do." Eric frowned, wondering where the trick was. "But no, I don't believe you."

"I swear it's true. I swear on my life. I promise you, as I soon as I find out what his plans are, I'll call and tell you. I don't want Kieron to win."

The line went dead, and Eric gazed at the phone until it went dark. "Yeah. And I'll believe that when I see it. You're nuts if you think I'm not telling everyone else about this." Despite his words, the threat of Kieron attacking Sees-the-Wind hit a little too close to home. In the morning, he'd talk to Lumbering Bear about getting his grandfather some physical protection.

Lady in Grey, Part 1

ERIC LED SUSAN and Karen through Lumbering Bear's home to the back room, where the Grey Lady stayed when she appeared in Kendrick these days. Only her bond to the Makah people allowed her to do so. They saw the Grey Lady waiting in the rocking chair as they entered the room.

Karen held back her gasp of dismay. The Grey Lady was barely visible. She was a half-shade of an old woman, a translucent shadow of her former self. The only thing that kept Karen from bursting into tears was the fact that the Lady's eyes were still grey. Susan put a hand on Karen's arm, both to support her and to be supported.

"Oh, it is not as bad as it looks, young ladies." The Grey Lady's voice was stronger than it seemed it could be from such an insubstantial form. "I am here only in part. There is much I need to maintain to protect our lands from the Nightmares." She gestured for Susan and Karen to sit on the bed. Eric remained by the door.

"We found Mary Stewart's diary—" Karen began.

Susan interrupted. "We know about Cora Mae and the Binding." She gave Karen an apologetic look. "I figure blunt is good right now."

"Yes," the Lady agreed. "Time is of the essence."

Karen looked at her hands and swallowed hard. It was time to put her money where her mouth was. "We know about the Binding. We know that you must Bind with a willing woman—at least, we believe it must be a woman—and we know it needs to happen soon."

The Grey Lady nodded, her eyes bright.

Karen glanced between the Grey Lady and Susan. Susan had her head bowed and her hands clasped. "We know who you need to Bond with."

"It's me." Susan raised her head. "I will Bind with the Grey Lady. I think it was always meant to be."

"Wait, what?" Karen felt relief and irritation flood through her. "What do you mean?"

"It's me—I know it's me. I've lost my purpose. I have no family. I love this city, and always have. I've fought for it so many times and sacrificed so much." Susan gestured to her clothing. "I wear nothing but grey, for crying out loud. I'm the one who is to Bind to, with, the Grey Lady. This last six months have pushed me toward it."

Karen looked at Eric who nodded. "You knew?"

Eric shrugged. "I guessed. I didn't know." He wasn't about to voice the memory he had of the Grey Lady talking about her next Binding.

"And?" The Grey Lady's voice was very soft as she gazed at Susan.

Susan turned from Karen to look the Lady in the eye. "And you see Alexander. You can be with Alexander if you choose to. Right?"

The Lady inclined her head. "Yes."

"Then it is meant to be. I will Bind with you. Here. Now." Susan stood and offered her hand.

Lady Grey shook her head. "Tomorrow is time enough. You have things to do today. To wrap up. To say good-bye."

"I have to get Changer's Claw, too." Eric shifted from his comfortable leaning pose to a readied stance. "I need to inform the council."

The Grey Lady touched Susan's still outstretched hand. "Go and do the things you need to do. Be sure this is what you want."

"I'm sure." Susan left the room, walking with the distracted air of someone thinking about everything that suddenly needed her attention.

"There's nothing special you need to do? No special alignment of the stars or anything?" Karen asked.

"The Binding needs nothing more than a willing person." Lady Grey smiled at Eric. "It doesn't need even Changer's Claw, though it makes the Makah feel more... involved. Yet, it has never been required. No special time of year. No elaborate ritual. Just the mingling of blood and light."

Karen did not move. The Lady gazed at her and waited. Finally, Karen asked, "Will she die?"

"Oh, no. She will live forever. Though, with each new Binding, her specific personality will become muted. But for the lifetime you will live, Susan and I will be one. You will see both of us in the one body." The Grey Lady tilted her head. "You may mourn her... and me. For neither of us will be the same. I, who have been Cora Mae, Mary Margaret, Elizabeth Brown, Sleeping Stone, and Falling Petals, as well as the Grey Lady, will now welcome Susan Moore in. Thus it has ever been. The Pact will be upheld."

"The Pact?"

Eric shifted, rubbing his hands on his jeans. "The Pact between her people and mine. Or, I guess between her people and the people of Kendrick." He paused. "Sees-the-Wind will die when this happens?"

The Grey Lady nodded. "Yes. Or, more to the point, I will not renew his life. He will continue to live until he dies."

"So, there's no worry that Kieron is going to use Luke Coleman to try to kill him?"

Karen gave him a sharp look. "What do you mean?"

"Luke called me last night," Eric replied. "Said that he wanted me to know he wasn't working with Kieron of his own free will. That Kieron was gloating about having a plan for Sees-the-Wind. And that he'd call and tell me as soon as he knew what it was. It's a lie, of course."

Karen turned to the Lady. "Could Kieron do something to you through Sees-the-Wind? Or to the barrier that's keeping the Nightmares out?"

"It is possible. Yes. Also, I believe this is a trap of some kind, but I do not have the eyes to see it." The Lady nodded to Eric. "Be careful. But protect your grandfather. He still has his role to play in all of this."

Karen fought with her emotions. She was almost disappointed she wasn't required to Bind to the Grey Lady. Almost as much as she was relieved. But losing Susan, or part of her, would hurt. She didn't know how to wrap her head about it. She fell back to what she knew—coordinating the plan of attack to save Kendrick. "The Ritual of Renewed Earth... what is it?"

"Ah. You have discovered that as well. I am pleased." Lady Grey shifted in the rocking chair, though it did not move. "Once the Binding is done, I will have the strength to rebuild the Veil. Though, I will need power. So much power that I cannot do it alone. I will need at least three from the city of Kendrick to funnel power to me. With it, I will rebuild what has been lost." She gazed at Karen. "I need you to find those people."

"That, I can do." Karen stood, pleased to have something to focus on. "Tomorrow. What time?"

"I suspect that Susan will be ready as early as noon." The Grey Lady turned to Eric. "Bring her, and those you trust, to the Pillar of Memory. That is as good of a place as they come."

Eric nodded. "Will do."

Then, the Grey Lady was gone, leaving Karen and Eric looking at each other. She shrugged. "Okay. I guess we have our marching orders. I'll bring Susan here tomorrow at noon."

"Cool." Eric let out a sigh. "Things are coming to a head, aren't they?"

"They always do."

***

Alexia watched Doc work on Corelli, writing blood runes over and around the bullet wounds. One of the lethal pieces of lead was still in Corelli, next to her heart. It was the wound Doc was most afraid of. Rightfully so. Though his blood magic was strong for a human, he was still merely mortal.

She looked up at Keth hovering in the background, muttering, "Don't die. Don't die. We need you."

Keth was also right. Corelli was needed. Alexia stood, waited until Doc moved out of the way, and waved a hand. Everyone but her stopped moving.

Alexia walked to the bed and sat at Corelli's side. "Only for you will I do this," she whispered.

She kissed Corelli's brow, letting her personal magic heal Corelli as much as she dared—not enough to allow the woman out of bed, but enough to allow her to live. She smiled as Corelli's eyes opened, and grinned as she realized where she was and at the strange sight of her non-member girlfriend at her side.

"Alexia?" Corelli tried to sit up.

Alexia held her down with a gentle hand. "I'm here."

"How?"

"I've always been here. I couldn't see you die. Not to that barbarian."

"You were at the duel?" Corelli's eyes widened and she shook her head. "I didn't see you."

"You weren't meant to."

"V'ger?"

"Dead." Alexia's voice was hard. "You couldn't stop the spell you wrought. He burned."

Corelli shuddered at the thought, and at her girlfriend's look of satisfaction. She glanced around the room again and realized what was wrong. "They're not moving."

"No." Alexia tilted her head. "They're fine. I'll release them soon. I just needed to save you."

Corelli flushed with pleasure, then with confusion. "Why? How?"

"You may be first in the Order, but you are also first in my heart." Alexia glanced at Keth. "I am selfish. I wasn't... I'm not ready to let you go." She looked back at Corelli. "But you're still too weak to go anywhere, do anything."

Again Corelli tried to sit up. "I have to."

Again, Alexia stopped her with a gentle hand. "No. I will help. Only for you will I do this. When I wake them, tell Keth to bring me the power stone. I'll be in the Colonel's Park at the chess tables. Don't allow her to ask you any questions. Take command immediately."

"How will you get out?" Corelli stopped and answered her own question. "They won't see you, will they?"

Alexia shook her head and stood. "No." She paused and looked away. "Please don't let this change things between us."

Corelli touched her hand. "Why would it?"

"I'm not human."

"And I'm a young mage who runs a magic order that is trying to save the city by allying with gargoyles, cranky witches, the Makah, and the fey." She raised Alexia's hand to lips, placing a kiss there. "Nothing is going to change. I love you."

Alexia turned back to Corelli and smoothed her hair. "And I, you." Then she was gone, walking away. As soon as she crossed the threshold, Keth and Doc continued their paused movements.

Keth was the first to see Corelli awake. "Doc!"

Doc turned and blinked with surprise. "Corelli, I thought..." He shook his head and hurried to her side. "Never mind what I thought, how do you feel?"

"Like I've been shot." Corelli locked eyes with Keth. "I need to speak with you and Sagan. What's the status of Rook?"

Doc stood up straight. "No, I—"

"You will do nothing. I am First in the Order, and I have some things that need doing now." Corelli didn't even look at him, but she saw Doc wince, then scowl.

"In a holding cell." Keth tilted her head. "He is to be cast out."

Corelli nodded, putting up with Doc's examination of his healing runes as she spoke. "We'll deal with that in a bit. Go get Sagan, please. We've got work to do. While you do, don't be quiet about my miraculous recovery. Laud Doc. Laud me. Make shit up. I don't care. Just make sure that everyone knows I'm awake, alive, and almost recovered, despite what he did."

Keth smiled a knowing smile. "Of course." She bowed to Corelli and left the room.

***

"Aaron, where are you? Okay, you aren't answering your phone. Call me as soon as you get this. It's important. Like city-saving important." David ended the call and walked through the doors of the Kendrick Historical Library.

Nicholas nodded to him from behind the librarian's counter. "Hello David. All alone?"

"Yes. 1851. Brotherhood of Light. Father Michael. Did he have a journal, or does the Brotherhood keep archives of events?" David paused. "Sorry. Distracted. Hello to you as well."

"That's a very good question." Nicholas put down his pen. "Let me see if I can help you."

"It is. I wish I thought of it sooner." David followed Nicholas to the card catalog. "No Chalice?"

"No. She left shortly after your group left yesterday." He flipped through the cards, looking for books by the Brotherhood of Light. "Hasn't been back."

"Huh. She followed me and Eric to Coleman's. I haven't seen her since." David rubbed his forehead. "That was such a stupid thing to do."

"What was?"

"Going to *Treasures & Trinkets*. I'm pretty sure Coleman's working with the enemy, and now they know we know about the Ritual of Renewed Earth. Sorta."

Nicholas straightened and headed for the stacks. "Why did you go there?"

"Karen suggested it." David followed, looking at the rows of books but not reading any of their titles. "Nicholas, this bibliotaph thing, it's not a me or her sort of thing, is it?"

"No. You, or her, or both, or neither." Nicholas stopped at a row of books. "I've been without an assistant before. For a short blissful time, I had several. But it is up to you and to the library, of course."

"The library?"

"This is the best I could do." Nicholas handed David two books. Both had plain brown leather covers. "And yes, the library. You don't think a magical library wouldn't have a say in who tends it, did you?"

David shook his head. "No. I guess not. The thing is, I don't think I want to become a librarian. Bibliotaph. Whatever. I think I'd rather do something more active. Like remaining with the police department."

Nicholas nodded. "I understand. It's what I thought you'd say."

"You're not mad?" David followed him back to the reading area.

"No. Like I said, I'd rather you want to be here than not." Nicholas shrugged. "Happy reading." He nodded to the books in David's hands. "I hope they help."

David nodded back. "Yeah. Me, too." He sat down at the nearest table and opened the first book. He discovered it to be an archival record of the Brotherhood of Light from late 1850 to early 1851.

***

Alexia was waiting for John at the *Teller's Fortune* when he arrived to open for the afternoon. He paused as he rounded the corner and saw her sitting on the front steps. Something about the way she sat, then regarded him as he approached, warned him that not all was well in the world.

Welcome to Kendrick, he thought. His meeting with the mayor had gone well enough, for all the news that had been shared. "Alex? You okay?" He pulled his keys from his pocket. "You're not on duty for another couple of hours—"

She stood, picking up the small picnic basket she had at her side. "Today, I don't work for you. Today is special."

"Oookay." John held the door open for her, then followed her inside, flipping on the lights.

"You might want to keep the shop closed for a couple of days."

He paused and turned the open sign back to closed, then locked the door. "Right. What's happened?" John set himself up behind the counter and watched her. Anything to make his 'never gonna get involved' employee act like this wasn't a good thing.

"Corelli almost died to make sure this got to the Grey Lady. In this case, I specifically represent her. Not the Order. Though, she is doing this in the name of the Order of the Sacred Eye. Do you understand?"

Alex didn't look like she normally did. She seemed taller, almost glowing and her eyes... they were dark orbs, with starlight in them. It was like looking into outer space. John slowly shook his head. "No. I don't."

Alex pushed the basket toward him across the counter. "Look at it, but do not touch it."

He opened the basket and saw a glowing quartz crystal as large as his fist within. John knew that it held immense power. "My, what pretty things you bring me."

"This is for the Grey Lady. She will use it in a ritual to seal the breach between worlds. It is from Corelli in the name of the Order of the Sacred Eye." Alexia gazed at, and through, him. "She almost died to make certain this needed artifact went to the right person. Do you understand?"

John was beginning to, and that was enough for him. "Yes, Alex. I do. Do you want me to take it... no." He said as she shook her head. "You'll give it to her."

"Yes."

"The Grey Lady will Bind with Susan Moore tomorrow at noon." John pulled a cigarette from his inner pocket, lit it and took a long drag, taking comfort in the familiar taste. He flipped on his smokeless ashtray. "That's a good enough time for you to give her the crystal. I'll introduce you then."

Alex smiled, and was the affable shop girl he'd hired once more. "She found someone to Bind to. Good." Her smile disappeared. "Then the breach can be sealed. I will lend my strength with the others in the name of Corelli."

"So, you know about that." John stared at her, but she didn't answer. "Right. So, don't take this the wrong way, but, what are you?"

"I am a Daughter of Night from the Gentle Lands, and I am not feeling very gentle right now."

John nodded as a hint of those star-filled eyes reappeared. "Yes. That is who you are..." He gestured with his cigarette. "*What* are you?"

"Ah..." The word was an exhale on the wind. Alexia looked down at the basket as she closed it and pulled it to her. She looked up and half-smiled. "I am as my namesake. I am a Defender. This city is not the first to have such an invasion of creatures from another realm, John. When the breach ripped in earnest, I stepped forward. I am prepared to do my duty."

"I'm probably going to hate the answer, but what is your duty?"

"You've read about cities and places that have been destroyed by horrifying disasters, yes?" She gazed at him and mirrored his nod. "When a breach cannot be sealed and the invasion is a foregone conclusion, we seal the breach in the only way we can. It kills all of the invaders and the people, and leaves a mystery for the ages. It also kills the Defender."

Alexia leaned over the counter, making John take an involuntary step back to bump into the wall. "I am the last resort. I am not supposed to get involved. But I'm not willing to let go of Corelli. It's why I've left her in her weakened state and why I represent her in this. I don't want her anywhere near what will happen next."

"You'll kill everyone?"

"Everyone."

"How?"

Alexia shrugged. "It will look like a natural disaster. Something like the Tunguska event, but on a smaller scale. In this case, I guess it would look like a volcano or a meteor strike. But there would be nothing left of Kendrick, and the breach would be sealed."

John took another long drag on his cigarette to buy himself time. He rubbed his cheek. "Alex, why are you telling me this?"

"Because someone needs to know the stakes. Someone needs to understand what I will do—must do—if the breach is not sealed in time." She turned away, taking the basket with her. "I'd rather not do this. I've grown fond of this life." Alexia stopped at the door. "I'll see you tomorrow."

Once Alexia was gone, John let himself sink to the floor, trembling with the effort to keep himself calm. Part of him wanted to tell Karen. Part of him wanted to run very far away. Part of him, the biggest part, wanted to see how this was all going to play out. "Nothing like a nuclear last resort to make things exciting."

Then he pushed himself to his feet. "What the hell is a Daughter of Night from the Gentle Lands?"

***

Chalice was angry. Oh, yes. She was very angry. That anger gave her the energy she needed to do and to be smart about it, too. She'd killed one Nightmare monster already; one of the few that had come through with some poor person's death. It had scuttled upon her by accident as she watched *Treasures & Trinkets*, waiting for Luke Coleman to come out.

He didn't sleep. At least, he didn't seem to. The light on his basement apartment never turned off. It was possible he was afraid of the dark, but Chalice didn't think that was the case. That was fine. She didn't need to sleep either. She wouldn't lose her quarry. Not now when it looked like he was leading her someplace.

More to the point, he was leading the enemy someplace deep in the early hours of the morning.

Chalice bared her teeth in a feral grin as Luke stopped in front of a small house and his dark passenger—her enemy, the leader Nightmare, invincible for the moment—detached from Luke's shadow and slithered in under the door. She watched as Luke hovered there, gazing at the house. When he turned on his heel and walked away, she was torn—the Nightmare was the enemy, but Luke was the one she could hurt right now. When the Veil was strengthened, when everyone attacked as one, ah, then it would be another story.

After hesitating a few seconds longer, she chose to follow Luke, to continue her surveillance of the thrall. The Nightmare enemy could only hurt humans in dreams, and this one had already woken up. She could see that by the light now illuminating the second story window.

Sliding from negative space to negative space, Chalice kept pace with Luke. Based on what she remembered, he was her best chance to kill the creature that had murdered her family. All she had to do was wait, watch, and make her move when the betrayal came.

***

Susan stood before Alexander's statue, holding his unmoving hand while she spoke on the phone. "...and my letter of resignation is on my desk. I needed to make it official because, otherwise, there'd be talk. I recommended you to take over for me. I know this may seem sudden, but it's been a long time coming. I don't know if you'll see me around town. You might. It's okay to say hello. I know I'm going to miss working with you, Monica. And I know you'll do a good job with the museum."

She looked up at Alexander's face. "The gargoyle statue in the basement. I'm going to have it moved and soon. Most likely Karen Wilson will be in charge of that. I left her number in my list of things for you to know. You might want to ask her if she wants to learn the ropes from the ground up. Or ask Gale. I know she's interested." Susan paused. "I guess there's not much more to say, except good luck. I wish I'd been able to talk to you before I left. I hope I see you around."

After ending the call, Susan stroked Alexander's stone cheek. "You knew this was going to happen, didn't you? That's why you pushed me to the library in my dream. You somehow figured out a way for us to be together again."

There wasn't a verbal answer, of course. But there was a sense of amusement and anticipation radiating from the statue.

"Just twelve more hours to go." Susan looked down at her phone as it vibrated a text message. "Karen's here. I'll see you soon."

***

As the two of them walked through the halls of the Kendrick Museum, Karen thought about the night she'd first met Susan. It was also the first night she'd met Sebastian. In a way, it felt like some undefined circle was being closed.

"I thought it was me who was supposed to Bind to the Lady." Karen's blurted words startled even her.

Susan shook her head with a half-smile. "No. You're meant for other things. The library, it seems. Or maybe this place." She opened her office door. "Thanks for coming so late."

Karen shrugged. "I wasn't sleeping. I'm a night owl."

Susan gestured to one box. "Those are for you. They're my journals and some other stuff." She gestured to a second box. "That's mine. I just don't know." She shrugged. "Keep them safe for me until I figure out my new life.?"

"Of course." Karen could see pictures and other small, sentimental things in the second box.

"I'm scared." Susan sighed with relief. She seemed to feel better now that she'd admitted the fear.

Karen tilted her head. "What are you afraid of? Losing yourself or...?"

"Yes. Losing myself. Losing Alexander. All this being a false fantasy."

"You don't have to go through with it. You know you don't."

Susan's eyes were bright. "But I *want* to. I want to so bad. Think of everything I'll see and do. And I'll be with Alexander again."

Karen nodded. "The Grey Lady told me that you would be you and you would share with those who had come before. That you... your specific you, would only be muted once the Grey Lady binds to another again. Who knows when that will be? The Lady told me that it would be longer than my lifetime. So, I won't really lose you."

"You'll never lose me." Susan handed her a set of keys. "Do you want my apartment?"

"What?" Karen looked down at the keys in her hand.

"It's on a monthly renewal, and I have a lot of money in the bank."

Karen shook her head. "I don't... But I'll take care of your stuff, if you want."

"It's too late for me to transfer the money to you..."

"You don't have to."

"I want to." Susan smiled. "You've been a good friend to me. Also, you're going to protect Alexander until I know where he needs to go."

"I can transfer the money for her," Reginald whispered over Karen's earpiece.

"I'll tell the Master of the City. He'll take care of it." Karen put a hand on Susan's arm. "Do you want me to stay with you tonight?"

Susan shook her head. "No. Tonight is for me. I just wanted to make sure the important things are safe. Do whatever you want with my apartment and the stuff inside. I'm pretty sure I won't need it anymore."

"Okay. I'll take care of it."

Then there was nothing left to say. Susan and Karen each took a box out to Karen's waiting car. John stood there, smoking. He nodded to Susan. "You ready?"

"I am now." Susan gave him a brief hug as he took her box. Then she gave Karen a bigger hug. "No tears tomorrow. I'm not dying. I'm doing something much more interesting."

Karen nodded, unable to speak. Susan gave Karen a kiss on the cheek, turned away, and re-entered the museum. Now, Karen understood Mary Stewart's fear and grief when Cora Mae stepped up to Bind to the Grey Lady. Karen continued to watch the museum until John touched her shoulder.

"You all right?"

Karen shook her head. "No, I don't think so, but I will be."

"Where to now?" John opened the car door for her.

"My place to stow some stuff... then dinner?"

John nodded. "That sounds good. You going to go back to the library before the Binding?"

"I might. To look up more on that ritual." Karen didn't add that she wanted to see if there was anything more about the Binding.

"Huh. Okay." John paused. "Would you look up something for me?"

"Sure." Karen waited for him to settle into the car. "What do you need?"

"Could you look up what a 'Daughter of Night from the Gentle Lands' is?"

Karen started the car and looked at him. "That's kinda specific."

He nodded. "It is. I'll tell you about it another time. Okay?"

She shook her head with a smile. "All right. Sounds like a great story to me."

"I hope so."

***

Elsewhere...

Griff paddled as fast as he could, but he knew it wasn't going to be fast enough to get to dry land. He had a choice; bail water or swim for it. The dark water with its unknown creatures held nothing but a choking death. He had to figure out how to bail water and paddle to shore at the same time.

The bucket at his feet was small, but it would do the job. He threw water out of the canoe for a count of ten, then paddled for a count of ten. The shore was getting closer. It would work. However, the next time he picked up the bucket, not only was it smaller, it had a hole in the bottom. There was so much water everywhere. He had no choice but to bail with one hand and to paddle with the other.

As soon as this started to work, Griff frowned. By the laws of physics, paddling one-handed should send him in circles instead of toward the shore. "I'm dreaming," Griff said then looked to the left. "Am I awake?" He looked right. "Am I awake?"

After considering what he knew, he shook his head. "I'm dreaming. That means this canoe is now a powerboat and is going to make it to land... now."

An answering bump of boat against land made him grin. "I'm dreaming. I'm in control. I'm..."

Griff opened his eyes on the dark bedroom. He glanced to his left and grunted at the time on the clock. "Nightmare almost got you that time." He sat up and looked around. Helen was still out of town. With no wife to cuddle back to sleep, he gave the rest of the evening up for a loss. He had to be up for the early morning shift anyway. After turning on the light, Griff pulled on a pair of comfy pants and headed downstairs to make coffee.

He was flipping through an old magazine and taking his first drink of coffee when the shadow man entered the kitchen. Griff put both the coffee and the magazine down. He looked left. "Am I awake?" He looked right. "Am I awake?" Nodding to himself, he answered the question. "Yes. I'm awake." Then he looked up at the shadow man again.

It was still there.

"But, I'm awake. You can't be here."

Kieron smiled. "Yet, here I am." Then he threw himself at Griff.

Griff's cries for help and his struggle against the Nightmare made flesh went unheeded by the night birds, and unheard by the rest of the still-sleeping world.

Lady in Grey, Part 2

ERIC WATCHED LUMBERING Bear's silhouette walk away. He had to shade his eyes to see that much in the sunrise light. He looked down at Changer's Claw when he felt the twins arrive. He didn't say anything for a long time. Just stared at the artifact he'd been entrusted with. It had once been part of an old whaling harpoon. Now, all that was left was the tip, made of sharp mussel shell blades and bone points. This was mounted on a carved club. While it was not used as a weapon, it could be.

He took care to keep his hands away from the sharpened edges of the Claw as he set it aside. "He asked me what I thought about those we've been working with. He asked me if they were worthy to see the ceremony. When I said, 'Yes,' he just accepted it. It was scary."

"Your words hold weight now." Thomasina took his hand in hers.

Thomas leaned against him. "You are shaman in all but name at this point."

Eric shook his head. "I'm not ready for that. What if I get it wrong, and my words sink like stones?"

"You will make mistakes."

"You will fall."

"But we will be there..."

"...to help you up again."

He let their childish voices cascade over him and sighed. Then he remembered the promise. "When will you change?"

Thomas shrugged. "At the moment of the Binding, we believe. We've never changed with the Grey Lady before—other than the change all of us go through in each Binding."

"Are you scared?" Eric glanced back and forth at their faces.

Thomasina nodded. "Yes. But excited, too. It's been a long time since the first change."

"We don't know what it will be like to be older." Thomas screwed up his young seeming face. "Or what emotions we'll feel."

"All of them." Eric laughed and hugged the twins to him. "But don't worry. I'll be here to help you through a lot of it." Then he looked at Thomasina. "Though I'll have to find someone else to help you with some of the girl stuff. Maybe Gale."

***

Nicholas shook his head. "I can't find anything about a "Daughter of Night" that's concrete. It's either poetic or vampire-related or Greek myth-related. As for the "Gentle Lands," there's the modern interpretation of Wales, Ireland, Scotland and the surrounding islands. In tales and legend, it sometimes refers to Lemuria—a mythical place where strange, ageless people lived. There were Dreamers who could dream your dream for you and make it a reality."

Karen made a face. "Weird. I don't think I'd want my dreams to be reality. They're too strange and nonsensical."

"I think the point was that these Dreamers could dream you a logical dream in reality." He paused. "If that makes any sense at all."

"What was the Greek myth related to the Daughter of Night?"

Nicholas shifted his books around. "Ah, here. Eris is the daughter of Nyx, also known as a Goddess of Night. Eris is a force of strife, discord, and chaos."

"That doesn't seem to match with the "Gentle Lands" concept."

"No, it doesn't." Nicholas closed the book. "The problem here is that there is no context. Both terms are too generic to match to a location, time, or culture. You'll have to get more information from John."

Karen nodded. "Yeah. Maybe he'll tell me why he asked." She stood and gathered an armful of books to put away. "I've got a couple other things to look for anyway."

"When you get back, I'd like to talk to you about something." Nicholas didn't look up from the book he was reading.

"All right." Karen could tell from the all-too-casual way he spoke that it was something important to him. "I'll be back soon."

She put each book back where it was supposed to go. Then, after a look through the card catalog, Karen found a couple more books by Elizabet Sampson and Cora Mae Steward. Either one could have more details about what happened with the Binding.

As Karen passed the Rare Book Room, there was the thump of a book hitting the floor. She paused. "Nicholas? Chalice?" Peeking into the room, she could see a book on the floor but no one nearby. She knew she wasn't supposed to go into the room but, at the same time, she couldn't leave the book just lying on the floor.

Karen almost dropped the book when she picked it up and read the title. "Raymond 'Griff' Griffith." She knew that name. He'd been her boss for six years at the Emergency Services Center. She put the book on the large central stand. There was no other book on it. She stared at the book, wanting to open it, to see what it was, but not daring to do so.

The book opened on its own and flipped to the last few pages. The title of the chapter was *The Death of Raymond Griffith.*

Karen leaned forward and began to read.

***

Nicholas found her like that just steps behind Sebastian. "There you are. This little guy almost broke a window to get... in." He stopped and saw the tears on her face. Bowing his head, he said, "I'm sorry. This is what I wanted to talk to you about."

Sebastian leaped to Karen's arms. She caught him without thinking about it. "The book fell. It fell. Then it opened itself up when I put it back." Karen gazed at him through a veil of tears. "Griff's dead. Kieron did it." Her face hardened as she hugged Sebastian tight. "And you knew."

Nicholas took a step backwards, raising his hands to ward her off. "No. The book must've just arrived. That's what this room is. That's why people aren't supposed to come in here. Not until they've been trained. I guess the Library's accepted you. I'm sorry this is how you found out. I didn't know. I've never seen this book before, nor read its last chapter."

Karen wiped at her tears. "I don't understand."

He thought for a moment and then shrugged. "Usually there's a better way to introduce prospective Bibliotaphs to one of the Library's most important secrets. When there's an unexpected or unusual death in Kendrick, that person's Lifebook appears here. Then it's the job of the Bibliotaph to read the last chapter and determine if someone needs to know, or to allow things to play out."

Nicholas sighed. "No book falls here without a purpose. The person who finds it was meant to find it. I'm just sorry this is how you found out about them... the room and your friend."

"Do I have a Lifebook?"

He nodded. "Yes. Somewhere in the Library. But you aren't supposed to read it. It changes things when you do." He paused. "I found out about you from Heather's book. That's how I started following you. Then I realized that you were also Speaks-for-the-City. I read about you in Sparks-of-the-Moon's book."

Karen winced at the memory of her murdered friend, and at the memory of the Makah Guardian who had died trying to protect Changer's Claw. "The Library's accepted me. What if I haven't accepted it?"

"Then you haven't. It was just making its choice clear. But, I'd rather you be here because you want to be here, and not because you think you have no choice."

"Is David going to work here?"

Nicholas hesitated, then shook his head. "He's going to remain with the police. But don't let that influence you. I can go without an assistant for a while."

Karen frowned. "Where's Chalice?"

Nicholas looked away. "Chasing a prophecy."

"I need to think about this more." Karen touched Griff's book. "And I need to call the SU. This wasn't a natural death. Kieron made sure to hurt Griff for as long as he could."

The Head Bibliotaph nodded. "Take all the time you need."

She looked at her watch. "Noon is coming up fast. Tell me this: is Cora Mae's Lifebook here?"

"In this room?" He looked around at the rows and rows of books. "No. She didn't die an unexpected or unusual death."

"Did she die?"

"I don't know. I don't think so. Not in the way you and I understand it. If you want, I can look for the book."

Karen shook her head. "Please do. It might give me some hints on what's about to happen to Susan. It would be handy to have—if it exists."

*　*　*

Aaron sat at the kitchen table as David put a cup of coffee in front of him and got one for himself. Next to Aaron's cup sat three books. David recognized two of them as being from the Library, and wondered again how the Kendrick Historical Library worked. He also wondered if he'd made the right decision.

Tapping the top book, the only one David didn't recognize, Aaron shrugged. "This was all I could find in our archives. It's not much." He sighed. "The Brotherhood of Light fights malevolent spirits. These Nightmare creatures are something else. There's very little we can do. But..." He held up a finger, paused to take a sip of coffee, then pulled the first book to him. "There is something here."

David leaned forward. "Those are archival books?"

"Those two are." Aaron flipped through the book in front of him. "This one is a personal journal of our doctor, Brother Joseph, from 1851. I found it by accident. But since it was from the time period you requested, I looked through it. There's one particular passage I noticed." He cleared his voice and read.

"*The rite Father Michael participated in was a success. While we did not have the skills to fight the fiends, our faith in the Lord preserved us. During the fight to protect the rite, those who prayed for God's protection were protected more than those who did not. Almost none of the Brotherhood of Light were harmed. It appeared that the fiends could not break the shield of faith, and even nearness to the faithful was painful for them.*

'However, we could not fight and pray at the same time. Should this sort of fight occur again, I would recommend that the Brotherhood of Light form a shield of faith about the Grey Lady, and those within the rite itself and allow the more secular factions to do the actual fighting.

'Though, in truth, the idea of this does not sit well with me. I am a physician, but I am also a warrior for the Light.'"

Aaron closed the book. "It goes on to talk about who was actually harmed from the Brotherhood, and who else fought on the side of good. But the bit about the shield of faith sounded important."

David put his cup down and steepled his fingers in thought. "Perhaps it's like what we're doing to protect our dreams. It's an act of will and belief. By giving everyone the tools to guard their dreams, the power of the Nightmares has lessened. The faith of the Brotherhood of Light, your faith, is so much stronger because you *do* fight evil spirits. You *know* so much more, thus your faith is that much more."

Aaron nodded. "Yes." He gazed at the closed book, following the faint cracks in its worn leather cover. "As much as I don't want to, I think the role of the Brotherhood in the upcoming Ritual of Renewed Earth is to be a shield rather than a sword."

"Yeah, I think it is." David glanced at the clock. "The Binding ritual should be happening soon."

"You're not going?" Aaron gave him a quizzical look.

David shook his head. "No. I wasn't invited. Just told of it. I know Karen and John will be there, and one of them will tell me or Mason what happened." He shrugged. "As interesting as it sounds, it's really not my place to be at something like that. I'm not even sure Karen or John would be there if it wasn't for Susan."

Aaron sat back. "I wonder what this new Grey Lady will be like."

"I think we're all wondering that. I hope she's the best parts of Susan and the Grey Lady that once was."

"From your lips to God's ears."

***

Eric led the small group of outsiders through the throng of his people up to the Pillar of Memory. He'd been surprised at seeing Alexia, but her words, "I have a gift for the Lady," made everything seem well again. He could hear Susan and Karen speaking quietly behind him. John had not said a word since they greeted each other.

"A lot of people here," Susan murmured.

"It's a momentous occasion." Karen patted their clasped hands. She glanced up at the nearly silent, waiting Makah people. "But, there's still time to back out if you want to."

Susan shook her head. "No. This is what I'm meant to do. What I want to do." Then she asked, "Did you dream last night?"

Karen thought back and shook her head. "I'm sure I did, but I don't remember..."

"I think, if you ever want to talk to me but can't find me, try to dream of me. That's how I found Alexander again." Susan looked up at the carved pillar of stone. "I made myself dream of him."

"Okay." She nodded and let go of Susan's hand, but remained at her side.

Eric handed Changer's Claw to Lumbering Bear. As the leader of the Makah people, he would perform the ceremony normally presided over by the tribe's shaman. While Sees-the-Wind still lived, Eric would not take his place. He stepped back and melted into the crowd until he was on its outside edge. From there, he would watch and see what everyone did.

Karen walked with Susan to Lumbering Bear. She touched Susan's arm. "I'll see you soon."

The huge man looked down at the smaller women. "Are you ready?"

"I am ready." Susan patted Karen's hand with a distracted smile, then turned to Lumbering Bear. "I am prepared for the Binding."

Lumbering Bear raised Changer's Claw and began to speak, capturing the crowd's attention.

No one saw Eric look down at his phone, then turn and sprint away, back toward his grandfather's workroom.

He's going after your grandfather now. Come quickly.

The text message was from a private number, but Eric knew it was from Luke Coleman. He also knew that it had to be a ruse to get him away from the Binding ceremony.

Eric bared his teeth as he ran. Apparently, Luke didn't know Eric was far from the only one who could bend the earth's power to his will. Not only that, there were Guardians in the crowd and they were more than a match for any Nightmare creature.

With the workroom in sight, standing next to several of the houses the Makah owned, Eric slowed and watched the area he approached. Nothing moved. Everyone was at the ceremony. And why not? This was a once-in-a-lifetime event. Eric hurried to the workroom door and burst in with a loud shout.

Eric hadn't expected anyone to be here. However, he didn't hesitate when he saw Luke standing over Jake, the Makah teen who had been guarding his grandfather during the ceremony. Eric grabbed the carved club hanging on the wall and charged Luke with another shout.

Luke jumped away from Jake, raising his hands. "I didn't hurt him! He's just unconscious." He circled away from Eric until he stood between the teenager and the door. Then he dropped his hands. "Be prepared. He's coming."

Eric looked around the workroom with the war club still raised. It was his grandfather's weapon, and he could feel the power in it. He backed up until he reached Sees-the-Wind. Relief flooded through him as he saw his grandfather's chest rise and fall in an easy rhythm. Slowly, he lowered the club. "Why are you helping?"

"He has no choice." The answer came from a shadow next to the door. Kieron moved sinuously away from his hiding spot. "It seems I no longer need to kill Sees-the-Wind. Though, I might anyway. For the sheer joy of it."

Eric hefted the war club high. "I'd like to see you try." Inside, he quaked with fear and mentally screamed for the twins to help.

Kieron laughed and advanced on him. "Your weapons cannot harm me."

"Wanna bet?" Eric met Kieron's advance with a hard swing of the war club, and was rewarded with the Nightmare's surprised gasp of pain. "How's that feel?"

Then there was no more time for talking. Kieron reacted like a wounded viper, lashing at Eric while dancing away from the one weapon in this room that could hurt him. Kieron's form shifted and morphed to suit him, manifesting shadow weapons that cut and struck as if they were solid.

Still, it was not enough to remain unscathed. The third time Eric landed a blow, part of Kieron's shadow form broke off and dissipated like smoke in the wind. "Now!" he cried.

Luke, who had crept up behind Eric, knocked him on the back of the head with a blackjack even as the teen turned too late to ward it off. Eric fell to his knees, his club clattering to the ground.

Luke raised the blackjack to knock Eric unconscious, but as he was bringing it down, a short, round, angry form tackled him from behind. Falling with a surprised cry, Luke tried to protect himself from hitting the floor and from the fists pummeling him. He failed on both counts.

Chalice, who had waited days for this chance, popped to her feet and kicked Luke hard in the stomach, even as a shadow sword burst through her chest. She turned her cry of pain into a laugh of triumph, and turned as Kieron pulled the sword back in confusion. "You have my blood on you. I can hurt you now."

"You..." Kieron breathed the word out, a dying man's last exhale.

"Me." She bent and picked up the fallen war club. "Finally." Wincing as she rubbed the wood against her bloody wound, Chalice stalked toward Kieron.

Kieron moved away, a step back for every step Chalice took. "You were dead."

"I bound myself to vengeance. For over fifty years I waited. I wait no more, you bastard!" Chalice rushed Kieron, swinging the club at him.

He jerked away from it—straight into her fist. Her flesh burned his shadow form wherever she touched him. For the first time since entering this world, Kieron was on the defensive against an enemy he barely understood. "Luke!"

Kieron's panicked cry was answered with the sound of a gunshot, followed by a second; both impossibly loud in the small workroom. Luke pulled himself to his feet as Chalice looked down in disbelief at the wounds in her chest. Grimacing, she took another step toward Kieron, then crumpled to her knees and fell to her side as blood flowed from her wounds.

Eric scrabbled dazedly toward Chalice and the war club, but he couldn't make his legs or arms do what he wanted them to do. There were multiple images of everything in front of him. He was aware that Chalice had tried to save him and was now badly hurt. He silently cried out for the twins again. This time, a pair of dark-haired teenagers appeared in the workroom in-between Chalice and Eric.

"We are here as the promise demands," they said in unison. They spread out, Thomasina went to Chalice's side and Thomas to Eric's side. Thomasina put a glowing hand on Chalice's unmoving body.

Thomas reached down to Eric, then stopped, leaping up and toward Sees-the-Wind's still form. He was still moving when the two projectiles aimed at the defenseless shaman— another bullet from Luke's gun and a shadow spear from Kieron—struck him full in the chest.

Thomas hit the ground next to Sees-the-Wind's pallet. He looked down, eyes wide in disbelief and fear, watching black shadow cracks split his form. Screaming as his body arched and exploded in light and sound. Thomasina's scream mirrored his, and she disappeared in the explosion.

"No." Eric's voice was weak as he reached for where he last saw Thomasina. Then, as Luke kicked him in the back of the head, darkness took him.

***

Karen watched the Pillar of Memory, watched as Susan and the Grey Lady, mingling blood and light in their clasped hands, walked away and into the distance. Even though the stone pillar was only a few feet away, it looked as if the women walked the length of a football field before they stopped moving. She could see the women facing each other, then bowing their heads together. They stood like that for a long, silent moment before they turned as one and began their long walk back to this reality.

Halfway home, there was the muffled sound of gunfire. Or two tires popping in secession. Both were possible, and Lumbering Bear gestured to a couple of people who fanned out, looking for the source of the noise.

Karen did not care. She only had eyes for Susan, who was now the Grey Lady. She could see only one woman walking back now. The closer she came, the more Karen recognized her. It was Susan. But she had white-blond hair and wore a long, grey dress with a matching jacket.

At the same time, it was the Grey Lady. Her walk was as elegant and stately as it always had been. Her eyes were the grey of river stones. When she stepped from wherever she'd been back to the ground in front of the Pillar of Memory, her power was clear. Karen dropped her eyes, confused, and unable to sort out her feelings. She looked up again as the Grey Lady stopped in front of her.

"Hello," the Grey Lady said.

Karen's heart gave a lurch. It was Susan, but it wasn't. "Hello."

They looked at each other and the Grey Lady offered Karen her hand. Then another one of those muffled gunshots reached them and a small child near the Pillar of Memory let out a terrified shriek. They turned to see a dark-haired teenage girl flicker in and out of existence. She was arched in agony with her head thrown back in a soundless scream.

"Thomasina..." The Grey Lady glided to the girl's side and reached out a hand. As soon as she touched Thomasina's flickering form, the girl became solid and gained a foothold in this reality. The scream gained in volume, then cut off as Thomasina collapsed to the grass, bleeding.

***

Elsewhere...

Vicki and Sees-the-Wind fought back-to-back, defending against and defeating the Nightmare monsters. Despite all of the time the old man had been with her, he never tired in the fight. And he never stopped trying to pull her out of her self-made hell. Though she had no control over it at this point. The Land of the Midnight Hunt had taken on a life all its own. Both Vicki and Sees-the-Wind had come to realize this.

As the last of the monsters fell and fled, Vicki leaned on her bat, panting. She'd learned to fight rather than flee her tormentors. "They just keep coming."

"We will keep fighting." Sees-the-Wind shifted from his warrior form back to his old man visage and put his hand axes back in their sheaths. He cocked his head to the side and listened. "They are preparing to rally again."

Vicki gazed up at the night sky and the moon in descent. "They don't have much time. Why would they rally now?"

A weak laugh came from one of the downed monsters—a twisted form of a man with a bird's head and claws for hands. The laughter gained strength as Vicki and her mentor approached. When the birdman saw them, it clacked its beak twice. "...You don't know."

"Know what?" Vicki hefted her bat as she flicked her teal hair from her sweaty face.

"The youngling. Kieron has the youngling now." Clacking his beak again, this time at Sees-the-Wind, the birdman let his tongue loll in a leer. "Kieron will use the blood of earth and light to subvert the Veil's mending."

Sees-the-Wind was on him at once, shaking the monster. "How do you know this?"

"Can you not feel it, warrior? Can you not feel the triumph of the Conqueror?"

Throwing the birdman to the ground, Sees-the-Wind stood, stretched out his arms and closed his eyes. After a silent moment, he opened his eyes and gazed at Vicki.

"What?" She drew him away from the monster as it laughed again. "What is it?"

"Kieron has Iron Eyes." Sees-the-Wind's gaze was impassive, and his face closed into a severe look of expectation. "I can no longer allow you the luxury of finding your own way out. I need you to deliver a message."

Vicki was no longer looking at him but over his shoulder. "They're back. We've got to get ready."

"I am ready." He grabbed her by the shoulders and gazed deep into her eyes. "Remember this, and tell everyone. Kendrick depends on it." Vicki heard Sees-the-Wind's message in her mind and felt it seared into her soul. Then he let her go. "Be brave, little warrior, and remember."

Vicki shook her head. "How am I going to get out of here? I can't. I haven't found..."

"Leave that to me."

The roar of the Nightmares' charge drowned out anything else he might have said. To her horror, Sees-the-Wind drove himself into the middle of the Nightmares' line, allowing himself to be completely surrounded. He was so tall and bright that none of the monsters noticed her. It was then that she realized what he was going to do.

Vicki didn't have time to even try to stop him before he dropped his weapons and clapped his hands above his head. The clap turned into an explosion, and she was thrown backwards into light.

Gifts, New and Old, Dark and Light

VICKI FELL, SCREAMING, into the light.

Arms wrapped around her, holding her tight as her scream died in her throat, and the light became a white and blue hospital room. In her ear, a young woman murmured, "It's okay. I got you. I'm here, just like I promised. I've been watching and waiting. It's okay."

The pain and weakness of unused muscles made her slump against the woman who laid her back down on the hospital bed. Vicki gazed up at her and recognized the Steward features. "Julie?"

The woman nodded. "I've been waiting. I'm so glad you came back to us."

"Where am I?" Vicki looked around the room with little jerks of her head, instinctively looking for the enemy.

"Mercy Hospital. Long term care." Julie sat down. "Are you all right? You were screaming."

Vicki remembered the message she needed to deliver. "No." She tried to get out of bed, but Julie stopped her. "I have to get a message out. I have to. Everything depends on it."

"What message?"

Vicki opened her mouth, then closed it again, shaking her head. "I need to tell my... father and anyone who's fighting the Nightmare monsters. I—" She stopped, not sure how to express her inability to trust a stranger with something this important.

Julie gazed at her, tilting her head. Then she nodded. "All right. You need our father and those fighting against Kieron. I will get them here."

"No. Wait. Just our father, Karen Wilson, Corelli from the Order of the Sacred Eye." Vicki thought about it. "Brother Amit and Brother Aaron from the Brotherhood of Light." She paused again, opened her mouth to say Walks-the-Ocean, then remembered that Anu had killed him in the same battle that put her in the coma. She shook her head, blinking sudden tears at the memory. "That's it."

Julie put a hand on her shoulder. "I'll let them know. I'll be right back."

Vicki wasn't surprised when Julie disappeared. She'd spent so long in her dream world with the impossible happening that one disappearance wasn't going to alarm her. Though, she wondered how that could happen in the real world.

***

Karen stood well outside the building where Chalice had been found, watching the buzz of people moving in and out. The Grey Lady stood with Alexia as both of them spoke with Thomasina and Chalice. Several Makah stood around the quartet—some asking questions, others obviously on guard. Karen hadn't gotten the whole story of what had happened, but what she did know wasn't good. Eric was gone, and Kieron was at fault.

No one knew for certain why Sees-the-Wind had died. There were no signs of damage to him or his pallet. No cuts or bruises. The whispered words said that it appeared he'd just stopped breathing. When the wailing and song mourning his death started, Karen left the room out of respect and an inability to not think about Sparks-of-the-Moon, the Makah Guardian whose death had introduced her to the Makah people as more than a local, indigenous curiosity.

Karen turned away from the small crowd, still unable get over the idea that the dark-haired girl was Thomasina. The last time she'd seen the twins was while she was remaking the Lady's Garden at 15th and White. *Where's Thomas? Why isn't he here? Is he a teenager now, too?* The thoughts tumbled over themselves in her mind.

Shaking her head, Karen walked toward a small copse of trees. There, she saw John was still on the phone with, presumably, Mason.

"Reginald?"

Her earpiece sprang to life. *"Yes, Karen?"*

Turning away from the scene, she walked a few paces away. "Can you find Eric?"

There was a pause. *"No. I'm sorry. He is hidden from me."*

Karen sensed that he wanted to say more, but was holding back. "You've been quiet lately. I mean, you answer whenever I talk to you, but... you haven't been very active."

Reginald paused. *"You told me that you didn't want me to take care of you. I've been trying to let that happen. I'm not very good at gauging when you need me or not."*

"Oh." Karen nodded to herself. "That makes sense."

"Also..." Now Reginald sounded both plaintive and a little angry. *"I don't dream. I don't know what you are fighting, or how to help you. All I know is that something is attacking, but*

I can't help because it's not attacking the city itself. Only the people."

"I didn't know. I'm sorry." Karen frowned. "I don't even know what a city dreaming would look like."

"There are parts of me that I know exist, but I know nothing about. The Historic Library is one. When you entered it, I sensed its importance to me. But that was it."

"How's that possible?"

Again, Reginald was quiet. Then he asked, *"Are you aware of how your heart beats at all times of the day? Or how your lungs breathe? The blood rushing through your veins?"*

Karen shook her head. "No."

"Even Julie Steward, who is part of me, has autonomy. I do not know what she thinks. Most times I know what she does. Sometimes I don't. But I learn from her. I suppose, she is as close to me dreaming as can be."

"She told me once that she was a part of you, but that she still had her own independent will." Karen looked up again. "Well, in the future, feel free to ask if you can help."

"If I can."

"If you can," she repeated then stepped back in alarm as Julie Steward suddenly appeared in front of her. "Uh, hello."

"Hello." Julie glanced around. "Vicki is awake. She is asking to see you, Amit, Aaron, Mason, and Corelli."

Karen blinked at her. "What? Now?"

"Yes." Then Julie was gone.

"I..." Karen stood there for a moment. "That was unexpected."

"Is there anything I can do?" Reginald sounded hopeful.

"Yes." Karen nodded to the air. "Try to make it so we all arrive at the hospital about the same time."

"I will do my best."

She walked over to John. He gazed at his phone with a frown of confusion, then looked up as she approached. "Apparently, Vicki is awake, and is asking for some people. I've got to go. I'm not sure how or why, but Julie told me."

John shook his head. "I was about to tell you that first part myself. Mason is on that list. But apparently I'm not. No matter. I need to stay here and see what I can learn from all this." He glanced at the Grey Lady, recognizing the serious look on her face.

"Probably a good idea. I'll call you as soon as I know anything." Karen gave him a kiss on the cheek before she hurried away.

***

John had mixed feelings as he watched Karen walk away. Vicki waking was an event in and of itself. But was she just a teenage girl now, or did the monster still lurk inside her? At this point, it was anyone's guess.

He didn't realize the Grey Lady was standing next to him until she spoke.

"We need to talk."

He turned to her, struck by the familiar—but not—face that looked at him. It was the Grey Lady. It was Susan. It was neither. It was both.

"How's Chalice?" He followed her as she walked away from the crowd of people Lumbering Bear was giving orders to.

"She will live. Thomasina had begun to heal her when she and Thomas were sundered." The Grey Lady stopped and turned to him with a swish of her long dress. "But that is not what we must speak of."

John glanced at her, then looked away at the wilderness of the Makah land. It was easier not to look at her and see Susan. "What's up?" He pulled out a cigarette, lit it, and enjoyed the first rush of smoke.

"Kieron has taken Iron Eyes. He will use him to rip the Veil in twain—whether or not I mend it. I need you to do something for me."

"I'm not going to like this, am I?"

The Lady shook her head. "No. But it's important, and you are one of the few that I believe has the strength of will to do it."

John bowed his head and gazed at the lazy drifts of smoke rising from his cigarette. "What is it?"

"Iron Eyes has the blood of the Makah and my people in him. He is the perfect conduit to destroy everything. I should have seen it sooner. I thought Sees-the-Wind was our greatest weakness."

"Get to the point."

"If Kieron cannot be stopped, the only other way to save Kendrick is to close the conduit."

John turned to her, locking gazes with those not-quite-familiar eyes. "You're hedging."

It was the Lady's turn to look away. "Yes."

"Speak plainly with me."

"If Kieron cannot be stopped, you will need to kill Iron Eyes as I mend the Veil and renew the earth. One of them—Kieron or Iron Eyes—must die."

John looked down at his cigarette, thinking. He raised it to his lips, inhaled, held it, then let the smoke dribble out of his mouth and nose before he nodded. "It's a hard thing you ask."

"I ask because it needs to be done, and you are one of the few who can do it." The Grey Lady glanced over her shoulder at Alexia, who still carried the small picnic basket. "You are one of the very few who knows what will happen if you don't."

"Sometimes I hate you." John's voice was soft. "Not because of what you're making me do, but because of what you're making me remember."

"If there were another way, I would take it."

"Right." He broke the cigarette in half and put the unused portion back in his inner jacket pocket. "I'll do it. I'll be your assassin. But only because I have no other choice."

"Thank you."

"Thank me when we survive this."

The Grey Lady put her hand on his arm. "With what Alexia has brought me, we have a chance of succeeding. Fear not. We may yet win the day. With a little help, I now have the power to mend the Veil."

John glanced over at Alexia. "Well, if we don't, no one will be around to blame you." He started to walk away. Then he turned back to the Lady. "You need to do something for me."

The Grey Lady quirked Susan's half-smile at him, but said nothing.

"You need to keep Karen out of the fight with Kieron."

"She is not a fighter."

"I know that. You know that. But she just lost a man she considered a father to that monster." John scowled. "His name was Griff. Now she wants Kieron's blood. So, you need to figure out a way that keeps her with you at the ritual. I don't want her..." He spread his hands wide. "...throwing herself at him in rage."

For a moment, the Lady was Susan. "Oh, no. Poor Griff."

"Poor Karen. Will you do as I ask?" John's face was hard. "It's my one condition."

The Grey Lady inclined her head as she wrapped her otherworldly serenity about herself once more. "I will do so. I will have her stay with me to coordinate my defense through

Sebastian and the gargoyles. The Mueller boys will need an adult with them to help."

John considered this. "Good." He turned to walk away, his head full of emotions he didn't want to think about.

"John..."

He stopped but didn't turn around, clenching and unclenching his fists. "What?" His voice was sharp with irritation.

"I have a gift for you."

He stiffened. "There's only one thing I want from you that we haven't already discussed."

"John Corso, would you do me the great honor of accepting this gift?"

Turning in a slow pivot, John saw the Lady holding out a Todari tarot card to him. He did not have to look at it to know it was the Two of Pentacles, the card he'd given her months ago to keep her alive. "You will not get it back."

"I know." The Lady smiled at him. "I give this card to you with my whole heart. I hope it helps you in your fight and restores your equilibrium. I hope we both survive what is coming, and have the chance to get to know each other once more."

John reached out and took the card from her. "That's a lot of hope for one gift, but I accept it, and also the hope for all those things." He gazed at the tarot card with something akin to love and obsession. It was beautiful.

The Two of Pentacles card showed a young woman wearing a peasant's dress as she planted flowers. Ignoring the fallen autumn leaves, she planted these flowers in a box protected by an overhang. Two of the blossoms were in the shape of pentacles. One flower was already planted. The second was being planted. The young woman's face shone with hope, even in the lateness of the year.

Tearing his gaze from it with an effort, he pulled a slender carrying case created for these cards from his tweed jacket. "Am I so out of balance?" he asked as he tucked the card away.

"I think we all are in some way. There will be many choices to make in the near future. Having someone with an even train of thought will be good for everyone."

John nodded. "Good to know. Uh, when will we be doing this ritual?"

"As soon as you find Kieron, I will do all I need to do. As long as he is distracted by taking the fight to him and rescuing

Iron Eyes, I should have all the time I need to perform the Ritual of Renewed Earth."

"Nothing like a deadline. All right. I'm off for real this time. Good-bye, Lady Grey."

"Good-bye, John."

***

Karen was the last to arrive at the hospital and make it up to the long-term care ward. As she walked into the waiting room, she saw David and Mason standing in one corner, Amit and Aaron nearby, and an old woman with long, wavy gray hair sitting in one of the battered chairs.

Stopping at the entrance to the area, she gave David a quizzical glance. He shrugged and gestured to Mason. Fair enough.

"Are we waiting for Corelli?" Karen kept her voice as neutral as possible. She was still coming to terms with the fact that perhaps Corelli wasn't the villain she had made the girl out to be.

The old woman answered in a quavery voice. "No. We were waiting for you."

Karen gave her a second look. "I don't think we've had the pleasure."

"No." The woman stood. "I'm Keth. I represent Corelli. She is too injured to come here. I will pass on whatever message needs to be passed on. Vicki has already been told."

"Will she be okay?"

Keth nodded. "Oh, yes. She will. She just did something very dangerous to make certain Kendrick would survive what's coming." The old woman raised a wrinkled hand. "A conversation for another time."

Julie walked up with an Indian man in a doctor's coat, who addressed the group of them. "I am Doctor Walia. I'm in charge of the coma patients here." He nodded to Amit. "Victoria has been awake for only a short time. It is only by the prestige of her visitors, and the legal nature of what put her in the hospital, that I am allowing this large of a group to see her so soon. You have ten minutes. Don't overtax her."

Doctor Walia turned and led them to room 731. "Ten minutes," he repeated as they filed in.

Julie walked to one side of the hospital bed and Amit to the other. Karen found her place at the foot of the bed while the rest milled about around the room, finding comfortable spots to stand and wait. Karen noted David was doing his best to stay behind everyone else, letting Mason's bulkier frame hide him. Then she remembered that it was his bullet that broke the connection between Anu and Vicki, and put her in the hospital.

Karen gazed at Vicki, searching her face for traces of Anu. Instead, she saw a waifish teen with blond roots and faded teal ends. The girl's dark eyes had a haunted, tired look; almost bruised against her pale skin. She watched as Vicki glanced around at the people watching her.

Amit leaned forward and offered a hand. He smiled as she took it. Squeezing gently, he said, "It's good to see you in the real world."

"You, too." Vicki took a breath and looked up to face her audience. "Thank you for coming. I know…" She stopped and shook her head. "Sees-the-Wind has been with me in my dreams for what seems like months. We've had a lot of time to talk. He protected me like Amit did. He—" Her voice caught and tears sprang to her eyes. "—he sacrificed himself to make sure I got out with his message. I don't know who the message is for, but I know the Grey Lady needs to know. And you guys do, too."

"What's the message?" Karen kept her voice soft to keep from startling the girl. She did not know Sees-the-Wind beyond the few meetings she'd had. Right now, Karen was more interested in saving Eric from Kieron. Anything Vicki could tell them might help.

Vicki closed her eyes as she spoke. "Sees-the-Wind said, *'The enemy intends to anchor Iron Eyes to the Veil and divert any energy fed into its renewal into tearing it down. It will bring about the merging of the two worlds, and the destruction of ours. This cannot be allowed to happen.'*" She opened her eyes. "I don't know what this means, but I promised him I would tell everyone."

"Well," Mason said, "this changes the plan of attack. We need to find Eric that much sooner, and before the ritual happens."

"We know one of the perpetrators. I'll see what the status of the search is." David left without waiting for an answer.

Karen bowed her head, wondering if David felt as guilty as she did for allowing Eric to go with him to question Luke Coleman, thus bringing the boy to the enemy's notice. She shook the thought off. There would be time enough for guilt after everything was done. Or they'd have much bigger problems to worry about.

"Is there anything else?" Julie asked.

Vicki turned to her. "Sees-the-Wind sacrificed himself. He killed so many of them to make sure they didn't come here. You need to know that."

"We know," Aaron said. "We won't forget."

Julie stood. "Thank you for coming. I think this was the message that needed to be told to you all at once. Do what you need to do."

Mason paused as the rest of the group began leaving the room. "What will you do, Julie?"

"As one of Vicki's legal guardians, I will remain here and see to Vicki's care until she can come home with me."

"One of Vicki's guardians?" Mason repeated softly.

"I, like you, father, rarely do anything halfway." Julie smiled, but it was a polite smile. "It's already been taken care of. Don't worry about it."

"Thank you." He paused and looked at Vicki. "I'm glad you're awake. It may take some time to get to know each other again."

Karen left the room to wait for Mason in the hallway. She didn't want to eavesdrop any more on what promised to be an awkward, painful family reunion. She didn't have to wait long. Doctor Walia shooed Mason out of Vicki's hospital room precisely at the ten-minute mark.

"Can I walk with you?"

Mason nodded, looking distracted.

"Is there anything I need to be doing right now? I mean, as your consultant on this case, I think I'm pretty much wrapped up." Karen paused as she saw David talking quietly with Aaron and Amit, causing Mason to stop with her. They appeared to be waiting for Mason as well.

"I'd like you to stay close to the Grey Lady." Mason's frown was more of concentration than irritation. "We knew the Grey Lady. We knew Susan Moore. We don't yet really know who the new Grey Lady is. Until the Veil is mended, you're still on the clock."

Karen nodded. "And Eric?"

"We'll find him."

"I want to be there."

Mason glanced at her, confused. Then his face cleared as he remembered the morning call. "I'll see what I can do. In the meantime, focus on the Grey Lady." He paused before continuing on to speak with the waiting men. "Get some sleep. You look worn out."

Karen's smile was perfunctory. "All right. I'll see you soon."

She headed down to her car in the underground parking lot. Her thoughts were all over the place. She did not like the fact that Kendrick's forces needed to be split to save everyone from Kieron and his monsters. First, Eric needed to be found and rescued. Hopefully with Kieron's painful death involved. Second, the Grey Lady needed to perform the Ritual of Renewed Earth to fix everything. Karen couldn't imagine that either would be an easy task.

"Karen Wilson."

The quavery voice came from her right. Karen lifted her head and saw Keth waiting by her car. "Oh, hello."

"I have a message for you from Corelli." Keth tilted her head to the side and watched Karen with a discerning eye.

"All right..." Karen waited.

"She said to tell you that the Order will be there to assist the Grey Lady in her ritual. They have done so in the past, and are willing to do so now—for the future."

"Thank you." Karen bit her lip. "Is Corelli really going to be okay?"

"She will be. It was..." Keth marshaled her thoughts. "Corelli now runs the Order of the Sacred Eye. V'ger is no more. That's all I can tell you."

"Dead?"

Keth nodded.

Karen sagged against her car. The knowledge that Corelli no longer worked for the man who had shot David, was partially responsible for Heather's death, and had participated in the ritual that had almost murdered her, did more than she thought it would to shift her perceptions and emotions. Karen realized that part of her undying grudge against Corelli was weighed down by her hatred of the Order's old guard. "Wow."

"Wow, indeed." Keth half-shrugged. "I need to go now."

"Give her my regards, please. Tell her that, maybe when she's well, we can have coffee. Okay?"

Keth peered at her for a moment, then nodded. "I will. We will see you when the Grey Lady calls."

***

"How are you?"

"Stronger than I've ever been, but I'll never be whole again." Thomasina looked straight ahead as she led Chalice by the hand through one of the many shortcuts she and her kind could take.

"Ah." Chalice understood the pain.

"They will worry for us." Thomasina's eyes were distant.

"Let them." Chalice kept her eyes on her feet, not watching where they were going. She didn't want her logic about roads to foul things up. "They've enough to distract them already with mourning for their dead and preparing for battle. Our job now is to make certain there *is* a battle."

The teen gazed down at the woman as they crossed through the hedge back onto the paved roads. "How did you get to be so..."

"Cranky?"

"No. Well, yes, but no. So strange. Your *blood* is of the light, but *you* are not of the light."

Chalice glanced around. She recognized where they were; the City Center in the greenest part of the Colonel's Park. Now, she led Thomasina. "Once upon a time, a Nightmare broke through a young girl's dream. It was met by one of you, a Watchguard, and there was a terrible fight that sent the Nightmare back to whence it came... but not before murdering all of the girl's family. Mortally wounded, the Watchguard crawled to the girl—who was not yet dead—and asked what she would do for vengeance. 'Anything.' was her answer. And the Watchguard was pleased. 'I will save you. 'Defender' I call you, but not claim you.' With that, the Watchguard poured itself into the girl's wounds, and became part of her blood."

Thomasina scanned the park as they walked across it. "You were the girl. That's why I was able to heal you."

"Bright one, aren't you?"

"There is more to the story."

"Of course there is." Chalice stopped before a darkened building. "The only part that matters now is the last part of a prophecy." She did not look away from *Treasures & Trinkets* as she recited the two lines. "'*Though it will be many years hence, and you will lose all that you have, you will find your vengeance. When the child of earth and light is captive and the Veil is torn, either you will take your vengeance or all will be lost to this world and the next.*'"

"It is a grim telling." Thomasina gazed at the building. "Iron Eyes is not here."

Chalice growled her frustration. "All right. I've got one more place to try. If that's not it, you'll have to do some of your super fey stuff to find him."

"If I can. He is in shadow now. Only if he is near may I sense him."

***

Elsewhere...

From the childish drawings on the wall, the basement room had once been a playroom for children. Now, it was a man's sanctuary with its large TV, small refrigerator, and comfortable furniture. Luke took a soda from the fridge and popped it open as he watched Kieron work.

Kieron had the unconscious Eric on his back, with his arms and legs spread-eagled. Tied down with both rope and shadow, Kieron had Eric's shirt open and was painting runic symbols on his chest. The shadowed symbols remained for a short time, then sunk into the boy's skin. Kieron repeated this over and over until he was satisfied. When he was done, he stood with a wobble.

"They actually hurt you." Luke tried to keep the hope out of his voice. He saw how Kieron was physically smaller than he once was.

"You wanted them to hurt me." The shadow man turned to him. "Didn't you, little doppelganger?"

Luke shook his head, then stopped, and shrugged. "Maybe. Then I'd be free to have Kendrick to myself, and do my own thing."

"That's better. Truth is always better." Kieron offered him his hand. "There is little better than an honest slave."

He accepted Kieron's hand, and realized his mistake too late. Luke raised his chin. "I am a good slave. You need me."

"You are, and I do," Kieron agreed. "But not in the way you believe." He yanked the doppelganger to him. "I am hurt, and you have exactly what I need. Pity that your creator will know when I'm done."

"What—no!" Luke's words turned into a scream as Kieron pulled Luke into him, subsuming the doppelganger in shadow until the two forms became one. Arched in agony,

Luke's scream cut off as the shadow mass expelled the desiccated form of a corpse.

The shadows pulled in on themselves, revealing a man's face—neither Luke's nor Kieron's—wreathed in wispy, shadow-like smoke. The body followed. Were it not for the shadow trails betraying his origins, Kieron now looked human. Until he opened his eyes.

He moved to the mirror behind the bar and gazed at the unfamiliar face through black orbs of moving shadow. "So, that's what the corpse looked like. Luke Coleman, you chose well. So much power, stolen from the battlefield...and all those memories." A demonic version of Paul Malloy's face smiled at himself in the mirror. "Todesengel, indeed."

Kieron turned back to the unconscious teen. "Time to get to work. They'll be coming for us soon."

A shadow knife appeared in his hand and he used it to make a single, shallow incision down Eric's body from sternum to navel. Eric barely moved. Kieron held a hand over Eric then reached into, and through, his chest. With a grunt of effort, Kieron pulled the first of his minions through to this side of the Veil.

Eric's eyes popped open as Kieron reached in his hand again. This time, as he pulled another monster through—one with too many eyes and too many tentacles—Eric opened his mouth in silent agony. He could do no more than that.

Blood for the Renewed Earth

THOMASINA STOPPED IN the middle of the dark, suburban street. "He's near." She started to walk forward again, but Chalice held her back. "What?"

Chalice pointed to the shadows around the Griffith house. "Those are alive. I should've realized he'd come back here. Can you feel the death energy?" She peered at shadows and shook her head. "Too many."

Nodding, Thomasina clenched her hands. "I'll tell the Grey Lady we've found him."

"I'll call in the troops. It's time." Chalice waited until Thomasina disappeared to speak aloud. "Nicholas, I think this is it. I just wanted to say thank you for everything. You were good to me. I appreciate that... and you." She gave a short bark of laughter. "If it's not the end, well, I'll tell you this to your face the next time I see you."

***

"Honey, wake up." John shook Karen's shoulder. "Chalice found Eric."

Karen sat up with a jerk and blinked sleep-filled eyes at him. "What time is it?"

"Just past three in the morning."

"Where is he?" She scrambled out of bed, bumping into the dresser as she shoved her foot into her jeans.

"David's called the SU in, and Lumbering Bear is coordinating the Makah and the Bacchanalia Coven. The Grey Lady needs you at 15th and White to coordinate the gargoyles with the Mueller boys."

She stared at him as she pulled her t-shirt down. "I'm going to get Eric, and I'm going to deal with Kieron."

"Not if you want to save the Grey Lady and Kendrick." John adjusted his jacket and checked his weapons.

"What do you mean?" Karen moved slower now, scowling as she put on her sneakers.

"I mean, the Brotherhood of Light will be on defense duty. That means the Order and the Gargoyles will be offensive protection for the Lady and her ritual. Sergeant Mueller is already on his way with the SU and the gargoyles have the Mueller twins. You're the only one who can talk to the gargoyles through Sebastian and the boys."

Karen sat still. It was a low blow to make her choose between protecting her friends and getting revenge. There really wasn't a choice when put in simple terms. She mentally called for Sebastian. *"Thunderbutt, is this true? Do I need to coordinate the gargoyles?"*

"Yes."

The small gargoyle appeared in the doorway and said no more. But Karen noticed that John and Sebastian specifically did not look at each other. They were up to something. "John."

"Yes?"

"Where will you be?"

John cleared his throat. "With the SU, coordinating everything through Mason on the phone. The Grey Lady can't complete the ritual until Kieron is dead or his link to the Veil is destroyed. If it isn't obvious, I need to tell him and he needs to send a signal."

"What aren't you telling me?" Her voice was soft.

"Whatever I don't know." He shrugged and would never regret the lie. "I gotta go. Kieron's power is growing."

Karen put her earpiece on. "Reginald?"

"Yes, Karen?"

"What's your status?"

"Kieron's power is growing. Parts of me are disappearing. I don't know what he's doing in them."

Karen scowled. So, John convinced the city to go along with him. "Fine." She stood and walked to John. "You be careful and make sure he's very dead. Bring Eric home safely."

"I will. You be careful, too." He paused and hugged her tight. "I love you, Karen Wilson." He kissed her on the cheek.

"I love you, John Corso." Karen did not like the way it sounded like they were saying good-bye forever.

The two of them left the *Teller's Fortune* without another word.

***

"Where's your mom?" Karen gazed down at the twins she now had charge of. She was glad that they had had the sense to at least arm themselves with small aluminum bats. Not that she wanted them to have to use their weapons. But better safe than sorry.

Devon raised his chin. "Mom's at home. Dad and Edmund said she needed to stay there where it was safe. We had to know she was okay."

"Edward said that, too." Daniel shrugged. "Are we going to have a bunker?"

"A bunker?" Karen looked between the two brown-haired boys as she shifted her backpack.

"Yeah. It's the only way to be safe. Generals stay in the bunker and give their troops orders." Daniel grinned at her with the excitement of a child prepared to play. "You're one of our troops. You get to advise us."

Karen wasn't certain that was exactly how things were going to go, but she didn't want to fight with them. However, the bunker sounded like a good idea. "Wait here."

She walked over to the Grey Lady, who gazed at the ritual defense the Brotherhood of Light and the Order of the Sacred Eye set up. They stood there in silence, watching the Order members, directed by Keth and an older black man, scatter to the edges of the hedge that was now almost six feet tall. The Brotherhood broke into seven pairs and set themselves in a loose, large circle around Karen and the Grey Lady. One of each pair knelt facing the Lady with their sword across their laps. The other of the pair stood with his back to them, his sword out and ready.

"Looks formidable," Karen said, keeping her voice low.

"Yes."

"Where do you want me and the boys?"

The Grey Lady looked around, then pointed to the side. "That is a good place."

"I don't suppose you could build me a little hedge fort or bunker? The boys think that we should have one."

The sound of Devon and Daniel's joyful shouts was her answer. When Karen looked, a small, one-room structure had grown out of the hedge. She watched as the boys ran inside to explore. "Are they going to be safe?"

"They, and you, will be as safe as can be. I wish it were closer to me, but right now it is easier to pull from what is already here. You'll recognize the chairs."

"*Karen, I need permission to operate on the Lady's land,*" Reginald's voice came over her earpiece. "*I cannot help you without it.*"

Karen nodded to air. "I'll ask." Turning back to the Lady, she saw that Alexia, Keth, and Aaron had joined them within the Brotherhood's protective circle, but stood to the side. "Reginald needs your permission to help."

The Grey Lady was Susan for a brief moment as she blinked in surprise. Then her confusion cleared, and she smiled. "Granted. So, that was your secret all this time," Susan murmured before she took up the mantle of the Lady once more. "It's time for you to join the boys. The gargoyles and my people are coming. The darkness harries them."

Karen ran for the hedge-born bunker. As soon as she entered, the door disappeared into a wall. There were several small windows to look out. As the trio of Keth, Alexia, and Aaron set themselves around the Grey Lady, holes in the hedge appeared. Gargoyles ran through or jumped the hedge. With them were a crazy menagerie of fantastical creatures intermixed with humans she had seen about town.

Winged beauties of light flew next to bestial half-goat men. A checker from the local grocery store paired up with a small dog-like gargoyle and a mailman. A huge stag pranced near Theodore and Theodora—the blond twins who were often messengers of the Grey Lady—and several small gnomes wielding knives.

The last to enter the garden was James, the Lady's polite butler Karen had met so long ago. "They are coming," he said as he took his place among the defenders.

Then the darkness fell upon them.

***

John parked where he was directed, and Sergeant Mueller took him to where David, Lamiel, and Lumbering Bear were coordinating the SU, the Guardians, and the Bacchanalia Coven. "The Coven has the area silenced somehow. So, whatever fighting we do will be quiet enough. Also we've been shown the Guardians, so we don't attack them. Fighting with werewolves. Imagine that."

"I can. We've done it before." John gave Mueller critical look. "Should you even be here? Didn't you just get out of the hospital a few weeks ago?"

"More like a couple of monthes ago. I've been on active duty for six weeks now. If my boys need to go into danger, then I need to make sure I do everything to keep them out of it."

"Karen will take care of them." John saw David look up and motion him over.

"I hope so." Mueller disappeared into the crowd of prepared SU officers in combat gear.

David handed John an earpiece. "Wear this. It's me and Mason. One of us needs to tell Mason when our mission is done. Eric is rescued, or Kieron is dead. Preferably both."

John put the earpiece in. "I'm here now, Mason." Before Mason had time to respond, Lumbering Bear shouted, "They're coming!" John saw the darkness surge out of the house and shadows. It revealed itself to be gibbering monsters armed with teeth and claws, stingers and tentacles. A cry went up from the officers and Makah warriors and a howl from the werewolf Guardians.

David thrust a bulletproof vest at John. "Put it on."

John let it fall to the pavement. "I don't need it."

Before either of them could enter the fray, Thomasina appeared with a bloodied Chalice at her side. "Come with us to save Eric. We need you."

David and John looked at each other, then they both moved as one to follow the women. "What happened to you?" David asked Chalice as she swung her blood-smeared war club at the nearest monster, braining it.

"My blood hurts them." She looked over her shoulder at John and David. "My blood can kill Kieron. Remember that."

***

Karen pulled her weapons, a butcher knife and a stun gun, from her backpack. They weren't much, but she wasn't supposed to be fighting. She watched as the darkness flowed over and through the hedge at the south end of the garden like malevolent fog. With it, came the shrieks and howls of the Nightmare monsters made flesh. "Get your bats ready. Reginald, tell me when you see breaks in the line."

"Will do."

A sudden light from center of the ritual circle made Karen flinch away. When she looked back, she saw the Grey Lady holding a large quartz crystal. The light emanated from it. Aaron was on one knee, facing the Lady's back, with his sword plunged into the ground. It looked like he was praying to the cross made by the hilt. Keth sat in a serene pose of meditation facing the Lady. Alexia stood tall and proud, chin high and her palm facing the Grey Lady.

Karen was surprised to see the pulsing light flowing from Alexia to the crystal. She blinked a couple times, and realized she could see light flowing from Aaron's sword hilt and from Keth herself to the Grey Lady.

"The center of the defense line is buckling."

Karen called to the boys over her shoulder, "Tell them the line is buckling in the center."

"I want to see." Devon held his arms out so he could be picked up.

"Only for a moment." She picked him up, and the small boy paled at the sight of the monsters and the supernatural defenders fighting. There were screams of pain mixed with howls of victory. "Okay? Enough?"

Devon nodded and Karen put him down, trying to think of something soothing to say. That flew out of her head as Daniel shrieked in terror. She looked back to see slick, grey-green tentacles worming their way into the bunker through the holes in the hedge. One of them had wrapped around Daniel's leg.

***

Thomasina led the way through the chaos of Nightmares fighting Guardians, officers shooting from behind cover, and shadows trying to choke and smother. Every time David stopped or turned to try to help someone in trouble, Chalice grabbed him. "If we don't get the kid or kill Kieron, *everyone* dies."

John helped Chalice wrangle David, feeling cold and unaffected. These weren't his people fighting and dying. These monsters weren't his goal. If everything he loved were to be saved, there was only one thing he needed to do. "The sooner we do what we need to do, the sooner this stops, David. Keep moving."

David pulled himself in and focused on Thomasina's back with a visible effort.

Leading her small group through the yard and into the house, Thomasina kept them in a serene bubble until they reached the basement steps. As soon as the basement door closed, the monsters were on them. Thomasina was thrown from the stairs by something John couldn't see while tentacles grabbed Chalice and David, yanking them to the floor. A creature with knives for hands reared up on a snake's body and stabbed at John with both blades. Its flat, eyeless head was studded with spikes.

The sound of gunfire was loud in the basement and John caught brief flashes of what was going on below him as he dodged and fought the creature with his bare fists. Thomasina was on the floor next to Eric, working on the shadowy rope around one wrist. David was backed into a corner by a brightly colored orange thing that was more mouth than body. He had his gun out. And Chalice... Chalice was screaming.

That was the last thing John saw before he zigged when he should've zagged and one of the snake creature's hand blades punched through his chest and pinned him to the wall.

***

Karen leapt forward and chopped at the tentacle, piercing it deep. It let go of Daniel's leg and disappeared back into the hedge. Where the tentacle had been, his jeans were corroded by acidic slime. "Get away from the back wall." She leaned toward the window to yell to the Grey Lady, and stared at what was outside.

The monsters had backed the defenders almost all the way to the ritual's outer defense line. The gargoyles, the Order, and the Brotherhood stood fast, but they could not stop the Nightmare monsters that attacked with suicidal intent. While Karen watched, something red with wings and too many clawed legs sprang up and over the line. Even as it screamed in pain and one of the Brothers cut it from stem to stern, it caught another one of the Brotherhood.

That man struggled in the monster's grip, spurting blood from a torn throat, and looked right at Karen. She knew him. It was Amit, the monk who had spent so much time in a coma and had befriended Vicki. She swore she could see him trying to say Vicki's name as he died.

"Karen, some of them are massing in the north. They're trying to sneak in."

"Devon, tell the gargoyles an attack is coming in from the north." Karen shouted out the window. "They're coming in from the north! Sneak attack from the north!" She had forgotten all about trying to get the Lady to shore up the bunker. The two pairs of defenders behind Aaron prepared themselves.

"Karen!"

She didn't know which of the boys screamed, but she turned with her stun gun already arcing. Stunning the first of the tentacles that had wormed itself through the hedge, Karen slashed at it with a panicked swing. The second tentacle knocked her knife away and grabbed for her. She dodged and zapped it as well.

"Reginald, help!"

"How?"

"Barriers. Fighting statues. Anything to keep this monster off us."

"*Yes. I can do that.*"

"Hurry!" Karen stunned a third tentacle and wondered how many charges her stun gun had.

***

John looked down at the blade in his chest and cocked his head. "That should hurt. I wonder if it will hurt later." He punched the snake monster in the head twice, and watched as it crumbled into shadowy dust. Looking down at the chest wound as it closed, he nodded to himself. "Huh. So that's how that card works. I don't care to try that again."

He turned in an unhurried pivot and surveyed the room. Thomasina was struggling with an invisible something around her neck, and Eric was still lying flat and unmoving on the floor. David had his gun to the mouth monster's head and shot it to no avail. John jumped down to the basement floor and realized the mouth monster had both of Eric's legs in its biggest mouth.

Kieron stepped toward John with his head tilted with curiosity. "You have power."

John blinked as he recognized the face Kieron now wore. Then he shrugged and nodded. "I do." He pulled his gun. "I don't like how I feel right now. This isn't me."

"Then give it to me. I know what to do with power."

Half-smiling with no joy, John shook his head. "No." He shot Kieron twice in the head and frowned as Kieron laughed.

"You can't hurt me. Nothing can."

"I can," Chalice shouted as she broke free of the power that held her. She did not hesitate. She rushed forward and leaped upon Kieron's back, pressing her bloodied body against him. "My blood can kill you!"

Kieron howled in agony and danced around, scrabbling at the furious woman clinging to him like a burr.

***

It was a fight Karen couldn't win. Too many tentacles were breaking through the hedge wall. Looking out the front window, she saw fleeing the bunker would be just as dangerous as staying within it. "Susan! Help!"

Karen thought the Grey Lady flicked a glance over at her, but she shouldn't be sure. There was no response, no shoring up of the wall. As she stunned another questing tentacle and made sure the boys, huddled in the corner behind the camp chairs, were safe enough, a high-pitched scream cut the air. Karen looked back at the ritual circle.

A tall, slender, white figure had broken through the Brotherhood's line. Even as its legs blackened and burned, it held Keth by the waist in huge hands. The old woman screamed again as her middle was crushed. She gestured one last time toward the Grey Lady then went limp. The Grey Lady rocked back on her heels with the force of the energy thrown at her, then reset her feet, fed now only by Aaron and Alexia.

Karen didn't have time to wonder why nothing approached Alexia. Something slithered up to her in a flash, wrapping around her waist and her arm holding her stun gun. Crying out in pain as it felt like her skin was boiling, Karen got flashes of statues—baby angels, colorful fishermen, wooden bears, even carved fish—charging into the garden.

"Sebastian!" Karen yelled even as the boys beat at the tentacle around her waist with their baseball bats. She shifted the stun gun to her other hand and shocked the smaller tentacle burning her arm. It let go, leaving behind melted and blistered skin.

Then all coherent thought left her as the tentacle around her waist opened its dozens of sucker mouths and bit down, chewing through the remains of her clothing to get to the tender flesh beneath.

***

John considered the scene before him. David was in the mouth of a monster. Thomasina fought with shadows. Kieron struggled to get Chalice off him and failed as she yelled, over and over, "My blood will kill him!" Eric, senseless, was still bound to the floor. John could see the glow of the ritual on him.

All of this would stop with Eric dead or Kieron dead. The easiest and fastest choice was clear.

He considered for a moment longer and took aim, not thinking about what he was doing. He let the Todari tarot cards—all thirty-nine of them—guide his movements. Even then, John did not close his eyes. If he was going to murder someone, he was going to do it with his eyes open. He owed them that much respect.

Flinching at each measured shot of his pistol, John refused to look away from his target.

***

There was a flash of grey through the window as Karen writhed on the grass she'd newly planted. The pain didn't stop so much as cease to be all consuming. She flailed wildly, with the knife she'd somehow retrieved, at everything around her.

"Stop! It's me! Stop!"

Sebastian's voice thundering through her mind pulled her back to coherence. Karen saw the gargoyle pulling the severed tentacle from her midsection. She still held the knife and wondered why the pain was fading. "Are we safe?"

Sebastian shook his head and pointed upward with one gore spattered claw.

The entire back hedge wall of the bunker bowed inward as something huge tore open the top back corner of their hiding place. Through it, Karen saw a single eyeball gaze down at them from above a jagged, beak-like mouth filled with too many teeth. It tore at the hedge wall and ceiling, forcing its way inside.

The twins screamed, "Mommy! Mommy!" as they clutched each other.

Karen added her panicked voice to theirs. "Reginald!" With Sebastian pressed to her, snarling up at the monster, she was unable to do anything to save herself or the children. "Reginald, please…" she whispered as a last prayer.

The monster leaned in and clacked its beak at her.

There was a great cracking and tearing of earth and stone as large concrete walls shot up around them, knocking the monster back. The walls continued rising until the opening at the ceiling was at least fifty feet above them.

"I'm here, Karen. Are you okay?"

Shaking, she looked at Devon and Daniel. Their clothing was torn, tears cleaned furrows in the dirt on their faces, and they both looked like children on the edge of hysteria. "You guys okay? Are you hurt?"

They looked at each other and nodded, afraid to speak.

"All right. I think we're safe for the moment. Okay?" Karen leaned back against the wall and heard a roar of triumph from the monsters. "I need to see." A hole the size and shape of a brick appeared next to her head.

Outside, the fight was down to the ritual circle. Fey creatures of myth and legend stood shoulder-to-shoulder with the Brotherhood of Light and the Order of the Sacred Eye. Karen saw Alexia standing in front of the Grey Lady. Aaron stood at the Lady's back. It looked as if only Alexia was feeding power to the crystal. Or perhaps, she was helping the Grey Lady hold it until the signal came. Karen couldn't tell.

A massive horned and scaled dog with glowing eyes pushed to the front of the pack at the north end of the garden. Karen saw Aaron step forward. She couldn't see his face, but she could tell he was bracing himself for the attack.

***

Despite being shot in the back four times, Chalice gave a triumphant cry and did not let go. Even as she coughed blood onto Kieron's neck, she followed up with her teeth, ripping flesh and shadow from her enemy.

John watched with a discerning eye. If Kieron didn't die soon, he *would* kill Eric. It was what he had to do.

Thomasina, no longer fighting invisible monsters, freed Eric's wrists and ankles. The shadows fell away at her touch. The mortal ropes took a little longer to deal with. As soon as the teen was free, she gathered his unresisting form to her and gazed at John. "Flee now. Get your friend and go. The end comes."

Despite all that had happened, John blinked in surprise as Thomasina disappeared with Eric in her arms. He turned back to Kieron, who had fallen to his knees, Chalice still atop him. Both struggled weakly against the other. John stepped toward them.

"Go!" Chalice, her face a mass of blood and torn flesh, spat over her shoulder. She grabbed Kieron by his head and twisted.

One of John's cards told him an explosion was coming. He turned back to David and pulled him from the dead monster's mouth. Everything below David's thighs was missing, but he still appeared to be breathing.

John threw him over his shoulder and ran up the stairs. He spoke in an emotionless voice as he did, "Eric is free. Kieron's about to die. Move everyone back now."

He had no idea if Mason heard or not. He hoped so, and that's all he could do now.

***

"The dog, Reginald. Get the dog before it attacks."

"I can't get my statues there. The monsters are protecting it."

It was true. There was an area of calm around the Nightmare dog as it dug its hind feet into the grass for purchase. Outside that serenity, the monsters were fighting with everything they had to keep the gargoyles and statues from swarming it.

"No," she whispered as the Nightmare and Aaron tensed, then sprang. The dog raced for the Grey Lady, shadows erupting from it as it moved. It leaped into the air, but was met by Aaron and his sword. The shadows wrapped about Aaron, hiding him as the dog howled its pain and anger. The darkness swelled into a bubble that engulfed them both. Then it contracted tight and disappeared in a crack of thunder.

Thomasina appeared within the ritual circle next to the Grey Lady. She had Eric in her arms. She dropped him from bloodied hands and collapsed on top of him.

The Grey Lady looked down, then back at Alexia, who gave her a single nod of assent. The Grey Lady knelt and placed the quartz crystal point first on the ground. She closed her eyes, then pushed. For a long moment, nothing happened. Then the world exploded in light and sound and beauty.

***

"Go!" John shouted as he fled the Griffith house with David over his shoulder. "Go! It's going to explode!" He waved off the officers as more took up his warning and echoed all around him. Most of the monsters were dead, wounded, or had disappeared. John ran toward the police barrier.

He didn't make it before the house exploded.

Tumbling to the ground, John was able to keep from injuring David any more as parts of the destroyed house rained down around them. He looked back as a crunching, sucking sound pulled the remains into the basement, pulverizing it, and everything in it.

John's ears popped as if he'd been in a climbing plane and he had a cold. The immense pain was a surprise; it was the first he'd felt since the fight began. He winced and watched everyone around him do the same. When he gazed back, he saw nothing more than a torn hole in the ground where the house had been.

Men and women in SU gear ran up to gather John, David, and everyone else from the destruction site. Relieved to see that there were already ambulances on the scene, John gave up David, walked to the nearest police car, and leaned against it. He pulled out a battered cigarette, lit it, and took a long inhale.

"Mason?" John didn't know if his earpiece was still working until the mayor answered.

"I'm here. Status?"

"Kieron's dead. House is destroyed. David's hurt bad. I don't know if he'll make it." John smiled as he saw John Mueller, bleeding but alive, get into the ambulance with David. "What happened with the Grey Lady?"

"Light, and a lot of it."

"Is Karen okay?"

"I don't know. I believe so. A sixty-foot wall appeared around her position. It was touch and go but I think she's all right."

John blew out smoke in a sigh of relief. "I'm heading that way right now."

***

"Edward and Edmund want in. The boys said they sounded a bit frantic. They're going to tear down the walls soon." Karen spoke to the air then smiled at her not-so-little gargoyle as she clambered to her feet. "You rescued me." She spoke to both Reginald and Sebastian at the same time.

"You need toothpaste?" Sebastian's mental voice was tinged with worry.

"Something. Not toothpaste." Holding her wounded arm up, Karen saw that the skin had not only been burned, there were small, circular hunks of flesh torn from it. Black lines spread out from each bite mark. It was a nasty wound. She wondered if it would ever heal. Just looking at it made her wonder how bad her waist was. And wonder why she wasn't feeling any pain right now.

The concrete walls sank back into the ground, and Karen could see all of the Nightmare monsters were dead.

Edward and Edmund swarmed into what was left of the hedge bunker. The boys lifted their arms up to be carried.

While Karen watched, she blinked at the darkness encroaching on her vision. Something was wrong. She spun around, looking for the Grey Lady, or someone who could help her. She reached toward those still alive in the ritual circle, then collapsed, her body convulsing as she fell into darkness, with Sebastian's mental cries following her down.

***

Elsewhere...

When the first of the books appeared in the rare books room of the Kendrick Historic Library, Nicholas did not wake up. It was only when a cascade of books tumbled to the floor from the central stand, in a crash too loud to have been made by mere books, that Nicholas woke with a jerk. He dressed as fast as he could and hurried downstairs.

Nicholas stopped when he saw the pile of books and winced as another couple appeared on the reading stand, only to slide off and add to the pile in both height and horror. It'd been years since he'd seen this kind of death. Even the fight against the Children of Anu, and before that, the fight with the Order of the Sacred Eye, had less death.

He entered the room and gathered the books into piles, shifting them from the floor and central stand to the table. One by one, he looked at their titles. Some names he knew. Most he did not.

Nicholas stopped when he came to the book titled *Chalice McGinn.* Hugging it tight to his chest, he sank to the floor, sobbing.

Beginning Again

"'...INVESTIGATORS ARE STILL looking into the gas main explosions from the night of the 19th. The destruction in the suburban neighborhood of Southwood was catastrophic. Called to the home of Raymond 'Griff' Griffith, the Kendrick police department was on hand to set up a quarantine zone. Still, the collateral damage was extensive. The cost to life and limb was even higher—'"

"No. Stop." David shook his head and gazed up at the hospital room ceiling. "I don't want to hear the list of the dead again. I can't."

"Okay. But you gotta hear this part." John Mueller shifted in his seat, swiped at the iPad screen, and read.

"'...Speculation includes terrorist activity on the part of a lone wolf because of the secondary explosion in the Northern Lights neighborhood. If it were not for the heroic measures taken by Detective David Hauberk and Sergeant John Mueller, the death toll might have been higher. While Sergeant Mueller sustained only mild injuries, Detective Hauberk suffered the loss of both legs...'"

"Christ," David muttered. "That's the third time in the last two weeks they've pointed out that I've lost my legs. I'm sure they wished me well again." He looked down at what was left of his legs. Everything from just above the knees down was gone. Even though he knew his legs were missing, his knees itched. It bothered him. The doctor told him he'd probably have phantom itches for the rest of his life.

Mueller put his iPad down. "Has HR been in to see you?"

"Yeah. And Disability." David scowled at his bandaged stumps, hidden by the non-offensive, sky-blue blanket. "At least another two to three weeks here. Then home care. Maybe. I may have to hire someone to help me. I don't think I can stand six more weeks of the hospital."

Mason stepped into the room with a small potted plant. He paused, looking between the two men, then held it up. "This one's from Olivia."

David half-smiled. "Hello."

Mason nodded. "Nice to see you." He looked everywhere but at David's missing legs and Mueller as he put the plant down and stuck his hands in his pockets.

David and Mueller exchanged a glance. Mueller stood. "I gotta go. I'll come see you tomorrow after my shift." He nodded to Mason. "Sir."

"Sergeant." Mason shifted, pulling his hands out of his pockets after Mueller left. He looked at David then down at the floor.

"Sir? Can I help you?" David frowned. "Please don't say I'm fired. As soon as I get out of here, I can use a chair while I'm waiting for my prosthetics. My body's a little ragged, but my mind isn't."

Mason moved to the chair at David's bedside. "Olivia tells me that I suck at being... at talking... sometimes. No, you're not fired. Far from it. I heard what you said about the home care. Olivia and I already talked about it. I know you live alone. I'd like you to move into my house until you're on your feet again.... Damn. I didn't mean to say it like that."

David laughed. It burst out of him tinged with hysteria and surprise. "On my feet again..."

Mason plowed forward. "Lord knows I have the room and the people working there. They've been feeling neglected since the eldest moved out. I'm not having another kid. Vicki's going to stay with Julie. We both think she'd be more comfortable there."

Stifling his laughter, David nodded. "Your wife is right. You do suck at talking sometimes, but I accept. I don't plan to call you Dad, either."

"Well, good." Mason's smile was brief. "You did a good thing there. You've faced horrors—true horrors. I don't think you're any less the cop you were because of that." He pointed at David's lack of legs. "A lot of good men died, and we need you more now than ever."

"Thank you. I appreciate that."

"You're welcome."

David sobered and took a breath. "How's everyone else?"

Mason gazed at his hands. "Some better than others. I just met the Brotherhood's current leader, Brother Jeffrey. I don't think we'll have as close a relationship with them for the near future."

"But they *will* work with us?"

"Yes. As long as they get to work with someone they know." Mason looked up. "Which means you and Mueller. Maybe Corso."

Leaning back against the bed, David nodded. "Well, I guess it's nice to still be needed."

***

"I feel like I slept through the apocalypse." Her steps careful, Corelli walked next to Alexia who kept her pace slow.

"You kinda did." Alexia smirked. "That's what you get for being shot on the eve of a great ritual event and having to spend weeks healing."

They sat on one of the benches in the garden of the Order's mansion. Corelli glanced up at her girlfriend and squeezed her hand. "I'd like to ask you a question. I'm only going to ask it once, and you don't have to answer it. Okay?"

Tensing, Alexia nodded as she returned Corelli's squeeze. "What is it?"

"That night everything happened. I slept like I've never slept before. And the dream was so wonderful. I almost didn't want to wake up." Corelli tilted her head and gazed at Alexia. "Was that you? If it was, why?"

Alexia was quiet for a long time. "Yes. It was me." She let her gaze drift to the flowers around them. "I knew what was going to happen was going to be bad. It was sort of an 'all or nothing' deal. I decided if it all went pear-shaped, the least I could do was make sure you had the best dream you could have before..." She stopped and shook her head. "Are you mad at me?"

"No." Corelli pulled Alexi into a hug. "Never. Thank you for thinking of me even when everything was bad." She let go and patted her legs. "Once more around the garden before you go to work. Doctor's orders. Then I need to meet with Sagan to figure out who the new First Circle will be."

Alexia stood, letting the tension drain away. "Okay, hon. Whatever you say."

"I'm going to hold you to that." Corelli stood and began to walk again.

"Please do."

***

Vicki looked up from petting Theron, Julie's large black and white cat, as the two little ghost girls ran from the kitchen, through the living room, and down the hall. Living with ghosts didn't bother her. It was the small children. She wasn't used to them, or to happy laughter.

Julie set a soda down next to her on the low table. "How are you today?"

Shrugging, Vicki petted Theron's white, roly-poly tummy. "Is the cat a ghost, too?"

"Why do you ask?"

"The girls..."

"Jessica and Erin."

"One of them ran into me yesterday. Not through me." Vicki shrugged again. "It surprised me."

Julie sat back and considered the pair. "To tell you the truth, I don't know. Theron was here when I arrived. The house had been taking care of him. He was the first thing they cared for. Does it matter?"

"No... yes. If the cat is a ghost, then I know it won't die on me."

"Ah." Julie leaned forward and clasped her hands in front of her. "I will never leave you, Vicki. I promise. I can't die unless the city itself dies. You don't have to worry about being alone anymore."

Standing in a sudden rush that made Theron squawk with indignation, Vicki grabbed her jacket. "I got to think about things. I mean, whatever I want is mine. I don't have to scrap and fight for food or clothing or anything anymore. What am I going to do with myself?"

"Go to school?"

Vicki grimace in distaste at the idea of formal schooling. "I appreciate all this... but I kinda thought Amit would help me." She stopped, turning her face away. "I'll be back later."

Julie nodded, remembering what it was like to be a young woman full of too many emotions, disappointment, and grief. "All right. Dinner's at seven."

Without answering, Vicki left the beautiful house on Yarrow Street and walked away. She didn't care where she was going. She just needed to go.

***

"I'm fine," Karen laughed as John escorted her to her car. "Yes, I'm scarred for life, and yes, apparently I'm allergic to monster venom, but I can walk to my car and drive it even."

"You've only been out of the hospital for a week." He opened her car door for her. "Don't push it. Seriously."

"Hon, I promise. It's why I'm driving and not walking. Skin is tough stuff. It grows back. I was going crazy in there. I *need* to go to my own apartment. Water the plants if they're still alive. Do the things that need doing when the world isn't going insane. Also you need your space." She hugged him with one arm before she slid into the car. "I promise. I'm just doing what I need to do. You need to focus on you. Besides," she tapped her purse, "you'll be with me anyway. The card will continue to heal me."

John bowed his head and kissed her. "All right. I'll stop smothering you. Mister Mayor wants to see me anyway."

"Give him my regards, and tell him I got the check. I'm happy to consult for the city but, man, I hope we have a break for a little while."

"I'll tell him." John shut the car door and stepped back.

Karen waved and drove away.

John gazed after her until she was out of sight. Then he took the short walk through the Colonel's Park to City Hall at the far end of the City Center Promenade. The building was so familiar now, he didn't have to stop and think about where he was going. Mason's secretary waved him into the mayor's office without a word.

He knocked on the doorframe and went in.

Mason stood with his hand out. "Come in, come in."

John noted the circles under Mason's eyes as they shook hands. He hoped that something hadn't broken in Kendrick so soon. "You rang?"

The mayor nodded. "Just needed to touch bases. You know how it is."

"Nothing is on fire?"

"Nothing supernatural." Mason gestured vaguely then gave him a keen once before sitting again. "But a mayor's job is never done. How are you? And how's Karen?"

"Slowly getting back to what constitutes as normal. She sends her regards, and thanks you for the check. Also she says that she wants some time off before the next crisis."

"Good. Good." He looked around the room but focused on nothing.

John narrowed his eyes at Mason's distracted air. "What's going on? What do you need?"

"Never one for small talk."

"Not really. Give."

Mason fidgeted with a pen. "No one has seen the Grey Lady since that night."

"Is that unusual? She tends to keep her own schedule."

"Yes, I know. But *no one* has seen her. The hedge at 15th and White is about ten feet tall and impossible to get through. Lumbering Bear isn't talking, and Eric hasn't been seen either."

"Does the hedge look healthy?" John rubbed his chin. "Yes."

"Have any of her people been seen?"

Mason paused then looked through the stack of papers on his desk. "Yes. The blond twins have been in the stores, and a couple of the more fantastical creatures have been spotted on the highest rooftops."

John shook his head. "Everything's fine. Don't go borrowing trouble."

"I can't help it. It's quiet. Too quiet."

"Except for the tears."

Mason's head shot up in alarm. "Tears?" Then he nodded, his face clearing as understanding dawned. "Tears. Yes, I'm sorry. I'm in work mode. The last of the officers' funerals was yesterday."

"Look. Just be happy the local rag wants to turn this into a paranoid conspiracy about terrorists."

Mason gave him a satisfied, if wry, smile. "Sometimes I do good work."

"That was you?" John nodded his approval. "Yeah, you do."

"Do you mind if we go over some stuff? Just to make sure I'm not missing anything?"

"Sure, no problem." John gave him a sly look. "Maybe I should charge you an expert's consultation fee."

"Please don't. I don't think the city budget could handle it."

***

"You look good." Thomasina touched the leather fringe on Eric's ceremonial outfit. Glancing at his face, she tilted her head. "Are you feeling well?"

Eric shifted his elaborate basket hat. "Nervous, I guess. This is officially it. I am the tribe's shaman. It's a lot of responsibility. Before, I could lean on Lumbering Bear, but now…" He shrugged. "It's all me."

"You won't be alone." Her playful smile faltered.

"Are *you* okay?"

It was her turn to shrug. "Thomas is gone. Were it not for the pact, the promise to stay with you, I would have died along with him. Instead, I'm stronger than I've ever been, but I'm... just me."

"You aren't alone." He put his hand on her shoulder. "I'm here. We'll be brave together."

"Have you chosen your new name or will you keep 'Iron Eyes'?"

Eric looked out his grandfather's—now his—workroom. "It will change. I've chosen 'Eric Standing Stone.' It will remind me of the Pillar of Memory, and of the true stories that must never be forgotten." He saw the council heading toward the building and stood.

Thomasina stood as well. "I will remember for you and your people, if you wish."

"Will I live as long as Sees-the-Wind did?"

"I don't know." She shook her head. "This is a new beginning for me as well. But, as you said, we'll be brave together as we face it."

Eric nodded and gave her a shy smile. "I guess we will."

***

It's clear to me that Brother Simon, who refused the mantle of Abbot, and was most comfortable with his birth name, Aaron, knew he was going to his death. From the letter left in his office, to all of his things neatly packed and arranged in his cell, to the request for personal good-byes to those within and outside the Brotherhood, he had made peace with himself and his anticipation of fulfilling his holy duty.

This does not stop me grieving for him. It is even harder on all of us without a body to bury.

I will pack all of his things and send them to our superiors. One thing of note from his letter struck me. I quote it here:

"...and it is my sincere wish that the Brotherhood of Light continue to openly work with the other supernatural factions of Kendrick. We know so much more about Kendrick and each other by sharing, rather than hiding, our arcane nature with the appropriate denizens of the city.

"If nothing else, I learned that lying, and pretending to be someone I'm not, hurt more feelings than benefited the Brotherhood. Lamiel still has not forgiven my transgressions against her and hers. Karen Wilson did forgive me, but it was clear she never forgot that our meeting and everything for the first year was a lie. ..."

I disagree with Brother Simon here. While I agree that we should continue to work with certain members of Kendrick, I disagree that we should share as much as we have. I disagree that hiding who and what we are is the wrong thing to do. I would rather we work with a very select few—Mason Steward, John Mueller, John Corso—and no others. I would rather we fall back into obscurity.

I will say as much in my report to my superiors. Then they will decide. The lesson I have taken from the case of Brother Simon is that to have too much interaction with the outside world is to invite confusion and unrest into the soul. Our job of protecting the world from malevolent spirits is too important—and too dangerous—for such to occur again.

Brother Jeffrey sat back and looked at his journal entry. He didn't want the mantle of Abbot for the Kendrick branch of the Brotherhood but he, most likely, did not have a choice. Either an Abbot would be sent, or his term as Abbot *pro tem* would become permanent. Either way, until that time, he would limit the Brotherhood to its core focus.

"Let the mayor call, should—when—the need arises. We have better things to do than play nursemaid to the likes of Kendrick's supernatural forces." He muttered and closed the book. "Then we'll see."

***

John didn't pause when he saw Alexia sitting on the bench outside *Teller's Fortune.* Instead, he walked up to the door and unlocked it. "Good. You're here. We need to talk about schedules."

Alexia gave him a sideways glance as she got up and followed him in. "I'm not fired?"

"Well, most bosses would fire a person who took off for two weeks—no call, no show."

"I—"

John continued his thought, running over whatever she might have said. "But I'm not that kind of boss. Besides, the store's been closed. I've gotten some cranky calls about it. From what I'm hearing, we're going to have a run on sage and quartz crystals."

She stared at him, frowning. "Why am I not fired?"

"Do you want to be fired?" He walked behind the counter and pulled several of his Todari carrying boxes from his ever-present messenger bag.

"No, but..." Alexia shook her head. "I don't understand."

John opened the back of one of the display cases. "Look. First, you aren't affected by these." He placed the Todari cards in the display case, one by one. Ten in this first one. Ten in the second one. Twenty in all. "Most people are gaga over them. And these are the benign ones. The rest are locked up elsewhere, or on my person."

Alexia glanced at the tarot cards as he set them up. Yes, they were powerful, but they weren't anything she hadn't seen before. Also, they weren't her focus. She walked up to the counter and looked down at them, trying to figure out what he wasn't saying.

"Second, if a last resort, stupidly powerful, being wants to be my employee, who am I to say no, as long as you get your work done?" John straightened, shifted to the next display case, and went to work on setting out the last ten of the Todari cards he usually had on display. "Besides, I need you to keep everything organized. I'm shit at that. I forget things." He flicked a glance at her. "You seem happy here."

"I am." Alexia cocked her head and gazed at him. She let a little of her true self shine through. "What's the third reason?"

John didn't say anything for several long minutes as he completed his task. When he stood, his face was as impassive as stone. "Third, I like having you around for when—not if—I complete my collection of Todari tarot cards." His voice was low and hard. "I don't know what will happen to me when I possess them all. I used the ones I had to fight the Nightmares. All of them. I didn't like what they did to me. I didn't like how I felt."

He shook his head as if to clear it. "That's not right. I didn't like the *memory* of how I felt. It wasn't human. It was all power and... I don't know how to describe it." John looked at her. "When that day comes, I need to know there's someone around who can deal with me if need be. Before I hurt those closest to me."

"You could just give them all to me now and be free."

John reared back as if she'd slapped him. "No. I can't. I don't want to. My job on this earth is to collect all those cards. I don't know why. I just know it is."

Alexia considered this. "All right. When you get the cards together, if you become an inhuman monster, I'll put you down. Deal?"

Amused, John nodded and put out his hand and said, "Deal," as they shook on it.

"So. The schedule?"

John shrugged. "I just thought you could make it up for my approval."

***

Karen faced the Kendrick Historic Library. She gazed at its arched windows and stone walls that reminded her of a church or a castle. "What do you think? Could this be home for a while?"

It was a rhetorical question she asked herself, but Sebastian and Reginald both answered her.

"I think it is a good place to try. The library is important to me. I'd like to learn more. If you don't mind." Reginald sounded curious and hopeful.

"He put a bowl of Snickers bars out on the main counter. Big ones." Sebastian gave her the mental image of him swimming in Snickers wrappers—empty ones.

Karen thought at Sebastian with affection, *"Always thinking with your stomach, eh?"* To Reginald she added, "I suppose so. It's not like I'm doing anything other than healing right now." Pushing one of the double doors open, she walked in with Sebastian at her heel.

Nicholas stood behind the main counter, tapping on a laptop. He looked up and smiled as she came over to the counter. "I wasn't sure you'd come back after..." He gestured at her arm.

"I had to heal a bit." Karen watched Sebastian out of the corner of her eye clamber up the side of the counter that had the bowl of Snickers bars waiting. "I heard about Chalice. I'm so sorry."

He nodded, and absentmindedly pushed the bowl of candy toward the small gargoyle. "I'm sorry, too. There were so many books that night."

"How long have you worked for the library?" The question came out of the immediate need to turn away from the loss, guilt, and grief Karen had been avoiding.

"Over twenty years. I've been the Head Bibliotaph for sixteen."

"Are you happy? Have they been good years?"

They both turned to watch Sebastian try to stuff an entire candy bar in his mouth at once. Nicholas nodded. "Yeah, I'm happy. I mean, it's not all rays and sunshine, but no job is. But it's a good job. We're here when we need to be, and that's important."

"You understand that if I work here, I don't just work for you. I work for the Master of the City, and the mayor may need some consultation work from me. This means I may have to drop everything at a moment's notice."

"I know all about Reginald being the city."

Karen furrowed her brow. "How?"

He shrugged, "I read your book. Parts of it anyway."

"Can I read yours?" Karen didn't try to keep the challenge out of her voice.

"If you can find it." Nicholas pulled the bowl of candy from Sebastian after he took a third Snickers bar. "Slow down. It's not like it's going out of style."

"So, you're okay with me coming and going at all hours?"

"Yes. I won't tell you all of the library's secrets. You good with that?"

"Yes." She gestured to Sebastian. "He'll eat you out of house and home if you have candy around."

"As long as he doesn't destroy anything, I don't care." Nicholas wagged a finger at the gargoyle. "You'll have to pull your weight around here, too."

Sebastian ignored him in favor of his candy bar.

Karen hesitated, then said, "I'm stubborn, nosy, and sometimes keep grudges I shouldn't."

Nicholas looked her in the eye. "Chalice McGinn worked for me for fifteen years. I think I can handle cranky."

That made Karen smile. "Okay. Last question for now."

"Yes?"

"Is this a paid position?"

He grinned. "Yes. It's not a lot, but it's enough to live on."

She doodled invisible patterns in the table. "I thought that, maybe, I could journal everything that's happened that I can remember since Reginald first called me. You know? So other people will have something to go on when I'm not around anymore."

Nicholas watched her doodle. "I think that will be good for you and the future."

"Okay then. I'd like to give it a shot."

"Right then, follow me. I'll start showing you around."

***

The two of them sat down at one of the front tables. "Now that all the boring, legal, and usual stuff is out of the way, we come to the core point of the Kendrick Historic Library." Nicholas stroked his salt and pepper beard for a moment. "My old mentor told me this: 'Never forget why we are here. We are here because people need us. When they find us, we are exactly what they are looking for—even if they don't know it themselves.' I'd like to add: What they are looking for may not be in this library. It may be that we give them the jumping off point to where they need to go. Or, sometimes, they just need a quiet place to read."

"How can you tell?" Karen was already thinking of all the things she needed to learn to help take care of the place.

"You listen." Nicholas tapped the table once. "You ask questions. But, most importantly, you listen."

Karen didn't get a chance to answer that as the one of the double doors opened. A teal-haired teenage girl slipped in and stopped, looking surprised at seeing someone she recognized in an unfamiliar place. "I can go...?" She addressed the half-question to Karen.

Karen and Nicholas exchanged a glance. He did not look surprised. In fact, Karen realized, he looked pleased with himself. It was something she was going to have to ask him about. Later.

"No." Karen shook her head. "Come on in. It's okay." She looked back at Nicholas. He nodded to her, encouraging her to go on. Karen stood. "What can we do for you today?"

Vicki continued to look like she was going to flee until Karen ushered her over to the front counter. "You work here?"

Karen nodded. "I do now."

Looking around at the rows and isles of books, Vicki sighed. "I've always loved books. But I couldn't keep any for myself. Julie told me I should get out of the house and stuff. And I found this place. I can't believe I never noticed it before."

"You are welcome here." Nicholas stood and headed to the back office. "Karen will show you around."

"Hope you're familiar with the Dewey Decimal System."

Vicki shook her head. "Nah. Just point me at the YA section."

Karen flushed. "I have to admit, I don't know where that is. Give me the name of one of your favorite authors, and I'll use that to find it...."

***

Elsewhere...

It was the hedged lot at 15th and White, known as the Lady's Garden to those in the know. It was also so much more. It was a place between worlds, where those of certain power could go.

The new Grey Lady sat up on Alexander's lap, cuddled close in a way that the old Grey Lady never would have. Times, and people, change.

"This is not what I thought it would be," she said.

The keystone gargoyle, currently of warm flesh and suede-like skin, chuckled. "It never is."

"We are not bound as Susan and you once were."

"No." His voice was low and musical, belying his huge size and strength. "But we are bound still."

"We, and all of our people now." Lady Grey looked up at him and cupped one broad cheek.

"That was unexpected."

"But needed."

Alexander shifted the Grey Lady into a standing position, then offered his hand to her as he stood. "We go where we have never been before, and your people are now welcome in the high places."

The two walked through the lush grass and fair skies of that other place. "Where are we going?"

"I have something to show you."

The shift from the place between worlds into the one known as reality was a smooth one. The Grey Lady looked up at him in surprise. Alexander said nothing. She looked back to the Lady's Garden, smiling at the statue of Alexander that protected all of the gargoyles in Kendrick. Around him, gargoyles and fey cavorted without a care.

"They do not see you as I do." The fey and gargoyles gave her their respect, but did not react to Alexander.

"No. That is our bond. It is better this way. Let the younger ones lead and find the right path now."

"How long have I been gone?" She shook her head. "I'm not yet used to how time moves around me now. I know of it, and understand it, intellectually..."

"Two weeks. Long enough that those who know have started coming to your people and mine to discover whether or not you still live."

The Grey Lady laughed. "Of course I do. My places of power are here." She stopped and nodded to herself. "It is time I take up my mantle of duty once more."

"Yes." They walked to Alexander's statue and he, a spirit of sorts in this place, walked into it and settled down. "But I am still here, and we may speak when we need—or want—to."

She gazed around the garden and began to build. Under her feet and Alexander's statue, a gazebo rose, building itself out of light until it was complete. Alexander's statue was at her back, a tea table and several chairs, properly arranged, were inside, with a wonderful view of the lot and the cottage that had also grown at her whim.

As the Grey Lady settled into place, James appeared from inside the cottage, carrying a tea set. The blond messenger twins, Theodore and Theodora, bounced into sight. They ran for the gazebo, laughing as they came.

"Lady!"

"You're back."

"We've missed you."

"But we've had new friends to play with."

The Grey Lady inclined her head. "Have you enjoyed yourselves?"

"We have."

"But we're happier you're home."

"As am I, dear ones." The Grey Lady smiled a gentle smile at James as he set up the afternoon repast. "Do I have any petitioners?"

"Yes, my Lady." He poured her tea and added the sugar.

"Send for them."

James had but to glance at the twins and they were gone, skipping through the hedge as if it wasn't there. "Anything else?"

The Grey Lady paused and considered. "Yes. Invite Karen Wilson to tea for tomorrow afternoon. I suspect we have much to talk about."

The quintessential butler bowed as he had ever since his creation, and returned to the cottage. With the new Lady Grey, he finally could have a phone in the house. He intended to use it and explore all of the new things that came with this new beginning.

KENDRICK'S HISTORIC LIBRARY ARCHIVES

The Fool's Path

IT WAS YET another perfect home with a perfect lawn and was the perfect target. John scowled at the tri-level house at the end of the cul-de-sac in Redmond's suburban hell. Sure, for some people, the Eastside was a great place to live in but you wouldn't want to visit. Unless you were craving boredom.

Or the perfect mark to rob.

John grinned as he crept close. He'd been told that this house was a treasure trove of sellable things. Rich had broken in a couple months back, stole some small things worth a whole lot. The pawnshop would do good business tonight.

He checked the backdoor and found it unlocked. Typical rich-bitch Microsoftie who thinks the world revolves around them. John slid his skinny sixteen-year-old frame—*lithe*, he liked to think—into the kitchen. It was filled with the contrast of his target's life: bachelor antique collector. Crappy pans were strewn about on the countertop while shining, embossed plates sat in neat, secure rows behind glass front kitchen cabinets.

John ignored all this. Too heavy to carry. Too easy to identify. He wanted the stuff in the office. Rich said he saw lot of small collectible things that were easy to pawn and hard to claim as an individual. The office was upstairs. Every step he took seemed to creak and crack, but with these newer houses, he knew it was his imagination.

His near constant grin was a scar in the dark. In his mind, he was hunting through a dangerous tomb for the magical idol that would bring him fame and fortune. John paused at the top of the stairs. Screw fame, he just wanted fortunes.

Nothing moved in the dark.

Four rooms split out from the landing. Three open and one closed. He could see a bathroom, a room with random crap—exercise equipment and a chest of drawers, and a room with a desk. That meant the closed door was the bedroom. No doubt, there were valuable trinkets in there, but so was the owner. Perhaps another day, if the take from the office was good.

Three quick quiet steps and he was inside the office. He blinked in the dim light. The room was bigger than he had assumed and there was a second, smaller room off the first. He could already see the bookcases filled with books and more. The grin returned and he examined the shelves in this room first. Just as he picked up a small and heavy metal statuette, a voice behind him spoke.

"Knocking would've been polite, you know."

Without thinking, John turned and hurled the statuette at the small figure standing in the doorway of the second office room. He followed it, throwing himself at his enemy, intending to bowl them over. Instead, he went flying and crashed into another stuffed bookshelf, some of the books crashing down on him. The last of these, as thick as a dictionary, landed on the back of his head with a blinding thump. It added to the already surreal moment of someone so small tossing him across the room.

John lay there, half covered with books, unable to make his body obey him. It was worse than being forced to play football in gym class, getting creamed by a jock with a shitty attitude and a desire to hurt him.

The figure moved to an overstuffed chair and sat. "What am I going to do with you?"

This time, he could tell the voice was definitely female. The sudden click and illumination of the lamp next to her gave John the impression of a small, dark-haired woman with tanned skin before he flinched way from the unexpected light. He groaned as he moved.

"I'm sorry about that. I didn't mean to hurt you. But, I've learned that to defend myself, I need to be very aggressive. I was serious though, knocking would've been the polite thing to do."

John sat up, wincing as everything hurt. He froze at the sight of the small woman holding a large pistol. This time, he noticed the silver streaking her hair. He always noticed the stupidest things when he was scared. "Uh, you don't need that. I promise."

"Liars always say, "I promise." No, I think I'll keep this. So, who are you?"

"John." He winced at the squeak in his voice then shifted until he had his back against the bookcase. This gave him a good view of the room. The most lethal things at hand were the books scattered around him. He could throw a couple and make a run for it.

"John what?" She didn't take her eyes off him. "I can shoot you before you grab a book. Trust me, I've been through this before."

He looked at her and saw not just the face of an old woman but the face of someone who'd been through the war.

Her eyes were dead. Her hand didn't tremble. "Corso. I'm John Corso."

"Well, John Corso, I'm Lina Yanin. You may call me Mrs. Yanin."

"Yes, ma'am." He had no idea why, but he knew respect and care was needed. It was probably the gun pointed at him.

"What are you doing here, young man?"

"Looking for something to steal and pawn." John paused, confused. He hadn't meant to say that.

"I think you're bored and angry and looking for something to fill your shitty life."

John blinked at her blunt words. He grimaced at the truth of them. "What's it to you?"

She ran her hand through her hair and sighed. "It... fuck it. It reminds me so much of me at your age." Lina peered at him, dark eyes hard and calculating. "You might be the one... Yes. I knew I didn't lock the backdoor. I usually do. Maybe." She stared at him for a dozen heartbeats longer. "I'll give you a choice. You can take whatever you want in the house except for the tarot card in the safe over there. If you take the card without my permission, well... let's just say you'll regret it for the rest of your short days."

John looked around until he saw a small safe on the bottom shelf of one of the bookcases. It was surrounded by books but it wasn't hidden. "Or what? You'll shoot me?"

With a bark of a laugh, she tossed the weapon to the side. "It's not even loaded. Then again, I don't need it to protect myself from the likes of you."

John surged to his feet. "Oh yeah?"

"Yeah."

The word, spoken with the flat tone of knowledge, and the books tumbled about him, made him pause. He grabbed an expensive looking crystal bell. "I can take this?"

Lina nodded. "Anything you can carry as long as you don't steal the tarot card in the safe."

"What's so special about the card? Why's it in the safe? And what choice? You said you'd give me a choice but you didn't tell me the second part." John put the crystal bell back on the shelf. He wasn't going to take it without knowing what else was on the plate.

"Smart kid. Last one didn't even notice that."

"Last...?"

"Your friend, Richard."

"He didn't say he met you."

"I know. He doesn't remember."

John scowled at her. "Why not?"

Lina smiled with too many teeth. "Magic."

"Bullshit."

"Eh? Was it bullshit that I threw you across the room, John Corso? Bullshit that you're respectful to me? Well, as respectful as a punk like you can be. Bullshit that you haven't tried to run? It's magic and it's all linked to the tarot cards I own."

Reluctant wonder crept through his mind and body. Magic? *Real* magic? Was it possible? "Tarot cards are bullshit."

"Of course they are. Most of them anyway. Not the cards I have. Not the Rinaldo Todari tarot cards. They're the real deal."

He stared at her, everything else in the room forgotten. "What's my other choice?"

"You can take anything in the house that you can carry... or you can take the one tarot card in the safe. That's your choice."

"There's more to it than that." John glanced at the safe. It was small enough to pick up and walk off with. Probably heavy, though. Or bolted to the shelves.

"There is. If you take the card—" She paused. "That's not right. If you *accept* the card, you'll be accepting a new purpose in life." Lina barked an abrupt laugh. "You'd be accepting a brand new life. One I don't recommend if I'm to be honest."

John leaned back against the bookshelf and crossed his arms. "I don't understand."

She gave a long sigh full of weariness. "I suppose not. And I need to tell you. There's magic in the card I want to give you. It can lead you to the other cards. It wants to. It changes things around you to help that happen."

"Why would you give it up, if it's magic? Did you call the cops? Is that what this is all about?" John wanted to leave. He tensed himself to go but he couldn't make his legs obey him.

"I'm tired, kid. Really tired. Even with it locked away, I can feel the Fool calling to me to continue the quest. I don't have it in me anymore."

"The Fool?"

"Yes," she breathed, her voice soft. "The first card in the Major Arcana. The Fool. *"A choice of life, a choice to be made. Choose your path carefully and nothing will lead you astray."*

Goosebumps crawled up the back of his neck at this last bit that Mrs. Yanin quoted. There was power in the words. He rubbed his arms as she finished it.

""*A decision is made, black or white. Think again. Are you wrong or right?*" What will your choice be, John Corso? Will you accept my gift or will you take what else is in the house?"

"I think I want the card." John examined his words. They were true words. The idea of holding magic in his hand was too much to give up.

"In the safe, there's a bundle of a thousand dollars in twenties next to the card. You can take that instead. You can walk away a thousand dollars richer and forget all about the Todari tarot cards."

He locked eyes with her. "Why would you say that?"

"Because it's a choice that will change your whole life. It will give you a purpose. It will be a burden."

"I can handle it." He lifted his chin. "I want the card."

"Are you sure?"

"Yes. I'm sure. I choose the Todari tarot card."

Lina relaxed in her chair and smiled. "Three times asked. You've got the will of a card collector. I'll give it to you. But that is the only thing you may take from the house today. Agreed?"

John nodded. "Agreed."

"The safe combination is 11-29-19-60." She paused and smiled a small smile of remembrance. "That was the day I accepted the Fool and the Fool's path as my own. I was so young and naïve then. I didn't know what I was doing."

"Well, I do." He stepped to the safe and knelt before it. He paused, his hand hovering over the safe dial. *Am I doing the right thing?*

"You can still choose to take the riches."

There was an ache in her voice that said she wanted him to choose the riches and leave the tarot card behind. At the same time, there was still hope in her tone that pleaded for him to take it. It was that ache... the one that said *don't choose the card...* that moved his hand.

John opened the safe and saw two things: a thin box a little bit bigger than a paperback book and a small pile of twenty dollar bills. Ignoring money for the first time in his life, John picked up the box. "I choose the tarot card."

"I give it to you with my own free will. It is your tarot card now. God help you."

"I don't need God's help." He stood and raised a hand to open the box.

"No!" Lina's voice was sharp. "Don't open it in front of me. Just go."

"Why?" He dropped his hand.

"You'll understand when you see the card. Just... please. Go now."

John narrowed his eyes as he scowled. "If this is a trick..."

"It's not. Just wait until you're on the doorstep to open it. You'll understand."

"Alright." Suddenly, he felt reluctant to leave. He didn't know why. Fear pooled in his stomach. "Anything else I should know?"

She nodded, looking even smaller and more frail. "The card is indestructible. All of them are. They're artifacts. They may be given away willingly or found or inherited, but never stolen, never forced from their owner, and never sold. If they are, the power of the card works against the false holder. It's a terrible thing to see." She pointed at the box in his hand. "That one will lead you to the rest. Each one has a different power."

"Do you know what each one does?"

"Some yes. Some no. That's something you'll have to learn on your own. There are many collectors, John Corso. You've entered their world now." She smiled at him. This time it was filled with joy. "I can't wait to see what they make of you. You may go now."

The fear and reluctance disappeared and a lightness descended. He nodded to her. "Thanks." He moved to the door and paused. "Will I see you again?"

"Oh yes. Of course. I have more than one Todari tarot card."

John half-smiled. "Okay then. Later." He turned and walked away. He left the house as he entered it—through the backdoor. However, on the back porch, underneath the flickering light, he paused and opened the card box.

All thoughts of this being a weird practical joke drained away as he looked at the most beautiful thing he'd ever seen. The vivid colors took his breath away.

The card was of a sailor in old fashioned clothes walking off a pier. The boat was already gone, sailing away in the distance. Sailor looked backwards instead of watching where he walked. Over his shoulder was a bag. Peeking out of it was a deck of cards. Tarot cards. Beneath the sailor, a dolphin breached the wild waves so he could step upon its back. On the pier, turned away, was a child in the same outfit as the sailor.

John knew, but he didn't know how he knew, that the card symbolized blind faith in the universe and that it was a card of new beginnings, but the abandonment of the old for the new. He walked away from Lina Yanin's house without watching where he walked in an unconscious parody of the card he held. It was mesmerizing. He continued to walk, swearing that he could see the waves move and the distant flags on the ship wave.

He walked without knowing how long or how far, caught in the spell of the Fool. Until a hand spun him around and a fist socked him in the jaw. John tumbled to the ground, losing the card as his head bounced off the pavement.

Blinking and dazed, he didn't recognize where he was or who had hit him. The man, blond with a craggy face, hunkered over him, going through his pockets with experienced hands. "Hey..." the protest turned into moan of pain as the mugger punched him again. This time, pain exploded in his nose and a warm gush of blood poured down his face and into his mouth.

The mugger opened John's wallet, pulled the small wad of cash from it, and stuffed that in his pocket. He dropped the wallet on top of John as he stepped away. "Not much cash. But what's this?" He hunkered again and picked up the Todari tarot card.

John sat up and reached for it. "No!" He got kicked in the side for his trouble.

"This might be worth something to someone."

Holding his side, John shook his head. "I won't give that to you. It's mine. You can't take it."

"Fuck off, kid." The mugger strode down the alley towards the street.

Hurt him, John thought towards the card. *Hurt him bad. You're mine.*

When it looked like the guy was going to get away, John grabbed his discarded wallet, forced himself to his feet, and stumbled after him. "Hey!"

The mugger looked over his shoulder, slipped on something, and tumbled into another person. That guy shoved him away with a curse. The mugger tripped on the sidewalk curb and hit the asphalt hard. John could only stare as the sound of squealing brakes ended in the mugger being hit from the side as he struggled to get out of the road.

John hurried to the mouth of the alleyway. A crowd gathered by the injured man and the driver was on the phone to emergency services. He looked down. At his feet was the Fool. Picking it up, he saw that it was as pristine as when he first looked at it, despite being knocked around and dropped in the muck a couple of times. He smiled at it. "So, that's what happens, eh?"

He put it back in the small carrying box, not wanting to be mesmerized by its beauty again. As he did, he saw a twenty dollar bill half under a newspaper. It was a mess but it would get him home. John looked around, wiping the blood from his mouth. He had no idea where he was or how long he'd been walking, staring at the Todari card. That was something he was going to have to be careful of in the future.

Again, he was compelled to look down. There was something about the newspaper... He picked it up and looked at it, scanning the headlines. It was the entertainment section of yesterday's paper. When he hit on it, he knew that all that had just happened—the walking, the mugging, the twenty dollar bill—all of it, had been so he would see this one tiny article.

Ignoring the sounds of the approaching ambulance and the babble of people, he read the first paragraph to himself. "Todari Art Presentation. Professor Raymond Bahl, the foremost expert on painter Rinaldo Todari, will be speaking at the Seattle Art Museum on Tuesday at 8 p.m. This free lecture is open to the public."

He stopped reading. That's all he needed to know. Someone at the lecture, probably Professor Bahl, was going to tell him more about the Todari tarot cards. Then he'll know what to do to get the next one. He walked with slow, pain filled steps away from the chaos of the accident and waved at an approaching taxi.

John grinned once more, still tasting blood, as the taxi passed him by. It felt good to have a purpose. To know he was meant to do great things. Magic was real and now he was a part of it.

Kelpie Storm

THE POLICE DIDN'T find Miriam's body. Susan knew the cops didn't believe her when she told them what happened on the beach; that a monster had dragged Miriam under the waves and almost killed Susan, too. Susan glared at the newest cop in front of her, knowing that the woman wouldn't believe her either. But, from the way her parents acted, it was talk to the cop or go back to the hospital.

"Miss Moore, I'm Sergeant Charlotte Gabrielle. I know you've told your story multiple times but I need you to tell it to me as if I haven't got the faintest idea of what you're talking about. Because, honestly, I'm coming into this case cold."

Susan gazed at the pretty black woman. The sergeant wasn't too tall and had a nice face. She figured the cop was probably a shrink. "I'm not crazy and it's not a story."

Sergeant Gabrielle nodded. "My apologies, Miss Moore. I need you to give me your... point of view of the events that happened to you and Miss Page."

"Call me Susan." Susan gazed at the older woman, suspicion and anger plain on her face. "Are you a doctor? You know, for crazy people." She waggled her finger in a circle at her temple.

Sergeant Gabrielle shook her head. "Just a cop, Susan. And you can call me Charlotte... or Lotte... if you like."

Anyone in authority who tries this hard to be a kid's friend isn't what they seem. Susan glared all the more, crossing her arms. "What's the S.U. stand for?" She pointed to the initials on Charlotte's badge.

"It means 'Special Unit.' I'm part of a special taskforce in the Kendrick Police Department to investigate unusual occurrences."

"Like a monster dragging my friend into the ocean?"

Charlotte tilted her head and nodded, her eyes brightening with interest as she leaned forward. "Yes. Most of the police believe she ran away and you're covering for her—"

"I'm not!"

She held up a hand. "I know. I believe you. Yes, teenagers run away. It happens. But, your case, and Miriam's disappearance, it doesn't fit the profile."

Susan sat back and considered this. "Why not?"

Charlotte reached out a hand towards, but didn't quite touch, the bandage on Susan's arm. "This."

She referred to the bite mark on Susan's arm where the monster had savaged her, trying to drag her into the water while Miriam laughed. Susan hugged herself tighter, aware of the lingering pain in her arm and didn't respond.

Charlotte pulled back, her posture straightening from the comforting, understanding person into the cop she was. "All right, we'll take it from the beginning." Her voice was crisp and neutral. "What I know is that you, Susan Moore, age 13, and Miriam Page, also age 13, were on the beach by Pier 3 on Saturday the 15th. Why don't you tell me what happened that night?"

Susan shrugged, feeling shy and resigned. She knew this nice woman wouldn't believe her but spoke anyway, her voice taking on the rote tone of someone who has told the same story too many times. "We were out storm watching. We like to watch the waves crashing. You don't really get to see that in the bay. Miriam pointed out a whitish horse that's trotting up the beach. She said it came out of the water. I didn't believe her. I mean, it was a really pretty horse and the storm gave its coat almost a bluish color. It seemed friendly enough. Came right up to us. Miriam put out a hand to pet its mane and then... she was on its back. I don't know how. It didn't have a saddle and she didn't know how to ride. I... was afraid. Horses scare me. They're big."

Charlotte nodded but didn't say anything. Susan blinked back tears that threatened to overwhelm her. Charlotte pulled a tissue from a nearby box and handed it to her. The sergeant still didn't speak but she did smile and nodded for Susan to continue.

Wiping at her eyes, Susan looked away from the cop and focused on the wall of family pictures. "Horses scare me," she repeated. "I stepped back and told Miriam to get down but she didn't look at me. She just laughed. She didn't seem like herself. She just pet the horse and laughed. And it kept getting closer to me. I could see something was wrong with it. Something bad. Its eyes didn't look right. I yelled at Miriam to get down again and then it...it bit me."

Susan rubbed the bandage covering her right forearm, the bite mark aching with the retelling. "It grabbed me with sharp teeth and shook me by my arm like a shark does. I yelled and screamed while it pulled me towards the water. Miriam just... it's like she wasn't there, wasn't seeing what was happening. I stabbed the monster in the eye with my thumb. That's how you get away from sharks that get you in the water." Susan thrust her left fist forward with her thumb out to the side. "I hurt it bad enough that it let me go. I ran. I ran away and left Miriam to die."

The tears came in a flood and Charlotte moved to Susan's side, gathering her up in motherly arms. "I believe you," she whispered as she rocked Susan against her. "I believe you and you did the only thing you could do against a monster like that."

Susan pulled back from Charlotte, wiping at her face. "You know what it was? You know?"

It was Charlotte's turn to pause and look uncomfortable before she said, "Kendrick's a special place and, sometimes, strange things happen. I think this is one of those times. It's why I was assigned to the case."

"But what was it? What killed Miriam?"

"It sounds like a kelpie... or some variation of one. We haven't had an incursion of such creatures in decades."

"Then you know! You'll get it and you'll tell everyone." Susan willed Charlotte to agree.

Charlotte pulled away from Susan, then moved back to her original seat, reassuming the role of the cop once more. She didn't look at Susan for a long moment. "Officially, either Miriam Page will be considered a runaway or someone attacked you two and you are too traumatized to remember what really happened."

"But, you said... kelpie."

Sadness filled Charlotte's eyes when she looked at Susan. "The world isn't ready to believe in some of the things that happen in Kendrick. And, really, you won't remember this in a few years. You'll come to believe that she ran away or that you two were attacked by a stranger. We'll try to get this monster but no one will ever know the real truth. You have to accept that. There is no other choice."

***

Susan refused to speak about the incident again. Not to her friends, her family, or the town reporter who came to see her. Instead, she stewed and researched the monster. Charlotte had given her a clue: the word "kelpie" and she wasn't going to just pretend that the monster didn't exist, no matter what the cops and newspapers said.

She went to the Kendrick Historical Library to find out everything they had on sea monsters, especially kelpies. There were so many sea legends and versions of kelpies, sirens, and mermaids that she didn't know what she was looking at. After hours upon hours of fruitless searching, the assistant librarian, Nicholas, suggested that, if she were looking for local sea legends to visit the Kendrick Museum. The curator, Mister Brownson, knew just about all there was to know about the Pacific Northwest and its history.

Armed with little more than her memory and a nebulous determination to get revenge on the monster that killed her friend, Susan headed to the museum with a purpose.

Housed in what was once the city hall, the Kendrick Museum was a great building of pillars and stone, scrollwork and statues. The top of the building was covered in gargoyle statues that they rotated on a regular basis to preserve the artwork as well as keep things interesting.

Open and free to the public, Susan was already familiar with the museum but had never arrived with such a purpose before. Ignoring the beautiful artwork, the city founders plaque, the sculptors' room filled with statues, and the mariner display, she headed straight to the Makah whaling exhibit. The room was large and filled with a myriad of ocean going tools, including boats, oars, and Makah ceremonial dress. The whole exhibit was deeply cluttered with the artifacts of daily life and the ceremonies around whale hunting.

Susan looked around the room, frowning. There was nothing about monster legends in the room. It was all daily life minutia, religious ceremony, and history. While some of the history was really cool, it wasn't what she wanted. If the Makah didn't have legends about sea monsters, she wasn't sure where she should look.

"Excuse me. Are you Susan Moore?"

The musical male voice came from behind her. When she looked, she saw a tall man from the Makah tribe in khakis and a button-up shirt open at the neck. The most striking thing about him was his light blue eyes. She had never seen a Makah man with blue eyes before. There was a nametag on his shirt that read: Mr. Brownson. She nodded.

"Nickolas from the Kendrick Historical Library gave me a call. He said that you were looking for legends of local monsters to write about for a school project?" He smiled at her, his head tilted with curiosity.

Susan nodded again. "Uh, yeah. I have a report due soon." It was the lie she'd come up with when the librarian had asked her why she was researching ways to try and kill a kelpie. "Local sea monsters," she added.

"I'm Charles Brownson but you can call me Charlie if you like. I'm the curator. I can help you. I'm the expert in all things historical around here."

Susan nodded again and tilted her head, unable to contain her curiosity. "You have blue eyes."

Charlie smiled, showing generous white teeth against his brown skin. "Yes. My great-grandmother was a settler. Mary Stewart. I'm directly related to one of the city's founders, Sergeant George Stewart. But both my parents are Makah."

Susan smiled. "Neat."

"So, local *sea* monsters?"

She nodded.

Charlie gestured for her to follow. "The only sea monster legends I know of are listed in the mariner and marina exhibits." They walked back through the main hallway towards the Mariner room. Susan noticed that the sculptors' exhibit had a bunch of large gargoyle statues with gem colored eyes as Charlie spoke. She turned away from that exhibit, making a mental note to come back and look at them another time.

"Legends of sea monsters have been around for ages. In the Makah tribe, there was a legend of a sea monster that stole children. In the modern day, most consider it a kelpie based on the description of the monster from the settler and sailor reports. It was a shapeshifter that was either a man with skin the color of a sea lion or a horse with a coat the color of the summer sky. This monster would come during a storm and lure the unwary to ride its back or lure young people with a siren song. Its magic was strong. Once you were caught by its glamour, there was almost nothing that could free you from the monster's trap. Only two things..."

Charlie led Susan to the mariner exhibit and showed her what looked to be a hooked knife with a bell-shaped bottom. It sat amongst the general work tools from the now defunct whaling industry. With whaling outlawed, no-one went whaling these days, except for the Makah, but that was for religion reasons and not greed. At least, that's what Susan had heard.

"One of the two things was this whaling spear tip. This tool wasn't used to kill whales but it was used to help harvest the blubber from the whale carcass. Legend says that a sailor saved his shipmate from the kelpie by stabbing it with this very tool. There's a discussion amongst my peers as to whether or not the weapon was effective because it's iron or because it's a weapon and things stabbed with it tend to bleed."

Susan stared at the tool. She saw that it would fit on top of a broom handle. It was exactly what she was looking for. It was exactly what she imagined it would take to kill a horse monster from the ocean. "What's the second thing?"

"Dried flowers. If the sea monster, we'll stick to calling it a kelpie—there've been many names for this legend including "Child-Thief-From-the-Sea" and "Sea-Horse-that-Walks-Like-a-Man" as well as "siren"—touches dried flowers, it's forced to shift into the form it's not in. If it's a horse, it shifts to a man. If it's a man, it shifts to a horse. It's this shifting that releases its victim from its captivating song."

For a moment, Susan didn't say anything. She just stared at the weapon, realizing she had no idea how she was going to get Charlie to loan it to her so she could kill the monster, the kelpie. Looking up at him, Susan tilted her head and asked, "When was the last time this monster was seen?"

Charlie shrugged. "A couple decades ago. Supposedly, it was trapped in a magic jar full of dried flowers."

The timing matched what Charlotte had told her. "Do you believe that?"

"I believe there's more to this world than we can comprehend." He looked at his watch. "And, I'm sorry, but I must make a phone call. Perhaps we'll talk again and you'll tell me about your report." Charlie nodded at her and walked off.

Susan couldn't believe her luck. It was as if the curator told her exactly what she needed to fight the monster and then left so she could take the weapon without having to ask him for it. She hesitated as she reached for the artifact. Stealing was a bad thing that only bad people did. Then Susan shook her head. Letting a monster go free to kill kids was worse. Besides, she was only borrowing the weapon. She'd return it after the monster was dead. Susan picked up the whaling spear tip and slipped it into her backpack before hurrying away.

***

Two days later, Susan was ready. She had her dried flowers from the craft store stuffed in both pockets of her raincoat and her makeshift weapon tied to the top of a broom handle. A storm was rolling in. She waited on the beach by Pier 3, trying to look like any other kid, just watching the ocean.

As the sun went down, Susan felt eyes watching her. She looked around and saw nothing but the rocky outcropping at the base of the beach. She turned her attention back to the ocean. The rainclouds darkened the sky as the wind whipped the placid bay into small, white-capped waves. "C'mon, you kelpie. I'm ready."

Of course she wasn't but it was too late to realize it as the neighing of a horse answered her wish. From the waterline, the same white-blue horse from weeks ago came trotting towards her. Susan stuffed a hand in her pocket as she stood, holding the makeshift spear. The horse slowed as it saw the weapon but it didn't stop. Instead, it moved into a stately walk, its head high as it chuffed towards, inviting her to come and ride.

Its right eye, the eye she had stuck her thumb into, was a milky white instead of an endless black. It was the same kelpie that had stolen Miriam. Its damaged eye was the proof. It was also proof that if she could hurt the monster, she could kill it.

Even though Susan knew it was a monster, she still had the urge to reach out to the horse and pet its flying mane. She stopped herself and flung a handful of dried flowers at it in a warding gesture. Most of them were caught by the wind—stems and all—to be blown away. But one caught in the horse's mane.

There was a blurring of the horse's form and then a young man stood there, a dried flower caught in his hair. "You know the old ways," the kelpie said as he pulled the flower from his hair and let the wind whisk it away.

"Where's my friend? Where's Miriam?" Susan was shaking, shocked that not only had the flowers worked but the kelpie could talk. She gripped her spear tighter.

"Miriam?" He tilted his head and smiled. "I don't know anyone with that name."

"You do. You stole her when you came with the last storm."

The kelpie put his hand to his injured eye. "You're the other one." For a moment, his handsome visage twisted into something feral, cruel, and angry. Then the look of hatred was gone and the monster shook his head, smiling once more. "I only see a beautiful young lady before me. One that I wish to show the world. Come ride with me and see the wonders of the sea and the stars and the rain. We will run forever, you and I. We will be together for always."

His voice dropped into a musical, sing-song tone that drew her in. Already, Susan could imagine what it would be like to ride the horse's back, to not be afraid of it or anything else ever again. She would know what the oceans looked like in ways that no one else could show her. And, even though part of her mind was screaming in terror, Susan dropped the spear with its stolen tip and took a step forward.

The kelpie nodded, offering her his hand. "We will travel the world, just you and I. We will be as one. It will be glorious."

All Susan knew at this point was the kelpie's voice. Miriam didn't matter. Her family didn't matter. The fact that it was pouring rain, and she was about to die, didn't matter. She reached out her hand to his and accepted her fate. A moment with him was worth her entire life.

An instant before their hands touched, a huge, grey shape tackled the kelpie from the side. At the same time, the words "*I choose you!*" reverberated in Susan's head. The shock of these two things broke the kelpie's mystical hold on Susan's mind and she stumbled back from the sudden, monstrous fight. Taking another step back and away from what her mind refused to believe, she tripped over the fallen spear and landed hard on her butt, biting her tongue in the process.

As bright pain and the taste of blood filled her mouth, Susan couldn't deny what she was seeing. The kelpie, back in horse form, was fighting with one of the huge gargoyle statues from the museum. Only, it wasn't a statue anymore. It was at least seven feet tall with skin that looked like it would feel like suede, large horns, golden eyes, and claws. It wrestled with the kelpie as the monster took large bites out of the gargoyle's hide.

Susan realized that the gargoyle—*Alexander*, she didn't know how she knew his name—was bleeding.

Alexander threw the kelpie away from him and crouched with his claws out. The kelpie moved with preternatural speed and bull rushed the gargoyle, bowling him over. As Alexander fell, he clawed at the horse's tender underbelly. The kelpie screamed an all too human scream and bucked, kicking Alexander in the face. The gargoyle fell back, his arms raised to protect from pummeling hooves.

Run!

Susan heard Alexander's voice in her head and knew that he was sacrificing his body to give her a chance to escape. She got up and grabbed her weapon, then charged the kelpie, stabbing it the side with the whaling spear tip. It went in far deeper than Susan had expected. The spear tip disappeared completely inside the monster's flesh. Again the kelpie screamed and whipped around, intending to trample Susan in its fury.

She did the only thing she could. She threw the second handful of flowers at it. The kelpie blurred and transformed back into a man shape. He staggered, unbalanced by the spear sticking out of his side. Still he charged at Susan, wild with fury.

The kelpie didn't make it.

Like before, an instant before the monster touched Susan, the huge, grey shape of Alexander tackled him from the side, tumbling the two of them to the ground as Susan scrambled away. With the spear tip in his side, the kelpie didn't appear to be able to transform back into his horse form. Alexander's claws shredded kelpie flesh before he literally tore the kelpie's head from the monster's body.

For a long moment, Alexander knelt over the kelpie's form, snarling at the kelpie's head. Then, like sea foam, both the kelpie's body and head dissolved into bubbles, water, and spindrift, leaving the gargoyle kneeling in the sand, covered in seawater as the spear hit the ground with an almost inaudible thunk.

Susan stood nearby, watching the gargoyle and what was left of the kelpie. She let herself crumple to the sand, kneeling like Alexander was, not sure that her legs would support her in her relief and realization that, if it weren't for the creature in front of her, she really would be dead right now.

She watched as Alexander stood and brushed sand and debris from him. He didn't look at her but she still heard his words in her head.

Are you well? Were you hurt?

"No." Susan shook her head. "Why...?" She paused, not sure what she was asking.

Why did I kill it? Because it was going to kill you. Why do I protect you? Because I've found you worthy. Why have I found you worthy? Because you were going to right a wrong even though you had no concept of what you were fighting. Alexander looked at her, his citrine eyes gleaming. *I choose you.*

Susan smiled, not completely certain what that meant, but she felt the care radiating from him. "Okay. Um. So, now what?"

He walked over to her and offered her his hand. She accepted it, standing up. She looked at her small human hand dwarfed by his huge, gargoyle one, but didn't pull back from him. Instead, she stroked the back of his hand with a fingertip. It was warm as a mug of hot chocolate and as soft as expensive leather.

Now, we get you home. May I carry you?

Susan nodded, then laughed as Alexander scooped her up. His wings opened as he launched himself into the sky. Clinging to him, she watched the ground speed by and realized that two people stood back from the beach, watching them. "People!"

I know. They're good people. Safe. They already know about me. They won't bother you. You are protected. I promise. You have nothing to fear. I am here for you, now and forever more.

Susan relaxed in Alexander's arms, knowing what he said was true. She didn't know how or why, but nothing would ever be the same. She thought about Miriam, her heart still hurting at the loss but pleased that the monster who took her would never do the same to another.

***

Nicholas and Charlie stood side-by-side in the shadow of Pier 3 about a hundred yards away from where the fight had been, watching Alexander fly away with Susan in his arms. They were silent for a long moment before Nicholas spoke.

"Well, that was unexpected."

"Sorta, but not really." Charlie headed towards the site of the dead kelpie, his eyes on Susan's makeshift spear. "Charity warned me that Alexander seemed fascinated with the girl."

Charity, a gargoyle the size of a full-grown corgi, loped ahead with her wings flattened to her side. She arrived at the spear long before the men. She didn't pick it up. Instead, she looked out at the sea and snarled, her curled lips revealing sharp canine-like teeth.

Nicholas followed. "I knew she was special. I mean, she did find my library. That only happens if people really have a need."

Charlie picked up the spear and untied the spear tip from the broom handle. "Legend tells that the kelpie isn't dead. It's just... asleep for a while. I wonder how long."

"I wish we could've imprisoned it." Nicholas huddled in his jacket against the rain. "After Susan came by, I went and found Miriam's Lifebook and read the last chapter. She bought the cursed jar from Coleman at *Treasures and Trinkets*. He told her that it was a wishing jar and that all she had to do was take it to the ocean and release the flowers."

"That man is a menace."

"He's not a man."

"You know what I mean." Charlie looked at the spear tip. It was covered in sand and ichor from the kelpie.

Without preamble, a tall woman in a long grey antique gown stood next to the two men. She had white hair piled high on her head and clear grey eyes. "I believe you are looking for this." She held out a small jar half filled with dried flowers.

Nicholas jumped back. "Holy shit!"

Charlie gave the woman a small bow. "Lady Grey. Thank you. I didn't know if you'd come." He accepted the jar. "What do I do?"

Lady Grey smiled at them. "Put some of the creature's blood into the jar, seal it, and make sure it doesn't get broken."

"Sorry, Lady Grey. Just not used to the sudden appearance thing." Nicholas ducked his head, rubbing the back of his neck.

"I understand. You've just watched a nightmare fight a gargoyle who then flew off with a young girl. I suppose my sudden arrival could've been handled more delicately but I wanted to make sure we got the creature's blood into the jar before it was washed away by the rain." There was a twinkle in the ageless woman's eyes as she spoke.

Charlie finished getting the monster's blood from the spear tip into the jar and closed it tight. "Nightmare?"

Lady Grey took the jar from Charlie. "Nightmare. A creature of darkness from my land that managed to make it through the Veil. It must have come through someone's night terror of the kelpie myth to be forced into that shape." The jar in her hand glowed briefly. "I've sealed it within. Please keep it safe." She offered it back to Charlie.

Nicholas shook his head as Charlie stuffed the jar in his jacket pocket. "So much to learn about Kendrick and its denizens."

"That's what we all say when we discover the real world of Kendrick." Charlie patted him on the back and paused as he turned to speak to Lady Grey.

The Lady was gone.

"Does she always do that?" Nicholas looked around, unease plain on his youthful face.

"No. But I suspect there's a lot going on right now. So, how's it feel to have seen the leader of the gargoyles bond with a human for the first time in a century, meet the Grey Lady of the Goodfolk, and watch a nightmare be killed and then captured... in that order?"

"Weird."

"It's only going to get weirder from here. And I'm going to bet that we both meet up with Miss Susan Moore again."

Nicholas nodded. "I suspect so."

Ley of the Land

THE BOY LOOKED up at the old man standing in the shadow of the stone totem pole. Sees-the-Wind gestured to his apprentice, Eric Iron Eyes. "Sit. Today is an important day."

Taking his favorite spot in the circle of sitting stones across from the pole, the ten-year-old looked up at the Pillar of Memory and wondered about it once more. Eric kept his tongue as his great grandfather, shaman of the tribe, sat next to the object of his fascination. As always, he could see the power radiating out from the pillar into the ground and the air. He knew that he was one of the few who could see this. It was one of the reasons he was chosen as apprentice.

"What do you see before you?"

Eric eyed Sees-the-Wind, looking for the trick in the question. Such deceptively simple questions always had complex answers. "I see you, Grandfather. Sitting next to the Pillar of Memory."

"Tell me about the Pillar of Memory."

The boy screwed up his face, trying to remember what he had been told about the sacred artifact. "It represents the oldest pact the Makah have with the outsiders. It's as wide as a man and twice as tall. It...is made of stone not from here. I see its connection to the land. Um..."

Sees-the-Wind tilted his head. "But what does that mean?"

"Which thing?"

"The pact. The stone not from here. What do these mean?"

Eric shook his head. "I don't know. No one ever really talks about it. Even when I ask. They just say to ask you."

The shaman nodded. "As it should be. Some knowledge is too dangerous to be known... and too precious to be forgotten."

Eric leaned forward. "You're going to tell me now?"

He gave his apprentice a brief smile—a white scar within a mass of deeply tanned wrinkles. "Yes. And you will need to remember everything I tell you." The smile disappeared. "This is a true thing and you *must* remember it."

Sees-the-Wind tapped the drum he used for storytelling, beating out the slow cadence for the tale to come.

"Long before the white man arrived to take our land as their own, the People were invaded by another. The Pillar of

Memory was once a huge, stone boulder that appeared one night during a storm of immense power. A great bolt of lightning struck the ground, opening it up, and allowing the boulder to rise from another world into ours. This was witnessed by the shaman and his apprentice.

"The boulder was more than mere rock. It was a gateway to another world. And out of that gateway came creatures of beauty and light; both terrible and marvelous. What we, the Makah people, did not know was that these creatures were fleeing a lost land. All we saw was the invasion of creatures we did not understand.

"For many years, a war was fought. For many years, the creatures of light and the Makah people were lost to a war to hold the land as ours. Until, one day, the shaman's apprentice fell into a hidden ravine and almost died. He was found by the greatest of the creatures of light—what looked to be a grey lady with a crown of white flames. Knowing he was done for, he said, 'Before you kill me, let me know your name so I may take it with me.'

"Seeing a man-child before her, the grey lady took pity upon the shaman's apprentice. Instead of killing him, she healed him and helped him from the ravine. When she touched him, she shared herself with him in the healing, it changed both of them, and both people knew more. He knew that she was their queen, and that they wanted nothing more than peace. And she knew the fear and misunderstanding the Makah had of her people.

"It was because of this meeting, the grey lady's kindness, and the shaman's apprentice's new understanding of what the creatures were that a healing between the two people could begin. From that day, the shaman's apprentice was the one to meet and speak with the creatures who called themselves the Good Folk. Out of this one act of kindness, the Pact was born.

"For many years, the Makah and the Good Folk lived in peace and harmony with the land. The more the Good Folk worked with the Makah, the more they looked human. Still made of light. Still not of this world. But kindred spirits. The Makah protected the Good Folk and the Good Folk protected the Makah."

"Who was the shaman apprentice?" Eric couldn't keep the question to himself any longer.

The old man stopped the beating of his drum and looked at his apprentice. "The name he took upon becoming the tribe's shaman was Sees-the-Wind."

Eric blinked at his elder for a moment. "You're named after him?"

Sees-the-Wind shook his head. "No, young one. I *am* him."

Laughter bubbled up before Eric could stop it. He shook his head. "You can't be. That would've been... hundreds of years ago. You're old, but—"

Eric's voice cut out as Sees-the-Wind seemed to grow tall and fierce, power rolling from him in waves that dwarfed even the power radiating out from the Pillar. "Do not mock me or our history! I do not lie. This is a true thing. One that *must* be remembered."

The boy found himself cowering on the ground even after Sees-the-Wind regained his old man's stature and demeanor. "I'm sorry," Eric whispered.

Sees-the-Wind nodded once. "Are you ready to hear more?"

He shifted back into a sitting position. "I am, Grandfather."

"As I grew into a man, I became the shaman of the tribe. I continued to be the ambassador to the Good Folk, and every year we renewed the Pact of Protection. Then one year, we—the Grey Lady and I—met on the anniversary of the Pact... and we both had had warnings, prophecies, of the coming white man. It was then that we spoke of our love of the land, and the worship of the bounty we had enjoyed. It was at this meeting that we knew we needed to do something more to protect that which we loved. We could not stop the coming tide, but we could make a safe harbor.

"It was the Grey Lady that proposed the Binding of our peoples and the sacrifice needed. One of each of us would give of ourselves to the other... and they would become one. It would bind us, both our people, to each other, and to the land. But, this Binding needed more than our approval. It needed the whole of each tribe to agree.

"This great decision was not easy. I offered myself to the Binding, but the Makah would not hear of it. A fierce debate raged for days until Falling Petals, the chief's youngest daughter, spoke up and offered herself. I wanted to deny this, for I had long loved Falling Petals. I wanted her as my wife. But the good of the people came before my selfish heart. In the end, her father and I both let her go.

"The Good Folk had also had a long debate, for it was the Grey Lady who offered herself to the Binding. Some of the Good Folk feared how it would change them because the Grey Lady was them. What happened to her, happened to all. But it was as the Grey Lady had foreseen. Her long sight was stronger than mine.

"The Binding was when the Good Folk gained substance... and it was when the Makah gained the Guardians who protect Changer's Claw and the other Makah artifacts. Changer's Claw was used in the Binding but I know not how. Only those in the Binding know."

Sees-the-Wind's voice grew silent in the face of Eric's growing questions. The boy tried very hard to keep his tongue, but his impatience almost overwhelmed him. The shaman's brief scar of a smile appeared and disappeared. "Ask your questions, boy."

"But, how are you alive still? How did the Binding give us Guardians? How did it give the Good Folk flesh? I don't understand." Eric fidgeted in his seat as he looked between his elder and the stone pillar. "And how did the Gateway boulder become a pillar?"

The old man nodded at each question. "These will be answered. Patience a little longer. And remember my words."

"The Binding was beyond anything I had ever seen. It was as if Falling Petals and the Grey Lady walked into the distance without leaving our sight. It was a ritual that all witnessed. They spoke together, they mingled blood and light, then walked towards the Gateway boulder... that is now the Pillar of Memory... and continued walking until they were almost too small to see. Then, where two walked forward, only one returned. The change was immediate. The Good Folk were more than light. There was a substance to them now.

"For the Makah, the change was... not immediate. The one who returned looked much like Falling Petals, though her hair was white and her clothing grey. She returned to us as Queen of the Good Folk, but also of the Makah people. She returned and offered herself to me as wife. The Grey Lady was Falling Petals and the Falling Petals was the Grey Lady. Both, it seemed, loved me, despite my flaws.

"I accepted this and for ten years, she lived with the Makah as one of them. She bore us three healthy sons and one beautiful girl. Every one of them was changed. Our children

were the first Guardians. While the blood doesn't always run true, every Guardian is of my blood. And every apprentice to me has been of our blood... the Grey Lady who was Falling Petals and mine.

"After ten years, the Grey Lady needed to return to her people. She offered me a gift of life and a choice. First, she gifted me with the ability to live as long as she did. Then, when it was time for a new Binding, she promised me the choice of whether or not to continue on with her. Since then, I have witnessed three Bindings."

"But why?" Eric's question burst out before he could stop it.

"Why what?"

"Why go on? Isn't she someone different now? The Grey Lady isn't Falling Petals anymore. Right? She doesn't even look Makah."

Sees-the-Wind bowed his head. "She is, and she is not. There are memories there. And, in the ley of the land as well as the people, I wanted to see the legacy I created. I wanted... to make sure that the sacrifice was worth it."

"Was it?"

For a long moment, Sees-the-Wind did not answer. Then he continued the true story that needed to be remembered, his drum beating out the slow cadence once more.

"My grandchildren were just born, proving the Guardian blood true, when the white man came. Colonel Reginald Kendrick and his true aid, Sergeant George Steward. They came to the land, and found it good. Unlike most who simply took what they wanted, Colonel Kendrick and Sergeant Steward traded and bartered for what they wanted. The Colonel wanted to found a new town that would be a safe haven for those who had fought in too many wars. Sergeant Steward and his entire family had pledged himself to the Colonel.

"It was from this that Kendrick was born of the People, the Land and Sea, the Good Folk, and the white man. I don't believe the Colonel ever really understood this, but I know the Sergeant did. He made himself an ambassador to the Makah. He respected our ways as much as he could understand. He even took one of the Makah as his wife. It was for this reason that the Grey Lady blessed him and his with the ability to sense the land and all within its borders.

"There were trials and tribulations, yes. There always are. But the Binding of the Makah and the Good Folk did protect the land we loved. It was Sergeant Steward's first born son, Marcus, who suggested that part of the Gateway stone be used to carve a statue of the Colonel to honor him. Marcus was touched by the land and by the Good Folk. He understood that using the Gateway stone, placed at the town's center, would permanently bind the city of Kendrick to the land itself.

"When the stone was carved, leaving the Pillar, one of the Good Folk known as the Maker came to me and asked if he could carve what was left into a monument to the Pact, and the sacrifices made. I, and the council, agreed. With one of my apprentices, the Maker crafted the Pillar of Memory you see now."

"And a lovely monument it is." The Grey Lady's voice, light and amused, broke the spell of the telling.

Eric jerked, startled by the woman's sudden appearance at his side. Sees-the-Wind did nothing more than still his drum and nod to the fey queen.

"You always did have a lovely storytelling voice... And I did wish to meet this one again." She gestured to one of the sitting stones that circled out from the Pillar. "May I?"

"You are always welcome to join me and mine, Lady Grey."

Eric watched as the Grey Lady sat upon the stone as if it were a throne, arranging her long, grey gown about her legs. He looked at the two eldest in the land, and saw a hint of the love the two of them had once shared in the mingling of glances. This was not the first time he had seen Lady Grey. The twins—Thomas and Thomasina—had once taken him to her secret home for tea. But that had been years ago, when he was just a baby.

"The twins will miss him when he's grown. Already, his iron eyes fail to see them from time to time."

Sees-the-Wind nodded. "Ever it is so with the young ones. They do not stay young for long."

Eric frowned as they talked around him. "How many?" he demanded. "How many apprentices have you had?"

The old man shook his head. "Many and many." He raised his chin and finished his telling.

"Binding the city of Kendrick to the land did more than protect the land. It gave safe harbor to many who can see

beyond this plain of existence. Powers grew as the city grew. As the city's borders grew, so did the borders we were all connected to. And where there is power, dark forces amass, drawn to it as a moth is to the flame.

"It became our duty to protect the land from more than those who came to claim it. Now, every year upon the anniversary of the Pact, it is renewed. The spirits are consulted. The dangers assessed. Plans for protection made. Responsibility assigned. There are many evil creatures that would dearly love to tear out the heart of Kendrick and consume it whole. Some of these creatures are already denizens of the city itself.

"The Makah and the Good Folk are the oldest guardians of the land, and it is a responsibility we will not shirk. We will protect the land we worship until we are no more."

Sees-the-Wind stopped for a moment and gazed at Eric. "That is the true story that *must* be remembered."

Eric looked between Sees-the-Wind and the Grey Lady. "Is it the anniversary of the Pact?"

"No. That comes in the fall, on the Autumn Equinox."

"When light becomes dark," the Grey Lady added with a secretive smile.

"Then, why are you here? It's not for me... is it?" Eric's voice held both a note of fear and pleasure.

She shook her head. "Not just for you, Iron Eyes." The Grey Lady turned her attention to Sees-the-Wind. "I have foreseen things."

The shaman glanced at the Lady with a question in his eyes, and Eric knew the question he was asking of her. "Let me stay. I'm his apprentice now." Eric knew the plea would be ignored, but he had to ask anyway.

"Terrible things." Her voice was neutral, neither permissive nor dismissive.

Sees-the-Wind nodded to her and shook his head at Eric. "Not this time. Soon. But not now." The old man gestured with his chin. "Go, and tell no one. We will speak again soon."

Knowing better than to argue, and still remembering the brief, terrible visage of the Shaman's anger, Eric nodded and slouched off with his hands in his pockets and his shoulders slumped.

The two eldest watched him go until he was out of sight. They sat together in companionable silence for a time. Then, Sees-the-Wind murmured, "Terrible things."

"Yes."

He nodded. "I've had troubling dreams lately."

"As have I."

"What have you seen, great Lady?"

"I have foreseen the end of me."

Sees-the-Wind gave her a sharp look, and saw no fear and no lie in her eyes. "A new Binding?"

"Perhaps. Perhaps not. The path is not clear, but the end of things... of me... as I am now is coming. Dormant powers rise. All of Kendrick is in danger."

"How soon?"

The Grey Lady looked into the distance again. "A few years. The blink of an eye. Iron Eyes is there, and is almost a man. It's why I wanted see him as he is now."

"There is time, then, to stop this?"

She shook her head with a sad smile. "No, dear one. What will be, will be."

He nodded. "When you end, so will I."

"Not necessarily." She stood in a smooth motion and crossed the circle to sit next to him. "I may not die. Just change."

Sees-the-Wind looked into her stone grey eyes and shook his head. "Binding or death. My end comes. I have seen too much. I do not appreciate a young man's youth anymore. The world has changed too much to be what the tribe and the land needs me to be."

She put an arm around his shoulders and pulled him to rest against her. "I have sensed this for a time. It's why I came now. A warning. And, the promise of respite. I did not understand why you chose to stay at the last Binding. You were tired then."

He rested against the warmth of her and pretended, just for a moment, she was Falling Petals once more. "It was not time yet." A pause. Then, "He has her eyes."

"Yes."

Sees-the-Wind pulled away and looked at her, searching her face, and seeing the same grey eyes his grandson—so many times removed—had.

Lady Grey smiled at him. "I, we, can see ourselves in him. It's why the twins love him so, and will mourn the loss of their childhood friend to maturity."

"He has her eyes, her temperament... and her talent."

"A worthy successor."

He nodded. "Finally." The weight of the ages lay in that single word. Then the shaman shook himself out of his melancholy. "But the foretelling. The rising power. What do we do?"

It was the Grey Lady's turn to be silent for a time. Sees-the-Wind did not interrupt her or press her with words. The two of them had had centuries to understand how the other thought and worked. The words would come in time.

When she spoke, the Grey Lady's voice was distant. "A girl will come who speaks for the city, for Kendrick. It will be a terrible day of theft and betrayal. Much hinges on what this girl does. Support her. Have the tribe support her. I believe through her, rather than my death, will my change come."

"She will Bind with you?"

The Lady shook her head, not a white hair falling out of place, "That will be for another. I cannot really see her yet, but she is a child of the city with a bond to the land. The path is unclear, but it is not the one who speaks for the city."

Sees-the-Wind took a long, slow breath. "I will know her when I see her?"

"Yes."

"Then I will trust my instincts."

"It is all we can do."

He reached out and took her hand in his, squeezing it gently. "Thank you for the warning... and for the promise. We will save you, but I admit, I look forward to my rest."

"As do we all, dear one."

They sat together for a very long time in the shadow of the Pillar of Memory. Both of them heard Iron Eyes sneak away with his companions. Neither of them said a thing.

***

"I have her eyes," Eric said with awe as he touched his face. He looked at Thomas and Thomasina for confirmation.

The dark haired twins glanced at each other, then as Thomas nodded, Thomasina spoke for them both. "Yes. You are their child through and through. The strongest we've felt in a long time. We believe the land senses the growing danger, and has gifted you with its bounty." She bit her lip. "It's one of the reasons we love you and why we helped you listen."

Eric nodded. "The Lady is in danger."

"Danger and more. The city, thus the land, is in danger." Thomasina sighed. "The Binding always changes us in some way."

"The Good Folk?"

"Yes. We are of the Lady, and she is us. She was one of the first... and the first to drive back the monsters."

Eric frowned as he looked at the twins. "Are the monsters coming here?"

Thomas nodded as Thomasina shrugged. "We think they might. They've ever searched for a way in. And, there's little else that concerns the Lady."

"What happens if she dies?"

The twins paused, silently consulting each other for a couple of moments. "We sleep," Thomasina finally answered. "We don't actually die, but we would sleep within the land for an age, unable to fulfill out part of the Pact with the Makah and with the land."

"I don't want you to go. You're my only friends."

Again, the wordless exchange. This time, Thomas spoke. "We can make you a promise. If the Lady survives the coming danger, when the Binding happens, we'll *change* for you. Just me and Thomasina. Not Theodore and Theodora."

"Change how?"

"Grow up with you."

"Be there for you," Thomasina added.

"Because I'll be the shaman of the tribe?" Eric looked between them.

Thomas shook his head. "Because you're our friend."

"And we need you as much as you need us." Thomasina grabbed his hand for a moment then pulled back into herself again.

"Promise me." Eric put out his hand, palm down. "Promise me you won't leave me."

Thomas and Thomasina placed their hands on top of his and spoke in unison. "We swear that we won't leave you for as long as we can. In this, we'll serve the Lady as best we can."

Eric felt the power of the promise binding the three of them together, and relaxed. "Thank you. I'll be brave when the danger comes with you at my side."

The twins nodded. "We will be brave together."

***

The Grey Lady looked up from her quiet reverie with Sees-the-Wind. "Those little scamps."

"What is it?" He tilted his head at her amused smile.

"It appears that yours and mine have bound themselves together. This... might change things."

"For good or ill?"

She gave a small shrug. "That remains to be seen. The wit and wisdom of youth often amazes me."

"The binding of the Good Folk and the Makah can never be bad. You and I have proven that." Sees-the-Wind nodded to her. "But it can make for unexpected happenings."

"Then we must wait and see." The Grey Lady smiled at him. "He really is our child, and may be the best hope for us all in the coming trials."

"Then may I train him to the best of my ability."

"It is all any of us can ask for and do."

The two smiled at each other, then settled comfortably together as they briefly became the young couple they once were. Husband and wife, hand in hand, in duty and love of the land.

Kendrick's Lady

"SO, THIS IS the house that killed my daughter." Mason stared at the Victorian house for a long time. He marveled at how much it blended into the neighborhood, even though it was the only Victorian on the block; a queen reigning over her less beautiful court. It was sheltered by evergreen trees and a perfectly aged white picket fence on all sides. He took another look at the two majestic turrets that gave it that feel of a storybook home before walking up to the front double door and knocking.

It was both shocking and expected when Julie opened the door. "Hi Dad. I've been expecting you. Please, come in."

He hesitated, looking at what appeared to be his daughter, suddenly alive. "Julie?"

"It'll all be explained over a nice cup of tea." She paused, then added. "The old rules of hospitality still hold here."

"Thank you." Mason took a breath to calm his frantically beating heart. He stepped over the threshold and looked at her. She was still beautiful, with the classic Steward features of black hair, light gray-colored eyes, and sharp cheekbones. "I thought... I heard you were lost to us."

"No." She stepped forward to hug him. "Not in the way that you might think."

He hugged his youngest daughter, savoring the warmth of her body and the pounding of her heart. She was alive. Alive, despite what the family's magic had told him. "Julie, how? What happened?"

"Please, come in. Let's talk."

Following her from the front door to the parlor, he could see she had continued the storybook motif inside with hardwood floors, crown moldings, overstuffed furniture and intricately detailed area rugs.

"This place..." He gestured to his surroundings. "It's exactly what I would have imagined for you if you could have built your own home. You always did love Victorian-style settings."

He sat down on the comfortable couch with his briefcase beside him but almost immediately jumped up again, his hand going for his pocket. Only his daughter's sharp words kept him from pulling a magical weapon.

"The rules of hospitality hold true in my home!"

His eyes stayed locked on the thing that had startled him: a pair of arms poking up from the floor—*just* arms and hands—holding a silver platter.

She remained seated in the chair she had chosen, watching both her father and what had surprised him. "The house will not harm you unless it feels that it or I are in danger. Please, Dad, let me explain. It's all right."

Mason sat back down and watched with cautious fascination. Out of the floor, the two arms carried a silver tea set. They flowed through the floor as if it were water. Their skin morphed to look like the part they traveled through: first tile, then wood, then carpet. He had the urge to touch one as it brought the silver tray to him. He wanted to see if the hand's skin felt like the floor or not. He reached out a hand toward it. "May I?"

Julie nodded. "Yes. No sudden moves. The house is still getting used to how humans act."

One hand held the service tray. Another gave Mason a cup of tea. He accepted it with one hand, holding out his other to touch. Obligingly, the hand stayed still and let its guest stroke the back of it. While that was happening, a third hand grew out of the carpet in front of him to steady the tray.

"It's warm and it feels like skin, even though it looks like carpet."

"Yes. Do you want sugar or milk for your tea?"

"Oh. Yes." He pulled his hand away from the one he had been examining and finished making his tea. When he was done, the hands, just two now, took the tea service back to the kitchen. He watched them with awe and curiosity. "Is that how the house manifests itself? Through those hands?"

"Yes." She sipped her tea.

He wrenched his attention back to his daughter. "According to the oracles, you're dead. But you seem very much alive to me. This house, the thing that was supposed to have killed you, is now in your name. Apparently, you bought it from a Reginald Kendrick? As in Colonel Reginald Kendrick?"

"My body is dead. I'm part of the house now and, consequently, part of Kendrick. As for the paperwork, the city has learned to mimic human ways as necessary. I'm sure it used the name Reginald Kendrick because that is its namesake."

He looked at her, so calm and serene. He was not sure just how to take her acceptance of the fact that she was dead but not. "Julie, what happened to you? How did this all come about?" He gestured to the room around them. "This place didn't exist twenty five years ago. Twenty years ago, it was a one-room shack. Fifteen, it was a small, nondescript house."

"Kendrick is growing up. This is just one of the ways it is exploring its environment. Manifesting itself here. The city is alive and this part of it is awake; specifically, self-aware. It was woken up by three acts: An act of violence, an act of nurturing, and an act of acceptance."

"Would you tell me about them?"

"If you will listen."

"May I record it for the family archives?"

She nodded. "Kendrick is aware of our family's history and duty. It's one of the reasons it chose me." She waited until he was ready, tape recorder out, pen and paper in hand to make notes, and to ask questions later. He was a thorough man, her father. It was something she sincerely appreciated about him.

"It started with an act of violence." Julie said. "These things always seem to start with blood."

***

He took his prize to the abandoned house on Yarrow Street, where he'd been squatting for a few weeks. When he first found it, he was certain it was a sign from God, telling him that this is where he was meant to be. The house was empty, but in surprisingly good condition for its unused state. He had fixed up one of the rooms for himself and the precious ones he'd bring back here to play with.

"We're home, and you've been such a good girl!" His voice was chipper as he carried the little girl through the empty house to the bedroom. It was sparse and immaculate with only a plastic covered mattress and a couple boxes placed neatly side-by-side. Dusty light streamed in through cracks in the shuttered window.

He put the doll down on the mattress and sat beside her. "We're gonna play now, okay? You like to play, don't you?"

"Yes," the doll's soft voice was barely a whisper.

"You're gonna be my doll and we're gonna have lots of fun together. Then, I'll take you home." He loved that look of shining hope on his dolls' faces. It made them so lovely. Of course, he also loved that look of fear and pain. There was nothing he did not love about his precious ones.

"I want to go home." Her eyes were liquid with held back tears.

"Now, now. What's the rule I taught you? Say it for me. Be a good doll."

"Dolls don't scream. Dolls don't cry. Dolls do as they're told and they don't die." She recited. Her voice was dull as the hope drained away. She pushed at the escaping tears with the backs of her hands.

"Right. Dolls do as they're told. We're gonna play doctor now. I'm gonna be the doctor. You're gonna be the patient." He reached over to the first box, pulling out a pair of scissors and a scalpel.

***

She had broken too quickly. It left him feeling cheated and dissatisfied. "Trash. Garbage. Broken. Nothing." He sneered at it. "You're nothing, you stupid doll. Nothing. Why'd you break so easily? Flawed. Bad. Filthy! Look at you. You did this on purpose just to piss me off. Well, you did, you stupid bitch. You happy now?"

He grabbed the broken doll by the foot and dragged her remains through the house, heedless of the bloody smears trailing after him. He didn't care about them. All that was important was to get this trash out of his sight and in the ground as quickly as possible. He did not want a broken doll in his house. "No. I have higher standards than that, and I will find a better doll than you." He dumped her into the already-prepared hole and used his fury to fill it as quick as he could.

When he returned to the bedroom, he didn't notice that the blood in the hallway and kitchen had disappeared. Instead, he scrubbed the mattress, the floor, and the wall behind the mattress. He ended this ritual by scouring himself raw in the bathroom, crying tears of shame, anger, and desire as the blood and dirt washed down the drain.

***

Weeks later, he found his doll again. This one was a little older and bigger, but that meant she would be stronger than the previous inferior one. She would last long enough to satisfy him. Not like the other one. Pushing away the irritating memory of the flawed doll, he petted the shining hair of the sleeping doll beside him, baring his teeth in a grotesque smile. She would be the perfect doll.

He was sad that he'd had to drug the girl but, unlike so many of the others, she had struggled, yelling for help when he pulled her from her bike. Judicious use of chloroform dealt with the problem quickly enough. It was a shame, because he liked to talk to his dolls as he took them back to the playhouse. It was a way of getting to know each other. He especially liked to teach them the rule. He recited it to himself.

He pulled around the back of his playhouse and got out, gently picking his precious one up and carried her inside. The house was immaculate as ever. He was always so careful to prepare for his playmates. As usual, all of the rooms were empty except for the bathroom and the playroom. The playroom was special. This is where he brought his doll.

After placing her on the plastic covered mattress, he sat next to his boxes of toys, admiring how they reflected the light. He would not force the girl awake. He wanted to watch her blissful slumber shift from confusion at waking into an unfamiliar place to outright fear. It was a rare thing for him; a special treat from his perfect doll.

He hummed his tune to himself until he realized that he wasn't humming alone. A sweeter, higher-pitched voice had joined his. Quickly, he looked to see if his doll was awake. She should not be and was not. Listening, he thought he could hear the rule repeated over and over in a whisper. Confused, he stood and looked around. The voice was louder now but he still could not make out the words. "Who's there?"

He picked up a knife from one of the boxes and started prowling through the empty house. The voice turned into a distinct giggle as it seemed to run from him, always sounding like it was in the next room. He stomped through the kitchen to the dining room, shouting, "Where are you? You don't belong here! This is for me and my doll."

Hearing the laugh behind him, he turned around to see a discarded pink ribbon on the floor. He knew it had not been there earlier. He picked it up and smelled it. It smelled like the last doll; the flawed one that had broken so quickly. He threw it down in disgust.

"Tony, don't yell. Tony, don't lie. Tony, do as you're told and you won't die."

The sweet, sing-song voice startled him, making him whirl around with his knife held high. In the doorway stood the flawed doll. She looked like she had when he'd first brought her here. He stared at her, speechless.

"But you lie all the time, don't you, Tony?" Her voice held a note of maliciousness that clashed with her angelic face.

"I threw you away. I buried you. You were broken." Tony watched as she turned and started skipping down the hallway toward the playroom where his precious one was, singing the bastardization of his rule. His sudden rage broke his paralysis. "No! You stay away from her. She's mine." He ran after the broken doll, skidding to a stop in the playroom. She stood between him and his perfect one. "Go away. You don't belong here. This place is mine and she's mine."

"No. You don't belong here. She doesn't belong to you. This isn't your house and the house doesn't like you." The girl crossed her arms.

With a furious roar, he lunged forward, intending to break her again. Then he was falling. He hit the floor hard, the knife in his hand skittering away. Looking back to see what he had tripped over, he saw that hands had grown out of the floor and gripped his ankles. More hands grew out of the floor around him, grabbing him and holding him down. Horrified, he screamed.

"Tony, don't scream. Tony, don't lie. Tony, do as you're told and you won't die." The doll's voice floated to him as the hands pulled him away from her. He screamed again as he saw one of the hands carrying his knife over to him. It flowed through the floor and stopped inches from him, poised in almost a questioning stance. Two hands clamped over his mouth to stop his screams. He looked to the broken doll, his eyes pleading for help.

"You screamed. You lied. The house doesn't like you. Now, you die." She turned from him to the still sleeping doll; his perfect one. He struggled like a trapped rat as the hands gripped him tighter. The hand with the knife stabbed him in the leg. The hands muffled his scream of pain, holding him in place. In his bucking struggles, he saw the hands carrying the mattress with his perfect doll from the room, followed by the flawed one, who shut the door behind her.

The rest of the hands pulled his toys from the boxes and advanced on him. Knives rose, poised above him. Garden shears opened and closed with hesitant jerks. Rubber tubing slithered along the ground toward him. Each toy was brought forward. The last thing he saw was the scalpel as it flashed towards his eyes.

***

"The little girl, Rachel, was found asleep on the mattress on the porch by someone passing by. When the police came, they found no evidence that anyone had been in the house for years. The house learned a lot from the murdered girl, Theresa, and from the child murderer. It learned the difference between innocence and guilt, as well as guile and revenge. It was the first time Kendrick had actually experienced these emotions for itself, and not through someone else secondhand." Julie gave her empty tea cup to one of the attentive hands.

"Rachel Samson? I heard about that. The papers said that the kidnapper must have been spooked at all of the press." Mason jumped at the sudden loud crash from the hallway. A statue rolled into view, and a black and white tuxedo cat sauntered in after it. "Oh. I half-expected the murdered girl." He watched as the hands appeared; some to pet the obviously spoiled feline and one to clean up the mess.

"Theresa is here somewhere. She's understandably shy of men. This is Theron, otherwise known as the fat cat."

Mason furrowed his brow. "How do you know what actually happened?"

"I know everything that has happened here since Kendrick manifested this place. I know a lot more about the city as well. It is part of my memory now." She held up a hand to forestall his further questions. "How and why is another story, and I'm getting to it. I promise. That was the act of violence. Next is the act of compassion."

***

The homeless man shuffled down the street. It was cold, gray, and rainy. This was not his usual neighborhood. In fact, he wasn't sure how he'd gotten here, but now that he was he kept walking, looking for shelter. It was an almost suburban neighborhood; too close to the city center to truly be suburban, and not close enough to the Gateway district to really worry about the police patrols those hoity-toity rich people insisted on having.

The sharp squawk of unhappiness caught his attention and he lifted his head, peering around. He kept walking and the high pitched squeaks got louder. He stopped at the yard of an unlighted house. The desperate call of the baby animal allowed him to hone in on it. "Oh, look at you." He said as he carefully reached under a bush and pulled out a bedraggled black and white kitten. "You poor thing. All alone, just like me." He held the shivering kitten close. "We need to get dry."

He walked up to the porch of the house. The door was locked. "Oh, come on, please? It's cold and we need to get dry. Please?" He tried the door again. This time it opened. "There. That's better." He stepped inside and closed the door behind him. The house was dark and empty, but unexpectedly warm. Perhaps someone had forgotten to turn off the utilities when they left. It was a good turn of fortune for him and his new friend. He stripped off the wet outer layers of his ragged clothing and spread them out to dry. His long johns were still dry. He tucked the kitten inside his shirt to warm it. He was rewarded with a purr from the tired baby.

He explored the house, looking to see if there was anything worth salvaging. The house was like a treasure chest. Everything he could want was here. There was a mattress and a blanket in one of the back bedrooms. The place still had running water. He bet it had electricity. A squeak from within his shirt informed him that his kitten was awake. The continued squeaks and urgent suckling on his fingertip when he petted it told him that the kitten was very hungry. "Let's see if there's anything to eat. I don't know if we're gonna be that lucky, Theron."

Pausing, he wondered at the name. He searched his patchy memory and came up with odd images of himself in front of a classroom. "Theron is Greek for hunter," he said to himself as he lost the hazy memory. "Good enough name for a cat." He rummaged around in the kitchen and let out a whoop of delight. He showed his prize to the kitten: a single can of chicken noodle soup. "We gonna eat tonight. You're my new good luck charm."

Fixing dinner consisted of opening the can with his old army field can opener and getting his trusty spoon from his bag. He mixed the soup up, then dipped a finger in and fed the kitten. Theron was clearly ravenous. So was he. However, he fed the kitten almost as much as he did himself. "You should be eating milk and wet cat food. Why'd your momma abandon you? Did you wander away and get lost? I get lost a lot. I don't remember too well."

After eating, he took the blanket and made it into a mound on the bed, nestling the kitten within. He decided to take advantage of the running water while he could and shower; his first in weeks. It warmed him inside and out. He never realized that the towel waiting for him after his shower hadn't been there before he went in. Same with the comb on the sink. In his mind, both had always been with him.

From the shower, he returned to the living room and put on all of the layers of clothing he wore to ward off the cold. He automatically packed up what he brought with him and headed out the door into the night. It was sad to leave the warm, dry place, but he had places to be, things to do, people to talk to. He paused at the sidewalk with the nagging feeling that he was forgetting something, but could not place what. After a moment of trying to remember, he looked around uncertainly. He wasn't sure how he'd got here on Yarrow Street, but he belonged in the City Center. He set off in that direction.

Inside the house, the kitten slept in the blissful warmth of a full belly and a soft bed. Tentative, the hands grew out of the floor and walls to examine the tiny creature that the man had taken such care of. Mimicking his motions, one of the hands stroked the kitten. It purred in response. More hands hovered about, watching and waiting.

When the kitten woke again and gave off its demanding squeak to be fed, the hands went into a flurry of motion. Two held the kitten, a third pet it and a fourth brought out milk in a shallow bowl. Theron messily ate his fill. Afterwards, the hands cleaned up the kitten, petting it until it went back to sleep. They placed the kitten back on the blanket and began to wait again.

***

"That was when the house started to learn the joy of caring for someone. The homeless man had been so kind and gentle with the kitten. It taught the house the good side of humanity."

"What happened to the homeless man? Do you know?"

"Kendrick takes care of him. He doesn't remember much. He lives in an almost perpetual state of now. He was once a favorite teacher at the high school. He taught Greek, Latin, Italian and Spanish. Greek history was his passion."

"Maybe I should get him some help."

"I don't know, Dad. Kendrick is very good to its favorites. I don't think he needs help. Despite the memory loss, the man is happy, and Kendrick makes sure to provide all he needs."

Mason hesitated a moment, then asked, "Are you happy?"

Julie nodded. "Happier than I ever was in life. Now, I know who I am and where I belong." Her father frowned at her, not understanding. "Let me explain. It finishes out the awakening of the house, why I'm here and what happened to me."

He nodded.

***

Julie turned right onto Yarrow Street from North Main. Her mind ticked over her errands for the day until something caught her eye: an ordinary-looking house, but there was something about it...

She slowed down to look at it, then pulled over to prevent an accident. Stepping out of the car, she knew that there was something very special about this place. It was the one Steward family gift she had and she had it in abundance: the ability to know when something of less than mundane nature was occurring near her. It was the only family gift she had received, and right now it was on high alert.

All thoughts of classes, studying, and errands were gone. She had to know more about the house. Her sharp eyes took in the details of it and saw its potential. A few more fir trees around the property line for privacy, some grooming to the overgrown lawn and a flowerbed to weed. The only thing missing was a "For Sale" sign on the front gate. She wanted this house. Staring at it for a long time, all she could think was that it was perfect. Just like that, she accepted the house and felt that the house had accepted her.

The decision made, she noted the address and got back in her car to continue her way to city hall. Instead of doing the errands she had previously planned, she would look up the title of the home, see if she could track down the owner and convince them to sell it to her. She would be persuasive, or she would get the rest of her family involved to be persuasive for her.

The next day, she returned on foot. It was less than three miles from the Steward estate to the house on Yarrow Street. She was used to taking long walks to work out her frustration. This particular frustration was the inability to find any paperwork on the house at all. Without that knowledge, she didn't know who to speak to about buying the house.

When she arrived, her eyes widened. The house and its yard had changed. There were more fir trees around its edge and the front lawn was beautifully groomed. Even the flowerbed was ready for planting. She knew this should not be possible. At the same time, growing up a Steward taught her that the word "impossible" did not seem to apply to the city of Kendrick.

Looking up and down the street, she noticed that there were a lot more fir trees at every house. In light of that, there was nothing unusual about her house. It fit right in. "Hey, kid!" She called to a boy down the way, "Do you know who lives here?"

"I don't know. I haven't seen anyone in there for a while."

"Okay. Thanks."

"You gonna move in?" He looked at her with a greater interest.

"I might." She smiled at him, turning back to the house. She watched as a black and white tuxedo cat sauntered to the porch from around back. It meowed a greeting at her, then plopped to its side in a sunbeam, exposing its furry white tummy in a clear come-pet-me invitation.

Without hesitation, she opened the gate and walked up to the cat. "Hello there. I'm Julie." She offered her hand for a sniff before tentatively petting the cat's soft fur. "Do you live here?" The cat meowed again, seeming to answer in the positive. "I wish I lived here. I really like this place. I'd like to look around inside."

As if on cue, the front door clicked open and swung outward. Julie stepped back, waiting for the person at the door to appear. After a moment, the cat got up and walked to the threshold. It meowed one last time over its shoulder and sauntered in.

Julie watched this with fascination. "Hello?" She called to the open door. "Is anyone there?"

Silence. Though, not an uncomfortable one. It felt anticipatory. She stepped on the porch and peeked inside. "Hello? Your door is open." Looking around, she saw that the place was bare. It made her smile. No one was living here—yet. She entered and closed the door behind her. The handle of the door was warm. She looked down to see that it was an ornate ivory handle; the kind she loved.

"Hello?" She called out into the silence again. When no answer came, she convinced herself that the wind must have opened the door at the same time as her comment. With a small laugh at herself, she began to explore the home. In each room, she stopped and imagined how she would decorate it; what colors and what furniture. She wished she had a notebook to jot down her ideas.

Her head brimmed with plans for what she would do with this place once it was hers as she walked back toward the front of the house, even more determined to own it now. Houses had auras, and she could tell that this one liked her as much as she liked it. However, as she entered the living room, all of her plans and ideas were forgotten. In the time that it took for her to investigate the rest of the house, somehow, someone had come in and decorated the living room exactly as she had imagined it.

She was frightened at first, uncertain of what was happening. She knew magic was at work here. She just did not know how, why, or who. But without anyone there to explain it, she was left studying the living room layout. In the back of her mind, she decided that she wanted to shift one of the tables and a lamp to see what it would look like.

Before she could take a step, hands grew out of the floor and wall and began to move the furniture as she wished.

"Holy crap!"

The hands froze at her surprised explicative.

Don't want?

Julie looked around. She realized that the question was more felt in her head than heard. "Just surprised."

Don't like?

She could feel the clear disappointment and realized it was coming from the house. "No. No. Just surprised." She repeated. "Please, go ahead and move the furniture. I'd like to see how it will look." The hands sprang into action again and moved the furniture to the spots she had considered.

Happy?

"Yes. It looks wonderful." She stepped into the living room and sat down on the edge of one of the overstuffed chairs. "What are you? Are you the spirit of the house?"

Kendrick.

"Kendrick? You mean the city of Kendrick?"

Yes.

Her heart sped up again. Her father had postulated that this could happen in the future. The city could manifest itself in some manner as part of its personal evolution, but he had never discussed this situation.

You're afraid. You don't like me?

"No. No. Surprised. Startled. I love this house. You. I really do. It's new. It's the sudden change. There is always surprise in change. Sometimes there's fear."

You like me?

"Yes. I do. Very much. I want to stay here. I want to live here forever. This place, you, makes me feel like I finally belong. I—I've never belonged with my family, but here it all seems so perfect." There was a long moment of nothing. She was afraid she had confused it with her blurt of enthusiasm. "Hello? I'm sorry if I—"

Tea?

"T?"

Would you like some tea?

"Oh. Yes. Thank you." She sat back in the chair, curious at what would happen next. She waited in silence, turning over the idea of her living in a house that literally had the personality of the city in it. The thought made her smile. Soon, the hands returned with a silver tea service and presented it to her. As she fixed the tea the way she liked it, she asked, "If you are the city, who owns this land? This house?"

I do.

"Did you do the paperwork for it? I couldn't find anything. No title. No permits. No history. Nothing for me to work from so I can own it legally." There was a long silence before the house answered her.

I still have much to learn about the way things are done in your world.

"I can tell you anything you want to know." She sipped her tea, enjoying its sweet citrus taste.

I am alone. I have my favorites, but I only watch them, helping them if they need it. They do not know me. I do not want to be alone any longer.

"I've always been alone. I've never fit in anywhere. Not in society. Not in school. Not even in my own family. I have almost none of their talents. They have never known what to make of me. I can't help them with their rituals, and we have nothing in common but blood."

You may stay here with me if you wish.

"Yes. I wish. I want it very much." She yawned sleepily. "It feels right."

Do you really wish to stay with me forever? I am able to make it happen.

"Yes. I do. I belong here. I can help you learn about the human world." One of the waiting hands took the mostly empty tea cup before it could fall from her nerveless fingers. Her head lolled to one side in a drugged sleep.

Then, more hands appeared around her, one petted her hair, and another stroked her arm. There was a silent communion as one of the hands produced a scalpel. A hand held her hair away from her face; another supported her head while the last hand slit her throat. The gush of blood was immediate and lethal.

The chair morphed into a dozen or more hands, supporting her unmoving body as they stretched her out on the floor, eyes closed with a smile on her lips. Quickly, the rushing blood slowed to a trickle and her breath stopped. Every drop of Julie's blood disappeared as soon as it touched the floor. When the blood stopped, the hands lifted her body up and carried it into the back part of the house through a glowing door that had not been there before.

**

"There was no pain. Almost no transition for me. I fell asleep. I died. The house, the city, Kendrick, absorbed me. I woke up in my bedroom. I was here, like this. This body of mine is a construct of the city; part of it. Just like this house is. But, it feels like it always did to me. Only now, I am more aware. I am part of the city. I may go anywhere the city exists. If I really want to, I may sit here and view any part of the city I wish. And I can go there."

Mason stared at his daughter, his pen still, his paper empty of notes. "You are the city now?"

"No. Kendrick is the city. I am just a part of that. A small, distinct part."

"I don't know what to say."

"Be happy for me, father. I finally have a purpose. I know what I need to do."

"What is that?"

"To help Kendrick learn. To protect him from those who would harm him."

"Him?"

"He is named after a man. Most people in the city think of the city in masculine terms. It affects him."

"This is astonishing. I knew our family had a calling, but I didn't realize it would extend to this. There's so much more the Steward family will be able to do now."

"No." The word was firm in its statement.

"No?" Mason gazed at Julie with a mixture of confusion and curiosity.

"The Steward family and its members are the acknowledged caretakers of Kendrick. But, they must continue as they have always done. I cannot allow anyone to harm or influence the city through this house. No one."

"But, Julie, this was meant to be." Mason said. "I looked at the satellite photos. This place came into being the year you were born. It grew up as you did. It..." He looked at the expression on her face and stopped. "Why not?"

"The city is alive. You know that. It has been self-aware for some time. But not on this level. It watches. It has its favorites and its enemies. Now, it is starting to experience emotions for itself firsthand. Real emotions. I can't allow anyone to manipulate that. Not even with the best intentions at heart. If a real problem arises, you can, of course, come and talk to me or call me. Or I may come to you to let you know of something going on. But, I have to be careful. Where one person may be altruistic, another may not be."

Mason wanted to argue. But he needed to think about this new information, and to consult with the family first. This changed things for everyone. Finally, he nodded. "All right. I see what you're saying. I need to go. To think about this."

She stood when he did. "Thank you, dad. I know it's not easy. Come back soon. Or invite me over."

He stifled his desire to protest and say that his home would always be her home, but he knew that was no longer true. This was her home now. "I will, kiddo. I will. I love you."

"I love you, too." They embraced and parted.

Mason walked down the walk and out the gate to his car. He paused a moment to look back at the home, taking in the gabled roof and conical turret tops. It really was the storybook home of his daughter's making. It made him both happy and sad, but he couldn't put his finger on why.

"Hello!" A chipper female voice brought him out of his thoughts. "Are you moving in? I'm Sandra Macintosh from next door." She stood on the sidewalk by her mailbox.

"Oh, no. I just came to visit my daughter."

"She must be 'Kendrick's Lady' now."

"What?" He was surprised at the woman's comment.

"The house. Most Victorian homes have a name. This one's called 'For Kendrick's Lady.' I guess that makes your daughter—"

"Julie."

"Julie." She continued, "Kendrick's Lady."

"I guess it does." Mason nodded, clenching his fists while keeping his face neutral to hide his pain as he looked back at the house, and the city that had claimed his daughter as its own.

Dick's Muse

"FOSSILS, MY ASS." Dick tossed the book on writing, written by an author more famous and successful than he, to the table. "Stories aren't like fossils to be grubbed over in the dirt." He told his pedigree Persian cat, Mr. Kitty, who had wandered over for a few good cuddles. "Stories are new friends and you have to talk to them. Get to know them. Love them. Get them to tell you their secrets." Dick smiled at the indulged cat in his lap. "Isn't that right, Mr. Kitty? Yes, Daddy's always right."

He sighed. It was not the stupid metaphor that was bothering him. Stupid metaphors could be forgiven. It was the writing exercise. It was eerily close to his personal situation. He, Richard Carter, known as Dick to his friends, had married the lovely Charity. They had a beautiful daughter, Haley, who was four and was currently at a friend's birthday party next door. Charity had gone insane, and was now in the Kendrick Asylum after trying to kill him. It was almost exactly the writing lead-in for the exercise.

Granted, there were differences: They were still married. There was never a court restraining order. It was not a prolonged period of stalking. The doctors had termed it a 'psychotic break,' and recommended that Charity be remanded to their expert custody for observation and treatment. After all, she had been an exemplary member of society up until the break and, with therapy, she could be again.

With another sigh, he pushed the protesting Mr. Kitty from his lap and went to the kitchen for a drink. He cracked open a diet soda, took a long swallow, and made an appreciative noise at the familiar sweet burn before returning to the living room. After a moment of aimless indecision, he picked up the TV remote. There was another pause as a silent debate waged in his head. This was his writing time and turning on the TV would destroy any thoughts of creative productivity for the rest of the day.

The real problem was that his stories, his beloved friends, were not speaking to him. Not like they normally did. He figured it was why he had been so restless since he arrived home. It was also why he had picked up that book on writing again. He obviously already knew how to write. He had sold five novels in the last three years. Still, it was good to keep up with what the other well-known authors were saying. Maybe he would write his own book on writing. People were always clamoring for it.

The TV clicked on as the decision to give it up for the day was made. *"... breaking story. There has been a mass escape from the Kendrick Mental Health Center today. It is a story stranger than fiction..."* The News woman in front of the familiar home for the criminally insane was saying. *"... One of the Kendrick Asylum orderlies simply opened all of the locked doors of the Asylum and let the inmates go. When asked why, as he was taken into custody, the orderly, Steve Bellingham, was reported to have said, 'She was right. She didn't belong here. So, I let her go.' Many of the escaped inmates have already been recaptured..."*

Dick stopped listening. For a moment, he stopped everything. No breathing. No heartbeat. No thinking. The remote control slipped from nerveless fingers and turned off the TV as it hit the floor. Suddenly, everything made sense. When he could think again, he took a deep breath and could smell it; her perfume. It was called 'Dorian' and both of them had been wickedly charmed by both the description and the scent.

"The only way to get rid of a temptation is to yield to it. Resist it and your soul grows sick with longing for the things it has forbidden itself. Inspired by the eternal, beautiful, wicked Dorian Gray—a Victorian fougere with three pale musks and dark sugared vanilla tea."

The woman's voice floated to him from the doorway of the living room reciting his thought to him as he had it. "It is considered a gender neutral scent, but it always smelled better on me."

He turned to look at his wife with growing horror and fear. "C-Charity."

"Yes, we're both here and we're both pissed. You have been a very naughty boy, Dick."

"I can explain."

"What's there to explain, Dick? You summoned a muse, me, and stuffed me in your wife's body because she wasn't doing it for you anymore. She wasn't inspiring you because she was taking care of the baby. No longer mistress, mother, muse, and maid. Just a tired mother and maid because you were too damn busy 'trying to write.'"

"That's not true. I helped out when I could." He backpedaled into his den as she advanced. He ran around behind his large cherry wood desk, pressing himself against the wall there. "I was going to let you go. I swear it. As soon as I finished this last book."

"Really..." She kicked away the throw rug revealing the remains of the ritual circle. Old blood, animal and menstrual, still stained the wood floor. "I see you were all ready to do so."

"Charity..." His hands were raised in a conciliatory gesture.

"My name is not Charity. It's Somnia. Charity's letting me take the lead on this one. No more lies, Dick. I'm a goddess. A minor one, but still a bloody goddess. I know your mind. I've been hearing your thoughts since you bound me to be your concubine muse. What better way to be inspired to than to fuck the stories out of me, eh?"

"What do you want? Do you want me to free you? I'll do it. I still have the book."

"I'm already free."

"What?"

"Free, Dick. You made a mistake. You let them take me away. For the last three years, I have been in a place where people don't always think you're crazy because they really are. You aren't the only person who can do rituals. I convinced a doctor to do one for me. I convinced him it was all I needed to set me on the right path. Him, a believer, and an artist. A real one. It took them a while to get all of the ingredients, but they finally did. They freed me a couple nights ago."

Understanding dawned in his eyes. That was when his friends had stopped talking to him. His well of plots and characters had mysteriously dried up. Since he was only editing his latest book, it was a livable, if disturbing, situation. He had grown used to his friends talking to him all the time.

"Friends, my ass." She closed and locked the den door. "They weren't your friends. They were kidnapped hostages. Do you realize because of you, no one in Kendrick has had a single worthy thought while driving in the last three years?"

"What? I don't understand."

"Of course, you don't, Dick. Do you have any idea which muse I am? No. You never bothered to ask. You just grabbed the first muse who came by and stuffed her in your unsuspecting wife's body. I had been in the middle of inspiring Mark Mullen on his nightly drive when you imprisoned me and stole his inspiration."

"Mark Mullen? I stole his inspiration?" He was impressed in spite of himself.

"I'm the bloody muse of the Zen drive. People all over the world worship me with lattes and sing their praises to me with the songs on the radio as they drive to and from work. I whisper hints on how to solve that problem at the office, what to get the wife for her birthday, and fill the special ones with stories to be told. Luckily for the world, I was able to halt your thievery at the borders of Kendrick."

"Mark Mullen." He murmured. "How was he able to keep writing?"

"Talent, which you don't have." She shrugged. "We minor muses like to talk to him."

"Why? Why him and not me?" The whine in his voice made him cringe more than his fear of the angry muse in his wife's body. But, before he died, he had to know why they had passed him over. "Why have you always talked to him and not me?"

"Because, you don't listen. You never have." Somnia stepped forward. "I don't think you get the picture, Dick. This isn't about you, your failings, or your wants. This about me and what I'm going to do to you for what you have done to me."

"But, you're free. You don't have to do anything to me."

"Yes. I do. You did this once to a muse. You'll do it again."

"I won't. I promise. I won't trap another muse. I won't ever write another word." They both knew this was a lie as soon as it left his lips.

She ignored his protests. "As much as I inspire people to great things, I also inspire them to think of, if not do, terrible things. Do you know how many people fantasize about torturing and murdering their bosses or co-workers on a daily basis as they drive home? They imagine it in great detail. It helps them cope. Sometimes, they imagine hurting themselves. Sometimes, they just have random insane thoughts. From now on, you will know about every horrible, painful thought..." She smiled at him. "...and you will experience each happening to you for the rest of your miserable life."

Dick's protests died before they were born. He forgot all about Somnia, his wife, and his unfinished novel as someone stabbed him through the hand with a pen and another person kicked him in the ass so hard he thought his tailbone was broken.

Somnia stepped from Charity's body. The two women looked at each other for a long moment before looking down at the man at their feet writhing in agony with breathless screams on his lips.

***

"I heard that he just went mad—like in one of his books. They found him curled up in his office, insane, and screaming that people were torturing him."

"I never liked his books. Just cheap knock-offs of Mark Mullen's novels."

"Wasn't it strange how Charity got well so quickly after she found out her husband had lost it? I mean, it's weird."

"I heard they found her shopping at the grocery store. She was very calm and sweet when they picked her up. They almost thought they had the wrong person. She was so willing to help. Maybe, she was never really crazy. Who hasn't daydreamed of killing their husband after the thousandth time they forgot to bring home the milk? I've also heard that writers are notoriously hard to live with. Maybe, she just snapped."

The other woman laughed. "I know Tony's come close to death a few times."

"It's good to have her home. I always liked her better than her husband. He always seemed so needy."

The two gossiping women waved and smiled at Charity as she arrived home from a walk with her young daughter. Charity returned both the smile and the wave. "She was always a better friend than Dick. I can't say I'm sorry that they've switched places.

A Card Given

JOHN CORSO SAT at the poker table; it wasn't where he wanted to be, but it was where he needed to be to get what he wanted. The traditional hexagonal poker table with green felt top was out of sorts with the flow of Japanese decorations of *Sushi-Ya*. But, there was no safer place to have a high stakes game of this particular caliber.

Of the other three men and one woman at the table, only the man across the felt from him mattered. Sandeep Gowda was an older Indian man with graying temples. He wore loose cloth trousers, a silky, mandarin-style shirt, and a waist sash complete with a ceremonial dagger. John, on the other hand, wore his usual khakis, rumpled button-up shirt, and tweed jacket. John appreciated what an odd contrast they were.

Akira Yamamoto, the dealer and one of the owners of *Sushi-Ya*, nodded to them. "Are you prepared?"

John glanced at his second, Mason, an older man in a business suit, then nodded. "I am."

Sandeep patted the leg of his second, Puja, a gorgeous Indian woman in a loose cotton dress, and nodded. "I am."

"Gentlemen and lady." Akira clapped his hands once. The tattooed men around the room left, sliding the rice paper doors closed behind them. "*Sushi-Ya* has agreed to host this game. All in this room are bound by the rules of hospitality. All in this room agreed to them. The game results are final." He bowed to the room. "Remember, you came to us."

John nodded to Akira. "I understand. I'm sure this will be a friendly game."

"I don't know about friendly." Sandeep shook his head. "Fair, though."

"A fair game, then." John fiddled with an unlit cigarette.

"Ante up, gentlemen." Akira's eyes crinkled into a mass of laugh lines.

Mason leaned to John. "Are you certain you want to do this? Really? Something this important... left to a game of chance?" He held a box out to John. It was about six by nine inches, and an inch tall.

"Poker is a game of skill, Mr. Steward." Sandeep's silky voice was filled with mirth. "I find it interesting that your second is the mayor of Kendrick himself." Sandeep gave Mason a respectful nod. Mason returned it, his mouth a firm line of disapproval.

"Not so much skill as luck, considering the rules we've agreed upon." John tucked the cigarette into an inner pocket before accepting the box. "And I find it interesting that your second is a slave." He gestured to the tattoo on the woman's collarbone.

Puja flushed as she handed a similar box to Sandeep. Then she pulled the collar of her dress closed, hiding the small star-shaped tattoo.

Sandeep's smile cut like a knife. "My property knows to keep my property safe... or pay the price."

The two of them looked at each other, both reluctant to be the first to reveal their bounty. John shook his head and opened his box, revealing the exquisite Todari tarot card within. It was the eighteenth Major Arcana, the Moon. As always, the vivid colors made him catch his breath. This image was of a crescent moon. Sitting on the inner curve of the crescent was a beautiful woman with long, flowing dark hair and a diaphanous white gown. Below her, on the edge of a lake, were two dogs howling and barking up at her as she looked off to the side, unconcerned. Crawling out of the lake from the other side was something that appeared to be a lobster.

"'Imagination, intuition, and dreams for you. But for one you love, bad luck may ensue. Unseen perils, possible woes. Deceptions abound with secret foes.'" John stroked the edge of the card with an affectionate finger. "'Storms are weathered, peace at a cost. Practicality wins, imagination is lost.'"

He held it out to Akira, speaking in a careful, formal tone of voice. "I give this card to you. It is my willing ante into this game."

Sandeep nodded, appreciative. Puja smiled at the dark-haired woman on the card. Opening his box, Sandeep revealed the Two of Pentacles from the Todari tarot deck. Not a Major Arcana card, but no less stunning.

John clenched his hands under the table to keep himself from grabbing at the card. He'd never seen it before tonight. Leaning forward, he drank in the vivid colors of its image.

The Two of Pentacles card showed a young woman wearing a peasant's dress as she planted flowers. Ignoring the fallen autumn leaves, she planted these flowers in a box protected by an overhang. Two of the blossoms were in the shape of pentacles. One pentacle flower was already planted.

The second was being planted. The young woman's face shone with hope, even in the lateness of the year.

John smiled and nodded. "That's the one. *'Harmony and agility in changing times. New projects are running too far behind.'* Although... *'Juggled events fall apart. Forced laughter, not of the heart. Messages in writing, letters to start.'"*

"I give this card to you." Sandeep handed the Two of Pentacles to Akira. "It's my willing ante into this game."

Akira accepted both cards with the gravitas of a priest. He took a moment to look at them both. "They are beautiful. I've never seen one in the flesh, much less two. Is it true? That they give you powers?"

"Yes." Sandeep nodded.

"They loan you their strength. Only the owners may share in it." John corrected.

"I would joke about being their owner now, but I know how many people have died trying to collect these artifacts." Akira's smile disappeared to be replaced with the non-expression he usually wore. "There will be three hands, no betting. I will gift the winner with these two exquisite Todari cards."

Akira placed the cards in front of him, face down. The effect was immediate. Everyone relaxed and focused on each other instead of the cards. Akira opened a new deck of mundane playing cards and began shuffling them.

"I was surprised to get your call and the offer of the game." Sandeep tapped the edge of the table twice with his ring. "How many Todari cards do you have now?"

John took of his glasses and started cleaning them. "Would you tell me how many you had if I asked?"

"Seven. Soon to be eight." Sandeep's pride at this number showed in his bright eyes.

John nodded, still cleaning his glasses. "A respectable number."

"And you?"

"Thirty-eight. Soon to be thirty-nine."

The Assamese man didn't try to hide his shock as he took a breath and stared at John. "So many. I knew you were the foremost collector... but I had no idea."

John put his glasses back on. "Most don't."

Akira dealt each man five cards. John looked at his hand. A busted straight. Low numbers. Nothing to do but ask for four cards. Sandeep asked for two. John glanced at his cards. Nothing again. Not even a pair.

Mason murmured under his breath. "This is going well."

"Trust me." John nodded to Akira.

Akira returned the nod. "Please reveal your cards."

Sandeep reveal a pair of aces against John's garbage hand. "Ha! This *is* off to a good start."

John sat back with a sigh and watched Akira gather up the cards. "This round to you."

"Tell me, what power will my new card give me. It reveals enemies, yes? That's what I've heard."

"It gives you visions of the future." John glanced from Puja to Sandeep and back again. Puja automatically pulled her collar closed to hide the slave tattoo. "What about the card I'll win? What will it give me?"

Sandeep scowled. "Visions of the future? Did you have a vision of this game?"

"Perhaps." John's face mirrored Akira's neutral expression. "The Two of Pentacles' power?"

"It mends that which had been sundered. It brings into balance those that need it." Sandeep gave John a quizzical glance.

"Interesting." He nodded, as if something had clicked into place.

Mason looked at John. "You didn't know?"

John kept his eyes on Sandeep even as Akira dealt the next hand of cards. "No."

"But..."

"Later." He picked up the cards Akira dealt. Aces over jacks. John signaled for one card, hoping to get a full house. He shook his head as it turned out be a four of spades. Looking at Sandeep's face, John could tell he wasn't happy.

Akira nodded to each man. "Reveal your cards."

Sandeep muttered curses under his breath as his pair of threes lost to John's hand. Akira swept the playing cards to him, and began shuffling the cards.

"That's one for me and one for you, Sandeep."

The dusky man nodded. "It is. It comes down to one hand. Are you certain you wish to do this?"

"Good question." Mason shook his head. "I must've been mad to agree to this game, much less to be your second."

"I'm sure. More sure now than ever." John's smile was hard, hiding his teeth.

Sandeep looked at the cards Akira was dealing and leaned forward. "Listen, John. I've changed my mind. Don't pick up those cards. We can quit the game together. Take our cards back." He glanced at Puja, his forehead moist with sudden desperation. "You can have her. Keep her, free her. It's your choice."

John shook his head. "I—"

"I'll kill her after this game if I lose that card. I told her so before we arrived." Sandeep shoved Puja out of her chair. "Beg for your life."

Puja tumbled to the floor. Instead of getting up, she crawled under the table to John's feet. Even as John pushed back from the table, the woman grasped his leg. "Please, please, Mister Corso. Please, he *will* kill me. He promised. You can save me and get your card back, too. I'll be your slave, your lover, whatever you want. I swear it."

"She's very skilled. Her mother sold her to me as a child. I've had her well-trained."

John looked down at her, his eyes hardening. She must have seen his rejection because Puja started to wail. "Please, God! Please!"

"That's not how this works. If we forfeit now, Akira owns both cards. Sandeep knows that. I will *not* lose them." Turning from her even as she clung to his leg, John picked up his cards.

"So be it." Sandeep nodded. "Puja!"

John stared at his cards without seeing them. He could feel Mason glaring daggers and refused to meet his friend's gaze. Sandeep smiled at his cards as Puja returned to her seat, her makeup smeared under tear-filled, bloodshot eyes.

"One." Sandeep slid a card to Akira and received one in return.

Again, John looked at two pair. Kings over tens. He glanced at Sandeep and knew the man had something. John slid one card to Akira and got one back. John didn't even look at it. He slid it into his hand and nodded to the dealer.

"Gentlemen, reveal your cards. Winner takes all."

Sandeep revealed a flush of hearts. Heart hammering in his chest, stomach sour with anxiety, John put his cards on the table without looking.

Sandeep slamming his fists on the table told John he had won. Looking down, he saw the full house, and collapsed back in his seat.

Sandeep stood. "You've won. And I'm a man of my word." He pulled the knife from his sash, grabbed Puja by the hair, and stabbed her twice as an alarm rang throughout the restaurant. John and Mason leaped from their seats even as

Akira tackled Sandeep, knocking him away from the bleeding woman.

John and Mason stood back as the tattooed wait staff dragged Sandeep out of the room. Akira prayed over Puja, pressing his hands to her wounds. John leaned forward as Akira's hands began to glow, and the woman took a shuddering breath.

"Thank God." John pulled the cigarette from his pocket and played with it.

Mason looked between them. "Did you know?"

"Later."

"'Later' better be a damn good story."

Puja opened her eyes and stared up at Akira. "I'm alive?"

"You are reborn." He touched the tattoo and it disappeared. "You died and were reborn a free woman."

"I don't... I can't... I've never..." Puja sobbed, babbling.

Akira pulled her into a fatherly hug. "Shhhh. We will care for you here until you're strong enough to fly in body and mind. The rules of hospitality apply to you, too. He cannot harm you further." Akira glanced up at John with unforgiving eyes. "Neither of them can."

John looked away, fiddling with his cigarette all the more.

As Akira called for one of the older women who worked at the restaurant, Mason nodded to Akira's healing hands. "That's new."

Akira watched Puja as she left the room. He took a towel from his apron and cleaned his hands until nothing of the girl's blood remained. "Not new. Old. No one may be harmed in this place. We take no sides, follow no leadership but our own. And we do not allow the Lost to be abandoned."

He returned to the poker table and picked up the two Todari cards. "Mister Corso, I gift these to you. You are their rightful owner."

John accepted them. "Thank you. I accept them in the spirit they are given."

"I am neutral, but I'm glad I did not need to gift those to that man." Akira's laugh lines reappeared, but there was no joy in his eyes. "And I now know what these cards are worth to you."

"Me, too." John put both cards into the small box.

**

"What in the Sam hell was that all about? Did you have vision of what would happen at the game?" Mason's driver opened the car door for the two of them.

"I did. But before that... I had a different vision." John took his battered cigarette from his pocket. "May I?"

Mason nodded and the two of them cracked the back windows. "At least you smoke those European cigarettes."

"That's because American cigarettes are shit."

"So, vision?"

John took a long drag and held it before exhaling toward the open window. "A vision that we need that card. It's going to sustain one of our allies."

"And the Moon? Did it tell you what would happen at the game?"

"Yes."

"Even what would happen to Puja?"

John wouldn't look at Mason. "I knew a woman would be hurt, but then the lobster pulled the woman away from the dog. So, I hoped."

"But you didn't know." Mason shook his head. "She could have died."

"There's only one woman I will give away a Todari card for, much less two of them. You know that."

Mason nodded. "I know. Karen. You're a cold man."

"You have no idea." John watched the passing scenery without seeing it as he smoked. As he did, he noticed his hands were still trembling.

"I'm slowly getting an idea." Mason sat quiet for a moment. "How is she doing?" His voice was carefully neutral.

"Karen?"

Mason nodded.

"She's... all right. Not hurt physically. But her heart... She's feeling the pressure of being the Master of the City's Representative. These last two years fighting the Children of Anu have taken their toll. So many people have died."

"That's not her fault."

"I know that. You know that. But she's been at the center of every major fight in the last few years. I used to think she was impetuous, naïve, and foolhardy, but now I know she's just trying to do what's right. And 'right' comes with the weight of responsibility. None of the factions blame her. Not the

Bacchanalia Coven, the Makah, the Brotherhood, the Special Unit. None of them. But she still feels the pain of every loss."

"Maybe that's why she's a good leader." Mason glanced at him. "And why she needs you."

"Yeah. So, I do what I have to. The hard times aren't over. I need to make sacrifices to protect her." John took a long drag, then let the smoke dribble out his nose and mouth. "She makes me willing to make those sacrifices. I didn't expect that. All in all, Mason, I'm a selfish bastard."

Mason gave him a half smile. "I know. But I'm glad she brings out the good in you."

"I don't know if there's any good to bring out."

"I'm sure there is. I have my family's legacy back, and Kendrick is safe for the moment, partly because of you." He thought for a moment. "I've done a lot I'm not proud of to protect my family and this city as well. So, if you say that card is worth what happened to keep Kendrick safe...who am I to judge?"

John gave him a tightlipped smile; unhappy but grateful.

The two of them sat in companionable silence for rest of the ride to the Steward estate. John smoked his cigarette and wondered if it would be worth it. Part of him cringed at the memory of condemning Puja to death. He was sure that was something that would come back to haunt him in time.

As the car stopped at the estate, Mason turned to him. "Nightcap and conversation?"

John shook his head. "Things to do, and miles to go before I sleep."

"You gonna tell me the whole story someday?"

"Maybe. I still don't know all of it myself. Can I get a lift elsewhere?"

Mason nodded. "Yes. Where?"

"Dock 14."

Mason gave John a careful look. "Really?"

"Really."

"Should I come with you?"

John shook his head. "I'd rather not."

Mason got out of the car as the door opened for him. "It's a good thing I trust you." He turned to his driver. "Dock 14 for John."

Waiting until the door was closed, John shook his head, his voice low. "You really shouldn't."

***

The last time John had been at Dock 14, they—he, Karen, and a rare alliance of various supernatural factions in Kendrick—had gathered a strike force bent on rescuing a kidnapped ally. They'd arrived too late. The Abbot, a good man, had been ritually beaten to death by the Children of Anu. John didn't like to remember what they'd found in that dark, dank cave. He walked down the beach to a driftwood log and sat on it, smoking, waiting, thinking.

Karen. The naïve young woman who had come into the supernatural world blind, because the Master of the City had chosen her as his representative. She had been brash, reckless, and fearless in her quest to stop the casual acceptance of the war that had raged hot and cold amongst the supernatural factions for decades. Now, she was a recognized leader among the hidden denizens of Kendrick. Betrayed, attacked, almost ritualistically murdered, she still held out hope that all could live in peace. Despite her losses, Karen never wavered from that belief.

How could a selfish, cynical man like him not love her? And she loved him back. He smiled, thinking about holding her as they talked about everything and nothing while Sebastian, the baby gargoyle who'd bonded himself to her, cavorted about the metaphysical book store. Yes, he would do a whole lot to protect her.

John dropped his cigarette when the Gray Lady appeared on the log next to him. She still wore the long, gray, high-necked gown she always wore, but now she looked old, translucent. "I wish you wouldn't do that."

"I apologize. I have little time or energy for the niceties of corporeal living." Her voice tickled his ear in a whisper.

John retrieved his fallen cigarette, dusted it off as he pulled the last of the tobacco from it, then put the filter in his pocket. "I had a dream," he said as he lit another cigarette.

"I know."

"I have a Todari card."

"You have many."

John watched the lapping waves with their small, white caps. Conversations with the Gray Lady were always like a game of riddles. The problem this time was the heavy feeling of doom, instead of the usual feeling of confusion. "The dream. It warned me of a coming danger."

"Yes."

"What danger?"

"Tell me your dream, John. I may be the Queen of the Fair Court, but I am not all-knowing."

John glanced at her, saw the weary, patient smile, and nodded. "Something was chasing me through a hallway of doors. It broke through every door I slammed shut. Except for the last one. The last one held. On it was a Todari tarot card, the Two of Pentacles. I touched the card, and light came from me to it. The card glowed and the door grew roots, sealing the door shut. All the while, the monster pounded and clawed at the wood."

"Did you see the monster?"

"No. But I knew that door was the last door, and if it got through... I would die."

She thought for a moment. "We are more than tied to the land. We're called 'the Goodfolk' because we're its guardians. But we are failing. Our places of power have been destroyed. They will take time to rebuild...if they can be rebuilt."

There was a sadness in her voice that broke his heart, and told him that he was doing the right thing, that he had made the right choice—no matter the pain. Taking the Todari carrying box out of his pocket, he opened it and looked on the beauty of the Two of Pentacles. It hurt him to have to give it up so soon. "Who is this for?"

The Gray Lady put her hand on his arm. "Me. If you would keep Karen and the rest safe."

Karen. How she had changed him and opened his world. "How will it help?" He took the Todari card out of the box, refusing to look at the Moon card beneath. He didn't want to see any more futures. Not tonight. Not for a long time.

"It will anchor me to the land. My hold is tenuous, the bindings sundered by the destruction of my keeps. The fair folk have ever been tied to the land and their places of power. When the Children destroyed them in their greed, they broke our protections. We, too, have our duty to those in Kendrick, though most never realize it." She paused. "They know the Veil is faltering. This will strengthen it for a time."

"They?"

"The Nightmares. The monsters on the other side of the Veil. The ones who would raze this land, and subject its denizens to unimaginable horrors. The portent of your dream."

"Until?" He held the Two of Pentacles up.

"Until I can find the one who will come after me."

John tore his gaze from the Todari tarot card to look at her. "You're dying?"

"Oh, John, dear *Collector*... how can you look at me and ask that question?" Her rebuke was gentle and amused. "Yes. I'm dying. I will be replaced by another with a love and link to the land. Just as I followed the one before me."

"You're being unusually forthcoming."

"Impending death and doom will do that."

"Can we stop... what's coming?"

"Yes. Perhaps. With help from good people like you."

Good. Was he good now? He'd always hidden his selfishness under a veneer of civility and the guise of a rumpled scholar. But now...

John nodded. He held the card out to her. "Lady Gray, would you do me the great honor of accepting this gift?"

"You may not get it back." Her voice was barely heard now, a whisper on the wind.

He grimaced at the thought, his heart pounding his ears, but kept his hand out, offering her the precious card. "I know. I risked another card for it earlier. I even... I did something horrible to get it. I give this card to you with my whole heart. I just hope it helps you and your people. I hope you survive. And... I hope what's coming won't be as bad as I think it's going to be."

"That's a lot of hope in one gift."

John's stomach turned over, the selfish beast within roaring with want. He forced his hand to remain extended to her. "Please, please accept it before my baser nature takes over."

The Gray Lady took the card from him. "I accept it with all that I am. I, too, hope for all of those same things. Thank you."

As soon as her hand took the card from his, her translucency filled in and she looked solid. Her presence became a weight, he could sense and his selfish beast was quieted for the time being, replaced with the satisfaction that the sacrifice was worth it. "Is there anything else I can do?"

She nodded. "Guard your dreams. Do whatever you can to guard your dreams and the dreams of those you love. The Nightmares are coming, and we don't have the strength to hold them back."

Author's Biography

JENNIFER BROZEK IS a Hugo Award-nominated editor and an award-winning author. Winner of the Australian Shadows Award for best edited publication, Jennifer has edited fifteen anthologies with more on the way, including the acclaimed *Chicks Dig Gaming* and *Shattered Shields* anthologies. Author of *Apocalypse Girl Dreaming, Industry Talk*, the *Karen Wilson Chronicles*, and the *Melissa Allen* series, she has more than sixty-five published short stories, and is the Creative Director of Apocalypse Ink Productions.

Jennifer is a freelance author for numerous RPG companies. Winner of the Scribe, Origins, and ENnie awards, her contributions to RPG sourcebooks include *Dragonlance, Colonial Gothic, Shadowrun, Serenity, Savage Worlds*, and *White Wolf SAS*. Jennifer is the author of the award winning YA *Battletech* novel, *The Nellus Academy Incident*, and *Shadowrun* novella, *Doc Wagon 19*. She has also written for the AAA MMO *Aion* and the award winning videogame, *Shadowrun Returns*.

When she is not writing her heart out, she is gallivanting around the Pacific Northwest in its wonderfully mercurial weather. Jennifer is a Director-at-Large of SFWA, and an active member of HWA and IAMTW. Read more about her at www.jenniferbrozek.com or follow her on Twitter at @JenniferBrozek.

Also From Apocalypse Ink Productions

If you enjoyed this book by Jennifer Brozek, you may enjoy one of these other Urban Fantasy books published by Apocalypse Ink Productions

FLOTSAM
TRILOGY

PETER M. BALL

The Flotsam Trilogy

My name's Keith Murphy. Danny Roark and I hunt down the dark things that prey on humans like you. Or we did, until what seemed like a routine assassination job went bad. Really bad. Now the end of the world is coming at us like a possessed freight train.

Running doesn't bother me. It's a fine survival trait. What bothers me is the 9mm bullet I swallowed—with the soul of my last victim trapped inside it. That botched job I mentioned. He was leader of the Raven Cult: bloodthirsty fools who won't let a little thing like death cramp their style. When Roark goes down, I'm left to figure out what the cult's survivors are planning.

It's a puzzle I've got to figure out before the Gloom gets too strong and the real monsters come through—ones my ragtag, mostly demonic, army can't handle. All this magic and end of the world stuff was Roark's department, not mine. I'll have to figure it out as I go. The end of the world's still coming, but it's got to go through me first.

The Flotsam Trilogy contains the novellas Exile, Frost, and Crusade as well as two more stories from the gold coast, "Local Heroes" and "Tithes."

Find this trilogy at http://www.apocalypse-ink.com or from Amazon, Barnes and Noble, or Drive Thru Fiction.

The Sheynan Trilogy

This dark urban fantasy adventure by Dylan Birtolo is an omnibus of three novels: *The Shadow Chaser*, *The Bringer of War*, and *The Torn Soul*, and features three new short stories.

The Shadow Chaser: Darien Yost is a young man haunted by blackouts and vividly realistic dreams. When mysterious strangers start to appear, claiming that he has a power which makes him unique, he finds himself entangled in their world; a world of shape shifters. Soon, he is thrust into the middle of a centuries long war, and must master his ability before either side claims him... as an asset or a casualty.

The Bringer of War: Months have passed, and the Arm of Gaia and the Shadows still struggle to control Darien's destiny, attempting to use him to tip the balance of their war. But Darien has embraced his power. He and his allies have gone on the offensive, hunting down those who are trying to enslave him. Meanwhile, another renegade shifter has appeared, trying to pull Darien away from his friends for reasons of her own.

The Torn Soul: Time is running out for Darien. As new players and new dangers enter the scene, Darien must confront his past, and convince the Arm of Gaia and the Shadows to work together against a new enemy—before his mind is lost to the Sheynan's curse.

Apocalypse Ink Productions is an independent press focused on dark speculative fiction and horror in its fiction line and online based writing education in its non-fiction line.

Please visit our website at http://www.apocalypse-ink.com to learn more about us, and to find information on other books— both digital and print—that we have available.

www.ingramcontent.com/pod-product-compliance
Lightning Source LLC
Chambersburg PA
CBHW070343030726
47504CB00001B/47